The Billy Palmer Chronicles

DEREK JOHNS has been a bookseller, editor and publisher and now works as a literary agent in London.

The Billy Palmer Chronicles

Derek Johns

BOOKS

First published by Portobello Books 2010
This paperback edition published 2011

Portobello Books
12 Addison Avenue
London W11 4QR

Part one ('Wintering') and part two ('Wakening') of this book were originally published by
Portobello Books as separate volumes: *Wintering* in 2007 and *Wakening* in 2008.

Copyright © Derek Johns 2007, 2008, 2010

The right of Derek Johns to be identified as the author of this work has been asserted
by him in accordance with the Copyright, Designs and Patents Act 1988

The author wishes to thank Methuen Publishing Limited for permission to quote
from Noël Coward's *Private Lives* (Copyright © The Estate of Noël Coward).

A CIP catalogue record is available from the British Library

9 8 7 6 5 4 3 2 1

ISBN 978 1 84627 214 1

www.portobellobooks.com

Designed by Richard Marston
Typeset in Joanna by Avon DataSet Ltd, Bidford on Avon, Warwickshire B50 4JH
Printed and bound in Great Britain by CPI Bookmarque, Croydon

Wintering

'If Winter comes, can Spring be far behind?'

Shelley, 'Ode to the West Wind'

One

Billy raised his face to the sun, seeking its warmth. He passed under a canopy of trees which for a few moments turned morning into evening.

'We're having an Indian summer,' said Jim.

'What's an Indian summer, Daddy?' said Sarah.

'It's a summer that comes just when you think summer is over.'

'Is there a Cowboy summer too?' said Billy.

His father didn't reply, and Billy turned to look at him. He was wheeling his bicycle, and this seemed to absorb all his attention.

The road was lined with stinging nettles, dock leaves and Queen Anne's lace. When it dipped steeply towards the village, Sarah asked to hold Jim's hand.

'Take your brother's,' he said.

'I don't want to.' She tossed her hair, and Billy took this as a signal to run ahead.

'You're old enough now not to hold hands,' said Jim. 'And don't dawdle.'

'I'm not dawdling, I'm walking.'

'Yes, and slowly. Do you want to be late on the first day at your new school?'

'I don't want to go to a new school,' she said. 'I liked the old one.'

'We've been through all that. You have to go to a new school, just as I have to go to a new job.'

Billy climbed a gate that opened onto an empty field. In the hazy distance he could see a hill that rose sheer out of the countryside, with a tower at the top.

'Dad!' he shouted. 'Look at this. Is it a castle?'

'That's Glastonbury Tor,' said Jim when he caught up.

'What is it?'

'What is it? It's a hill.'

'But it must be something.'

'Well, there are stories. I don't really know them. You'll have to ask your new teacher.'

Billy was transfixed. This was the strangest hill he had ever seen, an impossible hill.

'Can we go there?'

'How?' said Jim, pushing off again. 'There are no buses for miles around.'

Billy was the laggard now, stopping at every gate to catch sight of the tor. How many fields would he have to cross to get there – ten, twenty? But then there were the cows. Billy wasn't sure about cows.

The school was a grey limestone building no bigger than a house, its walls covered in scarlet Virginia creeper, its only decoration a wrought-iron porch. To reach it they had to cross a stone footbridge over a stream. Alongside the bridge was a ford, the water a foot or so deep.

'Sit on the steps and wait for Miss Shute,' said Jim. 'I must get on.' He wheeled his bicycle up the slope past the church and swung onto it. Billy watched his receding figure, trying not to feel abandoned.

As soon as his father was out of sight, he began to explore. There was a tiny yard, with no swings or anything. How different this was from his school in Bath, with its broad playing fields and troops of boys in blue blazers and caps. This strange new place would take some getting used to, the little school and the house without a garden.

'Daddy said we'd be late,' said Sarah, 'and there's nobody here. Can we go home?'

'Of course not. The teacher will be here soon.'

'Why is she called Miss Shute?'

'That's her name.'

'But why? It's a silly name.'

The door opened behind her, and a voice said, 'You must be the Palmer children.'

She was spare and pale, her greying hair tied in a bun, a plain black dress flapping around her ankles. They followed her through a hallway and into a classroom. It was very bare, containing only desks for twelve children, a table and a chair. Sitting beneath the blackboard was another woman dressed in black. She rose heavily as they entered.

'This is Miss Shute,' said Miss Shute.

Where the first was spare, the second was stout. They were different renderings of the same idea: even the features of their faces were the same; but one was all angles and the other all curves. Their wintry blue eyes rested on Billy and Sarah.

'We hope you will be happy here,' said the first Miss Shute. 'Where did you go to school before?'

'I went to the Unicorn School,' said Billy.

'And I went to St Mary's,' said Sarah.

'And what were your best subjects?'

'Reading and writing,' said Billy unhesitatingly.

'I don't know,' said Sarah. 'I liked them all.'

'Well, that's good.'

'I don't think I will be happy here,' said Sarah.

'Why do you say that, my child?' said the second Miss Shute.

'I don't think I like you.'

The Misses Shute looked at one another and sighed. 'I think you will grow to like us,' said the second. 'We may seem stern to you, but we're not really.'

'Billy, what did you read last at the Unicorn School?' said the first Miss Shute.

'*Treasure Island*, miss.'

'Did you like it?'

'Yes, a lot.'

'Then for your first lesson this morning you will write about your favourite character in *Treasure Island*. Who is that?'

'Jim Hawkins.'

'Very good. And what have you been reading, Sarah?'

'*The Water-Babies*,' said Sarah, shy now.

'And who do you like in *The Water-Babies*?'

Sarah considered for a moment and glanced at her brother for encouragement. 'Well... I quite like Ellie. But the one I really like is Mrs Doasyouwouldbedoneby.'

'Then your first task will be to copy out some pages about Mrs Doasyouwouldbedoneby and Mrs Bedonebyasyoudid. Is your hand-writing neat?'

'No.'

'Yes it is, Sarah,' said Billy. 'Mum's helped you with it.'

'No it isn't,' she insisted. 'It's... straggly.'

'We'll soon see,' said the first Miss Shute. 'Miss Shute will be your teacher, Sarah, and Billy, I will be yours. Assembly is in this classroom. I would like you both to stand at the front so that I may introduce you.'

There was a commotion in the hallway, and two boys burst into the

3

classroom. The first was very tall, a little older than Billy, and the second was about Sarah's age. They were both lean and bony, with shocks of ginger hair and large ears. Billy wondered whether everyone here came in twos.

'This is Frank and Ed Willmott,' said the first Miss Shute. Frank, the elder, looked Billy up and down before going to a desk at the back of the classroom. More children began to arrive.

'Why are there two Miss Shutes?' said Sarah to Billy.

'One for your class and one for mine.'

'Are they sisters?'

'They must be.'

'I think they're creepy.'

Twenty or so children filled the room. They whispered to one another and stole glances at Billy and Sarah. There was an air of informality that Billy was quite unused to. The boy who stood next to him was about his age. He had freckles and a sly smile, and repeatedly looked sidelong at him without saying anything. Miss Shute asked the children to close their eyes and say the Lord's Prayer. Billy sensed the other boy leaning towards him as he began. 'Our Father, who farts in heaven…' He opened his eyes and looked at the boy, whose face wore an expression of complicity. '… lead us not into detention, but deliver us from teacher.'

'We have two new children in the school today,' said Miss Shute. 'Billy and Sarah Palmer have come from Bath. We know you will make them feel at home here.'

The younger children, including Sarah and Ed, went to the second classroom, leaving four boys and six girls. 'Billy, please sit next to Alan,' said Miss Shute. The desks were constructed in pairs, with sloping tops, empty inkwells and pencils lying in grooves. Miss Shute gave Billy some paper. 'Alan, will you look after Billy?' she said to the freckled boy. 'I hope you will be friends.'

'Yes, miss,' said Alan. 'He looks all right.' And to Billy, 'You look all right, I reckon.'

He began composing his essay. 'I like Jim Hawkins best of all the people in Treasure Island because he is very brave,' he wrote. 'Also, he has the same name as my Dad.'

Miss Shute moved around the room, speaking to them one at a time. With ten children ranging in age between eight and eleven there

4

was no single set of lessons: each child was given something different to do. Billy shaded his eyes and looked over at Alan's piece of paper. His handwriting was rambling and effortful. 'Henry the Aith had six wives,' Billy read. 'They were not very good wives so he chopped of there heads.'

He looked around the room. The other children were talking freely, and not much work was getting done. Behind him, Frank Willmott and another boy were squabbling over possession of a rubber. Billy looked up at Miss Shute, who seemed quite unconcerned. After an hour or so she asked the children to stop what they were doing, and began reading from *Lorna Doone*. 'This is a good story,' whispered Alan. 'The Doones are a very bad lot, going around murdering people. But John Ridd'll take care of 'em.'

At morning break the children dashed into the yard, the boys and the girls occupying their separate territories. Frank Willmott laid a hand on Billy's shoulder and said, 'So, Billy Palmer, you have to run the gauntlet.'

'What's that?'

'It's what you have to do to be a member of the school. Come on, lads, let's show him.'

The other boys stood with their hands flat against the classroom wall.

'You go through four times,' said Frank. 'The first time you get rain, the second time you get lightning, the third time you get thunder, and the fourth time you get hailstones.' He took up a position at the other end. 'Now, run!'

Billy ducked and entered the tunnel created by the boys' arms. As he did so the first boy, Ed, slapped him on the back. Each in turn gave him a slap, the last and hardest being Frank's. 'Now, back to the front,' he said. Billy ran again, this time being rabbit-punched; the third time it was prods with the knee. He was soon hurting a lot, and tears were starting in his eyes. Frank's final blow, a punch in the stomach, was vicious. He was very strong, despite being so wiry, and he seemed to be enjoying himself.

The gauntlet broke up, and Billy tried to face Frank down. Tears were welling in his eyes, but he knew he mustn't wipe them away. He set his mouth firm.

'You are now a member of the school,' said Frank. 'But you have to tell us some things about yourself.'

'All right.'

'So you're from Bath. Why have you come here?'

'Because my dad's got a new job.'

'What's that, then?'

'It's in an outfitters in Wells. Selling clothes.'

'And what did he do before?'

'He sold cars.'

'What sort of cars?'

'Jaguars.'

Billy sensed a change in the attitude of the boys. This part of his initiation had suddenly become interesting.

'Your dad sold Jaguars?' said Frank.

'Yes,' said Billy. 'We had one too, a Mark Eight.'

'You mean you got to *ride* in a Mark Eight?' said Alan wonderingly.

'Yes. All the time.'

Frank considered this information for a moment. 'I think you're a liar,' he said, and the mood of the boys changed again.

'No I'm not,' said Billy. 'Ask my sister, she'll tell you.'

'Why hasn't he got his fancy Jaguar now, then?'

'I don't know,' said Billy. His father had never really explained.

'I think you're a liar, Billy Palmer. Liar, liar, pants on fire.'

'No I'm not!' shouted Billy. Why didn't he believe him? Of course they'd had a Jaguar. It was the best car of all.

'Cross your heart and hope to die.'

'Cross my heart and hope to die.'

'Well do it, then,' said Frank, a glint of menace in his eyes. 'Cross your heart.'

Billy did as he was told, while Frank looked at him sceptically. 'I'll get my sister to talk to yours,' he said. 'And if you're lying, you're for it.'

'I'm not. Sarah will tell you. She always wanted to sit in the front, but Dad wouldn't let her.'

Miss Shute appeared in the doorway and called the children back in. As they were crossing the yard Alan said to Billy in a low tone, 'I believe you. What colour was it?'

'Indigo blue.'

Alan whistled softly. 'Indigo blue,' he said with a faraway smile.

––––––

Jim cycled past the church hall and the village shop and out onto the Launcherley road. This journey of four miles into Wells would now be his daily lot, his daily penance, so different from the ten-minute drive to the showroom in Bath. The road skirted the hills, passing through flat farmland. It was harvest time. Never having thought very much about the countryside, he must now learn to understand it. He wondered how the kids were getting on. This school seemed hardly a school at all, more a place to leave children during the day. And those spinster sisters were very odd. Well, Billy and Sarah would have to make do, just as he would have to.

He cycled past apple orchards and open fields. A wood pigeon flew from a tangled hedge, startling him for a moment. He saw a large farm up ahead, and smelled the sweet, raw odour of silage. Then at a crest in the road the façade of Wells Cathedral came into sight. He had come here once with Margaret, just before they were married, to visit her Uncle Reg and his wife. It was really a market town, he thought, not a city; the great edifice at its centre gave it airs.

Reg's shop was in Market Place. Jim dismounted and pushed his bicycle along the cobbled street. At one end was a stone cross with a fountain, and at the other the Bishop's Eye, the gateway to the palace. This stately tranquillity made him uneasy.

A sign etched in gold above one of the shops read 'Underhill's', and below, 'Outfitters to the Scholars & Gentry of Wells'. The windows curved inwards towards a recessed door, and displayed school uniforms and dull men's clothes. Jim pushed his bike into a narrow, gloomy space.

'You can park it out the back,' said Reg, barely looking up as he spoke. Catching sight of himself in a mirror, Jim hastily removed his bicycle clips. In his tweed jacket and grey flannels he was hot and flustered after his ride. He swept back his wavy brown hair and took another look at himself, at the new assistant in Underhill's Outfitters.

'It'll be slow for a week or two,' said Reg. 'You've missed the back-to-school rush, for which you should be very grateful. And nobody's thinking about winter just yet. I need to do stocktaking and accounts, so I'm going to leave the customers to you.'

Reg was a small, fastidious man, his grey hair crinkly and glistening with Brylcreem. His eyes are too close together, thought Jim, squint eyes.

'Are the prices on everything?'

'There's a list,' said Reg, reaching into a drawer under the till. 'Here. Now, I don't want you trying to *sell* anything to anybody, understand? This isn't like what you're used to. If somebody wants something they'll buy it.'

Jim was good at selling. The last thing he'd sold was an XK150 Drophead. He had persuaded the buyer to take just about every extra going, from the Dunlop racing tyres to the wood-rim steering wheel. If Reg didn't want Jim to sell, then more fool him.

Reg went into the office at the back, leaving him alone in the shop. He looked at the price list, and tried to relate it to what was on display. Everything seemed to come in a shade of grey or brown – there was nothing remotely fashionable, no modern fabrics or bright colours. The dark wood of the fixtures oppressed him, and he stood at the front of the shop gazing out into the street, at the few people who passed by. Perhaps Mondays were always quiet, he thought. It was ages before the doorbell rang.

'I want a cap,' said his first customer. He was florid and thickset, a clod of a man.

'Yes, sir,' said Jim. 'What sort of cap?'

'One like this,' the man said, removing a worn flat cap from his head. He examined it through thick glasses, turning it over in his hands. 'Had this one twenty years.'

'What size is it?'

'Blowed if I know. The label went a long time ago.'

Jim went over to the display of caps. 'Try this,' he said, choosing the plainest. The man tried it on in front of the mirror.

'How much?'

Jim returned to the counter and the list. 'Seven and six,' he said.

'Got anything cheaper?'

Jim handed him another, almost identical cap.

'This one's six shillings.'

The man tried it on. 'I can't see any difference,' he said.

Jim took the caps back. He couldn't see any difference either. 'This one has a better quality lining,' he said involuntarily. 'It'll last longer.'

The man took them back and looked at the linings. 'I think you're right,' he said. 'I'll take it.'

At lunchtime Jim stepped out into the sunshine, breathing in the warm air with a sense of grateful relief. He walked through Penniless Porch, the towered archway that separated the town from the cathedral precincts, and onto the green. Sitting down on the grass he slowly ate his sandwiches, and then lay back and closed his eyes. He'd had one customer that morning, and had taken a trifling sum of money. Wondering how he was going to get through the afternoon, he drifted into sleep.

When he awoke it was to a thrilling, reverberant sound. The bells of the cathedral were ringing. But this was no ordinary bell-ringing: it was an intricate music, full of complex harmonies. It seemed to go on forever, oceanic, washing over him. When it ended he sat up, collected his things, and began to walk slowly back to the shop. He felt utterly stranded.

Margaret tidied the breakfast table and riddled the ashes in the stove. She wasn't sure whether she was daunted more by the prospect of her tasks or by the time stretching ahead of her. Certainly there would be many more chores than she had lately been used to. But then there would be little else. Hubert Fosse had lived in this cottage until his wife died, when he moved into an outbuilding at the back. The furniture consisted of the few sticks they had been allowed to hold onto, and things that Fosse had left behind. Margaret's sole indulgence was the Roberts radio she had hidden in the airing cupboard the day the receiver came to do the inventory. *The Light Programme* would be her society now.

She went out into the yard behind the house. Margaret had had a single brief conversation with Fosse since they moved in two days ago, and she felt she should try to get to know him. His farm was a small one, with twenty-odd Friesian cows, two pigs, and some chickens and geese. He was in the milking shed, washing down the stalls, and he stood awkwardly as Margaret entered, stretching his back. Margaret thought he was the ruddiest man she had ever seen. His bald scalp was peeling from the sun, and his white hair seemed to come from everywhere except the top of his head – from his ears, his nose, and, most dramatically, from his chest, overflowing the collar of his shirt. It was like a pelt.

'Good morning, Hubert,' said Margaret.

'Morning.'

'I was wondering whether I could be of any help to you.'

'You'll have enough to do, I guess, with your family.'

'Yes, I'm sure. But there'll be times, I expect. Did Uncle Reg tell you I was a land girl during the war?'

'No, he didn't.' He emptied a bucket of water across the floor and picked up a broom.

'It's a long time ago now, of course. But I know something about dairy farming. And I used to be able to milk.'

'Well, I could surely use a hand with the milking. But that means getting up at six.'

'I'm up at six these days anyway.'

'Then put your head around the shed door any morning,' he said, beginning to scrub. 'I can't pay you, though. All I can do is give you some milk.'

'That would be most welcome.'

Margaret sensed that the conversation was at an end. But as she turned to go, Hubert said, 'Maybe there are things I can do for you too. It must be hard, all this.'

'Thank you.' She looked away from him. 'Yes, it is hard. But much harder for Jim.' She wanted to go on, wanted to talk of the shame Jim felt over losing his business. She realized that she wanted to talk to someone very much. Instead, she simply wished Fosse good morning and stepped back into the yard. She stood for a moment gazing at the cottage. It was an odd sort of place, its roofs steeply gabled, the windows hung with white shutters. It's a gingerbread house, she thought. Well, it could be much worse. She entered the kitchen and opened the door of the larder. The shelves seemed very empty, and this reminder that she must replenish them came to her as a surprise.

Crossing the bridge by the school she looked out for Billy and Sarah, but they were in class. The village shop bore a sign that read 'Lyons Tea – The Tea of Teashop Fame'. She thought back to the tearooms in Bath, to lazy mornings spent nursing a cup of coffee and gossiping with her friends. The moment she entered, the tiny woman behind the counter said, 'Mrs Palmer, if I may guess. Welcome to the village.'

'Thank you.'

'We don't get many strangers here. Not that you're a stranger, of course. Bath is where you're coming from, now, isn't it?'

'That's right.'

'You'll find things a little slower here.'

Margaret looked around the shop, its shelves stacked high with groceries.

'I don't think I'll mind that,' she said.

'Good. Now what can I get you?'

Margaret hadn't really discussed housekeeping with Jim. It was one of the subjects that seemed difficult to broach at the moment. She would just have to see how much things cost.

'Do you have meat?' she asked.

'You get that from the butcher's van. You just have to flag him down one day and make an arrangement.' Margaret imagined herself roaming the lanes in search of a butcher. 'Capstone's his name. Come here tomorrow about eleven and I'll see if I can find him for you.'

She spent the rest of the morning doing the washing, and in the afternoon she fell asleep. When she awoke, for a moment she imagined herself to be in the airy bedroom at the big house in Bath. She had often slept in the afternoon there, but more from boredom than from the weariness she felt now. The children would be home from school soon. But first she would steal an hour at Mansfield Park. Henry Crawford had just proposed to Fanny Price, and Fanny had foolishly accepted.

Billy appeared a couple of minutes before Sarah. For a while he had tried to keep pace with her, but in the end he had given up and run on. He was halfway up the stairs when Margaret called him back.

'You must wait for your sister,' she said, 'and take care of her.'

'But she's so *slow*.'

'She's seven, Billy, and she shouldn't have to find her own way home.'

Sarah opened the door as Margaret was speaking. 'I can find my own way home,' she said. 'It's easy.'

'How was your first day at school?'

'It was horrible,' said Sarah. 'The Miss Shutes are *witches*.'

'No they're not,' said Billy, 'they're just old.'

'Yes they are. I saw their broom.'

'No you didn't.'

'I did,' said Sarah emphatically. 'It was in a cupboard.'

'Perhaps they use it for sweeping the floor,' said Margaret.

'It's a special flying broom.'

'You know there are good witches as well as wicked ones, don't you?'

Sarah looked at her mother with a grave expression. 'The Miss Shutes are very wicked,' she said.

Jim got home at six, and they sat down to eat. After supper Billy and Sarah went exploring in the farmyard.

'How did it go?' Margaret asked Jim.

'It was awful, Maggie,' he said. 'I'm not sure how I'm going to do this. Reg obviously dislikes me, for a start.'

'I'm sure he doesn't. He gave you a job, remember, when no one else would.'

'Yes, and he's going to lose no opportunity to remind me of that.'

Margaret sat down and kissed him on the cheek. 'Then you must gain his respect,' she said.

'And how do I do that?'

'I don't know… by doing a good job.'

'He more or less told me he doesn't want me to do a good job. A child could do it.'

He slumped into the armchair and picked up the newspaper, turning to the cartoons. Margaret stood and began to clear away the supper things. What will he do in the evenings? she wondered. The children would find things, and she would read. But Jim had spent his with the television and the record player. What was he going to do without Sergeant Bilko and Artie Shaw?

It was difficult to get Billy and Sarah to bed: it was still light, and they sensed that with their new surroundings should come new routines, new privileges. But it was barely ten by the time Jim went upstairs. Margaret read for a while longer before following him, and spent a long time in the bathroom. There was no mirror save for Jim's shaving mirror, and she was glad of that. In recent years she had become aware of changes in herself, of the ways in which her body had been betrayed by age and the children. She combed her hair slowly and splashed water over her face. Jim lay on his back in the half-light, gazing at the ceiling, and when she got in beside him she waited tensely for a moment. And as he had done every night for a long time now, he leaned over, kissed her lightly, and turned his back.

By the end of Billy's first week at school, he and Alan were friends. One morning Alan came by the farmhouse, and they set off across the fields. Billy hadn't been sure where he was able to go, but Alan wandered freely, so he simply followed. They walked through an apple orchard, and Alan told him that scrumping time would come soon.

'What's scrumping?'

'Stealing apples.'

'Is it allowed?' said Billy, feeling immediately foolish.

''Course it isn't. That's the point. We'll do it with Frank and the rest of the gang. He'll tell us when.'

They crossed a stile and came into the field where Fosse's cows were pastured.

'Will they chase us?' said Billy.

'Watch.'

Alan began to run straight at them. They scattered before him, and he ran back to Billy with an exultant expression on his face. 'See,' he said. 'Scaredy cows.'

At the top of Folly Lane there was a birch copse. Alan led the way to a place at the edge from where they could see the countryside stretching before them. It was criss-crossed by ditches that ran very straight alongside tracks and hedges.

'Are they canals?' said Billy.

'They're called rhynes.'

'Rinds?'

'No, rhynes. R-h-y-n-e-s.'

Glastonbury Tor dominated everything, a pyramid on the plain.

'So what do you know about the tor?' said Billy.

'It's where King Arthur's buried, isn't it?'

'King Arthur of the Round Table?'

'Yes.'

'I thought he lived in Camelot.'

'But he died here. Avalon, they called it.'

Billy's eyes returned to the tor. 'Have you been there?' he said.

'My dad took me in the milk lorry once. You can see for miles.'

'Do you think your dad would take me there?'

'Maybe.'

They lapsed into silence for a moment. Alan sucked on a blade of

13

grass and said, 'My dad says all this used to be under the sea, and Avalon was an island.'

'You mean when he was a kid?'

'No, a long time ago. Hundreds of years, maybe thousands.'

Billy gazed at the plain. How exciting, he thought, that all this might once have been under water. They would have needed a boat to get to school. But then the school would have been under water too. It was hard sometimes to account for things, for how strange the world seemed. He narrowed his eyes. 'Alan,' he said. 'You know when you see colours, like green and blue... do you think everybody sees the same thing?'

'How do you mean?'

'Well, how do I know that what I see as green you don't see as blue?'

Alan thought for a moment. 'We've got the same eyes, haven't we?'

Billy looked at him, then back towards the tor. It held his attention all the time. 'Come on,' he said suddenly. 'Race you back down the hill.'

———

At the weekend the cottage was eerily quiet. Billy was soon bored, and tried without success to interest first his sister and then his mother in playing games. His father ignored him, reading the newspaper from cover to cover and back again. Then just as Billy was giving up on him, he said, 'Let's do the British Grand Prix, shall we?'

'All right.'

They got out the Dinky toy set and the scale model of Aintree race-track that his father had helped Billy to construct a year or so before. Billy's Dinky toy cars had been his prize possession. Jim had bought him any number of them, including gift sets such as the racing cars and the sports cars. And since they had gone together to the British Grand Prix the previous summer, they had often re-enacted that marvellous day. The Jaguar people had given Jim passes for the paddock and the pits, and before the race they had been able to stroll about among the cars and meet the drivers, those nonchalant heroes in their white overalls and armoured helmets. Every moment of that day was seared on Billy's memory: the deafening noise, the acrid smell of petrol, the sheer exhilaration of it all.

They set up the track, placing the pits and the grandstands and the barriers in the right places.

'Who's in pole position?' said Jim.

'Stirling Moss,' said Billy, as he always did. 'With Mike Hawthorn beside him. Then Fangio and Brooks, and Collins at the back.' There were only five cars in the set, but these had always been enough to create the atmosphere they wanted. Jim waved a tiny flag, and Billy moved forward Moss's Vanwall and Hawthorn's Ferrari. At the first bend Hawthorn tried to edge past, but Moss turned sharply and entered the straight in front. Jim brought Fangio's Maserati and Brooks's Vanwall up behind; Collins would be relegated to last place throughout.

They completed two laps. 'We forgot the fire engine,' said Jim. But Billy went on, manoeuvring the cars one by one through bends and chicanes and down fast straights. He decided he would make things more interesting by having Fangio overtake Brooks and make ground on Moss and Hawthorn: this race wasn't coming alive as it used to. Then suddenly he crashed Moss's Vanwall into a barrier, flipping it over onto the floor. He sat for a moment surveying the havoc he had wrought.

'Dad,' he said, 'this isn't very exciting any more, is it?'

'Why not?'

'I don't know. It's not… real.'

'But we're remembering it, like it was at Aintree.'

Billy stood up. 'I think this is for kids,' he said. He looked at his father with an expression that mixed apology and defiance. And then he ran out of the door into the yard.

———————

Margaret got up at six and went quietly downstairs to the kitchen. She put on her oldest pair of slacks and one of Jim's jerseys, and tied her hair in a scarf. Hubert was leading the cows into the milking shed. 'You'll need wellingtons,' he said. 'I'll get my wife's.'

In the dark of the shed the cows loomed large and strange. She hadn't been near one for many years. They bellowed in their stalls, and shifted their feet uneasily. They want this over with, she thought, want to be rid of their load. She ran her hand down the coarse black hair of the nearest. They were so ponderous, and so docile. Hubert gave her a pair of wellingtons. 'The pail and stool are over there,' he said. 'You'll need a cup for the foremilk.'

Margaret placed the stool close to the haunches of the cow; its udder was swollen, and marbled with thick veins. She began tentatively, drawing a little milk from each teat into the cup, and then she placed the pail in its place and began to work. After a while she found her rhythm, and the cow became still, pacified by her touch. The milk seethed as it struck the metal. When the pail was full she took it over to the cooling machine and poured the milk into the reservoir at the top, watching it trickle over the iron corrugations and into the churn below.

When they were finished Hubert gave her a jug of milk, and she carried it out into the yard. On the way to the kitchen door she stopped to look at the pigs, Stan and Gertie. Gertie gave her a penetrating stare. They were revolting creatures, and yet there was something rather likeable about them.

Jim and Billy and Sarah were up by now.

'Look, warm milk,' said Sarah.

'It's not pasteurised,' said Jim.

'And nor was the milk you and I grew up on.'

'It tastes funny,' said Billy.

'Just drink it,' said Margaret. 'It'll do you good.'

———

The weather was changing as Jim set off for Wells, and by the time he arrived at the shop it was starting to rain. Towards the end of the previous week trade had picked up, but this Monday was as slow as his first, the pall lifted only by the arrival of a delivery from Askews in Bristol. Reg spent the morning checking the clothes against the despatch note, fussing over discrepancies. He was getting on Jim's nerves. Whenever Jim offered to do anything more than stand behind the counter and deal with customers he dismissed him, saying that it would take longer to explain than to do it himself. Jim's predecessor had been nineteen. If Reg had given him this job solely out of charity, then they would both have to accept the pretences that came with it.

He ate his sandwiches in the stockroom and listened to the rain. He must get out for a while. He hadn't brought a raincoat, so he turned up the collar of his jacket and thrust his hands in his pockets. A little way down Sadler Street was Goody's café, and he ducked through the door and into an airless room. Condensation ran down the windows, obscuring the world outside. He sat at a table in the corner and lit up a smoke, while a middle-aged woman bustled behind the counter. The menu tacked to the wall offered sausage, egg and chips and baked beans on toast. Jim would gladly have given his sandwiches a miss and eaten lunch here, but with what? The seven pounds a week from Underhill's would be stretched as it was.

A girl appeared through the door at the back, and came over to take his order. Jim hadn't set eyes on a young woman since he came to Wells: he seemed to come across only old people and children. Girls must be somewhere, he'd presumed. Well, here was one. He sat up a little straighter, all his senses suddenly alert.

'A cup of tea, please,' he said.

She smiled and turned back to the counter. There was something open and direct in her manner that Jim found appealing. And she had a gorgeous figure, with slim hips and full breasts that her apron couldn't hide. She returned with Jim's cup of tea. 'Anything else?' she said. Jim knew from the way she hesitated that she returned his interest. She had long dark hair that hadn't been permed or fooled about with, and her lipstick wasn't overdone. Her brown eyes drew Jim in. 'No thanks, love,' he said.

She began wiping down the other tables, and Jim made a show of looking away from her; but with the windows steamed up there wasn't really anywhere else to direct his gaze. He sipped his tea and dragged on his cigarette, wondering how best to arrange his arms and legs.

Jim attracted women, and he knew it. He'd never had any trouble. Well, the trouble had always been that there *was* no trouble. He'd strayed many times since he got married. It was easy when you had money and a car and reasons to be out in the evenings. The last one had been a receptionist at the showroom. That had got messy, and after she left, Jim swore he would stay faithful to Margaret. But that was a year ago now, and since then everything had changed.

Billy was settling into a routine at school. Miss Shute took a particular interest in him, and encouraged his reading. She seemed little concerned with other subjects, and this suited him very well. Books, and with them history, were what she cared about. Billy had been biding his time for a few days now, waiting for his moment.

'Miss, I'd like to know about Glastonbury Tor,' he said. 'And King Arthur.'

'A very good idea, Billy. Have you read about King Arthur?'

'No. I know he had a round table, and some knights. And Alan says he's buried in the tor.'

Miss Shute glanced across at Alan. 'Not in the tor, in the abbey.' She looked at Billy for a moment. 'I have just the book for you,' she said. She stepped into the tiny storeroom and returned with a sturdy, green-bound volume. *King Arthur and His Knights of the Round Table*, he read, by Roger Lancelyn Green. 'This will be your next book,' said Miss Shute. 'You must read about Arthur, and Lancelot and Guinevere, and Sir Gawain and the Green Knight, and Sir Galahad and the Holy Grail. This is our heritage, Billy. Do you know what that means?'

'No, miss.'

'It means our past, our history. These are the first stories of Britain. They're wonderful stories, too.'

Billy leafed through the book, gazing at the woodcut illustrations of these magnificent characters. The first chapter was called 'The Two Swords'. He began reading straight away.

At morning break the boys played 'it', racing around the little play-ground. No matter how hard Billy tried to tag Frank Willmott, his long skinny arm would reach out and tag him straight back. Frank's brother Ed came off worst. 'Titch', they called him, though he wasn't much smaller than Billy and Alan. When they stopped for a breather, Frank gave Billy one of his calculating looks.

'You're a swot,' he said.

'No I'm not.'

'And a crawler,' said Les Vowles, who seldom spoke except to echo Frank.

'You've always got your nose in a book.'

'So?'

'So... you're a swot.' Frank paused for a moment. 'What's that book, then, about King Arthur?'

'Well, it's about King Arthur. And his knights.'

'What happens?'

'I've only just started it. Arthur is brought up by Merlin, who's a wizard. Then he pulls a sword out of a stone, and that means he's going to be King of Britain.'

'Just for pulling a sword out of a stone?'

'It's a special sword. It's called Excalibur. And nobody else can pull it out.'

The other boys listened attentively to Billy. He had the sense that he was besting Frank, outwitting him. Who wouldn't want to read these stories of knights and swords and wizards and monsters? Frank looked at each of them in turn. 'Sounds like stuff and nonsense to me,' he said.

'Well it isn't,' said Billy. 'It's good.'

Frank suddenly turned on Les and punched him hard on the arm.

'Ow! What did you do that for?'

'Let's do the Davy Crockett song,' he said. He turned back to Billy. 'I bet you don't know the Davy Crockett song.'

'No.'

Frank smiled archly. 'Come on, lads,' he said, and with that the four boys began to sing:

> 'Born on a mountaintop in Tennessee,
> Killed his ma when he was only three,
> Killed his pa when he was only four,
> And now he's looking for his brother-in-law.
> Davy, Davy Crockett, king of the wild frontier.'

Eager to repeat the joke, they immediately began the verse again. Frank sang lustily, apparently sure of his renewed authority. Billy picked up the words and sang along too. As they filed back into the school, a truce seemed to have been called.

Billy and Sarah walked home at the end of the day, or rather, Sarah walked and Billy ran back and forth and in circles around her. They passed a house that was called Tanyard Cottage.

'Miss Vale lives there,' said Sarah. 'Trish says she's got a hundred cats.'

'A hundred? No she doesn't.'

'She does too.'

'Nobody has a hundred cats.' Billy leaned over the wall and looked into the weedy, overgrown garden. 'Where are they, then?' he said.

'They're all inside,' said Sarah, straining to see. 'She doesn't let them out, in case people steal them.'

Billy could see no sign of any cats. 'Let's ask Mum,' he said, and with that he ran off. For once Sarah followed, and they were both out of breath by the time they got home.

'Does Miss Vale have a hundred cats?' Sarah asked Margaret the moment they came into the kitchen.

'Who is Miss Vale?'

'She's got a hundred cats.'

'*Where* has she got a hundred cats?'

'She lives at Tanyard Cottage, Mum,' said Billy. 'You know, the tumbledown place on the road to school.'

Margaret looked from one to the other for a moment. 'Well, there's only one way to find out how many cats she's got. We'd best pay her a visit.'

'Oh, when?' said Sarah.

'On Saturday morning,' said Margaret decisively. 'It's about time we got to know our neighbours.'

On the way to Tanyard Cottage, Billy climbed the first gate, as he always did now, to take in the view of the tor. A curtain of rain was sweeping across the countryside, the sun breaking through here and there like the beams of a car's headlamps. They had to race to the cottage so as not to get caught in a shower.

They knocked on the door and waited, and after a few moments heard a voice call out 'Coming'.

She seemed to Billy to be old but somehow not old. She had a nest of red hair and piercing green eyes, and her face was caked with white powder. Her dress, a blue smock, was wrinkled and dirty.

'Hello, poppets,' she said.

'Miss Vale?' said Margaret.

'Yes.'

'My name's Margaret Palmer. We've just moved into Coombe.'

Miss Vale raised her hand distractedly and brushed her hair. 'Come in,' she said.

In the barely furnished sitting room Billy was almost overcome by the smell of pee. Did it come from Miss Vale, he wondered, or from the cats? Sarah looked about her, turning from one side to the other in search of any sign of them. Margaret laid her hands on Sarah's shoulders and set her straight.

'Would you like some tea?' said Miss Vale.

'That's very kind of you, but we've just had breakfast.'

They sat down.

'And where have you come from?'

'From Bath.'

'From Bath,' said Miss Vale pensively. 'I used to live in London. And lots of other places.' She paused, seeming to be about to say something more but then thinking better of it. Then she said, 'That was a long time ago, when I was a dancer.'

'You were a dancer?' said Sarah.

'I was a very good dancer.'

Billy sat staring at this colourful creature. In his experience old ladies were not dancers; indeed they weren't anything at all, except old.

'Have you got a hundred cats?' said Sarah in a hushed voice.

'Well, I'm really not sure.' Miss Vale looked about her as if to consider where they might be hiding. 'Shall we count them?'

'Yes, please,' said Sarah.

'They're in the other room,' she said, and rose from the chair. The three of them followed her to the door, which she flung open as if to reveal wonders.

They were everywhere, Miss Vale's cats, on chairs, on tables, in baskets and on the floor. The older ones stared vacantly, while the young ones tumbled towards them. Sarah gasped in astonishment, picking up a tabby kitten, and Billy began counting, a judicious expression forming on his features. 'Thirty-one,' he said eventually. 'No, thirty-two. I think.' Miss Vale cooed at them, appearing not to mind that they were tearing her furniture apart and neglecting the litter trays.

'This one seems to have taken a fancy for you, poppet,' she said to Sarah. 'Would you like to have it?'

'Oh, yes! Can I, Mummy?'

'I'm not sure. We should ask your father first.'

'Please, Mummy. Please.'

Sarah cradled the kitten in her arms, and it purred its way to sleep.

'Very well. But if your father objects it must come straight back, do you understand?'

'He'll love it. Is it a girl or a boy?'

'I've really no idea,' said Miss Vale. 'It's one or the other.'

'I think it's a girl.'

Billy looked at his sister. He was sure he would end up looking after this kitten, just like the hamster Sarah had insisted on having the year before.

'We should be going now,' said Margaret. 'Perhaps we could call on you another time?'

Jim returned to Goody's a few days after his first visit. The girl was there again, and her smile of recognition was intoxicating.

'What's your name?' he said when she brought him his tea.

'Liz,' she replied. 'Liz Burridge.'

'I'm Jim Palmer.'

'I know you are,' she said, fidgeting with her apron strings.

'You do? How's that?'

'Oh, people talk. And you're new around here.'

'What do they say?'

She glanced across at the woman behind the counter, who was looking at her disapprovingly. 'Perhaps I shouldn't say.'

'Well, you have to now, don't you?' he said, teasing her. 'What time do you get off work?'

'Half past five.'

'Me too. How about a drink in the Star?'

An expression of alarm crossed her face. 'Tonight?' she said.

'Why not?'

'I don't think I can.'

'Where's the harm in it?'

'I... I've got to cook supper for my mum and dad.'

'Another day, then.'

'I don't know. Perhaps.'

He paid for his cup of tea and stepped back out into the rain. Moody and irritable, he took up his position behind the counter in the shop. There was nothing for him nowadays, nothing to enjoy, nothing to look forward to.

Over the course of the next few days he found that his thoughts kept on returning to Liz Burridge, and on another damp morning he returned to Goody's determined to try again.

'How about tonight?' he said abruptly as she approached his table.

She tugged at her apron strings and looked out of the window. 'All right,' she said after a few moments.

22

He looked up at her in surprise. 'See you in the Star, then,' he said. 'Half past five.'

'Yes.'

She turned away, and Jim reached into his pocket for some change. He had less than he'd thought. Back in the shop, he spent the afternoon in a state of agitation. How was he going to explain his being late to Margaret? Supper would be on the table by six as usual. Well, he'd have to make something up. A boy from the Cathedral School came in and bought a couple of pairs of socks. Somehow the two shillings ended up in Jim's pocket, and he left the sale off the sheet. He was instantly dismayed by what he had done, but at the same time incapable of undoing it.

After Reg closed up the shop, Jim wheeled his bike to the Star Hotel and found an empty table away from the other drinkers. A blue smoke haze hung in the air, lit up by the last rays of the sun. The Star was where the commercial travellers went, and those farmers who could afford to stay on after market day and have a night away from their wives. There wasn't a woman in sight. When Liz arrived the drinkers stirred momentarily before lapsing back into their torpor. Jim ordered a pint of bitter and a cider.

'Cheers,' he said, and he levelled a candid look at her. There wasn't much she'd been able to do to her appearance since lunchtime, but clearly she had spent some time in front of a mirror. She seemed even prettier to him this evening.

'So what are these things people have been saying about me?' he said.

She smiled cagily, and smoothed down her black skirt. 'That you got into some sort of trouble. That you've come here to get away from it.'

'Is that so? And who exactly is saying these things?'

'That would be telling, wouldn't it?'

Jim took a draught of his beer and set down the glass. 'I'm a bankrupt, Liz, that's all. People don't seem to like bankrupts.'

'How did it happen?' Liz's expression had turned to one of concern.

'I was in the motor trade. I had the Jaguar franchise in Bath.'

'Classy,' she said.

'I had the Austin franchise before, but then I changed. And that's when things started to go wrong.'

'Why?'

'Oh, I don't know. Petrol rationing after Suez didn't help.'

She looked away for a moment, and then back at him. 'This is a bit of a comedown, then,' she said softly.

'Reg Underhill's? You could say that.'

In the corner a foxy-looking man was reading the *Sporting Life* and glancing across at them. Jim gave him a challenging look, and he promptly buried his face in the paper. He turned his attention back to Liz.

'What about you?' he said. 'You're not planning to spend the rest of your days in Goody's, I hope.'

'I'm going to nursing school in Bristol in the spring,' she said. 'I've been filling in since I left school.'

Christ, he thought, how old is she? He'd imagined she was at least twenty, but he must be wrong.

'Did you grow up around here?'

'I was born here. My father runs the International Stores.'

'Like it?'

She shrugged. 'It's no good for people my age. There's nothing to do except go to the Regal on Saturdays. I'll be glad to get out.'

'What goes on at the Regal?'

'Oh, the matinees, you know. Westerns and that. And then sometimes there's music. That's the best. Lonnie Donegan came here in the summer.'

'You like Lonnie Donegan?'

'Not as much as Tommy Steele and Cliff Richard.'

'Big bands are what I like,' said Jim. He gazed down into his glass. 'Glenn Miller, Benny Goodman.'

'Eddie Calvert's coming soon, I think.'

He gave her a mocking smile. 'Eddie Calvert. "Oh Mein Papa". He's all right, I suppose.'

They fell silent for a while.

'I expect you're married,' said Liz, looking away and then back at him in that unnervingly direct way.

'You expect right. Does that bother you?'

'Not if it doesn't bother you,' she said.

He looked into her eyes, and she held his gaze.

'Would you like to go to the Eddie Calvert concert?' he said.

'Yes,' she replied. 'I would.'

Two

At afternoon break, Frank gathered the older boys around him, with Ed tagging along as usual.

'It's scrumping time,' he said solemnly. 'Tomorrow morning, Alton's farm. Everybody in?'

The four of them nodded.

'Where's Alton's farm?' said Billy.

'It's on Southey Lane,' said Alan. 'I'll show you.'

The next morning Alan called by and they set off, heading in a direction that was new to Billy. There were apple orchards everywhere, the trees laden with red and green fruit.

'Do I need anything to carry the apples in?' he said.

'Just your pockets,' said Alan. 'It's not how many you can carry, it's just stealing them that's the fun.'

Frank and Ed and Les were already there, lounging against the wall of Alton's orchard. They climbed over and landed softly in the long grass among the windfall apples. 'The pigs like 'em,' said Ed, and he made a disgusting snuffling noise.

They broke up into two pairs, Frank and Ed and Billy and Alan, while Les was posted as guard. Under one of the smaller trees Ed straddled Frank's shoulders, and Frank raised himself to his full height. Ed began picking apples, first stuffing them into his pockets and then handing them down. Billy and Alan did the same, but Alan seemed very heavy on Billy's shoulders, and it wasn't long before they began to ache.

'I need a rest,' he said.

Alan clambered down. Their pockets were already bulging.

'Fagged so soon?' said Frank.

'Alan's heavier than Ed is,' said Billy.

'No he isn't. I'm just stronger than you, that's all.'

'Well, you're older.'

'Not by much.'

'Yeah,' said Les. 'Frank's stronger'n you. And he's not a crawler, either.'

Ed slipped from Frank's shoulders, and the boys stood in a circle.

Frank was carelessly tossing an apple in his hand, and suddenly he drew back his arm and hurled it at Billy, striking him on the leg. Before Billy knew it, Alan had picked up an apple and thrown it at Frank, narrowly missing his head. As if by some unspoken command, the boys immediately retreated behind the nearest trees, Billy and Alan on one side and Frank, Ed and Les on the other, and began pelting one another with apples.

'This is *war!*' shouted Alan elatedly.

The boys darted out to collect more apples, and then dodged back behind the trees. With only two on their side, Billy and Alan were getting the worst of it. Just as they were beginning to run out, Billy saw a man appear at the gate.

'Oi! What the hell do you lot think you're doing!' he shouted.

The barrage ceased. Frank turned and ran, followed by Ed and Les. 'Let's go the other way,' said Alan, and he and Billy sprinted uphill towards the wood. Behind them they heard Frank and Les arguing about where to get over the wall.

'Frank Willmott,' said the farmer sharply. 'I might have known. Wait till your father hears about this.'

Billy and Alan soon made it to the middle of the wood. They stopped to catch their breath, and Alan started laughing uncontrollably. 'We won, Billy!' he said. 'We won the war!'

He took an apple from his pocket, rubbed it against his shorts, and took a big bite. Straight away he grimaced, and threw the apple into the trees.

'They're not ripe yet,' he said.

'What shall we do with them then?'

'Take 'em home and hide them for a bit.'

Billy had three apples in each of his pockets. He gave Alan two, and they set off for home. Four apples seemed a modest haul, and it didn't occur to Billy to conceal them further. When he appeared in the kitchen his father took one look at him and said, 'What have you been up to?'

'Exploring with Alan.'

'And what have you got in your pockets?'

Billy produced one of the apples.

'Alan's dad gave it to me.'

Jim looked at him sternly. 'Are you quite sure about that?' he said.

26

'Yes.'

Billy always hated telling lies, especially flimsy ones like this.

'I wouldn't want it thought that any son of mine went around stealing things.'

'No,' said Billy weakly, heading for the stairs.

'That's understood, then,' said his father. 'No stealing.'

'Yes, Dad.'

'And no telling tales.'

Margaret invited Reg Underhill and his wife Winifred to dinner, feeling that they owed them an expression of gratitude, both for giving Jim a job and for finding the cottage. She had never known them very well: her father and Reg were not close.

She bought a chicken from Hubert, which in consideration for her feelings he killed and beheaded. But the business of plucking and preparing it seemed to take all day. And then there was the wood stove to deal with: she had by now mastered it for boiling and frying, but grilling was a problem, and roasting an unknown. She packed the children off to bed early, despite their loud protestations, and at half past seven their guests arrived.

Reg was driving back and forth in his shiny black car in an attempt to find a place to park that wasn't muddy. As he got out he took a handkerchief from his pocket and wiped the bonnet.

'What do you think?' he said to Jim, standing back to admire it. 'New from Harris Motors.'

It was a Standard Vanguard. Jim knew it was a 1957 model, and that Reg's describing it as new was at the very least misleading.

'Very nice,' said Jim.

'Now he's doing all right, is Harris.'

They sat around the kitchen table. Jim offered Reg a beer, and Winifred took in the cottage. Like her husband she was neat and sober in her appearance. And also like him, she was short and very broad in the beam.

'Well, this is cosy,' she said to Margaret.

'Oh, it's perfectly fine. We like it.' Margaret stooped to open the door of the stove, sure that the chicken was still quite raw. She pressed a fork into it, and pink juices flowed.

27

'How is Hubert these days?'

'It's hard to tell. He keeps himself to himself. But I'm helping him with the milking one or two days a week.'

'He needs to remarry,' said Reg. 'A man can't live without a woman, especially on a farm.'

'I don't think the marriage prospects are very good around here,' said Margaret. 'Especially for a man in his fifties.'

'And have you met any of your neighbours?' said Winifred.

'Just one, really, apart from people in the shop. A rather odd woman named Miss Vale.'

'Ah, Leonora Vale.' Winifred's eyes flashed mischievously. 'The scarlet woman of Coombe.'

'What do you know about her?'

'Well, she claims to have been in Isadora Duncan's dance school. Then I suppose Isadora got tangled up in that scarf, and that was an end of it.'

'What do you mean she got tangled up in a scarf?' said Reg.

'She was wearing a long scarf and sitting in a sports car, and when it started off the scarf got caught in the back wheel and broke her neck.'

Margaret decided she really must get to know Leonora Vale.

'What about the Latymers?' said Winifred.

'The people in Coombe Hall, you mean?'

'Yes. But I suppose you're unlikely to set eyes on them.'

'Who are they?'

'He owns the Charlton Cider company in Shepton Mallet,' said Reg. 'Married to someone half his age who used to be a television announcer.'

'She's nothing like half his age,' said Winifred.

'She's a rich man's floozy, that's what she is.'

Winifred's eyes flashed again. 'You're just jealous, that's all,' she said, and turned to Margaret. 'Anyway, they stay behind those high walls of theirs, and I don't know anyone who's even so much as spoken to them.'

Margaret busied herself with dinner, willing the chicken to cook. Too soon Jim and Reg had drunk all the beer, and there seemed little left to talk about. Margaret did what she could, but they remained stubbornly silent. She looked again at the chicken. A few hours earlier it had been strutting around the yard; now it seemed to be taking its revenge. Eventually she appealed to Winifred, who inspected it closely and suggested that it be quartered and fried. Jim carved it up and Margaret took out the largest pan. It was past nine by the time they ate.

Now and then Winifred cast her eyes across the table and made as if to speak, but then returned her attention to her plate. Eventually she said to Margaret, 'I expect you've been reading a lot. You always were a great reader.'

'I'm re-reading Jane Austen at the moment. I think I shall do that every few years from now on.'

'You know there's a mobile library, do you, that comes to the village once a month?'

'No, I didn't. Thank you for the tip.'

'On the subject of books,' said Reg, suddenly rousing himself, 'did you hear about the break-in at old man Pettigrew's?'

'You mean Pettigrew the printer?' said Jim.

'Yes. Has a big house out on Bristol Hill. The place was broken into the other night, and all they stole were his old books.'

'They were more than just old books, dear,' said Winifred. 'They were antique books, and Alf Pettigrew's pride and joy.'

'They were probably very valuable,' said Margaret. 'Even my Everyman editions of Austen are worth something these days.'

'Time was you never heard about robberies and that sort of thing in Wells,' said Reg. 'I don't know what we're coming to.'

'Oh, don't be silly,' said Winifred. 'Wells is as quiet as the grave.'

Reg hacked at his chicken crossly. 'It may be for you, Winnie,' he said, 'but you don't have to put up with the school-kids and the Teddy boys. It's bloody mayhem at times, I can tell you.'

Winifred ignored her husband, and turned to Margaret. 'There's an amateur theatrical society I make costumes for,' she said. 'We're putting on Noël Coward's *Private Lives* in March, and you'd be perfect for the part of Amanda. Would you like to come to the auditions?'

'That would be rather difficult,' said Margaret, 'with the children and everything.'

'Yes, dear, of course.'

'But thank you for asking.'

The evening drew on. After a while even Winifred turned in on herself. She doesn't want to risk saying the wrong thing, thought

29

Margaret, and it's so easy to say the wrong thing when things are so wrong in themselves.

Listening to the car drive away, Margaret realized she was exhausted. She started to clear the table, and suddenly burst into tears. Jim put his arms around her and stroked her hair. 'It's all right, Maggie,' he said. 'It's over now.'

———

Jim had been back to Goody's once, but it was awkward, and he decided he'd better find somewhere else to sit at lunchtime. The Eddie Calvert concert was still a week away, and he fought his impatience for it. Liz was occupying his thoughts to an alarming extent.

He walked up the High Street one day to the Star and settled into a chair with a pint of beer and the *Daily Express*. After a while the foxy-looking man he remembered from his evening with Liz entered and sat a few feet away. He began to read his *Sporting Life*, but then he folded it ostentatiously, as if trying to attract Jim's attention. Jim looked over, and the man nodded at him. Jim nodded back, but returned to his paper.

'Afternoon,' the man said, in Jim's direction but not exactly to him.

'Afternoon,' said Jim.

'Mind if I join you?'

Jim had no particular desire to talk, but was unable to summon the will to resist. 'If you like,' he said.

The man picked up his glass and paper and slid into a chair next to him.

'Gordon Towker,' he said.

'Jim Palmer.'

'Saw you here with the piece from Goody's the other day.'

Jim stiffened. 'Piece?' he said.

'You know, Liz Burridge. All right, isn't she?'

Jim was already regretting having spoken to him. He had a thin, sharp face, and a lipless mouth. He was losing his black hair, and what there was of it was plastered close to his skull. Jim looked at him for a moment without saying anything.

'Look here,' said Towker, 'I don't mean anything by it. She's just a bit of all right, that's all.'

'You could say that. I'm a married man, though.'

'Of course you are,' he said, with an expression Jim found hard to fathom.

They both took draughts of their beer.

'Working in Underhill's, then?' said Towker.

'That's right.'

'I've got a shop myself. On St Cuthbert Street.'

'What do you sell?'

'Oh, whatever comes along. Towker's Toys and Games, it's called. But I'll sell pretty much anything I think I can get rid of. Drop by some time and I'll show you around.'

'Thanks.'

They sat for a while looking at the other drinkers clustered by the bar.

'So what were you doing before you came here?' said Towker.

'I expect you know. Everyone else seems to.'

Towker smiled evasively. 'Yeah, I know. You had a Jaguar garage and it went bust.'

'So why ask?' said Jim.

'Just trying to be civil,' said Towker with a shrug.

'All right. I'm sorry.' Jim extended his hand and shook Towker's. 'Some people can be a bit funny about it, that's all.'

'Not me, mate. I know what it's like to be down on your luck.' Towker paused, and then added, 'I'm unlucky too.'

'You are?'

He tossed the *Sporting Life* onto a chair. 'Unlucky with the gee-gees, unlucky with the ladies. I even got sunk in the war.'

'You were in the navy?'

'Merchant marine. Atlantic convoys, and then the Murmansk Run. Froze my bollocks off.'

'Where were you sunk?'

'Off southern Ireland. We got picked up pretty quick by a destroyer, though. It wasn't so bad.'

'I was in Ireland during the war. Sat it out in an RAF signals camp in the north.'

'Everything was simple in those days,' said Towker. 'Not like now.'

'I suppose so,' said Jim. 'You wouldn't want to go back to them, though, would you?'

'Crikey, no.' Towker drained his glass. 'Well, nice to meet you.

31

Maybe I'll see you in here another day. And if you've ever got anything you want to sell, just let me know.'

'I haven't got a single thing to sell,' said Jim. 'But thanks for the offer.'

———————

On a grey, chilly morning, Margaret changed into the smartest skirt and jumper she still possessed and set off for Tanyard Cottage. She wanted to tell Leonora Vale what a success the kitten had been, that Sarah was now inseparable from it. She had christened it Lucy, even though none of them could tell what sex it was. It slept in a cardboard box by the stove, and was not permitted to leave the kitchen. Jim had seemed remarkably tolerant of it, but he drew the line at its sharing Sarah's bed.

Autumn was well along, and the leaves were turning. Margaret drew deeply on the cold, pure air. Mornings like this brought back memories of her days on the farm near Midsomer Norton during the war. That time seemed dream-like now. Everything had been potential: the war would end, they would win, a man would sweep her off her feet, and that would be that. And all those things happened; but that hadn't quite been that after all.

Miss Vale appeared not to recognize Margaret at first. Then she said, 'Come in, poppet,' and turned back into the house. The stench of the place seemed if anything stronger than it had been before. Miss Vale was wearing the same dirty blue smock she had worn on Margaret's first visit.

'Sarah loves her kitten,' she said as they sat down.

'Sarah?'

'My daughter. You gave her a kitten when we called last week.'

'Ah yes. Would she like some more?'

'Thank you, but I think perhaps one is enough.'

'One is never enough of anything. Surely you must know that.'

Margaret looked around the stuffy room. Everything about it expressed the solitariness of this woman. There was no decoration or memento that said who she was.

'I'm not sure,' said Margaret.

'Oh yes. The Platonic ideal. The unity of the whole. Would you like a cup of tea?'

'Thank you.'

Margaret followed her into the kitchen. The fire in the stove was almost out, and it took an age for the kettle to boil.

'You said the other day that you'd been a ballet dancer,' said Margaret after a while.

'Not ballet, *dance*. Ballet is a false and preposterous art, hardly an art at all.' Miss Vale shuffled about the kitchen as she spoke, and her hand shook slightly as she poured tea into the cups. 'Whereas dance is the expression of truth and beauty through the instrument of the human body.'

'Yes, of course.'

'That's what Isadora taught us, and she was the greatest dancer the world has ever known.'

'You actually studied with Isadora Duncan?'

'I was one of her earliest pupils. She tried to set up a school in England, but she failed, and my parents sent me to Berlin to join her there.'

'How old were you?'

'Oh, about eight, as I recall.'

Her hand went continually to her hair. Now and then she would fix her glittering eyes on Margaret's and hold them for the longest time.

'That's very young, hardly older than Sarah.'

'Well, things were different then. And my parents were devoted to Isadora and her ideas.'

'What was she like?'

'She was like an angel. She wasn't really one of us. When she danced in those gauzy dresses she was just other-worldly.'

They returned to the sitting room and sat down again in the lumpy armchairs.

'And she taught you?'

'Well, she did when she was there. But she was usually travelling, especially after she met Paris Singer. We were taught mostly by her governesses.'

'Who was Paris Singer?'

'The sewing-machine heir. He gave her all the money for the schools. They had a child, but he drowned, poor thing, along with her daughter.' She wrapped the smock closely around her waist, hugging herself as she did so.

'I had no idea. She seems to have had a tragic life.'

'She was beyond tragedy,' said Miss Vale emphatically. 'Everything was sacrificed to her art.'

'How long did you stay with her school?'

'Oh, eight years or more. I was teaching the younger ones myself by the time I left. We lived in a beautiful villa near Beaulieu for most of the time. Then a couple of years after war broke out Isadora moved the school to America, and I decided to go to London.'

Margaret hesitated for a moment, and then said, 'I do hope you don't mind my asking you all these questions.'

'Not at all, poppet. I can tell you're an artist too.'

'I'm not an artist, I'm afraid. I wish I could say I were.'

'You may not think so, but I see it in you,' said Miss Vale.

'I can't imagine how. I mean... it's very kind of you to say so; but I'm simply a wife and a mother.'

'Isadora was a wife and a mother.'

'And a great dancer, as you said.'

Miss Vale gazed at Margaret intently for a few moments. 'So what happened?' she said.

'What happened?'

'How did a family like yours come to be living at Fosse's Farm?'

Margaret hesitated and then said, 'Oh, my husband had some troubles.'

'What sort of troubles?'

'He had a business that failed.'

'And is he a good husband?'

She felt both discomfited and somehow gratified by this directness. 'Of course he is,' she said.

'Men are often not at their best when they're in trouble.'

'No, perhaps not. But he's a good man.'

'I've no doubt he is.'

Margaret returned her stare. 'I ought to be going,' she said. 'There's a lot to do.'

'You must come back,' said Leonora Vale. 'I like you.'

'Let's go to the pub,' said Jim one Sunday morning. 'I feel cooped up in here.'

Neither Margaret nor Sarah wanted to join them, so Jim and Billy set out alone for the Fourways Inn. Billy chose a place in the garden from where they could see the tor shimmering in the morning light. They sat quietly for a while. Lately there had been an awkwardness between them that neither knew how to dispel.

'Tell me what you've been reading in those books of yours,' said Jim at last.

'About Glastonbury?'

'Yes.'

Billy's face assumed an expression of great earnestness. He stroked his upper lip with his forefinger, composing himself.

'Well, there were Druids and people like that, when it was an island. Then there was Joseph. Not Jesus's father, another one. He was called Joseph of something. It's a hard word starting with A. Anyway, he brought the Holy Grail to Glastonbury.'

'What was the Holy Grail meant to be, exactly?'

'It was a cup. Jesus and the disciples had drunk from it. Then Joseph collected some of Jesus's blood in it, when he was on the cross. It was a special cup. He also had a stick, and when he stuck it in the ground it became a bush, with lots of flowers.'

'A hawthorn bush,' said Jim.

'You know that bit. It's still there, isn't it?'

'Well, a bush of some sort will be there.'

Billy waited for something more from his father, but it didn't come. 'Anyway,' he said eventually, 'Arthur's knights wanted to find the Holy Grail. They looked all over, and then Sir Galahad found it. But as soon as he found it he died and went to heaven.'

'What happened to the Holy Grail?'

'I think they lost it again. Only Sir Galahad really found it.'

Jim looked away into the distance. 'What do you think that means, that Galahad would die and go to heaven as soon as he found the Holy Grail?'

Billy screwed up his face and thought for a moment. 'It means he found it. He'd been looking for it for a long time. They all had. And then he found it.'

'So when you find what you're looking for, everything's over?'

'Yes, sort of.'

Jim turned away from him again. 'I'd say those stories about Joseph and Arthur and his lot are poppycock,' he said.

'No they're not.'

'They're myths, Billy. Do you know what a myth is? Something people make up so as to comfort themselves.'

'But what's wrong with that?'

Jim gazed down into his glass. 'What's wrong with it?' he said. 'It makes people content with what they've got.'

'Isn't that a good thing?'

'It depends. In the case of you and me, it's not a good thing at all.'

'Why?'

'Because we've got nothing, that's why.'

The expression on his father's face was hard now, and it frightened Billy.

'Let's go there and find out if those stories are true,' he said.

'We'd need a car.'

Billy glanced back at the tor. It seemed to be further away every time he looked at it.

'Why don't we have a car any more?' he said eventually.

'Because I don't sell them any more.'

'But lots of people who don't sell them have them, don't they?'

'Oh, I don't know what I'm saying.' Jim paused, and then tried again. 'We haven't got as much money as we used to.'

'Will we ever have one again?'

'I hope so.'

'I liked the smell of them. Especially the Jaguar.'

His father's features softened. 'I liked the smell of them too,' he said. 'All that walnut and leather.'

'If you sell a lot of clothes, perhaps we'll have enough money for one then.'

Jim sighed. 'I'd have to sell plenty of clothes to buy a Jaguar, Billy. A whole mountain of them.'

When Jim next dropped by the Star for a pint, Gordon Towker was sitting in the corner. He sat down beside him.

'Saintly Place,' said Towker.

'A saintly place?' said Jim. 'The Star?'

'No. In the three forty-five at Chepstow. Feel like a flutter?'

'I'm no good at betting,' said Jim. 'Never have been.'

'Well hang on while I phone through my bet. Then maybe you'd like to see the shop?'

Jim watched as Towker stalked out of the room and to the phone box. What a mug, he thought. Did anyone ever make any money betting on horses?

When Towker returned they walked to his shop. He unlocked the front door and swung the sign to 'open'. It was a sort of den, musty and with very little light, and cluttered from floor to ceiling. Jim noticed an old Dansette record player, a transistor radio, boxes of fireworks, and piles of *Picture Posts*, *Beanos* and *Dandys*. There were spare parts for bicycles, Subbuteo table-football games, Hornby train sets. And books, lots of them, some on shelves and others in stacks on the floor. Jim picked one up. *Young England*, it read on the cover, and inside, 'An Illustrated Annual for Boys Throughout the English-Speaking World'.

The stack of books toppled, and Jim made to pick them up. 'Where do you get this stuff?' he said.

'Oh, all over. People around here know what I'm in the market for.'

'Do you ever sell any of it?'

Towker looked hurt. 'What do you mean, do I ever sell any of it?' he said. 'How do you think I live?'

'Sorry. It's just that… well, there's a lot here.'

'Ever occurred to you that there are six bloody schools in this town?'

'Yes, but I thought they were for well-off kids.'

'You'd be surprised. Tight bastards, some people, even if they do send their kids to fancy schools.'

Jim looked above his head. Model aeroplanes hung by strings from the ceiling.

'I'll do all right this week,' said Towker, 'selling Halloween stuff. Then it's Guy Fawkes Night. And then before you know it it'll be Christmas. There's always something going on.'

Towker began to pick up the books. What did he do in here all day? Jim wondered.

'I'd better be getting back,' he said. 'Thanks for showing me around.'

'I'll be seeing you in the Star, then,' said Towker.

Farmer Alton had confronted Frank Willmott's father with the facts of his crime, and Frank had been given a thick ear. He had been surly with the other boys since. At break one morning Alan was telling them about the Biggles book he was reading. Billy could tell he was trying to mend things.

'It's called *Biggles Defies the Swastika*,' he said. 'It's fantastic. He gets trapped in Norway when the Jerries invade. He dresses up in a German uniform and pretends to be a Gestapo officer. Then he and Algy get caught by Biggles's enemy, Von somebody.'

'Do they get away?' said Les.

'Don't know yet, I haven't got that far.'

''Course they'll get away,' said Frank. 'It's Biggles, isn't it? He always wins in the end.'

'Anyway, it's smashing.'

Frank turned to Billy and said, 'What did your dad do in the war?'

'He was in the RAF,' said Billy.

'Oh yeah? My dad drove a tank. He was with Monty in North Africa. I bet he killed more Jerries than your dad did.'

'I don't know how many Jerries my dad killed. But he was really brave.'

'I bet my dad was braver than yours.'

'No he wasn't.'

'Yes he was.'

'He wasn't, so there.'

'Prove it.'

'How?'

'In a fight. You and me. The winner's dad is the bravest.'

Billy looked at Frank. He was in for a fight, he knew it: the time had come. But Frank was bigger and stronger, and he was bound to lose.

'All right, then,' he said.

The other boys backed away, chanting 'fight, fight, fight', and then 'oih, oih, oih'. Frank raised his fists, and Billy did the same. Suddenly Frank leaped forward and lashed out, catching Billy painfully on the side of the face. Billy had never used fists before: whenever he'd had fights at the Unicorn they'd always been wrestling bouts.

Frank moved in again, this time punching Billy in the chest. Billy quickly realized he was beaten, but knew too that he must not give up just yet. He launched himself at Frank, pushing him to the ground, and fell on top of him. But Frank simply rolled them both over, strad-dling Billy and twisting his arm behind his back.

'Submit?' he said.

Billy was wincing with pain, but he said nothing. Frank pressed his arm even further up his back.

'Submit?'

'Submit.'

Frank climbed off him, triumph lighting up his face. Billy got up and dusted himself off.

'So, my dad's braver than yours,' said Frank. 'That proves it.'

Billy said nothing. He looked at Alan as if to appeal for his support, but it was clear that Alan was unable to give it.

'You have to say it,' said Frank, 'otherwise I'll clock you one again. My dad's braver than yours.'

'All right,' said Billy. 'Your dad's braver than mine.' He turned away from the other boys and tried to hold back his tears.

The day before the concert, Jim set off for work and then abruptly turned back. He walked through the kitchen, muttered, 'forgot some-thing,' to Margaret, and went upstairs to the children's room. Taking Billy's Dinky toy sets from the cupboard, he hid them under his coat, and without another word left the house and set off for Wells.

During his lunch break, he went to the Star Hotel and looked in on the bar. Towker wasn't there, so he walked on to his shop. He was inside, leafing through an *Eagle* comic. Jim took out the Dinky toy-boxes and laid them on the counter.

'My boy's,' he said. 'He's grown out of them. What'll you give me?'

Towker opened the boxes. One contained the five racing cars and the other five sports cars, including an MG, an Austin Healey and a Jaguar XK120. Towker examined them closely. They were indestructi-ble, these cars, and didn't bear a single mark, despite the many accidents Billy had visited on them.

'Five bob,' said Towker.

'Each?'

'No, for both.'

'Come on, Towker, these things are valuable. They're gift sets, not just odd cars.'

39

'Seven.'

Jim looked down at the cars. He tried to remember what they had cost him three years ago or whenever it was he'd bought them. A lot more than seven shillings, certainly.

'Ten,' he said.

'Seven bob,' said Towker, turning his attention back to the *Eagle*. 'Take it or leave it.'

'Oh, all right then.'

Towker went into the back of the shop and returned with the money.

'Got anything else like these?'

Jim pocketed the coins. 'I'll talk to my boy and let you know,' he said.

He met Liz in the Crown for a drink before the concert. She had dolled herself up, with too much make-up and lacquer in her hair, and she was wearing a tight-fitting green dress. When she took off her coat Jim ran his eye down her lovely figure.

'Don't stare,' said Liz, smiling. 'It's rude.'

Jim shrugged. 'You look great, that's all,' he said. He watched her sip her cider. She was excited, he could tell. They walked to the Regal cinema. An oddly assorted crowd was gathering outside: middle-aged people, young couples, and even a lugubrious gang of Teddy boys. Jim brandished his tickets, and they made their way to their seats.

After a long wait the members of Eddie Calvert's band appeared and took up their places on the stage. There was a certain look to them all. They wore evening dress and slicked back their hair, and many of them had pencil moustaches. A chorus of four men and four women singers stepped out, flanking the musicians. Calvert himself bounded on stage, and immediately the band struck up the first number. A ripple of applause spread around the audience. Jim leaned over towards Liz and whispered, '"Zambesi".'

They ran through their repertoire in a way that seemed pretty mechanical to Jim, the band members standing for their solos, the singers crooning, Calvert lifting his eyebrows in time with the phrases he played on his trumpet. In the cha-cha rhythms of 'Cherry Pink and Apple Blossom White', Jim thought they might fly off his face. The melodies flowed, and Jim's thoughts drifted towards the music he loved, towards Jimmy Dorsey's 'Tiger Rag' and Count Basie's 'One O'Clock Jump'. This was so tame by comparison. He looked across at Liz, and saw that she was rapt. Whatever else, it was good to have a pretty girl at his side.

The concert ended with Calvert's signature tune, 'Oh Mein Papa', a dirge that had somehow been a number-one hit. Everyone applauded loudly, and the band took several bows. As they made their way out of the cinema Jim was aware of the excited chatter around him. Evidently this sort of thing was sufficiently rare in Wells to cause a stir.

He took Liz to the Swan Hotel, calculating that he had just about enough to cover dinner provided they didn't drink too much. They were shown to their table by a spotty youth in an ill-fitting suit, and Jim ordered two glasses of white wine.

'I've never been to the Swan,' said Liz. 'Well, I've never been to a restaurant, not what you'd call a proper restaurant anyway.'

'It's the best place in town,' said Jim.

'I expect you've been to lots of places like this.'

'I suppose I have. But not for a while.'

There were very few other diners, and Jim was glad they would not be overheard: the illicit pleasures of the evening were tinged with feelings of guilt and anxiety he was unable to banish.

'So you enjoyed it,' he said.

'I loved it. I mean, it's not Tommy Steele, but it's just so good to hear music, isn't it, real music?'

'The radio and records don't give you that… oh, I don't know, that shivery feeling.'

'Have you heard a lot of bands?'

'Not really. Bath was never much of a place for the kind of music I like. The best concert I ever went to was in London.'

'Who did you see?'

'Louis Armstrong, at the Palladium. Now that was a concert.'

Their food came. Jim was famished, and began eating straight away. He continued to do most of the talking throughout dinner. He was enjoying himself, enjoying impressing this girl with his stories. She made him feel he'd led an interesting life, that the state of affairs he now found himself in was merely temporary, and would one day add to his fund of anecdotes.

After dinner he walked Liz to her parents' house. All the lights were out. 'I don't suppose I can come in?' he said.

'No, I don't think that would be a good idea.' She hesitated for a moment, and then said, 'Next week they're away.'

Jim looked at her intently, and kissed her wide mouth. She held back for a moment, and then folded herself into him. He kissed her again, prolonging it until she broke off. 'Good night,' she said, and turned towards the door.

'Until next week, then,' said Jim.

Three

In the school yard there was a tacit understanding that since the fight some sort of order had been restored. But Billy was burning with resentment, certain that he was better than Frank, just not sure how to show it.

'Alan,' he said quietly as they leaned against the wall of the playground. 'Could we get to Glastonbury Tor, just you and me?'

'You mean walk?'

'No, it's too far. Could we hitch a ride?'

Alan's eyes gleamed. 'Sure. We could walk to the main road and stick out our thumbs. Somebody's bound to pick us up, I reckon.'

'We'll have to pretend to our parents that we're going somewhere else.'

'Easy. We're collecting pennies for the guy.'

Alan called for him at the weekend. Billy was sure this was the bravest thing he'd ever done. On the main road between Walton and Glastonbury there were very few cars in either direction, and none of them stopped. After half an hour they sat down at the side of the road and began to throw stones into a stream, turning back every time they heard the sound of a car.

'We're too little,' said Alan. 'They don't think we mean it.'

'What if we stand in the middle of the road?'

'No fear.'

They stared into the water.

'Why's it so important to go to the tor?' said Alan.

'I don't know... it's like Kirrin Island is for the Famous Five. It's a special place.'

'But why is it a special place?'

Billy looked towards the tor. It was encircled by mist today, and seemed to float in the air.

'What about all the stories?' he said. 'Why have so many things happened there? It must be the most special place in England.'

A pale blue Morris Minor appeared, and it slowed and came to a halt. For a moment Billy's spirits soared. The door opened and a woman stepped out.

'Crumbs,' said Alan. 'It's Mrs Hardie, the vicar's wife.'

'Alan Tyler?' said the woman. 'What on earth are you doing?'

'Just going for a walk,' said Alan.

'Then why were you trying to flag down a car?'

'We were tired,' said Billy.

Mrs Hardie frowned at them. 'Then you would do better to try getting a ride in the right direction. Come on, I'll take you home.'

From the moment Mrs Hardie's car pulled up outside the cottage it became impossible to maintain the deception of collecting pennies for the guy. His father sent Billy to his room, where he waited for ages before he heard footsteps on the stairs. Worse than any punishment was this time of dread, this time of rehearsing excuses and wondering what his father would say to him.

'Let's get two things straight,' said Jim, his face flushed with anger. 'Firstly, you don't lie to your mother and me about where you're going, and you never try to cadge lifts. God knows who might have picked you up: there are some very strange people around these days. And secondly, you must get out of your head this stupid idea of going to the tor. It's only a bloody hill, after all.'

Billy usually knew better than to answer back; but today he felt stubborn, and refused to be cowed.

'It's not just a hill,' he said. 'And those stories aren't poppycock, like you said.'

'Listen, young man. If I hear any more nonsense about the tor, it's going to be out of bounds for ever.'

Billy lay in bed that night unable to sleep, images of Glastonbury teeming in his mind. I will go there, he said to himself, I will go there.

Margaret stopped by Leonora Vale's cottage on the way to the village shop and gave her some fresh milk for the cats.

'How sweet of you.'

'What do you feed them, usually?'

'Oh, scraps, mostly. They take care of themselves. They are hunters, after all. You should see what some of them bring in. One dragged a vole back once.'

They went through the ritual of making tea. When they had sat down Miss Vale said, 'Well, how are you?'

Margaret was unable to suppress a sigh. 'I'm all right, I suppose,' she said. She looked across at Miss Vale, who was studying her closely. 'Well no, I'm not all right.' The ghost of a smile hovered around her mouth. 'Do you know the radio programme called *Mrs Dale's Diary*?'

'I listen to it every day.'

'You know how she's always saying, "I'm worried about Jim"?'

'And she has plenty to worry about.'

Margaret absently brushed cat hairs from her skirt. 'Well, I'm worried about Jim,' she said.

'Of course you are. Jim's worried about Jim.'

Margaret was startled. 'You know?'

'I don't know anything, except what I see in you. I've never set eyes on your husband. But he's lost, isn't he?'

With these words Margaret simply crumpled. It was as though all the anxiety and sadness of the past months were being released at once. Leonora Vale sat down beside her on the threadbare settee and put her arm around her shoulders. 'Now, poppet, you're going to tell me all about it,' she said. 'But first I think you need a little something.'

She went into the kitchen and returned with a hip flask, pouring dark brown liquid into the milky tea. 'Have a slug of that,' she said, and then she poured even more into her own cup. Margaret drank the bitter stuff and wiped her eyes. They sat in silence for a while, Leonora Vale watching Margaret thoughtfully.

'He's never had a strong sense of who he is, that's the problem. He sees himself as the world reflects him back.'

'Most people do.'

'But with Jim it's worse. Anyway, when things were going his way he was fine. Oh, he was arrogant sometimes; but he was settled in himself. Since the bankruptcy he seems… well, as you say, he's lost.'

'He needs your help.'

'But how do I give it to him? He's becoming a stranger to me. We don't…' Margaret looked up at her and knew that nothing less than the truth would do. 'We don't make love any more. We barely talk to each other.'

'Forgive me, but this is a very common experience. All men and women go through something like this at some time in their lives.'

45

'It's happened to you?'

Leonora Vale smiled wryly. 'It's happened to me,' she said. 'A few times.'

'You were married?'

'Just once. Marriage didn't seem the be all and end all in the world I lived in. But one man did persuade me to throw my lot in with him.'

'Who was he?'

'His name was Lawrence James. He was a choreographer.' She smiled again. 'He literally swept me off my feet.'

'How long were you married?'

'Four years. But we were often not even in the same place. And for him it was an open marriage.'

'Open?'

'He could sleep with whomever he pleased, and I wasn't to mind.'

'And did you mind?'

'I minded terribly. We were supposed to have yielded to an over-powering love for each other, a love that would be equal to anything. We were Tristan and Iseult. But it wasn't long before I knew he was making love to someone else.'

'How did you know?'

Leonora Vale gave her an enigmatic look. 'You just know, don't you?'

Margaret returned her gaze for a moment. 'I've usually known,' she said, 'when Jim has been seeing someone else.'

'Of course you have. They can't hide it.'

Margaret was getting a taste for her whisky-laced tea. She held the mug in both hands and rocked slowly back and forth. How strangely comforting was this eccentric woman.

When it was time to go, Leonora Vale walked with her to the gate. She took Margaret's head in her hands and gently kissed her forehead. 'You must talk to him,' she said.

It was becoming something of a habit now for Jim to go to the Star for a pint at lunchtime. At first he had promised himself this would be an occasional treat, but his need to get away from Reg and the shop, and for some sort of company, drove him there almost every day. Towker was always lounging around. Jim had become a little wary of him since he'd sold the Dinky toys, and sometimes he deliberately sat as far away from him as he could. He did so today, but soon Towker collected his pint and came over to join him.

'Afternoon,' he said.

'Hello,' said Jim.

Towker methodically rolled a cigarette. 'Everything all right?' he said eventually.

'As well as can be expected.'

'Hear you were at the Eddie Calvert concert.'

Jim sensed trouble looming. 'Yes, I was.'

'Good, was it?' He picked some shreds of tobacco from his lower lip.

'It was good for what it was. He's not exactly my sort of thing.'

'She enjoyed it, did she?'

Jim thought for a moment how best to handle this. Dismissively, he decided. 'Yes, she did. Calvert's a bit old-fashioned for her, though.'

'They just like being taken out though, don't they, women? Like being shown a good time.'

Towker took a silver lighter from his pocket and made several attempts to light his meagre cigarette. Jim tried to keep his temper. He knew he was fooling himself if he thought his seeing Liz might go unnoticed.

'Expensive, though,' said Towker when Jim didn't reply.

'Expensive?'

Towker finally lit the cigarette, and drew on it deeply. 'Women,' he said. 'Cost the bloody earth.'

'I suppose they do.'

Jim was about to drain his glass and stand up when Towker spoke again.

'I don't suppose you've got anything else to sell me like those Dinkys?'

'No, I haven't. I'll ask the boy some time, but nothing at the moment.'

Towker glanced across the room. Something held Jim back, he couldn't say what.

'But you could use some cash, I expect.'

'We all could.'

'Yeah, but you especially, if you don't mind my saying so. What's Underhill paying you?'

'I don't think that's any of your business.'

'Sorry. But you know what I mean – kids, and then a night out now and then.'

47

'Yes, I know what you mean.' Once again Jim made to leave, but stayed fast in his chair.

'You wouldn't want to do a freelance job, would you, on the side?'

Towker was by now looking thoroughly shifty. Jim felt a wave of revulsion pass over him. 'What sort of job?' he heard himself saying.

'Driving. Delivering something.'

'Why can't you do it yourself?'

'I don't have a car. Can't drive, anyway.'

'Well I don't have a car either, in case you hadn't noticed.'

'But you could get one, couldn't you? You could borrow one?'

Jim sat back wearily. 'What are you talking about?' he said.

'I've just got something needs delivering to London, that's all. Something I can't sell in the shop.'

'What is it?'

'Now that would be telling.'

'Yes it bloody well would. If you think I'm going to run an errand for you without even knowing what it is, you can think again.'

Towker sucked on his cigarette. 'Twenty quid,' he said.

'Twenty quid?'

'For a day's outing to London.'

Jim looked down at his hands. Twenty pounds was almost three weeks' wages.

'What if I said yes?' said Jim. 'What if I got hold of a car?'

Towker exhaled sharply. 'You come round to the lock-up,' he said, 'load some packages, drive them to an address I'll give you in Bloomsbury, and I give you twenty quid in cash.'

Jim looked angrily at Towker. 'Fuck off,' he said, and he stood up and strode out into the street.

———

Billy crept down the stairs and out into the yard. It was dark in the mornings now, an enveloping dark he hadn't known when they lived on the edge of a city. Hubert Fosse had set up hurricane lamps in the milking shed, which hissed and spat now and then. He had been washing down the cows, and they steamed in the dim light.

Billy stood in the doorway watching his mother rhythmically milking a cow. It was restless, and stamped its hind hooves. Margaret spoke

48

to it soothingly but was unable to calm it. Eventually she turned and saw him staring at her through the gloom.

'Billy?' she said.

'Hello, Mum.'

'Why are you down so early?'

'I couldn't sleep.'

She twisted herself around to look at him.

'Are you all right?'

Billy stood for a few moments without speaking. There were things he had wanted to tell someone for quite a while, but now that the moment had come he felt tongue-tied. Finally he said, 'Mum, what do you do when someone doesn't like you very much?'

Margaret stopped milking and turned on the stool to face him. 'Come here,' she said. Billy stepped towards her, and she held out her hands to him.

'Who doesn't like you?'

'There's a boy…' Billy took a deep breath. 'There's a boy called Frank Willmott at school. We had a fight. He said his dad was braver than mine.'

'Well that's exactly the sort of silly thing that boys say, isn't it? It doesn't mean anything.'

'But he really doesn't like me, Mum.'

She stroked Billy's hands in hers.

'Then you must be brave,' she said. 'Why do you think he doesn't like you?'

'I don't know. Because I read books. And because he thinks I'm a liar.'

'A liar?'

'Yes, when I talk about what we used to do before we came here.'

'I expect our old life must seem strange to someone like Frank Willmott,' said Margaret. 'You must think carefully about what you say. You haven't been boasting, have you?'

'No, Mum. But I did talk about the Jaguars.'

'Well there you are, then.' She raised a hand to his hair and brushed it back. 'Things are very different now, Billy. It's best to try to forget how they were before. You do like it here in the country, don't you?'

'Yes, I do. It's just that…' He looked at her questioningly. 'Mum, why did we come here? Why didn't we just stay where we were?'

49

His mother sighed. 'Your father explained that to you, Billy. He had to close the garage and find another job, and this is where he found one.'

'But why did he have to close the garage?'

'Well, because…' Margaret hesitated. 'Because he made some mistakes.'

Billy looked around the shed, at the cows that flanked them on all sides. 'I don't think Frank believes we ever had a garage,' he said.

'It doesn't matter. You'd be better off simply not talking about it. Try to talk to him about the things he's interested in.'

'I don't think he's interested in anything, except pushing other boys around.'

'Every school has its Frank, doesn't it? The Unicorn must have had a Frank.'

'I don't remember. There wasn't anyone who hated me there.'

She rested her hands on his shoulders. 'He doesn't hate you, Billy, no one hates you. He's just a boy. You have to show him that you're brave, and then he'll like you.'

'How do I show him I'm brave?'

'By being yourself. And by not getting into fights.'

'I didn't want to fight.'

'Then you should have turned your back.'

Billy looked down at the ground. 'I'll try,' he said. 'I'll try to be brave.'

'Good.' His mother hugged him, and stood up. 'Now, I have two more cows to milk. Why don't you go and lay the table for breakfast?'

Billy ran out into the yard. The faint light of dawn led him back to the cottage, where his father and sister were still asleep. The image of his mother patiently drawing milk from the cow's udder stayed vividly in his mind.

In the crowded bar of the Crown, Jim sat with Liz in a glazed silence. The knowledge that her parents' house stood empty not far away was strangely daunting to him. There didn't seem to be much to talk about, and they found themselves taking an excessive interest in the old photographs and prints on the walls. The publican glanced over at them now and then, smiling crookedly. We attract attention, Jim thought, there's no getting away from it. Did he seem that much older than her? Chewing his sausages and baked beans, he found himself thinking back to his conversation with Gordon Towker, to the things he'd said about women and money. They stepped out into the chilly night, and Jim took Liz by the hand as they walked to her home.

She ushered him into the sitting room, looking up at him shyly as he entered. There was a brown three-piece suite with white anti-macassars, a green-tiled fireplace, an ornate dark-wood clock on the mantelpiece, and a small Ekco television set. China cats and dogs sat on the surfaces of tables and shelves, along with photographs, mostly of Liz as a girl. She was an adored only child, it was easy to see.

'Tea?' she said.

'Have you got anything stronger?'

Liz went into the kitchen and reappeared with a bottle of Cyprus sherry.

'Tea, then,' said Jim.

When she returned she perched herself on the other end of the settee. Jim was tense, and unsure of himself. In the old days he would have been master of a situation like this. Eventually he laid down his cup and slid along the settee towards her, putting an arm around her shoulders and kissing her tentatively. She responded readily, raising a hand to his face and pressing her mouth to his. 'Let's go upstairs,' he said. He hated the grapplings of the settee, the awkward baring of a breast or raising of a skirt, the breaking off in a fluster so as to get to the bed. A man should undress a woman slowly and tenderly.

Liz led him up to her room. The bed was very narrow.

'What about your parents' room?'

'Oh no, I couldn't.'

She switched on the bedside lamp and turned to face him. They embraced and kissed again, and Jim began to take off her blouse and skirt. The outlines of her body were soft in the shadows, her skin creamy and warm. Jim suddenly felt a hunger he hadn't known in a long time. She lay on the bed, and he hurriedly undressed. When they were naked he forgot everything he had said to himself downstairs, everything he had ever known about this act except its culmination. His urgency made him clumsy, and Liz even had to remind him to put on a rubber. It was over very quickly.

They lay for a while, Jim resting his head on her shoulder, unable to look her in the eye. This was what you did with a tart, he thought, this

51

taking and using. But Liz was a sweet, trusting and inexperienced girl.

'It's all right,' she said, running her hand through his hair.

'No it's not, Liz. That might as well have been my first time.'

'Don't be silly.' She kissed him lightly.

Jim raised himself on his elbow and gazed down at her.

'Except my first time, I couldn't even get it up.'

She laughed, and kissed him again. 'Next time will be different,' she said.

He left soon after, and walked back to Underhill's to collect his bicycle. As he cycled out of town he rehearsed the conversation he would have with Margaret when he got home, the lies about another night out with the lads from the Star. He imagined her curled up by the fireplace with her book. And he wondered what she might be thinking, about him, about the children, about everything.

———

On Guy Fawkes Night they set off for the village. Billy insisted on holding the torch, even though there was a full moon and it really wasn't necessary. He shone it into the hedges and trees, and up into the sky. 'It's like an umbrella of light,' he said.

There was a crowd of people milling around under the apple trees, and at the top of the huge bonfire a gaunt-looking guy sat strapped to a chair. A group of children were chanting, 'Guy, guy, guy, Stick him up on high; Hang him on a lamp post, And leave him there to die.'

They saw the Misses Shute, and walked over to them.

'Well, Billy and Sarah,' said the thin Miss Shute. 'And Mr and Mrs Palmer. How nice to see you all.'

Seeing his teachers in this dramatic setting changed Billy's idea of them. They wore their long black dresses, as they always did, but there was something different about them here, an ease and a familiarity that was quite absent at school. Alan had told him they had been in the village for thirty years, an unimaginably long time.

'Do you think Miss Shute will ride on her broom tonight?' whispered Sarah to Billy.

'No, that's at Halloween. Anyway, she hasn't got a broom.'

'We didn't do anything at Halloween, did we? We used to have a pumpkin.'

'I don't think they have pumpkins around here.'

Billy and Sarah stayed close to their parents. Many of their friends were there, including Alan Tyler, but they all remained with their own families. Frank and Ed Willmott looked subdued as they stood by their father, who towered over them. He's the giant in *Jack and the Beanstalk*, thought Billy. He looked up at Jim, who though quite tall himself was overshadowed by Willmott. He hoped they wouldn't get into a fight.

A man took a long pole with a stuffed sock on the end, dipped it in a can of oil, and set a match to it. It leaped into flame, and he thrust it into the bonfire. It had been dry lately, and the wood kindled easily. Within less than a minute it was roaring, the guy and the chair consumed by the flames, and sparks flew into a sky turned suddenly bright orange. After the fire's first rush, people stepped forward with potatoes on sticks and laid them in the ashes. Then the fireworks began, rockets and cascades and roman candles.

'Can I light a firework?' said Sarah.

'No,' said Jim. 'But you can have a sparkler. I'll get you one.'

She ran in circles waving the sparkler, stopping now and then to watch rockets whoosh into the sky. Jim helped light and launch them: Mighty Atoms, Rockets, Silver Rains. He took a match to one that stood in a milk bottle, and it shot up and exploded into hundreds of points of light. Billy and Sarah gasped, and begged him to light another.

He straightened the rocket, lit the fuse and stood back. Just at that moment, the bottle gently tipped over onto its side. Jim lunged forwards in an attempt to right it, but he was too late, and it caught light and hurtled towards Sarah, grazing the side of her face as it went. She let out a cry of pain, and he dashed towards her, taking her head in his hands. There was a burn mark that seared her cheek and ear, and her hair was scorched. He picked her up and held her close to him. Her body was convulsed with crying.

'She's in shock,' he said to Margaret. 'We must get her to a doctor straight away.'

Margaret ran over to the Shute sisters. In the noise and confusion no one else was aware of what had happened.

'Dr Enright,' said the thin Miss Shute. 'His house is less than a mile away. Follow me.'

They hurried out into the road. Jim held Sarah tight and whispered to her soothingly, while Margaret grasped Billy's hand. By now Sarah was sobbing quietly, burying her face in Jim's chest. Billy looked on, wondering how brave he might have been had the rocket hit him rather than his sister.

Dr Enright was a soft-faced man in his sixties. He took one look at Sarah and led her into the surgery room that was attached to his house. He said almost nothing, tutting now and then to himself. Sarah squinted in the bright light while Enright took out some astringent and a cotton swab. 'This will sting, child,' he said, and Sarah recoiled and cried out again when he rubbed her cheek. Billy stood by, watching attentively.

'An inch to the right and she might have lost an eye,' said Enright. 'As it is, this will heal quickly. You are most fortunate.' He said this to Jim rather than to Sarah.

Jim let out a long, slow breath, and sat down on a chair. 'Thank God,' he said, holding his head in his hands.

'It wasn't your fault,' said Margaret. 'It could have happened to anyone.'

'Of course it was my fault, Maggie,' he said angrily. 'It was bloody stupid of me not to make sure the bottle was stable.'

'It's a dangerous night, Fireworks Night,' said Enright. 'I always expect a visitor or two. It's easy to be careless.'

Sarah was whimpering gently. Margaret took her up in her arms. 'It's all right now,' she said. 'Let's take you home.'

Enright ran them back to the cottage in his Alvis, Sarah sitting on Margaret's lap, Billy beside them.

'That's the last time I'm lighting any fireworks,' said his father.

———————

Jim and Billy set out early the following Saturday and cycled to Wells, Billy balancing precariously on the crossbar. They arrived at Reg's house before eight, and he gave Jim the keys to the Vanguard.

'I don't want you giving it any poke, now,' he said.

'I'll take it easy,' said Jim, 'I promise.'

Reg watched as Jim and Billy opened the doors and slid into the front seats.

'Do you really think you're going to get anything out of your Aunt Beatrice?' he said.

'I just want to make up, that's all.'

Reg eyed him thoughtfully. 'Well, good luck,' he said. As Jim engaged first gear and gingerly steered the car out into the road, he shouted, 'And no poke, now, do you hear?'

They drove through the half-light and came to a halt outside a lock-up garage. Billy saw a dim figure emerge from the scrubby wasteland on the other side of the road.

'Morning,' the man said. He surveyed the car. 'That'll do. Nice big boot.' Then he saw Billy sitting in the passenger seat, and looked quizzically at Jim.

'Don't worry about the boy,' said his father. 'He wants to see his great-aunt.'

Billy looked at the man and decided he didn't like him one little bit. And it wasn't true that he wanted to see Aunt Beatrice: his father had insisted that he come.

The man opened the doors of the lock-up and brought out six packages wrapped in paper and tied up with string. They were heavy, and by the time they were loaded into the boot of the car it sat notice-ably closer to the ground, the rear tyres subsiding a little into the tarmac. He gave Jim a scrap of paper.

'He'll be expecting you around lunchtime,' he said. 'He doesn't know your name, and he won't ask. All right?'

Jim looked up at him and nodded. 'Don't expect us back before seven or eight,' he said.

Sitting in the front seat of a car was a pleasure that Billy had imagined he would never know again. He watched the semaphore movements of his father's arms as he shifted the gears and swung the steering wheel. Wanting to play his part in this show of dexterity, he reached out to the dials of the radio and gave them a reverent touch.

'Don't fiddle,' said Jim sharply.

Billy looked across at him, and instantly the joy he had been feeling drained away. His father was hunched over the wheel, an anxious expression on his face. He was so unlike the relaxed and confident driver Billy had always known.

'About those packages,' he said. 'We're not delivering them, under-stand?'

'What do you mean?'

'I mean that as far as your mother and sister and great-aunt are concerned, we didn't pick up any packages and we're not dropping off any packages. Do I have to make it any plainer than that?'

'But we are.'

'Yes, Billy, you and I know that we are. But nobody else is to know. And if you tell anyone, you're for it. That man's a friend of mine, and I'm doing him a favour. But he doesn't want it talked about, and that's that.'

By now they were passing through the Georgian terraces of Bath. This was where they had once lived, in a big house with a Jaguar parked in the drive; this was where they had been happy. He folded his arms and fell silent.

London had always been something of a mystery to Jim, and it took a long time to find the place in Bloomsbury where they were going. He parked in Museum Street and they strolled to a bookshop. 'Bernard Smith, Antiquarian & Second-hand Bookseller' read the sign, and on the door a note said, 'Back in ten minutes'. Billy peered through the window, surveying the books on display. Macaulay's *History of England* stood in four uniform volumes, the *Memoirs* of Giacomo Casanova in twelve. There were sets of Shakespeare and George Bernard Shaw. He looked up and down the street: every second shop sold books or prints. There must be thousands of books here, he thought, tens of thousands.

A middle-aged man appeared, and looked at them warily. He was plump and dishevelled, his green corduroy jacket worn at the elbows, the lapels sprinkled with cigarette ash. He took a keyring from his pocket and opened the door. They followed him inside without a word passing between them.

'I'm delivering something,' said Jim as the bookseller turned on the lights. The spaces between the stacks of books were narrow, the shelves extending to the high ceiling.

'You would be the man from Somerset,' said Smith.

'I would be the man from the man from Somerset,' said Jim.

Smith opened up the till and inspected its contents. He laid a brown paper bag on the counter and took out a sandwich, biting into it hungrily.

'Well, you'd better bring them in,' he said.

Jim stepped back into the street and returned with two of the packages. By the time he had brought back the other four, Smith was inspecting the contents of the first package closely. He turned the pages of a book carefully, nodding his head in a bird-like way as he viewed them through the half-glasses on the end of his nose. Billy sensed this process was going to take a while, and he sat down on a stool. Smith leafed through the books one by one, now and then taking another bite of the sandwich and wiping his fingers carefully on a handkerchief before resuming. Billy wasn't able to see many of the titles, but he could read the names Defoe, Richardson, Smollett.

The silence was interrupted only by an occasional rasping sound as Smith cleared his throat. Eventually he looked up at Jim. 'Very fine,' he said, 'very fine indeed.' He disappeared for a moment and returned with an envelope. 'There's no need to open it. Your man and I have an understanding.'

Billy watched as Jim slipped the envelope into his jacket pocket. There was only one thing it could contain, surely, and that was money.

'Good day,' said Smith, and he began to carry the books into the back of the shop.

'Good day,' said Jim, grasping the handle of the door. Then he looked back. 'Is this a good business, books?'

Smith glanced up at him, taking the glasses from his nose.

'It is if you know what you're doing,' he said.

'I suppose that's true of any business.'

'I suppose it is.'

Jim gazed thoughtfully for a moment at the rows of books, and then nodded to Billy to step out into the street. As the door shut behind them, Billy wondered what on earth his father was up to.

Beatrice Palmer, Billy's maiden great-aunt, lived in a Victorian mansion block on the bank of the Thames. They parked near Putney Bridge and walked to the entrance, climbing two flights of stairs to the flat.

'Good afternoon, Jim,' said Beatrice, and to Billy, 'and you too, young man. How nice.'

'Hello, Aunt Bea.'

'Sit down and I'll make some tea.'

Beatrice was seventy now, and as elegant as always, in a blue and white polka-dot dress and black shoes. Jim followed her into the kitchen, and Billy went over to the balcony window. It was one of those brilliant afternoons when winter still seems benign, and a silvery light glinted on the surface of the river. They used to come here

57

every year to watch the Boat Race, Beatrice preparing a high tea that was practically a banquet, with sandwiches, jellies, cakes and scones. Today, however, she handed Jim a cup and Billy a glass of lemonade without ceremony. Jim sank into a plush red velvet armchair, and then struggled to sit up straight.

'I received your letter,' she said. 'What did you want to say to me?'

Jim looked over at Billy and said, 'Why don't you go out onto the balcony and watch the boats?'

It was mild enough to sit outside on the wicker chairs. Billy placed his lemonade on the table and gazed out at the pleasure boats gliding by. He looked back through the glass door at his father and great-aunt, and jammed it open a little with his foot so as to hear their conversation.

'I wanted to say I'm sorry, more or less,' said Jim.

Beatrice examined him critically. 'I think the moment for that has passed, don't you?' she said.

'I tried to apologize at the time.'

'Not very hard, as I recall.' She sipped her tea delicately.

'It was difficult.'

'It was indeed.'

'Aunt Bea, I know I didn't behave very well. But it wasn't *all* my fault.'

'Then whose fault was it, exactly?'

He seemed to cast about him for inspiration. 'It was the times. The credit squeeze. The rationing.'

'Jim, you made one miscalculation after another,' she said. 'Once you saw trouble looming you could quite easily have averted it. In the end the bank had no alternative but to call in your debts.'

His hands were gripping his knees tightly, and his expression was agitated. 'I'm sorry about your money, Aunt Bea,' he said. 'I would gladly repay it if I could.'

'You'll never be in a position to repay it, not in my lifetime.'

Jim glanced in Billy's direction, and Billy looked away.

'How is Margaret?' said Beatrice.

'Oh, fine. She seems to be coping.'

'I trust you understand how hard this must have been for her?'

'Of course I do.'

'I wonder about that.'

She stood up and crossed to the balcony door.

'Come back in, Billy,' she said. 'You'll catch cold.'

'I'm all right,' he said, not wanting to be drawn into this unsettling encounter.

'Tell me about your new school.'

Billy reluctantly stepped back into the room. 'It's very small,' he said. 'And I don't have to wear a uniform.'

'Do you like it?'

Billy shrugged, and looked at his father.

'You'd rather be back at the Unicorn, wouldn't you?'

'I suppose so,' said Billy. He had an impulse to talk about Frank Willmott, but then decided against it.

'But you miss your old life, I expect,' said Beatrice.

'Some things I miss.' He looked very directly at his great-aunt. 'I wish we had a car,' he said. 'Then we could all visit you like we used to. Today we're only borrowing Uncle Reg's Standard, and it's not much of a car anyway.'

'Billy, we've been through this a hundred times,' said Jim, setting down his teacup in a gesture of exasperation.

'Nevertheless the boy misses it,' said Beatrice. She patted her mouth with a napkin, and stood up to close the balcony door. Turning to face them again she said, 'I don't think I want you to come here again, Jim. If Margaret would like to bring the children she is welcome to.'

Billy looked at his father, who sat speechless in his chair.

'I'm sorry to have to say this in front of you, Billy,' she continued, 'but you must understand that there are some things in life that have consequences.'

Jim slowly got to his feet and motioned to Billy to follow him. Before he could make a move, Beatrice stepped across the room and kissed him on the cheek. He looked up at her, bewildered.

'I think you ought to be on your way home,' she said. 'It gets dark so early these days.'

They descended the stairs, and returned to the riverbank. Jim leaned against the wall, gazing vacantly into the water. A lighter was making its way upstream, pushing against the current. Billy looked up at Jim as though at a stranger. This day had made him feel afraid of his father. He watched the traffic crossing the bridge, and willed him to return to Reg's car. The trip was ruined now.

––––––

Whenever Billy had things on his mind he went for a walk. And he had things on his mind now, things that were difficult to understand. He clambered over the stile across the road and took in the familiar view. Seeing the countryside unfold below made him feel that it was there for him alone. The light was forever changing things, making the scene different every time he looked at it. Mostly it was like a great green carpet, but sometimes it was like old brown linoleum, and at others even a gold cloth. Always the tor loomed in the distance, a kind of sentinel.

From the first field he could see Coombe Hall, which was hidden from the road by a high wall and gates. It was a very large place, with a sweeping gravel drive, neatly tended lawns and gardens, and what looked like a dovecote at the back. Billy wondered who lived there, and why his father and mother had never spoken about them. In Bath he was always being taken to other people's houses, some quite as grand as this, where he dutifully played with children he didn't know or like while his parents sat talking for hours on end. Apart from Hubert Fosse and Miss Vale he knew no one here outside school. His mother seemed to want to get to know people, but his father showed no interest whatsoever.

What *was* his father interested in? he thought. And what was that strange day in London all about? He'd been told that Aunt Beatrice was particularly looking forward to seeing him; but when they arrived it seemed that she hadn't been expecting him at all. His father had wanted something from her, he was sure, something she was unwilling to give. And then there were the books, the secret books. Billy generally liked secrets; but this was not one he wanted to be in on.

He came to the ford by the school, and looked at the piece of rope that hung from a tree above it. He had often wondered whether he might be able to swing across to the other side, and now, seeing as there was no one watching him, he decided to give it a try. He stepped into the water, wading out to the middle. It was icy cold, and came up to his knees. He grabbed the rope and drew it back towards the bank. The bough of the tree creaked as he skimmed over the surface, but the rope didn't take him anywhere near the other side, and he found himself dangling in mid-air. He fell back into the stream and stumbled to the bank, where he stood trying to wring the water from his shorts.

He decided to walk up the Arminster road, and soon he came upon a very large farm, with outbuildings that extended in every direction. It was like a fort, but an abandoned one, after the Indians had laid siege to it and killed all the whites. As he was imagining the terrible scenes of the massacre he heard familiar voices, and he turned to see Frank and Les striding down the hill, looking purposeful. When they saw Billy they glanced at one another and smiled conspiratorially.

'Billy Palmer,' said Frank.

'Hello.' They were the last people Billy wanted to see, and he made to walk past them. But Frank and Les stepped across the road and barred his way.

'Where are you off to, then?' said Frank.

'Just exploring.'

'Well this is our patch, so you can explore somewhere else.' Frank folded his arms and stared at Billy, and Les did the same. Billy thought for a moment what to do. There was no point in trying to pass, but at the same time he didn't want to turn around meekly and walk back down, no doubt being closely followed. He saw a path a few yards away that appeared to lead towards the village.

'I'm going to the shop, anyway,' he said, 'to get some things for Mum.'

'Shop's not open on Sundays,' said Frank, and he and Les sniggered.

Billy cursed himself for making such a stupid mistake. 'Oh, I forgot,' he said.

'So you'd better turn back then, hadn't you, and run along home.' Frank looked down at the dark stains on Billy's shorts. 'Been wetting yourself?' he asked, and he and Les began sniggering again.

'I was trying to swing across the river by the school.'

'Me Tarzan, you Jane,' said Les. By now he and Frank were laughing out loud. Billy felt mortified, and stood gazing at the ground.

A van appeared, and honked loudly. Frank and Les stepped to one side of the road, and Billy to the other. As the van passed, Billy saw his chance, and began to run alongside it up the hill. He had run twenty yards or so before the others realized what he'd done. They shouted at him, and gave chase. Billy was a good runner, and he was spurred on both by fear and by a determination to show them what he was capable of. He ducked into a side road, which began to take him downhill again. His heart was bursting, but he kept on. Looking back, he saw that he was leaving Frank and Les behind. The rush of cold air on his face thrilled him, and he ran even faster.

When a bend in the road took him out of their sight, he vaulted a gate and ran back across an empty field, hiding behind a tree at the bottom. He heard Frank and Les carrying on along the road, shouting his name and threatening to get him. Billy stood gasping, his hand resting on the rough bark. He saw that the field below would bring him out onto the Coombe road, and he ran towards the stone wall. Jumping over it, he was suddenly back on home ground, on the road he took every day to school. He made himself slow down, tried to saunter along this familiar road. But he wasn't very good at sauntering, and as soon as he had got his breath back he started to run once again.

Margaret's anxieties about Jim were mounting. He was becoming increasingly withdrawn into himself, and liable to lose his temper over the smallest thing. The evenings were the worst, after the children had gone to bed and they sat alone. Jim had taken to the radio, but he fretted over it, moving the dial back and forth. Hilversum, Athlone, Luxembourg: it was as though he were seeking a world, not just something to listen to. Whistle and static pierced the air, snatches of foreign voices and bursts of music. It was difficult for Margaret to concentrate.

'Jim, let's talk,' she said.

He looked up and switched off the radio, and Margaret laid down her book. There was no settee in the room, and they sat opposite each other in upright chairs.

'What shall we talk about?' said Jim.

'I don't know. Anything. We don't seem to talk at all these days.'

He sighed. 'I'm sorry, Maggie,' he said. 'I'm not myself.'

Margaret gazed at him, suddenly afraid of what she wanted to say.

'I understand how hard this is for you,' she began. 'But I don't think you're going about things in the best way.'

'How do you mean?'

'I mean you're feeling sorry for yourself, and that can't lead anywhere.'

Jim picked up the radio again and toyed with it. 'I've a bloody right to feel sorry for myself,' he said.

'No, Jim, you haven't. Things have happened, and we all have to deal with them as best we can.'

'I *am* trying my best.' Jim looked at her peevishly. He was so like Billy when he was in this sort of mood, she thought, so easily hurt.

'I know you are,' she said. 'But don't you think it would be better if you shared things with me?'

He put down the radio again, and looked at his hands in the way he always did when he was at a loss.

'I sometimes think I don't know how,' he said.

Margaret felt suddenly overwhelmed by her tenderness for him. She stepped over and perched on the arm of his chair.

'Let's go to bed,' she said.

Margaret undressed while he was in the bathroom, leaving her nightgown on the chair. When Jim got into bed they embraced stiffly. He began to caress her, to kiss her neck and her breasts. The flush of arousal was strange to her. She felt Jim's fingers describe a circle around her navel and descend to her thighs. He touched her, gently at first and then firmly. And then suddenly he broke away.

'I'm sorry, Maggie,' he said. 'I suppose I'm not in the mood.'

She put her arms around his neck and pressed herself to him, but he shook her off and turned over. While his body was unresponsive, hers was jangling with desire and frustration. Burying her face in the pillow, she cried as soundlessly as she could.

Four

Winter closed in, and with it the margins of their life. It rained incessantly, and the farmyard became a sea of mud. The only warm rooms in the cottage were the kitchen and, when they lit a fire, the parlour. In the evenings Jim and Margaret would occupy the two armchairs while Billy and Sarah read or played games on the kitchen table. Billy had decided they should all play Monopoly, and in preparation had been trying to explain the rules to Sarah.

'The only way to learn properly is to play it,' said Jim as he sat listening to Sarah's insistent questions.

'So let's play now,' said Billy.

'It's late,' said Margaret. 'Monopoly takes ages. We'll play at the weekend if the weather hasn't changed.'

The weather didn't change, and Saturday morning was as dismal as any of the previous days. After breakfast Billy got out the Monopoly set, and began methodically to set it up.

'Dad, you must be banker,' he said.

'All right,' said Jim, laying aside yesterday's paper.

'What do you want to be, Sarah?'

'I want to be me.'

'I mean what token do you want to play with?'

'Oh.' She looked at the shiny silver tokens. 'I want the boot,' she said.

'And I want the racing car,' said Billy.

Jim took the top hat and Margaret the thimble. Sarah threw the dice first, and landed on Euston Road.

'Do you want to buy it?' said Jim.

'How much is it?'

'It says on the board. One hundred pounds.'

Sarah counted the money she'd been given. 'Yes, I will buy it,' she said. She handed Jim a hundred-pound note, and Jim gave her the card with its pale blue edge.

'You can charge me rent if I land there,' said Billy. 'Six pounds. And lots more if you get The Angel and Pentonville Road.'

'I want The Angel too,' said Sarah. 'It's a nice name.'

When she landed a fifty-pound doctor's fee she protested loudly. 'We didn't pay to go to the doctor when I had my firework burn,' she said.

'It's a game, Sarah,' said Billy. 'It's not meant to be real.'

'Come on, pay up,' said Jim.

Sarah tossed over a fifty-pound note, which Jim carefully banked. Billy looked across to the window. The rain streamed down the panes, and he could see no further than the other side of the yard.

'I'll swap you Oxford Street for Park Lane,' said Jim after a while. 'Plus seventy-five pounds.'

Billy looked at the dark blue card in front of him. They had driven along Park Lane on the way to the bookshop, and then into Oxford Street. This reminder made him shiver suddenly.

'I paid fifty more in the first place,' he said. 'You'll have to give me a lot more than that.'

'A hundred, then.'

'No.' Billy folded his arms and looked staunchly at his father.

'It isn't worth much to you without Mayfair,' said Jim.

'And Mayfair isn't worth much to you without Park Lane.'

'Come on, Billy, we need to move the game along. There's no point in playing unless we can start to buy houses and hotels.'

'So sell me Mayfair.'

'It's not for sale,' said Jim, and he threw the dice for his next move.

When it came to Sarah's turn she landed on Go To Jail. Billy took her boot and dumped it on the orange Jail square.

'I don't want to go to Jail,' she said. 'I haven't done anything wrong.'

'Well you have to,' said Billy. 'Those are the rules.'

'I am not going to Jail!'

'Yes you are. Anyway, you're already in it.'

Sarah took her boot and placed it on Water Works, which no one had yet bought.

'Sarah,' said Margaret, 'you have to play by the rules. Now put it back in Jail.'

'No I won't.' Sarah jiggled in her chair, swinging her legs rapidly back and forth.

'Then you can't play,' said Billy. 'We'll split up your properties and play without you.'

'Oh no you won't,' said Sarah, and she reached out and swept away the houses Billy had placed on Whitehall and Pall Mall. Billy stooped to pick them up from the floor.

'That's it,' he said flatly. 'You're disqualified. Isn't she, Dad?'

Jim took Sarah's hand. 'If you don't want to play, then go and read your comic,' he said. 'If you do want to play, you must go to Jail.'

Sarah slid off her chair, seized her Bunty comic, and ran up the stairs without a word. Margaret and Jim looked at one another, and Jim shrugged his shoulders.

'Let's carry on,' he said.

'I think I'll hand in my properties too,' said Margaret. 'You two play on.'

'But it'll be no fun then,' said Billy. 'I thought we were doing it together.'

Jim looked at his watch. 'It's already taken most of the morning,' he said. 'Let's pack it up.'

Billy placed all the pieces back in the box with an air of silent protest. When he entered the bedroom Sarah buried her head in her comic and ignored him. He opened the cupboard door, and a Dinky toy Land Rover fell to the floor. As he was putting it back among the other toys, he noticed that his racing-car and sports-car sets weren't there. He ran down the stairs to tell his mother.

'They must be there,' said Margaret. 'Where else could they be?'

'They're not,' said Billy. 'I don't know where they are.'

'When did you last play with them?'

'A long time ago, with Dad. When we did the British Grand Prix.'

'Jim,' said Margaret, 'have you seen them?'

Jim laid down his paper and stared blankly into space.

'I sold them,' he said finally.

'You sold them!' said Billy. 'But they were mine.'

'What on earth are you talking about?' said Margaret. 'You had no right at all to do that.'

Jim stood up and faced her. 'He's grown out of them,' he said. 'And we need money for food and clothes.'

'If we need money then you must say so. How could you sell Billy's toys without telling him?'

'For God's sake, Maggie,' said Jim angrily. 'Here I am doing my best to support you, and all you can do is criticize me. I've just about had it, I can tell you.'

66

'And so have I,' said Margaret. Abruptly she got her coat and scarf from the rack and opened the door. Rain billowed into the kitchen.

'Where are you going?' said Jim.

'For a walk.'

'It's pouring out there.'

'I couldn't care less.'

Margaret tied the scarf tightly around her head. 'You can get your own lunch,' she said, ducking out into the yard.

———————

Billy lay on the bed and stared up at the ceiling. Sarah glanced over towards him and then returned to her comic, sneezing loudly and wrapping herself in the eiderdown. Billy looked around the tiny room. Sometimes this house felt like a prison.

'Mum's gone out into the rain,' he said.

Sarah sat up and stared at him.

'Where's she gone?'

'I don't know. For a walk.'

'Why has she gone for a walk?'

'She's cross with Dad.'

'Why?'

'Because he sold my Dinky cars.'

'He did?' said Sarah breathlessly. She looked at the teddy bear that sat on her pillow. 'He wouldn't sell my toys, would he?'

'I don't know. I don't know what he'd do.'

Billy hopped off the bed and went over to the cupboard. He searched through its contents thoroughly.

'Nothing else seems to have gone,' he said.

'Why did Daddy sell your Dinkys?'

'To buy food and clothes, so he said.'

Sarah gazed out of the window and into the gloom. Billy looked at her and saw that tears were beginning to roll down her cheeks.

'Do you think they still love each other, Mummy and Daddy?' she said.

'I think so.' He stepped across to Sarah and put his arm awkwardly around her shoulders. 'Don't worry, things will be all right when she gets back.'

'But what if she doesn't come back?'

Billy looked at his sister, at her tear-stained cheeks. There was fear in her eyes.

'I wish we hadn't come here,' she said. She sat stiffly, not leaning towards Billy, and he took his arm away.

'It's all right,' he said. 'This is just a horrible day.'

'Mummy will come back, won't she?'

'Of course she will.'

He looked across the narrow room towards the landing. But what if she doesn't come back, he said to himself, and we're left with just Dad? He thought of Jim sitting alone downstairs. How could he have sold his Dinky toys without telling him? Suddenly he knew he must talk to him.

Jim was sitting at the kitchen table smoking.

'I hadn't grown out of them,' said Billy.

Jim stubbed out his cigarette violently. 'Yes you had,' he said. 'Remember the last time? You messed it up.'

'I hadn't grown out of them,' said Billy, trying to keep his voice steady. 'And they were mine.'

'Who paid for them?'

'But you gave them to me.'

'Don't you lecture me, my boy. Wait until you find out what it's like to try and make your way in this world.'

Billy stared at his father, who carried on pressing the stub of his cigarette into the ashtray even though it was long extinguished, and then turned and ran upstairs again. Back in the bedroom he pulled his copy of *Robinson Crusoe* from the shelf and lay down on the floor. He had got to the place where Crusoe first meets Man Friday. Flipping back the pages to when Crusoe was still alone, he began to read.

———————

Margaret's headscarf was no protection against the rain, and by the time she had gone a few hundred yards she was soaked. She was furious with Jim; he seemed to have lost his bearings completely. She pressed on, and it was only when Tanyard Cottage came into sight that it occurred to her to call on Leonora Vale.

'What on earth are you doing out in this weather, poppet?' she said as she opened the door.

'I just wanted to get away for a bit, that's all.'

'Come in, come in this instant.'

She gave Margaret a towel and went to put the kettle on. Margaret dried her hair and face, and accepted a mug of tea laced once again with the contents of the hip flask.

'That'll take care of you.'

'I'm sorry, Miss Vale,' said Margaret. 'I think I'm becoming a burden to you.'

'Nonsense. And you must call me Leonora. Now what's going on?'

Margaret gave her a guarded account of the morning's events, without directly referring to Jim's having sold the Dinky toys.

'You're cramped in that cottage,' said Leonora. 'You need more space. You in particular. You're letting your own life revolve entirely around theirs.'

'I thought that was what was expected of me.'

'What's expected is one thing,' said Leonora, with a dismissive wave of her hand. 'What's for the best is usually quite another.'

'I was brought up to think that doing what was expected of me would make me happy.'

'We all were. That doesn't mean we can't reach some conclusions of our own.'

Margaret gripped her mug tightly. The air in the house was as fusty as ever, but somehow she didn't mind as much now.

'Tell me about yourself,' said Leonora.

Margaret shrugged. 'There isn't much to tell,' she said.

'Then tell me a little.'

Margaret leaned back into the settee.

'Well, I was born and brought up in Bath,' she said. 'My father ran an insurance business. I was in the Land Army during the war, not far from here, near Midsomer Norton. And I went to work in my father's office when the war was over, as a secretary and receptionist.'

'And then you waited for Jim,' said Leonora dryly.

'And then I waited for Jim. We met at a motor-trade dance. He was the most handsome man I'd ever seen. It was completely obvious from the beginning that we would get married. I'm not sure it ever occurred to me to say no.'

'And soon you became a mother.'

'Very soon. And for a few years that was quite enough. Jim started to do well, started to expand the business, and we moved into a large

69

house. The children, the house, Jim's friends, the Rotary Club: that was my life.'

'Well, it was someone's life.'

'Yes. I wonder who she was?'

'You must do something of your own, something that has nothing to do with anyone else.'

'And what might that be?'

'Well, I've already said that I see an artist in you.'

Margaret looked down at her damp shoes and stockings. 'It's one thing to say you're an artist, and quite another to be one.'

'So be one.'

'Leonora, you are very kind, but I simply wouldn't know where to begin. I love reading. It's my great solace. But I could no more write than I could fly to the moon.'

'I don't think you can be sure about that.'

'I feel it.'

Leonora gazed at her for a few moments. 'I've always had trouble with my eyes,' she said. 'Would you read to me?'

'Of course, gladly. What would you like me to read?'

'What are you reading at the moment?'

'I'm about to start *Tess of the D'Urbervilles*.'

'Will you come here and read it aloud to me?'

———

Jim hadn't set eyes on Liz for nearly two weeks. He dropped by Goody's one day at lunchtime and asked her to have a drink that evening, and they met in the Anchor.

She was looking very lovely. He reached over and kissed her, but she pushed him away.

'Not here,' she said.

'I've missed you,' said Jim.

'I haven't been very far away. You could easily have come by.'

'It's been a difficult time,' he said.

'And not just for you. If a girl's just a one-night stand she'd like to know.'

'This is not a one-night stand, Liz,' he said, putting his arm around her. 'But there are problems, problems we've both known about from the beginning. Like where to go tonight. I suppose your parents are around?'

'Yes,' she said. She looked away, and then turned back and kissed him gently on the lips. 'I'm sorry.'

They sat quietly, holding hands under the table. I've got to work something out, Jim thought, got to find a place we can go. This is like being seventeen again.

He went up to order another round of drinks, and at that moment Gordon Towker walked in. He saw Jim and joined him at the bar.

'Can I buy you a drink?' he said.

Jim nodded over his shoulder. 'I'm with someone, thanks anyway.'

Towker's gaze followed Jim's, and he smiled nastily. 'Wouldn't want to barge in on the lovebirds,' he said.

'Another time, then.'

Jim picked up his beer and Liz's glass of wine and returned to his seat.

'Cheers,' he said.

'So you know him?' said Liz.

'Gordon Towker? He sort of picked me up in the Star.'

'You want to be careful with that man.' She looked across at him disapprovingly.

'Do I?'

'Yes. He's a strange one.'

'Strange how?'

She hesitated, sipping her wine. 'Well, for a start he was caught behind the swimming baths with a boy from the Blue School a while ago.'

Christ, thought Jim. 'What happened?' he said.

'Nothing. It was all hushed up.'

'Anything else I should know about him?'

Liz looked towards Towker again. It was clear that he knew he was being talked about.

'He's a bad lot, that's all,' she said.

Jim looked down at his hands. 'Let's change the subject,' he said. 'What's on at the pictures? We could go one day soon.'

'*A Town Like Alice*, I think it's called.'

'I know. It's set in Malaya during the war.'

She looked out across the dark, smoky room. 'Malaya,' she said. 'Sunshine. I could use some of that.'

He took a draught of beer. 'Shall we go somewhere else?' he said.

'Such as?'

Jim looked out of the window across Market Place. It was a bitter night. He thought of the set of keys Reg had recently given him.

'Let's go to the shop,' he said.

'To the shop?'

'Have you got a better idea?'

'And make a cosy nest out of school uniforms?'

Jim kissed her hard on the mouth. 'I want you, Liz,' he said.

She looked at him coolly. 'I'm not coming into Underhill's with you,' she said, and she stood up and began to put on her coat.

'Sit down, sweetheart.'

'I'm going home.' Her lips were pressed together, her eyes narrowed.

'Don't be angry, I'm only doing my best.'

'I'm not angry. I just want to be treated like a lady, that's all.'

She turned away from him and crossed to the door. Jim was intensely aware of Towker's having witnessed this scene. He stood up too quickly, knocking over the table and spilling the remains of their drinks. For a moment he thought to pick up the glasses, but instead he marched across the pub and out into the street. An icy wind was blowing, and Liz was nowhere in sight.

Alan had told Billy he was joining the Scouts, and Jim agreed that Billy could go along to the meeting to see whether he might want to join too. Everything was hushed in the cold night as they walked towards Walton. The Scout troop met in a wooden hut just off the main road. The Scoutmaster was a tall, slightly stooped man with a straggly moustache and a weak chin. Billy thought he looked ridiculous in his shorts and long socks held up by green garters.

'Welcome to the Walton troop, Tyler,' he said to Billy. 'This evening you will be sworn in as a tenderfoot.' He looked from Billy to Alan. 'And I hope your friend will be inspired to join us too.'

'He's Tyler,' said Billy, pointing to Alan. 'I'm Palmer.'

'Of course you are,' said the Scoutmaster. 'And I'm Wilkins. But you call me Scoutmaster, because that's what I am.'

The hut was very small. A single-bar electric fire gave out a faint heat, and a trestle-table stood on the bare floor, the Union Flag behind it. There were ten Scouts, ranging in age from eleven to fourteen or so, none of whom Billy knew. They seemed very sure of themselves, very pleased to be wearing their scarves and hats and badges. At a command from the Scoutmaster they formed two lines.

'Tyler,' said the Scoutmaster to Billy, 'you will join the Owl patrol. And Palmer, you can too, for this evening.'

Alan and Billy stood alongside the boys of Owl patrol, facing the Raven patrol on the other side.

'Scouts,' said the Scoutmaster sonorously. 'We will commence with the swearing in of the new boy. Come here, Tyler.'

Alan stepped forward, and the Scoutmaster looked from him to Billy for a moment. 'Yes, of course,' he said. 'Tyler.' He looked down the ranks of the two patrols. 'What do we ask a new Scout to swear to?'

In unison the boys said, 'To be loyal to God and the Queen, to help other people at all times, and to obey the Scout law.'

'Good,' said the Scoutmaster. 'Now, do you swear those things, Tyler?'

'What's the Scout law?' said Alan.

'We'll get to that later. Now do you swear?'

A titter went around the other boys.

'I swear,' said Alan.

'Good. Do you know the motto of the Scouts?'

'Yes,' said Alan. 'Be prepared.'

'And do you know the significance of those words?'

'Well, you have to be prepared in case of danger and that.'

'And what else has the initials B. P.?'

Alan thought for a moment. 'The petrol company,' he said.

'No, no,' said the Scoutmaster irritably. 'Baden-Powell. You know who he was, don't you?'

'He was the founder of the Scouts.'

'Quite right. The hero of Mafeking. Now, we will sing the Scout's Chorus. Ready?'

The boys held their breath for a moment, and then on a signal from the Scoutmaster the two patrol-leaders began to sing 'Een gonyâma, gonyâma!', to which the others responded with 'Invooboo. Yah bô! Yah bô! Invooboo.'

Alan turned to look at Billy, a sly smile forming around his mouth. Billy suppressed a smile of his own, and stood up straight.

'I expect you're wondering what that means, Tyler,' said the Scoutmaster.

'Yes, sir.'

73

'It means "He is a lion!" and "He is better than that. He is a hippopotamus!" '

'Why is a hippopotamus better than a lion?'

'Have you read Kipling?'

'No.'

'Read Kipling. Read Kim. Then you'll know.'

'Can we do Kim's game?' said the patrol-leader of the Owl patrol.

'Very well. Where are the things?'

There was a rush to a box under the trestle-table. 'I have to put them out,' said the Scoutmaster. 'You lot aren't allowed to see them.' He produced a tray, and then set out on it a number of small articles. Billy could see a button, a pencil, a cork, a walnut, and a couple of rags. The Scoutmaster made a show of hiding them under a cloth. Then he turned to the Scouts, taking a pencil and a piece of paper from his shirt pocket.

'I'm going to take away the cloth for one minute,' he said. 'You must try to memorize as many of these things as you can. I will then ask you to step up one at a time and whisper to me all the things you can remember.'

He whisked away the cloth, and the boys gathered around and peered at the tray. Billy's view was obscured by boys standing in front of him, but he was able to see about ten of the things, and he began to repeat to himself what they were. There followed a laborious process in which each of the boys went up to the Scoutmaster, who noted down their names and the things they had remembered. By the time it came to Billy's turn he had forgotten most of them.

'This is a silly game,' he said to Alan as he went back into line. 'If they've played it before, the others will remember what the things are anyway.'

The winner was the patrol-leader of Raven patrol. The Scoutmaster congratulated him. 'You must all learn to be observant,' he said. 'It's the most important thing.'

Billy leaned towards Alan. 'I thought being prepared was the most important thing,' he said.

'I don't think he knows what he's talking about.'

The boy next to them elbowed Alan hard. 'Shut up,' he said. 'Do you want to be a Scout or don't you?'

They listened quietly to the Scoutmaster telling them a long and

74

involved story about how a shepherd boy in the north somewhere had lured a murderer to his arrest, and ended with the Scout War Dance, in which the boys stepped forward and back and around in circles, all the while shouting the chorus they had sung earlier. Billy found it quite baffling, and was glad when it was over.

As they walked back through the dark towards home, Alan kicked a stone into the ditch and said, 'I don't think I want to be in the Scouts after all.'

'Nor do I,' said Billy, and they smiled at one another broadly.

The shop was dark and empty when Jim arrived. It was unlike Reg not to be there before him, and he wasn't sure for a moment what to do. He decided he had better open up. His keys were to the shop itself, but not to the office or the safe. He switched on the lights, turned the sign to 'open', and took up his place behind the counter. Ten minutes later the phone rang, but he was unable to get into the office to answer it. Something was wrong with all this. After a while the door opened, and Norman Elsworth from Herring's China Shop stepped inside. His movements were slow, his expression grave.

'Reg has had a stroke,' he said.

Jim slumped down on the stool by the till.

'Is it bad?' he said.

Elsworth nodded in response.

'Where is he?'

'In the Infirmary. Winnie's with him. She says she'll be by as soon as she can.'

'I'm sorry,' said Jim, staring across the room.

'So am I.'

After Elsworth had left, Jim took in the sombre aspect of the shop as though for the first time. He was stunned, quite unable to think things through. When Winifred arrived he stared at her, words failing him.

'How is he?' he said at last.

'He's unconscious,' she replied. 'He doesn't know yet what's happened.' She looked pale and exhausted.

'How bad is it?'

'They don't know yet. But at the very least he's not going to be able to come back here for a while.'

75

He tried to give her a hug, but the difference in their heights made it a clumsy gesture.

'I'm so sorry, Winnie,' he said.

'He'll be all right,' she said hollowly. 'Once I get him back home he'll be all right.'

'When can I visit him?'

'Not today. I'll let you know.'

They opened up the office, and Jim put change in the till. He passed the hours in a daze. He felt he should tell the customers about Reg, and several of them seemed to forget what it was they had come for and simply gave him their condolences. At half past five he shut up shop and put the takings into the night safe at the bank. As he cycled home he tried to think about the consequences of all this, but his thoughts strayed haphazardly. When Margaret asked him what might happen to the shop, he could answer only that he had no idea.

Winifred phoned him the next morning and told him that Reg was able to receive visitors.

'He won't be able to talk, though,' she said. 'He's going to need speech therapy before he can do that again.'

Jim hesitated, and then said, 'We should have a word about the shop, Winnie.'

'Yes. I'll come by tomorrow.'

The Infirmary stood back from the Glastonbury road, a large Victorian building with Gothic flourishes that made it look almost like a church. Jim hated hospitals, hated the odours of sickness and its cures, the echoing sounds of footsteps and the banging of doors. He'd had mercifully few occasions to step inside one except for when the children had been born, and even then he had felt an urge to get away as quickly as possible. A nurse directed him to Reg's ward. It was a large, green room with a dozen or so beds in it. Their occupants stared bleakly at this handsome man who would soon be able to turn around and go home.

The nurse had warned Jim that Reg would be practically unable to respond to him, and Jim wanted simply to register his presence and go. Reg lay quite inert, an oxygen mask over his nose and mouth. A faint sign of recognition showed in his eyes as Jim sat down next to the bed.

'Hello, Reg,' he said.

Reg nodded, and Jim wrestled with his unwillingness to say the obvious things.

'Comfortable, are you?'

Reg nodded again, and a strange, soft grunt came from beneath the mask.

'They'll have you out of here in no time, won't they?'

Reg turned to look away down the length of the ward. This is hopeless, thought Jim.

'I'll come back when you've got that bloody mask off,' he said. 'You look like Dan Dare.'

Jim thought he detected a hint of a smile, or perhaps it was a grimace. Reg's eyes had never smiled, only his mouth.

'Don't worry about the shop,' he said. Reg didn't respond, and he felt a sudden wave of anger pass over him. The cranky bastard had this coming, he thought, and he's left me high and dry. He made his apologies and left. In the frigid air outside he collected his bicycle from the shed and pushed out onto the road.

———

Winifred came by the shop the next morning. Jim made a cup of tea, and they sat on the hard chairs in the office, Jim listening out for the entrance of customers.

'He's paralysed down his left side,' said Winifred.

'Christ,' muttered Jim, and then, 'sorry, Winnie.'

She reached out and laid her hand on his. 'It's all right: that's exactly what I'd like to say.'

'Will he make a full recovery?'

Winifred shook her head. 'Nothing like,' she said. She looked around the cluttered room. 'He won't be coming back here, not ever.'

'What will you do?' he said.

'Well, I can either sell up or ask you to take it over.'

'Me?' he said, a note of alarm in his voice.

'Who else?'

'But I wouldn't know where to begin.'

'Of course you would. You've been working here for nearly three months now.'

'Winnie, with respect, Reg hardly involved me at all. I know nothing about buying stock and such things.'

77

She looked at him thoughtfully for a moment. 'It's up to you, Jim,' she said. 'If you want to take it over, then we'll agree on a salary and I'll do all I can to help. Otherwise I'm bound to sell the place, and there's no certainty that a buyer would want to keep you on.'

Jim stood up and scratched the back of his neck. He looked around him, from the dingy office to the stockroom and out into the deserted shop, and then back at Winifred.

'I'll have to think it over,' he said. 'You can rely on me to take care of the place for a while, at any rate.'

Winifred stood and gave him a peck on the cheek. 'Ring me on Monday,' she said.

She made to collect her things, and Jim held out her coat. She slipped her arms into it, buttoned it up, and smoothed down the lapels. 'Do think about it, Jim,' she said. 'And think about Margaret and the children.'

After she had gone, he stood disconsolately behind the counter. The empty gabardines and suits hung from their rails, mocking him. He had never felt so trapped in his life.

———

At the end of the school day Miss Shute asked Billy, Alan, Frank and two of the girls to stay behind. She sat them in the desks at the front.

'Next term you will all be taking your eleven-plus exam,' she said. 'I hope you understand what that means.'

'It's to see if we can go to grammar school,' said Audrey Purchase.

'That's right. If you pass you will go to the Blue School in Wells, which is a very old and very fine school.'

'And if we don't pass?' said Alan.

'Then you will go to the secondary modern school, which is also a fine school, but not as fine as the Blue School.'

'What will we have to do?' said Billy.

'We are going to have to do a little of everything,' said Miss Shute. 'At the beginning of term I will show you an old exam paper, so that you can see the sort of questions you'll be given. There will be reading, writing, arithmetic, science and art. Some children have to do French too, but you're excused that.'

'I'd like to learn French, miss,' said Billy.

'You'll do so if you go to the Blue School, Billy, as I'm sure you will.

But we are going to have to work hard next term, do you understand?'

Billy and Alan and Frank started walking home together. At the crossroads where Frank turned up the hill they stood for a few moments in a knot.

'I couldn't care less about the eleven-plus,' said Frank. 'My dad says the secondary school is good enough for anyone.'

'It depends what you want to do when you grow up,' said Billy.

'That's easy. I'm going to take over the farm.'

'What are you going to do, Billy?' said Alan.

He stood thinking for a moment. 'I'm going to be an explorer,' he said finally.

'And explore what?' said Frank.

'I don't know. I bet there are places in Africa and South America that haven't been explored.'

'Yeah, places not worth exploring,' said Frank. 'With lots of snakes and bugs.'

'I'll be an archaeologist, then.'

'A what?'

'An archaeologist. Someone who finds old forts and towns and things, under the ground.'

'Like the bloke who found the mummies,' said Alan.

'What mummies?' said Frank.

'You know, in Egypt. That king, Toot somebody.'

'He was cursed,' said Billy. 'The curse of the mummies.'

'What happened to him?' said Frank.

'He died.'

'Well of course he died. But how?'

'I think he was poisoned,' said Alan. 'That was the curse.'

'I'm not bloody well going to get poisoned,' said Frank. 'I'm going to stay where I belong.'

'Well I don't belong anywhere,' said Billy. 'So I'm going to explore and find things.' He began to run along the road towards Coombe, and then turned around. 'Are you coming?' he said. Alan shrugged his shoulders and made to follow him.

'You don't need to go to any school, then,' shouted Frank. 'You just need to get lost.'

————

Billy was going to be an explorer and an archaeologist. He hadn't understood this until the conversation with Frank and Alan, but now his conviction was unshakeable. He began to devour adventure stories set in faraway places. Through school or the mobile library he got hold of Rider Haggard's *King Solomon's Mines*, John Buchan's *Prester John*, Conan Doyle's *The Lost World*. He spent the long winter evenings lying on the floor by the fire, his imagination taking flight. When he went out walking through the fields he was no longer in Somerset but on the veld in South Africa. The stream that ran by the school was the Amazon. And the tor was Everest, the most challenging mountain in the world. At night he lay in bed listening to the sounds of Sarah's gentle breathing and inventing stories of his own, stories in which he was always the hero. And it was into this vivid world that new and strange sensations began to enter.

It had begun one morning, when he awoke to find that his penis was quite stiff. He touched it cautiously, but at that moment his mother called him to come down for breakfast. The stiffness quickly passed. When it happened again in the evening, as he lay waiting for sleep, it seemed even more strange and exciting. It must have something to do with all these daydreams, he thought. And over the next few nights, he found he could summon this change by thinking of mountains and waterfalls and jungles. The more he touched himself the nicer were the feelings he could bring on, until one night he simply couldn't stop, and after a while he experienced a strong tingling sensation, followed by a sense of happiness that stayed with him until he drifted into sleep.

This was a most extraordinary thing. Why hadn't anyone told him about it? Every night now he went through this secret ritual, and it seemed to him that every night it became more enjoyable, more comforting. But what was it? There was only one person he could ask.

Billy called at the Tyler farm the next morning, and he and Alan set off into the woods. They arrived at the place they had come to the first time they had been together, and sat down on the damp earth, gazing at the horizon.

'Alan,' said Billy. 'Are you having strange feelings?'

'What sort of strange feelings?'

'In your willy. Is it going stiff sometimes?'

Alan smirked. 'Sure,' he said. 'I've had them for a while.'

'So what happens?'

'I have a wank.'

'A wank?'

'Yeah, I give it a pull.'

Billy let out a sigh of relief. 'So do I,' he said.

'Everyone does,' said Alan. 'Frank even had a wanking circle at his place once, when his parents were out.'

'A circle?'

'Four of us sat on the floor in his room and pulled on our willies. Frank's got spunk, too.'

'What's spunk?'

'It's the sticky white stuff that makes babies. You know, the seed. We'll get it soon, I reckon.'

'It makes babies? How?'

Alan looked at Billy pityingly. 'Hasn't your dad told you the facts of life?' he said.

'No.'

'Well ask him. My dad told me ages ago. He tried to keep a straight face, but he couldn't.'

'So what did he say?'

'He said how babies are made. How you put your willy inside a girl.'

'Inside a girl?'

"Course. Then the spunk goes inside her tummy and makes a baby. It's like the cows and the pigs. You must have seen them doing it.'

Billy had never heard anything so improbable in his life. He thought of Sarah, of the little fold of skin that she peed out of. Was that where you put it? He gazed out across the countryside and wondered how he could find a way of asking his father. But no, he would ask his mother first.

That night as Billy lay in bed he thought of Sarah, and of Audrey at school, but he still couldn't make a connection between girls and these feelings he now so easily aroused. He thought instead of clouds scudding across a blue sky. And he thought that perhaps he wouldn't talk to his mother about this just yet.

———

Every few days now, Margaret would set off for Tanyard Cottage in the middle of the morning and read *Tess of the D'Urbervilles* to Leonora Vale.

It was something she had come to look forward to eagerly. Leonora would sit back in her chair, a dreamy expression softening her features. Margaret hadn't considered herself a good reader, but after a few chapters she became quite fluent, hesitating or stumbling less often. And after an hour or so of reading, they would talk for a while until it was time for Margaret to go home.

Leonora seemed to Margaret to be very bound up in the destiny of Tess Durbeyfield. Margaret had forgotten how highly wrought was Hardy's language, how mystical his imagery. After a few mornings she came to the chapter in which Tess's baby is taken ill. 'Poor Sorrow's campaign against sin, the world, and the devil was doomed to be of limited brilliancy,' she read, '– luckily perhaps for himself, considering his beginnings. In the blue of the morning that fragile soldier and servant breathed his last, and when the other children awoke they cried bitterly, and begged Sissy to have another pretty baby.' She paused and looked up, and saw that tears were streaming down Leonora's cheeks.

'It's terribly sad, isn't it?' said Margaret, not sure whether to go on.

Leonora took out a handkerchief.

'My baby's name was Astraea,' she said eventually. 'She died of meningitis just before her first birthday.'

Margaret set aside the book and looked at the rumpled figure sitting across from her. Leonora suddenly seemed very small and frail.

'I'm so sorry,' said Margaret. 'I had no idea.'

'Of course you hadn't, poppet,' said Leonora, blowing her nose loudly. She paused to collect herself. 'I was quite old, especially for those days – thirty-five.' She stared beyond Margaret. 'My dancing days were over, and I had no idea what to do. A man came along, a kind man I thought, and we had a child. But Astraea never had a chance, and after she died the man left me.'

Margaret thought of Billy and Sarah, and felt a shudder go through her. The death of a child was surely the worst thing of all.

Leonora gathered herself up and smiled. 'I'll put the kettle on again,' she said. 'How foolish of me to cry over something that happened more than twenty years ago.'

'It's not foolish at all,' said Margaret. 'Now let me make the tea.'

As Margaret walked back to the house, her thoughts dwelled on Leonora. The more she learned about her the more intriguing she became. She must have lived there alone for many years. What did she do with herself all day, an intelligent woman who had difficulty reading and whose only company, besides Margaret herself and the cats, was the radio? She was wandering in the middle of the road when suddenly from around the bend a large silver car shot towards her. She leaped into the ditch and fell awkwardly, covering herself in mud. The car screeched to a halt, and two people stepped out and ran back up the hill. Margaret stood brushing away the dirt.

'My dear young lady,' said the driver. 'I'm so awfully sorry.'

He was a rakish man in a fawn camel-hair coat and shiny brown shoes.

'It's perfectly all right,' she said. 'I was jaywalking.'

'And David was going too fast,' said the woman. 'I've told him a thousand times to drive more slowly around here.'

She was about Margaret's age, and wore a fox fur coat and an elaborate hat. Her oval face was carefully made-up. Like her companion, she seemed wholly out of place on this country road.

'May we offer you a lift?' said the man.

'That's very kind, but I live less than half a mile away, and in the wrong direction for you.'

'You live nearby?'

As he said this, it dawned on Margaret who they must be.

'At Fosse's Farm,' she said.

'Then we're neighbours. We live in Coombe Hall.' He thrust out his hand. 'David Latymer,' he said. 'This is my wife, Clare.'

They were flustering her, these sleek people. 'I had better get home and clean my coat,' she said.

'Of course,' said Latymer. 'But we must make this up to you. You must come for a drink one evening.'

'That would be very pleasant,' said Margaret, thinking that it would probably not be pleasant at all.

'What is your telephone number?'

'We're not on the phone.'

'Then we will send you a note,' said Clare. 'How nice to meet you.'

Five

The car stood in the yard like a magnificent black beast. Billy soaped its haunches gently, while Jim worked on the radiator grille. Since Winifred didn't drive, she had simply handed over the keys. To all intents, the Vanguard was now theirs.

'How big an engine has it got?' asked Billy.

'It's a two-litre.'

'What's a litre?'

'It's something like two pints.'

'Like pints of milk?'

'Yes.'

Billy tried to imagine four milk bottles under the bonnet.

'Can we see?'

'When we've finished washing it.'

All Billy's scorn for this car had vanished the moment his father drove it home. It was a car and it was theirs, and that was all that mattered. Jim splashed a bucket of water over the roof, and they shammied it dry. It shone brightly in the cold sunlight.

Jim opened up the bonnet and they looked inside. Strangely, Billy had never seen a car engine before, nor wondered what it might be like. His father was more interested in the lines of a car than its innards. The engine and the other mechanisms were weirdly complicated, pipes and wires and rubber tubes sprouting everywhere like the stems of an exotic plant.

'These are the four cylinders,' said Jim.

'The four pints.'

'That's right. The Jaguar had eight. Here's where you put in the oil, and that thing there is the windscreen washer refill.'

'What's this?' said Billy, pointing to a bulbous contraption with a stopper at its head.

'I think that's for the brake fluid.'

Jim closed the bonnet and brushed his hands on his trousers. 'She's all right, this one,' he said. He patted the car's front wing, and they stood back to admire it.

'So now can we go to the tor?' said Billy.

Jim's face darkened. 'The tor?' he said. 'We'll see.'

'But why not?'

'Do you have any idea how much petrol costs?'

'No.'

'Well it's bloody expensive. Just because we've got a car again doesn't mean we can go tearing off wherever we want. The main thing is that I can drive to work and back instead of freezing on that bike.'

'But the tor isn't that far away. Surely we can afford to go just once?'

Jim picked up the bucket. 'I'll be the judge of what we can afford,' he said, and he turned towards the house.

———————

It was a short step from reading aloud to Leonora Vale to auditioning at the Byre Amateur Theatrical Society, and one made possible by the car. As Margaret drove through the darkness to Wells she did her best to suppress the skittishness that had overtaken her.

The Byre Theatre was at the lower end of Chamberlain Street. As Margaret entered the foyer a very large woman appeared, holding out a hand stiffly in front of her. 'Diana Mogg,' she said loudly. 'You must be Margaret Palmer.'

She was about six feet tall, with a mane of white hair and eyes that swam behind the thick lenses of her glasses. She was both producer and director, apparently, and was a teacher at the Girls' Blue School. She led Margaret into the auditorium. Four people sitting in the front row turned and stood as they came down the aisle.

'Introductions,' said Diana Mogg. 'Michael Ford is playing Victor Prynne, Bert Dampler is Elyot Chase, Irene Beer is Louise, the maid, and Liz Burridge is Sybil Chase. This is Margaret Palmer, who we're auditioning for the part of Amanda Prynne.'

There was a general shaking of hands and nodding of heads.

'I'm sorry if this seems like an inquisition,' said Diana. 'We thought we had our Amanda, but she's moving, and has had to drop out.'

Margaret suddenly felt very vulnerable. She hadn't done anything like this since school. There was a catch in her throat, and she wished she could have a glass of water.

'We'll start with Victor and Amanda's first scene,' said Diana. 'You've read the play, I trust?'

Margaret brandished her French's acting edition of *Private Lives*. 'I can't say I'm familiar with it yet,' she said.

'Oh, never mind about that. If I give you the part, you'll soon be very familiar with it.'

Margaret and Michael Ford stepped up onto the stage, and stood awkwardly in the centre. 'Don't bother about stage directions,' said Diana. 'Just think about the words.'

Michael Ford was a good-looking young man with olive skin and very dark eyes that stared at her in a way that Margaret felt was not yet called for by the script.

'Now,' said Diana. 'You are on a hotel balcony in Deauville with your new husband. You are very rich, and you have nothing better to do than to indulge in idle chatter about whether it would be nicer to be in Paris. Your first husband, unbeknownst to you, is in the next room with his new wife, and you will soon bump into him. You are very beautiful, Margaret, and you are wearing a negligee.'

Michael laughed nervously, and then looked abruptly down at his script.

'Come on then, Victor,' said Diana.

Michael cleared his throat and spoke his first line. 'Mandy,' he said, to which Margaret replied, 'What?'

'Come outside, the view is wonderful.'

'I'm still damp from the bath. Wait a minute… I shall catch pneumonia, that's what I shall catch.'

Before Michael could speak his next line, Diana stood up and shouted 'Diaphragm!' Margaret looked down at her, startled by the interruption.

'Pardon?'

'Use your diaphragm. You're speaking from here,' she said, pointing to her throat, 'when you should be speaking from here.' With this she thumped her stomach very hard. 'Now go back to the beginning.'

Margaret breathed deeply and spoke her lines as clearly as she could. She had no idea how to use her diaphragm.

'God!' said Michael.

'I beg your pardon?'

'You look wonderful.'

'Thank you, darling.'

'Like a beautiful advertisement for something.'

'Nothing peculiar, I hope.'

'I can hardly believe it's true. You and I, here alone together, married!'

Margaret began to relax, and even to enjoy the banter of these frivolous characters. When they came to the end of the scene she looked down expectantly.

Diana turned to the others, paused for a moment, and said, 'I think we have our Amanda.'

Margaret heaved a sigh of relief, and Michael leaned across and kissed her on the cheek. 'Wonderful, darling,' he said.

They left the theatre and walked together to the Swan Hotel, where Michael insisted on buying the drinks. They were in ebullient mood, and only Liz Burridge seemed to Margaret to hold back.

'Now all we need is for someone to take over from Winnie Underhill on the costumes,' said Diana.

'I might have something in my wardrobe that would do,' said Margaret, thinking of an evening dress she had managed to hold on to.

'Good,' said Diana, gazing at her almost affectionately. 'Oh, Margaret,' she said, clapping her hands, 'you *are* Amanda!'

They sat in the armchairs chatting and scheming. This was Margaret's first night out since they had come to Coombe, and she was light-headed by now.

'We must do an article on the production in the New Year,' said Michael, 'to get the ball rolling.' He turned to Margaret. 'I'm on the *Wells Journal*. Features.'

'That must be very interesting.'

'Until I land a job with one of the nationals, yes.' He smiled at her artlessly. 'I'm going places, you see.'

Margaret and Billy and Sarah drove into Wells one morning to do some shopping for Christmas presents. To Billy the deliberations over what to buy and for whom and how much seemed endless, and he was glad when it was finally over and they could go to the Bishop's Palace. They wandered across to the gatehouse, and watched the ducks scoot about in the moat.

'Do you see that rope?' said Margaret. 'The swans tug on it when they're hungry, and it rings a bell.'

'How do they do that?' said Sarah.

'With their beaks.'

87

'Let's see them do it.'

'They don't seem to be around. We'll come back another day.'

Sarah looked crestfallen, and Margaret took her hand. They walked to the cathedral, and entered the door under the carved figures of the west face. The vaulted arches of the nave soared above them.

'This must be the biggest church in the world,' said Billy, his mouth agape as he craned to look upwards.

'One of the biggest, I'm sure.'

He stood absorbing the wonderful stillness of the place.

'Will we go to our church at Christmas?' he said.

'Would you like to?'

'Yes. It's Jesus's birthday. We went last Christmas, didn't we?'

Margaret gazed towards the quire without replying. She had never been in the least religious, but a place like this was a challenge to her unbelief. After a few moments she said, 'I need a cup of coffee before we go home. Would you two like a lemonade?'

They walked across the green, along Sadler Street and into Goody's café. The place was full of people, and very stuffy. The waitress seemed to recognize Margaret.

'This is Liz Burridge,' she said to the children. 'She's in the play with me.'

Liz smiled shyly without saying anything, and took their order. When she returned she spilled coffee into the saucer, and this seemed to distress her far more than it should have done. She fussed over it with a cloth.

'I'm so clumsy,' she said.

When she was out of earshot, Margaret said, 'She's a strange girl, that one. Goodness knows how she's going to carry off the part of Sybil.'

'Who's Sybil?' said Billy.

'She's a character in my play. She's a very chatty character.'

'She doesn't look very chatty to me.'

Jim found himself settling into his new routines. Winifred Underhill had been a great help at first, but now that Reg was back at home, she left Jim to his own devices. He quickly realized that running the shop was essentially no different from running the car showroom. Reg had been meticulous in his record-keeping, and it wasn't hard to work out who to speak to about what. While he reproached himself for it continually, Jim couldn't help but feel relieved at having the place to himself. He thought about taking on a junior, but decided it wasn't necessary provided his customers knew not to call at lunchtime. He still felt confined much of the time, but he told himself there was nothing to be done about that.

He had seen Liz once since the evening in the Anchor, and it had been strained. She had got him to promise that now that he had the use of a car, they would take a trip somewhere soon; but one way or another he hadn't set a date.

Since he could afford a shepherd's pie or a bowl of soup for lunch these days, he had taken to going to the Crown. One day as he was finishing off his pint of beer he glanced at a copy of the *Wells Journal* belonging to someone at the next table. The headline read, 'Three Wells Men Arrested for Book Theft'.

He quickly left the pub and bought a copy of the paper. Back in the shop he sat down and read the story.

'Three local men, and a bookseller in London, were arrested this week on charges of theft and receiving stolen goods. George Crocker and Arthur Trafford were charged with stealing a large number of antique books from the house of Mr Alfred Pettigrew, owner of Pettigrew's Printing Works. Gordon Towker, another local man, and Bernard Smith, a bookseller with premises near the British Museum, were charged with receiving stolen goods.

'Mr Pettigrew's house was broken into on the night of the 21st of September. Wells Police believe that Crocker and Trafford took away as many as thirty books, valued at more than a thousand pounds. It is alleged that Towker then took receipt of them and sold them on to Mr Smith. Police from the Theobalds Road station in west central London arrested Smith after an anonymous buyer reported his suspicion that a book Smith attempted to sell him came from Mr Pettigrew's collection. It would appear that Smith gave the police Towker's name, and that Towker in turn gave Wells Police the names of Crocker and Trafford.

'All four men have been released on bail, pending proceedings at Wells Assizes early in the New Year.'

Jim laid down the paper and sank back into his chair. You bloody fool, he thought. What on earth were you thinking of? He stared out into the shop, Towker's words coming back to him: 'He doesn't know your name, and he won't ask.'

Smith had clearly shopped Towker, and Towker had shopped the thieves. If Jim were going to receive a visit from the police, then surely it would have happened by now. What exactly had Towker said about how the books got to London? He looked down at his sweaty, fidgeting hands. There was nothing to do but sit it out, and stay out of Towker's way.

The bell on the front door rang, and Jim sprang up from his chair.

'Mr Palmer?' said his customer.

He couldn't have been thirty, but the top of his high domed head was quite bald except for a few sandy wisps. He had a girl's mouth and soft grey eyes.

'Winnie Underhill suggested I call by. My name's Bert Dampler. I work at the Regal. I'm in a play, *Private Lives*, and I'm going to need a suit.'

'My wife's in that play.'

'Yes, and we're very glad to have her.' He bobbed up and down as he spoke; if he weren't so deferential, Jim might have supposed he was spoiling for a fight.

'You're going to want something that looks like it's from the thirties.' Jim went across to the rack of suits. 'None of these were made for the casino at Deauville, I'm afraid,' he said. He took down the darkest suit he could find. 'This might be a bit big for you, but no doubt we can take up the hems and sleeves.'

Dampler went into the changing room and emerged a few moments later, his feet tripping over the trouser-ends. Jim knelt down to take them up, pinning them in place.

'Put your shoes back on and take a look in the mirror,' he said.

Dampler didn't look at all bad. 'You'll need a crisp white shirt and a dicky bow. What's your character's name?'

'Elyot Chase.'

'Well, Elyot, I think you cut a fine figure. That'll be eight pounds.'

Jim took up the sleeves of the jacket and made out an alterations slip. As he was handing it to Dampler he said, 'So my wife's got a future on the stage, has she?'

'Well, we've only seen her in the audition so far. But she's perfect for the part. She's smart, your wife.'

'Yes,' said Jim. 'I suppose she is.'

———

Billy missed the television, and Alan had told him there were children's matinees at the Regal. Alan persuaded his father to drive them in the milk lorry to Wells one day, and they went to see *Flash Gordon*. A queue of boys waited patiently outside the cinema. They bought gobstoppers and sat in the dim light waiting for the films to start.

Billy had seen *Flash Gordon* on television, but on the cinema screen it seemed rather flimsy. Flash's rocket fizzed as it streaked towards the planet Mongo. Ming the Merciless had unleashed a deadly purple dust on the Earth, and had to be stopped. Billy watched as Flash and Dr Zarkov fought their way into Ming's palace, where the evil scientist was experimenting on his victims in a glass tube. There were four short films, by the end of which Flash had managed to save the Earth. As they stepped back into the foyer Billy said, 'That wasn't very good, was it?'

'They're old films,' said Alan. He looked at the posters advertising forthcoming attractions. 'They should have some newer stuff here.'

'There's a *Hopalong Cassidy* programme on after Christmas,' said Billy. 'It says so outside.'

'He's not much better,' said Alan.

They went out into the street, and stood wondering what to do until Alan's father returned to pick them up.

'Let's go and see the Blue School,' said Billy.

They asked someone the way, and walked along Princes Road until they came upon a weathered brick building that stood back a little from the street.

'It's red!' said Alan.

'I don't think it's called the Blue School for that reason,' said Billy.

'Maybe they see it as blue when we see it as red,' said Alan with a smile.

As they were walking back, Billy looked down a side road and saw a black Standard Vanguard parked to one side. It was exactly the same as theirs. He turned towards it, and as he came nearer he saw from the number plate that it was indeed theirs. But his father had driven to

Bath that morning, saying he had some business to do. Billy signalled to Alan to stay back, and slowly approached the car. Through the rear window he could see the outlines of two heads, one of them clearly his father's. They appeared to be having an animated conversation. After a few moments his father leaned across and kissed the other person. The kiss lasted a long time, and involved many movements of their arms and hands. Billy stood stock still, not sure what to do. As the figures disengaged, he saw that the other person was the waitress at Goody's, Liz Burridge. His father was stroking her cheek now. Billy looked at the wing mirror, and knew that if he were to stay where he was any longer then his father might see him. He turned and ran, grabbing at Alan as he passed and gesturing to him to follow.

An invitation arrived from the Latymers. Margaret was inclined not to accept it, but Jim was curious about these people, and persuaded her to go. There was no mention of the children, so Margaret asked Hubert Fosse to look in on them.

Jim pressed the button on the entryphone, and within a few seconds the gates swung open to reveal Coombe Hall. It was odd to think that this place was almost directly across the road from the farm: there was no trace of it at all from the road.

A silver Bentley stood on the gravel outside the front door. Jim took in the house and its extensive grounds and said, 'They must be millionaires.'

David Latymer appeared from behind the double doors, and stood under the portico as they approached.

'How very good to see you,' he said. He was wearing brown corduroy trousers and a yellow cashmere jumper. He shook Jim's hand and kissed Margaret's, and led them through a hallway to an enormous room at the back. Clare Latymer raised herself from a chaise longue, laying down a copy of Country Life. They've rehearsed this, thought Jim, this 'rich people at their leisure' act.

'A cocktail?' said David.

Jim had never been one for fancy drinks. He hesitated for a moment.

'I usually have a dry martini at this hour,' said David.

'Thank you,' said Jim, not sure whether he had any choice.

David left the room for a moment, and Margaret complimented Clare on the house.

'We found it soon after David bought the company,' she said. 'We needed somewhere for when we're not in London.' She waved her cigarette in the air, in a gesture that encompassed the entire place. The room they were in was cluttered with furniture. Above the marble fireplace a large and ornate mirror lent Jim a view of Clare's elegant back.

David returned with a tray that bore four glasses, a bottle of gin, a bottle of white vermouth, a silver shaker and some green olives.

'The secret of a good martini is to keep everything in the fridge, even the cocktail sticks,' he said. 'That way you don't dilute it with ice.'

Jim had drunk a martini or two in London. They were lethal. Men in the City would down two or even three before lunch every day, and somehow conduct themselves through the afternoon without forfeiting either their own fortunes or those of their clients. David flourished the shaker and poured out a cloudy liquid. He then pressed two olives onto each cocktail stick and rested them against the sides of the glasses. His movements were very precise and at the same time very casual.

'Cheers!' he said when he had passed around the glasses. 'To our new neighbours.'

They sat down on the two settees, David and Clare on one and Jim and Margaret on the other. The fire crackled, and an ormolu clock above it chimed six o'clock.

'I nearly ran over your lovely wife,' said David to Jim. 'I'm extremely glad I didn't. If I may say so, my dear chap, you are a lucky man.'

Jim took a sip of his martini. It was like being plunged into a cold bath, the chill running all the way down to the pit of his stomach. He eyed David Latymer over his glass. His thick grey hair contrasted with jet black eyebrows that arched above very pale blue eyes. He's a phoney, thought Jim. But then, weren't all rich people phoney? He reminded himself that not so long ago he too had been well off. But not like this.

'I'm lucky in some ways,' he said. He glanced over at Clare, who had hooked her legs under her in such a way as to show off her slim ankles. She had been studying him closely. They can't work us out, Jim thought. Either that or she fancies me.

'Forgive me, Jim, if I say that we know something about you. Only the sort of things one picks up here and there, of course. And having now met you, I have no doubt at all that your fortunes will change for the better before too long.'

One day perhaps, Jim thought, people won't talk to me as though I have some incurable disease.

'Tell me about your own business,' he said.

David set down his martini glass and scooped up a handful of peanuts. 'I own the cider company in Shepton, Charlton Cider,' he said.

'But you're not from around here?'

'No, no, from London. I bought the company five years ago. It wasn't doing very well in those days.'

'And now?'

'Oh, very nicely.'

Clare Latymer stood up and suggested to Margaret that she show her around the house. Jim looked at the two women, at the contrast between the artificiality of Clare and the simplicity of Margaret. I know which one I prefer, he thought.

As they left the room, David topped up Jim's glass. This stuff was beginning to befuddle him, and he would have to be careful what he said.

'So,' said David. 'What's your plan for restoring your fortunes?'

'I'm not sure I have one. I probably won't be discharged from bankruptcy for several years, and until then I'm a bit stuck.'

'All right, so you can't be a director of a company. That doesn't mean to say you can't improve your lot.'

Jim shrugged. 'I applied for any number of jobs, and as soon as I mentioned I was a bankrupt, people went quiet on me.'

'Well, that's simple prejudice, isn't it? You speculated to accumulate, and it didn't quite work out.'

'Not quite.'

'I expect you're a good salesman.'

'I used to be.'

'That's my background, sales. I could sell anything to anyone.' David leaned back into the deep cushions.

'Well, I'm selling now, in a way.'

'You want to set your sights a little higher than that though, don't you?'

'Sure I do. I haven't quite worked out how, that's all.'

94

A large Golden Labrador entered the room and flopped down in front of the fire. David reached down to pat its head.

'It's a seduction, isn't it, selling?' he said. 'You have to make the other person want *you*, as much as what you're selling them. And you have to start by putting yourself in their shoes.'

'Of course.'

'And you know what you must do before you can put yourself in their shoes?'

Jim thought for a moment. The gin was already going to his head.

'You have to take off your own shoes!' said David triumphantly. 'You have to forget who you are, and see who they are.'

'Yes,' said Jim vaguely.

'They're not just buying a product, they're buying a *feeling* about themselves.' There was an evangelical glint in David Latymer's eyes. Jim was beginning to feel very uncomfortable. He put down his drink, promising himself he wouldn't touch it again, and prayed for the return of Clare and Margaret.

'I think you should come and see me some time soon, at the cider factory.'

Jim wasn't sure what he meant by this. Was he thinking of offering him a job, or simply planning to resume the lecture?

'Thank you,' he said. 'I've never seen cider being made.'

David waved his hand dismissively. 'Oh, you can see how it's made, if you like,' he said. 'But personally, I'm more interested in how it ends up down people's throats.'

By the time Clare and Margaret returned, Jim was disliking David Latymer intensely.

'What a magnificent house,' said Margaret.

'Thank you,' said David. 'It does us during the week.'

'We usually spend our weekends in town,' said Clare. 'We're only here now because David has to be at the office in Shepton early tomorrow morning.'

Jim made to get up, and reeled back into the settee. 'We ought to be going,' he said, trying to cover his embarrassment. 'We've taken up quite enough of your time.'

They walked back through the house, and under the portico he breathed in the fresh air deeply. He extended his hand to David Latymer, who shook it forcefully. He's not sober either, he thought.

'Happy Christmas,' said Clare.

'And to you,' said Margaret. She glanced at Jim. 'I think we had better get home,' she said, 'and rescue poor Hubert from the children.'

It was while Billy was re-enacting the battle of the Alamo in the hay-shed that he came upon the bicycle. It was a bitterly cold day, far too cold to play outside. The bike was a dark green Raleigh Junior, and it looked fairly new. What was it doing there, he wondered, so hidden away? With numb hands he pulled it out from behind a bale, brushed off the hay, and swung his leg over the crossbar. It was exactly the right size for him. Scarcely able to contain his excitement, he laid it down on the ground and raced across to the house. Jim and Margaret were sitting at the kitchen table reading separate sheets of the newspaper.

'Dad, Mum!' he shouted. 'There's a bike in the hayshed!'

His father and mother glanced at one another.

'Well, young man,' said Jim, carefully putting together the pages of the paper, 'we'd better go and investigate, hadn't we?'

Billy practically dragged him back to the hayshed. He picked up the bike, and mounted it once again.

'It seems to be a boy's bike,' said Jim, running his hand along the handlebars. 'I wonder whose it is?'

Billy looked up at him, and watched his features break into a smile.

'Happy Christmas, Billy,' he said. 'I think it's come early this year.'

'Oh, Dad! You mean it's for me?'

'Of course it's for you. It's high time you had a set of wheels.'

Out in the yard Jim said, 'The secret is to keep moving forward. If you slow down you'll fall off.' Billy got on, and Jim placed one hand on his shoulder and the other on the back of the frame. 'We'll start doing it together,' he said. 'If you feel yourself falling then jam on the brakes and put your foot out.'

They pushed off, Billy gripping the handlebars. After a few yards Jim let go, and for a moment Billy felt suddenly, terrifyingly free before he clattered to the ground, the bike skidding out from under him. He got up, brushed off his grazed hands, and stood it upright again. They repeated the manoeuvre, Jim holding on for longer, and this time Billy was able to come gently to a standstill and stay in the saddle.

'Try going down the yard,' said Jim. 'It slopes a bit.'

Billy turned the bicycle to face towards the road, and Jim set him off. He quickly gained speed, and now his only thought was to hang on. 'Brake!' shouted his father. He pulled on the brakes, but too hard, and his momentum hurled him over the handlebars and into the ditch.

Jim raced towards him. 'You bloody fool,' he said. 'I told you to brake, not upend it.'

Billy looked up at him dazedly, wondering how he could have known how hard to brake when he'd never ridden a bike before.

'Are you all right?'

'I think so,' he said.

'Well there's no blood, just a bruise on your forehead.'

His father leaned forward and inspected his face closely. Billy pulled back and pushed away his hand.

'What's the matter?' said Jim.

Anger surged through him, with this man who always took things away just as he seemed to be giving them, who always spoiled things with his petty rages. Jim's head being so close to his like this reminded Billy of two other heads, those in the car in Wells. For a moment he considered telling his father that he knew about Liz Burridge. But he thought better of it, and got unsteadily to his feet.

'Nothing's the matter,' he said finally. 'It hurts, that's all.'

———

On the last day at school before the Christmas holidays, the Misses Shute took all the children to church.

'We do this every year,' said Alan. 'It's a special service, just for us.'

A large yew tree dominated the churchyard, and here and there were the gravestones of the children's ancestors. St Peter's Church was small and neat, its grey walls glistening after a night of rain. The children took up their places in the pews in the same positions as they had in the classroom, and Billy sat near the back with Alan, Frank, Les and Ed. The air in the church was if anything colder than outside, and with every whisper from the children came the ghost of a cloud.

The Reverend Harry Hardie watched as they settled, resting his hands on the lectern and raising himself on the balls of his feet now and then.

'Welcome, children,' he said at last, 'to our school Christmas service. We shall sing some hymns and carols, and we shall ask ourselves what is the meaning of Christmas.'

Billy had never set eyes on the vicar before. He had a long grey beard, a reedy voice, and a rather startled expression.

'So, children, what is the meaning of Christmas?'

'Presents,' murmured Alan to Billy, and Les said quite audibly, 'Dad getting drunk.' Frank elbowed Les and told him to shut up.

'Christmas was when Our Lord Jesus was born, who came into the world to save us from our sins. Now where was Jesus born?'

Four or five hands shot up, and the vicar nodded at Sarah. 'In Bethlehem,' she said.

'Quite right. But Joseph and Mary didn't live there, did they, they lived in Nazareth. Why did they have to go to Bethlehem?'

This time the only hand that went up was Frank's. Billy had never seen him volunteer an answer to anything.

'They had to pay some taxes,' he said.

'Almost right, Frank,' said the vicar. 'Very good. They had to *register* for taxes, because Joseph was born there. And what happened when they got to Bethlehem?'

Several hands went up again. 'There was no room at the inn,' said Audrey.

'There was no room anywhere. Too many people had come to the town. So they found refuge in a stall for animals. And where did they put the baby Jesus?'

'In a manger,' said Frank before anyone else could speak.

'Yes. And what is a manger?'

'It's a trough, that animals eat out of.'

Billy looked across at Frank. He was eager and attentive, quite different from the boy who sat at the back of the schoolroom doodling or throwing paper aeroplanes.

'Meanwhile,' continued the vicar, 'in the hills outside the town, there were some shepherds tending their flocks. And an angel appeared to them.'

'And the angel told them the son of God had been born in Bethlehem,' said Frank, 'and they should go and see him.'

They sang some carols, and finally 'Jerusalem'. As they filed out, Harry Hardie shook the children by the hand and wished them a happy Christmas. Back in the playground they had a few minutes before lessons began again.

'That hymn, "Jerusalem",' said Frank to the other boys, 'you know what it's saying, don't you?'

They looked at one another, uncertain what Frank was getting at.

'That Jesus came here, to England.'

'No he didn't,' said Alan.

'He did. With Joseph of Arimathea.'

At this Billy's ears pricked up. 'You mean the one who planted the hawthorn stick at Glastonbury?' he said.

'Yeah.'

'But he didn't come until after Jesus died. He had Jesus's blood in the Holy Grail.'

'He came before too, that's what my dad says. He reckons Joseph was a tin trader, and came to Cornwall with Jesus. Then they came up around here.'

This struck Billy as the most extraordinary thing, and that it should come from Frank made it all the more so.

'When Jesus was young?'

'Probably. Before he went into the wilderness, anyway.'

Miss Shute called them to their lessons, and they dashed back into the classroom. 'You don't know everything about Glastonbury,' said Frank as they were sitting down.

'I never said I did,' said Billy. 'Maybe you can tell me more some time.'

———

Margaret had bought Leonora Vale a geranium, and she and Billy and Sarah walked to Tanyard Cottage to give it to her. Leonora was wearing a green plaid skirt and a red jumper, as though in anticipation of this Christmas call.

'You don't seem to have very much in the way of plants,' said Margaret. 'I thought this might brighten things up.'

'Oh, my plants are in the garden,' said Leonora. 'Not that there's much to see at the moment.'

All Billy had seen of Leonora's garden was a tangled patch at the front.

'Perhaps we could see it anyway?' said his mother.

99

Leonora led them through the room where the cats lived, and out of the back door. They stepped into a walled garden that Billy had never imagined could possibly be there. Though it was in its winter drab, this was a beautifully tended place. There were small apple and greengage trees trained against the walls, gnarled espaliers with lichen-covered branches, and row upon row of what in a few months would be a wonderful assortment of vegetables. At the end were a greenhouse and a rickety shed.

'It's a secret garden,' said Billy.

'Yes,' said Leonora, 'that's exactly what it is. And now you too know the secret.'

They walked slowly down the path between the vegetable patch and the flower border.

'Potatoes, beans, onions, carrots, cabbages, parsnips,' said Leonora in a kind of litany. 'And over here there will be larkspur, helichrysum, tulips and roses.' They went inside the greenhouse and stood on the chilly stone floor, gazing up at the glass roof. 'Those are peach and nectarine,' said Leonora, pointing to spindly branches that clung to the wooden struts. There were a couple of cracked panes, but this entire space seemed to be cared for in a way that the house simply wasn't. They walked across to the shed, and Billy peeked in at the jumble of tools and pots and cans. He picked up one half of a broken pair of shears.

'What's this?' he asked.

'Oh, they're my non-secateurs,' said Leonora, smiling.

'But there's only one of them,' said Billy.

Leonora patted Billy on the head and said, 'Now you've ruined my little joke.'

'You are a sly one, Leonora,' said Margaret. 'You've kept this all to yourself.'

'As it should be. You know what Voltaire said, don't you?'

'No.'

'Well, he said simply that we must cultivate our garden. But what he was really saying was that the world's troubles would be greatly eased if we did.'

'I wish I had a garden like this,' said Margaret. 'I did once, I suppose, but I had other people to look after it.'

'Then it wasn't really yours.'

They went back into the house, and Leonora put the kettle on.

'What are you doing on Christmas Day?' said Margaret.

'What I do every day, poppet. Why?'

'Would you like to come to our house for dinner?'

The first rehearsal of *Private Lives* took place on a very cold evening. Margaret drove carefully on her way into Wells, her desire not to be late wrestling with her fears about ice on the road. The others were all there by the time she arrived.

'We will do the first two scenes,' said Diana Mogg. 'Now, remember how important these are in establishing the characters and their relationships. All four of you are in an unsettled state. You are *giddy*.'

Margaret sat in the front row watching Bert Dampler and Liz Burridge rehearse the first scene. Liz projected more strongly than Margaret had thought she might. Bert on the other hand seemed too wet. He could manage a certain kind of flippancy, but there was something unconvincing about him in the end: she simply couldn't imagine him being rich. Which set her to wondering whether anyone would find *her* convincing as a rich woman. Well, she would just have to put it on. And the more her character was described by Elyot and Sybil Chase as being uncontrolled, wicked and unfaithful, the more determined she became to play it to the hilt.

'I don't believe I'm a bit like what you think I am,' she said as she took her turn on the stage.

'How do you mean?'

'I was never a poor child.'

'Figure of speech, that's all.'

'I suffered a good deal, and had my heart broken. But it wasn't an innocent, girlish heart. It was jagged with sophistication. I've always been sophisticated, far too knowing. That caused many of my rows with Elyot. I irritated him because he knew I could see through him.'

They came to the end of the scene. 'Good, Margaret,' said Diana. 'Now, Michael, you must be altogether more cynical. You don't really love Amanda, you've just persuaded yourself that you *should* love her. Let's try it again.'

They went back to the beginning, and this time Michael was better. He's feeling his way into it, thought Margaret, as we all are. As the evening wore on, she began to sense a determination in herself to make this as good as it could be. And she sensed something else, something she hadn't felt for a long time, which both exhilarated and appalled her: she began to feel the sharp promptings of ambition.

At the end of the rehearsal they all went to the Swan Hotel again. The euphoria of the audition evening was replaced now by a mood of realism, and an intimation that this apparently shallow play about selfish and foolish people would in fact be harder to bring off than they had supposed. Margaret made a point of sitting next to Liz.

'You're very good,' she said. 'You've got Sybil's...' She broke off, trying to find the right word. The one she wanted to use was 'insecurity', but she didn't dare say it. In the end she said 'gaiety', which was not what she meant at all.

'You're very good too,' said Liz. 'You must have had lots of experience.'

'Experience of acting?'

Liz looked away for a moment. 'I mean you really *are* sophisticated. The rest of us...' At this point she leaned towards Margaret, and spoke softly. 'The rest of us are just country people. But you know what it's like to be well off, to have style.'

Margaret wondered what Liz had been told about her, and was certain it must have been exaggerated. She was beginning to think that Liz's remarks might betray some sort of resentment.

'I think style is one of those things you can't buy,' said Margaret. 'You either have it or you don't. And may I say that I think you have it yourself.'

The evening broke up, and Margaret drove home. Gliding along the Launcherley road she felt for a few moments weightless, and abstracted from her life. What would it be like, she wondered, to be free of all this, of her responsibilities to Jim and the children, to her life as she knew it? She let her imagination carry her away. She was an actress on the West End stage, and Michael Ford her leading man and her lover. In her suite in the Savoy Hotel, she sat reading her notices and savouring the triumph of the opening night. Such thoughts quickly shamed her, and she set them aside. But she was unable to deny them, or to suppress them entirely.

Later, as she sat with Jim in the parlour, she found herself returning to the script, unable to leave it aside. She laughed out loud at one point.

'What's that?' said Jim.

'Oh, it's just Coward's way with words, that's all. "Certain women should be struck regularly, like gongs." That shouldn't be funny at all, but it is.'

'You're enjoying it, then?'

'I'm enjoying it very much.'

Jim put down the newspaper. 'Bert Dampler came into the shop the other day. He doesn't look the part, somehow.'

'Oh, he'll do. But I'm bound to say that we women are better than the men.'

'Who's playing the other woman?'

'A girl called Liz Burridge. She's a waitress in Goody's café. She's very young, but she's definitely got something.'

'Liz Burridge?' said Jim.

'Yes, do you know her?'

'Well, I've bumped into her in Goody's.' He picked up his newspaper. 'I see Macmillan's in trouble again,' he said.

Six

On Christmas morning Jim set off in the car with Billy and Sarah to collect Leonora Vale. In the confined space Billy smelled the faint scent of urine that seemed to follow her everywhere, and he was now certain that it came from her rather than the cats. She really was a very strange person, seeming at some times to be very wise and at others very silly. He couldn't remember anyone outside the family ever being invited to Christmas dinner before, and he wondered what it was about Miss Vale that his mother found so fascinating.

'Happy Christmas!' she said when they arrived, handing Margaret an exuberantly wrapped bottle of whisky.

'Leonora, you shouldn't,' said Margaret.

'Oh, I think she should,' said Jim, smiling easily and taking the bottle from Margaret's hand.

The turkey from Alton's farm took hours to cook, but this time Margaret was prepared.

'And what did Father Christmas give you, poppet?' said Leonora to Sarah as they sat down to eat.

'There's no such thing as Father Christmas,' said Sarah emphatically. 'I've known that for ages.'

'You've known it since last Christmas,' said Jim.

'I always knew.'

'No you didn't,' said Billy. 'You used to ask me how he could get down so many chimneys in one night.'

Jim proposed a toast, and they drank to what he called 'companionship'.

'How is the play coming along?' said Leonora to Margaret.

'We've only had one rehearsal. But it's fun. And harder than I thought it would be.'

'Ah, Noël was always a deceiver. He made everything look so easy, when it wasn't at all.'

'Noël?' said Jim. 'You knew Noël Coward?'

'When we were very young, yes. We spent a few weekends together at Hambleton Hall, with Mrs Astley Cooper. She was a friend of Noël's boyfriend, Philip Streatfield.'

'I thought Noël was a boy's name,' said Billy.

'It is,' said Leonora.

'But only girls have boyfriends.'

Leonora swept her hand through her hair and gave his mother a supplicating look.

'He was a friend who happened to be a boy,' said Margaret.

'Yes,' said Leonora. 'We were all children really, no more than eighteen or so.'

'What was he like?' said Billy.

Leonora looked at Billy and Sarah as if considering how much she could say. 'He was so young, so impressionable. He would follow Mrs Cooper around with a notebook, jotting down her bon mots.'

'What's a bonmow?'

'It's something clever that people say. Like "only mad dogs and Englishmen go out in the midday sun".'

'That's not clever at all,' said Sarah. 'Cats go out in the midday sun too. Lucy does.'

'How is Lucy?'

'She's got fleas,' she said, jamming her knife into a roast potato and sending it flying off her plate.

'So did you get to know Coward well?' said Margaret, rescuing the potato and cutting it up.

'Not well. I spent perhaps three or four weekends with him. And of course there was always such a houseful. One saw other people at meals and drinks, and played games in the evenings. But the men were usually off hunting during the day.'

'Not Coward, surely?'

'Well, let's just say he wasn't quite as fastidious about hunting as Oscar Wilde.'

'Are you going to tell us you knew Oscar Wilde too?' said Jim.

Leonora laid her hand on his. 'Now, now, young man,' she said. 'I'm not that old.'

After dinner Billy and Sarah listened to Wilfred Pickles on the radio, visiting a children's hospital. Jim poured shots of whisky for himself and Margaret and Leonora, and later he drove Leonora home. When he returned he said to Margaret, 'She's a queer fish, your Miss Vale, but she's all right, I think.'

'She smells like a fish,' said Sarah.

'She smells like pee,' said Billy.

Margaret's eyes flashed suddenly. 'If I hear one more word like that from either of you, you'll spend the rest of Christmas in your room.'

Billy stared at his mother, astonished by the vehemence of her words.

'I'm sorry,' she said, beginning to stack the dishes. 'I think Leonora's a treasure, that's all.'

———

As Jim sat quietly in the Crown, he heard a voice from behind him say, 'I've been looking for you everywhere.'

'You only had to come to the shop,' said Jim.

'You and I need to have a word,' said Towker. 'Let's take a walk.'

They went out into Market Place, and began walking towards the gates of the palace. Towker was in an agitated state, and he pressed ahead of Jim and into the grounds.

'You've heard I've been arrested,' he said when they were alone. 'Receiving stolen goods.'

'What's that got to do with me?' said Jim.

'Come off it, Palmer,' said Towker harshly. He flicked away his cigarette butt. 'Smith grassed on me.'

Jim thrust his hands into his coat pockets. 'I was doing a favour for a friend,' he said. 'I was going to London anyway, and you asked me to drop off a few packages.'

'Very decent, I'm sure.'

Jim felt a shiver of fear run through him.

Towker glanced edgily around. 'Look,' he said at last, 'there's no reason why you need come into this. Smith couldn't care less. But I'm going to need a favour.'

Jim let out a slow breath and watched it mist in the still air. 'What sort of favour?' he said.

'Friend of mine needs a job.'

'I'm not an employment agency.'

'Just for a few weeks. He wants to get into the fashion business in London, and he needs someone to show him the ropes.'

Jim looked down at his feet. So, he thought, it's come to this. 'I'm supposed to give him the benefit of my vast experience, then, am I?' he said.

'It's simple,' said Towker. 'He spends a few weeks helping you out, you show him how the place works, and then you write a nice reference on Underhill's notepaper.'

'I don't need any help.'

Towker looked at him levelly. 'I think you do,' he said.

The cathedral loomed palely in the moonlight. Jim and Liz sat a little apart on the bench, not touching or even looking at one another. The cold evening air, which might have drawn them together, somehow caused them to huddle in their own spaces.

'Why didn't you tell me you were in the play?' he said.

'Why should I? There's lots of things I do that you don't know about.'

'But after Margaret's audition?'

'We haven't seen each other since then, remember?'

'It's Christmas. There's a lot going on.'

Liz turned and looked at him very directly. 'Jim, you're a nice man and all that, but I'm not sure this was a good idea.'

'Maybe we shouldn't see each other again.'

She sat in silence for a few moments. 'Is that what you want?' she said at last.

He gazed towards the cathedral. What did he want, really? He wished he knew.

'No, Liz, it isn't,' he said.

She shifted along the bench and rested her head on his shoulder. 'It isn't what I want either,' she said. 'But I'm in a play with your wife.'

He looked down at her, and Margaret's description flashed through his mind: 'She's very young, but she's definitely got something.' His thoughts drifted to Margaret. Here he was again, neglecting his wife and his children, chasing after someone who would soon enough pass out of his life. Was this what he wanted, really?

She took his hand and entwined his fingers in hers. 'Do you have the keys to the shop?' she said.

The new term began, and the children shivered in the barely heated classroom, the boys at the back etching patterns into the ice on the inside of the windows. A new sense of purpose had been instilled in those who would be taking the eleven-plus. Miss Shute was firmer now, less willing to indulge their whims, and to Billy the classroom was a place of work in a way it had never been before. In the playground the boys tore around for a few minutes to get warm, and then congregated in the far corner.

'I've been thinking about what you said before Christmas,' said Billy to Frank. 'About how Jesus came around here. I think you're right. It makes sense, doesn't it?'

'I expect so,' said Frank a little warily.

'Just think of all the things that have happened at Glastonbury. It was because Jesus went there and made it a holy place.'

'I didn't say he went to Glastonbury. Just around here somewhere.'

'But he must have come to Glastonbury. That's where Joseph of Arimathea came.'

Frank rested his long back against the wall and eyed Billy thoughtfully. 'My dad would know,' he said. 'You could talk to him about it.'

'Could I?'

'Don't see why not. Come back with me after school and we'll ask him.'

As Billy and Frank and Ed walked along the Arminster road a bank of dark clouds massed above them. The boys looked up expectantly.

'It's going to snow,' said Frank.

'Oh, great!' said Billy. 'I want to see what it looks like in the country.'

The Willmott farm was a ramshackle place. The mud in the yard was covered with a rime of frost that the afternoon sun had left untouched. Paint peeled from the doors and windows, and there was a closed-in feeling to it. Billy felt apprehensive about entering this house full of giants. They went into the kitchen, and Frank's mother looked up from the stove.

'This is Billy Palmer,' said Frank. 'He wants to talk to Dad about Jesus.'

Mrs Willmott gazed fixedly at Billy. Like her husband and sons she was tall and rangy. 'Any boy who wants to know about Our Lord is welcome in this household,' she said.

Billy sat at the kitchen table while Frank went in search of his father. It was very like the kitchen at home, plain and dark; but there was a sadness about it, and about the whole house, that Billy sensed strongly and couldn't shake off.

Matthew Willmott stooped as he entered the kitchen. He was surely the largest man Billy had ever seen, his shirt-cuffs hanging open around his forearms and his trousers barely stretching to his ankles. He had the same reddish skin as Hubert Fosse, and his carrot-coloured hair shot up into the air above his forehead. Billy watched closely as he sat down on a wooden chair that disappeared under him.

'So, young man,' he said, 'you want to know about Jesus in Somerset, do you?'

'Yes, sir,' said Billy.

'You're a believer, then.'

'A believer?'

'You believe in God and Our Lord Jesus Christ.'

'Of course I do.'

Willmott shifted his weight and reached out for the teapot. 'Don't see you in church, though, do we?' he said.

'My dad and mum don't go very much.'

'Are they believers?'

'I think so.'

Willmott poured tea into a large mug and took a noisy draught from it. He looked at him in the sceptical way that Billy had come to know so well from Frank. 'Families should go to church together,' he said. 'Now, what can I tell you?'

'Frank said that when we sing "Jerusalem" we're singing about Jesus coming to England.'

'That's right,' said Willmott, burying his face again in the mug.

'Well, I know about Joseph of Arimathea, and I know all about King Arthur and everyone…'

'Those Arthurian stories are nonsense,' said Willmott, cutting Billy off. 'The only stories that are true are the ones in the Good Book.'

'You mean you don't think there was a King Arthur?'

'I think there were some heathen louts who latched on to the story of the Holy Grail, that's what I think.'

Billy wasn't sure what to make of this, but he knew that if he wanted to learn about Jesus in Somerset he'd better not contradict this frightening man. 'Will you tell me about Joseph and Jesus coming to England?' he asked quietly.

Willmott wiped his mouth with the back of his hand and sat back in the creaking chair.

'They came to St Just, in Cornwall, first,' he said. 'Joseph was Mary's uncle. Jesus disappears from the Gospels between the age of twelve and thirty. There must have been many things he did. One of them was to come to England with Joseph.'

'Joseph was a tin trader?'

'Yes. He was a Pharisee, a rich merchant. Cornwall was the best place in the world then for tin. And when they were done in Cornwall, they sailed up the coast to the River Axe, and came to Priddy.'

'Where's Priddy?'

'Just north of Wookey Hole, where the caves are.'

'And what did they do there?'

'Traded for lead. There's lead everywhere around here.'

'Did they leave any sign that they'd been there?'

'Our Lord didn't need to leave any sign. His very existence was a sign.'

'So how do you know?'

Willmott looked sternly at Billy. 'I just know, that's all,' he said. He put his mug down firmly on the table, the noise ringing around the room, and then nodded wordlessly at his wife, who refilled it from the teapot.

Billy considered for a moment. 'And then they came to Glaston-bury,' he said.

'No, Jesus never came to Glastonbury. Joseph came back after Jesus died.'

'Well I think Jesus must have come to Glastonbury. It's such a holy place.'

'Fine words, young man, but he didn't.'

Billy looked around the room, at the cobwebs in the corners of the ceiling and the ashes on the floor, and a thought occurred to him.

'You know when in the Bible the devil takes Jesus to the top of a hill, don't you?'

'"The devil taketh him up into an exceeding high mountain, and sheweth him all the kingdoms of the world, and the glory of them",' said Willmott.

'Well I bet that mountain was Glastonbury Tor.'

Willmott harrumphed loudly. 'That was in Galilee,' he said.

'But how do you know?'

Willmott leaned towards Billy. 'I know because it says so in the Good Book.' He reached out his arm and Billy flinched, but Willmott only rested a hand on his. 'You may be mistaken about a few things, young Palmer, but I like your sincerity. There isn't enough of that around.'

The first flakes of snow had begun to fall. Frank looked towards the window and said to Billy and Ed, 'Let's go outside. Race you.'

They dashed out into the yard, where they stood with their arms outstretched and their mouths open, gathering as many flakes as they could. Suddenly there was a flash of lightning, and a few seconds later a roll of thunder. Billy had never known thunder and lightning with snow before. What had started as a flurry soon became a blizzard, obscuring the house and the barns and making the boys' figures indistinct. Frank whooped with joy. 'It's a sign, Billy,' he said. 'I think you're right about Jesus and Glastonbury. I think he's sending us a sign.' He scooped up a handful of snow and packed it tightly. 'And here's another sign,' he said, and threw the snowball at Billy, hitting him square on the chest. Billy threw one back at Frank, which exploded on the top of his head.

'Signs and wonders!' Frank shouted exultantly. 'Signs and wonders.'

———————

Billy sheltered at the Willmott farm until the storm abated, and then began to trudge home. It was dark and the sky was rapidly clearing, bright stars taking the place of snowflakes above his head. The snow was deep on the ground by now, and for the last half-mile he felt as though he were wading. But none of this mattered to Billy. He was in an exalted state. The knowledge that Jesus had come to Glastonbury, and that he, Billy Palmer, had been the first to understand this, was thrilling. It put all his troubles in an entirely different perspective, his being at odds with Frank Willmott, his fearing that his father was a liar. What did any of that matter when he had solved the great mystery of Jesus's life?

The farm and the cottage eventually came into sight. The moment he stepped into the kitchen, everyone looked up.

'Where on earth have you been?' said Margaret.

'At the Willmott farm,' said Billy. 'Sarah was supposed to tell you. I was all right.'

'You said you were going to look for Jesus,' said Sarah.

Billy turned to Jim. 'Jesus came to Glastonbury Tor, Dad,' he said. 'I know it.'

'Is that what Matthew Willmott's been telling you?'

'No, I said it. And it's true.'

His father shook his head, but said nothing.

In bed that night Billy imagined Jesus and Joseph on the tor. It was a long time before he fell asleep. And when he awoke in the morning it was to a scene that was utterly transformed, dazzling in the bright sunshine.

'There'll be no school for you two this morning,' said Margaret as she shovelled snow away from the doorway.

'And no work for me,' said Jim. 'I'm going to have to phone Winnie, though.' He gazed out of the window.

'Can I come too?' said Billy.

Jim looked back at him. 'If you like,' he said.

'I'll get my wellingtons.'

Out in the yard, Billy struggled in the deep snow.

'Are you sure you want to do this?' said Jim.

'Of course. It's fun.'

There were just two colours in the world, blue and white. The snow lay in drifts in the fields, piled up against walls and hedges, and in the places where cows and sheep usually grazed there was a smooth emptiness. Billy ran his hand along gateposts and branches, brushing off their delicate fronds. The landscape below them was a great white sheet, the tor a pillow someone had left under it.

'It's so quiet, Dad,' he said.

'That's what happens when it snows. Remember "Silent Night"?'

'Silent Day, that's what this is.'

It took them a long time to get to the village, and then Jim had to dig his way into the telephone box. Billy wanted to stay out as long as possible, and persuaded his father to sit with him on the wall of the bridge over the stream. There was a frill of ice at the edge of the water.

'Do you think the river might freeze over?' said Billy.

'No, it runs too fast.'

'That's a shame. We could have gone ice skating, like we used to in Bath.'

'You'll go ice skating again one day.'

Billy looked down at the grey water. 'Are we going to live here for ever now, until I grow up?' he said.

'For ever is a little longer than when you grow up, Billy.'

'But you know what I mean.'

'Yes, I know what you mean. Well, I'm not sure. We'll have to see how this job goes.'

'Is it a good job?'

Jim shrugged his shoulders and pulled out a packet of cigarettes. 'It's all right,' he said. 'It's better than no job at all.'

'Not as good as the Jaguar job, though.'

'No, not anything like as good as that.'

Billy looked behind him at the school, which stood as quiet as on a Sunday, and then back at his father. The thought of his Dinky toys returned, as it had so often lately. His father might not be able to sell real Jaguars any more, but that hadn't stopped him from selling toy ones. He felt an urge to challenge his father's explanations for things, his easy turning aside of the questions Billy wanted answers to.

'Dad,' he said, 'why did you have to close the garage? Mum said you made some mistakes.'

His father lit a cigarette. He inhaled deeply and said, 'Did she now? Well, she was probably right.'

'What happened, then?'

Jim looked at the cigarette in his cold hand. 'If you want to know the truth, I was a bloody fool. I wanted too much.'

'Too much what?'

'Oh, too much money, too many things, too many envious looks from other people. The usual.'

'So that's why you had to close the garage?'

'I had to close the garage because I wanted to sell something that not enough people wanted to buy. If I'd stuck with Austins I'd have been fine. But then you and I wouldn't have been able to ride around in that Mark Eight, would we?'

'I'm glad we've got a car again now, even if it's only a Standard.'

'So am I.' Jim paused for a moment. 'I suppose we have a few things to be glad about, don't we?' he said. 'But it's still not enough.'

Billy studied his father closely as he gazed into the distance.

'I want to leave my mark,' Jim continued. 'I don't want to have to ask myself one day what it was all about.'

'I'm going to leave my mark,' said Billy. 'I'm going to be a famous explorer.'

Jim flicked cigarette ash into the water. 'I'm sure you are,' he said.

When the bell rang early in the morning, Jim's heart sank. He knew very well who this must be.

He was a thin, languid young man. The features of his face were finely drawn, but his upper lip seemed to have trouble closing over his lower. He was smoking a cigarette, and held his hand away from his body in a gesture that Jim suspected he had learned from some film.

'I'm Tony Lewis,' he said. 'Nuncle sent me.'

'Nuncle?'

'Gordon Towker. Mr Towker to you.'

He was probably about seventeen or eighteen. Along with his attempt at an air of sophistication came a contemptuous gaze. He looked around the shop.

'So this is where I'm going to learn about the fashion business, is it?' he said.

'No,' said Jim. 'This is where you're going to learn about selling clothes.'

'An important distinction.'

'Yes. And let's get one or two other things straight while we're at it. I'm doing you a favour, and I expect you to be suitably grateful. There won't be much for you to do, but I want it done properly. Understood?'

'Of course, Jimmy. You don't mind if I call you Jimmy, do you?'

'I do, actually.'

Lewis looked at him calculatingly. 'Still I think I'll call you Jimmy,' he said. 'Actually.'

Jim had come across men like Lewis in the war, but none as nancy as this. He was in for a difficult few weeks, he was quite sure.

'I'm going to show you the stock sheet and where everything is,' he said, trying to suppress his rising anger. 'Which is more than Reg Underhill did for me, I can tell you.'

He spent the morning showing Tony Lewis around. The boy

showed no sign of having registered anything Jim told him. After a while he sat down on the stool and put his feet up on the counter. He leaned back his head and blew a perfect smoke ring into the air. Jim hadn't seen anyone do that for years.

'I'm going to London, you know,' said Lewis.

'So I hear.'

'I'm going to work for Hardy Amies.'

'You are?'

'Well, he doesn't know it yet. But he will.' He blew another smoke ring. 'Then, when I've conquered the London scene, I'll go to Paris and work for Pierre Cardin.'

'You seem to have it all worked out.'

'Yes I have, *actually*.'

'So what are you waiting for?'

'You know very well what I'm waiting for. A year's experience in the trade.'

'A year?' said Jim plaintively.

'Well, that's what it'll say on the reference you're going to write me.'

'I'll write anything you want me to now, today.'

'Not so hasty, Jimmy. There are things I can learn here. But don't worry, I won't be in your way for very long.'

Jim had no intention of leaving Lewis in the shop at lunchtime, and he emptied the till and prepared to lock up as usual for an hour. As he was about to put the takings in the safe, Lewis said, 'I'll need some money.'

'That wasn't part of the deal,' said Jim.

'I don't mean wages. Pocket money.' He reached out a long arm and whisked away two pound notes. 'That'll do,' he said. 'Fivers are so diffi-cult to change, don't you find?'

Jim thought for a moment about trying to take them back, but decided against it.

'So what's with you and Gordon Towker, then?' he said.

'Me and Nuncle?' said Lewis. 'Oh, we're just friends.'

'Nothing more than that?'

A look of distaste came over Lewis's features. 'Gordon Towker?' he said. 'I wouldn't touch him with a bargepole.' Then he looked directly at Jim. 'But a man like you, well that would be a very different matter.'

Jim and Margaret drove to the New Year's Eve party at the Moggs' house in Wells quite late in the evening. They had once again relied on Hubert Fosse to take care of the children, and didn't want him to have to stay too long.

'He seemed a bit fed up about it this time,' said Margaret.

'He shouldn't be,' said Jim. 'I gave him the whisky bottle as we were leaving.'

'I wonder how many people we'll know.'

'You'll know one person and I'll know no one.'

'I hope you're going to enter into the spirit of it.'

'I'll be the life and soul of the party,' said Jim with a wry smile.

The Moggs lived in a large house off the Cheddar road. When they arrived, Diana greeted them boisterously.

'Ah, Amanda Prynne and her current consort,' she said; and to Jim, 'how very good to meet you.'

Peter Mogg was a doctor at Melborne House, and most of the guests were either doctors or teachers. Michael Ford was the only other member of the *Private Lives* cast, and along with him, Jim and Margaret were the youngest people there. An elderly man introduced himself as Robert Erwin, the headmaster of the Boys' Blue School.

'Our boy should be joining you next year,' said Jim.

'It's highly competitive these days,' said Erwin. 'I'm afraid it's not enough just to pass the eleven-plus. He'll have to come to the school for interview.'

Margaret was approached by Michael, and Jim watched her out of the corner of his eye. He hadn't seen his wife like this for a long time now, and he was struck by how much at ease she seemed. She's spent the past months holed up in a tiny cottage, he thought, with only me, the children and Hubert Fosse for company. No wonder she's reached out to Leonora Vale and the theatrical society.

A man came up to Erwin, and in turn was introduced to Jim as Jack Oakley, the owner of the Regal.

'I met your Bert Dampler the other day,' said Jim. 'He's in a play with my wife.'

'Yes, of course.' He leaned towards Jim and said, 'I fancy that young man's future lies *behind* the stage rather than on it.'

He was in his sixties, slightly stooped, with sharp, inquisitive green eyes and terrible teeth. His smile was faintly mischievous, but he closed it down quickly, as though to conceal the ruin of his mouth.

'Are you a cinema-goer?' he said.

'Well, I used to be, but it's difficult now, living in the country.'

'People are watching more and more television these days,' said Oakley. 'It's getting harder to compete.'

'You should show the sort of films you can't see on television, like Hitchcock's.'

'I'm afraid they might go over the heads of some of my customers,' said Oakley. 'Ealing comedies are what go down well here, them and war films.'

Before long Diana Mogg clapped her hands and announced that it was one minute to twelve. She turned on the radio, and as Big Ben started to chime, Jim and Margaret joined the others in counting down to midnight.

'Happy New Year!' said Jim, and he kissed Margaret and held her to him. 'Happy nineteen fifty-nine.'

She rested her head against his shoulder. 'It'll be a better year,' she said, 'won't it?'

'I can't see how it can be any worse.'

They were home by half past twelve. Hubert sat rather still in the most comfortable chair, and Jim could tell at a glance that the level of the whisky bottle had dropped precipitously. He walked him across the yard and made sure he was safe inside his rooms. When he went upstairs, Margaret was standing by the bed in her slip.

The dim light accentuated the lines of her body. He eased the straps over her shoulders, and the slip fell to the floor. Margaret wrapped her arms around his neck.

'Get under the blankets, sweetheart,' he said.

She pressed herself to him. 'No,' she said. 'I want to see you.'

'When we were together, did you really think I was unfaithful to you?' said Amanda Prynne.

'Yes, practically every day,' said Elyot Chase.

'I thought you were too; often I used to torture myself with visions of your bouncing around on divans with awful widows.'

117

'Why widows?'

'I was thinking of Claire Lavenham really.'

'Oh, Claire.'

'What did you say "Oh, Claire" like that for? It sounded far too careless to me.'

'What a lovely creature she was.'

Diana Mogg sprang up from her seat, crying, 'Bert, you must be *wistful* when you say that. The whole point of this scene is to maintain the tension between Elyot and Amanda, the feeling that they are still in love but still distrust one another too. *Wistful* now, Bert. Try it again.'

They were only a few weeks away from the first night, and a sense of urgency was beginning to creep in. Margaret found herself more and more exasperated by Bert and Michael's failure to understand the essence of the play. For her part, Margaret had immersed herself in it to a degree she found a little disconcerting. She so much wanted it to be a success now. She and Diana had tacitly joined forces, and Margaret had become in effect the deputy director. She urged the others on, prompted them when they stumbled over their lines, and made her own suggestions about tone and emphasis. Into the dark and empty space of the theatre she ushered visions of the balcony at Deauville and the apartment in Paris that were almost startling in their clarity. And then she had to remind herself that she had never even been abroad.

The cast dispersed at the end of the rehearsal, and Margaret and Liz found themselves the only ones inclined to go to the Swan for a drink.

'The men aren't strong enough,' said Margaret as they sat down by the fireplace.

'When are they ever?' said Liz.

'Maybe Coward meant the women to be more interesting than the men. But when we come to a line such as "Elyot and me, we were like two violent acids bubbling about in a nasty matrimonial bottle", I'm reminded that Bert Dampler hasn't got a clue what a matrimonial bottle might be like.'

Liz smiled. 'None of the rest of us have,' she said. 'Remember you're the only married person in the cast.'

'Yes, of course,' said Margaret, sighing. 'I'm being too hard on them. And it's not as though we're much better.' She looked across at Liz, at the supple figure sitting rather too straight in the leather armchair. 'What about you, Liz? Do you have a boyfriend?'

Liz looked into the fire and then abruptly back at Margaret. 'Nobody special,' she said. 'Why do you ask?'

Margaret shrugged. 'I'm sorry, I'm just curious. You're such an attractive girl. I'm surprised Michael or Bert haven't been hanging around you.'

'Michael did make a pass once, but I don't care for him. He thinks he's a charmer. I don't like that.'

'What *do* you like in men?'

Liz shifted uneasily in her chair. She was avoiding Margaret's gaze now.

'I like a man to be attentive, but not smarmy,' she said at last.

'Don't we all.'

They sat silent then, Liz apparently mesmerized by the flames of the fire. Margaret realized that she barely knew her.

'What are your plans, Liz?' she said. 'What are you going to do with your life?'

'I'm going to nursing school in Bristol after Easter.'

'I couldn't imagine you staying at Goody's for very long.'

'That's just a way of filling in time. They weren't able to take me last September.'

'Do you know Bristol?'

'I've been there once, for the interview.'

'It'll be very different from here.'

Liz looked up at Margaret again. 'I want it to be as different as possible,' she said.

———

When the very cold weather was over, trade became brisker in the shop. Jim had mastered the essentials, and was quietly satisfied that there appeared to have been no falling off in takings since Reg's stroke. All he needed now was to see the back of Tony Lewis, and then he could begin to prepare for the spring and summer consignments.

One morning Norman Elsworth from Herrings came in looking for a new jacket.

'When are you going to wear it?' said Jim.

'Every day,' said Elsworth.

'To tweed or not to tweed, then, that is the question,' said Lewis.

Elsworth gave him a sour look. 'I can make up my own mind, thank you,' he said.

119

Jim took out a couple of jackets, one in plain grey and the other in a Prince of Wales check. 'Too fancy,' said Elsworth of the second, and he tried on the grey one. It was a little tight in the shoulders, and after a few moments' straightening, Jim suggested he try a larger size.

'Very dapper, I'm sure,' said Lewis. He stood behind the counter with his arms akimbo, turning his head this way and that.

'It's perfect,' said Jim. 'And it'll serve for any occasion.'

'Jackets are longer this season,' said Lewis, 'with softer shoulder padding and slim-cut lapels.'

'They may be in Savile Row,' said Jim, 'but in Market Place in Wells this is how they are.'

Elsworth paid for his jacket and left. As soon as he was out of the door, Jim turned on Lewis.

'I can put up with your doing sweet fuck-all around here,' he said, 'but I won't tolerate that kind of talk with customers, understand?'

'I don't think Nuncle would like to hear you speaking to me in that way.'

'Well Nuncle isn't here, is he?'

'Not at this very moment, no.'

Lewis stared impassively at Jim. What do people think is going on in here? Jim wondered. It must be obvious that there was something odd about this arrangement, especially since he continued to close the place at lunchtime. He went into the office and began drawing up an order to send to Askews. Out in the shop he could hear Lewis chuckling for no one's benefit but his own.

Billy sat across the desk from the headmaster, his father and mother on either side of him. Robert Erwin seemed fantastically old, his wrinkly face and wild white hair making him look like a ghost.

'So, Billy,' he said, 'you want to come to the Blue School.'

'Yes, sir.'

'First you have to pass your eleven-plus, as you know.'

'I'm taking it soon.'

'We are able to offer places on the understanding that they may be claimed if you pass. But we need to know a little about boys before we can do that.'

Billy looked expectantly at the headmaster, who was reading from a sheaf of papers, and then cast his eyes around the room. In a corner stood a huge globe, the biggest he'd ever seen, and he had to resist the impulse to get up and give it a spin. He looked back across the leather-topped desk at the man who held his fate in his hands.

'Your teacher gives you high praise, young man,' he said. 'You're particularly interested in literature and history.'

'Yes, sir.'

He laid down the papers and took off his glasses. 'What are you reading now?' he said.

'*Kidnapped*, sir.'

'Ah, David Balfour. Boys like David Balfour, don't they?'

'Well, he's a boy like us.'

'He's scarcely a boy, as I recall. He must be sixteen or so.'

'But he's not a grown-up.'

Erwin looked at him thoughtfully for a few moments.

'So what do you think of Bonnie Prince Charlie?' he said.

'I haven't got that far.'

'Oh, he's not in it. But surely Alan Breck talks about him?'

'Was he the one who tried to get Scotland back from the English?'

'Precisely.'

'Then I think he's all right, sir. I think Scotland should have its own king.'

Erwin nodded as if to express agreement. 'Do you now?' he said. 'And what about Wales?'

'Wales too. Some people think King Arthur was from Wales.'

'But you don't?'

'No, sir. He was from here.'

He picked up the papers again and put on his glasses. After a few moments he said, 'So what do you want to be when you grow up?'

Before Billy could answer, his father said, 'His head's full of ideas, Mr Erwin, like all boys'.'

'I want to be an explorer,' said Billy, a note of defiance entering his voice. His head wasn't full of ideas at all; it just had one.

'What kind of explorer?'

'I don't know. Just someone who explores new places.'

'And where would you like to explore?'

Billy considered this question carefully, gazing once again at the globe.

'I think there are bits of China that haven't been explored,' he said at last.

'Not even by the Chinese?'

'I don't mean by the Chinese. I mean by us, the English.'

'So a place hasn't been explored until the English have been there?'

'Not properly, sir. After all, we invented exploration, didn't we?'

Erwin smiled weakly, and Jim shifted in his seat.

'There have been a few Scots explorers too, you know,' said Erwin.

'Oh, they count too.'

He looked benignly at Billy. 'You seem well disposed towards the Scots,' he said. 'You must have guessed that I'm one myself.'

'No, sir, I didn't.'

'All the better then.'

On the way home they stopped at the village shop, and Margaret bought groceries while Jim and Billy sat in the car. A young woman passed by pushing a pram, and Jim wound down the window.

'Good morning, Mrs Burnham,' he said. 'How's the baby?'

'Teething,' said the woman wearily. 'There's not a wink of sleep to be had.'

As she walked on, it dawned on Billy that now was the time. He had intended to ask his mother, but today he felt bold enough to talk to his father. 'Dad,' he said. 'Will you tell me about babies, one day?'

Jim twisted in his seat to face Billy. 'If you want,' he said, and then, 'I suppose I should have done before now, shouldn't I?'

Jim suggested that Margaret drive home alone, so that he and Billy could take a walk. As they crossed the footbridge, Jim said, 'So you're getting hard sometimes, I expect.'

'Yes,' said Billy.

'You're dreaming about girls.'

'No, not really. I'm dreaming about mountains.'

'Girls and mountains have a lot in common.'

'Do they?'

Jim smiled and said, 'No, not really.'

They began to ascend the slope towards home, and then Jim said, 'So you know what you do with it?'

'Some boys have told me, but it seems strange.'

'It does at first,' said Jim. 'Then soon it doesn't at all.'

'So what happens after you've put it inside a girl?'

'Well, she has an egg in her.'

'An egg? You mean like a chicken's egg?'

'Well, it doesn't have a shell. But it's an egg. And it's fertilized by the man's seed. Then it grows into a baby, and nine months later it's born.'

They stopped at a gate and looked across at the tor. 'It may sound odd,' said Jim, 'but it's actually very nice. It's so nice that people do it all the time, even when they aren't making babies. You don't just put your willy inside her, you kiss her and touch her all over.'

Billy sensed that a moment had arrived, an opportunity to talk to his father properly.

'If people do it when they're not making babies,' he said, 'do they do it even when they're not married?'

Jim looked away from him and shifted his weight uneasily. 'Sometimes,' he said.

'Have you done it with other people, with people who aren't Mum?'

'I'm not sure that's any of your concern.'

'But I want to know the facts of life,' said Billy insistently. 'That's what they're called, aren't they?'

His father remained silent for a long time. 'Well then, yes I have,' he said. 'But there's no reason your mother should know, understand?'

'Do you do it with Liz Burridge?'

The instant the words were out of his mouth he regretted them. His father turned on him angrily.

'Who said anything about Liz Burridge?' he demanded.

Billy looked away. 'I saw you,' he said.

'You saw me what?'

'I saw you in the car with her, when I went to the Regal. You said you were going to Bath.'

Jim let out a sound that was something between a sigh and a groan. He hung his head and said nothing.

'I'm sorry,' said Billy. 'I wasn't sneaking. We just went to look at the Blue School, and I saw the car.'

Jim looked at Billy for a few moments. 'I'm the one who should be sorry,' he said. 'I'm the one who should be bloody sorry.'

———

Jim told himself over and over that he shouldn't see Liz again, but something always drew him back. He took her to Shepton Mallet for dinner, reckoning that to be seen with her in Wells was too risky now. The King's Arms was a pretty inn set back from a quiet square away from the centre of the town. Through the leaded windows a soft yellow light beckoned them in. In the bar the wooden beams were hung with brass tankards and horseshoes. They sat drinking white wine and studying the ornate menu, Jim watching Liz closely as she ordered. She was ill at ease with this sort of formality, it was plain to see. They went through to the dining room and sat at a candle-lit table by the window.

'The woman must always sit facing into the room,' said Jim.

'Why's that?'

'So that she may be admired by the other diners.'

She smiled, and relaxed into her chair.

'I'm going to London next week,' she said, 'for the first time.'

'What are you going to do there?'

'My mother's taking me on a shopping trip. She's going to kit me out for Bristol.'

'I'd forgotten about Bristol. How long is it now?'

'Two months.'

'Selfridges,' said Jim. 'That's the place for good clothes at reasonable prices.'

'You sound like an advert,' she said, smiling mischievously.

'Do I? Maybe I'm spending too much time in that shop.'

'You're spending all your time in that shop. It's your job.'

'Don't remind me.'

Their prawn cocktail starters arrived. As she picked up her fork, Liz said, 'There's a man over there who keeps staring at us.'

'Men are always staring at us,' said Jim. 'They're jealous.'

'I don't think this one's got any reason to be jealous. The woman he's with is a stunner.'

They returned to talk of London, to the things Liz might cram into a single day there. Then she looked beyond him and whispered, 'He's coming over.'

'My dear Jim,' said the man. Jim turned in his chair to see the elegant figure of David Latymer.

'Hello, David.'

There was an awkward silence. 'This is Liz Burridge,' he said.

'How do you do, young lady,' said Latymer. His pale eyes scrutinized Liz closely.

'Liz is the daughter of a friend from Wells.'

'And you've decided to explore the delights of Shepton.'

'It's very nice,' said Liz.

'It's quiet. It doesn't have the tourist attractions of Wells. And that suits us very well.' With this he gestured towards the table he was sitting at, and Jim looked across to see Clare Latymer waving at him. He smiled tightly.

'Well, I should leave you to your tête-à-tête,' said Latymer. He bowed to Liz, nodded at Jim, and returned to his wife.

'Who was that?' said Liz as soon as he was out of earshot.

'David Latymer. He owns the Charlton Cider Company. They live in the big house near ours. That's when they're not in their mansion in London.'

'He's got rich written all over him.'

Their conversation became uneasy. Jim was drinking a lot, and he reminded himself that he would have to drive home in the dark. Eventually Liz said, 'They're leaving.'

'That's torn it,' he said after they'd gone.

'Will they tell your wife?'

'No. We never see them. It's just that… oh, I don't know: there seems nowhere we can go these days.'

She laid a hand on his, and stroked it with her thumb. 'We'll find places,' she said.

They returned to the lounge after dinner, and Jim ordered a whisky. The other diners had left, and though it was barely half past nine they had the place to themselves. Jim swirled the liquor in the heavy glass.

'Do you know what I think, Liz?' he said suddenly. 'I think I'm a failure.'

She looked at him with a startled expression. 'Just because you're not as rich as David Latymer?'

'No, that's not what I mean. I've messed up my life.'

'You've had some problems, that's all.'

He looked at her thoughtfully. 'I've had a barrow-load of problems, Liz. And whose fault is that?'

'But you said it was the times, the rationing and that.'

'Did I now?' he said wearily. He watched the light reflecting off the amber liquid in his glass. 'Well, I've always been good at finding other things or other people to blame.'

She looked away from him. 'And I suppose you think you're a failure as a husband too?' she said.

He gazed at her profile, at the soft mouth and the lovely line that described her throat and neck. 'Maybe,' he said. 'How do you measure that, though? Does the fact that I'm here with you rather than at home with my wife mean I've failed as a husband?'

She turned towards him. 'Only you can know that,' she said.

Jim weaved his way back to Wells, knowing he shouldn't be behind the wheel. Market Place was silent beneath the towers of the cathedral, and the key screeched in the door of the shop as he opened it. He left the lights off, and they felt their way towards the office. Closing the door behind them, he turned to Liz and took her in his arms. They made love in the clumsy sort of way he hated, and soon they were saying good night out in the street. He didn't offer to escort her home, but got straight in the car and drove out onto the Glastonbury road.

The whisky was doing strange things to his eyes. The familiar road seemed now to veer in unexpected directions, and to fork into two when he knew very well that it shouldn't. He slowed down, but still the road deceived him, causing him to turn too sharply or not sharply enough. Near Launcherley Farm a dog appeared from nowhere and ran in front of him. He jammed on the brakes, and having come to a halt he was suddenly afraid of going on.

He opened the door and got out, inhaling the frosty air deeply. Reaching back into the car he switched off the engine and the lights, and lit a match to a cigarette. He felt swathed in the dark silence, and consoled by it. Consoled for being a bankrupt, for being an adulterer, for being a lousy father. He stood there for a long time, leaning against the side of the car, his eyes fixed on the intermittent glow of the cigarette.

———

'We just weren't thinking,' said Margaret.

Dr Enright looked at her in a way that she took to be mildly reproving. How could she explain that it had been the first time in months?

'How old are you?'

'Thirty-six.'

'We'll need to do some tests, then. One must be careful later in life.'

So this was later in life, thought Margaret. How odd: she felt as though she were just beginning.

'Where would you like to have it?'

'Is there any choice?'

'There's Wells Infirmary or home. I wouldn't recommend home, of course; but some women prefer it.'

'The Infirmary,' said Margaret. 'I had Billy and Sarah in hospital.'

'Good. I will refer you to Dr Morton.'

She walked home very slowly. The snows had cleared, and winter's grip was loosening. She leaned against a gate and looked towards Glastonbury. What would the children think, she wondered, of the idea of another brother or sister? And what would Jim think? As she considered this she knew she wouldn't tell him, at least not for a while. Her hand went to the place. Jim had had his secrets, and she would have hers.

Billy and Sarah were already home by the time she returned.

'Where have you been, Mummy?' said Sarah.

'To the doctor's.'

'Are you ill?'

'I've got a funny tummy.'

'Let me rub it.'

Margaret sat down at the kitchen table while Sarah stroked her awkwardly. She put a hand up to Sarah's hair, and drew her to her breast. She will be thrilled, of course, she thought. And she will be a great help, especially when she's older. Margaret so much wanted to tell her now. But she must wait. And Jim must wait too.

———

Margaret sat in Leonora's sitting room reading the last pages of Tess of the D'Urbervilles. The fire had gone out, and the room felt cold and cheerless.

'I've seen many more tears on the faces of beautiful women than on plain ones,' said Leonora eventually.

'Is that fate?' said Margaret.

'Everything's fate, poppet.'

She went into the kitchen to make a cup of tea, and when she returned Margaret noticed that the sole of one of her shoes was flapping loosely.

'Your shoes are in a terrible state,' she said.

Leonora looked down abstractedly. 'Well, I hardly notice.'

'You need a new pair,' said Margaret firmly. 'Something warm and dry for these chilly days.'

'I don't recall the last time I bought a pair of shoes,' said Leonora. 'In fact I don't recall the last time I bought anything that wasn't from the village shop.'

'Then I think a shopping trip is called for. Let's go to Wells on Saturday.'

They drove into town on a damp, windswept morning. The streets were quiet for a Saturday, the shops empty. Leonora bought a pair of suede bootees with sheepskin linings, and then they went to Browne's nursery to buy seeds. 'I'll start them in the greenhouse,' she said, 'and then put them in the garden in the spring.'

Margaret noticed that very soon Leonora began to show signs of fatigue. 'Let's go to the tearooms for a coffee,' she said.

Leonora sat down gratefully at the table, and smoothed the gingham tablecloth. 'I'm quite worn out,' she said.

'You're not used to it,' said Margaret. 'You must get out more. I think we should make this a regular occurrence.'

Margaret ordered coffee, and a cake for Leonora. She looked around the room, at the other women sipping their tea. She was the youngest person there by twenty years, and she felt as though she were intruding on some sort of communion.

'The play must be getting close,' said Leonora.

'Yes,' she replied, and then she smiled ruefully. 'I think it's turning me into a shrew.'

'Why a shrew?'

'Oh, I don't know. I want it to be perfect, and of course it can't be. So I'm taking it out on the others.'

'Drama is exacting,' said Leonora. 'There's no point if it isn't, even in amateur productions.'

'That's what I think.'

'I saw it once, years ago. Not the original, though. That would have been something.'

'Who was in the original?'

128

'Larry Olivier was Victor, and your part was played by Gertrude Lawrence. Coward wrote the play with her in mind. And he played Elyot Chase himself.'

'It's very intricate. It must have taken him a long time.'

Leonora snorted. 'He wrote it in four days, in a hotel room in Shanghai. He was laid up with flu.'

'That's extraordinary.'

'Not really. The characters were all based on his cronies. Elyot and Amanda were the Castlerosses, a famously tempestuous couple.'

Margaret held her cup in both hands and gazed into it. 'He's so good on love, isn't he? He knows how frail it is.'

'Frail? That's an odd word to use.'

Margaret put down her cup and pushed it away from her. 'My husband's having an affair,' she said calmly. 'I've had my suspicions for a while, but now I think I know who it is.'

Leonora looked at her directly. 'I thought things were better between you,' she said.

'So did I. It's strange that it's only now that I can sense it. He might have had a dozen affairs in the autumn for all I knew. But in the past weeks he hasn't been able to hide it.'

'And who is she?'

Margaret looked down at the tablecloth. 'Ah, well that's rather awkward,' she said. 'If I'm right, that is. It's one of my fellow cast members, a girl called Liz Burridge.'

'And who is Liz Burridge?'

'She's a child, really. She can't be more than eighteen or nineteen. She works at Goody's café down the street, and she's going to be a nurse.'

'She sounds about right,' said Leonora tartly. She put her hand on Margaret's. 'I'm sorry, I shouldn't have said that.'

'You can say anything you wish. She's pretty and very impressionable. About right, just as you say.'

She dropped Leonora off on the way home. As she entered the kitchen she sensed a stillness in the place. Billy was reading in the children's room, Jim sat in the parlour, and Sarah was playing half-heartedly with her cookery set.

'Did you buy anything for me?' said Sarah.

'No I didn't. This was for Leonora, as you very well know.'

Sarah rested her chin in her hands and looked at her mother sulkily.

'What have you been making?' said Margaret.

'I can't make anything without you, can I? Daddy's no help at all.'

Margaret went into the parlour and gave Jim a kiss on the cheek. 'You're all very glum this morning,' she said.

'Are we? That's because we haven't had you around.'

She brushed her hand through his thick hair. How does she see him? she wondered. Does Liz Burridge see an attentive man, or does she see what I see: a man who needs attention?

Seven

It was weeks now since they'd got the car, and throughout that time the matter of the tor, and of their going there, seemed to Billy to be something he dare not speak of. It was very clear to him that his father could afford the petrol if he wished. He was denying Billy the thing he most wanted. But why? His bafflement only increased when one day Jim suggested they all go to the caves at Wookey Hole. Billy told himself this must be some sort of step along the way, some sort of test perhaps. And anyway, he was excited by the prospect of this trip. His imagination was fired by the idea of a river flowing underground, of caves where people used to live. Impatient for it, he decided the day before that he would go up into the hills between the village and Wells to try and see where the caves were.

He was quite steady on his bike now, and went further than he had ever done before. The ride into the village was downhill practically all the way, and he felt like a bird swooping in on it, the cold air blowing his hair flat against the top of his head. A bridleway led off Dark Lane, and he dumped the bike in the bushes and set off. The sun was low and watery, and he wondered how far he would be able to see. Following a path that rose steeply through a wood, he came out on the edge of a stony field. A fox slunk out of the trees, doubling back the moment it saw him.

On the far side of the field was a beech covert. All Billy had to do was to get to the other side of it for the view of Wells to open up. The cathedral dominated everything. He tried to picture what it must have looked like hundreds of years ago, when the cathedral was first built. No wonder people went to churches like this: they were so much bigger and grander than anything else.

The Mendip Hills curled gently around the town. Wookey Hole was just beyond Wells, he'd been told, but where? The haze made things indistinct, and for now he would just have to imagine it. He was desperately disappointed. Why did he have to rely on his father to go to places like Glastonbury and the caves? He turned back into the covert and ran across the field, telling himself that at least now he had some idea of where he was going.

That night, like so many nights now, he lay awake for ages. Images of caves and rivers coursed through his mind. Unable to settle, he crept down the stairs to get a glass of milk. The stairs creaked, and as he climbed them again, a candle appeared in the doorway of his parents' room.

'Billy?' said his mother.

'I can't sleep,' he said. 'I'm too excited.'

She rested a hand on his shoulder. 'You don't want to be tired in the morning, do you?' she said. 'Go back to bed and count sheep.'

'That never works.'

'Count the stars, then.'

The next morning they set off early. Sarah was reluctant to go.

'There's three big caves,' said Billy, 'and one of them has a witch in it.'

'That's Miss Shute,' said Sarah. 'That's where she lives.'

'I do wish you'd stop talking about your teacher in that way,' said Jim. 'She is not a witch, do you understand?'

She folded her arms and stared out of the car window.

'And I don't want any pouting from you, young lady.'

'I'm not pouting, I'm feeling my teeth with my tongue.'

'No you're not,' said Billy, 'you're pouting. You always do when you're told off.'

'You stay out of this,' said Jim.

'Why? She's always spoiling things.'

'No I'm not,' said Sarah.

Jim pulled over and turned in his seat to face them. 'Look,' he said, 'if you two can't stop squabbling we'll just go home.'

Billy looked away from his father. Why was he so cross, he wondered, on this of all days? He glanced appealingly at Margaret, who gave him the tight-lipped expression she always used when arguments broke out.

They walked past the paper mill to the entrance of the caves, and stood looking out over the river as it gushed from the side of the cliff. 'They used to chase animals over these cliffs,' said Jim, 'and then come down here to get them.'

'Then what did they do?' said Sarah.

'Eat them, of course.'

'Yuck!'

'We eat animals, don't we?' said Billy. 'We'll probably eat bits of Stan and Gertie one day.'

'No we won't!' said Sarah. 'I'll never eat Gertie, ever.'

There were half a dozen other people on their tour, including three who spoke in strange accents and wore brightly coloured clothes.

'They're Americans,' said Jim. 'That's how they dress.'

Billy stared at the boy, who was a couple of years older than him. He wore a red jacket, blue trousers, and yellow socks. Billy had never seen yellow socks before, not even on a girl. He couldn't take his eyes off them.

The guide gathered them together and began his talk, and then they ducked into the strange gloom of the first chamber. Electric lights hung here and there, picking out the deep reds and browns and blacks of the rocks. There was water dripping from above, and the damp chilled Billy, even though it was warmer here than outside.

'I don't think I want to stay in here for very long,' said Sarah.

Margaret held her hand. 'You'll be fine,' she said. 'This is going to be exciting.'

In a larger, deeper chamber the river flowed gently by. The water was astonishingly clear, throwing off a ghostly green light. Billy slipped on the wet stone, and clutched at a rock to right himself.

'This is the Witch's Kitchen,' said the guide. He shone his torch at a huge stalagmite that grew out of the floor of the cave. 'And there she is, turned to stone when a monk sprinkled her with holy water.' The rock looked remarkably like a witch's head, with a bonnet, a hooked nose, and a gaping mouth.

They went on to the last chamber, a broad space with a low arced ceiling. The water seemed very still, more like a lake than a river.

'This is as far as we can go,' said the guide. 'But divers have discovered many more chambers, including one that's a hundred feet high.'

'Can you swim there?' said Billy.

'You can if you're a very experienced diver.'

Billy stood at the water's edge, gazing into the depths. People had been down there, he thought, explorers. How far could you get? If you went on for long enough surely you would come to the very source of the river. And then beyond that, the centre of the earth. If there was nowhere left to explore above ground, then he could always come to places like this.

He turned around, and saw that he had been left behind. Setting off for the entrance, he cast his gaze back one last time towards the river. And at that moment the lights in the cave went out.

Billy stood immobile, in absolute darkness. He was completely disorientated, and unsure what to do. He took a few halting steps, and then shouted, 'Dad!' His voice echoed around the cave, but there was no answering call. It occurred to him that he should feel afraid, but somehow he didn't. The dark and the silence were magical: he had never experienced such an absence of things. He stretched out his arms and whirled slowly around. What an extraordinary feeling this was, one of complete peace and freedom. He came to a stop, and called his father once again.

He had no idea how long it was before he saw the beam of a torch and heard voices approaching, but he sensed it had been a while.

'I'm here,' he said.

'Where?' said his father's voice.

'Here, somewhere.'

The torch came nearer. 'Bloody electricity cuts,' Billy heard the guide say. 'We just can't have this.'

As they came up to him, he was dazzled by the light.

'What were you thinking of?' said his father. 'Why didn't you keep up?'

'I liked it down here.'

'I don't care how much you liked it. You've given your mother and me the fright of our lives. You have to think of other people. You can't stay in your daydream world all the time.'

Billy stared at his father's face, which was strangely distorted in the torchlight. Who was he to talk about thinking of other people? He felt the grip of Jim's hands on his arms. It was so tight it hurt. And then he noticed that his father's cheeks were wet.

'Did you get dripped on?'

Jim put a hand up to his face. 'Have you never seen a man cry before?' he said.

Billy could only shake his head.

'Well sometimes we do. Just like everyone else.'

At school the next morning, Billy found it quite impossible to concentrate. The memory of his adventure in the caves crowded out everything else. Miss Shute gathered together the five children who would be taking the eleven-plus and sat them at the front of the class.

'Today we're going to do equations,' she said. 'Now, does anyone know what an equation is?'

Alan Tyler's hand shot up.

'Yes, Alan?'

'It's a line that goes around the middle of the world, miss.'

'No, that's the *equator*. Anyone else?'

The children's hands stayed down.

'Very well. An equation is something that equals something else.' She turned to the blackboard and chalked the number four, then a line below it, and below that a two. Then she drew two short parallel lines next to them.

'Four over two equals something, doesn't it, children?' she said. 'What is that?'

They studied the blackboard. It was obvious to Billy that this was as puzzling to everyone else as it was to him.

'Four over two equals two, doesn't it?' said Miss Shute. 'In other words, two into four equals two.' She chalked a two on the other side of the parallel lines. 'Now, let's make it a little more difficult, shall we?'

'It's difficult enough already, miss,' said Audrey.

'All will become clear. Now, if I write four over two here, and eight over four there, what does that mean?'

'That four over two equals eight over four,' said Billy.

'Quite right. And why does it?'

Billy looked at the numbers on the board. 'Because four into eight is also two,' he said after a few moments.

'Excellent. So, you see how an equation may balance out numbers that seem much larger and smaller than each other.'

In the playground at morning break Alan said to the other boys, 'I don't think I get it, this equations thing.'

'But we've only just started,' said Billy. 'We'll get the hang of it.'

'It's all right for you,' said Les. 'You're a swot.'

At this Frank turned on Les. 'No he isn't,' he said. He looked at Billy, and then again at Les, this time with a faintly menacing expression.

'You know what I think?' he said. 'I think Billy Palmer's all right, that's what I do.'

Jim and Liz sat on a bench in the recreation ground, looking across to the bandstand and the deserted croquet lawn. The first shoots of spring were appearing, and the air seemed almost balmy. He had wondered how to do this, whether to take her out one last time, write her a letter, or what. In the end this seemed the best solution. She had a day off from Goody's, and he asked her to meet him here at lunchtime.

'Say it, then,' she said.

'You do understand, don't you?'

'All I understand is that you've had your fun, and now you must run along home to your wife.'

Jim watched the children playing on the swings and slides, wondering how to reply. He heard a little boy say to his mother, 'I want all those other children to get off the roundabout before I get on.'

'I really care for you,' he said finally.

'I hate those words, "care for",' she said. 'They mean you don't love me.'

'I never said I loved you, Liz. I never used that word, and nor did you.'

She gazed into the distance. 'Do you love your wife?' she said.

'Yes,' said Jim unhesitatingly.

'Then why go looking for someone else? Why chase after me?' She bit her lower lip. 'This was a mistake,' she said.

'I'm sorry. I made it happen.'

She shrugged her shoulders and shifted on the bench.

'Will you say anything to her?'

'No. Why?'

'I don't know. Don't men fall on their knees and confess the error of their ways?'

'Not this one.'

'That sounds cynical.'

'Well it's not meant to be. It's just who I am, that's all. I've never been one for fancy words.'

She stood up, hesitated, and then bent down to give him a kiss on the cheek.

'See you at the first night, then.'

'That's what everyone seems to be saying at the moment.'

She turned and hurried away towards the palace moat. Jim watched her figure recede, and then looked back at the children in the playground. The little boy who wanted the roundabout to himself was sobbing now, his mother trying to calm him. Jim stared beyond them. What has this been about, he wondered, and why is it always this way? Why, when the moment came for parting, did they seem to feel something and he nothing at all? Slowly he raised himself and turned in the opposite direction.

'Let's invite Leonora and Hubert to supper,' said Margaret one day as they sat at the kitchen table.

Jim looked at her doubtfully. 'That's the silliest idea I've ever heard,' he said. 'What on earth would they say to each other?'

Margaret shrugged. 'I don't know,' she said. 'But they're both alone, aren't they?'

'They've lived within a stone's throw of each other for ages, and if they had wanted to get acquainted they'd have done so by now.'

'Yes, but it's only a year since Mary Fosse died.'

Jim looked across the yard to the outbuilding where Hubert lived. Perhaps he was being ungenerous.

'Very well,' he said.

She arranged a date for the following week. Billy and Sarah were promised they would be able to stay up at least until their guests arrived, and when the evening came around there was an air of expectancy in the house. Jim set out the bottle of whisky that Leonora had given them at Christmas, which had remained untouched since Hubert's last encounter with it on New Year's Eve.

Hubert wore a clean white shirt that was buttoned up to the neck, and he had shaved for the first time in days; there were nicks and scratches around his chin. As Jim made him a whisky and water, he sat stiffly in the chair staring at his large red hands.

'Have you heard about the new people at Perridge Farm?' said Jim.

'I've heard they plan to bring in Charolais,' said Hubert.

'Charolais?'

'It's a French breed of cattle. Some people seem to have got it into their heads that British breeds won't do.'

'Are French cows better, then?' said Billy.

'They certainly aren't, young man. You can't beat a British cow.'

Leonora had insisted on walking up the hill, and she was wheezing by the time she arrived at the house. Sarah took her coat and scarf, dancing around her in attendance. Since there weren't enough chairs in the parlour, Jim and Hubert came through into the kitchen and everyone sat at the table. Margaret sent Billy and Sarah off to bed, and began to prepare the meal.

'So when did you two last see each other?' said Jim a little too heartily.

'At Mary's funeral,' said Hubert.

'It was a very fine funeral, too,' said Leonora. 'Harry Hardie did her proud.'

'Right he did. He always had a soft spot for her.' Hubert drank his whisky, and Jim took the glass and topped it up.

'How about you, then, Leonora?' said Hubert. 'Life treating you all right?'

'Yes, thank you. My life has improved considerably lately, thanks to my new friends.'

Jim placed a tall white jug in the middle of the table. Hubert grasped it, and then set it down again. Watching him, Margaret recalled that the jug was one of the things that had come with the house.

'Mary used to say it was like a swan,' he said. He took it in his hand again and poured water for the others. 'She loved swans.'

'You used to walk together along the rhynes down at Redlake, didn't you, Hubert?' said Leonora.

'A long time ago, yes. She loved it down there, the marshes and ditches. You'd see bitterns and grebes and mallard ducks, hundreds of them.'

'I expect you still do,' said Jim.

'I haven't been down there for years.'

There was the sound of footsteps on the stairs. Sarah appeared, her nightgown hitched up around her knees, her eyes blinking in the light of the kitchen.

'My leg hurts, Mummy,' she said. 'Can I have some magic cream?'

Margaret went to the cupboard where she kept her hand cream, and sat Sarah on her lap.

'Where does it hurt?'

Sarah thought for a moment, and then pointed at the shin of her left leg. 'There,' she said.

'I get terrible pains in my legs,' said Leonora. 'It's all that dancing I used to do. It's caught up with me.'

Sarah watched her mother rub some cream into her skin. 'How can dancing catch up with you?' she said.

'It's an expression, sweetheart,' said Jim.

'What's an expression?'

'It's a way of saying things,' said Margaret. 'Now, back to bed.'

'But my leg still hurts.'

'Then lie on your other side.'

The evening fell rather flat after Sarah left the kitchen. Hubert cradled his whisky glass, becoming increasingly maudlin. The others tried to find things to talk about, but their consideration for Hubert made them tongue-tied. There was very little to be said that might engage him, and much that might exclude him. In the end Jim took him off to the parlour while Margaret and Leonora remained at the kitchen table.

'He's the loneliest man I've ever known,' said Leonora after they'd gone.

'He's alone.'

She looked at Margaret thoughtfully. 'He's much more than alone,' she said.

On the way back to the shop after lunch one day, Jim bought a copy of the *Wells Journal*, and a headline at the bottom of the front page caught his eye. 'Verdicts in Pettigrew Case', it ran. Tony Lewis was lounging outside, and Jim opened up, shut the office door behind him, and sat down to read the story.

'The trial of four men accused of stealing and receiving books owned by Mr Alfred Pettigrew took place this week at Wells Assizes. Mr Justice Bonington handed down sentences on George Crocker, Arthur Trafford and Gordon Towker. Crocker and Trafford were given custodial sentences of twelve months for robbery. Towker was given a three-month suspended sentence for receiving stolen goods. In the case of Bernard Smith, the London bookseller who attempted to sell on the books, the judge stated that there was reasonable doubt as to whether he was aware the books were stolen, but that he should have taken the trouble to inquire as to their provenance. He was let off with a reprimand.

'In the case of Gordon Towker, however, Mr Justice Bonington concluded that he must have known that the books were stolen. Towker will be obliged to report to Wells police station once a month for the next year. In his summing up, Mr Justice Bonington remarked that the fact that none of the men had a previous criminal record had led him to treat them leniently. When contacted by our reporter, Mr Pettigrew pronounced himself satisfied with the outcome, but particularly satisfied that he had recovered all the books in good condition.'

Jim tossed the paper aside, dragged the heavy Olympia typewriter from its shelf, and inserted a piece of Underhill's notepaper into it. Laboriously he began to type. 'To Whom It May Concern,' he wrote. 'Mr Anthony Lewis worked as my assistant in Underhill's Outfitters from January 1958 to March 1959. He was an exemplary employee, hard-working and conscientious, and displayed a keen interest in all aspects of the clothing trade. I would have no hesitation in recommending him to a future employer, and I wish him the best of luck in his future endeavours. James Palmer, Manager.'

He drew the piece of paper out of the typewriter, signed it, and went through into the shop.

'Here,' he said. 'A little billet-doux.'

Lewis took the note from him. 'I didn't think you knew any French,' he said.

'I know a damn sight more than you think.'

Lewis read the reference. 'Very elegant,' he said. 'You should try your hand at writing some time.'

'I'll stay with what I know,' said Jim.

Lewis folded the piece of paper and put it in the breast pocket of his jacket. It stuck out like a trophy.

'You'll be going now, then,' said Jim.

'Yes, I suppose I will.'

They stared at one another for a few moments. Then just as Jim was about to turn away, Lewis stepped forward and planted a kiss firmly on his lips. Jim reared back, wiping his mouth with the sleeve of his cardigan.

'Bye-bye, Jimmy,' said Lewis. 'Thanks for the memories.'

'Get out,' said Jim, and he strode back into the office.

In the weeks since Billy had confronted his father over Liz Burridge he had sensed a distinct change. Jim had not scolded him once, except when he got lost in the caves at Wookey Hole, and even then he'd been crying at the same time. But nor had he really talked to Billy, at least not about anything that mattered very much. His father was distant, bound up in his own thoughts. Was he still seeing that girl, and would his mother find out? He wished there were someone he could confide in.

When Leonora Vale opened the front door of Tanyard Cottage, Billy said, 'I was wondering if you needed any help planting seeds in the garden?'

She looked at him for a few moments. 'Perhaps it's time to take some out of the greenhouse and plant them outside,' she said.

They went through the house to the walled garden at the back. The cats stirred as they passed, and a kitten leaped onto his shorts. Gently unhooking its claws, he set it down on the floor.

The garden was in much the same state as when Billy had last seen it, a sort of garden-in-waiting. Leonora opened the greenhouse door and they stepped inside.

'Now, let me see,' she said. 'I think we'll start with the peonies.'

She handed him a flowerpot and, carrying another herself, led the way to a border of soil that lay beside the wall of the house.

'We'll need a trowel,' she said. 'There's one in the shed.'

He searched among the clutter and found a small spade which he took to be a trowel.

'Now, dig a small hole here, about three inches deep,' said Leonora. She watched as he did so. 'How did you know how much I hate kneeling nowadays?'

Billy took a pot from her and sprinkled some of the seed-laden earth into the hole he had dug. Then he dug more holes and distributed the rest of the seeds among them.

'Pat them down,' said Leonora, 'and spread some of the soil you've dug up over them.'

When the job was done she went into the kitchen to make tea. She gave Billy a glass of milk, and they sat down.

'So,' said Leonora. 'What have you been doing lately?'

'We went to Wookey Hole, to the caves. I got lost in the dark.'

'That sounds very brave.'

'Yes, it was.'

Billy took a gulp of milk and wiped his upper lip. He looked at Leonora hesitantly, and decided that now was the moment to take the plunge.

'You know those seeds we planted,' he said. 'Do they need eggs?'

'Eggs?'

'Yes. I thought seeds went with eggs, that they needed each other to make...' His voice trailed off.

'To reproduce, you mean.'

'Yes, to reproduce.'

Leonora laid down her cup. 'There are different kinds of reproduction, Billy,' she said. 'Plants don't have eggs, only animals.'

'And we're animals, aren't we?'

'We are.'

'So we couldn't do it with just seeds, then,' he said. 'We need seeds and eggs.'

She looked at him with a puzzled expression. 'That's right,' she said.

'But wouldn't it be better if we could. I mean, wouldn't it be easier if we didn't need both?'

'That depends,' she said. 'It would certainly be simpler.'

Billy looked at his empty glass. He felt vaguely disappointed by Leonora Vale's response to this problem, and thought it best to leave things there. 'I'd better go home,' he said. 'They'll be expecting me for lunch.'

She saw him to the door.

'Thank you, Billy,' she said. 'You've been a great help.'

'That's all right. It was fun.'

'Perhaps you should be a gardener when you grow up.'

'Oh no, I'm going to be an explorer.'

'Ah. More exciting.'

'Yes, much more.'

It was a year since Jim had been declared bankrupt, and he had to report to the County Court in Bath. Margaret went with him, and he was grateful for her company. Except for his passing through on the way to London, he hadn't been back to Bath since they left.

The cavernous room was full of people who were clearly in some sort of trouble, and Jim wished he were not numbered among them. They had to wait a long time, but eventually John Marshall appeared and led them into a small cubicle in which there was just enough space for Jim and Margaret to sit across the desk from him.

Marshall was in his forties. His hair and suit and tie were very black, his shirt and his papery skin very white. He made a show of looking for Jim's file, and opened it carefully. Then he sat back in his chair and smiled at them.

'Thank you for taking the trouble to come,' he said.

Jim remembered him as not a bad sort of bloke. He'd been as accommodating as he could at the time of the proceedings, and had even looked the other way on occasion. His manner was excessively courteous, and it was typical that he should thank Jim for taking the trouble to do something he was legally bound to.

'So how have you been?' said Marshall.

'Fine,' said Jim.

'Now let's see, we last spoke just before you moved to Coombe, and took up the job at Underhill's Outfitters in Wells.'

'In August.'

'And you're still at Underhill's?'

'I'm running the place,' said Jim. 'The proprietor had a stroke towards the end of the year.'

'I'm so sorry. And he's a relative of yours, Mrs Palmer, I believe?'

'He's my uncle,' said Margaret. 'He's been at home for some time now, looked after by his wife.'

Marshall turned to Jim. 'So you have new responsibilities?' he said.

'I do indeed.'

'Good, good,' he said. He looked down at the file again. 'And you're still living at Fosse's Farm?'

'That's right.'

'How are the children taking to the country?'

'Very well,' said Margaret. 'Especially our son.'

'A country childhood is a fine thing,' said Marshall. 'I don't mean…

well, I don't mean anything really. A country childhood is a fine thing, though.'

'Mr Marshall,' said Jim, leaning forward, 'how long do you think it might be before I can get discharged?'

'Well, as I said at the time, that's impossible to say. It may be only three or four years, it may be longer.'

'Time off for good behaviour?'

'Something like that. It's a serious thing, bankruptcy. I think you would do well to remember that. It's a breach of trust.'

'I know it's a serious thing,' said Jim, flushing suddenly. 'I knew it at the time, and I know it even better now.'

'I'm sure you do.' He closed the file with an air of finality. 'Until this time next year, then,' he said.

Out in the street, brilliant sunshine lit up the stone of the town.

'Let's go for a walk,' said Margaret.

'I don't know, Maggie. I'm not sure I want to be seen walking around this place.'

She took his hand in hers. 'You've nothing to be ashamed of,' she said. 'Let's go to the river.'

'I know I've nothing to be ashamed of,' said Jim. 'It's other people I'm worried about. "Breach of trust" indeed. Who does he think he is?'

Margaret squeezed his hand. 'He's just doing his job, that's all.'

'Just doing his job of persecuting people for trying to make the best of themselves.'

They walked towards Pulteney Bridge, and stood looking over the river and the horseshoe of the falls. Margaret turned to face him.

'You still don't really understand, do you?' she said.

'Understand what?'

'Why you failed.'

'I do, Maggie,' he said. 'I understand a lot better than you think.'

'Do you?'

He gazed down into the rushing water below.

'Just because I'm too bloody proud to admit it doesn't mean I don't know I made mistakes. But breach of trust? I won't accept that.'

'Then you must be trustworthy,' said Margaret, a flash of anger lighting up her face.

He looked at her for a few moments, and then twined his arm

144

around her waist. She knows, he thought, of course she does. Knows about Liz, and others before her.

'Yes,' he said softly.

———————

Billy had never been to a funeral before, and in the car on the way to London he tried to imagine what it might be like. He conjured up images of long hearses and hundreds of people dressed in black. Not that they themselves were in black, since, as his mother had pointed out, they possessed almost nothing suitable for such an occasion. Billy looked down at the grey flannels his father had given him. They were his first ever pair of long trousers, and they felt very strange: it was almost like being in bed.

'She should count herself lucky we're coming at all,' said Jim.

'Why, Daddy?' asked Sarah.

'Because she wrote me out of her will, that's why.'

'What does that mean?'

'It means she gave all her money to some charity or other.'

Margaret laid a hand on his arm and said, 'Let it be, Jim.'

So that was why his father had been so grumpy these past few days, thought Billy: he must have hoped for some of Aunt Bea's money.

In the chapel in Brompton Cemetery they found themselves among far fewer people than Billy had supposed. He looked around him, and didn't recognize anyone. He knew that Beatrice had never married, and that his father's own parents had died before he was born; but nonetheless it seemed odd that he should know no one here at all.

Above his head a plaque read, 'I am the resurrection and the life; he who believes in me, though he die, yet shall he live.' The service droned on, and Billy found himself gazing at Beatrice's coffin. Did he believe in heaven, in life after death? He wasn't sure. Jesus had lived on after the crucifixion, but then he was Jesus. Did everyone go to heaven? It would be very full by now if they did. But then most people didn't go to church very often; his own family seemed to go only when they absolutely had to. Could you not go to church and still go to heaven? He decided it would be wise to go at least a few times a year, just in case.

Out in the cemetery fleeting clouds chased the sun, and the wind caught his mother's skirt and lifted it above her knees. They stood over the grave and looked on as the coffin was lowered into the earth. Magpies flitted among the gravestones, playing tag. A stone near Billy bore an inscription that read, 'On earth one gentle soul the less, in heaven one angel more'. That would be how everyone fitted into heaven – they became angels. Frank Willmott had told him there were people who argued over how many angels could dance on the head of a pin. Six, that was what Frank's dad reckoned.

As the gravedigger shovelled soil over the coffin, Billy tried to hold on to his memories of Aunt Bea. The best were the Boat Races and the teas. And then there were the times she came down on the train from London to stay with them, bringing presents whatever the time of year. Since his father had no sisters she was always Aunt Bea, even though she was really a great-aunt. Now there was no one left in his father's family. He looked across at Jim, who stood with his head bowed. Billy could tell he was angry with his aunt; but clearly he was sad too. Anger and sadness seemed to go together so often, he thought.

'Did she leave us anything at all?' he said when they were back in the car.

'Billy, please…' said his mother.

'But I've just remembered: she always said I could have the binoculars.'

'You'll be getting a few things, and so will Sarah,' said Jim. 'But not me.'

On a blustery morning Jim looked out of the kitchen window and said, 'I feel like going for a walk. Billy, why don't you show me your hiding places?'

Running towards Southey Hill, Billy called to his father to keep up. The rain clouds raced them along Folly Lane and into the wood.

'This is where we play Cowboys and Indians,' he said. 'There's lots of trees to hide behind.'

Even now the wood was dense and green, the ground carpeted with ivy. The deeply rutted track was slippery with mud, and now and again they had to leap over puddles.

'Why do you think this is called Folly Wood?' asked Billy.

'I don't know. Someone must have done something foolish up here.'

'Something foolish?'

'That's what a folly means, a foolish thing. Or it can mean a building that's been made for no reason, like a tower without a castle
around it.'

'A foolish tower?'

'But I think it's more likely that someone did something foolish
here.'

They came out into an open field. Billy looked ahead, and the tor
was in sight again. It was always there, Glastonbury Tor: it followed
him everywhere he went.

'It's not that far after all, is it?' said his father.

'What?'

'The tor.'

'Not as far as Wookey Hole.'

'How about the weekend after Mum's play, then?'

Billy gazed at it longingly, and then looked up at Jim. That he had so
casually suggested this now struck Billy as being just as unfair as his
having denied it to him for so long.

'I'm not sure,' he said.

Billy was as astonished by his words as his father clearly was.

'You're not sure? But you've talked of nothing else for ages.'

He stood silent for a few moments, struggling with his strangely
conflicting feelings.

'I'll think about it,' he said.

Jim scratched his chin with his fingertips.

'All right, then. You think about it.'

'I hate this wig,' said Liz. It was very long and very blonde, and quite
altered her looks. 'Do I have to wear it?'

'But that's how Coward saw Sybil,' said Margaret. 'Anyway, you
know what they say, gentlemen prefer blondes.'

'If I knew any gentlemen that might be different,' said Liz sourly.

There was less than half an hour to go, and make-up was just about
done. Margaret looked in the mirror and told herself for the hundredth
time to be steady. This was something they were doing for fun, which
would be seen only by their families and friends, but which nonetheless
had sorely tested their modest talents. How absurd her daydreams
seemed now, her thoughts of a career on the stage, of fame and freedom.

'And as for this ridiculous dress,' said Liz. She stood up and smoothed down the bright red summer outfit she had been given to wear. 'I feel like I'm at Butlins, not in a smart hotel in France.'

'You look fine,' said Margaret. 'Stop fretting.'

'It's all right for you, you're as cool as a cucumber.'

'I'm as wound up as you. I'm just trying to unwind, that's all.'

Liz sat down again and looked unhappily at her reflection in the mirror. 'I'm sorry,' she said. 'I'll shut up.'

'Don't shut up, for goodness' sake,' said Margaret. 'You've got hundreds of lines to speak any minute.'

She touched the black silk of the negligee she would be wearing in the first scene, feeling for the bump that had just recently appeared. Soon, she said to herself. I will tell him soon.

Diana Mogg came into the dressing room and placed her hands on their shoulders.

'All set?' she said.

'As set as a jelly,' said Liz.

'Good, good,' said Diana.

Margaret looked up at her. Clearly nothing would be allowed to perturb her invincible calm.

'How are the men?' she said.

'The men are looking very... shiny,' said Diana. She smiled at their reflections, and suddenly they were all giggling.

Diana gave them both a peck on the cheek. 'Break a leg,' she said.

There was a buzz of excitement and trepidation in the car.

'How do you feel about Margaret's name being up in lights, Jim?' said Leonora.

'About time too, I say.'

'Will Mummy's name really be in lights?' said Sarah.

'No,' said Jim. 'It's just a way of saying that she'll be on the stage.'

'I've never seen a play.'

'Yes you have. You've seen nativity plays at Christmas.'

'They're not plays,' said Sarah. 'They're just dressing up.'

They dropped Leonora at the theatre and walked to the Underhills' house. Jim pushed the wheelchair on the way back, Reg making odd noises now and then that Winifred interpreted.

'He says this is his first night out in months,' she said.

They waited in the bar, and Jim drank a pint of bitter rather too fast. Billy ran continually to the door of the auditorium to peek at the stage.

'Nothing's happening,' he said.

'I bet a lot's happening behind that curtain,' said Jim.

A bell sounded, and people began to move towards their seats. Billy and Sarah rushed to the front.

'They're numbered,' said Jim. 'We're over here.'

'I won't be able to see,' said Sarah.

'You can sit on my lap, then.'

The lights dimmed and the curtain rose. The set was two balconies side by side, with terrace furniture and bright orange and white awnings. Liz Burridge appeared on one of them, and called back, 'Elli, Elli dear, do come out. It's so lovely.' Jim barely recognized her. Bert Dampler's voice could be heard from offstage saying, 'Just a minute.' After a pause he joined Liz. 'Not so bad,' he said, to which she replied, 'It's heavenly. Look at the lights of that yacht reflected in the water. Oh dear, I'm so happy.'

When Margaret appeared on the other balcony, Sarah whispered, 'That's Mummy.'

'I know it is, sweetheart,' said Jim. 'Now shush.'

It was a strange sensation seeing his wife wearing not very much and being referred to as 'darling' by another man.

'I wish I knew you better,' said Michael Ford.

'It's just as well you don't,' replied Margaret. 'The "woman" – in italics – should always retain a certain amount of alluring feminine mystery for the "man" – also in italics.'

'What about the man?' said Michael. 'Isn't he allowed to have any mystery?'

'Absolutely none. Transparent as glass.'

The actors did their best, and there were moments when Jim could imagine that this was something more than a brave and good-natured effort. Margaret held his eye throughout, sometimes for her acting, but mostly because she was his wife. The applause at the end seemed to him to express relief as much as enthusiasm. When Margaret emerged from backstage he gave her a fond embrace.

'You were great,' he said. 'I knew you would be.'

Jim needed to do some stocktaking in the shop, and he suggested that Billy come along with him one Saturday morning and spend some time exploring Wells while he worked. It was raining, and a fierce wind was blowing. They passed the Infirmary on the way into town.

'I fancy we'll be spending some time in that place soon,' said Jim.

'Why?'

'I have a feeling your mother has something to tell us. She thinks I haven't guessed, but I have.'

'What?' said Billy, confused now.

'Well, how would you feel about having another brother or sister?'

'Another one? Now?'

'Yes, now.'

Billy gazed out of the window at the windswept streets. This was the last thing he might have expected.

'I'd like a brother,' he said.

'I thought you'd say that.'

'Which would you like?'

Jim sighed. 'Oh, I don't mind,' he said, 'a boy or a girl. I'll have to make some changes whichever it is.'

'Changes?'

They pulled up outside the shop, and Jim turned towards Billy. 'I'll have to be around a bit more,' he said.

Billy looked back at his father. Why had it taken this news about a new baby for him to say this; why hadn't he said it ages ago?

'That'll be good.'

He spent the morning wandering around the town. With any luck, this would soon be his place too. He stood on the pavement outside the Blue School. It was huge compared to his present school, but still smaller than the Unicorn. He'd get used to it, he was sure.

When his father had finished the stocktaking they had lunch in the Anchor. As they were driving out of the town Jim said, 'We could go now, if you like.'

Billy looked ahead, at the outlines of Glastonbury Tor.

'Yes,' he said. 'Let's go now.'

The hill loomed larger and larger in the windscreen as they approached. It seemed to change shape, too, as though it were a living thing. Eventually it dominated their view, shutting out everything else. Billy craned his neck so as to keep the top of it in sight.

Jim turned into a road that led up the side, and pulled the car over as close to the hedge as possible. Billy raced ahead up the steep slope. As they neared the summit the rain eased, but the cold wind still tore through their coats. Billy ran around the tower, which was all that remained of the church that had once stood there.

'It's freezing up here,' said Jim, wrapping his collar around his chin.

'It's great!' shouted Billy. 'Look, over there is Wells. And that must be where we live, can you see?'

Billy was sure he had never seen anything like it before. This must be the way things looked from an aeroplane. Everything took on a different aspect from up here, everything fitted together in a way that could be understood. To the north lay Wells and the Mendips, with Alfred's Tower beyond, to the west the Bristol Channel, and to the south the flat expanse of the Levels. He tried to point out some of the landmarks, but the wind robbed him of his words.

'Let's go inside,' said Jim. But as they sought shelter, they discovered that the tower acted as a kind of wind tunnel, and they were blown out of the other side. Billy ran around to the entrance again, and this time he careered through, unable to stop himself. Jim tried it too, almost losing his footing as he was swept out of the tower and down the hill. It was exhilarating. They ran through the tower time and again, the wind rushing in their ears, Billy sprawling on the ground and shrieking with laughter.

'Where's the hawthorn bush?' he asked when they were getting their breath back.

'Over there, I think,' said Jim. 'On Wearyall Hill. We'll go there another day, and to the abbey.'

'Oh, I don't care,' said Billy. 'This is the best, the tor.'

They stood for a few moments surveying the landscape, and then Billy broke away to run through the tower once more.

Wakening

'To wake the soul by tender strokes of art'

Pope, Prologue to Addison's *Cato*

One

Billy sat in Goody's café poring over the map of Morocco. It was a map of wonders, of mountains and gorges and dunes, of places with beautiful names like Zagora and Taroudant. There were green palm trees, and everywhere the symbol that indicated a kasbah. What exactly was a kasbah? Billy wondered. He had been reading Walter Harris's *Morocco That Was*, an account of his time there at the turn of the century. Was it possible to travel in that way now, without a classical education and a private income? At Bristol he had been immersed in Robert Byron and Peter Fleming when he should have been reading the Brontës and Mrs Gaskell. Byron's 'stony, black lustred' Persia and Fleming's news from Tartary had captured his imagination. Now it was Morocco that had caught him in its spell, a place that was not so far away but which nonetheless seemed utterly remote. And he had fastened upon it all of his hopes for the future. He must go to Morocco to discover who he was.

He looked out of the window at the bleak February day. In a while he would be home, and his parents would learn that he had dropped out. There would be a scene, he knew very well. But he had determined on this course some time ago, and it was too late to turn back now. The conversation with his professor had settled it for him. 'You have a sentimental response to literature, Palmer,' he had said. 'You lack rigour.' Billy had held his tongue, but that had been the moment when he knew he wanted no further part of it. He would listen to no homilies about the right way to read: he would read as he wished, just as he would live as he wished.

What he wished for now was to be able to go straight to Marrakesh, but that would require money, and he must work for a while first. He looked down again at the map. From Marrakesh you had to cross the Atlas Mountains and keep heading south for the dunes. And then there was nothing but sand until Timbuktu.

He watched his father's cigarette smoke as it coiled towards the ceiling. There was something mesmerizing about it.

'I'm going anyway,' he said.

Jim brushed a piece of lint from the lapel of his suit and looked at Margaret for help.

'But you would have had all the time in the world to travel after your degree,' she said.

'I can't wait that long, Mum. I'm bored to death in Bristol. And what good is an English degree anyway?'

'You'd have found that out if you'd got one,' said Jim. He stared at Billy in dismay. 'What are you going to do with your life anyway? Become a gypsy?'

'I'll work in a bookshop in London for a while. Save some money. Then when I come back from Morocco, we'll see.'

Jim stood up and went into the kitchen. He returned carrying a bottle of whisky and a single glass. 'You're doing exactly the sort of thing I did,' he said. 'I thought sons were supposed to learn from their fathers' mistakes.'

'Let's not get onto the subject of your mistakes,' said Margaret.

'Cheers,' Jim said ironically. 'Here's to my eldest son's brilliant career.' He drained the glass in one gulp. 'You were going to be a teacher,' he said. 'You were going to make something of yourself.'

Billy heard the familiar tones of self-pity in his father's voice. Whose life was it they were talking about, Jim's or his?

'I was never going to be a teacher, Dad,' he replied. 'I only said that because I had no idea at all what I wanted to do.'

'Well you fooled me.' Jim stalked out of the room again. Billy and his mother looked at one another for a few moments without speaking.

'You know,' said Margaret at last, 'for once your father is right. Life without a degree may be much less fulfilling than you think.'

He crossed the room and sat beside her on the sofa.

'You don't understand,' he said. 'I've never been out of the country. There's a whole world out there.'

His mother sighed, and then leaned over to kiss him on the cheek. 'Perhaps I understand better than you think,' she said. 'I've always regretted the fact that I've never been abroad. I used to daydream about going to France.'

'You can go to France. I don't know why Dad hasn't taken you. He's doing well enough these days.'

'We've talked about it. But I'm thinking of when your father and I were your age. We simply didn't have any choices to make then.'

'There was a war on,' intoned Billy, repeating a phrase he must have heard a thousand times. He gazed at her earnestly. 'Well, this is my war,' he said. 'This is my adventure. I'll suffocate if I don't go now.'

'Then you must go.'

He raised himself up. 'I'm going for a walk with Tom,' he said. 'I'll come back to say goodbye.'

Sarah was hovering in the hallway, taking an unnatural interest in the newspaper.

'We've got to talk,' she whispered.

Billy followed her up the stairs.

'What's going on?' she said as she closed her bedroom door behind them.

'I've dropped out.'

'Wow! What are you going to do?'

'Work in a bookshop for a while, probably, to earn some money. Then go to Morocco. But it's not what I'm going to do, it's what I'm going to be.'

'What's that?'

'A free spirit.'

'Great. That's what I'm going to be too.'

'You already are.'

'I am, aren't I?'

He looked at her fondly. She was always getting into trouble these days, hanging around with boys, smoking and drinking. She drove their father wild with anger sometimes, and Billy was forever coming to her defence.

'Lee's joining a band in London,' she said, 'and he's asked me to stay with him in the Easter holidays. We can get together.'

'Of course. But let me get settled first.'

He went into Tom's room and hauled him off the floor, where he was playing with his Scalextric.

'Let's go outside,' he said. 'I've got something to tell you.'

They walked up Priory Road, Tom holding his hand. He seemed very young for eight; but then he was the youngest by far, and loved to distraction by the rest of the family. Billy had hated leaving him when he went to Bristol, and hated even more the idea of leaving him again now.

They passed the Regal. 'Dad's spelled the name of that film wrong,' said Tom.

Billy looked up at the marquee. 'It's called Bullitt,' he said. 'It doesn't have any bullets in it. Or maybe it does. It has a car chase that's meant to be very exciting.'

He halted for a moment to look at the cinema, the place where he had spent so many Saturdays helping out while he was at school. It was an ugly block of a building with a few art deco touches. For his father it represented respectability after the lost years in the wake of his bankruptcy. Billy heard Jim's words echoing in his mind, about sons learning from their fathers' mistakes. What had he learned from his own father? His impulse was invariably to do precisely the opposite of what Jim expected.

In Market Place the stalls were set out on the cobblestones. How quaint Wells seemed now. It was as though the clocks had stopped fifty years ago, five hundred even. They sat on a bench overlooking the moat of the Bishop's Palace and watched the swans glide by.

'I'm going away,' said Billy.

'But you went away before.'

'This is different. I'm going to travel.'

'Where will you go?'

'To a place called Morocco.'

'Where's that?'

'In Africa. Well, at the top of Africa. There's a city called Marrakesh that has a big square with snake charmers and storytellers. And oranges. And camels.'

'I'd like to ride on a camel.' Tom looked up at him quizzically. 'But why are you going there?'

'Why?' Billy fell silent for a few moments. 'Well, I've always wanted to travel. And there's something about the desert. It's going as far as you can go. And it's empty and silent.'

Tom's face assumed a baffled expression.

'I'm not explaining it very well, am I?' said Billy.

'Not really.'

'OK. When I was a kid, not much older than you, I wanted to climb

Glastonbury Tor. For a long time Dad wouldn't let me, and it seemed impossibly difficult. Ever since then I've wanted to do something impossible. Going to the desert is that thing.'

He ruffled Tom's hair. Was this really why he wanted to go to Morocco? It was only as he uttered the words that this justification had occurred to him. He looked up at the towers of the cathedral, and quite suddenly the boldness he had been feeling drained out of him.

He stood by the side of the Bath road, his thumb pointing resolutely east. Having hitch-hiked often enough before, he knew not to expect quick results. But he had left it late today, and darkness would come in a couple of hours. His departure had been delayed by one thing after another, as though neither he nor his family could quite believe he was going. It was very cold, and he fastened the top button of his combat jacket. After a stream of cars had coursed by, eventually a flat-bed lorry pulled over. Billy ran towards it, only to find that the cab already contained three men.

'On the back,' said the driver.

He slung his duffel bag onto the platform, and sat leaning against a roughly bundled tarpaulin. There was no guard-rail, and he set his hands firmly to either side of him so as to stay in place as the lorry negotiated the winding road. The countryside unfolded backwards, making this familiar road seem new. Good, he thought: I want everything to be new.

They dropped him off at the junction with the motorway. As he stood on the slip-road he could sense the light fading. No one would pick him up in the dark. He shivered in the icy air. The expressions on the faces of the drivers as they accelerated past him were impassive, grim even. But eventually a Ford Zephyr drew up, the driver leaning across to push open the door.

'London?' said Billy.

'Hop in.'

He was about fifty, balding and with a jowly face. 'Where in London?' he said.

'I don't really know.'

'You don't know?'

'Where are you going?'

'Home, me. Stepney.'

'Where's that?'

'The East End. But you don't want to go there, I can tell you.'

Billy looked out of the window as the car gathered pace. He hadn't thought much about where he would stay. It began to dawn on him just how impulsive his decision had really been: he hadn't planned anything at all.

'What do you do in Stepney?' he asked.

'I work for Ford's, in Dagenham. That's what gives me this smart car.'

'Right.'

'And what are you going to do?'

'I want to work in a bookshop.'

'Oh well, in that case Foyles is your best bet.'

'I suppose so. It's not my idea of a bookshop, somehow.'

'But it's big. There'll be more chance of a vacancy.'

Their conversation faltered very soon, and as darkness fell, Billy took to wondering what he might expect. He hadn't been to London for a couple of years now, and he had never felt very easy there. It was simply the place you went to when you dropped out. But now it began to loom in his imagination, this vast city that he knew so little about.

They drove on, the traffic becoming steadily heavier as they approached the city. It was night by the time they arrived, and Oxford Street was deserted. The driver pulled over, and pointed down a road to his right.

'It's just a few yards,' he said. 'But you'll need to find somewhere to stay.'

'Yes. Where?'

'The university's that way. There have to be rooms. Look in a newsagent's window.'

Billy thanked him, and walked down Charing Cross Road. Immediately Foyles came into view, a large building with red lettering running along the length of its frontage. 'The World's Largest Bookshop', it read. Gazing into its windows at the books on display, he began to feel that his quest was taking shape, becoming real. Foyles gave him something solid he could attach his hopes to. It was where he would begin.

He turned back in the direction of the university, looking for a newsagent, but found none. Unsure where to go, he kept on walking, quickly losing any sense of direction. The city was very quiet; he must simply be in the wrong part of it. Coming to a large square, he sat down on a bench and gazed up at the phosphorescent orange of the sky. The reality of his situation oppressed him now: here he was in a place where he knew almost no one, had nowhere to stay, and had very little money. A wave of exhaustion washed over him, and suddenly he knew that this bench was as far as he was going. He laid out his sleeping bag, climbed inside it fully clothed, and within minutes he was asleep.

He awoke feeling stiff and cold, and went in search of breakfast. Russell Square had been his shelter for the night, he discovered, and by the Tube station he found a greasy spoon that was open. He ate a vast breakfast, and afterwards found a newsagent with a board full of hand-written signs. 'Room to let in Store Street,' he read. 'Three pounds a week. Share of bathroom.' He noted the address, and asked a passer-by to direct him. Across the road from a café called Lino's he found the door. It was ages before anyone answered the bell.

'Yes?' said a woman. Her face was indistinct, and Billy's first impression was of a halo of grey hair.

'It's about the room,' said Billy.

'Come in, then,' she said.

He stepped inside the door and into a narrow hallway.

'You're a student,' said the woman, as if stating an incontrovertible truth.

'Yes,' said Billy. The moment he uttered this he realized that it was no longer true. But if he wasn't a student, what was he?

'Follow me.'

She was quite tall, and wore an oriental robe. Her movements were graceful and unhurried, and it seemed to Billy that their ascent of the stairs was interminable. Eventually they came to a door, which she opened tentatively.

'I'm not going to make any excuses for it,' she said. 'It is only three pounds a week, after all.'

It was very small, containing a bed, a chair and a chest of drawers. There was a sink at the far end and a single-ring stove. The meter bore a large sign that read 'Shillings only'. It was a lonely room. But then what could he expect? Billy pressed his hand down onto the mattress and turned to the landlady.

'I'll take it,' he said.

She showed him the bathroom, took his first week's rent, and gave him a key. He locked the door and lay down on the bed, gazing at the unshaded light bulb above his head. At least I'm in London, he thought; at least I've begun.

———————

He went out later for a bite to eat, and spent the evening in his room, reading. The next morning he went for a walk. Shunning the places where the tourists went, he headed east, and found himself exploring Clerkenwell and Blackfriars. He came upon the river, and leaned over the stone balustrade. The pleasure boats cut swathes across the river, the sunlight flaring on the water. He walked back along the embankment, and then got lost in Covent Garden. The market was silent now, the arcades empty. On this Sunday morning London was somnolent. As he stood wondering which street to take, he felt lost in more ways than one. Since the moment he had left home he had been assailed by a sense that he had cut himself adrift. He chose a direction at random, and it led him into a maze of backstreets. It was ages before he found his way to the boarding house, and by then he felt utterly dispirited.

He left it until mid-morning the next day before going to Foyles. Charing Cross Road was bustling now, London had come alive. The boy behind the counter directed him to an office where a woman took down his details.

'Miss Foyle interviews all candidates personally,' she said. 'She is available tomorrow afternoon at three.'

When he returned, he found Christina Foyle's office at the very top of the store. She sat stonily behind her desk, reading Billy's application form.

'How old are you?' she asked.

'Nineteen. I'll be twenty in May.'

'That's a very bad age.' She looked at him over her glasses. 'Why aren't you at university still?'

'I... I left. It wasn't what I wanted.'

'It seems to me that young people want far too much these days.'

She fussed with her glasses case for a few moments. 'And what makes you think working in a bookshop is what you want?'

Billy shrugged his shoulders. 'I just love books,' he said.

'We have a rule about staff reading books: not on the company's time.'

'I don't mean…'

She snapped the case shut. 'We don't have any vacancies at the moment,' she said. 'We'll keep your name on file.'

Out in the street, Billy felt dazed by this conversation. She hadn't given him a chance to explain himself. But then, how *was* he going to explain himself? He had better get his story straight. He walked past the other bookshops nearby, and decided he needed some time before he tried anywhere else. He wandered aimlessly among the crowds, beginning to feel overwhelmed. The city was frenetic now, so different from the place he had arrived in a couple of days ago. Everyone except him seemed to have something to do and somewhere to go. He turned back towards the boarding house, and the sanctuary of his room. And then, lying idly on his bed, he wished he had someone to talk to.

The next morning he tried Better Books, which was just across the road from Foyles. The man he spoke to shook his head regretfully. 'We've recently been taken over,' he said. 'I'll be letting people go, not taking them on.'

He walked down the street, trying one bookshop after another, and being turned away from every one. All his hopes seemed absurd now, his assumption that finding a job would be easy, that he would be seized upon as the sort of person anyone would be grateful to hire. It began to rain, a steady drizzle, and by the time Billy reached the boarding house he was soaked. He spent a sleepless night, wondering how long this search would take and how long he could endure it.

The following day he tried the antiquarian bookshops in Museum Street. Looking into one of the shop-fronts at the first editions of Joyce and Eliot, it dawned on him that this was the place he and his father had come to a few months after they had moved to Glastonbury. Jim had borrowed a car and they had picked up some packages from a shady-looking man in Wells and delivered them to a shop in this very street. Billy looked up and down and saw a sign that read 'Bernard Smith: Antiquarian & Second-hand Bookseller'. That was the place. The books had been stolen, as Billy had sensed at the time and later understood. His father had said he was doing a favour for a friend, but Billy had known even then that he was doing it for money. He stood in front of the window of Smith's shop and considered going in, but then thought better of it.

He had no luck with any of the other shops in the street. And then, in the late afternoon, he came across a bookshop he hadn't seen before, hidden away just a few doors up from Foyles. He peered through the window into a narrow space in which display tables nudged against the bookshelves. It was with a sense of trepidation that he entered Collet's and asked to see the manager.

He sat behind his typewriter, a man with a jutting jaw and a pipe clamped in his mouth. His moustache was a motley of grey and yellow.

'You've dropped out,' he said, a smile of self-satisfaction creasing his face. 'I can always tell.'

'Well... yes.'

'This place is full of drop-outs,' he said. 'Drop-outs, Maoists, anarcho-syndicalists – we've got the lot here.'

'I want to work with books.'

'Of course you do.' He rattled the stem of his pipe against his teeth and swept ash from his bright-red cardigan. 'Fiction?'

'Yes, fiction mostly.'

'Someone's leaving the fiction department at the end of the week. Going to Cuba, so he reckons.'

'I didn't think you could get into Cuba without being invited.'

'You can't,' said the manager, and he burst into a high-pitched giggle. When he had regained his composure he said, 'Andrew Wilson. Pleased to have you with us.'

They shook hands, and Billy realized that he had a job. Wilson led him to the fiction department, and introduced him to the woman who ran it.

'Beverley Hoskins, Billy Palmer,' he said. 'He's starting next Monday, taking over from Kevin.'

She was probably about thirty, and very plump. She smiled and said, 'I look forward to working with you.'

'Me too,' said Billy enthusiastically.

The days until he started at Collet's were hard to get through. He passed the shop often enough, staring at the window displays and wishing himself already there. He tramped the streets, criss-crossing the city, setting out his coordinates. London was vast, inexhaustible.

When he wasn't out walking, he sat by the gas fire in his room, reading Durrell's *Justine*. The fire hissed, and in its glowing reticulations he conjured images of Alexandria, its 'thousand dust-tormented streets'. How odd it was, he thought, that he could be so easily transported by a book to one great city when another lay on his doorstep and yet seemed nonetheless remote.

Eventually the following Monday came around. At half past nine Billy reported to Andrew Wilson, who told him to find Beverley. 'You'll have to do the donkey work,' he said. 'She's not the most agile.' Wondering how important agility might be in bookselling, he went off in search of her.

She stood behind the counter, going through stock cards. Her dark-brown woollen dress went all the way to the floor, seeming both to conceal and accentuate her girth. She smiled her shy smile, and set Billy to work opening boxes of books. They bore the black and orange Penguin imprint, and there were lots of them.

'Just put them on the shelves,' she said, 'moving books up where you need to. Put as many face-out as you can: it's nicer that way.'

Billy began to work, checking off the titles against the despatch note. He was surprised to find how many authors he had never heard of who, judging from the numbers of their books, must be quite popular. It was hard work stacking the shelves, and he began to see what Wilson meant by agility. In the middle of the morning Beverley brought him a cup of coffee, and then suggested she introduce him to the staff. There were three other assistants on the ground floor, who looked after the hardbacks, the crime books, the science fiction and the poetry, and downstairs three more. The basement had an air of studiousness, its signs indicating politics, economics, sociology and history. The other assistants were either very young or very old, and they seemed friendly enough. He said hello to them in turn. And then he saw a ghost.

He was the whitest person Billy had ever seen. Behind thick glasses his eyes blinked continually, as though he were staring at the sun. They were a dull pink colour, and quite unsettling.

'Peter Burns,' he said. 'No relation to Robbie.' He glanced away as he shook Billy's hand, as though at someone else, and then looked back. His eyes seemed fathomless. Throughout the rest of the morning the image of this strange creature kept recurring to Billy, and he found himself glancing down the stairs now and then so as to try to catch sight of him.

He finished stacking the Penguins, and Beverley asked him to mind the counter for a while. The customers came and went, generally handing over their books without a word. Then a military-looking man stepped towards him.

'You don't seem to have Pole's *The Valley of Bones*,' he said.

'Let me see,' said Billy. 'Pole?'

'Yes. Anthony Pole.'

He went to the shelves, but could see no books by anyone called Pole. Returning to the counter he looked at the stock cards, and drew a blank there too.

'No, we haven't,' he said. 'Perhaps I could order it for you.'

'No matter,' said the man. 'I'll go to Foyles. You really ought to have all the Poles, you know.'

Beverley returned a few minutes later, and Billy decided he had better report this encounter. As he was describing it, she put her hand to her mouth.

'Oh, Billy,' she said. 'Follow me.'

They went to the shelves, and Beverley took up a book and handed it to him. *The Kindly Ones*, Billy read, by Anthony Powell.

'It's pronounced "Pole",' she said, her eyes glistening with mirth. 'He's writing a series of novels called *A Dance to the Music of Time*. He's famous.'

Billy's cheeks flushed. 'Of course,' he said. 'I just didn't know how the name was pronounced. I'll go after him and explain.'

'Don't be silly. We haven't got *The Valley of Bones* anyway – it's reprinting.'

'I'm sorry.'

Beverley laid a hand on his arm. 'Don't be,' she said. 'This is your first day, after all. You'll learn soon enough.'

———

'Come and have tea,' said the landlady, Mrs Allingham. 'I always invite my young men to tea. And they always seem to be young men, not young ladies: girls prefer sharing flats.'

He had seen her glide about the house, always in her oriental silks, and was struck by her elegance and composure. But nothing had prepared him for the sight of her rooms. From the drabness of the hallway he stepped into a tropical den. Everything was bamboo and lacquer and porcelain. A brilliantly coloured folding screen took up one corner, its peacock's eye staring balefully out. This was another world entirely.

Mrs Allingham invited him to sit in a carved-wood chair, and poured the tea. Billy looked into his cup to see a faintly green liquid, half a dozen large leaves resting on the bottom. She didn't offer him milk.

'You'll be wondering where all this comes from, of course,' she said.

'Yes.'

'Malaya. Or Malaysia as they call it now.'

'You lived there?'

'For most of my life.' She sipped her tea, holding the cup in both hands. 'My husband was a rubber planter.'

'What's it like?'

'Oh, I loved it. The jungle isn't anything like what most people imagine. It's clean and bright. And everything is very simple, at least for an Englishwoman with servants and not very much to do.'

'Why did you come back?'

'My husband died. Men don't last long in the tropics. We had to come home during the war, of course; and then we returned in forty-six. But it wasn't the same – one could see that independence was coming.'

She laid down her cup and brushed back a strand of long grey hair. Her fine-boned face was a tracery of lines, around her eyes and mouth, across her cheeks and forehead.

'But I've invited you to tea to find out all about you,' she said, 'not talk about myself.'

'About me?'

'Of course.' Her eyes sparkled mischievously. 'You told me a little white lie, didn't you?'

'Yes. How did you know I'm not a student any more?'

'You don't keep student hours.'

'No, I suppose I don't.'

'So what do you do?'

'I work in a bookshop, Collet's. I've just started.'

'Well, that's a very fine thing to do. And you'll write a novel, won't you?'

'No. I'm not a writer. I want to travel. But I need to spend a few months in London first.'

She poured more tea, the pithy leaves circling in Billy's cup. 'And what about your family?'

Billy had been hoping he could forget about his family for a while. In the dusky light of Mrs Allingham's sitting room he found it hard to summon anything he wanted to say.

'It's just a family,' he said. 'You know.'

'There's no such thing as "just a family". What does your father do?'

Billy sighed, and took another sip of tea. 'He owns a cinema in Wells, in Somerset,' he said.

'Is that interesting?'

'I used to work there on Saturdays. It depends on what film is showing.'

'And your mother?'

'My mother...' Billy paused for a moment. What did he want to say about her? 'My mother is a saint.'

'And by that you mean that your father is a sinner?'

Billy fell silent, not sure how to reply, and an awkwardness came over them. Finally he said, 'I don't suppose my father is any more of a sinner than anyone else. But he went bankrupt when I was ten, and we had a difficult time for a few years before he was able to get a decent job again.'

'And your mother held things together.'

'Yes. It's what mothers do, isn't it?'

———

By the end of his first week, Billy had grasped the basic elements of his job. And indeed they were very basic, involving far more physical work than he had imagined. Beverley dealt with the publishers' reps, while Billy lugged books from the stockroom and filled the shelves. He spent at least some time behind the counter, and enjoyed displaying the knowledge he already possessed about books and writers.

But there was so much he didn't know, so much he hadn't read.

On the Friday he bumped into Peter Burns as he was leaving the shop to get some lunch.

'Fancy a bite?' said Peter.

They walked under an archway that led them into Soho. In Old Compton Street they entered a café called 2i's. 'Home of the Stars', read the sign. Sitting down at a plastic-covered table, they shouted at one another over the hubbub of conversation and the screech of the tall silver coffee machine.

'Have you ever seen any stars in here?' said Billy.

'They used to have music downstairs. I think the word "stars" is used rather loosely.'

Peter was studying the menu in a way that wholly obscured his face, holding it about three inches away. He squinted, and turned the card this way and that. But when the waitress arrived he said simply, 'The usual,' and to Billy, 'spaghetti bolognese.'

Billy looked around the steamy room. The other diners were mostly young, but smart, the men's hair tidy and the women in miniskirts and tight jumpers. It seemed an odd sort of place for Peter to come to.

'So how's it going?' asked Peter.

Billy set out his knife and fork and smoothed down the napkin. 'Fine,' he said. 'I'm enjoying it.'

'Beverley's all right. And Wilson is just about tolerable.' Peter blew his nose loudly and then began excavating it with his handkerchief.

'How long have you worked there?'

'Two years. I went there because of its traditions, but they're all gone now.'

'What traditions?'

'Radical ones. The original Collet's was on the site of a place they called the "bomb shop", because of its connections with anarchists. Then in the thirties the owner started bringing in communist literature from Russia.'

'But Wilson told me you were all radicals even now.'

'Well, I am. And maybe Philip Walters, though I suspect he's a backslider.'

'So what are your politics?'

'Oh, I'm a Marxist,' he said airily.

'Are you a member of the Party?'

'Of course not. The CP in this country is a bunch of lackeys.'

For so mild-mannered a person, Peter was very declamatory in his speech. Billy had stayed out of politics at Bristol. But there was something about this strange young man that he felt himself drawn to.

Their spaghetti arrived, and they tucked into it hungrily.

'Surely Marxism has failed,' said Billy after a few moments.

Peter wiped his nose with the sleeve of his shirt. 'It's not Marxism that's failed,' he said, 'it's Russian-style communism.'

'Aren't they the same thing?'

'Not at all. Marxism has never been put into practice, it's never been given a chance.'

'So what *have* they got in Russia?'

Peter tapped his fork on the side of his plate. 'They've got a corrupt form of the dictatorship of the proletariat,' he said. 'Only it's the dictatorship of Brezhnev and his gang.'

'Wasn't that bound to happen? Doesn't communism go against the grain of human nature?'

Peter snorted. 'Human nature!' he exclaimed. 'That's precisely the point. Human nature isn't some fixed, immutable thing – it's socially and historically conditioned.'

'Is it?'

'Of course it is. The reason communism hasn't worked in Russia is that people are still alienated, from their work and from the things their work creates. But Marx foresaw all this. He knew there would have to be an intermediate stage, a period of socialism, before true communism can establish itself.'

Billy chewed on his spaghetti. He had heard this kind of speechifying before, and didn't believe a word of it. He looked across the room. A blonde girl wearing a long velvet coat and a feather boa sat down in a booth.

'Why do you come here?' he said.

Peter smiled broadly. 'I like to keep my eye on the bourgeoisie.'

They sat for a while gazing at the girls. It seemed very clear to Billy what Peter meant by 'the bourgeoisie', and he wondered whether his own yearnings were as plain to see as his companion's.

After a while Peter said, 'What about you? What are you interested in?'

Billy looked down at his empty plate, and then out of the window. 'I want to see the world,' he said.

172

'That sounds pretty corny, if you don't mind my saying so.'

'I suppose it does. But I don't know how else to put it.'

'So you're going to do the Englishman abroad thing, are you, and look loftily upon the natives?'

Billy smiled. Talking to Peter was nothing if not bracing. 'I'm going to be a traveller,' he said. 'I'm going to go to Morocco and disappear into it.'

'You mean not come back?'

'No, I mean become invisible, and try to absorb things.'

Peter pushed his glasses up the bridge of his nose. 'Well I don't want to go anywhere,' he said. 'Right here will do me. I just want here to be as different as possible.'

The weekends were long and lonely, and Billy filled them as best he could with reading and walking. He had no money for the pleasures of the city, his bookshop wage taken up by rent and food. It was already clear that saving for Morocco was going to be difficult. And knowing almost no one in London, he was wholly dependent on the people he met in the shop. Billy sensed a friendship forming with Peter, but he seemed preoccupied with his political activities. He spoke of his selling the New Left Review on street corners as a kind of crusade.

There was in fact one person Billy knew in London, but he hadn't seen him since he was Tom's age. Len Haskell was his mother's brother, and he had cut off Billy's family after Jim had gone bankrupt. Billy had never understood why he had reacted in this way. His father had owned a Jaguar showroom that went bust, and for several years afterwards he had worked in a clothes outfitters in Wells. With the cinema he had got himself back on his feet. But Len had never relented. When Billy called home one day his mother gave him Len's number, urging him to phone and to try to mend things. And eventually, with nothing better to do, he did phone, and arranged to go to the house on a Sunday morning.

He took a bus, which lurched through Camden Town and up the hill to South End Green, where he found the little terraced house on Constantine Road. The net curtains in the bay window were drawn back, and a middle-aged man peered out. When he opened the door, Billy set eyes on someone quite other than the slim, dark uncle he had known as a boy. He was portly, his hair turning to grey, his complexion florid. As he led Billy into the sitting room the soles of his leather slippers rapped on the floor.

'You're tall, like your dad,' Len said as he lowered himself into an armchair, gesturing to Billy to take the sofa.

'I suppose so.' Billy looked around the room, at the heavy furniture and flock wallpaper. Len's wife had died many years ago, and Billy had never known her. The room they sat in seemed careworn and neglected.

'And how is he treating that sister of mine these days?'

'Oh, well, I think.'

Len pulled on the wings of his waistcoat. It was shiny and gold, and lent an odd splash of colour to the scene.

'Better than he has done, I hope.'

'He's doing his best. You know he owns a cinema now.'

'I heard.'

'He was the manager for a few years, and then he borrowed some money from the bank and bought it from the owner.'

'Always very good at tapping people for a loan, your dad. Sherry?'

'Thank you.'

Len lifted himself from the chair and padded into the kitchen. While he was gone, Billy inspected the framed photographs on the mantelpiece. They seemed very old, studio shots of Len and his wife Betty. He stepped over to the window and gazed out into the overgrown garden. A dog was barking furiously somewhere nearby, and it jangled Billy's nerves. He hadn't expected to enjoy this visit; but nor had he expected his uncle to seem quite so stern.

'So what are you doing in London?' said Len when he returned.

'I'm working in a bookshop.'

'Interesting?'

'Yes. I love being surrounded by books.'

'Like your mother.' He poured out the sherry, spilling some of it onto the tray. 'But she never had the time to read, not properly. Should have married someone who could read too.'

Billy knew he must change the subject. 'How about your work?' he asked.

Len harrumphed into his sherry. 'My work is the same as it ever was, and as it ever will be.'

'Insurance.'

Len nodded gravely. 'Insurance,' he replied. 'Against a rainy day.'

Billy sat wondering what to say next. Before he could muster anything, however, his uncle spoke again.

'You could stay here,' he said.

Billy looked at him in surprise. The expression on Len's face had softened, and what Billy had taken to be bitterness had turned to something more like melancholy.

'Thank you,' he murmured. 'I... The boarding house is very close to the shop.'

Len shrugged his shoulders. 'Just a thought,' he said. 'The spare room's quite large. Take a look at it before you go if you like.'

When, twenty minutes later, Billy left the house, he realized that he hadn't seen the room after all, that his uncle's offer had completely gone out of his mind, and that Len hadn't mentioned it again. He looked back at the bay window, remembering the dreariness of the room behind the curtains, and knew he would not be seeing his uncle again, not for a while at least. He thought of his mother, of the disappointment she would feel. Why hadn't she tried to mend things with Len herself? he wondered. His father had sworn he would never speak to him again, and, as was so often the case, it was his will that had prevailed. Perhaps he should return after all, and try to persuade Len to visit Wells. Perhaps he shouldn't always accept his father's ideas about their family.

In South End Green he sat in a corner café eating a sandwich and wondering what to do next. He had heard that Hampstead Heath was a good place to walk, the nearest thing to the countryside that London had to offer. Finding the road that led up to Parliament Hill, he came out onto a blustery knoll that gave him a broad view of the city. Kites flew in circles, children screaming at their fathers to keep them in the air. London was laid out before him, and Billy could see for the first time the way the landmarks stood in relation to each other. The Centre Point office block, which he passed every day on his way to work, loomed incongruously above the surrounding buildings; the Post Office tower seemed from here to be like a toy rocket; and the dome of St Paul's winked at him in the sunlight, a light that seemed at last to hold some promise of spring.

He walked between the ponds, and found himself in Highgate. Soon he saw the wrought-iron gates of a cemetery, and he wandered inside. There was something about the place that suited his mood, the doleful expressions of the stone angels and the tombstones that bore heavy phrases such as 'fell asleep' and 'passed away'. And then he came upon a tomb quite unlike anything else, a solid block of stone with a great shaggy head above it. 'Workers of all lands unite,' said the inscription, and below, 'The philosophers have only interpreted the world in different ways; the point is to change it'. Billy looked up again at the brooding visage of Marx, and thought of Peter. The point is to change it. But how?

———

At coffee break the next morning he told Peter about his explorations.

'That's Orwell's café in South End Green,' he replied.

'I don't think it was called that.'

'No, no,' he said impatiently. 'It's where he wrote *Keep the Aspidistra Flying*. Terrible book. He just wasn't a novelist.'

Peter took out his handkerchief and blew his nose loudly. He was always doing this, thought Billy, even though he seemed not to have a cold.

'What about *Animal Farm* and *Nineteen Eighty-four*?'

'Manifestos,' said Peter, 'not novels.'

'You can read them that way, I suppose. But don't you think they hold up as stories?'

'Maybe.' Peter stuck the handkerchief back in his pocket. 'We had a joker in here recently looking for Orwell's restaurant guide.'

'Restaurant guide?'

'Yes. *Dining Out In Paris And London*.' Peter smirked, and then said, 'So you're a fan of Orwell's?'

'Yes.'

'Then it seems to me you've got the makings of a revolutionary consciousness. There's an International Socialists' meeting in support of Dubček and the reformers this week. Want to come?'

'OK,' he said. 'Thank you.'

A few days later they went to the meeting at Conway Hall, going through a pillared foyer lined with wooden pews into a crowded room. Eventually they found spaces at a table at the back in which to sit.

There was almost no one over twenty-five. Most of them were young men, their uniforms of jeans and baggy sweaters worn with pride. There were a few young women, and Billy couldn't help but notice the way Peter's eyes rested on them. An older man banged his shoe on a table and called for silence.

'Welcome to the meeting,' he said, 'whether you're a member of the IS or not. We're here to express our solidarity with Alexander Dubček and his supporters. For those of you who've had your heads in the sand lately, after the atrocious events of last autumn, Novotný has had to concede the party leadership to Dubček, and the chance of reform is within their grasp. Last week the editors of *Literarni Listi* were reinstated. And Dubček is holed up in his rooms reading.'

A cheer went up from many in the audience.

'Yes, Czechoslovakia has a leader who can read!' went on the speaker. 'Who has the humility to believe that there are things he can learn if he is to lead his country into a brave future. A man who knows that the idea that socialism and democracy can't coexist is a bourgeois myth, that the crimes of Stalinism have nothing to do with true socialism.'

He was warming to his theme. 'Now Dubček must purge the party,' he went on, 'must clear out the apparatchiks. There must be a new political order. Once democratic socialism has been established in Czechoslovakia it can sweep the Eastern bloc. Then the fascists in America and the West will no longer be able to say that the project has failed. It hasn't even begun!'

Peter shouted, 'Let the revolution come!' Billy looked across at him. His whiteness, usually so pallid, seemed now to shine. He was clearly galvanized by the moment.

Other speakers came and went, and there were interventions from the floor. But everyone was in essential agreement, and the atmosphere was friendly and relaxed. The meeting broke up, and they stepped out into the night.

'So, what did you think?' said Peter as they crossed the square.

'It was interesting.'

'Only "interesting"?'

Billy paused, and then said, 'I don't know what it accomplished. Will your meeting here in London change anything on the streets of Prague?'

'It's about solidarity, about showing the world that we're watching.'

'Does Brezhnev care who's watching?'

'He will,' said Peter with an air of determination. 'Look, if you want to see what action can do, the next Grosvenor Square demo is the Saturday after next. Fancy taking part?'

'Like the one last autumn, marching on the American Embassy?'

'Yes. Except this time we're going to occupy it.'

'I'm going to a talk at the Royal Geographical Society that day. I'll meet you afterwards if you like.'

Peter gave him a withering stare. 'You're not with us, are you?' he said.

'No, I don't think I am.'

Andrew Wilson yanked the steering wheel of the minivan to the right, and they swung into Gower Mews. From the moment Billy had slid into the passenger seat, Wilson had been doing a fine impression of a complete madman, racing around the streets of London, cutting up cyclists and other drivers with relish. His pipe stuck out at a jaunty angle, and there was a gleam in his eye.

'Let's say hello to Pat and George,' he said.

A sign on a door at the end of the mews read 'William Heinemann, Trade Counter'. They entered to find two middle-aged men, one of them typing with two fingers and the other calling out the titles and quantities of books.

'Afternoon, gentlemen,' said Wilson.

The men replied without breaking off from their tasks. It was clear to Billy that some sort of ritual was being enacted. Wilson handed one of them an order form.

'How's business, then, Andrew?' the man asked.

'Could be worse.'

'Could be better too, I expect.'

'Could be better. Especially if it'd stop raining.'

The man returned with about a dozen books cradled in his arms. 'You know what you lot are always saying about the weather, don't you?' he said. 'If it's raining customers stay at home, and if the sun's shining they go out and do something more exciting than buying books.'

'It's an unalterable law of bookselling,' said Wilson.

He signed for the books, and they made their way back to the van and along the Euston Road. Billy was glad of this invitation to get away from the shop for a couple of hours and tour the publishers' trade counters, and glad too of the opportunity to get to know Wilson.

'Have you always been at Collet's?' he asked.

'No, I used to work at Foyles. Well, I grew up at Foyles, learned my trade there. But that was when old William was alive.'

'I had an interview with Christina before I came to you.'

'Battle-axe,' said Wilson.

Billy looked out of the window at the traffic halted all around. 'Why are there so many bookshops in the Charing Cross Road?' he asked.

Wilson adjusted the pipe in his mouth. 'I don't know,' he said. 'It's like districts in medieval towns, isn't it? Booksellers attract each other. A couple of hundred years ago they were all near St Paul's.'

'What was bookselling like in those days, when you started?'

'Not much different.' Wilson engaged first gear, and the minivan sprang forward a few yards before coming to an abrupt stop once again. 'Better Books tried to change it, but it didn't stick. They decided it would be a good idea to have silver bookshelves, so you couldn't see them. Bloody eyesore, it was.'

'That's not much of a change.'

'Oh, they did more than that. They had poetry readings and events and things. They even had tables with typewriters on them, so that writers could bash out their stuff.'

'That's a good idea.'

Wilson jammed the gear-stick forward once again. 'Writers should stay out of bookshops,' he said.

They stopped at the Collins trade counter in York Way, and then headed north. The rain lashed the windscreen, the wipers scraping back and forth. They pulled up outside a circular building and ascended an outside staircase to the first floor.

'The Old Piano Factory,' said Wilson. 'Duckworth's.'

The place was a litter of desks, chairs, papers and books. No one took any notice of them, continuing to go about their work with an air of nonchalance that Billy sensed was at least partly for show. Behind the desks were row upon row of book stacks. Wilson strode towards them, and was quickly lost from Billy's sight. An owlish-looking man in heavy black spectacles glanced up at him.

'New boy?' he said.

Billy nodded.

'You'd better go and see what Wilson's up to back there. Whenever he comes I have to go in afterwards and measure the dust on the books.'

'The dust?'

'The best form of stock control I know.' He thrust out his hand. 'My name's Colin Haycraft.'

'Billy Palmer.' He looked around him. 'This is what I always imagined a publishing house would look like.'

'Well this is about the only one that does, nowadays. The big publishers don't clutter their offices with anything so unsightly as books.'

Wilson returned, and dumped a pile of books onto one of the desks. He nodded at Haycraft. 'You're in danger of having to reprint this one,' he said, holding up a Greek history.

'No fear,' replied Haycraft. 'I'm sure demand will dwindle nicely soon.'

Back in the minivan, Billy sat thinking about these people he now found himself among. He had always thought of books as the repository of all that was worth preserving, and booksellers as their custodians. But there was something a little odd about Wilson and the others. There they were, surrounded by all the knowledge of the world, and yet in their different ways they seemed unworldly. But books could take you only so far. This was why he was going to Morocco, why he was no longer content just to read about it. This was why he was different from them.

Two

The man at the podium in the Royal Geographical Society was gaunt and ill-looking. Gavin Maxwell was famous for his island off the coast of Skye, and the otters he had raised there. But today he was talking about the Glaoui, a Berber tribe who until a few years ago had practically ruled Morocco. Maxwell coughed frequently, and gulped water from a tall glass. His voice was thin and reedy, his tones aristocratic. *Lords of the Atlas* his book was called, and he told an extraordinary story, of two brothers who had parlayed their control of the main pass over the Atlas Mountains into control of the entire country, and under the very noses of the French.

The slides projected behind Maxwell showed a fortress in the mountains, palaces in Marrakesh and Fez, and warriors on horseback dressed in colourful robes, their rifles pointing at the sky. It seemed scarcely possible that the last of the Glaoui brothers had died, and Morocco had secured its independence, only twelve years before.

Billy looked around the auditorium and up at the gallery. This was the shrine of British exploration, made famous by Livingstone and Stanley, by Scott and Shackleton. Billy looked back at Maxwell. He had apparently been a spy, a racing driver, a poet and a painter. As he spoke now, Billy could see the colours and hear the sounds of Africa in his words. He longed to be there. And then he remembered that he had less than ten pounds to his name.

After the lecture he tried to seek out Maxwell. There were so many things he wanted to ask him, about what life was like in Marrakesh, about how far you could go into the desert. But Maxwell had been spirited away to a private room, and a woman told Billy he would not be able to follow.

Disheartened, he strolled across Hyde Park and towards the café in Marylebone where Peter had said he would meet him after the march. Since the evening at Conway Hall they had kept off the subject of politics. A bond was forming between them, it was clear, but not one that grew out of shared interests.

He found the café, and ordered a cup of coffee. He had no idea when to expect Peter, especially given his ambition to occupy the embassy. In the event it was past six when he appeared, and when he did so he made an appalling sight. As he reeled across the room, Billy saw that there was blood matting his hair and trickling down his forehead.

Billy leaped up from his chair and led Peter to the table. 'What happened?' he asked.

'Bastards charged us,' replied Peter, sitting down heavily. His glasses were askew, and he took them off and put his hand to his face. He stared at the blood on his fingertips with an expression of utter perplexity.

'The police?'

'Yes. On horseback. One of them hit me with his truncheon. It was a riot. There were people lying on the ground all over the place.'

His words came in a halting sort of way, and he took deep breaths as he spoke. Billy looked again at the wound on the side of his head.

'This is terrible,' he said. 'You need to have that looked at straight away. Let's get a bus to my place.' He knew little about first aid, and could think only of Mrs Allingham. She would know what to do.

They boarded a bus, facing down the stares of the other passengers. Peter was clearly in great pain. He sat looking into space, groaning now and then and feeling the wound with his fingertips.

'Leave it alone,' said Billy.

Mrs Allingham ushered them into her rooms, and immediately set about boiling water and tearing strips from an old sheet.

'You foolish boy,' she muttered. 'There are better ways of making your point.'

She tended Peter's head, washing it thoroughly and winding bandage after bandage around it. 'You must see a doctor soon,' she said. 'Head wounds can be very dangerous.'

Peter was beginning to register his surroundings now, his eyes taking in the scene. 'Have I been transported to Vietnam?' he said with a puzzled smile.

'No,' said Mrs Allingham. 'You're exactly where you ought to be. And your next stop must be a doctor's surgery.'

'I'm all right.'

'No, you're not. Now, I'll make a cup of tea, and then Billy will take you to see my doctor. I'll give you his address and phone number. You may have to call him out at this time on a weekend, though.'

After dutifully drinking Mrs Allingham's tea, they went up to Billy's room. Peter sat down in the armchair. 'I don't need a doctor,' he said. 'I'll be fine.'

'Are you sure?'

'Yes.' He looked up at Billy, his eyes glinting. 'I did it,' he said. 'I showed those bastards what for!'

Sarah had said she would meet him in Portobello Road, which turned out to be very long. Eventually he found her at a stall, wearing a new coat.

'How do I look?' she said, twirling around.

'You look great.' He kissed her on the cheek. 'How could you afford it?'

'Dad gave me some money for the trip. I'll be almost broke now, but I couldn't not buy it, could I?'

'No, you couldn't not buy it.'

It was good to see her, to see a familiar face after all this time. Since they were children she had always been able to draw him out of himself, into the here and now.

'Where are you staying?' he asked.

'In Earls Court. Lee's band has a crash-pad there. I'll be here for two weeks. I'm so excited!'

It was Saturday morning, and the place was thronged with people enjoying the spring sunshine. They weaved their way down the hill, past places selling clothes and fruit and vegetables. Sarah was clearly entranced by it. The other shoppers were mostly young, their clothes brightly coloured, their hair flowing freely. This was the very heart of things, thought Billy, this was where it was at.

'You should buy something too,' said Sarah. 'You've had that awful jacket since you were at school.'

Billy looked down at himself, at the combat jacket and jeans he had worn every day since he had arrived in London. 'I'm not much interested in clothes,' he said.

'Well, I think you should get interested. How are you going to find a girlfriend looking like that?'

Billy felt suddenly wounded by his sister's words. He hadn't had a

183

girlfriend in a long time, and by now this seemed unnatural. No matter how often he told himself there were other things he wanted, this absence from his life was something he felt keenly.

'Let's have a drink,' he said, and they stepped into a crowded pub. He struggled towards the bar, while Sarah found a corner seat and claimed it.

'So, what are you going to get up to while you're here?' he asked when they were settled.

'I'm going to hang out with Lee and the band. They're throwing a party for my birthday next weekend. You must come.'

Billy hadn't met Lee. He was surprised that his parents had permitted Sarah to stay with him, and wondered what sort of story she had told them.

'What's the band called?' he asked.

'The Tricksters. They're influenced by the Stones.'

'How are they doing?'

'They've only just formed. They've done some gigs in Bath and Bristol, and they've got their London debut soon.'

'What does Lee play?'

'Lead guitar. He's great.'

She sipped her orange juice and sat back against the worn velvet of the seat. They gazed out across the smoke-filled room, and then Billy said, 'How are things at home?'

Sarah looked down into her glass. 'They're OK,' she said quietly.

'And what does that mean?' He looked at her intently. 'Come on, how are things really?'

She hesitated, and then said, 'Dad's been impossible lately.'

'Why?'

'I don't know. I think he's… I think he's got problems at the cinema.'

Billy sighed deeply. 'You mean it's not doing very well.'

She nodded. 'And he's driving Mum crazy.'

His thoughts turned to his mother, to the woman who had 'held things together' after the bankruptcy. She had gone through so much then, so much hardship and uncertainty. Surely she would never have to do so again?

'How is she?' he asked.

'All right, otherwise. Wants to go back into the acting, now that Tom's a bit older.'

184

'Good. She needs to get out of the house.'

'But let's not talk about home. How are *you*?'

Billy shrugged his shoulders. 'OK,' he said. 'The bookshop's sort of interesting. But I don't want to be in London, I want to be in Marrakesh. London's too much, in a way, there's too much to take in.'

'I think you're mad. London's wonderful. I wish I could live here.'

'You will one day.'

'*One* day, yes. When I'm too old to enjoy it.'

Billy smiled, and looked across the room. Was life something that was always lived in the next place? Perhaps he should forget about Morocco and make the best of things where he was. Perhaps he should try to make a go of bookselling. But even as he had this thought he knew it was out of the question.

'I've made a friend, anyway,' he said.

'Who's that?'

'His name's Peter Burns. He's an albino and a Marxist.'

'Cool.'

'He was in the Grosvenor Square demo and got hit on the head by a policeman's truncheon.'

'Everyone's talking about Grosvenor Square. Was he really there?'

'Yes. He asked me to go with him.'

'And of course you didn't.'

'Why do you say that?'

Sarah's face assumed an expression of mild reproach, but she said nothing.

'OK,' said Billy. 'But I'm going to do something of my own. Just you wait and see.'

———

Billy and Peter had agreed they could afford to go to 2i's for lunch twice a week. They usually sat at a table at the back, studying the other diners.

'What sort of stuff do you read?' said Peter one day.

'Oh, a lot of fiction. The last good book I read was *Catch-22*.'

Peter sniffed. 'American,' he said.

'Not everything American is bad, you know. Anyway, what's *Catch-22* if not an anti-war book?'

'Can't say I've bothered to read it.'

Their lasagne arrived. 'So what are you reading at the moment?' said Billy.

'*One-Dimensional Man*, by Herbert Marcuse.'

'Oh, him.'

'You're not a fan, I take it?'

'I've barely read him. His books seem impenetrable.'

'He says we're living one-dimensional lives, and that our capacity for independent thought is withering away.' As he spoke, Peter placed his elbows firmly on the table and steepled his fingers. 'It's a sort of update on Marx's false consciousness,' he continued. 'Though I don't think Marcuse is a true Marxist, not an orthodox one anyway.'

'Ideas have to develop, don't they?' said Billy. 'Things change.'

'I suppose so.' The bandage on Peter's head was lopsided, and he raised a hand to straighten it. 'I thought *Eros and Civilization* was pretty good.'

'What was that about?'

'Oh, the fact that people should be able to screw around without the state interfering.'

Billy looked across the café, at the young men and women who talked earnestly to one another amid the steam and the shouts of the waiters. 'Isn't that happening anyway?' he said.

Peter's expression turned gloomy. 'I suppose so,' he said. 'Don't ask me.'

Billy looked at his friend, and then back across the room. 'Do you have a girlfriend?' he asked tentatively.

'What do you think?'

'I don't think anything.'

'What sort of girl is going to go out with me?'

'What do you mean?'

Peter laid down his fork with an air of finality. 'I'm a freak, Billy,' he said.

'Of course you're not a freak.'

'Oh no? Look at me. I'm a weirdo. At least, that's what they called me at school.'

'School doesn't count. I'm sure no one calls you a weirdo now.'

'They don't *call* me one.'

Billy looked away again, strangely disturbed by this turn in the conversation. Then he found himself blurting out the words, 'I've never slept with a girl.'

'Well, that makes two of us.'

He looked once again at Peter, who was gazing wistfully at a table of girls nearby, and felt a powerful urge to talk about himself. His virginity was by now a matter of great embarrassment to him. He would be twenty in a few weeks' time, and furthermore his sister, who was barely seventeen, was surely sleeping with her boyfriend. But now was not the moment for such confidences.

'We need to meet some girls,' he said lightly.

'And how do we do that?'

'My sister's having a party next week. You're invited.'

'How come?'

'Because I've invited you.'

_____

The band's crash-pad was in Earls Court, a basement flat just around the corner from the Tube station. Billy and Peter had a drink in a pub nearby beforehand, loosening themselves up. By the time they arrived the place was crowded, the air already sweetened by dope. Sarah hugged Billy excitedly.

He had told her he was bringing Peter, and she was very solicitous, introducing him to her friends as the hero of Grosvenor Square. And then she took Billy by the hand and led him into the kitchen.

'This is Lee,' she said shyly.

He was a willowy figure, with long eyelashes above piercing blue eyes, and sculpted lips.

'Heard a lot about you,' he said.

'How are things going with the band?'

Lee grinned. 'Well enough,' he said. 'It takes time.'

Another boy joined them, brandishing a beer bottle.

'This is Julian,' said Lee, 'our singer.'

Julian thrust out his hand in a curious gesture, pointing it at the floor. 'Julian Saunders,' he said. He looked Billy up and down. 'Anyone ever call you Bill?'

'Billy's my name.'

'Billy the Kid.'

With that Julian turned on his heel and went over to kiss a girl. He wrapped his arms around her neck, almost throttling her with the beer bottle.

'Don't mind him,' said Lee. 'It's just an act.'

Cream's 'Strange Brew' echoed around the room, spacey and dizzy-making. Many people were just lounging around listening to it. Peter was talking to a girl who sat in a corner. As Billy approached them she said, 'I am I and you are not I.'

'I can't fault your reasoning,' said Peter, smiling.

'You are very white,' she said, as though noticing him now for the first time.

'And you are very high.'

'High and white,' she said, and she began to chant the words repeatedly, 'high and white.' Then she giggled, and burped. 'I like you,' she said. Peter took this as an invitation to sit next to her. As he did so, for an instant his easy smile vanished, to be replaced by a scowl of pain. Billy hesitated for a few moments, but Peter's smile returned as quickly as it had left. He went looking for someone else to talk to.

'This is Art, our drummer,' said Lee, introducing him to a boy wearing overalls and unfashionably short hair.

'Sarah tells me you're influenced by the Stones,' said Billy.

'Are we? Fucked if I know.'

A little later the fourth member of the band, whom Billy had not yet met, pulled out an acoustic guitar and called for the record player to be turned off. He began singing 'Like a Rolling Stone'. People started joining in, and Billy did so too. He heard the strains of Peter's voice above the others', and watched him wailing out the words. And then suddenly Peter let out a cry, and held his head in his hands. Billy rushed across the room to his side.

'What is it?' he said.

Peter couldn't speak, but simply groaned.

'Get up,' said Billy. 'I'm taking you home.'

Peter got unsteadily to his feet. The room had fallen silent now, and people looked on aghast. It was clear that he was in a bad way. He leaned on Billy for support, and they crossed to the door. Billy kissed Sarah hurriedly, and they stepped out into the night.

'You must see a doctor,' he said. 'This is crazy.'

'I hate doctors,' said Peter through gritted teeth. 'I spent my entire childhood being prodded by them.'

They took the Tube to Angel, and then walked to the flat Peter shared with two others from the bookshop. Once they were inside, Peter's pain seemed to ease.

'It was like nothing I've ever known,' he said, wiping snot from his nose. 'Like another blow to the head.' He sat down, but immediately stood again and ran to the bathroom. Billy heard the sounds of vomiting. He turned to Philip, one of Peter's flatmates. 'He's got to be made to see a doctor,' he said.

Philip made a despairing gesture with the palms of his hands. 'Ever tried telling him something he doesn't want to hear?'

Peter emerged from the bathroom. 'I'm going to bed,' he said. 'Thanks, Billy. See you on Monday.'

Out on the street the air was almost balmy, the first night Billy could remember since he arrived in London that wasn't cold. He walked westwards, towards King's Cross and home. The image of a policeman's truncheon crashing down on Peter's head kept coming into his mind. Sarah had described Peter as the hero of Grosvenor Square. Was he a hero, or was he a dreamer who had discovered the hard way that the world could be unkind?

———

As the weeks passed he became more settled in the bookshop. In the course of placing thousands of books on the shelves he had become familiar with them, at least with their authors and titles and blurbs. He knew how to deal with customers, and Beverley gave him more and more responsibility. And in his own reading he was striking out too. One day, when he and Beverley were talking about writers, she said, 'You've never really told me what you like to read.'

'I suppose not.'

'I think it's about time you and I got to know each other better. Shall we have a drink after work?'

They went to the French House pub and sat in a niche at the back, surrounded by photographs of actors and boxers. The place was quiet at half-past five, but steadily filled up with what Billy thought of as the bohemian element of Soho. He liked to imagine glamorous lives for these people, in the theatre, in films, in photography and design. He knew that in all likelihood they were bit-part players, but nonetheless they were a lot more colourful than the sort of people he knew. A fat man asked in a fruity voice for a vodka and tonic, and then surveyed the room as though to invite applause.

'Coming up, George,' said the girl behind the bar.

'And a nice chaser of *you*,' said the man, his eyes sparkling merrily.

'So,' said Beverley, placing her wineglass on the table, 'what *do* you read?'

'Oh, the usual. I think my own reading's only just beginning. At school and university you read what you're told to. The classics, the stuff they think is good for you.'

'They're classics for a reason.'

'You sound like my mother.'

'God forbid I should sound like anyone's mother!'

'I don't mean...' Billy's voice trailed off. There *was* something motherly about her, and it wasn't just that she was so large. 'I don't mean you're as old as my mother, or anything.'

'Good,' she said. 'I'm actually quite young, you know.'

They fell silent, and after a few moments Billy said, 'I haven't really answered your question, have I, about what I read.'

'No.'

He paused, trying to summon the right words.

'I think I'm looking to books to tell me how to live, who to be. Does that make any sense?'

'Of course.'

'Since their authors have presumably lived more than I have.' He looked across the room. 'There's this character in Bellow's *Seize the Day* who's obviously got it all wrong...'

'Tommy Wilhelm.'

'Yes. He's absurd, and childish. Yet by the end of the book he's come to some sort of awareness of this, he's grown. I'd like to think that I grew with him.'

'In the end you need more than books to tell you how to live, though.'

'I know. I've been reading a lot of travel books, and all they do is make me want to get away.'

She caressed her glass. 'I give you three months,' she said.

'Three months?' said Billy, startled.

'You'll be on your way soon enough. You're restless. And you've got more going for you than most.'

'Have I?'

'Of course.' She leaned towards him. 'You're bright, Billy,' she said. 'You've got it up here.' With this she tapped the side of her head, and then sat back again.

'I don't feel very bright,' he said. 'To be honest, I can't see a future for myself at all at the moment. I've dropped out, I have no qualifications, and I don't know anyone.'

'Nonsense. If you can't make your way on your wits and your charm, then there's something wrong with you.'

Billy smiled wryly. 'What charm?' he said.

'You're more attractive than you think.'

He looked down into his glass, and then at Beverley. The wine had lit up her face, and she was smiling in a way that was almost winsome. It dawned on him that her interest might not be so motherly after all.

'I suppose I am restless,' he said, attempting to get the conversation back on track. 'But I'm learning things. It's enough.'

'For now,' said Beverley, finishing his sentence for him.

The Tricksters' London debut was in the upstairs room of a pub near their flat in Earls Court. While the band members made their preparations, Sarah ordered pints of beer at the bar.

'I can't not drink with them,' she whispered to Billy. 'They expect it.'

He saw Julian coming down the stairs. 'How long have they been together?' he asked.

'Lee and Julian have been together for ages, but Andy and Art joined only a couple of months ago. They started out doing gigs at college.'

They made their way upstairs. The room was cluttered with amplifiers, speakers, wires and drums. The band took up their places, the guitarists tuning up, Art making a few precursory strokes, Julian tapping the microphone and counting into it. There were twenty or so people in the audience, of whom Billy recognized several from the party.

'Evening,' said Julian. 'Thanks for coming. We're going to play you a few... a few tunes. All our own work, as they say. The first song's called "Trick On You". A one, a two, a three, a four...'

The guitars and drums crashed in, and Julian cupped the mike in both hands. 'Trick on you,' he sang, 'I'm gonna play a trick on you, Gonna sneak up behind you, And play a trick on you.' Julian had a good voice, but he was forced to shout to make himself heard above the instruments. There was enthusiastic applause at the end of the song, and a cheer from Sarah. Billy placed his glass on the floor between his feet and clapped loudly.

The set came to an end, and they trooped back down to the bar.

'What do you think?' said Sarah.

'They're good,' said Billy, 'especially Lee. I like his voice when he comes in. He should do it more often.'

'Julian won't let him.'

'I'm not surprised.'

Lee joined them. 'You play like Clapton,' said Billy.

'Yeah? He's God, man.'

'No, he isn't,' said Julian, 'Jimi's God.'

'There are too many fucking gods around here if you ask me,' said Art. 'I'm going to find me some nymphs.' With this he turned and left the group, going to sit with a couple of girls who had been in the audience and were now eyeing them up.

During the second set Billy looked across at his sister now and then, at the smile of adoration that lingered on her lips. Why was it that Sarah had always gone straight for what she wanted, while he had taken the roundabout way? Was it as simple a matter as character? He thought of Peter's conviction that character didn't exist, or at least that it was formed by experience. And then he thought of Sarah at the age of two, of five, of ten: she had always been like this. He recalled how as a child she used to love eating overripe bananas. 'Lovely and bad,' she said of them, 'lovely and bad.' When, as he was leaving the pub, he turned back to see her kissing Lee, he felt a strange mixture of concern and jealousy.

———

Mrs Allingham was ghosting through the hallway one evening when Billy returned from work.

'How is your friend?' she said.

'I think he's OK. He keeps on having headaches, though.'

'What did the doctor say?'

'He hasn't seen one.'

She stood for a few moments as though lost in thought, and then beckoned him into her rooms. When they were seated she said, 'He must see a doctor.'

'I know. I've tried to get him to go, but he refuses.'

'He's wilful.'

'Yes.'

She stood and went into the kitchen, returning with a bottle of white wine. Without asking Billy whether he would like some, she poured two glasses and handed one to him. Billy tasted it, and it was very sweet.

'Some people find the problems of the world easier to bear than their own,' she said.

'I hadn't thought of it that way.'

'You don't, I take it.'

'My problem is not with the world, but finding my place in it.'

'Well, that's the problem of youth.'

She stared into the fireplace, and Billy took the opportunity to study her closely. He realized after all this time that she was beautiful, a desiccated beauty.

'I have this urge to know the world,' he said. 'All of it.'

'That would take a long time.'

'At least I know where I want to start.'

'And where is that?'

'Morocco. Marrakesh.'

'Why there?'

'I read a book about it, and it caught me.'

She sipped her wine delicately. 'The desert is very clean,' she said, 'like the jungle.'

'I want to see the shifting sands.'

'How is your French?'

'Passable.'

'You must know the language if you're going to be a traveller rather than a tourist.'

He placed his glass on the table. 'I'll brush up,' he said.

'When will you go?'

'When I can afford it.'

'I think you should be more definite than that.'

'Soon, then. I'll go soon.'

———————

'Sarah's been arrested,' Billy heard his father saying down the crackling line.

193

'What?' He turned to face the back of the hallway, cradling the phone closer to his ear. All his fears for his sister welled up inside him.

'Possession of Class B drugs. She's in Holloway Prison. What the hell's she been up to, Billy?'

'Can we see her?'

'Your mother and I are coming up tomorrow. Visiting time is eleven. You must be there too.'

'Of course.' Billy ran through his mind the excuses he might use with Wilson. 'I'll see you there.'

Holloway Prison was a crenellated affair reminiscent of the Tower of London. Billy shuddered as he entered the gates. His parents were already there, sitting on a bench in the waiting room. They stood when they saw him, and he kissed his mother and shook his father's hand. Their faces were lined with tension and fatigue. None of them said anything very much, and after a few minutes a warder led them into the visitors' room.

There were no iron grilles or glass panels, as Billy had somehow expected. Sarah sat at a long table, between two other women. The moment she saw them she burst into tears. Margaret held her in her arms, stroking her hair and whispering reassurances. Eventually they all sat down.

'It was horrible,' she said, wiping the tears from her cheeks. 'They just burst in, at midnight.'

'Were you taking anything at the time?' Jim asked.

Sarah shook her head. 'They found cannabis in the kitchen. They knew what they were looking for. If they hadn't found anything on us they'd have planted it.'

'So you've been smoking cannabis, have you?'

'Dad,' said Billy, trying to contain the anger he felt with his father, 'of course she's been smoking cannabis. Practically everyone smokes cannabis. It's harmless.'

'When I want your opinion I'll ask for it.' He turned again to Sarah. 'What's it like in here, sweetheart?' he asked.

Sarah groaned. 'I'm in a ward with nine other women. One of them's a child molester, or so they say.'

Jim let out a long, slow breath. 'A child molester?'

'We have to queue for everything – meals, baths, toilets. The warders come around four times a day and call out our names, just to make sure we're still there.' She looked around the high-ceilinged room. 'Where else would we be?'

'Are the warders all right?' asked Margaret.

'They're OK. Well, one of them's a witch.' She took a deep breath, and Billy could see she was taking courage from their presence. 'They strip-searched me when I arrived,' she said indignantly. 'Felt me up.'

'What about the others in the flat?' Jim asked.

'They're in Wormwood Scrubs, I think.'

'But what about your friend? Isn't she here?'

Sarah hesitated, and Billy said, 'She'd gone to her parents' for a few days, hadn't she?'

Sarah nodded. Jim stared at her intently, but remained silent.

'When do you come up for trial?' Margaret asked.

'I haven't been told yet.'

Billy banged his fist quietly on the table. 'They've no right to keep her here,' he said. 'It's a disgrace. Just because she's smoked some dope?'

His father gazed at Sarah, trying to muster more words. 'This is where they hanged Ruth Ellis,' he said eventually.

'Jim, for goodness' sake...' said Margaret.

'I'm sorry.' He looked down at his hands. 'It's just the thought of my own daughter, in a place like this.'

'She's in a place like this because the system stinks,' said Billy, 'and for no other reason.'

'Let's not get excited,' said Margaret. 'Sarah, you'll be out of here in no time. Your father will talk to the police, and we'll have you home very soon.'

Sarah leaned across and hugged her mother. 'I'll be strong,' she said. 'I promise.'

Out in the street the wind swept them towards the car. As soon as they were under way Jim said, 'There is no girlfriend, is there? She's shacked up with a boy.'

Billy stared at the back of his father's head. There was nothing for it but to speak the truth.

'His name's Lee,' he said. 'He's very nice.'

'So nice that he gets himself and my daughter arrested.'

Billy sat silent now. He had said everything there was to say, and wasn't about to get into a pointless argument with his father. Margaret turned to face him.

'I'm sure you were keeping an eye on her,' she said.

'I was. But you know what she's like.'

His mother looked at him sorrowfully. 'Yes,' she said, 'I know what she's like.'

He sought the tranquillity of Hampstead Heath as often as he could. It was easy to lose himself in the woodlands and grassy spaces. But always he found his thoughts turning inwards. He was beginning to have doubts about Morocco. It seemed very remote, in every way. And what would he find if he did get there? Would everything somehow fall into place?

In time his walks became longer and further-reaching. And as well as his yearning to get away there was something else, something harder to define, which he could only describe as a wish to be understood. No one in his life really understood him, not his parents, not his sister, not Peter, not Mrs Allingham – no one. Surely there was someone who could tell him who he was and that it was all right? And as often as he recognized the impossibility of this, his longing for it always returned.

One Sunday morning, as he sat on a bench gazing at the first, improbably colourful rhododendrons near Kenwood House, his thoughts turned to Len Haskell. He knew better than to expect wisdom from Len; but he was family, he knew where Billy had come from. He walked back across the heath towards South End Green and the little house.

Len was unshaven and unkempt, and Billy sensed that he was the worse for a few drinks the previous night. He offered him a cup of coffee, and Billy stood staring out across the garden while he made it. Storm clouds were racing across the sky, and the first drops of rain speckled the windowpanes. Len returned to the sitting room and handed Billy a mug. He took a sip of the sharp, sour liquid.

'You made it just in time,' said Len.

Billy looked back out of the window. The rain was pelting down now. 'We could do with some sunshine,' he said.

'We'll get it soon enough. You know what they say about the English weather, don't you – if you don't like it, just wait a few minutes.'

Billy tried his coffee again, but it tasted no better. 'Len,' he said, 'weren't you in North Africa during the war?'

'That's right. Why?'

'I want to go to Morocco.'

'Well, I never went there. We only got as far as Alexandria and Tobruk.'

'What was it like?'

'What was it like? It was a bloody nightmare. Hot as hell, sand in your eyes, Rommel's lot pounding away.'

'But wasn't it beautiful?'

'Not where I was, at any rate.' Len slurped his coffee and put down the mug. 'Maybe Morocco's different.'

'It's where the Sahara begins. The dunes.'

'It was flat in Libya. The only things that broke it up were the oases.'

'How long were you there?'

'About six months. Then they shipped us off to Sicily.'

'The sky must be big in the desert.'

'Big and blue. Always blue, day after day. Never a cloud in sight, as I recall.'

'I think I'd like that.'

'You would for a week or two.' He gestured towards the window. 'Then you'd start hoping for some of that stuff.'

Billy laced his fingers around the mug. 'Would I?' he said. 'I'm not so sure.'

———————

Billy and Peter sat in the French House as though at a wake.

'It's not who pulled the trigger that matters,' said Peter. 'They're all in it up to their necks – the FBI, the CIA, LBJ.'

Billy couldn't help but find this succession of acronyms faintly comical, despite their occasion. The news of Martin Luther King's assassination had reached them only a couple of hours earlier. They had planned this night out several days ago, but now that they were here, Peter was morose and angry. Billy wanted to change the subject, but he knew his friend well enough now to sense that this would take some time.

'There'll be the usual inquest and the usual whitewash,' continued Peter. 'The killer was acting alone; he just felt like popping off a nigger; et cetera, et cetera.'

197

'Maybe not, this time,' said Billy half-heartedly.

Peter sniffed, as he always did when Billy said something he disagreed with but couldn't be bothered to contradict. They sat in silence for a while, Billy looking sidelong at Peter now and then. He had taken off his bandages, and there was little trace of his wound. But he'd had another dreadful headache only a few days ago, and Billy continued to worry about him. Peter shrugged off any enquiry about his condition with the assurance that he was fine, that a headache never did anyone any harm.

'Let's get drunk,' he said at last.

Billy looked at him in astonishment. He had never seen Peter have more than one drink at a time.

'Really?'

'Yes,' said Peter determinedly. 'I feel like getting drunk.'

'Getting drunk costs money,' said Billy, delving into his pockets to see how much he had.

'It's on me.'

With that Peter stepped up to the bar and ordered a bottle of wine. He splashed the glasses full, and raised his in a toast. 'To the revolution,' he said dully.

Billy studied Peter's face for signs of the irony he detected in his tone. It was always hard to tell anything from Peter's features: he had a very inexpressive face.

They sat drinking their way through the bottle, and then another. Billy was hungry by now, but something told him to let Peter dictate the course of the evening. He was also a little drunk, as Peter had intended, and when they stood to leave he was unsteady on his feet. They made their way outside, and wandered up Dean Street. Soho was in full swing by now, the coffee shops, restaurants and bars all doing a brisk trade. Outside the Phoenix strip club a bouncer said, 'Come on in, lads. Lovely girls.' Billy looked at the posters, at the girls in their sequins and not much else. He had never been to a strip club, and was sure that if they did so now they would be fleeced. Peter was on the same sort of wage as he was, and Billy had no intention of ruining him. After a while the only thing to do seemed to be to go to another pub.

They found one near Piccadilly Circus, and Peter ordered another bottle of wine, ignoring Billy's protestations. When they turned away from the bar, Billy saw that two girls were looking in their direction.

Before he knew it, Peter had marched across to them, placing the wine bottle on their table in a stagy way. Billy followed in his footsteps, and they sat down opposite the girls.

'Good evening, ladies,' said Peter grandly. 'My friend and I were admiring your...' He smiled vaguely, casting about him for words. 'We were admiring your *coiffures*.'

'Our what?' said one of the girls.

'Your *hair*, dear ladies.'

She ran her hand through her long blonde hair. 'All right, ain't it?'

'It truly is.'

Billy was appalled by this awful impression of David Niven on which his friend had embarked. He had never seen anything like it.

'Yours isn't so bad either,' said the other girl. 'Do you get it bleached?'

'This, my dear, is my natural colouring. Where I come from, the Barbary Coast, everyone looks like this.'

'The what coast?'

'Barbary.'

'Is that anything like the South Coast, then?'

The other girl, who was dark-haired and much prettier than the blonde, leaned towards her friend and said, 'No, it's like the Costa del Sol, that's what it is.'

'I am descended from slaves,' said Peter, settling into his assumed accent now.

'White slaves, that'd be,' said the blonde.

'The term "white slaves" strictly speaking refers only to females,' said Peter. 'For the delectation of the Moors.'

'What's the moors got to do with it?'

The dark girl nudged her friend. 'I think he's talking about the Moors murderers,' she said. 'Is he creepy, or what?'

'He isn't creepy,' said Billy. 'He's just a bit drunk.'

The girls directed their attention towards him now. 'So handsome's got a tongue too,' said the blonde.

'Look, let me buy you both a drink. My friend's had a bad day and he's letting go, that's all.'

'Perhaps he should let go somewhere else,' said the dark girl. 'Or maybe he shouldn't be allowed to let go anywhere.'

Billy stood up. 'Come on, Peter,' he said. 'We're leaving.'

'But what about the bottle of wine?'

Billy picked it up. 'We'll finish it at my place,' he said.

Peter got slowly to his feet. Billy grasped him by the arm, and they made for the door.

'Nice meeting you, boys,' said the blonde. 'Come and see us again some time.'

Out on the street they leaned against the wall of the pub, breathing in the night air deeply.

'You've got to work on your chat-up lines,' said Billy.

Peter hiccuped, and tried to bring him into focus. 'Have I?' he said. 'I thought that was a pretty good one.'

―――――

He met his father for lunch in a Chinese restaurant around the corner from the magistrate's court in Bow Street. It had been two weeks since Sarah's arrest, and only now was she coming up for trial. Billy had been fuming over all this, and when he'd gone back to Holloway to visit her a second time, he couldn't help but vent his anger at one of the warders. He'd been told to leave immediately, and had sat on the bus going home in a state of rage. But now, with his father, he was anxious to appear unconcerned.

'They'll let her off,' he said. 'It's her first offence, after all.'

'I hope you're right.'

They toyed with their chop suey, both too wound up to eat. After a while Jim said, 'I think I'm in trouble again myself.'

'How do you mean?

Jim laid down his chopsticks and pulled a packet of cigarettes from his pocket.

'The Regal. It isn't paying.'

Sarah had alerted Billy to this, but he decided he had better act dumb.

'I thought it was doing fine,' he said.

'*Was*, yes.' Jim lit up, and directed the smoke away from Billy and the table. 'But not now. Television's just too strong a draw these days. And the costs of running a single cinema don't add up any more. At this rate I'm going to have to sell to Rank or somebody.'

Billy finished eating. He stared at Jim, uncertain how to handle this unexpected turn in the conversation.

'Are you sure about this?' he asked.

His father looked reflectively at his cigarette. 'I'm scared, Billy,' he said.

He had never seen his father like this. His image of him had always been one of a man who was sure of himself, irrespective of whether he was right or not. But Jim had messed up before. Billy had been too young then to understand what was going on. Now things were different, and he looked at a man who seemed vulnerable and uncertain. Billy was suddenly assailed by a sense of dread.

'If you have to sell out, will you get enough to repay the bank?' he asked.

Jim pursed his lips. 'Probably,' he said. 'But keeping up the mortgage payments on the house wouldn't be easy on the kind of wages I'd have if I were just managing it for somebody else.'

Billy recalled the day they had moved into their new house, the happiness they had all felt. At last he and Sarah and Tom had their own rooms, and weren't falling over one another all the time. Soon Sarah would leave home, and this would surely mean that Jim and Margaret and Tom could live in a smaller place. But Jim's pride was at stake again, and Billy knew what a force that was.

'What can you do to improve things?'

'I can let people go, so I don't have to pay them. It might come down to me and the projectionist. Oh, and the ice-cream girl – she's on commission.'

'Should you be showing different kinds of films?'

Jim smiled wanly. 'That's what you always used to say when you spent your Saturdays there. You know Wells, Billy – the West End it isn't.' He called for the bill and stubbed out his cigarette. Looking up at Billy, he said, 'How are things with you, then? Still in London.'

'It looks as though I'll be here for a while. My piggy bank isn't very full.'

'Can't you apply for some kind of job in Marrakesh and then go out to it?'

'I have no idea what that would be. Anyway, I don't really want a job there, I want to have some time and freedom.'

Jim smiled again. 'Freedom, eh?' he said. 'I remember that. When you find it, hold on to it, that's my advice.'

He paid the bill, and they walked to the court. There was a long wait before they were led into the visitors' gallery. Sarah and the band sat on the front bench, facing three magistrates. The chief magistrate summoned the police officer who had made the arrests, and everyone sat through a leaden and self-justifying account of what had happened. The accused had drawn attention to themselves by their rowdy behaviour, he said. Billy found this very hard to believe, given the evidence of Sarah's birthday party, which even as he left it was subsiding into a mood of introspection and languor.

The defendants pleaded guilty, and the chief magistrate pronounced his sentence. They were all put on conditional discharge. In view of her age, Sarah's condition was that she should return home to her family. Jim sighed audibly as the magistrate spoke the words.

They were reunited with her in the lobby, in a way that seemed to Billy rather confused. Sarah appeared from one door as they were coming through another. A policeman asked Jim who he was, and gave him a piece of paper to sign. It was all very perfunctory. Jim put his arms around her and held her tightly. She searched her father's face for signs of the censure she was surely expecting, and found none.

'Come on, sweetheart,' he said. 'I'm taking you home.'

Three

A few days after the trial, Lee appeared in the bookshop.

'I was around the corner in Denmark Street,' he said, 'looking at guitars. Then I saw the sign, and thought I'd drop by.'

Billy was glad to see him. 'Do you have time for a drink?' he asked.

He arranged with Beverley to take lunch early, and they walked to the Coach and Horses.

'What a lark!' said Lee as they sat down with their pints. 'Now we really are like the Stones – busted!'

'I don't think Sarah thought it was much of a lark.'

'I didn't have a chance to talk to her at all.'

'She had a terrible time in Holloway, banged up with a lot of crazies. What was it like for you?'

'We were in the Scrubs. It was a gas. We were all in the same cell. We practised close-harmony singing, until they shut us up.'

'Well, you had a better time than she did.'

Lee looked at him earnestly and said, 'Is she OK? I don't suppose I'll see her for a while.'

'I think you can assume she'll be under lock and key. Are you going back to Wells any time soon?'

'No, we're going to Cornwall. We're going to get it together in the country.'

'Cornwall? Why there?'

'There's this old sawmill someone's turned into a recording studio. It sounds amazing. We're going to make our demo tape there.'

'Is the place really set up for that sort of thing?'

'Apparently. Julian's been there – it's not far from where his family live – and he says it's got the lot: four-track recording, a big control room. And it's much cheaper than the London studios.'

Billy had been wondering how they paid for things, especially since none of them appeared to have a job. 'How cheap is cheap?' he asked.

'Fifty pounds a week all in.'

'That doesn't sound very cheap to me.'

'Julian's paying for it.'

Billy gazed out of the window. The street was flooded with sunshine, and London seemed at last to have shaken off its winter blues. 'I've never been to Cornwall,' he said.

'Why don't you come, then?'

'Me? But I'm not a musician.'

'No, but you can help us out a bit. We can pretend you're the roadie. It'd be fun.'

'When are you going?'

'Two weeks' time.'

Billy thought for a moment. Would Wilson let him off for a few days? He'd been there only a couple of months. 'I'd love to,' he said. 'I'll see if I can get the time off.' He looked across at Lee, and a smile stole over his features. If he couldn't yet leave for Morocco, nonetheless he could still have an adventure.

Mrs Allingham invited all her boarders to what she termed a 'soirée'. Billy had generally kept out of the way of his fellow guests; but clearly he was going to have to talk to them now. With the exception of two middle-aged men whose occupations he could only guess at, everyone in the house appeared to be a student.

There were eight people in Mrs Allingham's bower, two or three having gone missing. She served the very sweet white wine she had given Billy, and handed around little skewers of diced beef and chicken. 'Dip them in the peanut sauce,' she said. 'They're delicious. Satay.' Billy wasn't sure whether 'satay' was what they were called, or some kind of salutation.

'Now, we have two literary types,' she said after a while. She turned to Billy. 'Have you met Simon?'

Billy shook hands with a fair-haired young man wearing baggy brown cords and a jersey with holes at the elbows. He had seen him on the landing, and had nodded cursorily, but they hadn't spoken.

'Simon is studying something very refined,' said Mrs Allingham. 'I don't recall what it is, though.'

'Medieval Italian literature,' said Simon, smiling. 'That means Dante and Petrarch, basically.'

'Very refined,' she said, waving her hand in the air and turning to talk to someone else.

'The Divine Comedy,' said Billy.

'Very divine, as Mrs Allingham would say. Not very comedic, however, at least not in the way we understand it.'

'Petrarch I know nothing about.'

'He was famous for his sonnets. He wrote them to someone he called Laura. Dante had his Beatrice and Petrarch his Laura. Except that Petrarch probably made up Laura.'

'Dante didn't make up Beatrice?'

'Not quite. He just made of her what he wanted.'

As they were speaking, one of the middle-aged boarders approached them.

'John Abbott,' he said, holding out his hand. 'Pleased to meet you.'

Billy and Simon shook his hand, and talk of Dante and Beatrice was shut down.

'At the university, are you?' he asked.

'He is,' said Billy. 'I work in a bookshop.'

'Do you now? I work in a shop myself, selling televisions.'

'That must be interesting,' said Billy idly.

'It certainly is. It's a booming market, I can tell you.'

'I don't watch it,' said Simon.

'Well, you should. I can fix you up with a nice Pye portable, cheap. There are educational programmes as well as the rubbish, you know.'

'I'm getting enough education as it is,' said Simon, smiling ruefully.

Billy felt a sudden urge to get away, and it dawned on him that it was Simon he wanted to get away from, not John. This encounter with someone who was studying something lofty had unsettled him. Very soon he made his excuses and returned to his room. He sat in his armchair reading, listening to the footsteps of his fellow boarders as one by one they made their escape from Mrs Allingham's rooms.

Wilson sent Billy down to the basement for a few days. Philip was on holiday, and another assistant, Geoff, had what he described as pneumonia.

'Pandemonia more like,' said Peter. 'He should stay off the weed.'

The stock was completely new to Billy. By now he knew the fiction shelves from top to bottom, but here he relied on Peter to guide him. And then, after the second day, Billy realized that Peter seemed to be relying on him, asking him to do all the unpacking and shelving, and to mark the stock cards. Billy was by now accustomed to Peter's way of reading, which was to hold books within a couple of inches of his face. But now he sensed that something was different. And then there were the times when Peter would go to the lavatory and not return for twenty minutes or more. Billy began to watch his friend closely, sure that something was wrong, or at least more wrong than he had supposed. The next morning, when a box of Peregrine books was delivered, he decided to try something out. As he was unpacking he handed Peter a book opened to a particular page.

'I'm with Leavis on Spenser,' he said. 'Look what he says here about *The Faerie Queen*.'

Peter took the book from him and inspected the page. He smiled, and handed it back to Billy. 'Me too,' he said. 'He doesn't like Milton very much either.'

Billy tossed the book onto the counter. 'This isn't a Leavis,' he said. 'Look, Peter, come on, admit it: you can't read properly, can you?'

Peter looked at him blankly for a few moments, and sat down on the stool.

'It's double vision,' he said. 'I've been guessing for a week or more. It's a wonder nobody's noticed. You won't tell Wilson, will you? Please don't.'

'Oh, Peter!' said Billy. 'Do you mean to say that you're losing your sight and yet you still won't go and see a doctor?'

'I know. It's stupid. I'm sorry. I'm afraid, that's all.'

'Are you more afraid of doctors than you are of going blind?'

He looked up. 'I can't do it on my own,' he said.

Billy stared at his friend, his heightened sense of concern vying with exasperation over Peter's inability to take care of himself. He made Peter promise that they would together go to a doctor the very next day.

They went to the surgery near Peter's flat in Islington, and waited ages before he was permitted to register. The earliest appointment he could get was a week away. By then, Billy would be in Cornwall.

'You will be sure to go, won't you?'

'Yes, Billy. I promise.'

'Whose bright idea was it to go down on the Saturday of bank holiday weekend?' said Art, drumming his fingers on the steering wheel.

They were stuck in a traffic jam in the middle of Bodmin, and there was no end in sight to what had already been a frazzling journey. Billy was wedged between Art and Lee in the front of the Dormobile, and behind them the band's entire kit – amplifiers, drums, guitars, as well as rucksacks and suitcases – was stacked to the roof. Julian and Andy, the bass guitarist, had gone ahead the previous day in Julian's car, and to Billy the Dormobile felt like the band's packhorse.

Shortly before St Austell they turned south, and were soon descending a hill into the village of Golant. They came to a broad estuary, and parked the van facing onto it. There was a green MGB already there. 'Julian's,' said Lee. 'We're supposed to call him from here.'

While Lee went in search of the phone box, Billy walked across a single-track railway line to the water's edge. Boats were moored everywhere, yachts and dinghies. Seagulls wheeled above him, cackling derisively. On the far side of the estuary the thickly wooded riverbank rose steeply into a bright blue sky. Billy stretched, glad to be free of the van and to taste the salt air. How far away was the sea? Not far, surely.

After a few minutes they heard the sound of an outboard, and saw a small boat approaching, towing a flat barge. Julian and Andy waved at them, and came alongside the quay and tied up. They loaded the contents of the van onto the barge and set off downriver, Billy marvelling at the strangeness of it all.

'You can't get there any other way except along the railway line,' shouted Julian above the din of the motor.

'Where does it go?'

'It's for transporting china clay down to the docks at Fowey. There's only one train a day.'

They soon turned towards the bank, and drifted under a bridge into a small creek. Ahead of them Billy saw a large, square building, with a verandah at the front. It nestled in the trees, flanked by tall pampas grass. Julian steered the boat to the jetty, and they arrived at the Sawmill.

It seemed the most improbable place for a recording studio. But as Billy discovered when they carried the amps and the instruments up the slope, it really was one. The control room was dominated by a console that sprouted buttons and lights. Beyond it was a room with bare stone walls and floor, in which microphones stood like stick-men in a child's drawing, and wires snaked all around. They set up the amps and drums, and placed the guitars against the walls.

The resident sound engineer was called Gord, and he made tea for them all. They sat on the verandah looking out over the creek. 'Isn't this a hoot?' said Lee, and Julian and Andy started making hooting noises, which then turned into a choo-choo riff. They were exhilarated, by the craziness of there even being such a place, let alone by their having it all to themselves.

Lee and Billy fixed supper, doing their best with sausages and mash. As darkness closed in, they set off down the railway line to the village and the pub. The Fisherman's Arms was a tiny nook, with a wrought-iron fireplace and an upright piano. The walls were hung with photos of Golant and Fowey in the past, of sturdy fishermen and their boats and nets. At the bar sat a man of about sixty wearing a smelly old coat. He scowled as the boys entered, and stroked his moustache.

'He was here last night,' said Julian. 'Calls himself the Major. Thinks he owns the place.'

They sat down at a table, and Andy and Art began to roll cigarettes, drawing out the ritual as though they were rolling joints. Julian went over to the piano and started singing 'Ballad of a Thin Man'. 'Because something is happening here,' he sang, 'But you don't know what it is, Do you, Mr Jones?' His fingers crashed down on the keys, and he ratcheted up the performance, making ironical faces as he did so. Then out of the corner of his eye Billy saw the Major step down from his stool and approach the piano. Without a word he grasped the lid in one hand and brought it down forcefully, Julian managing to withdraw his fingers just in time.

'This is for music,' said the Major furiously, and he swung on his heel and returned to his place. Julian clearly thought about raising the lid again, but came back to the table instead, muttering 'Fuck you' under his breath. The others sat staring at the Major, before Lee said, 'Anyone heard Dylan's latest?'

'*John Wesley Harding*?' said Julian. 'He's gone soft.'

'No, he hasn't. He's gone back to his roots.'

'You can't go back,' said Julian emphatically, swilling his beer in the mug.

'So why did he go electric in the first place?' said Andy.

'He went electric because the world's become a noisier place,' said Lee, 'and he didn't want to be drowned out.'

'Nah,' said Julian. 'He went electric because he started tripping on acid.'

They went on like this for an hour or so, scoring points off each other. When they stood to leave, Julian went up to the bar to buy a bottle of whisky to take back to the Sawmill. As Billy held the door for the others he saw Julian flick open his lighter and put it to a cigarette. Then, leaving the flame burning, he reached down and held it under the hem of the Major's coat. Facing the other way, and in his cups by now, the Major had no idea what was going on. A wisp of smoke curled up into the air.

''Night, all,' said Julian. He sauntered towards the door, and gave Billy a wink as he stepped outside. The last thing Billy saw as he closed the door behind him was the Major leaping from his stool and shouting, 'Fire!'

The next morning the band set up in the studio, preparing to record their songs. Never having done this before, they relied on Gord to direct things. Billy sat with him in the control room, looking through the glass door to see them going about their work with expressions of anxious intent.

'They need to lighten up,' said Gord. 'Need to get used to being in a studio. We shouldn't try to record anything today.'

When they did come to record, there were frequent intermissions during which everyone crowded into the control room to hear what they had just played. The novelty of it was clearly intoxicating, and they grinned from ear to ear as they listened to themselves.

'There's a lot of bleed in this studio, I should tell you,' said Gord. 'The bottom end of Art's drums is bleeding into Andy's acoustic, and Andy's guitar delay is bleeding into Art's drum track. But that's no bad thing – it makes it sound real.'

Billy had no role to play, and after a while he began to feel bored and cooped up in the control room. He decided he would go for a walk, and set off down the railway line towards Fowey.

The china clay docks were vast, great sheds and hoppers lining the quay. The ships moored alongside seemed vast too, their names and ports of registration hinting at Poland and Sweden and Italy. Billy walked through a landscape blanketed by a film of clay, quite at odds with the bright colours of spring on the far bank. And then he found himself in the town, strolling down a narrow, winding street. The houses were washed in pinks and blues and yellows. The wares of a ship's chandler spilled out into the road, and then there were clothes shops and fishmongers and cafés the size of broom cupboards. Whenever cars appeared, the pedestrians stood with their backs to the walls to let them gingerly pass.

He came out into the main square, and walked over to the railing to look across the harbour. The water dazzled in the sunlight, and Billy shaded his eyes so as to look out to sea. He turned around, to see that the town sloped steeply upwards, its roofs piled on top of one another. Directly in front of him was a pub, The King of Prussia, with a bow window like the prow of a ship. He went inside, bought a half of beer, and sat down in a corner.

There was something almost too pretty about Fowey, he thought. This was the Cornwall of the postcards, a place where fishermen mended their nets and hailed one another gruffly as they passed, where the publican wore tattoos all the way up his arms. But it was also a gateway to the world. The Italian ship would pass within a few miles of Morocco on its way home. Perhaps he could ask for a passage, or stow away? But, no, he must do things properly, and he must be patient. By the end of the summer, surely, he could make his plans and go.

The days passed, the band spending their time in the studio, Billy taking walks in the woods or reading on the verandah. At low tide the creek was a stretch of sheeny mud, the water having receded even beyond the bridge, the boat and the barge lying stranded by the jetty. The rhythms of life in the Sawmill were in some ways fixed by the tides, and Billy liked this notion very much.

'It's my birthday today,' he said one morning over breakfast.

'How old?' asked Lee.

'Twenty. No more teens.'

'We must have a party, then.'

'Yeah,' said Julian. 'Let's get some booze in. How are we doing for dope?'

'We've got plenty,' said Art. 'I had a nice chat with my man in Notting Hill just before we left.'

They spent the morning in the studio, and then went into Fowey to plunder the off-licence. It was Julian who paid, as always, casually peeling five-pound notes from a wad in his back pocket.

'Thanks,' said Billy.

'It's not all for you, birthday boy.'

In the evening they sat at the table on the verandah, drinking and passing around joints.

'All we need now is a few chicks,' said Art.

'Some hope,' replied Julian.

Billy looked out across the water. 'I'm spending my birthday up a creek,' he said.

They talked on for a long while, until Billy decided he needed some air. Lee followed him, and they sat on the bench. The moon was full, and its reflection lay in the black water just in front of them, seeming to be within touching distance.

'Do you know the story of the Moonrakers?' Billy asked.

'No.'

'They were some Wiltshire yokels raking a pond for kegs of smuggled brandy. When the excise men caught them they feigned idiocy and said they were trying to rake the moon out of the pond.'

Lee gazed up at the moon in the sky and then at the one in the creek. 'When I was in Kathmandu a kid asked me if we have the same moon in England as they have there.'

'You were in Kathmandu?'

'Sure, on the trail.'

'What was it like?'

'Pretty rough in lots of ways. But beautiful too.'

Billy looked thoughtfully at Lee. He had been to Kathmandu, had been somewhere utterly remote. Suddenly he saw him in a different way.

'What happened?' he asked.

'What happened?'

'I mean, how did you feel when you were there? Did it change you?'

Lee looked up at the moon again. 'That's hard to say,' he replied. 'I don't think you can know if you're changed, at least not until later.'

'I feel changed by places,' said Billy. 'I feel changed by this place.'

'In what way?'

'Oh, I don't know. It's so peaceful compared to London.'

'Is peacefulness what you're looking for, then?'

'Sometimes. And other times adventure. Both, really.'

They fell silent. Lee glanced back at the house, and then at Billy. 'I miss Sarah,' he said.

'She misses you.'

'I really mean it. I'm in love with your sister.'

Billy took some deep breaths, trying to sober up. 'Shouldn't you be trying to forget about her?' he said. 'She's still at school, after all, and you're miles away in London.'

'I can't forget about her. She's so lovely, so sweet-natured.'

Billy smiled. 'You should see her when she's in a temper,' he said.

'I can't believe she has a temper.' Lee turned towards the water again, his expression wistful and grave.

'I'm sorry,' said Billy. 'Nowadays you probably know her better than I do.'

'I've got to find a way to see her again.'

'There are other things you've got to do first, though. We should turn in – you need to be in good voice tomorrow in the studio.'

'I suppose so.' He put his arm around Billy's shoulders. 'Happy birthday,' he said.

His week was drawing to a close. Reckoning that it would take two days to hitch back to London – one as far as Wells, and the other the rest of the way – Billy planned to leave on Saturday. On the Friday morning they all took the boat into Fowey, tying up at the quay and setting off for the pub. There was a billiard table, and they competed with one another in their ineptitude. Billy felt at ease with them now, accepted, and he was sorry to be leaving. They returned to the Sawmill, Billy trailing his hand in the water.

As they ducked under the bridge he saw a girl strolling down the grass slope towards the jetty.

'Rachel!' said Julian. 'What the hell's she doing here?'

Lee turned to Billy and whispered, 'Julian's ex.'

He watched as the girl sat down on the bench. She had long dark hair, and was wearing a flowery dress with puffed sleeves.

'Hello, boys,' she said as they came alongside.

'What brings you here?' Julian asked.

She sat with her hands resting palms-down on the bench, rocking one leg on the other. Her boots were brown suede, and went up to her knees.

'I was visiting my parents, of course,' she replied. 'Your dad told mine you were here.'

They clambered out of the boat, and Julian gave the girl a chaste kiss. The others nodded in greeting, and Julian introduced her to Billy. She was pretty in a mournful kind of way, her lower lip drooping a little, her eyes shrouded with too much kohl.

'How long do you want to stick around?' asked Julian.

'Oh, I have to drive back to London today. You can make me lunch, and then I've got to go.'

They walked up to the house, and pottered around in the kitchen preparing salads and setting out bread and cheese. The atmosphere was strained, and it seemed clear to Billy that Rachel's presence was not entirely welcome. Billy found his eyes returning to her often, to this colourful figure who had landed in their midst. When they were washing up he said, 'I've got to get back to London too. I don't suppose I could ask you for a lift?'

She looked at him appraisingly. 'Well, if you don't suppose so, then I don't think I can,' she said. 'But if you *do* suppose so, then of course I can.'

———

Rachel's red 2CV was parked alongside the band's van. They unfastened the catches of the canvas roof and drove off in a cloud of smoke from the exhaust. Going up the hill out of the village the car stuttered now and then, and Billy wondered how it would get them all the way to London. But Rachel seemed a good driver, manipulating the strange gear-lever and swinging the steering wheel from side to side on the narrow lanes. Soon they were on the main road heading towards Truro.

'So how did you come to know the band?' Rachel asked.

'My sister's a friend of Lee's.'

'Y'know, they're not good enough,' she said, pulling out to over-take a lorry. 'Oh, they can sing and play. But they need to write better songs.'

'They'll do it, won't they, if they take it seriously?'

'I'm not so sure. I've known Julian since school, and he's never taken anything seriously in his entire life.'

Billy braced himself as they took a bend a little too fast. 'And what do you do?' he asked.

'Do?' she replied. 'I don't *do* anything. I'm a poet.'

'Ah.'

'OK,' she said, softening. 'I *do* poetry. And you?'

'I work in a bookshop.'

'Great.'

'Not very. It's Collet's, on the Charing Cross Road. Do you know it?'

'I know where it is. I used to go into Better Books, until it became like everywhere else.'

'I've heard about the good old days of Better Books. They sound fun.'

'I went to a Stevie Smith reading there once.'

'I'm afraid I don't know her work.'

'She's my heroine. She writes poems that are down-to-earth.'

It was strange hearing her use a phrase such as 'down-to-earth', since that was the last thing she herself seemed to be. Presumably her family had money, like Julian's, which enabled her not to 'do' anything. He had been turning to face her now and then, and couldn't decide whether she was beautiful or not. There were moments when she seemed lovely, and moments when she seemed pouty and plain. He looked at her hands as they gripped the steering wheel. There were heavy silver rings on several of her fingers, and her nails were very long and bright red.

'What sort of stuff do *you* read?' she said.

'Oh, novels. I've been trying to discover new writers lately. I've been reading a wonderful book by Saul Bellow, *Seize the Day*. Heller, Nabokov, Baldwin.'

'They're all men.'

'Yes, I suppose they are. What about you? Besides Stevie Smith?'

She smiled sardonically. 'They're all women,' she said. 'American mostly – Sylvia Plath, Marianne Moore, Anne Sexton.'

'I need to read more poetry. I seem to be a prosy sort of person.'

'Do you know the difference between prose and poetry?'

'No, what?'

'Prose is words in the best order, and poetry is the best words in the best order.'

214

They stopped on the edge of Dartmoor for a cup of tea, and Billy took the opportunity to study her more closely. The kohl was definitely a mistake – she would look so much better without it. Her eyes were a deep green colour with flecks of brown, and he found himself looking at them closely.

'Where did you go to university?' Billy asked.

'I didn't. Went to a *lycée* in Avignon for a year. University's no place to be if you want to be a writer.'

'University's no place to be if you want to be a *reader*.'

'You too?'

'Oh, I went to Bristol for a year and a term. But I dropped out in February.'

'Good for you.'

This was the first time Billy had been congratulated on a decision the wisdom of which he was now beginning to doubt. 'I hope so,' he replied.

The journey was exhausting in the noisy little car, and the darkness put an end to their conversation. It was midnight by the time they reached London. Rachel pulled up at the bottom of Queensway.

'I live at the top of the street,' she said. 'Near the Porchester baths.'

'I can get the Tube home from here.' He grabbed his duffel bag from the back seat. 'Thanks for the lift,' he said. 'Perhaps you'd like to have a drink some time?'

'Sure,' she replied casually. She took a pen from her bag and wrote her phone number on the palm of his hand. Billy was struck by what he took to be the intimacy of this gesture. 'Give me a ring,' she said.

———

'You've missed all the fun,' said Peter at their coffee break on Monday morning.

'What fun?'

'In Paris. There's a revolution going on!'

Peter was at his most animated, his hair uncombed, his fingers continually pushing his glasses up the bridge of his nose.

'What's happening?'

'The students have occupied the universities, and they're closed down. There's fighting in the streets. But the thing is, the people are behind them – they're giving them food and blankets.'

Billy hadn't seen a newspaper in Cornwall or since he got back, and this news struck him as extraordinary. Perhaps Peter's prophecies were about to become real after all.

'There's this guy called Dany Cohn-Bendit who's leading them. He's got red hair!'

'He doesn't sound very French.'

'He's originally German. And a Jew.'

'It's true, Billy,' said Philip, sensing his scepticism. 'This time something's really changing. It's not just a student protest.'

'It's going to spread all across the country,' said Peter. 'And then to Germany. Just you wait and see.'

'And what about here?'

'Here?' Peter looked puzzled for a moment. 'Oh, we're not ready for it here.'

Billy went back to work, taking over from Beverley at the counter.

'They're all in a tizzy down there,' she said. 'No one's doing anything except nattering and arguing.'

'It sounds pretty exciting.'

'Is it?' She looked down the stairs to the basement. 'It's just boys being boys, that's all.'

It was a slow morning, as Mondays always were. Billy wanted to find out from Peter what the doctor had said, but would have to wait until lunchtime. He found his thoughts drifting towards Rachel. How many days should he let go by before he called her? It was ages since he'd last gone out with a girl, almost a year. Where would they meet? And how much would it cost to take her to dinner? He was lost in these thoughts when he became aware of a thump from the basement. There was a cry, and then Philip appeared at the top of the stairs.

'Peter's collapsed!' he said.

Billy raced down the steps, to find Peter sprawled on the floor. He had been carrying a pile of books, and they were strewn across the room. He was unconscious, and breathing only shallowly. Billy ran back up the stairs to find Andrew Wilson, but Philip had already got to him, and he was on the phone asking for an ambulance. They returned together to the basement, and crowded around Peter's inert body.

'Don't touch him,' said Wilson. 'Wait for the ambulance to arrive.'

It was ten excruciating minutes before it did, during which time Wilson closed the shop and the rest of the staff hung around not knowing what to do. Billy kneeled at Peter's side, looking for signs of movement or recovery, but seeing none. When the ambulance men arrived they stood back, and gently Peter was laid out on the stretcher. Billy followed them up the stairs.

'I'm coming with you,' he said.

'Against the rules,' replied one of the men.

'Where are you taking him, then?'

'The Middlesex.'

Billy turned back into the shop and asked Wilson if he could take time to go to the hospital. 'Of course,' he said, visibly shaken. Billy set off up the street, following the sound of the siren.

At the hospital he waited for a long time before anyone was able to speak to him. Finally a doctor came to the desk, and the duty nurse nodded in Billy's direction.

'Are you a relative?' he asked.

'No. I'm a friend.'

'Do you know where to contact his family?'

Billy realized that Peter had never spoken of his family, nor indeed about his past at all. Why had he never asked?

'I'll ask the manager of the bookshop where we both work,' he said. 'What is it, Doctor? What can you tell me?'

'He's had a stroke brought on by a subarachnoid brain haemorrhage.'

'What's that?'

'It's a leaking of blood over the surface of the brain, under a layer called the arachnoid.'

A horrible vision of spiders flooded Billy's mind.

'We're going to do an angiogram. He will almost certainly need surgery, and quickly. Has he suffered from high blood pressure?'

'Not as far as I know.'

'There are signs of a wound.'

'Yes. Could the stroke have been caused by a blow to the head?'

'Certainly.'

'Then that's what did it. He was in the Grosvenor Square demonstration, and a policeman hit him on the head with his truncheon.'

The doctor drew in a sharp breath. 'Why on earth didn't his GP refer him immediately?' he asked.

'Because he didn't have a GP,' replied Billy. 'I'm not sure whether he's seen a doctor since it happened. I tried...'

Billy felt suddenly overwhelmed with anxiety. He sat down on a chair.

'This is madness,' said the doctor. 'To have sustained a wound like that and not to have done anything about it?'

'I know.'

The doctor squared his shoulders and became businesslike again. 'I'd be grateful if you would try to let a relative know where he is.'

'Of course. I'll go to the bookshop now.' He stood and turned to leave, and then looked back again. 'When can I see him?' he asked.

'That depends on the success of the operation. Call the front desk when you have contact details for a relative, and the nurse will let you know.'

Billy walked slowly back to the bookshop, all sense of urgency having left him. It was open again, and he went straight to Wilson's office and gave him an account of what he had learned.

'Who can we get in touch with?' he asked.

Wilson threw down his pipe in a gesture of what seemed very like hopelessness.

'His parents are both dead,' he said. 'That's all I know. He's alone, Billy. He's completely alone.'

For several days, thoughts of Peter and Rachel contended in his mind. The only news from the hospital was that Peter had been operated on but remained in a coma. There was no point in visiting him until he regained consciousness. Billy wondered whether anyone besides him had attempted to do so. And when he called Rachel, she had seemed so offhand that he began to doubt whether he wanted to get together with her at all. He was scarcely in the mood for a date, given his feelings of guilt over Peter. He should have dragged him to a doctor much sooner: it was obvious that he had needed help. He went through his hours at the bookshop in a daze of worry and self-reproach.

The evening of his drink with Rachel came around, and they met in a pub on Westbourne Park Road, not far from where she lived. They sat awkwardly at a table near the door, Rachel continually looking up as people came and went.

'Have you heard any news from the Sawmill?' Billy asked.

'No. I don't expect to. Julian and I... well, I don't really know why

I went there. We're not in touch these days. I suppose I was curious about this place he'd found.'

'You said you were at school with him. Where?'

Rachel slid a fingertip around the top of her wineglass, as if trying to set it humming. 'It was in St Ives,' she said. 'A private school called Penhaligon's, where everyone's father was a painter or a writer.'

'And which is yours?'

'A painter. He does naive seascapes.'

'And Julian's father?'

She smiled. 'A writer. Adrian Saunders. He writes stories of naval battles in the Napoleonic Wars. You must have them in the shop.'

'Of course. I hadn't made the connection. They sell pretty steadily. Before the Mast, and other titles I can't remember.'

'Behind the Mast?' she said. 'Up the Crow's Nest?' She picked up her drink. 'I'm sorry, I'm being facetious.'

For a few moments he watched her in silence, and then he said, 'So what led you to poetry?'

'Oh, life.' She looked up at a stylish couple who were just coming through the door. When she failed to elaborate, Billy felt a wave of irritation pass over him.

'And poetry is what you do every day?'

She looked at him candidly. 'I was being provoking when I said that,' she said. 'I work part time in the gallery that sells my father's stuff.'

'Ah,' said Billy, feeling he had won a concession from her at last.

They went to a Greek restaurant, and ordered houmous and taramasalata and squid. This was a classier kind of place than Billy was used to, and he was relieved not to have to shout above the strains of bouzouki music and Zorba-like exclamations from the waiters.

'Now your story,' said Rachel.

Her directness was unnerving, and Billy found himself unsure how to reply.

'You have one, I presume?' she said.

'A sort of one.' He looked up at her. She was wearing too much kohl again, and it was smudged around her left eye, giving her a slightly piratical appearance. 'I'm quite ordinary compared to you.'

'I don't see how you can possibly say that. You barely know me.'

'OK. But your father's a painter and mine runs a provincial cinema. You're a poet and I work in a crummy bookshop.'

'It sounds to me as though you've got an inferiority complex.'

'Does it, now?'

She extended a hand to cover his. 'I'm sorry,' she said. 'I can be annoying, I know. Let's start again.'

Billy felt electrified by the touch of her hand. Suddenly he felt an urge to talk about himself, an urge he had suppressed for what seemed a long time now.

'My family is ordinary,' he said. 'I don't mean that bloody-mindedly. It just is. My father bought a car dealership in Bath after the war, and for a few years it went very well. Then he over-extended himself, and went bankrupt. We moved to a farmhouse in the middle of nowhere in Somerset, and I went to a school the size of this restaurant. Later I went to a place called the Wells Blue School, and after my father took over the cinema we moved to Wells.'

'A country childhood.'

'I was much happier there than I had been in Bath. I was free.'

'We lived in the country, on a clifftop near St Ives. I used to walk for hours along the paths.'

'So you know what it's like, then, to be able to get away, to be yourself.'

'Yes, I do.'

Their moussaka arrived, and they fell silent for a few moments.

'Go on,' she said.

'So we lived in Wells. Do you know it?' She shook her head. 'It's a market town, but it has a beautiful cathedral. The school was pretty small even there. I read a lot, and did English at A-level. Then I went to Bristol.'

'And lasted a year.'

'A little more than a year.' He put down his fork and took a sip of wine. 'I'm wondering now whether I should have stayed.'

'Not if you still feel the way you did just a week or so ago.'

'I suppose so. I want to travel. But after that I don't know where I'm going.'

'Do any of us? I've no idea.'

'But you've got a vocation.'

She smiled wryly. 'We'll see about that,' she said. 'I've got a *calling*, shall we say.'

'Is there any difference?'

'One's a fancier word than the other.'

The conversation turned to writers, and to the ones they liked. As had been clear in the car, there was a great gulf between his reading and hers. Billy spoke again of Saul Bellow, whose novels he was now devouring. Then he sensed that he was boring her, and said, 'I must read some contemporary poetry. I stopped at Eliot and Auden.'

'There's a reading at the Indica bookshop next week. A friend of mine is one of the poets on the programme. Want to come?'

'Thank you.'

'I'm not sure what you'll think of it. She reads to the accompaniment of a saxophone.'

Billy gazed into her eyes, and all his doubts about this girl fell away. He wanted to see her again, and soon.

He went to the hospital for news, and was told that Peter was still unconscious.

'I'd like to see him anyway,' he said. 'Is that possible?'

The nurse led him down corridors and up stairs, and eventually they came to a room containing just two beds. One was empty, and in the other lay Peter. He had an oxygen mask clamped over his face, and was hooked up to fearsome-looking machines by wires that were attached to his head. His hair had been shaved off, and there was a gash along his skull where the surgeon had operated.

'I'll leave you alone for a few minutes,' said the nurse.

He sat down in a chair by the bed, and took Peter's hand in his. It seemed very warm, unnaturally so. In his terrible repose, Peter seemed far away, in another world. Was anything going on in that normally fervent mind? A graph on one of the machines showed a steady rising and falling of brainwaves or some such. Billy found himself stroking Peter's hand, and then raising his own to his face to brush away tears. He stood up, kissed Peter's forehead, and turned to leave the room. Then quickly he retraced his steps down the corridors and out into the street.

As he was climbing the stairs of the boarding house, he came upon Simon. On an impulse he said, 'Would you like to have a drink?'

'Absolutely.'

They went to the College Arms across the street.

'You look done in,' said Simon as they sat down.

Billy raised his fingertips to his temples, kneading them wearily.

'I've just been seeing a friend in hospital,' he said. He told Simon about Peter, about the demo and its aftermath, realizing after a minute or two that he was talking compulsively.

'That's awful,' said Simon.

'Yes, it is.' He picked up his glass. 'But enough of this. Cheers.'

They drank their beer, and Billy looked at his companion. He was very scruffy, his hair sticking out at odd angles; but there was the light of a keen intelligence in his eyes.

'Tell me more about your studies,' he said. 'Our television salesman put paid to that.'

Simon smiled. 'Do you really want to know?'

'Yes. Tell me about Dante and Beatrice.'

'It's a pretty well-known story.'

'Not to me, it isn't.'

'I'm sorry. I don't mean…'

'I know you don't.'

'OK. Well, you know that Dante was inspired to write *The Divine Comedy* by his love for her?'

'Yes, more or less.'

'He first saw her when they were about nine. Then when they were grown up, Dante fell in love. But he had no chance of marrying her, or even meeting her properly. So he wrote poems. He pretended they were to someone else, a screen-love. Then he collected them in a book called *La Vita Nuova*, the new life.'

'A screen-love?'

'Yes. It was a convention of the time. You concealed who it was you really loved by writing apparently to someone else.'

'How odd.'

'Not really. The rules about courtship and marriage were very strict.'

'And *The Divine Comedy* came later.'

'Yes. After Beatrice had died young. But the earlier poems are more about the opposition between real and ideal love, about how lovers project on to their loved ones what it is they themselves desire, rather than what may be there.'

Billy's thoughts strayed to Rachel. What was it he was feeling for her? A sort of fascination, a sort of awe. Was this the way men were fated always to feel about women?

'If you want to know more about Dante and Beatrice,' said Simon, 'then come to a lecture. Outsiders are always welcome, and I've got a good tutor.'

The thought of stepping back into a lecture room made Billy shudder. 'Thanks,' he said. 'I'll think about it.'

The Indica bookshop was in Southampton Row. Its window displayed poetry and art books, and inside there were imports from America, from publishers such as New Directions and City Lights. Rachel introduced him to her friend, Dolly. She was dark like Rachel, but cultivated a more bohemian look. Her hair fell in ringlets around her face, and there were gold bangles on her wrists. The long black dress she wore set off her figure, and Billy found it difficult to keep his eyes away from her breasts.

She was one of three poets reading that night. The bookshop had laid on wine, which they drank from plastic cups, and people mingled and chatted for about half an hour before things got under way. They went from the bookshop itself into a room at the back, where the walls were lined with posters and paintings and the ceiling was covered with a strange silver material that shimmered whenever the door opened and closed. There were folding chairs set up in rows, and a single chair facing them at the front. A foppish-looking man with blond hair and horn-rimmed glasses stood and introduced the first poet. He was American, and he read his poems in a deep bass voice. Dolly was on next, and as she approached the front, so did a man holding a saxophone. Dolly coughed a couple of times and took a swig of wine, while the sax player tootled up and down the scales.

'I'm going to read a poem called "Cascade",' she said, and she rustled the pieces of paper in her hand.

'The music vibrated through my vagina,' she began, 'As though it were one of the instruments.' She paused, and the sax player sounded a few stricken notes. 'I felt myself becoming an orchestra, Becoming multicoloured. The sound ran through my hair like a celestial comb, It ran down my spine like a lover's caress.' The sax player did his thing again. 'I was a cascade of blue-green rainfall, I was a sonority of light.' She looked up, and the sax player remained silent. Someone in the front row began to clap.

Rachel leaned towards him. 'I think you'll find that owed rather a lot to Anaïs Nin,' she said.

Dolly carried on, the imagery of her poems becoming increasingly sexualized, her voice increasingly breathy. The sax player remained on hand, and contributed random notes now and then. Billy's thoughts drifted continually to Rachel, and now and then he stole glances at her. She seemed to be taking a supercilious kind of pleasure in the evening. He wondered what her poems were like, and whether he would get to hear them. It was one thing to criticize others' work, and quite another to stand up and read out your own.

They went to an Italian restaurant for something to eat, and Billy spent much of the meal worrying whether he was expected to pay for it. The dinner at the Greek place had cleaned him out. But it was Rachel who asked for the bill, saying, 'My turn.'

As they stepped outside into the street, Billy began to wonder when to say goodnight. Should he walk her to the Tube station? Should he buy her a nightcap in a pub? But she cut off his deliberations, turning to him and saying, 'Do you want to come back to my place?'

Her place was miles away, whereas his was just around the corner. She must know this, he thought. His pulses raced, and without thinking he said yes. She hailed a taxi, and very soon they were pulling up outside a block of flats in Bayswater.

The flat was enormous, and seemed all the more so for being bereft of furniture. Rachel led him into a sitting room that contained a single sofa, a coffee table and lots of books, mostly in piles on the floor. 'I don't know how long I'll be here,' she said, anticipating Billy's enquiry. Above the sofa was a poster advertising the famous poetry reading at the Albert Hall in 1965, when Ginsberg and others had read to thousands of people. Billy had heard about it, and wondered how poetry had sounded in a space so vast and so formal.

'Coffee?' said Rachel.

'Thank you.'

She went into the kitchen, and Billy followed her, leaning against the door pillar while she put on the kettle.

'Bloody cockroaches,' she said, taking off a shoe and slamming it down on the counter.

They returned to the sitting room, and sat on the sofa drinking their coffee.

'Were you at the Albert Hall?' he asked.

'God, no. I was still at school.'

224

She lay back against the cushions, and Billy sat immobile, cradling his mug in both hands. Rachel looked at him very directly, and suddenly he understood with absolute clarity that the moment had arrived. He put down his mug and leaned across to kiss her. She reached up and put a hand around his neck, pulling him towards her. Within a few moments they were all arms and legs, lips and tongues. There was nothing romantic about it, just a rush of blood and a powerful desire not so much for Rachel as to get it done, to rid himself of his shameful condition.

'I haven't got anything with me,' he said, breaking off.

'Do you imagine I'm not on the Pill?'

She stood up and took his hand, leading him into the bedroom. Like the sitting room it was almost bare, the bed and a clothes basket being the only things in it. The bed was rumpled, unmade since the previous night. She began to take off her clothes. Billy did the same, feeling that really they ought to be taking off each other's clothes. When she lay back he saw how boyish her figure was. Her dark pubic hair was a shock to him – the girls in *Parade* lacked such profusions. He lay beside her, and she rolled over and straddled him, immediately seizing his penis in her hand and sliding it inside her. She ran her hands through her hair, and Billy reached up to touch her nipples. 'Suck them,' she said, and she leaned forward towards him. They were very dark and very erect, and he felt like a baby at the teat. She rocked back and forth, and Billy felt himself getting close. He grasped her arms and rolled over, staying inside her as they fell. As he looked down on her, she smiled for the first time. 'Come, Billy,' she said. 'Come in me.'

When it was over they lay side by side, the fingers of one hand entwined.

'You don't have to ask,' she said. 'I seldom come myself.'

'Why?'

She shrugged. 'I don't know. Don't let go, I suppose.'

'You could take a little more time,' said Billy. 'And not jump on me.'

'OK, I won't jump on you next time.'

Billy stared up at the ceiling, and the thought that there would be a next time gave him as much pleasure as the thing they had just done. He smiled to himself, the smile of a loon.

Four

It was Wilson who told him that Peter was dead. A kind of fatalism had stolen over Billy in the previous week, as Peter remained in a coma, and all he felt now was an absence of feeling.

He asked for a few hours off, and walked back to his room. Recollections of Peter came in no particular order, the image of him lying unconscious in the hospital bed merging with that of him being drunk and lordly in Soho. It was Peter's passions he recalled most clearly, his denunciations of things he didn't believe in and his certainty about the things he did. However sceptical Billy might have been about Peter's ideas, he was bound to respect them. A few days earlier the news of Robert Kennedy's assassination had broken. Well, this was murder too, plain and simple. But what was to be done about it? If Billy had been with him in Grosvenor Square he might have been able to identify the policeman who had hit him. But he hadn't, and he knew that any attempt to seek justice would be futile.

Wilson had tracked down a cousin in Essex, and a funeral was hastily arranged. It took place on a warm Sunday afternoon in a crematorium in Kentish Town. The only mourners were the cousin, a woman of about forty, and the bookshop staff, and this made Billy feel even more desolate than ever. There was the pretence of a Christian service, and Billy wondered what Peter would have made of it, Peter whose great hero had described religion as the opiate of the masses. The sentiments expressed by the priest and Wilson and the cousin were cloying, and Billy longed for it to be over. When at last it was, he took his leave quickly, walking towards Hampstead Heath and solitude.

He found himself in South End Green, and then heading towards Len Haskell's house. The net curtain was drawn back again, and a few moments later Len was at the door. He led Billy to the sitting room and went off to the kitchen to put on the kettle.

'Dreadful business,' he said when Billy told him Peter's story.

'Yes, dreadful.'

'I should have offered you something stronger.'

'No, that's all right.'

'I suppose it's no use me saying he shouldn't have been in Grosvenor Square in the first place?'

'No, it's no use saying that.' Why was he repeating Len's words like this? What was it *he* wanted to say? He looked at the photographs on the mantelpiece. 'What was it like when your wife died?' he asked.

'It was the end of things,' said Len with a kind of vehemence.

'I'm sorry. I think I'm being selfish. I don't want to bring back painful memories.'

'They never go away.'

He looked at his uncle thoughtfully. 'What really happened between you and Dad?' he said after a while.

Len took a digestive biscuit and crunched it between his teeth. 'Your dad?' he replied. 'We just didn't get along. We're different, that's all.'

'But you haven't seen him or even Mum for years.'

Len sighed. 'It wasn't about the bankruptcy,' he said. 'It was about Jim's philandering. But I don't know how much you know about that.'

Billy's thoughts went back to the day he had discovered his father with the waitress from Goody's. They had been in the car, parked in a back street in Wells, and Billy had crept up on them and seen them kissing. It was one of the worst moments of his life.

'I expect I know more than you think,' he said.

'I expect you do. Maggie should have stuck up for herself, should have told him it wasn't on.'

'I don't think that would have been very easy for her. My father is a hard person to confront.'

'Maybe not. Is he still fooling around these days?'

'I don't think so. He has other things on his mind at the moment.'

'What sort of things?'

Billy hesitated, and then said, 'He's got money problems again, so he says.'

A grim smile came to Len's lips. 'He can't hang on to it,' he said, 'that's his problem.'

'I don't think it's the same thing as with the garage, though. Seems to me he's a victim of changing times.'

'Well, we're all that.'

Billy placed his cup on the table. 'Why don't you go and visit them?' he said. 'Isn't it time to let bygones be bygones?'

'I'll think about it,' said Len. 'He'd have to invite me, though, not Maggie.'

'I'll talk to him.'

'You talk to him. If he's willing to bury the hatchet, then so am I.' He looked at Billy, and then said, 'I'm sorry – unfortunate choice of words.'

Billy shrugged his shoulders. 'Peter isn't being buried,' he said. 'He's being scattered across Epping Forest.'

He had spoken to Rachel in the days after Peter's death, but had not seen her again. Memories of their night, of her dark hair falling across his face as he caressed her breasts, kept returning to him. But their physical coupling had not led to the sort of intimacy he had expected. She had remained out of reach, had resisted him even. So it was almost as a stranger that he greeted her outside Hampstead Tube station one evening, kissing her on the cheek and then thinking he should have kissed her lips.

It was truly summer now, the evenings long and lazy. They walked to the Poetry Society, and joined a crowd that was made up entirely of women.

'Men should read Stevie,' said Rachel. 'They would understand women better if they did.'

She had been referring to her as 'Stevie' all along, as a friend would. It seemed clear to Billy that there was an element of love in Rachel's feelings about her.

She couldn't have been more different from Dolly, a little woman in her sixties wearing a pinafore dress with a lacy white collar, her greying hair swept severely back from her forehead. She chatted for a long while before reading from her latest collection, a book called The Frog Prince. Her poems were simple and direct, and she sang them beautifully. Billy looked across at Rachel, who clasped her hands together on her lap and gazed at the poet dreamily. He had never seen such a softness in her.

There was one poem in particular that moved Billy, and from the first lines he felt himself to be possessed by it.

Rise from your bed of languor
Rise from your bed of dismay
Your Friends will not come tomorrow
As they did not come today

You must rely on yourself, they said,
You must rely on yourself,
Oh but I find this pill so bitter said the poor man
As he took it from the shelf

Crying, Oh sweet Death come to me
Come to me for company,
Sweet Death it is only you I can
Constrain for company.

After the reading Rachel queued to have the poet sign her copy of the book, lingering for a few moments in conversation until the woman behind her coughed politely. They stepped out into the warm night, and Billy suggested they walk to the heath. He took her hand in his, and they strolled towards Parliament Hill.

Sitting on a bench, Rachel rested her head on his shoulder. London glistened below them in the soft evening light.

'So when am I going to read some of your poems?' he said.

She rubbed her cheek against the cotton of his shirt. 'I don't know. Some time.'

'What are they like? What do you write about?'

'Oh, things. Feelings.'

He kissed the top of her head. 'You're being evasive again,' he said gently.

'I know.' She sat up, brushing her hair away from her face. 'The truth is, I haven't written very much. I... I'm not sure how good I am.'

'But you're starting out. And technique matters in poetry. Don't be hard on yourself.'

She curled herself into him again. 'I *am* hard on myself,' she said, 'as I ought to be. Sometimes I feel like a fraud.'

'Why a fraud?'

'Because I tell people I'm a poet when I've got a few half-decent poems in a notebook and that's it.'

'Then write more.'

'Oh, Billy, you don't know how hard it is. Have you ever tried to write?'

'Nothing more than essays.'

'Then you don't know. A poet has to look in the mirror every day.'

'Let me read those poems,' he said. 'Let's go home, and then some time soon let me read your poems.'

In the bed in her flat he whispered the little banalities of love. Was he in love with her? Or was it simply that the mask had slipped and she had come to seem vulnerable like himself? For the moment all that mattered was that they were falling asleep in each other's arms.

The bookshop was a forlorn place in the days and weeks after Peter's funeral. Billy recalled thinking that he had looked like a ghost the first time he had set eyes on him. Well, he was a ghost now, and seemed to be everywhere. Billy had been so bound up in his own ideas about Peter that he hadn't noticed the effect he had had on others. The basement was gloomy nowadays without the light of his ardour.

Billy's days were gloomy too. He was sad for himself, but sadder for the memory of Peter. As Wilson had said, he had been completely alone. He had surrendered himself to his cause, and in doing so had found meaning and a sort of companionship. But these were surely no substitute for friendship, and love. Peter's loneliness weighed heavily upon him.

When one day Lee bounded into the bookshop, Billy welcomed him like an emissary from the world outside. They went to 2i's for lunch, sitting at the table at the back that Billy and Peter had often claimed for themselves.

'How's it going?' Billy asked.

'Oh, OK.' Lee took up his knife and fork and began to tap them on the table, setting up a brief syncopation. Then he put them down again and said, 'We're not getting anywhere, though.'

'Why not?'

'Our demo tape keeps coming back from people. We've sent it to all the labels – EMI, Decca – and no one wants to talk to us.'

'The tape you made in the Sawmill?'

'Yeah. We thought it was great then. But when I listen to it now I'm not so sure.'

'Do you have any gigs coming up?'

'Just one, in a pub in Fulham.'

'So what are you up to?'

'Nothing much. And Julian reckons he can't afford to pay us any more. We'll have to get jobs again.'

'I'm sorry.'

'Oh, we'll figure it out.' He looked up at Billy, hesitated for a moment, and then said, 'How's Sarah?'

'Fine, as far as I know. It's hard for us to talk on the phone.'

'I tried calling, but your dad wouldn't let me speak to her.'

'That's not really surprising.'

'I know. But I miss her. You couldn't get a message to her, could you?'

'What sort of message?'

'That I'd like to see her. We're not at the place in Earls Court now, but I could give you a number.'

'Are you sure? Remember what I said when we were in Cornwall? And Dad was pretty definite about Sarah having no contact with you.'

'Please, Billy. I miss her.'

He looked at Lee for a few moments. 'OK,' he said. 'I'm going there for a weekend soon. Write your number down on a piece of paper and I'll give it to her.'

On his way back to the bookshop, Billy stopped by a newsagent. He glanced at a newspaper, and read a few paragraphs about Russian tank movements on the Czech border. He thought about buying it so as to read the rest of the story, but he had got out of the habit of buying papers, and put it back on the shelf. As he walked back to the shop, he felt the powerful presence of Peter beside him.

Rachel lay back on the bed, her hair splashed over the pillows, and he kissed her mouth.

'Would you want to go to Marrakesh with me?' he asked.

'I don't know you well enough to travel with you, Billy.'

He took a strand of her hair in his fingers. 'I suppose not,' he said.

'Why Marrakesh?'

'I've wanted to go there for ages. It sounds wonderful.'

'A friend of mine went to Tangier once. She said it was a dump.'

'Marrakesh is near the mountains and the desert. And then there's nothing for hundreds of miles.'

She took his fingers away from her hair and stroked them in hers. 'Sounds to me as though you've got the bug,' she said.

'Yes, I have.'

'Then you must go.'

'But how? I don't have any money.'

'Well if you're going to think like that, you'll never go anywhere.'

He fell back onto the bed, and swept a hand across his forehead. 'You really wouldn't come with me?' he said.

'Billy, I don't know what you think is going on here, but we're not together, not yet at least.'

He looked at their naked bodies. They had made love, and by now this seemed to him an apt expression for what it was they were doing.

'Not together?' he said.

'I mean we're not in a relationship.'

'No?'

'Don't be obtuse. We've slept together half a dozen times.'

'And that doesn't mean anything?'

'I didn't say that.'

'Well, I think we're together. I think I'm in love with you.'

She raised herself on one elbow. 'Oh, you silly boy,' she said. 'Stop talking about "love". Let's just have fun.'

A shiver of hurt went through him. 'Well, if that's the way you feel…' he said.

She leaned over and kissed him. 'You're too serious, Billy,' she said. 'Now, are you going to make the coffee or am I?'

He went home for the weekend, and he and Sarah dropped by Goody's café.

'He's getting worse,' said Sarah.

'How?'

'Oh, shouting at us over nothing at all. Going to the pub by himself and coming back drunk.'

'Drunk?' Nothing that Sarah had said so far surprised him; but Jim had never really been a drinker.

'Well, not falling-over drunk. But definitely the worse for wear.'

Billy looked around the café. Goody's had been taken over by teenagers in recent years, the shoppers going to the tearooms around the corner.

'Have you talked to Mum about him?'

'We talk all the time. She's beside herself with worry. But she never seems to say anything to him. When things get difficult she just retreats into Tom's world.'

She picked up a spoon, carving patterns in the sugar and then erasing them.

'I'd better talk to him, then,' said Billy.

'Oh, please do. We're all at the end of our tethers.'

Billy pulled a piece of paper from his pocket.

'I've got a message for you, from Lee.'

Sarah sat up straight, dropping the spoon into the sugar bowl. 'You *do*?' she said.

'He came into the shop the other day. He says he misses you, and tried to call, but Dad wouldn't let him talk to you.'

'He *did*? Dad never told me.'

'Well, of course he didn't.'

'Is this a letter?' she said, grabbing it from his hand.

'No, it's just his phone number.'

She turned in her seat. 'There's a phone box just over there. Can you lend me sixpence?'

Billy gave her the money, and immediately she was gone, dashing down the street. He sat drinking his coffee and wondering what he would say to his father. At supper the night before, he had sensed the tension in the air. This was his first return home since going to London, and he was having difficulty in picking up the signals his family were sending out.

It was only a minute or two before Sarah returned, looking crestfallen. 'He's not there,' she said. 'I'll have to go out later and try again.'

Billy studied her face for a few moments. She was seventeen now, but how often did he still see the seven-year-old Sarah in her, the little girl who had been so lost when they went to live in the farmhouse, and so lonely.

233

They finished their drinks, and Billy decided he might as well go to the Regal now, while Sarah returned to the house. Outside the cinema a poster was headed 'Coming Soon', and showed the helmet of an astronaut. '2001: *A Space Odyssey*', it read. As Billy entered the foyer he saw Bert Dampler, the assistant manager.

'Hello,' said Billy. 'What are you doing behind the counter?'

'Amy left a couple of weeks ago,' he replied. 'I'm doing this every day now.'

Billy looked at his shiny bald head and girlish features. He hadn't changed a bit since Billy used to come here as a boy. Bert was a young-old man who seemed perfectly happy to live out his life within the narrow compass of the town.

'Dad in his office?' Billy asked.

'Yes. Just go on up.'

Billy knocked on the door, and his father called to him to come in. It was a tiny room, cluttered with canisters of film.

'Come to view the wreckage, have you?' said Jim.

'What wreckage?'

His father extended an arm and swept it around the room. 'The *Marie Celeste* of the cinema world,' he said.

Billy sat down in a chair.

'Is it that bad?'

'It's even worse now than it was when we came up to London. I've had to let go of Amy and Colin.'

'Who does that leave?'

'Me, Bert and Stan.'

'Can you manage?'

'Oh, I'll manage,' said Jim. 'I've done so before and I'll do so again.'

'But, Dad,' said Billy, a note of irritation entering his voice, 'you're not confronting reality. If the economics of how cinemas run are changing, surely you must do something about it?'

'Not confronting reality, eh? Funny, but I seem to have heard those words somewhere before.'

'Well perhaps there's a reason for that.'

'Oh, yes? And what would that be?'

His father's face was suffused with rage now, a rage Billy knew was directed not at him but at everything. How dreadfully familiar this expression was, how often he had cowered before it in the past.

'Have you talked to the Rank people?' he said quietly.

Jim raised his feet up onto the desk and took out a cigarette. 'Not yet,' he said. 'I'm going to see how the summer goes. There's some good films coming up.'

'2001,' said Billy.

'And *The Odd Couple*, with Jack Lemmon and Walter Matthau. Supposed to be hilarious. It had better be – we could do with a few laughs around here.'

Billy stood up and crossed to the window. The matinee westerns had ended, and people were leaving the cinema and walking up the road. They were kids, mostly, boys in posses of four or five. He turned back to his father.

'Why don't you at least talk to the Rank people?' he said. 'No harm can come of it. You could give the impression you're thinking of taking a new direction, or something.'

Jim tipped ash from his cigarette. 'The only new direction I'll be taking is towards the Labour Exchange,' he said.

Billy left his father to stew, and walked back to the house. Immediately he heard voices raised in the sitting room.

'You're not to see him again,' his mother was saying. 'Your father forbade it, and that's that.'

'But why?' said Sarah. 'Just because we got busted?'

'Because you're seventeen and he's twenty-one. Because you're still a child.'

'Is that what you think of me?'

'Oh, Sarah,' said Margaret. 'Just be patient. Why are you and your brother in such a hurry to grow up?'

Billy padded silently up to his room and closed the door behind him. It was going to be an age before Sunday afternoon came around and he could take the train back to London.

———

He knocked on the door of Rachel's flat, and to his astonishment found that it was Julian who opened it.

'Hi, Bill,' he said.

'Julian!'

He was wearing a lacy white shirt that was open practically to his navel, and he looked very pale. There was a hint of make-up on his face.

235

'Come on in,' he said. 'I was just passing.'

They went through to the sitting room, and after a few moments Rachel appeared, holding two glasses of wine. She handed one to Julian, and turned to Billy.

'Wine?' she said.

'I thought we were going out.'

'We are. Later. Wine?'

'OK, thanks.'

She went back into the kitchen, and returned with another glass and a stool. Julian sprawled on the sofa, and Rachel motioned to Billy to sit next to him. She placed the stool on the other side of the coffee table, and sat with her long bare legs crossed, one foot hooked behind the other.

'How's tricks?' said Julian.

'All right,' Billy replied. 'Same as usual, really. What about you?'

Julian sat up and took a swig from the glass. 'We're breaking up,' he said. 'The band, I mean.'

'I'm sorry.'

He made a sour face. 'They weren't that great,' he said. 'I can do better on my own.'

'On your own?'

'Yeah. Singer-songwriter. Just me, my songs and an acoustic guitar.'

'What about Lee?'

'He's going back to the record shop in Bath where he worked before.'

'He must be disappointed.'

'I expect he is.'

Rachel had been sitting in silence, fiddling with her hair. When there was a pause in the conversation she said, 'Julian was picking up a book from me. Baudelaire.'

Julian grinned. 'Got to get my lyrics from somewhere,' he said.

'*Les Fleurs du mal*,' said Rachel. 'Weird.' She stood up and crossed the room, beginning to hunt through the piles of books against the wall. When she found the Baudelaire she placed it on the sofa beside Julian. He picked it up, leafed through it briefly, and then set it down again.

'So what are you two up to tonight?' he asked.

'We were just going to get something to eat,' said Billy. 'Maybe at the Greek place.'

'Disgusting stuff, Greek food. Don't know how you can stick it.'

Billy shrugged. 'We like it,' he said.

'We?' Julian turned to Rachel. 'I thought you hated it too.'

Rachel tossed her hair. 'Well I've changed my mind, haven't I?'

'A lady's prerogative.'

'Fuck off, Julian.'

He looked from Rachel to Billy, and then said, 'That's exactly what I was thinking of doing.' Raising himself from the sofa, he stepped around the coffee table. Rachel remained sitting on the stool, and he bent to kiss her, aiming for her lips. At the last moment she turned her cheek, and Julian's kiss landed on her ear.

''Bye, love,' he said, and to Billy, 'See you around.'

When he had gone, Rachel went to get the wine bottle and refilled their glasses. She sat next to Billy, leaning into him, and he put his arm around her shoulders.

'What was that all about?' he said.

'What was what all about?'

'Him. Julian.'

'I told you – he was collecting a book.'

Billy looked across the room, and then down at Rachel. All he could see of her was a tangle of hair. He took her hand in his.

'So how are you?' he said.

'I wrote a poem today.'

'You did? That's great.'

'We'll see.'

'Can I read it?'

'Not yet. It needs to ferment.'

'I'd like to, when it's fermented.'

'It might take a while.' She straightened herself, and then said, 'Shall we go to the Greek?'

'Are you sure you want to?'

'Oh, don't take any notice of Julian. Half of what he says is for effect, and the other half is lies.'

Simon gulped at his beer and placed the glass on the pub table, splashing some down the side. He was in a state of high excitement.

'I'm working on Petrarch's influence on Chaucer,' he said. 'It's extraordinary that no one seems to have done it before.'

'What's the evidence?' Billy asked.

'Chaucer refers to Petrarch in a poem, as the poet of the laurel crown. And he was in Florence shortly before Petrarch died. I'm sure they must have met.'

'The laurel crown?'

'Yes. Petrarch was the first poet laureate since the ancients. He went to Rome from Avignon to receive it.'

'Isn't Chaucer's stuff very different from Petrarch's?'

'That's what I'm working on. I think the influences are clearer than anyone has realized.'

Billy looked around the pub. It was a Monday evening, and the College Arms was empty save for themselves and a couple who were canoodling in an alcove.

'Did you say he lived in Avignon?' he asked.

'Yes. That's where he met, or imagined, Laura.'

'My girlfriend spent a year in Avignon.'

'I want to go there later in the summer.'

Billy's thoughts turned to Rachel, and to the strange evening they had spent a few days earlier. 'You were talking recently about the way lovers project the things they want on to their loved ones,' he said, 'whether those things are there or not.'

'Yes.'

'So that means that to be in love, you have to love two people.'

'Sort of.'

'Do you think they ever meet, those two people?'

'How do you mean?'

'Do you think that who she is and who you want her to be can coincide?'

Simon looked down into his glass. 'To be honest, I've no idea,' he said. 'I don't think I've ever been in love.'

'I can't tell whether I am or not. Sometimes I think so, and other times...'

'Don't we have to look at our parents to see what happens after a while?'

'Our parents? Are we really going to learn anything from them?'

'Well we ought to, surely.'

Billy cast his mind back to the weekend at home, to his father's rage and his mother's anxieties. 'Perhaps,' he said.

Rachel invited him to a party at Dolly's house near Ladbroke Grove. It turned out to be very grand, the biggest place he'd set foot in for a long while. He had somehow not expected Dolly to be rich. They went out into the garden, which was thronged with people, and were offered glasses of champagne by a black boy wearing a kaftan.

Dolly kissed Rachel, and held out a hand to Billy.

'So this is the young man,' she said, looking him up and down.

'The young man?' said Rachel.

'The young man you've been shagging. You have, haven't you?'

Billy felt his face colouring. Dolly might be unembarrassable, but he was not. Rachel twined an arm in his and said, 'And a very good shag he is too.' They both giggled, and Billy took a deep swallow of champagne.

They joined some people who were sitting on the lawn, and Billy half attended to their conversation, which veered from art to music to gossip. A paisley-shirted boy was holding court with four girls, talking about how he knew Donovan, how they were such good friends. They all seemed impossibly smart and sure of themselves. He lay back on the grass and watched the clouds scud across the sky, and then he closed his eyes. When eventually he sat up again, he realized that Rachel had disappeared. Dolly was sitting close by, watching him with a faintly amused expression.

'She saw Julian,' she said, 'and went off to talk to him.'

'Julian? He's here?'

'Apparently.'

He looked back towards the house, wondering what to do. The boy who had handed him the champagne came around offering hash brownies. Dolly took one for him and one for herself.

'So you and Rachel are having a good time?' she asked.

Billy bit into the brownie. 'Yes, we are,' he said. But as he spoke the words, he wondered whether they were really true.

'Has she shown you her poems?'

'Not yet. I keep asking to see them.'

Dolly arched her eyebrows. 'I wonder why?' she said. 'Perhaps because they don't exist?'

'Don't exist? What do you mean?'

She smiled, and made a show of inspecting her brownie closely.

'I have a feeling she hasn't written a single word.'

'How do you know?'

'I just know, that's all. It's obvious.'

'Not to me it isn't.'

'Well you're not a poet.'

Billy had an urge to say that she wasn't a poet either. There was something malicious in her expression now, and he knew he must get away from her. He stood up and walked across to the house, looking for Rachel. It was getting dark, and people were drifting back inside. Threading his way in and out of the rooms, he became aware that he was beginning to feel unwell. The hash brownie had been stronger than he'd realized. He sat down, and held his head in his hands. Suddenly he was overcome by nausea, and he stood and headed up the stairs. Feeling frightened as well as ill, he opened several doors in search of a bathroom.

Then he saw two figures emerging from a room at the far end of the corridor. Strange things were happening to his eyes, but he could tell that one of them was a boy in a lacy white shirt and the other a girl with long dark hair, hair she was in the process of brushing. He stood stock still, and then turned and ran back down the stairs. Stumbling out of the house, he was immediately dazzled by the streetlights. They seemed to be going around in circles, like a Catherine wheel. He climbed over a wall and lay down in a garden, but that only seemed to make things worse. After a while he decided the best thing to do was to sit up. One of the party guests, a middle-aged man, passed by him, and asked if he was all right.

'I just feel sick, that's all.'

'You had one of Dolly's hash brownies, I expect.'

'Yes.'

The man smiled. 'She makes the deadliest I know. The best thing you can do is get home and have some vitamin C.'

———

Sitting alone in the cinema in Leicester Square, half watching the images that flickered before him, Billy felt overcome by grief. He had lost a friend, and now he had lost a lover. Was life about something more than loss, and being lost? Two lovers kissed on the screen, and his thoughts returned once more to Rachel. She had been his first love, and would always be. But could he be sure that it had really been love, something more than just sex? When he had spoken of love she had said he was being silly. And then there was Julian. She wasn't over him, and hadn't been during the entire time she and Billy had been seeing each other.

When the film ended he stepped out into the warm evening and headed towards the river. The water was calm, untroubled by boats, and it lapped gently against the walls of the embankment. He looked across to the Festival Hall. A realization had been dawning for some time, and now he knew what he must do. His father needed him, and he had a duty to perform. Before he could think about going to Morocco, he must go home again. He walked slowly back to the boarding house and picked up the phone in the hallway.

Jim's voice sounded very distant on the other end of the line. 'What was that?' he asked.

'I said I'm coming home. I'd like to help you out in the cinema for a while, do some of the things Amy and Colin used to do.'

'You are? What's brought this on?'

'Nothing, Dad. I just think I can give you a hand.'

When he put down the phone he knocked on Mrs Allingham's door. She invited him in, and he sat down on one of the carved-wood chairs.

'I'll be leaving soon,' he said, 'once I've worked out my notice at the bookshop.'

'You're going to Morocco?'

'No, I'm going home. My father's got problems in the cinema, and I'm going to help out.'

'That seems very noble of you.'

'Does it? Perhaps. I thought I wanted to escape my family, but now I see that you can't do that, you shouldn't even try.'

'Blood is thicker, as they say.'

'Yes, it seems it is.'

Five

He lay in his bed, gazing around the room. The film posters had remained on the walls, Ursula Andress in Dr No and Julie Christie in *Darling*, and the shelves were filled with books by Orwell and Huxley and Hemingway. It was a teenager's room still. Sarah knocked on his door and said, 'Bathroom's free.'

'Do you always take this long?'

'I was only in there for five minutes.'

'Twenty, more like.'

'Well do you want to use it or not? Dad'll need it soon.'

He threw back the bedclothes and got up, grabbing his wash-bag. The bathroom looked as though three people had tried to use it at once, wet towels lying on the floor, shampoo and deodorant bottles standing open. Billy glanced through the steam at his reflection in the mirror, and his heart sank. What on earth had possessed him to come home again?

On the way to the cinema Jim said, 'So it didn't work out in London, then?'

'I didn't say that.'

They walked on in silence for a few minutes.

'What am I going to pay you?'

'I don't know. Pocket money. How about two pounds a week?'

'Are you sure?'

'The whole point of this is to *save* money, Dad.'

Jim looked ahead as the Regal came into view. 'All right,' he said. 'Two pounds a week it is.'

Bert Dampler was opening up as they arrived. They went through the foyer and into the auditorium, turning on lights as they did so. The floor was strewn with sweet wrappers, and the ashtrays in the arms of the seats were full of cigarette butts. Billy breathed in the stale air and said, 'I suppose this is where I start. I'll get the Hoover.'

He spent all morning cleaning the place, and then went home with his father for lunch. At half past one they returned to the cinema and prepared for the afternoon screening of 2001. Stan, the projectionist, had arrived, and was sorting out the reels of film. Stan was the longest-serving member of staff, having been there for years even before Jim took over. He was in his early sixties now, prematurely aged, and he shuffled around the place silently, exchanging only the most necessary words with the others.

Bert emptied a bag of change into the till and looked expectantly towards the door. Afternoon screenings on Mondays were never exactly crowded, but today there were just two people, a middle-aged man and a boy of about fifteen. Billy stood at the door of the auditorium and tore their tickets in half. When the film started, he dropped into a seat in the back row. The image of the spaceship preparing to dock at its station was stunning, the Strauss waltz crazy yet brilliantly apt. For an hour or more Billy sat spellbound, before it occurred to him that in fact he was working. He slipped back out into the foyer, to see his father talking to Bert. Jim turned towards Billy and said, 'I'm heading home for a while. I'll do the evening showing, and you can knock off once this one's over.'

'Is there anything I can do?'

'There's a consignment of chocolate bars that needs checking and putting on the shelves. Bert can show you.'

Billy spent a while at the sweet counter, and then went back into the auditorium. He had entirely lost the thread of the film, and simply surrendered himself to its images. The final scenes, in which the pilot flew through a kinetic corridor of light, were thrilling and terrifying. When it was over, Bert opened the doors, and the two paying customers stood and made their way out into the day.

'This one's so long we can only do two showings,' said Bert. 'Now I have to stick around until half past seven.'

'I'll stay with you.'

'Don't bother. There's nothing needs doing except minding the place. Stan'll go to the pub for his usual pint. Why don't you go with him?'

In all the years that his father had managed the cinema and Billy had helped out, he had never really talked to Stan. When he appeared from the projection room, Billy suggested he buy him a drink. The expression on Stan's face seemed to say that this could only mean trouble. They walked to the Rose & Crown, and sat down with their pints.

'So, how are you keeping these days?' said Billy.

'All right, I suppose.' Stan took a cigarette from behind his ear and rolled it back and forth between his fingers. Eventually he picked up a box of matches and lit it. 'I'm the one person your dad can't do without.'

'And he knows it.'

'Won't help me if he has to close the place down, though, will it?'

'He won't have to close it down.'

'Oh, no?'

'The worst that could happen is that he'd have to sell it.'

'Yes, to Rank. And the first thing they'll do is sack everyone and put in their own people.'

'You think so?'

'I've heard stories of the like.'

Billy watched as Stan smoked his cigarette. He did so very intently, as if he were trying to extract as much pleasure from it as he possibly could.

'Let's see what we can do over the summer,' said Billy. 'Maybe we can drum up some business somehow.'

'Best of luck,' said Stan. 'The place is doomed, and we all know it.'

———

Sitting next to the director in the front row of seats in the Byre Theatre, Billy watched as his mother crossed the stage. Thomas More had just resigned as Lord Chancellor, and he and his wife were having a domestic moment.

'Luxury!' said his mother.

'Well, it's a luxury while it lasts…' replied More. 'There's not much sport in it for you, is there?… Alice, the money from the bishops. I wish – oh, heaven, how I wish I could take it! But I can't.'

'I didn't think you would.'

'Alice, there *are* reasons.'

'We couldn't come so deep into your confidence as to know these reasons why a man in poverty can't take four thousand pounds?'

The scene unfolded, More's daughter entering the fray. This was an early rehearsal of *A Man for all Seasons*, and the actors still read from their scripts. Afterwards Billy and Margaret walked to Cathedral Green and sat down on a bench. Wells was radiant in the evening light. He looked up at the west face of the cathedral and tried to tell himself that he was simply on his summer holidays.

244

'You were great, Mum,' he said.

'Oh, nonsense. I only got the part because I'm the right age. But I'm enjoying it nonetheless.'

He hadn't been alone with his mother like this since he returned. Sitting with her now in this lovely place gave him an unfamiliar sense of ease.

'How do you think Sarah is?' said Margaret.

Billy shrugged his shoulders. 'Fine, I think.'

'Not pining after that boy.'

'Oh, I'm certain she's doing that. But her exam results are more important than Lee, surely?'

'She thinks she did well.'

'She would.' Billy looked away towards the Dean's Gate. 'And Tom?' he said.

Margaret smiled. 'Tom is a treasure. It's his birthday next month. Don't forget.'

It was the middle of August, and he had been home for ten days. How long would he have to stay?

'You haven't talked much about London,' said his mother.

'I suppose not.'

'Did she hurt you, that girl?'

Billy looked down at his hands. 'Yes, I think she did.'

'You can't expect things to go smoothly at first. It's as much about discovering how to be with someone as anything else.'

'There are men my age who are married.'

'And do you suppose that's necessarily a good thing?' She turned towards him. 'Better to take these things slowly,' she said. 'You have lots of time.'

'Do I?'

'Of course you do.' She stood up, and smoothed down her skirt. 'They'll be expecting us back,' she said.

They walked across the grass, and Billy glanced at his mother. There was one member of the family of whom they hadn't spoken a word.

'Mum...' he began. 'Let's go to the Swan and have a drink.'

'If you like.'

They found chairs by the fireplace, and Billy set down two glasses of wine on the table.

'We haven't talked about Dad at all since I came home,' he said.

'No.'

'He's in trouble again, isn't he?'

His mother looked away from him. 'Yes,' she said.

'And this time it's harder, because he's older.'

'A lot of things get harder as you get older.'

'How is he with you?'

She looked up at him. 'I'm losing him again,' she said. 'He's drifting away, as he did after the bankruptcy. I don't know how to pull him back to me.'

'Can't you talk to him?'

She smiled wearily. 'You know what he's like,' she said. 'When he's in difficulty his main concern is to hide it, to pretend nothing's wrong. He shuts down.'

'But he's admitted to me that things aren't going well.'

'Perhaps it's easier for him to admit such things to you than to me.'

He looked at her intently. 'He's going to have to sell, Mum,' he said. 'The sooner he realizes it the better.'

'Oh, I think he knows that,' she replied. 'He'll do it in his own way and his own time.'

'No. He'll do it when his obligations to other people demand it. And if there's anyone who can tell him when that should be, it's me.'

She swirled the wine in her glass, and her face set suddenly firm.

'No, Billy,' she said. 'That's my task. He's my husband, and he must answer to me.'

'He's never done so before,' said Billy exasperatedly.

'Perhaps that's because I haven't been strong enough.'

'Don't be so hard on yourself, and so easy on him.'

She watched as the wine drained down the glass again, its rivulets glinting in the candlelight.

'I sometimes think I've spent an entire marriage being easy on him,' she said. 'And where has it got me?'

Billy had never heard such a note of bitterness in his mother's voice. He touched her hand. 'Things are going to have to change, Mum,' he said. 'And the first thing that's going to change is him.'

He backed the Vauxhall out of the garage, and Sarah hopped in.

'If Dad knew what I was doing he'd kill me,' she said.

'We're going to Bath to buy you the new John Mayall album,' replied Billy. 'You couldn't get it here, remember?'

'Right.'

They drove out of Wells in silence, Sarah gnawing at her fingernails and then fiddling with the radio. In the city, Billy parked in a new multi-storey car park, and they walked to the record shop. Lee's features broke into a broad smile as they stepped through the door. He and Sarah kissed and hugged each other, and they went outside.

'I'll see you in a couple of hours,' said Billy.

'Are you sure?' replied his sister.

'Of course. Where shall I meet you?'

'In the George,' said Lee.

They set off in their different directions, Billy heading towards The Circus. He had very mixed feelings about this city of his birth. Until he was ten years old he had lived in a large house near the London Road and gone to a private school with the sons of Bath's elite. Then had come his father's bankruptcy, and their move to the country. He had seldom returned since, and during the years of his growing up, Bath had become a tourist attraction. He sat down on a bench near the botanical gardens, wondering how Sarah and Lee were getting on. It was mad of him to have agreed to drive her here, but she had been pestering him ever since he came home.

He walked back into the centre, and sat in a café eating a sandwich and reading the paper. The Russians had finally invaded Czechoslovakia, and Dubček's brave experiment was over. Billy thought of Peter, and was somehow glad he wasn't alive to witness it. What was all this protest around the world amounting to, really? He set the newspaper aside. This reminder of Peter had sent a shaft of pain through him. If only he were here now, arguing and gesticulating. But moments ago, Billy had been telling himself he was glad he wasn't here.

He looked at his watch, and saw that it was time to collect Sarah. Telling himself to snap out of this melancholy mood, he walked to the George. Lee and Sarah were sitting at a table in the furthest reaches of the pub, entwined in one another. Billy sat down, and they untangled themselves.

'What do you want to drink?' said Lee.

'Just a half of bitter, thanks.'

247

When Lee returned to the table, Billy said, 'Things all right in the shop?'

'They're fine. The manager said he'd take me back once, but not twice.'

'And what about your music?'

'I'm talking to another band. They're more bluesy. I'm hoping I can join them soon.'

As they were speaking, Billy became aware that someone had approached them. He looked up to see the lean figure of Bert Dampler.

'Hello,' said Bert.

'Hello. What are you doing here?'

'Taking my mother to lunch.' He gestured across the room to a woman who was waving at them. 'You remember my mother, don't you? She lives here.'

'Of course,' said Billy.

'What about you?'

'Sarah's buying an album. This is Lee, a friend who works in a record shop here.'

They nodded at one another, and Bert said to Sarah, 'Don't see much of you these days.'

'I don't seem to go to the pictures very often.'

'Nothing much on for teenagers. There's a shocker coming soon though, *Rosemary's Baby*.'

'Maybe I'll come along for that one.'

Bert returned to his mother, and the three of them went outside and said their farewells. Billy walked a few yards down the street and looked into a shop window. When Sarah caught up with him there were tears in her eyes.

'I won't see him again for ages,' she said. 'It's so unfair.'

They returned to the car, and Billy drove back towards Wells. Sarah continued to sniffle throughout the journey, staring silently out of the window.

'I told Lee when we were in Cornwall that he should try to get over you,' said Billy.

She turned on him. 'You did? Why?'

'Because it's hopeless, Sarah. You're here and he's there, and Dad's forbidden you to see each other.'

'He's not very far away now. I could take the bus.'

'But you'll need excuses. And Dad will suspect you're up to something.'

'It's all right for you,' she said, folding her arms. 'You're not in love.'

'Do you think I don't know how you feel?' he said, his voice suddenly tinged with anger. 'Do you think I don't miss Rachel?'

'Sorry.' She pulled out her handkerchief again. 'But you did say you weren't sure you were in love with her.'

'I *said* I wasn't sure. Now I think maybe I was.'

'Then you know how I feel about Lee.'

'Yes, I do. But that doesn't mean it's a good thing for us to see them again.'

'Why not?'

'Because there's no future in it,' he said earnestly. 'Because Lee is older than you and Rachel is mixed up.'

Sarah looked back at him. 'That's what boys always say about girls when they don't understand them,' she said.

Billy smiled. 'OK,' he said. 'Rachel is still in love with someone else.'

'Lee isn't, though. He's in love with me.'

Billy brought the car to a halt at a junction, and looked across at his sister, hunched in the passenger seat. 'Guess what I've just realized?' he said. 'You forgot to buy the record.'

'Can't remember the last time I went to the pictures,' said Len. '*Lawrence of Arabia*, probably.'

'Is there a cinema near you?' asked Jim, refilling Len's wineglass and his own.

'There's an Odeon just up the road. But going by yourself's no fun.'

Margaret stood and began to clear away the plates. 'Coffee?' she said.

'No thanks, Maggie.'

Sarah and Tom had already got down from the table, and Billy and Len and Jim sat toying with their glasses while Margaret went into the kitchen.

'Business not so good, then?' said Len.

'It's been better.'

'Got the place properly insured?'

'Of course I've got the place insured.' Jim picked up his glass, ignoring the stare Billy had been directing at him for several minutes

249

now. He had clearly been fortifying himself since before Billy had collected Len from the station, and had been drinking steadily and purposefully throughout lunch.

'You can get insurance against the collapse of businesses these days,' said Len.

'Who said anything about collapse?'

Len shrugged, and knocked back more wine himself. His face was shiny with sweat, and he took a handkerchief from his pocket now and then to wipe his brow. 'I don't mean anything by it,' he said. 'Just trying to be helpful.'

'I've got all the help I need, thanks.'

'That's all right, then.'

Billy looked from one to the other, deciding that he'd had enough of this. 'Let me take you for a walk around the town,' he said to Len. 'You haven't seen it in a long time.'

'Is it any different?'

'Well, no. It's just a nice place to walk.'

At the last moment, Margaret said she would come with them. They walked to Market Place.

'That's where Dad once worked,' said Billy, pointing to a shop whose sign read 'Underhill's: Outfitters to the Scholars & Gentry of Wells'.

They passed through Penniless Porch and into Cathedral Green.

'Hasn't changed, has he?' said Len.

'Now that's not fair,' replied Margaret. 'Not everything is Jim's fault. Life can be hard.'

They strolled across the grass towards the Deanery.

'I'm sorry I haven't been in touch,' said Len after a while.

Margaret placed her arm in her brother's. 'What matters is that you're here now,' she said.

'I'll come again, if you want me to.'

'Only if you want to. But you're going to have to try harder with Jim. You two rub each other up the wrong way.'

'Always have.'

'That doesn't mean to say you always have to.'

Billy turned to look at his mother and uncle. It had been difficult to persuade Jim to invite Len to Sunday lunch, and by now he was convinced it had been a mistake.

'This is the most beautiful façade of any in England,' he said, gazing up at the west face of the cathedral.

'It could do with a good clean,' said Len.

They returned to the house, and Billy drove Len to the station. When he got back he found his father slumped in his armchair, a half-empty bottle of red wine beside him.

'That was a great success, then,' said Billy.

'Is that my fault? I invited him into my home, and all he could do was gloat over my problems.'

'He didn't gloat, Dad. As he said, he was trying to be helpful.'

'Funny way of being helpful.'

'Oh, for God's sake!' said Billy. 'When are you going to face up to your responsibilities?'

'I am facing up to them. I'm running a business.'

'Yes, running it into the ground.'

Jim took a swig of wine. 'If you don't like the way I'm doing things you can clear off again,' he said.

'You seem to be forgetting that I'm trying to be helpful.'

His father looked at him with a strange expression that mingled resentment and fear.

'And you seem to be forgetting that I'm your father,' he said.

———

As the summer drifted on, Billy found himself mostly doing the evening shift in the cinema. During the days he reread his Conrads and Lawrences, and took long walks out towards Glastonbury and Shepton Mallet. At home, Jim's brooding discontent hung over everything, a discontent that occasionally found its expression in furious rows over very little. An uneasy peace existed between father and son, one that neither appeared to have any wish to breach.

Strangely it was Sarah who got on Billy's nerves the most. There were the typhoons in the bathroom, the constant refrain of 'Piece of my Heart' from her bedroom, the entreaties repeated every few days to find another reason for a trip to Bath.

Within a month or so of coming home, he was bored stiff. There was no sign of an upturn in his father's fortunes, and he began to wonder how much longer he ought to stick around. Part of the problem was that he had no friends in Wells any more. And then one day he

251

bumped into Roger Sealy in the High Street. Sealy had been the scally-wag of his year at the Blue School, a little kid with curly red hair and a nose for trouble. Billy hadn't seen him since before he'd gone to Bristol, and they arranged to meet one evening for a drink.

'Did you know the school is moving?' said Roger when they sat down. 'The old building's being given to the Operatic Society.'

'No, I didn't.'

'Sad, eh?'

'I suppose so. Can't say I ever had a great love of the place.'

'Nor did I, but you know – nostalgia and all that. We had some good times there.'

'Yes, we did.'

'Remember when the Beak caught us smoking in Lovers Walk?'

Billy smiled. He had smoked twenty cigarettes in an hour as a dare, and had been ill for days afterwards. But it had cured him of smoking for ever.

'And when we broke into the school at night,' continued Roger, 'and hung girls' panties and nylons from the chandeliers in the assembly room?'

'My sister still wonders where those panties went.'

'We had fun, that's what we had.'

'So what are you doing now?'

'Apprentice printer at Pettigrew's.'

'How is it?'

Roger pulled a face. 'It's a job, isn't it? I'm getting married soon.'

'Congratulations. Who to?'

'Pauline Trudgian. Remember her?'

Billy shook his head.

'I was going out with her when we were in the sixth form. You must remember her. She had pigtails and glasses then, but she was always gorgeous underneath.'

'Yes, I remember now. You claimed to have slept with her the night before her sixteenth birthday.'

'Well I did.'

Billy gazed across the room. This conversation was heading exactly where he knew it would, nowhere at all.

'So what about you?' said Roger. 'We all thought you were going to be a professor or something.'

Billy picked up his glass and took a long draught of beer.

'I dropped out of Bristol and went to work in a bookshop in London,' he said finally. 'Then my dad needed some help in the Regal, so I've come home for a while.'

'And after this?'

'I don't know. I want to travel.'

Roger looked at him with a perplexed expression. 'And where's it leading?' he said.

'Where's it leading? That's a very good question.'

'What's the answer, then?'

Billy looked up at him. 'I wish I knew,' he said. He gazed across the pub at the other drinkers. 'Don't you wonder sometimes what it's all about?'

'What what's all about?'

'Life, I mean.'

'It's about getting set up and getting on, isn't it?'

'But once you've set yourself up. Once you're established as a printer and you and Pauline have got kids...'

'That'll do me.'

Billy knocked back the rest of his beer. What was the point in musing aloud like this? Roger Sealy was one of the lucky ones, for whom it was all quite simple. Why did life seem to Billy so complicated?

Billy and Tom sat watching *Dr Who*, Tom making great play of hiding behind the sofa whenever the Daleks appeared. In half an hour Billy would need to set off to the cinema for the evening showing. Margaret had left for the theatre, and his father hadn't yet returned for supper. When eventually he appeared in the hallway it was clear that he'd been drinking.

'Sarah!' he roared. 'I want a word with you. Now.'

He came into the sitting room, looked hazily at Billy, and said, 'You too.'

Billy switched off the television and told Tom to go to his room. He knew very well what this must be about. His father went into the kitchen, and reappeared holding a whisky bottle and a glass.

'Looks to me as though you've had enough,' said Billy.

'Does it, young man? Well I'll be the judge of that.'

Sarah appeared and sat down on the sofa, folding her arms.

'You lied to me, both of you,' said Jim. 'I told you never to see that boy again, and what do you do but have a little tryst behind my back.'

'You've got no right to say I can't see him,' said Sarah.

'While you're living in my house I've got every right to. But the thing I don't like about this is that my son and my daughter lied to me.'

'Don't be so bloody sanctimonious, Dad,' said Billy. 'They had lunch together. If it had been anything more, I wouldn't have taken her.'

Jim looked at him with bleary eyes. 'But she'd have gone, wouldn't she?' he said. 'She'd have jumped back into his bed at the first chance.'

'You're disgusting,' said Sarah. 'I'm not listening to any more of this.'

She stood up and marched out of the room, banging the door hard behind her. Jim placed the glass and bottle on the coffee table and sat down heavily.

'I don't want my daughter to be a tramp, that's all,' he said.

Billy's own anger had been kindling, and suddenly it caught light. 'Do you know what you are?' he said. 'You're a hypocrite.'

Jim looked up at him in surprise, and took a slug of whisky. 'Just listen to the preacher,' he said.

'I'm serious. Do you think Mum didn't know about all the girl-friends when we were kids, the receptionists in the showroom, the waitress at Goody's?'

His father rested his elbows on his knees and looked vaguely across the room. The expression on his face was turning from anger to confusion.

'So I made some mistakes,' he said.

'You certainly did. One after another.'

'But Sarah's seventeen, and she's a girl.'

'Listen to yourself, Dad. What were your little sweethearts, if not girls?'

'There hasn't been anyone for years.'

'And that makes everything all right? That means Mum can just forget all the hurt, just pretend nothing happened?' He was furious now, all the repressed anger he felt towards his father spilling out. 'You're so bloody selfish you can't see anyone else, can you? You haven't got a clue about what other people might be feeling.'

Billy got up and stepped across to the table, picking up the bottle and glass and placing them on the sideboard. He sat down again and stared at his father in silence. Tears were starting in Jim's eyes.

'You don't know what it's like yet, Billy,' he said. 'You get married, you think you're in heaven for a while. Then a kid comes along, and suddenly you're second in the queue. She's too tired, she's got aches in all the wrong places. A girl makes eyes at you, and you're helpless.'

'You're not helpless,' said Billy. 'That's the point.' He sat rigidly in his chair, refusing to be softened by his father's distress.

'Have you never felt helpless?'

'Not over a girl, no.'

'Well just wait till you are. Then you can lecture me.'

'I'm not lecturing you about what you did ten years ago, I'm lecturing you about hypocrisy now.'

Jim took out a handkerchief and wiped the tears from his cheeks. 'It's easy for you to talk about hypocrisy,' he said. 'You haven't lived, haven't had to make compromises.'

'I know it when I see it.'

'Talk to me about hypocrisy in twenty years' time.'

'I will. But in the meantime I think you owe Sarah an apology.'

His father looked up at him, clearer-eyed now. 'Maybe I do,' he said. 'But don't you think a father has a right to be concerned about his daughter sometimes?'

Billy stared at his father, his anger subsiding now. 'Concern is one thing,' he replied. 'Constraint is another.'

The man from the Rank Organisation, Malcolm Dent, was very sleek, in a beige summer suit and a striped tie. Jim walked him around the Regal, Bert and Billy following at a respectful distance. Then they closed up and went to the Swan for lunch. At the corner table they sat studying menus and sipping water. Billy felt profoundly uncomfortable, but his father had insisted he join them.

'Baron Rank would like Wells,' said Dent. 'Old-fashioned values, that's what he believes in.'

'Perhaps Wells is just *too* old-fashioned,' said Jim. 'Perhaps we need some new ideas here.'

'Baron Rank is a traditionalist in his values, but has always been forward-thinking as a businessman.'

'So how did he create his empire, then?'

'By degrees. When he started, the scene was dominated by American films and distributors. But what he's most proud of is Pinewood, and the films that are made there.'

'*Brief Encounter*,' said Billy.

'Yes, *Great Expectations*, and many others.'

'And now you've taken over the Carry On films,' said Bert.

'Family-friendly films,' said Dent. 'Always family-friendly. And now perhaps you'd like to join the Rank family yourself?'

'Perhaps,' said Jim. 'This is just an exploratory conversation, you understand.'

'Naturally.'

Their first course arrived. Billy could sense his father willing Dent to order something other than water to drink, but no such word came from his lips.

'Economies of scale,' he said. 'That's what you're missing. You're paying through the nose for the films you're showing. If you were part of the Rank Organisation you'd save hugely on your costs.'

'But we'd just be a cog in a wheel,' said Jim.

'A vital cog in a very big wheel.'

After lunch, Bert and Billy returned to the cinema to open it up for the afternoon showing of *The Odd Couple*.

'What do you think?' said Billy.

'I think he's got no choice.'

'And what will that mean for you and Stan?'

'He's made a promise he would insist on us keeping our jobs. Whether he can deliver on it's another matter.'

'It wouldn't make sense to do anything else, would it? And Stan's close to retirement.'

'We'll see.'

Stan had arrived, and was fussing over the reels. There was a good audience for a weekday afternoon, about fifteen people. When his father came back, Billy followed him up the stairs to the office.

'So?' he said.

'So what?'

'Is he interested?'

'Of course he's interested. Now we have to do a little fandango for a while, that's all. They're not getting this place for nothing.'

'This is where I used to go to school,' said Billy.

He and Tom were sitting on the stone wall of a footbridge, below which flowed the bright water of a stream.

'It's a house, not a school,' said Tom.

'It used to be a school.'

Billy gazed at the little building, clad in the scarlet Virginia creeper he remembered from his first weeks there. What had then been the playground was now occupied by a small boat on a trailer. The sea was miles away, and he wondered when it was ever afloat.

'What did you learn there?' Tom asked.

'Oh, lots of things. About King Arthur and his knights for one.'

'King Arthur?'

'Yes. He's buried in the abbey at Glastonbury, or so they say.'

'I haven't been to Glastonbury for ages. Can we go now? Can we climb the tor?'

Billy smiled at his brother. He hadn't intended this to be a sentimental journey, but now that it was turning out that way he didn't mind at all. He had been two years older than Tom was now when they had come to the village of Coombe, and from the moment he had first set eyes on the tor he had known he was in a magical place. Would Tom sense that magic too? He couldn't remember the last time they had taken him to Glastonbury: he must have been very small.

They walked back to the car, and Billy drove down the narrow lane that led to the Glastonbury road. Memories of the harvest season ten years ago, of his early explorations, came back to him with extraordinary clarity. He had been a townie, and had had to learn the ways of the country. Now he was a townie again, and the landscape seemed to him once more charged with mystery and possibility.

They parked near the tor, and began the long climb up its western slope. There was a hazy light today, and it wasn't possible to make out many of the landmarks. They sat down on the grass and looked northwards towards Wells.

'Where is King Arthur?' said Tom.

Billy gestured behind them. 'In the grounds of the abbey,' he replied. 'We'll go there later.'

'So did you come here a lot?'

257

'No. Remember, I told you, Dad wouldn't let me. And we didn't have a car.'

'Didn't have a car?'

'Not everyone has a car, you know.'

'But we do.'

'Yes.'

Billy lay down and closed his eyes, thinking back to the windy spring day when he and his father had first come to the tor. The distance from Coombe had seemed too great to cross until then, but now it was utterly abolished, by the car, by the passage of time. It was hard to recall how much he had yearned to come here, and how long his father had refused his yearning. Was his wanting to go to the dunes nothing more than an act of revenge?

He sat up. 'I'll have to be leaving again soon,' he said.

'To ride the camels.'

'No, back to London, at least at first.'

'When will you go?'

Billy shaded his eyes, looking for the farmhouse where they once lived. 'I don't know,' he said. 'I have to help Dad for a bit longer.'

'After you've gone, I'll help him.'

'You'll have to wait until you're a little older. Then you can do what I used to, working on Saturdays.'

'I'd like that. I'd get to see all the films.'

'Not the grown-up ones, you wouldn't.'

'I'd sneak in.'

Billy smiled at his little brother. 'I expect you would,' he said.

Jim parked near Marble Arch, and they walked to the offices of the Rank Organisation. Malcolm Dent led them across the lobby and into a lift. His office was small and neat, and it was immediately clear that he was not in fact very senior.

'Mr Voysey will call us when he's ready,' he said.

They waited for fifteen minutes, Dent making small talk for a while and then falling silent, moving pieces of paper around on his desk. Eventually he led them into a much larger office, and a brisk man in a dark suit stepped around his desk and shook their hands.

'Do sit down,' he said. 'I trust Malcolm has been looking after you?'

'Yes, thank you.'

Billy looked across at his father, and sensed his discomfort. In the car he had been talking of how hard a bargain he had struck with them. But now he was clearly intimidated by the grandeur of his surroundings and the easy elegance of his new employers. Billy fiddled with his collar, wishing he could take off his tie. He hadn't worn one in years, and it was like having a noose around his neck.

Voysey crossed his legs and inspected a highly polished shoe.

'Welcome,' he said. 'Welcome in more ways than one. We have the papers here for you to sign. And once you've done so, you will be a member of the Rank family.'

Jim smiled weakly. 'I look forward to that,' he said.

'Good, good. And then we'll have your cinema brushed up in no time at all. They'll be flocking to it.'

'I'm sure they will.'

'Malcolm will be supervising the refurbishment. And reviewing your staff arrangements, of course.'

'We've discussed all that.'

'Yes, I know. And naturally we want to do our best by your people. We can't guarantee anything, however.'

'I've entered into this determined that I'll keep my team.'

'Quite right too.' Voysey stood and crossed to the desk, returning with a sheaf of papers. He placed them on the coffee table in front of Jim. 'Would you like a pen?' he said.

Jim produced a fountain pen from his pocket and inspected the contracts. After a minute or so he signed both copies. Voysey took one and left the other on the table.

'Congratulations!' he said. 'This deserves a drink. Malcolm?'

They raised their glasses of sweet sherry in a toast to the future of the Regal. After ten more minutes of pleasantries they were back out on the street, Jim clutching the pieces of paper that foretold his future.

'Right, drink,' he said. 'And not bloody sherry.'

They found a pub on the Edgware Road, and Jim ordered large whiskies.

'Thank God that's over,' he said as he sat down.

'That part of it's over, anyway.'

'Come on, Billy, knock it off.'

'Sorry.'

'You know what? I'm relieved. Now someone else can worry about balancing the books.'

'They'll balance. These people know all about that sort of thing. But what about your books? Are you going to be OK?'

Jim knocked back his whisky and set down the glass on the table. 'The purchase price pays off the bank, with a bit to spare,' he said. 'And we can manage on what they're going to pay me.'

'Good.'

'This isn't like last time. I've learned a thing or two since then.'

Billy looked thoughtfully at his father. Perhaps he *had* learned things since the bankruptcy after all. It was so easy to think of him as being feckless; maybe by now this was unfair. Jim took a chequebook from his pocket and wrote in it, handing a cheque to Billy. It was made out to him, and for a hundred pounds.

'What's this?'

'Arrears.'

'What do you mean?'

'I mean you've worked in the cinema for two months for beer money, and this is what I owe you.'

Billy had never seen such a sum. 'Thank you,' he said.

'Now go and spend it. Go to Morocco, if that's what you want.'

———

Margaret strode across the stage and embraced her husband. In this scene, which formed the emotional climax of the play, she was by turns tender, indignant and hurt. Thomas More would soon be ascending the scaffold, the most illustrious victim so far of Henry's whims. And before the rigged trial commenced, he was saying his farewells to his family. Billy watched from his place in the front row. By now he had become very involved, helping his mother with her lines at home and turning up towards the end of rehearsals. Tonight they walked from the theatre to the Swan, and sat with their coffees and brandies looking out towards the cathedral.

'She was a brave woman, Alice More,' said Billy.

'She was devoted to her husband, and she never wavered in that.'

'She's not the only woman devoted to her husband.'

Margaret looked down into the brandy glass, her face flushing. After a few moments of silence Billy said, 'What was Dad like when you first met him?'

She smiled. 'Cocky. He never had any doubt I would marry him.'

'And did you have any doubt?'

'No, of course not. There was a kind of madness in the air. The war was over, and if you were young you got hitched as soon as you could. It was only two months from when Jim and I first met that we were walking up the aisle.'

'And then the madness passed.'

'Yes.' She looked up at him. 'I know you think I've been indulgent,' she said, 'that I've let Jim get away with too much. But he's not a bad man, Billy.'

'What does that mean, not a bad man? How many people are bad, really? He's just weak.'

She took a sip of brandy. 'I did think of leaving him once,' she said, 'if I'm honest.'

'When was that?'

'The first time he strayed. I was carrying you.'

Billy thought back to the confrontation with his father, to the words about finding himself second in the queue. 'It wouldn't have been very easy, to leave then,' he said.

She looked up at him, her face darkening. 'It would have been impossible,' she said. 'It would have been ruinous.' She sighed, and composed herself once again. 'But enough of all this. Are you ready for Saturday?'

He looked at her steadily, wondering whether to press her further, and realizing that he mustn't. 'I've got my passport and my train ticket as far as Madrid,' he said. 'Then I'll improvise.'

'How long do you think you'll be gone?'

'Until my money runs out.'

'And then?'

'I'm not thinking about "then", Mum. I'm going to have an adventure at last.'

Six

Billy woke to the muezzin's plaintive call to prayer, drifting across the rooftops from the mosque. He opened the shutters of the tiny window onto the faint light of a Moroccan dawn. He had arrived at Marrakesh station in the dark, after an exhausting three-day journey, and this was his first sight of the city. He could see very little, though – a patch of sky, a wall, and a single cypress tree. He turned back into the room, surveying the mattress on the floor and the leather-covered chest that were its only furniture. He dressed hurriedly, stepped out onto the balcony, and looked down into the courtyard. In the daylight he could see how dilapidated the house was, tiles broken or missing, the fountain clogged with dirty water. The young man who had greeted him last night, Adil, called to him to go up to the terrace on the roof, where he would bring breakfast.

Billy found the staircase, and went up to the top of the house. From the terrace he could see all across the city. The minarets were the only tall buildings, the rest being an apparently continuous structure faced with baked red mud. Adil brought him bread and honey and sweet mint tea, and he sat down on a rickety chair to eat it. Once the voices from the mosques had subsided, all he could hear was the disputatious chatter of tiny birds.

'You are tired,' said Adil. His French was fluent, and Billy knew he would have to work hard to keep up with him.

'Yes. It's been a long journey.'

'You must rest today, not try to do too much. I have to walk to my home soon, through the souks, and will take you if you like. Then you must spend the rest of the day here.'

He was a young man, in his early twenties, Billy guessed, his manner courteous and grave. He wore a striped and hooded gown that went down to his sandals. His complexion was pale, his forehead high, his face long and thin.

The driver of the horse-drawn carriage Billy had taken from the station had brought him here, through a maze of dark alleyways, assuring him that he knew a place that was clean and cheap. Billy had made himself a promise not to resist blandishments or invitations of any kind. He would be a traveller, and would give himself up to whatever experiences might present themselves. But as it turned out he had made a good start. The Dar el Magdaz was indeed very cheap, and Adil very welcoming.

Billy walked over to the other side of the terrace, and behind an awning he saw a startling sight, a great wall of snow-covered mountains that rose up, as it seemed, out of the southern edge of the city. His very first glimpse of mountains had been of the Pyrenees, from the train to Madrid. But this was an altogether grander sight. It made Glastonbury Tor seem like a bump.

'The Atlas,' said Adil.

'But they're so close.'

'They seem closer than they are.'

'And beyond them, the Sahara, no?' How extraordinary, that he should now be so close to his ultimate goal.

A couple of hours later, Adil led Billy out into the alley and towards the souks. The narrow streets were teeming with people, all of them moving quickly, looking intent on their destinations. A donkey-cart appeared, and they had to stand back for a few moments to let it pass. It was piled high with sheepskins, which gave off a tremendous stench. A blind man stood at a corner, his hand held crookedly out, utterly immobile and silent. Now and then Billy lost track of Adil in the crowd, and had to hurry to catch up with him.

They entered a covered passageway, and Adil turned to him. 'This is where the souks begin,' he said. 'You must never worry about getting lost in here. It is important to get lost. Eventually you will see a familiar place, and be able to find your way out.'

They strolled along the main street of the souk, surrounded at first by textiles, then by carpets, then by jewellery. The aroma of spices filled the air. Billy felt almost overwhelmed by this riotous assault on his senses.

Above their heads was an iron trellis that almost entirely shaded them from the sun. There was one kiosk after another, all jammed into the tight space, all offering the same things. How did they ever sell enough to make a living, wondered Billy, given how many of them there were? The faces of the merchants seemed to come in two kinds, the pale ones, like Adil's, and the darker ones, the faces of the mountains and the desert. Then there was the occasional Negroid face, a reminder of Africa. They looked at Billy without curiosity, and none made any attempt to accost him, perhaps because he was with Adil, perhaps because he was clearly too young and too poor.

Something jarred Billy's back, and he turned to see four men carrying a stretcher at shoulder height. For a moment he wondered what it was, before realizing from the outline beneath the colourful rug that it was a body. The bier continued on its way, its bearers shoving people aside as they went.

They passed stalls selling slippers and leather goods, and came out into the sunlight.

'When you return,' said Adil, 'look up now and then, and go always south. Now, I will show you the loveliest place in Marrakesh.'

They crossed an open space, weaving past piles of rubble and rubbish, and came to the entrance of a building that, from the outside, was as plain as any Billy had seen. Walking down a long corridor, they came out into a courtyard. Along two sides ran columned arcades, and in the middle was a shallow pool. Every inch of the surface of the walls was decorated with carved wood, stucco or tiles, and it was exquisitely beautiful.

'This is the *mederssa*,' said Adil, 'the Koranic school. There are *mederssas* everywhere in Morocco, of course, but I believe this is the most beautiful.'

'This is where boys came to learn the Koran?'

'Yes. As many as eight hundred, all living in tiny cells on the upper floors.'

'Eight hundred?'

'Yes. They were only boys, after all.'

'And they studied the Koran all the time?'

'All the time, and only the Koran. No other books were permitted. There are still many places in the country where you will find boys receiving a Koranic education. We are a very traditional society even now.'

'What about you?'

'Me?' Adil smiled. 'I am studying engineering at the university.'

'Ah.' Billy felt suddenly very humble. From the moment he had met Adil the previous night he had known that he was intelligent and thoughtful. But now he understood that Adil's work at the hostel was rather like his own in the cinema.

They sat on chairs under an arcade, absorbing the atmosphere of the place. Tourists came and went, their cameras devouring the scene, and Billy gazed above their heads at the delicate tracery of the carvings. Someone had said that the French described Morocco as the 'nearest of the far lands'. For the first twenty years of his life, Billy had not left his own shores. Now he found himself in a place as exotic as any he could possibly imagine. The sun rose above the rooftop, drenching him with its warmth. He closed his eyes, scarcely able to contain his excitement.

He sat in the Café de France, writing in his notebook and occasionally taking a sip of cold coffee. He had found his place, somewhere he could sit for hours on end, watching the world go by. The main square, the Djemaa el Fna, stretched away into the distance, crisscrossed by people on foot, in carts, on bicycles, and the occasional moped. Here and there were snake charmers and magicians, but Billy knew that the real show in the Djemaa got started only in the evening. Now and then, beggars with sad, haunted faces would step up to him from the street, holding out their bowls, only to be shooed away by the waiters. The children were more persistent, extending their hands in supplication, saying 'eat, eat' repeatedly, their sadness turning to laughter in a moment.

The men sitting at the other tables took little notice of him, speaking to one another in low, guttural tones. They greeted one another in a highly ritualized way, kissing four times on the cheek, bowing slightly, their right hand placed on their stomach. Billy revelled in his invisibility, scribbling in his notebook and then gazing out across the square, his mind empty save for the impressions of the moment.

A young couple arrived, looking around and then settling on the next table. Billy knew they were American before they uttered a word. The girl was very blonde, with a square face and cool blue eyes, and the boy very dark. Billy had read about the hippy trail in Morocco, but these two were altogether too eager and fresh-faced to be dope-heads. They ordered tea and sat studying a guidebook, writing postcards, and counting their money. Billy did his best to ignore them, but after a while the girl turned to him and said, 'Sorry to disturb you, but my pen's run out. Can I borrow yours?'

Billy handed her the pen, and a few minutes later she gave it back.

'What are you writing?' she asked, her eyes resting on the notebook.

'Oh, nothing. A journal. Of sorts.'

'There's a lot here to write about.'

'Yes, there is.'

'Are you staying long?'

She was very direct in her manner, a kind of earnestness imbuing her every word and gesture. Billy could sense that he wasn't going to be able to shake her for a while.

'I've only just arrived,' he said. 'I'm not sure how long I'm going to stay.'

'My name's Erin,' said the girl. 'And this is Brad.'

'Hi,' said the boy. 'Glad to meet you.'

'Would you like to join us?'

Billy smiled. 'I'll lose my table,' he said. 'Let's just move them closer together.'

'You're British?' said Brad.

'Yes. And you're American.'

'I guess we stand out.'

'No, I didn't say that.' He paused for a moment. 'Have you been here long?'

'In Marrakesh, just a couple of days. But we've been travelling in Morocco for more than a week. Started in Casablanca, and then went on to Fez.'

'What's Fez like?'

'It seems kind of... I don't know, kind of older. There's more going on here.'

'And where are you going next?'

'Oh, back to Casablanca, before we go to Senegal.'

'What will you be doing there?'

'We've joined the Peace Corps,' said Erin, a hint of pride in her voice. 'We're going to help with rural development.'

'What does that involve?'

Before she replied, they picked up their things and moved the two feet to Billy's table.

'The main crop is groundnuts,' said Brad. 'But they don't know how to export them. We're going to be part of a programme that'll help them to do that.'

'Sounds exciting,' said Billy.

'It is.'

Erin reached out to the notebook and opened it at the first page.

'Erin!' said Brad. 'That's private.'

She smiled. 'The storks in their lavish nests,' she read. 'That's good. You're a writer.'

Billy gently extracted the book from her hands. 'No, I'm not,' he said. 'I'm a traveller.'

As he was placing the notebook on the ground beside him, the air was suddenly rent by the call of a muezzin, summoning the faithful to afternoon prayer. They watched as the men in the café paid their bills and walked across to the mosque. It quickly filled up, and many of them had to lay out prayer-mats in the square. They faced east, bowing repeatedly, their foreheads touching the ground, their hands wrung together.

'It's a shame we can't go into the mosques,' said Brad.

'It's a shame *women* can't go into the mosques, even their own,' replied Erin.

'Things are different here.'

'They sure are.' She turned to Billy. 'We've been thinking of eating at one of the food stalls in the square, but we haven't taken the plunge yet.'

'Nor have I.'

'We could go together one evening, maybe.'

'Sure,' said Billy. 'Let's do that. I'm invited to someone's house tonight, but perhaps tomorrow.'

'You're invited to someone's house?' said Erin. 'Neat! How did you manage that?'

'There's a student who's the sort of caretaker at the place I'm staying. His family live in the old city, and they've asked me to supper.'

'Great. Tell us about it tomorrow night. Shall we meet here around seven?'

———

'First we must go to the *hammam*, the baths,' said Adil. 'Westerners are not usually allowed into them, but you are with me.'

They were walking through the souks, past pyramids of spices and piles of figs and dates and oranges. It was early evening, and the narrow streets were crowded with people. Everyone seemed more interested in one another than in buying anything from the stalls. Billy found himself thinking back to Market Place in Wells, and more recently to Portobello Road. But these memories seemed to be in black and white, so pale were they in comparison to the colour and intensity of Marrakesh.

Beyond the souks they walked along alleyways in which children played hopscotch and kicked small bundles of twine. Eventually they came to a recessed doorway and entered into a dark space. Adil exchanged a few words with the porter, and Billy saw a note change hands. The porter looked at Billy and gestured to him to enter.

As his eyes became used to the light, he saw that he was in a sort of ante-room, in which men's gowns hung from hooks and slippers were placed neatly under a bench.

'Take off everything but your underpants,' said Adil, 'and then take two of those buckets and a bar of soap.'

They stepped through a wooden door into another room, Billy feeling both apprehensive and excited about what was going to happen. Tendrils of steam floated in the air. A man took his buckets and filled one with hot water and the other with tepid. Adil led him into a third room, and as he entered it, Billy was smothered by what felt like a blanket of humid heat. He could just make out the figures of men sitting against the walls, dozing or chatting.

'Sit here,' said Adil. 'Now we must sweat.'

They sat in silence for a long time, Billy gradually succumbing to an easy torpor. Men came and went, their brown bodies looming in the milky light. Billy looked down at his own whiteness, and then he noticed that his sweat was dark with dirt.

'You Westerners never really get clean,' said Adil, 'for all the baths you take. You must sweat it out, it's the only way.'

Billy washed himself with the soap and water, and then a masseur came up and took hold of his arm. Leading him into yet another room, he sat him down and began to knead his shoulders and arms. Now and then Billy heard a loud cracking noise, and pain shot through him. The masseur smiled enigmatically, turning him this way and that, manipulating his limbs firmly. There was a physical intimacy to all of this that made Billy feel very uncomfortable.

The man lay on the floor, his knees arched, and motioned to Billy to lie on his back on top of him. Billy wondered what he was expected to do, but then the masseur grabbed him and draped his body across his own. The small of his back was now resting on the fulcrum of the masseur's knees. For a few moments he was terrified, convinced his back would break. The masseur held onto his arms, and Billy swayed in the air, willing it to end. When it did, the masseur stood up, took a bucket of water in his hand, and splashed it over him. It was icy cold, and shocked him into a new alertness. Adil appeared and said, 'You are now as clean as an Arab.'

As they walked towards the house, Billy felt a sense of physical exhilaration he hadn't known in a long time, his skin caressed by the warm evening air. He was almost dizzy with pleasure.

Adil's house was small and bare, and it was immediately clear that his family were poor. Billy was greeted by his mother, who wore a veil, and his sister, who was probably about eighteen and who revealed her pretty face. Adil and Billy sat down on cushions beside a low table, and Adil began to pour tea, tasting it and then returning it to the copper pot. He did this several times before deciding it was properly brewed and handing Billy a small tumbler. Adil's mother and sister stood above them, watching silently.

'Where is your father?' Billy asked.

'My father is sadly dead. He died of cancer two years ago.'

'I'm sorry.'

'I am the head of the family now.'

With this he nodded at the women, and they turned towards the kitchen. Billy looked around the room. The walls were roughly plastered and stained here and there. There was no decoration except for the rug on the floor and the red cloth that covered the table. Adil's sister brought in what looked liked tall earthenware hats, and Adil took away their lids to reveal dishes of beef and chicken and couscous.

'You must eat with your hand, with your right hand,' said Adil. 'Wait until it cools a little.'

Billy looked up at the women, who stood near the door, and wondered whether they would be eating with them. 'Will your mother and sister join us?' he said.

'They will eat later.'

The beef was stewed with prunes and the chicken with lemon, and they were both delicious. Billy observed how Adil ate, and did his best to follow, but made a dreadful mess nonetheless. After the meat came sweets, slabs of fudge and honey pastries, and then the women brought ewers of water and towels. Adil lay back against the wall and said, 'What do think of Marrakesh?'

'It's fascinating. I've never been anywhere other than England before. I can't really believe I'm here.'

'I've been to France, but never to England.'

'Were you studying there?'

'No, I just wanted to see where our masters came from.'

'They're not your masters now.'

'Perhaps not. But their trace remains.'

'Colonialism is over for all of us, surely?'

'Colonialism is a state of mind,' said Adil, 'no matter who might be occupying the barracks.' He sipped his tea. 'The French left us some things. But it was robbery nonetheless.'

'The British were worse, I'm sorry to say.'

'They were more successful, that was the only difference. And more practical. The French had the idea they were civilizing us, bringing us the great gift of their culture. Still, they were not so cruel here as in Algeria.'

'So what now for Morocco?'

'What now? Modernization, of course. But we will never do more than scratch the surface. We are old here, very old.'

'I want to see something of the country,' said Billy. 'The mountains and the desert.'

'You will see how the Berbers live. We Arabs are colonizers too: this country is really theirs.'

'I've been reading about the Glaoui tribe. I want to go to their fortress.'

'It's abandoned now, and crumbling. But, yes, you must see it. Telouet, it's called. And then you can go to the desert.'

'I want to go as far as I can.'

'Then that is the edge of the desert, unless you are thinking of taking a camel train.'

———

He met Erin and Brad in the Café de France, and they sat drinking mint tea for a while before venturing into the Djemaa el Fna. At night the scene in the big square seemed almost apocalyptic, a confusion of noise, smoke, incense and light. Africans in white robes danced ecstatically to the sound of drums and castanets, the red tassels of their caps whirling in the air. The storytellers held their audiences spellbound, leaping from one spot to another within the tight circles of people, staring intently at them for greater effect. And the snake charmers played their lutes and cajoled rather than charmed the vipers and cobras into their lazy routines.

They strolled past the food stalls, gazing at the kebabs of meat and chicken and fish that lay ready for the brazier, and resisting the hustle of the touts. Eventually, and for no particular reason, they chose a stall and seated themselves on a bench. Tilley lamps hung above their heads, gathering smoke into their beams.

'The cheapest thing to have is a soup they call *harira*,' said Erin. 'It's kind of thick, with bits of lamb in it.'

'OK,' said Billy.

The waiter was clearly disappointed by the meagreness of their order, and pleaded with them to have some meat. Eventually he gave up, and tossed a basket of bread onto their table with an air of profound displeasure. Billy looked around him. The instruments of the various entertainers clashed with one another constantly, so that no single melody prevailed.

'Isn't this great?' said Brad.

'It's astonishing,' replied Billy.

'Just think, this must be what the place looked like a thousand years ago.'

Their soup arrived, and they picked up their spoons and began to eat. It was spicy and nourishing.

'So what have you seen so far?' Erin asked.

'Oh, not much in the way of the sights,' replied Billy. 'I've been soaking up the atmosphere.'

'You mean you haven't been to the Saadian Tombs, and places like that?'

'Not yet.'

'That's weird!'

'Do you think so?'

'Let's go there tomorrow. I want to see them again anyway. The Saadians were a dynasty of sultans, and their tombs were only rediscovered at the beginning of the century.'

271

'I know I ought to see these places…' said Billy.

'Let's do it, then.' Erin paused for a moment, laying down her spoon. Then she said, 'Hey, you know what? We're like Port and Kit and Tunner in *The Sheltering Sky*.'

'Oh, God!' said Brad. 'Does that mean I have to die horribly of fever?'

'And I have to have an affair with Billy.' She looked at him mischievously. 'Have you read it?' she asked.

'Yes,' he replied. 'Port dies, Kit goes crazy, and Tunner's left behind. And all because they wanted to see the desert.'

The air around them seemed newly charged, and not by the noise of the square. Billy was conscious that Erin looked at him now and then in a very candid sort of way. Had she meant anything by her remarks about the characters in the book? Suddenly he found himself weighing his words carefully.

'So where did you two meet?' he asked.

'At NYU,' replied Brad. 'We were both studying international relations.'

'And what do you plan on doing after the Peace Corps?'

'Oh, we're going to be in the State Department. We've already applied. And you?'

'I don't know. I'm not thinking beyond Morocco at the moment.'

'What did you do in England?'

'I dropped out of university and went to work in a bookshop in London.'

'You're going to turn that journal into a book, aren't you?' said Erin. 'You're going to be a famous travel writer.'

'Sure.' He smiled ironically. 'I'll send you a signed copy.'

Billy loved the city in the early morning, when the streets were watered and still gleamed in the sunlight, and the only other people up were the merchants and workers. He walked from the hostel to the Café de France, along the now-familiar alley. A man brushed past him carrying four chickens upside down. At first Billy thought they were dead, but then he realized they were alive but motionless, resigned to their fate. Cyclists weaved past him, tinkling their bells continually.

He sat at his favourite table in the café, ordered coffee and bread, and opened his journal. He had by now filled twenty pages with his impressions and thoughts. He had no idea whether he would ever attempt to put them into order, but for the moment he was content with these random jottings.

He saw a blonde woman heading across the square towards him, and laid down his notebook. Erin was alone.

'Where's Brad?' he asked.

'He's sick. He reckons it was the harira, but I'm OK, and so, it seems, are you.'

'I'm sorry.'

'He gets sick easy. I worry about how he's going to be in Senegal.'

She joined him for a coffee, and they walked to the tombs. The street took them through a district of artisans, and everywhere men scurried about, wearing blue overalls and skullcaps and looking intent on their business. In a little workshop two of them inspected a piece of ancient machinery, divining its secrets and then bringing it suddenly to life.

They arrived at the entrance to the tombs, and saw that a queue had already formed.

'I hate seeing places with gaggles of tourists,' said Billy. 'Let's come back later.'

'Where shall we go now?' asked Erin.

'Let's go to the Aguedal Gardens. They're just south of here. I've wanted to go there for a while. Apparently there are wonderful views of the Atlas.'

Walking past the palace, they stepped through a tall gate and were presented with what appeared to be an endless vista of trees and paths. They strolled through orchards of figs and lemons, the paths bordered by shallow channels in which green-tinted water eddied about. Ahead of them, shrouded in haze, lay the Atlas Mountains. After a while they sat down on a tiled patio.

'That's where I'm going next,' said Billy, pointing to the mountains.

'When?'

'Tomorrow.'

'How will you get there?'

'There are buses that take you so far. And then you hitch.'

'They say hitching in Morocco is dangerous.'

'Do they? I can't imagine why. People are so friendly.'

'How far will you go?'

He raised his hand to shield his eyes. 'To the desert, I hope,' he said.

'And what are you going to find in the desert?'

'I've no idea, but I feel drawn to it.'

'Sounds kind of spiritual.'

'Is it? I'm the least spiritual person I know.'

'But you're a dreamer.'

'Perhaps.'

They sat listening to the babble of water in the channel below them. After a while Billy said, 'So what do you dream about?'

She thought for a moment. 'About doing something useful, I guess,' she said. 'Something that helps the world.'

'Is the world ready to be helped?'

'Of course. What do you think we'll be doing in Senegal?'

'I'm sorry.'

'What hope is there if we in the West don't help those less fortunate than ourselves?'

'I just wonder...' He fell silent.

'You just wonder what?' Erin asked.

He looked down at his scuffed shoes. 'I suppose I wonder whether it's really our responsibility,' he said. 'I'm not doubting your good intentions. But wouldn't it be better if Africa could solve its own problems?'

'Well it can't. And, anyway, we created them in the first place, by stealing their people and their resources.'

'So you're giving something back now?'

'Yes,' said Erin firmly. 'That's exactly what I'm doing.'

They met again in the early evening, and Brad was still ill.

'At this rate we're going to have to change our plans,' said Erin. 'He can't go to Senegal like this.'

'That's too bad.'

She looked out across the square. 'Let's go to Yacout for dinner,' she said.

'What's Yacout?'

'It's a palace restaurant, a little north from here, I think.'

'Sounds expensive.'

'It's on me. My old man's just sent me some funds.'

274

'Are you sure?'

'Yes. Let's go.'

They hailed a carriage, which took them to a part of the city Billy hadn't yet explored. A young man led them up some steps and to a table in the corner of a pillared room, where they sat side by side on a low banquette. The walls were faced with brightly coloured tiles and carved cedarwood, tall teapots and vases standing against them.

'Neat, huh?' said Erin.

'I feel like a sultan.'

'I think you'd make a very good sultan. I'd like to see you in some flowing robes.'

'Like Lawrence of Arabia.'

'Yeah. Maybe you should get an outfit for when you go south.'

'I'd be taken for a Berber.'

'Wouldn't that be fun?'

'Not if I can't speak a word of the language.'

A waiter brought tea, and told them what they would be eating. There was a lot, one course following another in rapid succession. The centrepiece was a *pastilla*, a pigeon pie, which the waiter was very proud of, but which Billy found far too sweet for his taste. A group of musicians sat cross-legged in the middle of the room, making lovely, melancholy music with a lute, a single-string fiddle and a drum.

As they ate and talked, Erin now and then placed her hand on his arm to accentuate something she was saying. His mind returned to what she had said about Kit and Tunner in Bowles's book. Was she being flirtatious? It was hard to tell. And was he attracted to her? That was hard to tell too. But when a woman was being attentive like this, it was easy to respond in kind.

'You're a loner, Billy,' she said during a lull in the music.

'I suppose I am.'

'Don't you want to be with people?'

'I *am* with people. I'm with you.'

'You know what I mean. You're not *with* me.'

Billy sipped the strong, gritty coffee that had been set in front of them.

'I did ask someone to come here with me, but she said no.'

'Ah, so you're not a monk after all.'

'No.'

275

'Why didn't she say yes?'

'Because there was someone else.'

She was gazing at him now, resting languidly against the cushions. 'There often is,' she said.

'I wouldn't know. The truth is I don't know much about women.'

'Men don't.'

'Do women know more about men?'

'Oh, sure,' she said.

Billy knew that some sort of line had now been crossed. He put down his cup and said, 'Perhaps we should be getting back. Brad will be wondering where we've got to.'

'Oh, Brad,' she said. 'He's such a kid.' She toyed with her bracelet. 'I guess I'm going to marry him, though.'

They stepped back into the street, and he said, 'Let's walk. Let's just see where we end up.'

They walked along ill-lit alleyways, Erin linking her arm in his, and before long Billy recognized the way.

'This is my place,' he said after a while.

'Can I come in?'

'I don't know. I suppose so.'

'You don't sound too sure.'

Before he could answer, Erin raised herself on her toes and kissed him.

'I have one night before the rest of my life begins,' she said.

'So do I.'

'What shall we do with it?'

'I think we should sleep.'

'I guessed you'd say that.'

He wrapped his arms around her. 'I hope things go well in Senegal,' he said.

'They will.' She nuzzled her face against his neck. 'And I hope you find what you're looking for in the desert.'

At the door of the hostel he turned to watch Erin's figure dwindling into the darkness. He thought of Rachel for a moment. Perhaps he just wasn't ready yet for women. Erin turned to wave, and he waved back. No, he wasn't ready yet.

———

Billy gave his duffel bag and sleeping bag to the driver, who threw them on to the roof of the bus. Then he got in, hauling himself past the other passengers, all of whom stared at him with open curiosity, and into a window seat at the back. An hour or so after they were due to leave, the driver gunned the engine and they set off. Black smoke from the exhaust blew through the open window as they pulled out into the road. They followed the ramparts of the old city for a while, the driver sweeping past the bicycles and carts and mobylettes, and soon they were on their way south. For a long time the country was flat and the road straight, lined with trees painted white at their bases. Then they came to the foothills, and to terraces of cactus and walnut trees.

Billy sat with his knees braced hard against the seat in front, gazing out of the window at the changing scenery. Soon they began to ascend into the mountains, the landscape becoming harsher as they rose. As the bus negotiated the winding road, he had glimpses back into the valley from which they had come, and of the snow-capped peaks where they were going. In Marrakesh he had felt he could almost reach out and touch these noble mountains. Now they were just the other side of a pane of glass. He smiled at his reflection in the window. He was on the road, he was doing what he had wanted to do for so long. He was a traveller.

From the mountain pass the bus began to descend again, and then turned sharply to the left onto a dirt track. It rattled and shook, and Billy hung on to his seat. Eventually they came to the village of Telouet, where Billy and most of the other passengers disembarked.

There was a little café at the roadside, and he ate some couscous and drank gallons of water. He asked the waiter where the Glaoui fortress was. The man had only a few words of French, and he pointed vaguely east. Slinging his bag over his shoulder, Billy set off down the dusty road.

The fortress quickly came into view, a vast, brutish structure that dominated the valley. Billy arrived at its forecourt and looked up at the massive doors. There was no sign of life, so he knocked and waited. A few minutes later one of the doors was drawn back, and Billy was confronted by an African who seemed to be built on the same scale as the fortress.

'I'd like to look around, please,' he said.

The courtyard was full of piles of rubble, and had many doors leading off it. The African beckoned to Billy to follow him, and led him into a large reception room. The walls were lined with carved wood, of the kind Billy had seen in the *medersa* in Marrakesh, but like everything else in this place they were disintegrating. There were gaping holes through which Billy could see the countryside beyond.

'It was abandoned in nineteen fifty-six, when T'hami el Glaoui died,' said the African, 'and remains unfinished.'

They ascended some stairs to the roof, and from here Billy could see how the fortress had been constructed from stone as well as earth. But everything was crumbling. How quickly the great legacy of the Glaoui had been effaced.

'It is unsafe to go any further,' said the African. 'We must go back.'

A hawk flew above them, crying sharply.

'How do I get to Zagora from here?' Billy asked.

'You must go to Ouarzazate first. How far are you going?'

'To the dunes.'

'*Insha'Allah*,' he said gravely.

'*Insha'Allah*?'

'If God wills it.'

Billy looked up at the smooth, dark face of the African. There was a kind of serenity about him, the keeper of this ruined place.

'I hope He wills it,' he said.

The African bowed. '*Insha'Allah*,' he said again.

———

The owner of the café gave him a room for the night, and in the morning Billy caught a bus to Ouarzazate. Beyond the mountains the landscape changed again, rocky escarpments running alongside the road, their honey-yellow colour contrasting brilliantly with the blue of the sky. Ouarzazate was a dusty, shabby place, and he lost no time in getting on a bus to Zagora. By late afternoon he had crossed another high pass and was in the valley of the Draa River. Palm trees stretched into the distance, and at the roadside men and children stood holding out boxes of dates. This was Berber country now; the faces were nut-brown and weathered, the garments and headdresses gaudily coloured.

Like Ouarzazate, Zagora consisted of a single long street with houses on either side. Billy found a room, and in the evening went out for something to eat. He found a cheap café that was used by workmen, and sat beneath a faded portrait of the king, eating a meagre chicken tagine. He must be the only foreigner for miles around, he thought, and this made him feel oddly proud. His French was of little use by now, and he was more alone than ever. But this was a deeply satisfying sort of loneliness.

The nights were cool now and, having left his jacket in his duffel bag, he shivered as he walked back to the hostel. His room was a cell, with no electric light, and he read by candlelight for a while before turning in. He spent a restless night, images of the dunes coming always to his mind. He was so close now.

Not being sure of the buses from Zagora onwards, he walked to the end of the town and stuck out his thumb. Many who passed took this as a sign to honk their horns and cry out to him from their lorries and vans. A Peugeot estate car already containing five people pulled up, and the driver asked him in halting French where he was heading. Billy had read about these taxis that plied the roads, picking up and setting down people where they wished. He would have taken it if there had been anywhere to put his bags, but in the end he waved it on. Then after an hour or so a Bleriot lorry pulled up, and the driver said simply, 'Tagounite.'

Billy knew from the map that this was very near M'Hamid and the end of the made-up road, so he stowed his bags in the back of the lorry and opened the passenger door. With a grinding of gears they drove out of the town and towards the sun. The driver stroked his black beard and said in French, 'Tourist?'

'Traveller,' he replied, but it was clear that this distinction was lost.

The driver pointed at himself and said, 'Goats.' Billy turned to look through the rear window, and saw that the platform was covered in straw and littered with dung.

'Good,' he replied meaninglessly.

'Goats good.'

They drove on in silence, the road passing through a scrubby land-scape that was not quite desert, an escarpment ahead of them clearly forming the last barrier before the dunes. After a couple of hours a divide in the hills began to appear, and they gained height again so as to pass through it. Billy drew in his breath, and very soon beheld a country of sand. Just a few miles away was the edge of the desert.

'Dunes,' he said, pointing.

'You go there?'

He nodded. They drove on for a while, the outlines of the desert becoming clearer all the time. Then Billy saw a wooden sign off to the left, which read simply 'To the dunes'.

'Stop here, please,' he shouted.

The driver put his foot on the brakes, and they came to rest.

'Thank you.'

The man looked at him with a blank expression, stroking his beard again. 'Money,' he said.

'Money? But I was hitching.'

He raised his hands in the air, clearly not understanding the word 'hitching'. 'Money,' he repeated.

Bill reached into his pocket and pulled out a tattered note. The man took it, and gestured with his fingers to indicate that it wasn't enough. Billy gave him another note, and then opened the door and retrieved his bags. The driver engaged gear and drove off. As the lorry disappeared from Billy's sight, he looked up and down the road, which was by now empty and silent. The sign to the dunes beckoned him, and he began to walk along the hard sandy track in the direction it indicated.

It was midday, and fiercely hot. In Marrakesh the October air had been kind, but here for the first time he felt the power of the sun. Having no hat, he shaded his eyes and gazed towards the dunes. Now that he was on foot he could see that they were nothing like as close as he had supposed. He thought about turning back, but pressed on. He was nearly there.

He walked all day, and into the cool of the evening. With the sun behind him he could make out the lines of the dunes quite clearly now, and could sense that he was making progress. Eventually the deep blue of evening gave way to the black of night, and he lay down by the side of the track, exhausted. The stars pulsed in the sky, brighter than he had ever seen them. Except for the occasional howl of a dog, there was utter silence. Billy ran sand through his fingers, sand that by now was quite cold.

Now that he was so close, all the reasons for his coming here seemed to elude him. What was this crazy journey into nothingness all about? He recalled the things he had said to Tom and to Erin. How strange that such a strong determination had led him to this. What was it he wanted, really, from this barren place? What was it he lacked that the desert might supply? Tormented by doubts, he lay waiting for sleep to come.

He slept badly, the sand draining the warmth from his sleeping bag. Now and then he stood up and clapped himself with his arms, but when he lay down again the sand felt colder than snow. The night wore on, Billy dozing, turning on his side so as to keep his back as warm as he could. And then he was dreaming that his shoulder was being gently shaken. He opened his eyes, and in the starlight he saw three figures bending over him. He jumped to his feet, his heart pounding. One of the figures spoke quietly and soothingly, in a language he could tell was not Arabic, and which must be a Berber dialect. He smiled, and pointed into the distance. Billy resisted the urge to run away, and said in French, 'The dunes.'

The man repeated the word, clearly understanding it. He gestured to Billy to follow, and having no other idea in his head, Billy did so. They walked for about a mile, and then he saw a light. Soon they came upon a camp, three tents in a circle around a fire. One of the men called softly, and then there was an answering call. The man turned to Billy and made drinking and eating gestures. Now that he was no longer afraid, he realized he was weak with hunger.

They sat by the fire. A teapot hung from a wooden tripod, and a woman picked it up and poured mint tea into a cup, handing it to him. She went away and returned with bread and olives. Billy looked around him. In the firelight he could see that the tents were made of a dark sacking material, held up by wooden frames. The benches and the beds were covered with rugs and cushions, and pots and pans hung from struts above his head.

The woman was joined by another, and then by wide-eyed children. They watched Billy as he ate, encouraging him and smiling when he made a sign of satisfaction. He could now see the men's faces, and they were deeply lined, their eyes hooded and black. Billy made appreciative noises in French, knowing that the words would not be understood, but hoping that at least the sentiments might. He felt a strange mixture of exhaustion and exhilaration. That these people should have found him and taken him in like this seemed somehow miraculous.

After a while the man who had first shaken him awake took his hand and led him away from the tents. There was enough light now for

Billy to see a herd of camels tethered nearby. The man spoke a command to one of them and it sat down, its front legs seeming to collapse under it, its hind legs following. Billy swung himself over the leather saddle and grabbed the boss with one hand and the reins with the other. The camel rose, hind legs first, pitching him forward and then back, and now he was astride it, high in the air. It made a sobbing sound, and flared its nostrils as though trying to identify this new passenger.

The other men mounted their camels, and one of them took Billy's reins, leading him on. The loping stride was more comfortable than he had imagined, and he held the boss of the saddle in a relaxed grip. Ahead of him the line of the dunes was clear in the pale light. The camel train speeded up, and now Billy tightened his grip. When they reached the edge of the dunes the softer sand slowed the camels down, and Billy found himself able to concentrate wholly on the scene. The ridges and hollows undulated far into the distance.

The leader dismounted, and Billy's camel went through the awkward movements of sitting down. Billy leaped onto the sand and raced up the slope of the dune. One of the men shouted at him, and gestured towards the ridge. There the sand was firmer, and Billy made better progress towards the summit. When he reached it, he could see an interminable expanse ahead of him. He sat down, looking at the place where the sun was about to rise. When it did so it changed the scene instantly, creating shadows that no sooner had they formed began to ebb away. A light wind was blowing, and Billy watched as the line of the ridge gradually shifted, grain by grain.

The sun blinded him now, shining, as it seemed, only for him. The Berbers had remained below, and he was sublimely alone. He sat enthralled by the strange world now wakening. When the sun was up he stood and made to walk back down the ridge. Then suddenly he turned, and ran down the slope. His shoes filled with sand, and as they became heavier he lost his balance and tumbled forward. A cry of exultation broke from his lips. He picked himself up, smiled at the guides, and remounted his camel, turning towards the north. He had gone as far as he could go.

Westering

'But westward, look, the land is bright.'

Clough, 'Say Not the Struggle Naught Availeth'

One

Billy was wakened by the mastodon roar of the garbage truck, cutting its swathe through the West Village. Alice stirred beside him, placing her arm protectively over her head. He slipped out of bed and into the bathroom, standing for ages under the jet of the shower. Alice was still asleep by the time he had dressed, and he kissed her hair and quietly let himself out of the apartment.

It was a bitterly cold day, the kind Billy had barely imagined before he came to live here. This was a cold that sliced through him, that emptied his head of every thought save the warmth of the home he had just left and the coffee shop on Broadway he was heading for. The sign in the window advertised breakfast all day. Billy picked up his bagel and slid into a booth at the back, as far as possible from the draught. He and Alice used to eat breakfast together, but there seemed no time for that these days. They used to make love in the mornings too.

The offices of the magazine were in a building above the Strand Bookstore. As he waited for the elevator he looked idly at the name-plates of the other companies there: Puppetmaster Trading, Inc., Forgiven Ministries, The Robin Hood Foundation. Billy had once asked his editor what The Robin Hood Foundation might be. 'You're the Brit,' he had said. 'You tell me. But if it's robbing from the rich to give to the poor, it's sure in the right city.'

The place was dark and silent, and he switched on the lights and brewed the first of what would be the day's endless pots of coffee. The offices of *Narratives* magazine were about as functional as they could possibly be, a few desks and typewriters, a lot of papers and books. Heating ducts snaked around the big room, entwined here and there with electric wiring. The windows faced an air shaft, and let in very little light even on a summer's day. Billy sat down at his desk and polished his glasses with his handkerchief.

Four days ago had been press day, when final galleys were due to go off to the printers, and as usual they were behind schedule. Being late was an article of the editor's faith. In the past fifteen months they had published three issues, which would be unremarkable if not for the fact that the magazine was a quarterly.

Billy surveyed the piles of paper on his desk. Everything he was responsible for was ready to go except the story he had been wrapping up, which he would walk down to the printers at lunchtime. He raised his eyes to look at the editor's desk, which was strewn with pages of the John Gregory Dunne piece he had been working on. Billy stepped across the room and inspected the heavily marked galleys. Dan Blessing wasn't so much an editor as a re-write man. For him editing was a test of wills as much as anything else, a way to pit his strength against that of his contributor. Who would prevail? was the question he implicitly posed.

The Dunne piece was about the experience of adapting his novel *True Confessions* into a movie. Dan had wanted him to write about Hollywood as Fitzgerald or Faulkner would have done, as a kind of living hell in which only booze could see writers through. But Dunne lived in California, and was just as much a screenwriter as a novelist. He was also a man of decided opinions. It would be early afternoon before Dan could talk to him on the phone about his latest edit, and a long time after that before they were likely to have a final version.

Megan appeared in the doorway, and headed straight for the coffee pot.

'Feeling strong today?' she said.

'Sure. As soon as I've taken a dozen amphetamines I'll be ready for anything.'

She sat at her desk, resting her elbows on the empty surface. Megan looked after subscriptions and accounts, and times like this were always hard for her. She had no part to play except to give false assurances to the fulfilment house about the schedule, promising them that everything would be fine. For the bookstores and news-stands it didn't really matter how many issues came out in a year; but for subscribers who had paid twenty dollars it mattered a great deal. Megan started to chew her long dark hair. It's only ten o'clock, thought Billy, and Megan is already chewing her hair.

Blessing had no teaching assignments today, and had promised he would be in early. Billy got to work on the story, glancing at the clock now and then despite himself. At noon Blessing arrived, puffing loudly.

'Hi,' he said, dropping his satchels on the floor.

'Hi.'

Megan remained silent, apparently intent on the accounts books.

'How're we doing?'

'Fine. Are you done with the Dunne?'

'Almost.'

'And you finished the Glass piece yesterday, didn't you?'

'I wouldn't say I *finished* it...'

Dan Blessing was a stocky, grizzled man of forty or so, his beard shot through with white. He had founded *Narratives* magazine as a complement to teaching creative writing at New York University, and the early issues contained much apprentice work. Then he began to approach established writers, and before long he had a literary magazine to rival any. When Billy arrived in New York a couple of years ago he had introductions to several editors – George Plimpton at *The Paris Review*, Rust Hills at *Esquire* – but it was Blessing who had given him a job. As deputy editor he was one of the two full-time members of staff. An editorial assistant came in now and then, usually one of Blessing's students, and there was a contributing editor, Wendell Price. Price was wholly unpredictable, dropping by when he felt like it. Billy called him 'the Cowboy', for his boots and for the fact that he was always talking about writers from the west. There was no sign of him today.

Billy gathered up the manuscript and went back down to the street. The wind carried him along Broadway towards the printers the magazine used. Mostly their printers worked with local newspapers and businesses, and Billy had often wondered what they made of the stuff in *Narratives*. Dino, the guy who did most of their work, smiled and took the pages from him.

'Yesterday, right?' he said.

'The day before.'

'I'll see what I can do.'

'I need it by five, Dino.'

Two years in New York had sharpened up Billy's talk. He recalled going into a pizza parlour in his first days and saying, 'May I have a slice of pizza, please?' Over the course of the next few weeks he had come to understand that there were seven redundant words in that sentence, 'slice' being the only one he needed. The strange blend of courtesy and abrasiveness that characterized so many exchanges here had taken some getting used to.

When he returned to the office Blessing was on the phone, clearly speaking to Dunne. He was using his most ingratiating tone, the one he reserved for famous people.

'But the cadence is better,' he was saying.

Billy could hear only one side of the conversation, but it was clear that Dunne had his own ideas about cadence.

'OK, you're right.'

They went on like this for a while, until finally Blessing put down the phone. 'I'm going to need a few more hours on this,' he said.

'That means tomorrow before we can get the whole issue off to the printers.'

Blessing looked at Megan inquiringly.

'I'll see what I can do,' she said, shrugging her shoulders.

Billy knew what was coming next.

'Read it after me,' said Blessing. 'I may have missed a few things.'

By early evening he had the galleys back from the printers and was reading the Dunne piece. It was excellent, as he knew it would be, and needed nothing like the surgery Blessing had administered. They went through it once more, and then Billy headed to the Chinese takeout for some noodles. Megan had long since left, and he had called Alice to say he would be late. Maybe this wouldn't be an all-nighter, as he had earlier feared: maybe he would be home by midnight.

'Good work,' Blessing said eventually. 'I think we brought out the darkness in the story, don't you?'

Billy looked towards the window and the pitch black of the air shaft. 'We certainly did,' he said.

———

Alice sat on the sofa and wrapped the robe tightly around herself. She picked up the remote control and turned on the television, switching quickly from one channel to the next. There was one inanity after another – game shows, reruns of old sitcoms, talk shows in which people voiced their grievances and their prejudices, and always the ads, blaring at what seemed twice the volume of the programmes themselves. She turned it off again and gazed out of the window. It was very cold outside, she could tell, but she hated being trapped in the apartment like this. She found a copy of the *Voice* and looked at the listings. There was a film called *Mephisto* at Cinema Village, and she had heard good things about it. Slowly she dressed, putting on layer after layer, and went out into the street.

Walking past the brownstone houses, with their wrought-iron railings and window boxes, she thought how extraordinarily fortunate she had been to land this rent-controlled apartment when she first came to New York: if she hadn't, they would be living in outer Queens. Her father had arranged it through a friend of his. And now that they safely occupied it, all they had to do was live there the rest of their lives. Either that or get work that paid decently.

She had once said of her work as a set designer that it was 'on-and-off, except that sometimes it's off-and-off'. Certainly it was off Broadway, in the theatres of SoHo and the Village. The Schuberts and the unions had a lock on Broadway, and there was no way she could get work uptown. She hadn't had a job for over a month now, and time hung heavily on her hands.

The film was powerful and unsettling. Klaus Brandauer played an actor in Berlin in the thirties who is co-opted and eventually corrupted by the Nazis. The general to whom he is beholden seemed to use the word 'actor' as a term of contempt. She found her thoughts drifting back to her own acting career, at Yale and in repertory. She had been quite sure she was destined to be an actor, quite sure she would be onstage herself rather than behind it. Then came audition after audition, and rejection after rejection, in New York and San Francisco and Chicago. When was the moment she realized she wasn't strong enough for it? Was it when Mamet turned her down for the Atlantic company? Well, it didn't matter now.

She called Paul from a phone in the lobby of the cinema and asked if he were free for a drink. They agreed to meet in the Minetta Tavern, and she arrived fifteen minutes before he did. She sat looking out onto the street, at the nail bar, the smoke shop, the body art salon. She wished she had lived here in the sixties, when the Provincetown Playhouse was still open and Bob Dylan was singing at the Bitter End. New York was a hard and unforgiving place nowadays, a place in which everyone seemed to be out for themselves.

Paul Czernowski arrived, unwrapping a long red scarf from around his neck.

'God, it's cold,' he said. 'I wasn't made for this.'

'What were you made for?'

'Much more and I'm moving to Key West.'

'Not a lot of theatre down there.'

'Don't worry about me, sweetheart – I'll be a gigolo.'

They ordered a bottle of red wine. Paul smiled his pretty smile, and they clinked glasses. No longer young, he kept himself in good shape. He was small and wiry, his neat moustache turning to grey, his crew-cut hair still jet black.

'I bring good news,' he said.

'Yes?'

'We're heading back to the Public. A new production of *Long Day's Journey*.'

'That's great. When do we start?'

'Next week.'

'Who's the director?'

'Geraldine Fitzgerald.'

'She's good.'

'And tough, so I hear.'

'Well, we're good too.'

Paul sipped his wine. 'So what have you been up to?' he said.

Alice sighed. 'Nothing much. Being out of work doesn't get any easier.'

'How's Billy?'

'Oh, fine. Working all hours. We never seem to get it right, some-how. When he's working late I'm often at home, unless it's the other way around.'

Paul looked across the room. What would I do without him? she thought. Most of her recent commissions had come through Paul. They worked well together. But she shouldn't rely on him in the way she had come to.

'I'd better re-read the play,' she said.

'I thought you knew it off by heart.'

'Once. A long time ago.'

'Here's to a long day's journey, then,' he said. 'Here's to many long days' journeys.'

———

They usually slept late on Saturday mornings and went to the Lion's Head for brunch. Now that the latest issue of the magazine was finally done, Billy could relax a little. Sitting at a table near the window, he stretched luxuriantly.

'Tom called,' he said. 'He's coming to New York and wants to stay.'

'Stay?' said Alice. 'You mean with us?'

'Yes. He can sleep on the sofa for a while, surely?'

'Billy, the apartment's not big enough for you and me, let alone him too.'

She was toying with the menu, her thin, nervous fingers caressing it lightly. Her auburn hair was up this morning, the way Billy liked it, revealing the lovely line of her neck.

'A few days, then, before I find him a cheap place somewhere nearby.'

'I guess so.'

They ordered eggs and bacon and sat drinking their coffee.

'So what's he coming for?' said Alice after a while.

'To take pictures. He wants to start a New York portfolio.'

'Alfred Stieglitz watch out.'

'Come on, Alice. He's talented. You've seen some of the photographs he took in Thailand.'

'Sure he's talented. He just needs to channel his talents, that's all.'

'He's twenty-one. He's a kid.'

Billy had never quite understood why Alice was so wary of his little brother. They needed to get to know each other better, and maybe Tom's visit would help this along. But Alice had been cranky about everything lately.

'How's it going with *Long Day's Journey?*' he asked.

'We've got to finish the model by next week so as to show it to the director.'

Their eggs arrived, and a plate of toast.

'I hope there are no toasters in it,' he said.

She smiled. 'No. Just a lot of glasses.'

'Well, if you need help getting hold of them, let me know.'

'The Public has plenty of glasses.'

Back in the autumn Alice had worked on a production of *True West*. As was often the case, she did the props as well as the sets. One of the characters steals a lot of toasters, and there's a scene in which he decides to make toast in all of them. Billy and Alice had spent a morning scouring the city for old toasters, and after a while the enterprise

293

had come to seem as absurd as the scene itself. Both of them knew even then that the adventure of the toasters would enter into the mythology of their marriage.

Alice waved at the waitress and asked for more coffee. 'Mom and Dad want us to go up for a weekend sometime soon,' she said.

'They do? Christmas seems like only yesterday.'

She reached across the table and placed her hand on his. 'I'll be nice to your family so long as you're nice to mine.'

'Sorry.'

When they had finished brunch they stepped out onto the street. A white sun hung low above the rooftops.

'Shall we take a walk?' said Billy.

'It's too cold,' replied Alice, linking her arm in his and leaning into him. 'Let's get some food in. I feel like making a fancy dinner tonight.'

They walked to Balducci's. The produce in the store lay in glistening rows of green and red and yellow and black. This was a temple of food, a year-round Thanksgiving. If there was anywhere that spoke to Billy of the abundance of his adopted country it was this place in which food was not simply set out but somehow enshrined. They bought aubergines and mozzarella cheese and freshly made tomato sauce.

'Eggplant parmigian,' said Alice.

'Suits me.' He kissed her on the cheek, and thought not for the first time how good America was to him.

On his way to the offices of Farrar, Straus & Giroux he crossed Union Square, weaving his way among the bums and the drug addicts. This was practically a no-go area, and in the heart of the city at that. New York was a place of stark contrasts, of wealth and poverty, of beauty and squalor. A man wearing a filthy, tattered bandage on his hand was ranting to another, who sat staring glassy-eyed into the distance. 'She was cryin' but she wanted to kill me,' he was saying. 'Why was she cryin'? Maybe she was sad at the thought of me dead. Which is what she wanted.' He spat, and wiped his mouth with the bandage. 'Fucken dames.'

Matt Goldschmidt, the editor he was having lunch with, met him in the lobby, and they walked to a restaurant a couple of blocks away. Billy had heard that Goldschmidt was doing interesting things, and wanted to get to know him. It was an important part of Billy's job to learn from editors and agents what books were coming up, so as to consider whether to buy extracts for the magazine.

They ordered Bloody Marys and cob salads. Billy looked around the room, pausing for a moment to consider how much of his life he seemed to spend in cafés and restaurants nowadays. He glanced back at his guest. Goldschmidt was skinny and dark, and wore spectacles so large they were like a visor. There was a contained intensity about him that set Billy on edge.

'How long have you been at *Narratives*?' he said.

'Two years.'

'And before that?'

'I worked in bookstores in London, and then for a little magazine called *The Bystander*. You wouldn't have heard of it – it was aptly named.'

'And what brought you here?'

'My wife is American. We met in London, when she was studying set design. She had to come back, and eventually I followed.'

Goldschmidt twirled a plastic straw in his fingers. 'And how's life on *Narratives*?' he said.

'Blessing is hard to take sometimes, but we're doing some good things.'

'The last issue was strong.'

'Dan has a knack, there's no doubt about it. And for me it's great experience. I feel I'm in the middle of things.'

'So what can I tell you about?'

Their salads arrived, and the waitress refilled their water glasses.

'Well, what's coming up. I mean next year. We like to run extracts at least a few months ahead of publication of the books.'

Goldschmidt turned his attention to the salad, picking at it and setting the cheese to one side. 'We don't exactly have many new voices at the moment,' he said. 'How about some Coretta Smith?'

'Blessing doesn't do poets.'

'But these are essays.'

'OK. But Blessing doesn't really do *women*. Well, he does a few, but they tend to write like men in drag.'

Goldschmidt didn't smile, and Billy decided he'd said the wrong thing.

'How about Mario Vargas Llosa?'

'I haven't read him.'

'He has a new novel coming called *Aunt Julia and the Scriptwriter*.'

'Sounds intriguing.'

'He's brilliant. He's in the next wave of Latin American writing after Márquez.'

'Will you send me a galley?'

'Sure.'

They ate their salads, Goldschmidt leaving most of his on the plate, and ordered coffee.

'So, are you going to stay here?' he said after a while.

'In New York?'

'Yeah. In the US of A.'

'That's the plan. I like it here. Britain is pretty dull by comparison.'

'Is it? I've never been.'

'There's more going on here. There's an electricity in the air.'

Goldschmidt looked out of the window at the bustle of the street. 'We're wired in this city,' he said. 'We're wired and we're weird.'

———

Alice stood back from the model and looked at Paul and the director.

'What do you think, Geraldine?' said Paul.

The director peered at the scale model of the Tyrones' summer house.

'I like it,' she said. 'You've solved the problems of the thrust stage pretty well.'

'It's not ideal for interiors, but I think this works,' said Alice.

'What about the books?' asked Paul.

O'Neill had been very particular in his stage directions about the books – James Tyrone was a reader of everything from Shakespeare to Schopenhauer. But the production had an all-black cast, and Alice wasn't sure how to handle this. Did it have an all-black cast so as give work to black actors, or to bring out some hidden aspect of the play?

'We want all the books O'Neill specified,' said the director.

She left them, and Alice and Paul went for a coffee in the foyer. The Public Theater was a huge place, a Renaissance palace containing five stages. Paul handed her a cappuccino and sat down heavily.

'Thank God for that,' he said. 'Now we can get going.'

'She seemed sweetly reasonable to me.'

296

'I don't know why I got so worked up about it. I figured that since her *Mass Appeal* has been such a hit, she'd be a bitch.'

'You think all women directors are bitches.'

'There aren't exactly many of them.'

'Not nearly enough.'

Alice wrapped her hands around her cup. It was always chilly in this place in the winter, and the only time she ever warmed up was when she was painting scenes. She looked at her watch. It was past ten in the evening, and she must call Billy and let him know she was on her way. She felt terribly weary. It had taken all day to put the finishing touches to the model, and then the director had said she couldn't meet until after dinner. She went back to the office to collect her coat. Billy answered the phone after the first ring. 'I'll fix some pasta,' he said.

She stepped out onto Lafayette, tightening the scarf around her neck and burying her hands deep in her pockets. The streets were empty on this frigid night, and she walked quickly in the direction of home, her head down, her eyes unseeing. When she entered the apartment Billy handed her a glass of wine.

'How did it go?' he said.

'She liked it.'

'Great.'

'Remember what I said about glasses?'

'Yes?'

'Well, it's books too.' She drew the script out of her bag. 'Balzac, Zola, Stendhal, Nietzsche, Marx, Engels... the list is endless. You're going to have to help me out, Billy.'

'The Strand will have them.'

'No, these have to have fine bindings.'

'They have those too.'

She lay down on the sofa, kicking off her shoes. Billy put some water on to boil and cracked open an egg. Alice wasn't sure whether she was hungry, but Billy seemed determined to play the chef.

'How was your day?' she said.

'Fine. I had lunch with that editor at FSG I was telling you about.'

'What's he like?'

'He's an intellectual. They have them at FSG.'

'And they don't have them at other houses?'

Alice had been urging Billy for a while to get into book publishing.

She couldn't see any future for him at *Narratives*, and Blessing paid him a pittance. But Billy was curiously resistant to the idea, and sentimental, it seemed to her, about the magazine.

He ladled out the spaghetti carbonara and grated some cheese over it. Alice dragged herself to the table, and sat twisting her fork in the pasta.

'You should take some other editors to lunch,' she said.

Billy looked at her sharply. 'Alice, I'm not looking for a job.'

She shrugged, and laid down her fork. 'OK,' she said.

'It's like a slice of fruit cake,' said Tom, training his camera on the Flatiron Building. He dashed across the street and into the park for a different perspective, one camera in his hands and another slung over his shoulder. Who was it, thought Billy, that used to run around Paris, always on the move for the best shot?

They continued up Fifth Avenue, Billy pointing out the sights as they went along. Tom was clearly entranced by New York. It was a glittering winter's day, and the geometry of the city seemed sharper than ever. Billy thought back to his own first day here, holding Alice's hand and wondering whether this was somewhere he could actually live. Two years later, and at times like this, New York still had the power to thrill him.

They walked on towards the Plaza Hotel. 'Let's have a drink,' said Billy.

The place was quiet at this early hour, and they sat in wing armchairs in a dark corner. Billy ordered manhattans.

'We should be drinking mint juleps, but that's a summer drink.'

'Why mint juleps?'

'Because that's what Gatsby and Daisy drank here.'

'You're always bringing things back to books,' said Tom.

'OK then, this is the bar where Cary Grant gets lifted in *North by Northwest*.'

'That I do remember.'

Billy studied his brother as they spoke. Maybe it was the light in here, but he seemed gaunt. He hadn't seen Tom since he left London, and he had changed. He'd always been lean, but now he seemed shadowy somehow. There was a lot Billy wanted to know about him, but he'd been delayed so late last night that they'd barely had a chance to talk.

'So, what are you going to get up to here?' he said.

Tom swept his long black hair away from his forehead and nodded towards his cameras. 'I'm going to take pictures,' he said. 'Hundreds of them.'

'Buildings? People?'

'Anything that takes my fancy.'

'And what will you do with them?'

'You're sounding like Dad already. I'll sell them, of course. I've got plenty of contacts. My old tutor at St Martin's says he's going to help me out.'

'So no job then, as such.'

'This is a job, Billy. You're one to talk.'

They raised their glasses, and Billy said, 'To New York, then. To its bright surfaces and dark mysteries.'

Tom looked at him thoughtfully. 'You seem right at home here,' he said.

'Do I? I suppose so. Sometimes I think I'll never quite fit in.'

'Will you ever go back?'

'I'm not thinking about that at the moment. And I'm not sure Alice would want to.'

'You'll become an American.'

'No, never.' Billy watched as a white-haired couple stepped haltingly into the room. 'I'll always be English,' he said. He put down his glass. 'And how are things in England?'

'How are things?'

'How are things at home?'

Tom took a long slug of his drink. 'Sarah's wedding is all anyone's talking about,' he said. 'You are coming, aren't you?'

'Sure. Alice can't, but I'll be there. Let's hope she sticks this one out.'

'He's as dull as ditchwater.'

'Very different from Lee, I expect.'

'I was only a kid when she was with Lee. But yes, very different, I'm sure.'

'She needs to settle down. She is thirty now.'

'Is that some kind of frontier, thirty?'

Billy considered for a moment. 'For me it was,' he said. 'I was just fooling around in my twenties.'

Tom drained his glass, and Billy noticed how quickly he had done so. 'Well, I'm barely into my twenties,' he said, 'and I intend to do a lot of fooling around. What do you do for kicks in this town?'

Billy smiled. 'Oh, we occasionally go to the movies.'

'Great,' said Tom. 'I'll be seeing you.'

———

Wendell Price breezed into the office one day and suggested to Billy they have a drink. Heading for the Irish pub that Wendell favoured, they made their way along Fourteenth Street. It was a few days before the clocks were due to go forward, but winter still held the city tight in its grip. Flaherty's was a spit-and-sawdust bar, the kind e. e. cummings had described as 'snug and evil'. The other drinkers had the look of having been entrenched for some time. They ordered beers and whisky chasers. Wendell sat on one chair and put his feet up on another, his boots glinting in the lamplight.

'Read Carver's latest?' he said.

'I've got a galley, but no, not yet.'

'More low-rent tragedies. But fucking brilliant. There's a story about a guy who puts all his furniture out on the front lawn. His wife has left him, or something, you never find out. Then a young couple drop by, thinking it's a yard sale, and they end up dancing.'

'He's good at leaving things out.'

'The mark of a writer.'

Wendell knocked back his whisky and belched. His stringy blond hair hung down below his collar, and he was wearing a red bandanna. At first Billy had been suspicious of this Wild West routine, but as he'd got to know him he realized it was genuine. Wendell had grown up on a farm in Montana: he was the real thing.

'We're getting copies of the latest issue from the printers tomorrow,' said Billy.

'Great.'

'There's nothing in it from you, by the way.'

Wendell raised his hands in a gesture of surrender. 'I'm just your scout,' he said.

'Done any scouting lately?'

Wendell took his feet down from the chair and looked around the room. 'There's a guy called Harry Aitken,' he said. 'Has a collection of stories coming in the fall called *Solitudes*.'

'Too late, you know that. We need to hear about things a year ahead.'

'OK.' He wiped his mouth with the back of his hand. 'What have you come up with? Any teabag writers?'

'Teabag?'

'Brits.'

Billy laughed. 'You know how limited Dan's interest is in British writers,' he said.

Wendell gave him a sidelong look. 'So are we doing OK?' he asked. 'The magazine, I mean. Are we solvent?'

'Just about. But take away the NEA grant and we'd be sunk.'

'We're a cultural institution.'

'I'm surprised you can even get your tongue around those words, let alone believe them.'

'What are we, then?'

'We're a little magazine, like dozens of others.'

Wendell leaned towards Billy confidentially. 'I hear Blessing's up for a job at Iowa,' he said.

'Are you serious? He'd never leave New York.'

'Oh no? His kids are getting to school age.'

'But Iowa?'

'It is the leading creative writing school in the country, after all.'

Billy looked down into his beer glass. 'What would that mean for the magazine?' he said.

Wendell drew his finger across his throat.

'You'd better be wrong about that,' said Billy. He was taken aback by the low vehemence of his words.

'I just heard it, that's all.'

'You'd better be wrong.'

———————

Alice took the elevator to the top floor of Lord & Taylor and stepped into the canteen. Ellen waved from across the room, and she headed towards her.

'Hi!' said Ellen brightly. She stood to give Alice a hug, and then ran her eye up and down her appraisingly. 'You look tired.'

They sat down. 'I'm in the middle of a job at the Public. *Long Day's Journey into Night.* It's exhausting.'

'Let's have a drink. I have *so* much to tell you.'

Ellen Tardelli took her sunglasses away from the top of her head and ran her hand through her dark hair. Replacing the glasses, she looked at Alice with a gleam in her eye. When did she ever *not* have lots to tell? thought Alice. Her best friend since Yale, Ellen was a constant source of gossip and good humour.

They ordered white wine spritzers and glanced at the menu. 'So?' said Alice. 'What's new?'

'You know I just went to Milan.'

'Yes. How was it?'

'Oh, the usual. The fall collections are pretty dull if you ask me. But...'

'But?'

Ellen smiled coquettishly. 'We did it!' she said.

Alice kneaded her eyes with her fingertips. 'You and who did what?' she said.

'Me and Mike.'

'Oh, Ellen! Sleeping with your boss?'

'It's been heading that way for a while.'

'Yes, and I thought you were supposed to be trying to head it off.'

'Why, for God's sakes? He's a dish.'

'You don't need me to tell you why. You just never sleep with the boss, that's all.'

'It's not like I'm doing it to get ahead or anything. I just fancy the guy. And he's single.'

'OK, I'm not saying you're a whore. It's just impractical. Before you know it you'll be fighting, and what will that mean for things here at work?'

'Don't be such a killjoy. Sure it won't last. But, hell, the trip was great!'

Alice gazed at her friend reflectively. Why was she being so strait-laced about this? Ellen was a good-time girl, she had always known this. How often in the past had her high spirits dragged Alice out of some trough of despair?

'Good luck, then,' she said. 'Have fun while it lasts.'

'I will.'

They ordered, and when the waitress was gone Ellen said, 'And how is it with you and Billy?'

'Fine. He's working all hours, and we hardly ever see each other. But fine.'

'Fine *because* you never see each other, or fine in spite of it?'

Alice took a sip of her drink and paused to gaze around the room. The canteen was crowded with shoppers, all of them women. 'Fine in spite of it,' she said. She looked levelly at Ellen, as if to say that this was her last word on the subject. 'His younger brother is staying with us.'

'And how's that?'

'It's OK for a few days, I guess. Except I don't think a few days is what he has in mind.'

'What's he here for?'

'To take pictures. He's a budding photographer.'

'Sounds good.'

'Oh, he's all right. I'd only met him a couple of times before. He seems a little out of it to me, though. Spent too much time on the hippy trail.'

'It's funny, the way you married a Brit.'

'Funny?'

'I mean it's not as though you've been a lifelong Anglophile.'

'I'm not sure I *am* an Anglophile. I just spent a few months in London and fell in love with an Englishman.'

'In my book that makes you an Anglophile.'

Billy woke up early and went to the kitchen for some orange juice. Tom was sprawled fully clothed on the sofa, and the tiny living room was once again pervaded by the fetid odour it had taken on since he came to stay. Billy took a shower, and by the time he returned to the bedroom Alice was awake.

'What time did he come home?' she said.

'I've no idea.'

'What's he been doing, Billy? He sleeps practically all day.'

He sat down on the bed. 'He's young and in New York,' he said. 'Let's not worry about him.'

'He looks like a street person.'

Billy sighed deeply. 'He looks like a student, which is what he was until a few months ago.'

Alice raised herself on one elbow and took the glass from Billy's hand. 'He needs to find somewhere else to go,' she said. 'It's been over a week, and he's getting on my nerves.'

'OK. I'll tell him.'

When they were dressed Billy suggested to Tom they walk to SoHo. The cobbled streets and cast-iron buildings immediately caught Tom's attention, and he was once again busy with his cameras. Billy was struck by his continual restlessness, his hands always in motion, his eyes always scanning the scene.

'I love the patterns the fire escapes make,' he said. 'Maybe I'll call my New York collection "Zig-Zags".'

They went into a coffee shop to warm up.

'SoHo's amazing,' said Tom. 'Why didn't you tell me about it before?'

'I suppose I don't come down here very often. It was pretty much a wasteland until a few years ago, when the artists and galleries started moving in.'

'It's great. I'm going to spend all day here.'

Billy ordered coffee, and then turned back to face his brother.

'Tom,' he said, 'you need to find somewhere else to stay. The apartment's too small for all three of us, and Alice is getting tired of clearing up after you.'

His brother looked at him sheepishly. 'I'm sorry if I'm in the way,' he said.

'I'll check out a couple of places on my way home.'

Billy spent the rest of the day reading, and in the late afternoon he and Alice went to see *Reds*. Warren Beatty had made a three-hour homage to John Reed, the writer who had reported from the Russian Revolution, and Jack Nicholson was playing Eugene O'Neill. The film was overblown, but it put them in a romantic mood over supper. Alice took out a Leonard Cohen record, and they curled up on the sofa. Billy leaned down to kiss her, and the kiss didn't seem to come to an end. She began undoing the buttons of his shirt, and suddenly he was aroused. They took off each other's clothes, and lay naked on the rug.

'What if Tom comes back?' he said.

'He won't, not yet. And I don't care if he does.'

They hadn't made love anywhere but the bed for ages, and Billy felt the sort of excitement he remembered from their early days. Alice's body was slender, her hips a little bony and her breasts flat. But from the day he had first set eyes on her Billy had loved her willowy beauty. When it was over he held her tight in his arms for a long time.

'I'm getting chilly,' she said at last, kissing his ear. 'Let's put on our robes and listen to the Cohen again.'

They went to bed early, and soon fell asleep. It seemed only minutes before Billy heard the sound of the key in the door, but it must have been a few hours. Tom was groaning loudly, and Billy got up and stepped into the living room.

He was in a dreadful state, his face bruised and bloody and his clothes torn.

'What the hell happened?' said Billy.

'I got beaten up.'

'Where?'

'Oh, over in the East Village somewhere.'

Alice appeared, and went to inspect Tom's face.

'Sit down,' she said, 'and I'll fix you up. Billy, you must take him to the hospital.'

Billy was appalled by the sight of his brother. 'Who did it?' he said.

'Just some guys, Puerto Rican or something.'

Alice boiled some water and dipped a facecloth into it.

'Where exactly in the East Village?' she asked.

'I don't know. Somewhere near Tompkins Square.'

She wiped his face, and then stood up and turned to Billy. 'Your brother is using drugs,' she said. 'I'm surprised you haven't figured it out for yourself.'

Billy looked from Alice to Tom. 'Well?'

'Hey, it's just charley. It's not crack or heroin or anything.'

'You've been buying cocaine in Tompkins Square?'

Tom shrugged. 'I can take care of myself.'

'Well, clearly you can't. How long have you been taking cocaine?'

'Knock it off, Billy. It doesn't do any harm.'

Billy studied his brother closely, and noticed once again the hollowness in his cheeks. 'Let's get you to the hospital,' he said.

They bought their tickets and crossed the concourse to the gate. Alice looked up from the marble floor of Grand Central to the zodiac constellation of the ceiling. Ever since she was a child this vaulted space had awed her, this gateway to the city. And whenever she passed through it nowadays, it was always on a journey back to that childhood. Her parents had lived in Greenwich since she was born, and now she and Billy made the pilgrimage home every few weeks or so. This tremendous building spoke to her of order and familiarity.

It was Friday evening, and the commuters were flocking to the trains. They were lucky to get seats, and once settled they averted their eyes from the sullen faces of those standing in the aisles. At Greenwich station Alice's father picked them up. The air inside the Lincoln was stuffy, Hal clearly having left the engine running while he waited. There was still a brushstroke of daylight, and Alice could see that daffodils and crocuses lined the roadside. They chattered above the swish of the tyres as they made their way towards the house.

Barbara was standing in the porch as they turned into the drive. Alice threw her bag over her shoulder and hugged her mother.

'It's been such a long time,' said Barbara.

'We've been busy.'

'That's good. Now come on in. Hi, Billy. Give your mother-in-law a kiss.'

They went inside, and Alice and Billy dumped their things on the bed in her room. When they came downstairs Hal was mixing martinis at the bar. Alice sat on the sofa. 'I'll have a diet coke, Dad,' she said.

'So, how are the two intellectuals?' said Hal, handing Billy a vessel of liquor.

'Oh, thinking hard.'

'Glad to hear it.'

Barbara went into the kitchen, and Alice decided she had better offer to help. Barbara had baked a ham, and the potatoes and beans and squash needed putting on.

'You look tired, dear,' she said.

'That's what everyone seems to be telling me. We're building the sets right now, and that's the worst part.'

'Weren't you in that play once?'

'I played Mary Tyrone, the long-suffering wife.'

'Of course.' Barbara stood watching the pans bubble and boil. 'I've never understood about long-suffering wives,' she said. 'Why don't they just ask their husbands to change their ways?'

Alice looked at her mother, at her skinny arms and claw-like hands. She had put on some make-up for the evening, but her greying hair was wispy and wouldn't be tamed by the barrettes, and she seemed suddenly old. She fussed over the pans, and then asked Alice to check on the table. In the dining room Alice saw that it was already immaculately laid. It had probably been that way for hours.

They sat down to eat, Hal carving the ham and Barbara piling vegetables onto their plates.

'I see Mr Reagan is out of hospital,' she said.

'Is he?'

Barbara paused in the act of spooning out mashed potato. 'Do you know what he said to Nancy? It was the funniest thing.'

'Honey, I forgot to duck,' said Billy, looking ironically at Alice.

'To think that he could retain his sense of humour in a situation like that.'

'He could retain his sense of humour in a nuclear war,' said Billy.

'How do you mean, dear?'

'Let's just say I don't think he has much imagination.'

'He has something a lot better than that,' said Hal. He had finished carving the ham, and was holding his martini glass in his hand again. Since he usually made a pitcher of the stuff, Alice could never quite keep track of how much he was drinking. But his face was already suffused with pink. He looks like a big baby, she thought, with his curly fair hair and his jowls, a big alcoholic baby.

'And what's better than imagination?' said Billy.

'Vision. Ideals.'

Alice frowned at Billy, willing him not to rise to the bait. They'd had an absurd argument at Christmas over Reagan, when he wasn't even president yet.

'We're thinking of doing an issue of the magazine on him,' said Billy.

'Yeah?'

'Yes. "Writers Against Reagan", we're planning to call it.'

Hal stuffed some ham into his mouth. 'Against what exactly,' he said through his food.

'Oh, doubling the defence budget while at the same time cutting social programmes, that kind of thing.'

'Can we talk about something else?' said Alice.

'Sure,' said Billy, turning again towards Hal. 'How are the Mets doing?'

'They're still in spring training.'

Alice was by now glaring at Billy. Why was he always doing this? Why did he goad her father in this way? She looked from one to the other, Billy tall and slim, his wavy brown hair falling over his forehead, her father short and burly. They were so utterly different, the two of them – why didn't Billy simply accept the fact?

'The ham's delicious, Mom,' she said.

'Thank you. Your aunt Patsy sent it.'

'How is Patsy? I haven't talked to her lately.'

'She's fine, but the arthritis is getting to her, poor thing. She's coming to stay for Memorial Day weekend.'

'Great.'

'I hope we'll see the two of you then as well.'

The grandfather clock began to chime eight, and Alice paused to listen to it. 'You're seeing us now,' she said. 'We've only just arrived.'

Billy gazed around the room, at the American Gothic of the National Arts Club. There was red flock wallpaper, a gilded mirror, and quite a few muddy landscape paintings. A vast chandelier hung threateningly above his head.

'He didn't become *that* famous after *Portnoy*, did he?' he overheard someone saying.

'Of course not,' a woman replied. 'He's exaggerating for comic effect.'

Billy looked across to the corner where Philip Roth had taken up his position. He was a dark, sardonic presence, seemingly abstracted from this celebration of his latest novel. The protagonist of *Zuckerman Unbound* was a young novelist who has just rocketed to fame for a novel called *Carnovsky*, and all the talk at the party seemed to be about whether Roth was a raging satirist or just a raging narcissist.

Billy saw Matt Goldschmidt, and walked over to say hello.

'Nice party,' he said.

'Roth had to be brought here practically at gunpoint.'

'He doesn't exactly look at ease.'

The publisher, Roger Straus, clapped his hands and called for silence. He was silver-haired and brassy-tongued, and his speech was short and to the point. There was a moment when everyone present waited to see whether Roth would respond, but when it became clear that he wouldn't, the hubbub quickly resumed. Billy saw Dan Blessing out of the corner of his eye.

'So, what's this I hear about Blessing going to Iowa?' said Goldschmidt.

Billy froze in the act of bringing his glass to his lips. 'Tell me,' he said.

'He was out there last week, apparently.'

Billy recalled Blessing's being away for a couple of days without saying where he was. But that happened often enough for him not to remark on it.

'I've heard nothing,' said Billy, trying to appear unconcerned.

'I'd check it out if I were you.'

A reviewer on the New York Times Book Review approached them, and their conversation veered once again towards Roth. But Billy was unable to concentrate, and his eyes tracked the room in search of Dan Blessing. When he saw him he excused himself and joined Blessing at the bar.

'Dan, can we have a word?'

Blessing looked at him quizzically. 'Sure,' he said. 'What's on your mind?'

Billy looked around him, and then said quietly, 'I'm hearing you're going to Iowa. Is that true?'

'Who says so?'

'People who are in a position to know things.'

Blessing looked away from him. 'OK,' he said. 'I've talked to them.'

'And?'

'And I'm thinking about it.'

'What would it mean for the magazine?'

'It's too early to tell. Anyways, I may not take it.'

'When is it going to be not too early to tell? When are your staff going to be let in on this?'

'Lighten up, Billy. We'd figure something out.'

'We would?'

'Sure. Look, I need a few weeks to think it over. Let's talk again then.'

Billy turned to face the room, the writers and critics and editors. This was his world now, and he loved it. Feeling suddenly quite sick, he set down his glass and went out into the street for some air.

The spring sunshine lit up the red brick of the buildings, and the spindly trees on the sidewalk that had been struggling for life in the winter were once again flush with green. SoHo was already crowded with people heading for galleries and shops. The Julian Schnabel exhibition was a hit, and it was difficult to view the huge paintings unobstructed. They stood in front of a work that wasn't so much a painting as a wall of broken crockery.

'Did he have a row with his wife in the kitchen?' said Billy.

'It's thrilling,' replied Alice. 'It engulfs you.'

'It'll engulf us even more when it falls off the wall.'

She turned to look at him. He had been strangely uncommunicative these past few days, and now it seemed the only things he communicated were complaints.

'Do you want to do this or not?' she said.

Billy shrugged his shoulders. 'Sure,' he said. 'Let's take a look at this velvet one over here.'

They spent an hour in the gallery, by the end of which Billy was showing clear signs of impatience. 'Let's get some lunch,' he said as they stepped out into the street.

They found a diner and ordered omelettes.

'You have no visual sense at all,' said Alice.

'Has it taken this long for you to figure that out?'

'No. I'm just reminded of it, that's all.'

'I'm a words man.'

'Yes. But that doesn't mean you can't try to appreciate other things.'

'Alice, you know I do.'

'So why are you doing such a good impression of a philistine?'

'Philistine? Just because I think Julian Schnabel is probably a con artist?'

'Yes, philistine.'

Billy emptied his glass of water. 'Maybe I'm not exactly at my best at the moment,' he said.

Alice reached across the table to take his hand. 'What's up, Billy?' she said.

He looked across the room, and then returned her gaze. 'Blessing's going to Iowa.'

'To Iowa?'

'It's the best writing school in the country. It just happens to be a thousand miles away.'

'Is this for sure?'

'I don't know. He's talking to them, he says. But it all adds up. And if he goes, I don't see how the magazine can carry on.'

She let out a heavy sigh. 'This is serious,' she said.

'It sure is.'

'So what are you going to do?'

'I don't know. Wait until he lets me know for certain. Maybe he'll want to continue publishing the magazine from here. Maybe it'll even be good for me. But I have a feeling it won't.'

She looked at him searchingly. 'You mustn't wait, Billy,' she said. 'You must start talking to people now about another job.'

'I guess so. After I get back from England.'

'But that's three weeks away.'

He grasped her hand tightly. 'I'll wait until Blessing decides before I do anything. But as soon as I know for sure, I'll start making calls.'

Alice looked down at the knot of their fingers. 'Don't leave it too long, Billy,' she said. 'Please.'

Two

He pushed the trolley into the arrivals hall, looking around in search of his sister. Sarah waved from behind a line of people, and Billy moved towards her. They embraced, and then took stock of one another.

'You look different,' he said.

'And you don't.'

They walked to the car park, and Billy threw his suitcase into the boot of Sarah's ancient Mini. As she drove out of the airport he kept glancing across at her, trying to work out how and why she seemed so changed from two years ago. She had filled out a little, and her blonde hair was cut quite short. When she returned his gaze, her green eyes seemed milder than he remembered.

'Good flight?' she said.

'On Laker? There's no such thing. I'm here, that's the main thing.'

'Thank you for coming.'

'Not at all.' For a moment he was about to say that it was time he came home anyway, but he managed to stop himself. 'Are you all set?' he asked instead.

'Well, I am. I don't know about anyone else.'

'Where's John?'

'He's coming down tomorrow. He's got some things he needs to wrap up first.'

'He seems a busy man.'

'Yes, he is.'

They were on the motorway now, and Billy began to take in his surroundings. Everything seemed so small – the cars, the houses, even the office buildings. On the plane he had heard English voices for the first time in ages, and they struck him as being strangled somehow, lacking the broad vowels of America. He had been away a long time.

'So how are you?' she said. Whenever she looked at him she was unable to restrain a smile. Did he strike her as being funny, or was she just glad to see him?

'Apart from being stiff and sleepless, I'm fine.'

'New York agrees with you, then.'

'It does.'

She rested her hands on the top of the wheel, and they chugged along in the slow lane, lorries roaring past. 'You've got a slight accent,' she said. 'Just as Tom said.'

'Is he OK?'

'You'll have to see for yourself. I can't tell any more.'

'Is he working?'

'He thinks he is.'

The road was lined with fields now, and after a while they rose through pillow-like hills dotted with sheep and cows. This was England, this was where he was from. In the bright May sunshine it seemed impossibly lovely, as though it had been staged.

'And Dad and Mum?' he said.

'They're fine. Mum seems remarkably calm, considering. I suppose second weddings are different.'

Billy looked out across the countryside, recalling Sarah's first wedding. It had been in the same church, St Cuthbert's in Wells; but there the similarities ended. Sarah had married her teenage sweetheart Lee, a guitarist in a band, and it had lasted less than three years. Now, having drifted through many relationships, she was about to marry an accountant.

'What about Dad?'

Sarah pulled out to overtake a car that was travelling even more slowly than theirs. 'What do you want to know?' she said. Looking across at the wing mirror as she pulled back into the inside lane, she turned towards him. 'Do you want the good stuff first, or the bad?'

'The good stuff.'

'He's in the pink. This promotion has been very good for him. He spends a lot of time touring the cinemas all the way down to Cornwall.'

'And the bad?'

She looked at him resignedly. 'Guess,' she said.

'Who is it this time?'

'She works in the office.'

'And how do you know about her?'

'He's called her out of hours just once or twice too often.'

'So Mum knows?'

'Of course she does. It was she who told me.'

'What's she going to do?'

Sarah arched an eyebrow and remained silent.

'OK,' said Billy. 'How long then before it's over?'

'It's been going on for about three months, apparently. Shall we say another three?'

Billy looked away from her. 'That would be about right,' he said.

They drove for a couple of hours before turning off the motorway and threading their way through Somerset towards Wells. Billy wound down his window and breathed in the country air. Eventually they descended the hill into the tiny city, and he saw the square towers of the cathedral. Passing Market Place, he caught sight of the stalls set out on the cobblestones and the gateway to the Bishop's Palace beyond. As they made their way along Priory Road he became aware that he was steeling himself for the days ahead. He was coming home.

———

The wind caught Sarah's train, and it snaked around John's ankles. Tom had been trying to set up a shot, and Margaret had to disentangle the bride and groom before he could do so. Billy sat on the low wall of the churchyard. He hadn't yet been introduced to John Causley, and he was trying to consider what he thought of him. He was ten years older than Sarah. Billy thought of Lee, and of the men who had passed through Sarah's life since, and the contrast could scarcely be greater. Causley had a house and an accountancy firm in Barnet. Sarah had finally decided to settle down.

After Tom had taken what seemed like a thousand photos, they walked to the Swan. Their father hadn't stinted, and the champagne flowed. Billy saw Bert Dampler, and shook his hand.

'How does it feel to be back?' said Bert.

'A little strange, if I'm honest.'

'This must seem parochial compared to New York.'

'New York has its own problems.'

'Wouldn't suit me, I can tell you.'

Bert glanced around the room. His bald head was shinier than ever these days, his girl's mouth softer. He had been practising for middle age ever since his twenties, and now he had finally achieved it.

'How's the cinema business?' said Billy.

'It's good. And since Jim became area manager it's even better.'

Bert had worked at the Regal practically all his life, and now that Billy's father had moved up, he was in charge. Billy reminded himself for the hundredth time not to betray any sign of greater worldliness in anything he said. Wells was a world too.

'What's on at the moment, then?' he said.

'*Raiders of the Lost Ark*. It's packing them in.'

Billy's mother joined them.

'Great wedding,' said Bert.

'Yes,' replied Margaret. She turned to Billy. 'She had a wedding once before, but perhaps this time she'll also have a marriage.'

'It was more than just a wedding, Mum.' His thoughts went back to that day eleven years ago. He had been fond of Lee. But they'd both been too young, and Lee had had too much yet to do. Billy wondered what had become of him now, but knew better than to ask.

Jim approached, and put an arm around Billy's shoulders. A cigar dangled from his fingers. He coughed a couple of times, and took a swig of champagne.

'What do you think?' he said.

'Very elegant.'

'Not bad, eh? I wanted to do her proud. She's made the right decision this time.'

Except for a certain grey pallor, his father looked very spry. Billy reminded himself that Jim would be sixty this year. It was hard to credit, that he was old enough himself to have a father of sixty. They hadn't had a chance to talk properly, caught up as they were in preparations for the wedding, and he wondered when they would. As Jim moved off to speak to someone else, Billy glanced around the room. He knew very few people here outside his own family. He decided to slip outside, and stepped onto Cathedral Green. This was a medieval place, bounded by the Dean's Gate, the chapter house and the façade of the cathedral. A group of American tourists passed by, their eyes and their cameras eager to take in this improbably old and beautiful place. Billy sat on the bench, and as he did so the bells began to ring. This wonderful, symphonic sound had accompanied him on many a day when he was a kid, walking between home, the Blue School, the Regal and Goody's café. He closed his eyes and let the music wash over him, and then he became aware that someone was sliding onto the bench. Tom had had the same idea.

'It's still a bit chilly for sitting out,' he said.

'I needed some air.'

'Me too.'

'You must be tired after taking all those photos.'

'It was a hoot. Now I'm a real photographer – I've done a wedding!'

Tom looked as cadaverous as he had when he came to stay. He shifted on the bench, moving first his legs and then his arms, unable to keep still.

'How are you?' said Billy.

Tom raised his hand to shade his eyes. 'Fine,' he said. 'Dandy.'

'We were worried about you.'

'Don't be. I'm a big boy now.'

'When are you heading back to London?'

'Tomorrow morning. A day down here is about all I can take nowadays.'

'Well, you did your bit.'

Tom inspected his thumbnail and brought it to his mouth. His nails were bitten to the quick. 'She's sold out,' he said.

'Don't say that. Remember what I told you in New York, about turning thirty?'

'OK. But remember what I told you, about your sounding more like Dad every day.'

'Do I?'

'Sometimes.'

'I'll try not to.'

They returned to the reception, and Billy was finally introduced to John.

'So you're the bookish one,' he said.

'Yes. Do you read much yourself?'

'Oh, the occasional thriller. I'd be a sore disappointment to you, I'm afraid.'

He was a fleshy sort of man, packed into a pale blue suit. He had clearly been at the booze in the past couple of hours, and his face glistened with sweat. Billy recalled Tom's assessment of him as being as dull as ditchwater. All he cared about was that Sarah should be happy. But looking at the man who was now his brother-in-law, he felt a sense of relief that he wouldn't be seeing very much of him. Maybe Tom's response was simply more honest.

316

Uncertain what to say, Billy replied, 'You're not a disappointment at all. We're all very happy for you both.'

The words sounded dreadfully hollow. But John Causley beamed, and grasped his hand. 'Nice to be welcomed into the family,' he said.

———————

'So where's it leading, this magazine thing?' said Jim. His voice sounded quite hoarse to Billy. Maybe he had just been talking a lot recently.

'It's not leading anywhere,' replied Billy. 'It's what it is, what I do.'

It was two days after the wedding, and they sat in the bar of the Anchor, tumblers of whisky set in front of them. Margaret was at a rehearsal of her amateur theatrical company, and this was the first moment Billy had had alone with his father.

'Ever going to be any money in it?'

Billy took his glass in his hand and swirled it about, creating a liquid incandescence.

'I've never been interested in making money, Dad, you know that.'

'What about when kids come along?'

'I'll face that when it happens.'

Jim took out a lighter and lit up what must have been his fortieth cigarette of the day. He had always been a heavy smoker, but to Billy this now seemed excessive. Some people smoked for something to do with their hands; but Jim seemed to smoke for something to do with his life. He drew deeply on the cigarette.

'How about your work?' said Billy. 'It sounds as though it's going well.'

Jim rapped his fingers on the wooden table. 'The Rank people have been good to me,' he said. 'I've got a nice office in Bristol, a smart car, and when I feel like it I take a little trip to the cinemas down west just to make sure everything's all right.'

'You deserve it.'

'I do.'

Billy looked out across the room, thinking back to his father's bankruptcy and the years of trying to make good since. Of course he deserved it. But Billy sometimes wondered how much he was aware of what had happened to him, of the mistakes he had made. By the time you're sixty you ought to have acquired a kind of self-knowledge. Had his father? He wasn't sure.

'So this'll see you through to retirement, then.'

Jim tipped ash from his cigarette and emptied his glass. 'This is it for me, Billy,' he said. 'Five years more. Another round?'

'I'll get them.'

As he stood at the bar, Billy surveyed the room. It hadn't changed in the past twenty years, its low beams still catching people's heads, a fire crackling whatever the time of year. This was where they'd had lunch before going to Glastonbury Tor for the first time. It had been one of the great days of Billy's childhood, and looking back now it seemed like the day he and his father began to understand each other. He glanced across at Jim, who was stubbing out his cigarette and reaching into his pocket for another one. He recalled Tom's words about his becoming more and more like his father. Tom was quite wrong, of course: the differences between them could scarcely be greater.

'Mum seems well,' he said as he returned to his seat.

'She's got a great life, your mother. Completely bound up in the theatre these days. They've got some very strange play in the works at the moment, something about a police inspector and some mad critics.'

'So she's not lonely when you're away?'

'Lonely? She's got more friends than I've ever had.'

'I wasn't thinking of friends,' he said. 'I was thinking of her and you.'

Jim coughed, and took a swig of whisky. 'We're all right, your mother and I,' he said. 'Never been better.'

Billy looked down into his glass, wondering how much more he should say. Was there any point in bringing up this latest affair? Jim would deny it, as he always did, and the companionship they felt now would be lost. In a couple of days Billy would be on a plane to New York, and soon enough after that, Jim's affair would surely be over. What purpose was served by reproaching him for it?

'I wonder how Sarah and John are getting on in Jamaica?' he said.

'Lucky sods,' said Jim. 'We had to make do with Torquay.'

Billy smiled. 'And Alice and I went straight back to work.'

Margaret and Billy were having a bowl of soup when the phone rang. He could tell from the way she clutched at the phone that it was bad news, and from the conversation that it must be about Tom.

'He's had some kind of seizure,' she said as she returned to the table. 'Brought on by drugs.'

'Oh, God!' said Billy. He thought back to the night in New York when Tom was beaten up by drug dealers. He had decided to say nothing more of it at the time. Why hadn't he taken it more seriously?

His mother stood gazing absently at him, wringing her hands. 'We must go to London straight away.'

Jim was in Exeter, and Margaret asked Bert to drive them to the station. On the journey to London they sat in silence, watching the landscape unfold. From Paddington they took a taxi to the Royal Free Hospital, and a nurse showed them to Tom's bed.

He was asleep, and looked awful, his cheeks hollowed out, his complexion deathly pale. Margaret asked to talk to the doctor, and they waited at the bedside until he arrived.

'What can you tell us?' she asked, raising herself from the chair.

'Well, it's cocaine mainly, combined with alcohol on this occasion.'

'On this occasion?'

'Your son has a serious drug problem, Mrs Palmer.'

Margaret sat down again, and looked up at the doctor. 'What is it doing to him?' she said.

'It's wasting him.' He looked down at his clipboard. 'Forgive me,' he said. 'I don't mean to use emotive terms.'

'What can be done?' asked Billy.

'Well, he has to stop using cocaine. There's no specific antidote – he just needs to find a way to come off it. He's been taking larger and larger doses. The levels of dopamine and serotonin in his brain have risen significantly, and the cells have been adapting to the imbalances.' He paused for a moment. 'I'm sorry to be technical,' he continued, 'but it's important to understand what has been happening.'

'How easy will it be for him to stop using it?' said Billy.

'That depends. He's going to need some kind of therapy. The only way to overcome this is with the support of other people. And family...' With this he turned to face Margaret. 'Family may not be able to give the kind of support that's needed.'

'Are you talking about a clinic?'

'Not necessarily.' A nurse came up to him and whispered something in his ear. 'I'm afraid I have to attend to another patient,' he said. 'Let's talk again tomorrow.'

Billy gazed down at his brother. His body seemed very thin beneath the bedclothes.

'Let's go,' he said. 'He isn't likely to wake up any time soon. We'll come back in the morning.'

Margaret looked sorrowfully at Tom, and leaned over to kiss his forehead. She had held back her tears, but now they flowed freely down her cheeks. Billy took her in his arms.

'He's going to be OK,' he said. 'He's young and he can get over this.'

By now she was sobbing, and Billy held her tight. 'Come on, Mum,' he said gently. 'Let's get out of here.'

Tom had been staying at Sarah's flat, and the nurse gave them his keys. They walked the short distance to Belsize Park. The place was half-empty, Sarah being in the process of selling up and moving into John's house. There was a bed and a sofa, though, and that would be enough for a night. Billy found a bottle of brandy and poured them large measures.

'Here, drink some of this,' he said.

They sat side by side on the sofa, Margaret trying to compose herself. After a while she said, 'Did you have any inkling?'

Billy sighed. 'He scored some drugs when he was staying with us,' he said. 'I didn't think anything of it then. I'm sorry now that I didn't.'

'You know, I don't think there's been a moment in the past thirty-odd years when I haven't worried about one or other of you.'

'Oh, Mum, please don't say that.'

'It's true. You'll find out for yourself one day.'

He took her hand in his. There was something terribly distressing about his mother's words, and now it was him who had to fight back tears.

'It's been hard for you,' he said.

'No harder than for most.' She looked up at him, and then raised a hand and stroked his cheek. 'You've been wonderful children really. It's just me. I can't help but worry about things.'

'Of course it's been harder for you than for most,' said Billy. 'You had to hold things together after the bankruptcy. Dad hadn't got a clue, not for ages.'

'That's not fair. It was just as hard for him.'

'Perhaps.' He thought of all the things he wanted to say, about his father's affairs, about his selfishness and thoughtlessness. Was this latest girlfriend with him in Exeter? They'd been unable to get hold of him, and had to leave a message at the office.

'Anyway it's been fine for a long time now, at least since he sold the cinema.'

'His responsibilities extend beyond providing you with a home.'

She breathed in deeply, and took a sip of brandy. 'I'll be the judge of Jim's responsibilities,' she said.

He went to the window. It was raining now, and all he could think of as he stood watching it fall was how lucky Sarah had been to have had a fine day for the wedding.

'I'll go and buy some food,' he said eventually.

'I couldn't eat anything, not at the moment.'

'Well, you must.' He turned back to face her. 'Let me worry about you for a change,' he said. 'It's about time.'

Billy reached the doorway in Coptic Street and rang the bell. The little sign remained where it had always been, Sellotaped to the wall and reading 'The Bystander, a magazine of the Arts'. He heard Roy Urquhart's scratchy voice say, 'It's open,' and then, after a few moments, the sound of the buzzer. Even after all these years, Urquhart had still not quite got the hang of it.

He sat behind his desk in the upstairs room, a halo of light from the single window obscuring his features. Standing up, he extended his left hand to shake Billy's, his wounded right hand remaining at his side. It had often amused Billy to observe how people reacted to this, the boldness of Urquhart's gesture unsettling them and causing them to wonder for a moment whether in fact handshakes were always this way, whether they had confused their left with their right.

'Sit down,' he said. 'Can't really offer you anything at this hour, I'm afraid.'

'I'm fine,' said Billy.

Urquhart's grey eyes settled on him.

'How's the American?'

'I'm not an American, Roy. You should hear what they say about me. I'm the Brit, the teabag, the Limey.'

'They still say "Limey"? I thought that went out after the war.'

'They say it when they want to make a point.'

321

'But you're glad you went?'

'I'm very glad I went.'

He looked around the room. It made the *Narratives* office seem tidy, strewn as it was with manuscripts, drawings and review copies of books. *The Bystander* tackled everything: art, poetry, memoir, travel. Every issue was a ragbag or a cornucopia, depending on your point of view. In his six years there Billy had tried to introduce more contemporary fiction, but Urquhart had been resistant. He recalled trying to persuade him to publish a story from Ian McEwan's first collection. 'They're dirty,' was all Urquhart had replied.

'I could make a cup of coffee?'

'I'm fine, really,' said Billy, thinking back to the metallic tang of Urquhart's peculiar blend of Camp Coffee, powdered milk and sugar.

'Well, how does Merrie England strike you?'

'As being not very merrie.'

'No?'

Billy made a face. 'Thatcherism, race riots in Brixton...'

'Oh, things don't change that much.'

They don't in this room at least, he thought.

Urquhart searched in the desk drawer for his lighter. 'And how about your magazine? What's it called again?'

'*Narratives.*'

'Ah, yes. A nicely capacious word.'

'It's doing fine. We have a grant that makes your Arts Council stipend look like pocket money.'

'They know about patronage, the Americans.'

'They're richer.'

Billy thought for a moment about telling him of Blessing's possible departure, but decided not to.

'Perhaps I could find a rich American of my own,' said Urquhart.

'You must know lots of rich people.'

'Yes, rich and thick, as they say.'

'Are you doing all right, though?'

Urquhart lit his cigarette at the third attempt. 'I'm folding it up, Billy,' he said.

'Surely not?'

'Why not? I'm old, and no one wants my sort of stuff any more.'

'But you can't. *The Bystander* is an institution.' As he uttered the words he remembered that this was exactly what Wendell Price had said about *Narratives*.

'Literary magazines have their day,' said Urquhart. 'There's no point in rambling on if no one's listening. Look at Connolly and *Horizon*. Ten years. I've had almost thirty.'

Billy gazed at the little desk in the corner where he had worked for such a long time, and a wave of nostalgia caught him up. He should have stayed two years, no more. But he liked it here, and it was only when he met Alice that it occurred to him to move on.

He looked at his watch. 'I must be pushing off,' he said. 'I have to go and see my brother. I'm sorry this is so brief.'

Urquhart stood up and went to the door.

'It's good to see you looking so well,' he said. 'You will stay in touch, I hope, even after the magazine has gone. Next time let's have lunch at the Garrick. I'm running out of people to take there these days.'

———

The walls of the hospital waiting room were covered with signs about pregnancy testing and cancer research. An elderly man with a patch over one eye repeatedly looked his way, his expression gloomy and resentful. Billy stood and crossed to the window, looking out over the wet grass towards Pond Street. Eventually he heard Tom's voice. A nurse was fussing over him as though he were a small boy, straightening his collar and brushing back his hair.

'Here he is, then,' she said. 'All set to go back into the big wide world. Aren't you, dear?'

Tom smiled ruefully. He looked gaunt and pained, but oddly serene. He shook Billy's hand, and submitted to a kiss from the nurse. Billy took his bag and they stepped out into the damp, balmy day. On the walk to Sarah's flat he glanced at his brother now and then as though at an invalid, but Tom only looked back at him with a vaguely defiant stare. In the flat Billy made a cup of tea while his brother unpacked his few things.

'You stayed on,' said Tom. 'Thanks.'

'It's only a couple of days. We couldn't have Mum hanging around in London all this time with nothing to do but worry.'

'She'll be worrying just as much at home.'

'Yes, I suppose she will.'

323

He handed Tom a mug and sat down on the sofa. Tom squatted on the floor, holding the mug in both hands.

'Do you want to talk about it?' said Billy.

'About what?'

'About everything, Tom. About how you got to be in this state.'

'Am I in a state?'

'Yes.'

Tom sipped at his tea and made a face. He placed the mug on the floor and leaned his head back against the wall.

'Have you ever wondered what the point of everything is?' he said.

'Often.'

'What is it, then?'

Billy smiled. 'For me, for you?'

'For all of us. What are people doing with their lives, spending their days in meaningless jobs and their evenings watching television?'

'There's no use worrying about "people". The question is, what are you doing with your life?'

Tom looked up at him. 'I don't know, Billy,' he said. 'I tell myself I'm above it all. I take pictures of what others are doing and think this makes me somehow better than them. But I'm not, am I?'

'You're better than a lot of people. But surely you shouldn't be thinking that way?'

'When I'm looking at the world through the lens of a camera it seems to make sense. Then when I look at it with my own eyes it doesn't any more.'

'Maybe we're both observers. Maybe we both have to distance ourselves from life, you through photographs and me through words.'

Tom picked up his mug again. 'How funny,' he said, 'the idea that you and I should be the same.'

'Funny?'

'Yes.' He looked back at him. 'Maybe it was the difference in our ages, but you always seemed as remote as Dad.'

'Oh, Tom, really?' Billy looked down at his hands. He had always supposed himself to be a model brother. The thought that he might share some of the responsibility for Tom's unhappiness was hard to bear.

'I'm not blaming you or anything. It's just the way it was. I was only seven when you went off to university, remember.'

Billy sighed. 'I did try to be in touch,' he said.

324

'It wasn't about being in touch. It's not your fault, like I said. All I'm saying is maybe we need to get to know each other again. But you're on the other side of the Atlantic.'

'Come to New York. Come and live there for a while.'

Tom smiled ironically. 'So as to get to know my big brother?'

Billy gazed at him. Before he came to visit, Billy hadn't seen Tom for two years. During that time he had become a man. It dawned on him that he didn't know his brother at all.

'Come back again for a while at least,' he said. 'You liked it, didn't you?'

'I loved it.'

'Just stay out of the East Village this time.'

'I'm done with that,' he said. 'I'm going to clean myself up.'

'Where will you go, then?'

'Back home, for a while.'

'You told me that a day at home was enough nowadays.'

'That was before. And there are other people I need to get to know besides you.'

'Dad.'

'Yeah. Where is he, anyway?'

'He's coming up tomorrow. He had something on down in Exeter, and Mum told him to wait until it was done.'

'I suppose I'm going to get a lecture.'

'Probably. You could give him one too, though.'

'On what?'

'Oh, I don't know. On being a father.'

'It's a bit late for that, isn't it?'

'Why? Surely you never stop being a father?'

Tom hugged his knees. 'Like you never stop being a son,' he said.

'No. Or a brother.'

Three

'Fox,' barked the voice on the other end of the line.

'Mr Fox, my name's Billy Palmer, of *Narratives* magazine. I was wondering whether I could talk to you about Truman Capote.'

'A lot of people want to talk to me about Truman.'

'Perhaps I could buy you lunch?'

'You're English, right?'

'Yes.'

'But I thought *Narratives* was American.'

'It is.' Billy cradled the receiver in his shoulder and looked across the room at Dan Blessing, who had put him up to this call. 'Since the Bicentennial there's been an amnesty, and they've let a few of us in.'

He heard the sound of laughter coming down the wires. 'Meet me at the Racquet Club one day,' said Fox. 'Twelve thirty. Next Tuesday suit you?'

A few days later Billy took the subway uptown. As the train ground its way along, he glanced briefly at the predominantly black and brown faces, and thought of what Joe Fox had said about his being English. He was no different from most people in this city. Hardly anyone was from New York: this was the place you *came* to.

Joe Fox was a tall man in his mid-fifties with a pleasingly open face and a ready smile. His black hair was still slick from the shower. 'I lost again,' he said as he shook Billy's hand. 'I must remember to bend my knees.'

They walked to the back of the marbled lobby and ascended some stairs to the dining room, sitting in an airy space surrounded by men who looked fit and prosperous and wholly at their ease. Joe Fox ordered a bourbon and soda, and Billy considered how to approach this conversation. He had been apprehensive about meeting this famous Random House editor, and was trying to work out what to make of the contrast between the gruffness of his tone and the friend-liness of his manner.

'OK,' said Fox, 'I'm buying you lunch because I liked the sound of your voice. But don't expect me to tell you anything about Truman Capote you want to know.'

'Not many people in New York like the sound of my voice,' said Billy. 'Mostly they think I'm a stuck-up Brit.'

'My ancestors were stuck-up Brits. I can forgive you.' He looked down at the menu. 'What are you going to eat?'

'I'll have a club sandwich,' said Billy.

'Good choice,' said Fox, and when the waiter had moved away, 'the only choice here, in fact.'

Billy cleared his throat and said, 'Mr Fox, I was wondering whether Truman Capote would agree to give *Narratives* a chapter from his new novel.'

Fox smiled broadly, a smile that creased his face and lit it up. 'You're kidding, right?' he said.

'Well, no…'

'Good try.' He sank a large measure of bourbon. 'Ever since those chapters appeared in *Esquire* I've been telling Truman he made a lousy mistake.'

'But it was just the "Côte Basque" chapter that upset people, wasn't it?'

'Not the point. I don't like the idea of writers giving magazines work-in-progress.'

'I'm afraid that's one of the main things we do.'

'I know.'

'Then it's good of you to give me lunch, when you could have told me over the phone.'

'As I said, I liked the sound of your voice.' Fox looked at him keenly. 'Listen,' he said, 'I don't mean to be unhelpful. The thing is, I'm not sure how much more of this book Truman has actually written.'

'But the extracts were published five years ago.'

'Exactly. First there was the bullshit about John O'Shea stealing some of it…'

'Who was he?'

'A lover. Then there's the rather more significant fact that Truman hasn't been in a state to write much lately.'

'I'm sorry to hear that.'

Fox looked across the room. 'I shouldn't really be telling you this,' he said.

'I'll keep it to myself.'

'Oh, it's not exactly a secret. It's just that I'm his editor and his friend. At least I used to be his friend, before he started fucking himself up.'

Their sandwiches arrived, and Fox ordered another bourbon for himself and a glass of wine for Billy.

'Tell you what I'll do,' he said. 'Jim Schlesinger has some new stories. I'll ask him if he wants to show them to you.'

'That's very kind.'

'It's nothing. Now where are those drinks?'

———————

Alice sat in the stalls with Paul and the director and the production manager, watching the actors intently as they went through the technical rehearsal. All the usual questions ran through her mind: was the set serving the drama; were the actors making best use of it; did the lighting create the right kind of atmosphere? The play was *Entertaining Mr Sloane*, and they sat in the auditorium of the Cherry Lane. This tiny theatre was just around the corner from Alice's apartment, and she loved working here, despite the constraints of space and money.

Orton's stage directions were very few, starting with, 'A room. Evening', and later describing the room as being in a house in the middle of a rubbish dump. Alice had never seen a production, but in designing the set she had cast her mind back to Billy's flat in Kilburn, to its air of seediness and neglect. She often had reasons to be thankful for her time in London.

Onstage, the actor playing Sloane was beating up the old man, Kemp. The director stood and clapped his hands.

'You need to be further behind the sofa,' he said. 'That way you can kick out more viciously. And the audience will feel it all the more painfully for not being able to see exactly what you're doing to him.'

The actors took up their positions and began again. Alice had been worried about the positioning of the sofa, feeling that it took the actors too close to the front of the stage in many of the scenes.

'We need to move it,' she said.

'But then there won't be enough room for Kemp to fall down.'

'Let me see.'

She climbed up onto the stage. 'Let's just shift this end back,' she said. 'That way their entrances from the door will be easier.'

They carried on, until the scene in which the actor playing Kath, the raddled seductress, loses her false teeth. This had given Barbara Bryne no end of problems. How did you put false teeth into your mouth when you had a set of your own already there? Alice had hollowed out the teeth as much as she could without breaking them, but they were still causing difficulties.

She watched as Bryne played out the final ludicrous scene, in which she negotiates with her brother the joint ownership of Sloane while her father lies dead upstairs, murdered by Sloane himself. When it was over she invited Paul back to the apartment for a drink.

'I love it,' he said. 'It's truly weird.'

'You just love the guy playing Sloane.'

'He's a hunk. But I love the undercurrent of perversion that runs through it.'

'Don't get too excited, now.'

Paul smiled, and sat back into the sofa. 'I think we've got a job after this one,' he said.

'What?'

'It's a new production of a play by Wally Shawn, The Hotel Play. Apparently it has a cast of eighty.'

'Eighty? Where's it being produced?'

'At La Mama.'

'But there isn't space for eighty actors there.'

'Not all at once.'

She handed Paul a glass of wine and sat down beside him. Another job, she thought with relief, another few weeks of work and pay. Maybe this year was going to be better than she had feared.

'Do you know what sort of set they want?'

'Something minimal.'

'Let's think Shakespeare, then.'

'Shakespeare?'

'I mean Elizabethan Shakespeare. When they didn't really have sets.'

Paul looked alarmed. 'You want to do us out of work?' he said.

'Will it make any difference to what we get paid?'

'I guess not.'

She stood up and crossed to the kitchen. 'Let's make the actors the set,' she said. 'Let's try some human scenery.'

329

'I talked to Lish,' said Wendell. 'There's a new DeLillo. *The Names*. It's about an American who gets mixed up with a murderous cult in Greece and Jerusalem and Lahore.'

'When's it being published?' asked Blessing.

'Not till next spring. Gordon's sending me a manuscript.'

'Great. So what else have we got?'

Blessing turned to Billy, and to Kate Trenton, the assistant who had been helping them out lately. They were seated around the desk that doubled as a conference table, their yellow notepads stained with coffee rings, a bottle of whisky standing at Wendell's elbow.

'I've read the Vargas Llosa,' said Billy. 'I think we should go for it. Apparently Aunt Julia is based on his own aunt, and he married her.'

'You can marry your own aunt?' asked Kate.

'Maybe you can in Peru.'

'You know he once had a fist fight with Márquez, don't you?' said Blessing.

'No.'

'Like Vidal and Mailer,' said Wendell.

'More evenly matched.'

'If you need to fill pages there's that story by your new protégé, Dan,' said Kate. 'What's the guy's name?'

'We don't need to fill pages,' said Blessing. 'That's precisely what we don't need to do.'

'OK.'

'But we do,' said Billy. 'We have half an issue, and two weeks until press day.'

Blessing leaned back in his chair and then forward again, placing his folded arms on the desk.

'It doesn't matter about the press date,' he said.

'That's what you always say.'

'No, Billy. This time it doesn't matter because this is the last issue of the magazine.'

He looked at each of them in turn, a challenging expression on his face.

Billy tossed his pen onto the desk. 'Well, that's wonderful news,' he said.

'You've known this was coming.'

'I've known it because I heard it on the street.'

'We talked about it.'

'I confronted you.'

Blessing took hold of the neck of the bottle and poured some whisky into his coffee cup. 'I can't not accept this job,' he said. 'It's a great opportunity, and I need to spend some time away from New York.'

'You may need to,' said Billy. 'The rest of us need to stay, and earn a living.'

'You'll be fine.'

'Yes? Thanks for the vote of confidence.'

Blessing took a swig from the cup. 'I'll talk to people,' he said. 'I'll put the word out.' He turned to Wendell. 'And it's about time you wrote that novel, instead of just talking about it.'

'I *am* writing it.'

'What's it called? *American Decameron?*'

'Yeah.'

'A hundred stories sounds like a lot for you.'

'Fuck you, Dan,' said Wendell. He picked up the bottle and the notepad and stood up. 'You won't be getting an invitation to my launch party, I can tell you that now.'

'Sit down, Wendell,' said Billy. 'All right, Dan. When do we wrap up, and how long are you going to pay us for?'

'We wrap up when we wrap the issue, and I pay you until then. We make the last one a classic.'

'Well, if we're going to make it a classic, I suggest you start looking for some stuff of your own. Don't rely on the rest of us to put this one together.'

Alice gazed across the water to the boathouse, and then at the statue of her namesake, standing in Wonderland. She raised her face to the sun, which by now was bright and hot. It was Memorial Day weekend, and she and Billy had taken a walk in Central Park. Having eluded the clutches of her parents, they were having a weekend in the city. Here among the lawns and the trees it was possible briefly to escape its steady, insistent thrum.

'So Tom is better?' she said.

'Much, apparently. He's spending some time at home. According to Mum, he's over it.'

'That's good.' She took Billy's hand. 'He needs a girlfriend.'

'Oh, he's had lots of those.'

'He needs someone steady.'

A file of joggers passed by. On the walk here they had dodged the cyclists and the skateboarders and the young parents pushing their racing buggies. When was it that the things New Yorkers did at the weekend had become as competitive as the things they did during the week?

'Alice . . .' said Billy hesitantly, 'I've got something to tell you.'

She searched his face.

'Well?'

'Wendell was right about Blessing. He is going to Iowa, and he's closing the magazine.'

She looked away into the distance. 'So that's it, then,' she said.

'We're putting together one more issue. My guess is that by the end of June we'll be shutting up the office.'

She glanced back at him. She had known in her heart that this was coming, and she had wanted Billy to quit the magazine for a while now; but nonetheless this news came as a shock.

'So what will you do?'

'Exactly what you've been telling me to do. Call the publishing houses.'

'Good.'

'And Blessing says he'll make some calls for me himself.'

'I wouldn't count on that.'

'I won't.'

'So what about that guy from Random House you met recently?'

'Joe Fox? Sure, I'll call him next week.'

A St Bernard on a long lead came up to them and began to sniff her shoes. It was strange how many dogs there were in this city in which most people lived in apartments. In Alice's view only farmers and blind people needed dogs. The owner of the St Bernard reeled him in, and apologized.

'No problem,' she said. 'He's beautiful.'

The dog looked at her expectantly, as though wanting more compliments. Its owner, a young man in jeans and a Grateful Dead T-shirt, seemed also to be wanting something more. But she had no intention of reaching out and stroking it. After a few moments they moved on.

332

'What about other houses?' said Alice once they were alone again.

'Sure. FSG. Penguin. Harper. I know people in most of them by now.'

'Is it going to be hard?'

Billy took off his glasses and wiped them clean. 'I don't know,' he said. 'I may have to go back to the bottom of the ladder.'

Alice resisted the impulse to say that that was where he was anyway. She thought of the job she and Paul had coming up at La Mama, and of the fact that after this there was no more work in prospect. When she married Billy her father had described him as being utterly impractical. Could two people struggling in the arts really make a go of it? Maybe she should have married her college boyfriend after all. He was working for Merrill Lynch now, doing something she couldn't even begin to understand. And then there was the simple fact that Billy was the first man she had ever truly loved. Even as she had returned to New York, three short months after they met, she knew she wanted to share her life with him.

She twined her arm in his. 'You're going to be fine,' she said. 'You're a good editor.'

Billy leaned across and kissed her cheek. 'In this city you have to be better than good,' he said.

During the last two weeks in the life of *Narratives* magazine the atmosphere in the office was laden with gloom. Blessing made very few appearances, and, as Billy had guessed, it was down to him and Wendell and Kate to put the final issue together. Megan had already quit, which meant that Billy had to deal with the fulfilment house and the distributor. The issue had some good things in it, but it was far from being the classic that Blessing had spoken of. At the end of his last day there, Billy suggested to Wendell that they drown their sorrows in the pub.

'How's the job search going?' asked Wendell when they were settled.

'Not well. It's tough out there. When I left London I thought I was escaping a recession. Now I'm told there's one here too.'

'It's not that bad. You should have been here a few years ago, when the city was broke.'

'I certainly shouldn't have been here then.' He gazed into his glass. 'Alice is really on my case at the moment. She says I'm not trying hard enough.'

333

'She's your wife. That's what she's supposed to say.'

'I guess so.'

He thought back to the last conversation they had had about it. Alice's anxiety was spilling out now. Knocking back his drink, he offered Wendell another, and went up to the bar. As he waited he looked around at their fellow drinkers. They had the look of men under water, their gestures strangely exaggerated and slowed.

'How about you?' he said when he returned to the table.

'I'll probably head back home. Finish the novel, like Blessing said.'

'How far into it are you?'

Wendell looked away from him evasively. Then he picked up his glass and tossed the whisky down his throat. 'It's an ambitious project,' he said.

'I'm sure it is. A hundred stories?'

'All of contemporary American life in a hundred stories. Dos Passos step aside.'

'You're a real writer, Wendell. That story you showed me was great.'

'Thanks. I can do the odd story. It's threading them together that's the problem.'

'I'd be happy to read anything you want.'

'Sure. What I need is time. Some friends have a place on a lake. Maybe I'll hole up there for a while. But I'm not convinced that writers should hide away like that.'

'No?'

'Remember what Roth said about American writers having their hands full trying to make American reality credible?'

'Well, you're trying.'

Wendell looked down at his empty glass, and then upended it so as to capture the last dregs of whisky on his lips. 'What I mean is that in order to describe American reality you have to be in the middle of it, and a house on a lake is not where American reality is happening.'

'Some kind of reality is happening there, surely?'

'Yeah, fishing.' Wendell looked at him squarely. 'I'll take care of myself,' he said. 'It's you I'm worried about. Editorial jobs in New York are like gold dust.'

'I'd better get back to panning, then.'

Wendell wrapped his fingers around his glass. 'Have you ever written anything?' he said.

Billy smiled. 'I wrote a journal when I was travelling in Morocco. And when I was at *The Bystander* I wrote a terrible novel.'

'What happened to it?'

'It's in ashes, like many a lost masterpiece.'

Now it was Billy who languished in the apartment, wondering how to fill his days. Not one of the publishers he had called had so much as asked him to drop by, let alone held out any hope that there might be a vacancy. He took long walks, up to Central Park and down to the Battery, and brooded. Had his American adventure come to an abrupt end? Would he have to go back to working in a bookstore? One day he passed the social security office on Seventh Avenue, and the sight of it made him shudder. To have to stand in a dole queue seemed to represent the end of everything he had hoped for when he came here. Would it come to his having to return to England? But he was married now, his life extended beyond his work. Except that it didn't, really, not at the moment – things with Alice were very strained. She seemed to be blaming him for the closing of *Narratives* somehow. Certainly she was blaming him for not having acted sooner.

He arranged to see Matt Goldschmidt, and made his way one morning to the FSG office in Union Square. Sitting in the tiny cubicle Goldschmidt occupied, Billy gazed out of the window towards the towers of the World Trade Center. New York, he thought, where the streets are paved with gold.

'You have to get into editorial at the very bottom, you know,' Goldschmidt was saying.

'That's been made very clear to me.'

'The pay's lousy, the work is humdrum, and then after a couple of years, if you're lucky, they make you an associate editor and you get to do the work someone higher up should really be doing.'

'It sounds irresistible.'

'I'm sorry,' said Goldschmidt with a shrug. 'But you shouldn't harbour any illusions.'

'I don't.'

'This is a small place, and things don't open up very often. You should try the big houses.'

'I have. I've tried pretty much everywhere.'

'Random?'

'I'm seeing Joe Fox next week.'

'He's a great guy, and a great editor. Does he need an assistant?'

'No, not as far as I'm aware. I met him when I tried to persuade him to give me something by Capote, and now he's invited me for a drink.'

'I hope it leads to something.'

When Billy left the building he wandered over to the Strand Bookstore, and spent an hour browsing idly. Nothing seemed to catch his interest at the moment – his mind was blank. He recalled times like this in his past, when he first came to New York, and years ago when he first went to London, after he dropped out of university. But he had been full of wild hopes then, hopes that were quite untethered to reality. He was thirty-three now, and no longer young. No longer young, and knowing about only one thing, books. His life until now had always been contingent, accidental even – he had never really had a grand design. And now he seemed to have had his worst accident so far.

Joe Fox handed Billy a gin and tonic.

'It was designed for artists,' he said.

Billy looked up to the ceiling, which was about forty feet away, and then out of the vast windows and across the park. This was the grandest apartment he had ever seen.

'Why the "Gainsborough" Studios?' said Alice. 'Why not the "Winslow Homer" or something?'

Fox sat down beside her on the sofa. 'You're American,' he said. 'You know we still have a collective inferiority complex when it comes to the Brits.'

'Maybe a hundred years ago,' said Billy. 'But haven't you got over it by now?'

'We pretend we have.'

Billy sipped his drink, which seemed to be nine parts gin and one part tonic.

'You mentioned you have British ancestors,' he said.

'I'm descended from George Fox, the founder of the Quakers. Not that very much Quaker spirit has survived in me.'

'That's quite something, to be able to trace your ancestors back that far. I've lost track of mine beyond my grandparents.'

'I wouldn't especially recommend having illustrious ancestors.'

Billy looked around the room again. 'You don't have them on the walls.'

'Oh, there's a rogues' gallery in my place in the country,' said Fox. 'I keep them out there, like idiot cousins.' He reached across and took Alice's hand. 'Now tell me about yourselves,' he said. 'Where did you meet?'

'In London,' said Alice. 'I was studying stage design there.'

'And then you dragged him back here.'

'I didn't need to be dragged,' said Billy. 'I wanted to come.'

'You were on that magazine – what was it called?'

'*The Bystander.*'

'Right. I seem to recall meeting Roy Urquhart once, at a party in Chelsea.'

'He's the last of a breed.'

'Don't say that. I consider myself one of that breed too.'

'I'm sorry…'

'I guess he's a few years older than I am, though, when I come to think of it.'

'He's closing down the magazine.'

'So you're some kind of literary Jonah, it seems.'

Billy shrugged. 'I hope not,' he said.

'I'm kidding. But you need a job, right?'

'Yes.'

'There's an editorial assistant's job opening up at our place. But you'd have to take a step down. How old are you?'

Billy hesitated for a moment. 'Twenty-eight,' he said.

Alice had raised her glass to her lips, but she stopped in mid-motion and turned to glare at him. What was five years? thought Billy. Random House would surely not give an entry-level job to someone of thirty-three.

'Can you live on twelve thousand dollars a year?' asked Fox.

Since this was two thousand dollars more than Blessing was paying him, Billy found this easy to answer. 'Sure,' he said.

'Someone with your experience ought to be able to move up pretty quickly. But editorial jobs don't come along very often.'

'Who should I talk to about an interview?'

'Leave it to me. I'll call you tomorrow.'

They stayed for another half an hour, and then Billy and Alice left, walking along Central Park South to the subway station.

'Twenty-eight?' said Alice. 'What did you think you were doing?'

'Do you want me to get a job at Random House or don't you?'

'I don't want you to lie.'

'It was a white lie.'

'There's no such thing'

'Alice, I need a job.'

They crossed the street, and when they reached the other side she took her hand away from his. On the subway Billy felt both self-justifying and foolish, and couldn't think what to say next. After they had sat in silence for a while he said, 'He's straight out of *The Philadelphia Story*, isn't he?'

'I guess so. The question is whether he's the Cary Grant character or the Jimmy Stewart.'

Alice and Ellen went to see a French film, *Diva*, at Film Forum. It was pretentious and silly, and they left halfway through. As they strolled arm-in-arm up Thompson, a street person came up to them, smiling extravagantly. 'Ladies, spare a buck to go toward my new Cadillac?' he said. Alice smiled in return and gave him a quarter.

'Bums are getting smarter and smarter,' said Ellen after he'd gone. 'He probably *does* have a Cadillac fund.'

By now summer had clamped the city in its stifling embrace. They took refuge from the heat in a bar.

'How's work?' said Alice.

'Fine. I'm spending all my time on winter buying. I'm never in season, always one foot in the next.'

'So what will the well-dressed Manhattanite be wearing this winter?'

'Oh, cardigans, not pullovers. Plaid kilts. Cullottes.'

'Cullottes?'

'Sure. Except Calvin Klein calls them "split skirts".'

'I must pick mine up right away,' said Alice with a wry smile.

Ellen touched her hand. 'I'll get you some knock-offs,' she said.

Alice crossed her legs, pausing for a moment to run her hand down her calves and consider whether she needed to shave them again. 'And are things still on with Mike?' she said.

'Sure. He's taking me to Bar Harbor for a long weekend.' She leaned in towards Alice. 'He's great in bed.'

'I don't think I want to hear about it.'

'Oh, you married girls! When's the last time you and Billy had sex?'

'Last night, since you ask.'

'Touché.'

'It's not Billy in bed I'm worried about.'

Ellen squeezed a slice of lime into her drink. 'Well?' she said.

'He's lost his job.'

'Oh no! Why didn't you tell me?'

'I just have. I've only known myself for a couple of weeks.'

'How come?'

'The magazine's closing down. And just at a time when I have one more play in prospect and then that's it for the summer.'

'What's he going to do?'

'He has an interview at Random House. Editorial assistant.'

'Random House would be great.'

'Yes, it would. But it's a very junior position, and he's lied about his age, saying they wouldn't give it to him otherwise.'

'Everyone lies about their age.'

'No they don't. I don't.' She ran a fingertip down the side of the icy glass, drawing a line in the condensation. 'You know, they tell you that marriage helps you to share your burdens. What they don't say is that it doubles them in the first place.'

'Wait till you have kids.'

Alice licked her fingertip. 'Kids?' she said. 'Not yet awhile.'

'You're thirty-one, Alice.'

'Thirty-one and broke. It's OK for you, with your big salary and expense account. Spare a thought for us girls down in the trenches.'

'The trenches of Greenwich Village,' said Ellen archly. 'It's hell down here.'

———

Billy stepped into the lobby of the Random House building and took the elevator to the eleventh floor. Sitting in reception, he looked around at the books on display. This was the publisher of Capote and Vidal, Mailer and Styron. It had published the first American edition of *Ulysses*, and Faulkner, O'Neill, Shaw. The idea that he might be a part of it seemed both absurdly remote and tantalizingly close.

As the minutes went by he pulled from his pocket a copy of the résumé he had sent them. He must be clear about this revised version of himself he was about to create. Losing five years of his life had not been a simple matter, especially since he had to add on two, the years he would now claim he had spent finishing his degree at Bristol when in fact he had dropped out and mouldered away in bookshops.

Eventually Russell Williams came to collect him, and led him down a corridor to his office. He was in his late thirties, Billy guessed, barely older than himself. His hair was sparse and gingery and his face sharply delineated. He wore a tweed jacket of the kind Billy had never set eyes on in America, and a burgundy woollen tie. He sat down behind his desk and picked up Billy's résumé.

'You're a fiction man,' he said.

'I suppose so.'

'I don't do any fiction myself.' He waved airily at the shelves, and Billy turned to see a book about the Federalist Papers, a biography of Aaron Burr, and a couple of Civil War histories.

'Mr Fox told me you don't. I've always read history and biography as well as fiction. I would welcome the opportunity to be involved in them professionally.'

Williams's eyes returned to the résumé. 'So, let's see. You read English at Bristol, worked in a bookstore, and then you went into magazines. That's a pretty good apprenticeship.'

'It was.'

Williams laid down the piece of paper and took off his glasses. There was a donnish air about him that Billy guessed had been carefully cultivated.

'It's not very glamorous down here in History Corner,' he said. 'All the star editors are at the other end of the hall. I just get on with my stuff, and they leave me alone. I don't suppose my books ever make any money for the house, but they get good reviews.'

'I'm not interested in glamour.'

'No?'

'I'm interested in words, and ideas.'

'If you were behind this desk, what kind of books would you want to publish?'

'Well, I have to say that it would be mostly fiction, and literary biography. But that's some way in the future, isn't it?'

'That depends. We have kids here fresh out of Harvard and Princeton who think they can be Maxwell Perkins inside a couple of years but who'll soon be heading for law school. You strike me as being different.'

Billy found himself staring out of the window, at the other high buildings clustered around. Was Williams saying that he intended to hire him?

'I'm supposed to give you a typing test,' he said.

'I can type. About forty words a minute.'

'I'll take your word for it.' He put on his glasses again. 'Joe said I should hire you.'

'That's kind of him.'

'I'm interviewing other people.'

'Of course.'

'I'll let you know something next week.'

Williams stood and shook Billy's hand. Out in the street he craned his neck to look back up at this citadel of American publishing, willing Russell Williams to give him the job. This felt like his last shot. If it didn't work out, he really would have to consider going back to a bookstore.

———

If Alice could be said to have a second home it was Pearl Paint, the artists' materials store that spread across four floors of a big building on Canal Street. She had lost count of the number of hours she had spent there over the years, buying everything from sketchbooks and drafting pens to erasers and dividers. And paint, gallons of it. Today she and Paul were doing just that, buying paint to finish off the balcony area of the set of The Hotel Play. Alice's idea of 'human scenery' had not gone very far. The play required two levels, one for the hotel's lobby and bar and another for guest rooms, and for a short play it demanded a great deal of set design and construction. Alice couldn't help but think of the whole enterprise as being an act of self-indulgence on Shawn's part. The cast list contained many famous names, other playwrights and friends of Shawn's, many of whom would be on stage for a few moments at most. And having read the play through a few times now, she sort of didn't get it. What was Shawn trying to say in this seedy hotel in the tropics?

They crossed Canal Street, lugging the cans of paint, passing rows of tiny emporia selling cheap jewellery, clothes and hi-fi equipment. Canal Street was thronged day and night, New York's oriental bazaar. Everyone was buying and selling, delivering and collecting. All this stuff, thought Alice: what was it for?

'God, these are heavy,' she said.

'Just feel the heft,' said Paul. 'We won't be coming back here for a while now.'

The thought that there was no more work in prospect had haunted Alice throughout this production. She and Billy had no plans for the summer, and a long, hot emptiness beckoned. How would she fill it?

They paused at the corner of Broadway and set the cans of paint on the ground. A young man weaved past them, making eyes at Paul.

'Cute,' he said, watching him recede into the crowd.

'Is he? I never know with gays what's cute and what isn't.'

'Leave that to me, sweetheart.' He smiled, but fleetingly. 'Soon it isn't going to matter one way or the other.'

'How do you mean?'

'Haven't you read about this thing they're calling the "gay virus"?'

'No.'

'Five guys in LA have it. Some of them are airline stewards, and they reckon it's come over from somewhere in Africa.'

'A gay virus? How is that possible?'

'Don't ask me. But it's scary as hell. When I think of all the tricks I've had over the years...'

'I thought you were taking it easy nowadays.'

'Nowadays, yes. But what about my murky past?'

They picked up the cans again and headed up the street. Paul was right, Alice thought: they must make the most of this play. And surely it wouldn't be too long before the fall productions got underway. She must find reasons to be cheerful.

———

The waiting was agonizing. Williams had said he would let him know 'next week', but as next week became this week, and this week dragged on, Billy began to lose hope. He prowled the city, hanging out in bookstores and coffee shops. At home the strain was even worse, and he and Alice were barely speaking to one another. For the first time it dawned on Billy that marriage was something more than an expression of love, of preference. Only now was he beginning to understand that it was a compact, a practical arrangement. He had never given any thought to providing for Alice, and considered this an absurdly old-fashioned notion; but nonetheless his pride and his sense of who he was had been gravely threatened in the past couple of weeks.

At five thirty on the Friday the call finally came, and Williams offered him the job. As soon as Alice returned home they headed for Chumley's to celebrate. He drank far too much, and spent the weekend recovering. It was with a strange sense of unreality that on Monday morning he returned to the Random House building and asked to see Russell Williams.

'I'm not going to introduce you to everyone on the floor,' said Williams. 'You'll only forget their names. But you should meet Ivan Moskovitz. He sits at the next desk, and he can show you the ropes.'

Williams called out Moskovitz's name, and a short, dark figure appeared at the door. His head seemed far too big for his body, and his frizzy black hair shot out in all directions. He thrust out a hand and gripped Billy's firmly.

'Ivan works for Sandy McIntyre,' said Williams, 'who edits some hardcovers for Random and some paperbacks for Vintage.'

'Welcome to hard times,' said Moskovitz.

'We're going to need to transmit a manuscript today,' said Williams. 'Ivan, will you let Billy know what's involved?'

'Sure. Follow me.'

Moskovitz sat right behind Billy, his the last in a long row of identical desks bearing electric typewriters, phones and jumbles of papers. He took a form from a drawer.

'You're basically putting the manuscript into copy-editing,' he said, 'where the Gorgon and her sisters will fix it up and prepare it for the typesetter. But you've worked on magazines, right? You know the drill.'

'We didn't have forms.' Billy looked up at his new workmate. 'Who's the Gorgon?'

'Betty Schmidt, the head of copy-editing.'

They went through the materials and information Billy would need

343

in order to transmit the manuscript. While they were doing so, Joe Fox joined them.

'You made it,' he said.

'Thanks to you, it seems, yes.'

'Good.' He turned to Moskovitz. 'You don't have anything to eat, do you, Ivan?'

'No, Joe. Sorry.'

Joe moved on, and Moskovitz turned to Billy. 'He's always on the scrounge,' he said. 'You'd think the guy was poor or something.'

'Maybe he's being sociable.'

In the middle of the morning Moskovitz said, 'I'll show you the kitchen and the water cooler. Let's get a cup of coffee.' They walked along the corridor and into a small, airless room. Moskovitz poured coffee into two mugs and handed one to Billy.

'Williams asked me to show you the ropes,' he said, 'so let me tell you how it works around here.' He slurped his coffee. 'First you have to understand that this is the Mom and Pop show.'

'And who are they?'

'Anne Freedgood, the editor of Vintage, is Mom, and Jason Epstein, the editorial director, is Pop.'

Billy knew quite a lot about Epstein already. As well as being the chief editor at Random House he was a founder of *The New York Review of Books*, and one of the great and the good.

'You have to get around those two if you want to get on,' continued Moskovitz. 'And the first thing you'll need to do is to dump that dopey boss of yours and work with someone who's involved with Vintage.'

'Is that what they think of Williams?'

'It's what I think of Williams.'

Moskovitz had a habit of jutting his jaw whenever he made a statement, and this gave him a pugnacious aspect.

'So I've come in at the wrong entrance, have I?'

'I wouldn't say that. You'll need to work the room, though.' He looked across at the door, and then back at Billy. 'There's an associate editor who's thinking of leaving,' he said quietly. 'He has the one office that's likely to be vacated any time soon. My name is on that door when he does.'

'Good luck, then.'

'Good luck?' said Moskovitz. 'Luck doesn't have anything to do with it.'

Hal turned the steaks on the barbecue and wiped sweat from his brow. 'I'm frying too,' he said. 'This is the hottest Fourth of July I can remember.'

Billy and Alice had taken the train that morning, and now they sat with Hal and Barbara in the shade of a sycamore tree behind the house. Billy swigged beer from a can.

'Will you fetch the salads, dear?' said Barbara.

He stood and walked across to the house, his flip-flops setting up a drumbeat on the hard, sere lawn. When he returned, Barbara was saying to Alice, 'Isn't it marvellous?' She turned to Billy. 'It's just marvellous that you're at Random House.'

'Yes, it is.'

'Such a famous name. And owned by such a nice man. The one who used to be on *What's My Line?*'

'Bennett Cerf,' said Billy. 'But he's dead now. It's owned by a newspaperman.'

'That's right, Bennett Cerf. He always wore a bow tie, as I recall.'

'What are they paying you?' said Hal.

'Twelve thousand a year, to start with.'

'Twelve thousand?' Hal took off his aviator sunglasses and rubbed the bridge of his nose with his thumb and forefinger. 'We pay our entry-level people twice that much.'

'Random House isn't a hedge fund, Dad,' said Alice. 'It's a publishing house.'

'It makes money, though, doesn't it? What about the dictionary?'

'That's the reference division,' said Billy. 'I'm doing history books.'

Hal raised his beer can to his lips. 'Here's to history, then,' he said.

'It's a good day to be toasting history.'

'Two hundred and five years since we threw off the yoke of British oppression.'

'Of which I am a daily reminder.'

'Oh, you're not so bad. For a Brit.' Hal smiled. Considering how much he drank, he had very white teeth. 'I was thinking about the Declaration this morning as I was reading the paper. You know when it says, "Life, liberty and the pursuit of happiness"?'

'Yes.'

'Jefferson's original words were, "Life, liberty and the pursuit of property". But they changed it.'

'Why?'

Hal shrugged. 'I don't know. Maybe they thought they amounted to the same thing.'

Billy looked back at the colonial-style house with its shingled walls and gabled roofs. Even though he could scarcely imagine living this way himself, there was something very seductive about it, the abundance, the ease.

'And what about you, Alice?' said Barbara.

'My work? I'm through. On the breadline. My last job finished a week ago.'

'You should take a rest.'

'I *have* to take a rest.'

'There must be lots of plays coming up though, dear. I was reading about them just the other day. Someone's turning *Nicholas Nickleby* into a play.'

'That's on Broadway, Mom. I've tried uptown, but it's a closed shop. The unions.'

'I thought we broke the unions decades ago,' said Hal.

'*We?*' said Alice sourly. 'You were at the barricades?'

'You know what I mean.'

'Now, now,' said Barbara. 'It's a holiday, everyone, remember?' She took her glass of wine in her hand. 'Here's to the pursuit of happiness.'

They ate lunch, and then dozed and read. In the cool of the evening Billy and Alice took a walk in the woods.

'Maybe you should spend some time up here this summer,' said Billy. 'Get away from the city.'

'They'd drive me crazy. You know that.' She linked her arm in his. 'A beach is what I'd like, a long, white beach.'

'Coney Island?' said Billy, smiling.

'I was thinking more of Antigua.'

'Maybe we can go somewhere in the fall, if we don't spend anything for a while.'

'Maybe.' She gazed up into the canopy of trees. 'I do want to be comfortable, Billy,' she said. 'I just don't want to have to make compromises along the way.'

'We'll be comfortable,' he said. 'I'll see to it.'

She looked up at him earnestly. 'I've been thinking about what you said so as to get this job, about your age and your degree and everything. Maybe I was being unfair.'

He hugged her close to him and kissed her neck. 'It was worth it, Alice,' he said. 'It doesn't make me a liar. It's what you have to do.'

'I guess so.'

'As your mother said, it's marvellous that I'm at Random House. I feel I've arrived. Anything's possible there. I just have to make it happen.'

'You're sounding like an American.'

'I'm an honorary American. I'm married to an American and I'm living in America.'

'So you are.'

Four

In the taxi on the way to the restaurant Billy turned to Joe Fox and said, 'So what's the story with Jack Henry Abbott?'

'A long one,' replied Joe. 'Wait till we're sitting down.'

He had expected Elaine's to be smarter than it was. The gingham-covered tables were set out on a tiled floor, and faded frescoes covered the walls. There were photos of the many famous writers and actors who were regulars there, and peeling posters for old films and plays. Elaine greeted them and led them to a table. She was plump and dark, and her brown eyes gazed at them through large round glasses that perched on the tip of her nose.

'Bourbon?' she said to Joe, and he nodded in reply. 'And what about your guest?' Bourbon was a taste Billy hadn't acquired, and he asked for a glass of wine.

'So tell me about Abbott,' he said.

'Well, you know we just published his book, In the Belly of the Beast.'

'Yes. I saw a rave review in the Times. "Fiercely visionary", or some such.'

'He's a career criminal. Spent most of his adult life in jails across the country. And murdered one of his fellow inmates in one of them.'

'And he was taken up by Mailer?'

'He wrote to him while Norman was writing The Executioner's Song, saying that if Mailer needed to know about life behind bars, he would tell him. His letters were sort of brutal and ecstatic. Norman loved them, thought he'd found a new Genet.'

Their drinks arrived, and Joe stirred his and placed the cocktail stick in the corner of his mouth.

'And Mailer tipped off Random House?' said Billy.

'He tipped off Bob Silvers at the New York Review, and Bob told Jason.'

'Now he's murdered someone else.'

'That's the way it seems. So much for the redemptive powers of being published and praised.' Joe took the cocktail stick out of his mouth and inspected the bite marks he had made in it. Then he turned to Billy and said, 'What are you doing in the summer?'

'Nothing. I can't take a vacation this early. And we're low in funds.'

'You and Alice should come out to my place in Sagaponack for a long weekend.'

'Where's that?'

'The Hamptons. I bought a house there years ago for a song, before it started to become fashionable. Come on out there sometime soon.'

'Thank you. We'd love to.'

As they were returning to the office, Billy looked out of the window at the storefronts flashing by and thought with satisfaction of the turn his life had recently taken. He was at the centre of things now. It was hard to credit, the way he had travelled within a couple of years from a dusty magazine in Bloomsbury to the heart of literary America. It was only when he returned to his desk, to the scrawled notes from Russell Williams asking him to do some quite menial tasks, that he recalled that he hadn't quite arrived yet after all.

———

Alice and Paul descended the steps of the Public Theater and crossed the street. Their interview with Joseph Papp, the director, hadn't been encouraging. There was a new production of *Antigone* slated for November, but no decision yet about who might be designing it.

The day was searingly hot and humid. When summer took hold like this, the city overwhelmed Alice. Everything seemed intensified – the noises louder, the crowds thicker, the buildings looming ever larger. Air conditioners and the exhausts of buses blew yet more hot air onto the sidewalks. New York was an inferno.

They ducked into a café on Astor Place for iced tea, relishing the cool and the dark.

'That's it for me, then,' said Paul. 'Fire Island here I come. I guess I'll stay out there till Labor Day.'

'Lucky you.'

'I'm going to be as chaste as a virgin, though.'

'Yes?'

'Yeah.' He leaned towards Alice. 'I had some tests last week, and I'm waiting for the results.'

'What tests?'

'For the virus, of course. I'm not going to sleep easy until I know whether I'm positive.'

'Of course. I'm sorry.'

'They're calling it GRID now.'

'Meaning?'

'Gay-Related Immune Deficiency.' An expression of disgust came over Paul's features. 'And now the religious nutcases are saying it's God's retribution against us.'

'Well, that's obviously nonsense.'

'Doesn't stop people saying it.'

They sat in silence for a while, and then Paul said, 'So what will you do?'

'I've no idea. Billy can't take any time off yet. One of his colleagues has invited us out to the Hamptons, but that'll just be a weekend.'

'Hey, don't knock it. A lot of people would kill for a weekend in the Hamptons.'

Alice crunched ice between her teeth. 'I guess so,' she said. 'But what about the six weeks either side of it, stuck here in the city?'

'Make the most of it. Go to some galleries.'

'Maybe.' She looked up at him. 'Right now I can't get out of my mind that phrase Peter Brook used about the stage, the empty space. He should talk to me – I know all about empty spaces.'

Paul reached across the table and took her hand. 'We're going to be fine,' he said. 'This is a temporary lull.'

'To follow the last one.'

'You need cheering up. Aren't you happy about Billy's new job?'

'Sure. He's completely immersed in it. But it's demanding. He brings manuscripts home to read and edit in the evenings and at weekends. At the magazine he used to do all that in the office.'

'Does he appreciate how that is for you?'

'I think so. But it's still a fact.' She looked out of the window at the colourful street. 'How come work always seems to be feast or famine?' she said. 'Why can't it be steady?'

'You know the answer to that,' replied Paul. 'If you want a steady job you can have it.' He waved at the waitress. 'How about the one this girl's got?'

They drank another tea and then Alice headed for the apartment. It was three o'clock, and Billy wouldn't be home for hours. She looked on the shelves for the book by Peter Brook, and turned to the pages about Stanislavski and the Actors Studio. Were things better then? At Yale her professor always used to say there was no Golden Age. But of course there was: the Golden Age was always the age just before yours. She kicked off her sandals and curled up in the armchair. It was a short book, and even though she had read it a dozen times it would neatly fill her own space, the space between now and Billy's return.

The pattern of their life seemed to Alice profoundly changed. In the past she had many times observed, in a tone that was wry but also uncomplaining, that their work caused them to lead lives that often seemed quite separate, that glanced off each other's. Now, in the torpid heat of summer, her own life seemed not so much to glance off Billy's as to touch it only when his life determined it would. On a Sunday afternoon she lay on the sofa, her half-read copy of To the Lighthouse lying open and face-down on her stomach, watching Billy as he worked.

'How's the battle of Midway coming along?' she said.

'Three aircraft carriers and two battleship sunk so far,' replied Billy without looking up.

'So we're going to win.'

'We won, Alice, remember?'

'My memory of that particular occasion is a little vague.'

Billy set down his pencil and looked across at her. 'I have to get this done by tonight,' he said. 'It's going to press next week.'

'How long's it going to take?'

Billy took off his glasses and rubbed his eyes. 'I don't know. Three hours, maybe four.'

'That's the rest of the day,' she said, sitting up. 'And I'm getting a little tired of the Ramsays.'

Billy stepped across to the kitchen and poured himself a glass of water. When he had emptied it he said, 'What would you like to do? Go to a movie?'

'There's nothing on at the moment. But I feel cooped up.'

'Let's go to the White Horse for a drink. Give me another hour.'

By the time they sat down on stools in the bar, Alice was feeling this was merely a gesture on Billy's part. She looked up at the signs advertising Guinness and Newcastle Brown Ale. The White Horse was the closest thing New York had to an English pub, and in his first few months in the city Billy had often drifted here when he was feeling homesick. His suggesting they come here now simply made Alice feel even more inconsequential than ever. She sat gazing into the gilded mirror, not at herself so much as at the two of them.

'Next weekend we'll be at Joe's place in Sagaponack,' said Billy.

She looked back from the reflection of him to the original. 'I don't need to be humoured,' she said.

He reached out and touched her arm. 'I know,' he said. 'I've been there myself, haven't I?'

'But it's me who's there now.'

'I know that too.' He dropped his hand and curled it around his glass. 'You know what I think?' he said.

'Funnily enough, I have no idea what you think.'

Billy sighed. 'I think you need something else besides the theatre.'

'You mean quit?'

'No, I mean something *else*. For the times when there's no theatre work.'

'I could temp.'

'No, Alice,' he said earnestly. 'You're misunderstanding me. Isn't there some other kind of design work you'd like to do that can fill times like this?'

She looked away from him, and then down at herself. Her dress was bunched up around her knees, and she smoothed it out. 'I have to be ready to take these set design jobs at short notice,' she said, 'you know that. Other things would get in the way.'

'It was just a thought.'

'I guess I could apply to the Broadway theatres for scene painting work. But that's just manual labour, and I do enough of it already.'

'Forget it,' he said. 'I'm sorry. By September you'll be at the Public again.'

'Maybe. Even that's not a sure thing.'

'How about going back to some of your own work?'

'My own work?'

'The watercolours you used to do.'

'In our place?'

Billy raised his eyebrows. 'I'm just trying to be helpful,' he said.

'Thanks,' she said morosely. 'You're being a great help.'

Their conversation stalled, and they contented themselves with watching other people. Alice couldn't decide whether she had been unfair on Billy. His being wrapped up in his work like this was in some ways good to see. But was this their future she was staring at, a future in which he fulfilled himself while she lost her way? And what would happen when they wanted a child? That seemed unimaginable at the moment. But maybe it was the answer, maybe it was the something else Billy had talked about. A child was not 'something else', though. For the moment she would simply call more theatres in her search for work.

———————

The Hamptons Jitney dropped them off in Bridgehampton, and Joe Fox waved at them from a battered Volvo. They drove for ten minutes through flat farmland, the fields green with potato plants or yellow with corn. Just past the Sagaponack General Store they turned into a side road to the house. Like many they had seen, it was built of wooden shingles weathered to grey. There was a tang of salt in the air, but the sea remained out of sight. Joe showed them to their room and then fixed a drink. As they sat down in the garden chairs, Billy let out a sigh of contentment.

'What a beautiful place,' he said.

'It's where I decompress,' said Joe.

'How far away is the beach?'

'Fifteen minutes' walk. But I usually take the car. We'll go there tomorrow.' He turned to Alice. 'Now, house rules. Guests do the cooking and I do the dishes.'

'Fine with me.'

'Some people are coming over for dinner tomorrow night.'

'Who?'

'Jim Schlesinger, but without his wife, who's in Paris. And Jack Traub and his wife Dawn. Traub is at Harper & Row, and she's a poet.'

'I've heard of Traub but not met him.'

They sat outside until supper, and turned in early. The next morning Joe drove them to the beach. The sea was calm, and the spangly water lapped at their feet. Sand dunes lined the way, topped with sparse tufts of grass. The bathers weren't quite out yet, and the joggers and dog-walkers had the beach to themselves for now. They passed a marshy pond, and Billy said, 'Ever do any fishing?'

'Only at the fish store,' replied Joe. 'I don't need any excuses to stare into space.'

They spent the late afternoon preparing supper, Joe hanging around so as to tell them where everything was. When Alice made to season the lamb he said, 'You know that salt you're using? It's sugar.' At six on the dot Jim Schlesinger arrived. He was a compact man with a military bearing and a neatly trimmed white moustache. He greeted Joe perfunctorily and made straight for the fridge, taking out bottles of vodka and vermouth that stood in the freezer compartment. Nodding to Billy and Alice, he took a small plastic vial from his pocket and placed it on the counter.

'Ever drunk a Gibson?' he said.

'No.'

'It's a dry martini with cocktail onions instead of olives or a twist.'

'He carries those onions with him wherever he goes,' said Joe. 'God forbid he might go without his Gibson.'

Jack and Dawn Traub arrived, and they gathered in the garden. Jack Traub was a moon-faced man of about fifty with a mass of curly greying hair. His wife was probably fifteen years younger, her green eyes staring down a beaky nose, her lips seeming to be clamped together except when she spoke. Billy and Alice assumed the roles of hosts, making drinks and now and then checking on the food. The conversation fixed on the subject of writers and publishers, of who was up and who was down, of which writer had just changed agents and which reviewer had dished his rival's book in the New York Times. Billy found it hard to keep up. He looked across the garden towards the pampas grass, thinking that this was really a New York conversation, just happening a hundred miles east. Glancing at Alice he realized she was taking no part in it at all, appearing to be using the dinner preparations as a reason to absent herself.

They stayed out until late into the night. The conversation, so lively and gossipy earlier, became desultory as they sat looking up at the stars. After their guests had gone Joe ordered Billy and Alice to bed, and turned his attentions to the dishes.

'I guess that wasn't much fun for you,' said Billy as they lay waiting for sleep to come.

'It was fine,' she said. 'But this is your world, not mine.'

'I'm sorry.'

'Don't be. As I said, it's fine. In a couple of weeks we'll be at my parents for the weekend, and we can talk about something other than books.'

She turned over. Billy lay awake for a long time, exhilarated by the sense that once again Joe Fox had placed him at the centre of things. A dozen or more famous writers had houses within a stone's throw of this one, and it appeared that they were all at one time or another guests here. Would he be invited back? He hoped so.

In the morning Joe took Billy for another walk, while Alice remained at the house.

'Let's see if Bob Gottlieb is around this weekend,' he said.

'Bob Gottlieb of Knopf?'

'Yes. He sometimes stays at a friend's place.'

Billy had for some time wanted to meet Gottlieb. He was a legendary editor, who had published *Catch-22* and many other famous books. They approached a house in the lee of the dunes that was constructed on stilts. Joe led the way up the outside staircase and looked through a window. Turning to Billy, he pressed a finger to his lips and gestured with the other hand for him to descend again. When they were back on the sand he said, 'I don't think we'll bother them at the moment. They're knitting.'

They walked away from the house in silence, and once they were back on the beach Joe said, 'You know, there's a young British editor at Knopf on some kind of exchange programme, and I'm sure Bob said she was at Bristol University. She must be about your age, maybe a little younger. Her name's Clare Rowley. Ever come across her?'

Billy raised a hand to shade his eyes from the sun. 'I don't recall her, no,' he said.

'You two should get together. I'll arrange it.'

Billy's hand stayed at his brow, shielding him from Joe's gaze. A flush of heat had passed through him that had nothing to do with the sun. Of course, he thought – something like this was bound to happen. He lowered his hand and turned towards Joe.

'Thanks,' he said. 'I'd like to meet her.'

———

'Random House, huh?' said Wendell. 'The big time.'

'It's certainly big,' replied Billy. 'But I'm the lowliest of the low.'

355

'Just remember where you were at the last time we talked.'

'Sure. I have a lot to be grateful for.'

They were having lunch in a steakhouse a couple of blocks from the office. Wendell was back in New York briefly, and Billy was glad to see him.

'Alice must be pleased.'

'I hope so. She's not so pleased about my bringing work home, though.'

'That's part of the deal, I guess.'

'So it seems. Things would be easier if she were working too, but she's got nothing on at the moment.'

Wendell tugged at the bandanna that was tied around his neck. 'Complicated business, marriage,' he said.

'And what would you know about it?'

'Hey, I was married once.'

'You were? I had no idea.'

'For six weeks.' Wendell smiled ruefully.

'What happened?'

'I snored too much, apparently.'

Billy laughed. 'Are you serious?'

'That's what she said.' Wendell looked down at his plate. He had practically finished his rib-eye steak in the time it had taken Billy to pick up his knife and fork.

'So, how's the novel coming along?'

'I've done six chapters. Only ninety-four to go.'

'Did you go to the place on the lake?'

'No. I figured I was better off in Butte. It's not a bad town. You should come visit sometime.'

'Maybe I'll come and edit your book.'

'Great. When do I sign a contract?'

'When you finish, and when I become an editor. Shall we say two years?'

'Two years? Christ, I'm going to need longer than that. Dos Passos took nearly ten.'

'You'd better get onto it, then.'

'Let's see which happens first, me finishing my book or you making editor.'

Back in the office, Billy called Alice. She sounded very distant, and he wondered whether he had woken her up from a nap. When he replaced the phone he gazed down the corridor, thinking back to what Wendell had said about marriage being complicated. He so much wanted them both to be fulfilled and happy; but this constant balancing act made that seem a remote prospect. He must simply be more considerate. Certainly he wasn't going to hold back now at Random House. 'The big time', Wendell had called it. One day, maybe.

From Christopher Street to the Erie Lackawanna in Hoboken was no distance at all. Alice had never been here before, and was visiting Ellen's new apartment for the first time. As she walked away from the station she looked back at Manhattan. It seemed almost within touching distance, just across the Hudson. She had been surprised when Ellen said she was moving out here. But as she faced the brownstone, looking up at its wide stoop and the brass fittings on the front door, she began to see why.

'Hi!' said Ellen, ushering her inside. 'Welcome to Jersey.'

'This isn't my idea of New Jersey at all.'

'All my designer friends are moving here.'

The apartment consisted of a long corridor with rooms set off it. At the far end was a light, airy space with big windows that overlooked the waterfront. Alice thought of Marlon Brando. This was where he had tried to be a contender.

'They call them "railroad" apartments,' said Ellen. 'You can see why.'

'It's wonderful. But what are you going to do with all these rooms?'

'I don't know. I just like the idea of being able to walk in my home.'

Ellen made some lemonade, and they sat together on the sofa.

'I'm going to need about three times as much furniture as I had in my old place,' said Ellen. 'You'll have to help me choose it.'

After a while they went out, walking towards the campus of the college. From the grounds they were able to see Manhattan from its lower tip all the way up to the Empire State. The windows of the skyscrapers were lit up by the afternoon sun, flashing like the beams of giant lighthouses. They sat on a bench, watching the show.

'How are things with Mike?' said Alice. 'Still on?'

'Absolutely. We're going to Barcelona together in two weeks' time. I've never been.'

'And how is it when you're at work?'

'A little weird, I guess. We tend to avoid each other as much as we can.'

'Does anyone suspect?'

'Oh, I'm sure they do. People like to *suspect*, don't they? But I don't think anyone's really figured it out. We're pretty careful.'

'It sounds as though it's getting serious.'

'Does it?'

Alice looked away to watch a tugboat gliding down the river. 'How long's it been now? Six months?'

'Not that long. Five maybe.'

'Longer than a fling, anyway.'

Ellen toyed with her bracelet. 'Still on the dole?' she asked after a few moments.

'Yes. And no prospect of getting off it.'

'You've been here before, Alice. Something always turns up.'

'Something always *used* to turn up.' She looked back at her friend. 'Billy says I should be thinking about something else.'

'But the theatre's your lifeblood.'

'As well as, not instead of.'

'What would that be?'

'I don't know. Maybe I should do a course at FIT.'

'Forget it, sister. You're far too pure for the fashion world.'

'Am I pure? Is that what you think?'

Ellen shuffled along the bench and placed her arm around Alice's shoulders.

'You haven't got a clue,' she said, smiling. 'You'd hate the world of commerce. Remember all those things you've said about your dad over the years?'

'That's different. Dad's business is about money and nothing else.'

'All business is about money and nothing else in the end.'

'Is it?'

'We're fooling ourselves if we think any different.'

'Then I'll stick to the theatre.'

'You stick to the theatre, Alice. It's your home.'

When an hour or so later she emerged from the subway station, she walked south towards Canal Street and Pearl Paint. All her watercolours stuff was back in Greenwich, in the attic. She wandered around the store, looking at easels and paper and paint sets. Could she see herself setting up on a sidewalk somewhere, painting brownstones and being stared at by people as they stepped around her? She turned and hurriedly left the building. All that was in the past now.

———

In the dog days of late August, shortly before the Labor Day holiday, the office was eerily quiet. Almost all the editors, and most of the assistants too, had fled the city. Russell Williams was wrapping things up with Billy before heading for Vermont.

'I haven't had time to write the cover copy for the Midway book,' he said. 'Will you do it and get it to Betty by early next week?'

'Sure.'

'And then there's a monster that needs feeding.'

He stepped over to the shelves and picked up a manuscript that appeared to be nearly a thousand pages long.

'This is John Blueeyes's book,' he said, 'about the Long Walk. Have I told you anything about it?'

'No, I don't think so.'

'OK. Blueeyes is a Navajo, or at least mostly Navajo. Do you know anything about the Long Walk?'

'Not a thing, I'm afraid.'

'Toward the end of the Civil War the army forcibly marched eight thousand Navajo from their homeland in Arizona to a reservation in New Mexico. Plenty of historians have written about it, but Blueeyes considers himself the only one really qualified to do so. He's a cuss, but I think this is a significant book. I've done a preliminary reading, and it needs cutting by at least a quarter.'

'And you want me to do it?'

'I'd like you to read it while I'm away. Then we can talk about it some more.'

Billy took the manuscript and laid it on the floor beside him, thinking not for the first time that the responsibilities Williams was giving him so early on were gratifying but also a little onerous.

'I guess that's it,' said Williams. 'Take it easy for a couple of weeks, why don't you? Everyone else is.'

The next day Billy leafed through the Midway book again and began to write the copy. This battle that represented the turning point

359

in the Pacific war had entered into American mythology, and he wanted to get it right. He had spoken of himself as an honorary American, but at times like this he was intensely aware that he had not been born and brought up here, that he was still a foreigner. He'd had an absurd argument once with an author over his use of the phrase 'the lay of the land'. 'It's "the lie of the land",' Billy had insisted, 'it's intransitive.' The author had replied that he couldn't care less whether it was intransitive, that this was what Americans said, and who was Billy to lecture him about it?

Ivan Moskovitz was still around, and by now he and Billy had fallen into the habit of meeting in the kitchen over a cup of coffee and catching up. The associate editor whose office Ivan coveted had resigned, but Ivan had been told that for the time being no decision would be made about his successor. This had done nothing to blunt the edge of mordancy in his voice whenever he spoke of their colleagues.

'Did you see the piece in the *Times* this morning about Jack Henry Abbott?' he said.

'Yes.'

'They must be squirming over it, Jason and Erroll.'

'Erroll edited the book?'

'Yeah. Look, it's not his fault. He just did what Jason asked him to do.'

'And it's not exactly Jason's fault either that the guy's committed another murder.'

Ivan aimed a paper cup at the garbage can. 'It's all down to Mailer in the end,' he said. 'All that "hipster" bullshit, all that romanticizing violence.'

'It's what he's always done.'

'It sure is. But now he's fallen into the classic liberal trap. People like Mailer don't know anything about people like Abbott. He should read his Dostoevsky again – he knew what life in the gutter was like.'

'Can you blame him for responding to Abbott's voice, though? He's a powerful writer.'

'Don't get me wrong – the book's great. But that's not the point.'

'Surely it *is* the point,' said Billy. 'Publishers aren't the guardians of people's morals. If a book is good, then print it.'

'So there's no such thing as an immoral book?'

'I'm not saying that. If Abbott had urged people to commit murder, then that would be different. But he didn't.'

'He just described it lovingly.'

Billy emptied his mug. 'You'd have edited it, though, wouldn't you, if Jason had asked you instead of Erroll?'

Ivan smiled knowingly. 'Of course I would,' he said.

'Sushi is one of my great discoveries here,' said Clare Rowley. She stirred some wasabi into the soy sauce and then daintily dipped a slice of raw tuna into it.

'For me it's been bagels,' said Billy. 'With cream cheese.'

'Not very good for you.'

'A lot of things in New York aren't very good for you.'

She smiled, and he took another opportunity to study her. She was very dark, with long flowing hair and deep brown eyes. Her skin was tanned, and set off by the white cotton of her dress. She looked more like an Italian than an Englishwoman.

'So tell me how you came to be here,' he said.

'I'm at Jonathan Cape. Tom Maschler, the publisher there, is good friends with Bob Gottleib, and they arranged for me to swap with an editor at Knopf for a couple of months.'

'Good idea.'

'American publishing isn't so much different from British publishing. It just seems a hundred times bigger, that's all.'

'That's because Random House is actually many houses, rather than one.'

'I know. It's still a little overwhelming, though.'

He couldn't help but observe the way she ate this rather tricky food, handling her chopsticks as though she were brought up on them, and then wiping her lips with a napkin after every bite.

'And what's going on up at Knopf these days?'

'We just got in copies of Updike's latest this morning. Everyone's very excited.'

'*Rabbit is Rich*.'

'Are you an Updike fan?'

'I'm not sure. His sentences are wonderful. He's sort of the poet of American surfaces. But compared with Bellow and Roth...?' He left the question hanging in the air, not sure of the answer.

'He's good on sex,' she said.

'It's his subject in the end, isn't it?' replied Billy, suddenly unable to meet her gaze.

'So, how about you?' she said after a few moments. 'You've been here a while.'

'About two and a half years. My wife is American, and I followed her here.'

'You're lucky.'

'Am I?' He paused. 'You know what E. B. White said? "No one should come to New York to live unless he is willing to be lucky."'

'I like the "willing".'

'A colleague of mine says that luck has nothing to do with it.'

'Maybe we should talk about chance rather than luck.'

The waitress poured them more tea, and Clare took her cup in her hand. Her forefinger pointed away from it, and, as it seemed to Billy, towards him.

'Joe Fox told me you'd been at Bristol,' she said.

Billy had been preparing for this moment. In a way, he'd been preparing for it ever since Joe first mentioned Clare, on the beach at Sagaponack.

'You know what they say about people reinventing themselves when they come to America?' he said.

She put down the cup. 'So you *didn't* go to Bristol,' she said smiling.

'I did. But I didn't stay. I dropped out after a year and a term.'

'But you told Random House you graduated.'

'Yes.'

He waited while she sipped at her tea again.

'Good for you,' she said finally. 'Be lucky.'

He sat back in his chair, the tension draining from his body.

'I told them more than that,' he said. 'I told them I'm twenty-eight when I'm actually thirty-three.'

She giggled now, and raised her hand to cover her mouth.

'Anything else I should know about you?' she said. 'I wouldn't want to say the wrong thing to anyone.'

'That's it. A little rearranging. Fact is I've spent the past thirteen years in the book world, in bookshops, magazines, and now publishing. I think I've earned this break.'

'I'm sure you have.'

'All I need to do now is to catch up.'

'Catch up?'

'Become an editor. Be settled by the time I'm forty.'

'By the time you're thirty-five, you mean.'

'Maybe by then I'll be able to admit to my little deception.'

'Well,' she said, 'your secret is safe with me.'

A friend of Alice's offered them a weekend in his cabin in the Catskills, and they eagerly accepted. As Billy drove the rented car up the Thruway, Alice reflected that this was really their summer vacation. The heat of August had given way to the gentler warmth of September. The seasons changed so fast, she thought: soon it would be fall, and the trees would be turning. In Woodstock they stopped at a store and bought provisions. From there the directions were vague, and it took them an hour or so to find the right road, and then a couple of detours before they saw the track that led to the cabin.

'This is great,' said Alice. 'The middle of nowhere.'

It was an authentic log cabin, dating from the 1850s. It stood on the shore of a small lake, and there wasn't another building or sign of life anywhere. Alice jumped out of the car and ran towards the jetty. A rowboat was tied up there, its oars tidily stowed. Looking back at the cabin, she saw that it had a porch that ran the length of its frontage, with rocking chairs and a hammock. An ornate wind chime hung motionless in the still afternoon air.

Inside, the place was furnished and decorated in a simple, almost spartan way, the only colour coming from a few rugs on the floor. They unloaded the car and went for a swim, skinny-dipping in the cold water. Alice brushed her hair away from her face and looked around the perimeter of the lake. There was nothing but trees – maples, birches and elms – and all of them a deep, dark green. She breathed in the pure air gratefully.

Billy set up the barbecue, and while he cooked the chicken Alice boiled water for the corn and potatoes. They ate on the porch, using their fingers instead of knives and forks.

'Would you like to live in the country, someday?' she said.

'I spent the happiest days of my childhood in the country. But now… I don't know.'

'I don't mean any time soon. What with our work and all. But someday?'

Billy smiled. He licked his fingers and put his plate on the deck. 'Someday,' he said. 'But what would we do?'

'How about running a little bookstore?'

'You're talking to the wrong person, Alice. I did my time in bookstores.'

'But up here it would be different. It'd be a community thing.'

'And it would go broke in no time at all.'

She took a sip of wine. 'I know I'm being impractical,' she said. 'But I can dream, can't I?'

'Sure.'

They sat for a while listening to the cicadas and the occasional hoot of a screech owl. Then Alice turned to Billy and said, 'The thing that would change it all would be kids.'

Billy held her gaze for a few moments. They hadn't talked about children for a long time now.

'Yes,' he said. 'But we're not ready to think about that yet, are we?'

'Maybe we *should* be thinking about it.'

'Now?'

'No. But soon. I shouldn't leave it much longer than another couple of years.'

'A couple of years? Alice, I'm earning twelve thousand dollars a year and you're out of work. We're going to need longer than that.'

She looked out across the lake. The light was beginning to fade now, and the sky had turned the pale blue it becomes just before it begins to darken.

'How much longer?' she said.

'I don't know. Five years?'

'I'll be thirty-six.'

'That's OK, isn't it?'

'It starts getting riskier by then.'

Billy stood and picked up their plates. He kissed Alice on the cheek and stepped back into the cabin. Rocking back and forth in her chair, Alice stared up at the treetops. He doesn't want to talk about it, she thought, and maybe he's right. But sometime soon he will have to talk about it.

Billy passed through the rooms of Si Newhouse's brownstone, nodding at his colleagues but more intrigued by the paintings. Newhouse, the owner of Random House, was a collector of modern art, and the walls of the big rooms were covered in paintings by Rauschenberg, Johns, Twombly and Rothko. It felt more like being in a gallery than in someone's home.

The party was celebrating publication of Fran Lebowitz's new book *Social Studies*, a witty account of New York life. It was the sort of gathering that Billy, as an editorial assistant, would generally not be invited to, but Joe Fox had slipped him in. He recognized many people, editors and critics, but somehow didn't feel easy about approaching them. As he was standing in front of one of Rothko's field paintings, trying as Alice had often urged him to surrender himself to it, a voice said, 'It shimmers, doesn't it?' He turned to see Clare Rowley. She was leaning forward, an empty champagne flute in her hand.

'It's sort of depthless,' he replied.

'It draws you in.'

'My wife says I have no visual sense at all.'

'It's another language, art.'

'A foreign language, to me at least.'

She looked down into her glass and then across the room. 'Do you know anyone here?' she said.

'No. Just the people from the office.'

'I don't know a soul. I was thinking of leaving. Are you hungry?'

'I could be.'

'There's a Thai place nearby.'

'Let's go, then.'

They said a few goodbyes, and then descended the stairs and stepped out into the street. It was a beautiful late summer evening, and a hazy dusk was just beginning to cloak the city. They walked up Lexington Avenue for a few blocks and entered the restaurant. The maître d' beamed at Clare and led them to a corner table.

'You come here often,' said Billy.

'I live nearby, and it's become my canteen. I'm gorging on all the foods I won't be able to find back in London.'

'How much longer will you be here?'

'Just two weeks. I'm feeling sad already.'

Billy raised his glass. 'To the rest of your New York adventure, then,' he said.

'Thank you.' She smiled, revealing her very even teeth. She was once again wearing a dress that showed off her tawny skin. Billy looked away, telling himself as he had over their lunch that he must not appear too appreciative of this alarmingly attractive woman.

'New York is still an adventure for me,' he said, 'even after all this time.'

'You're seeing it through the eyes of someone else.'

'Someone else?'

'The Billy you've created for the purpose.'

'The young Billy, you mean.'

'Young, yes. But more than just that. This place seems to do that to people – it causes them to slough off their old skin.'

'You too?'

'Oh, I'm not here long enough for that. But if I were to stay, then yes, probably.'

'I wonder whether I'll slough off this new skin in time, too, or whether this is it now.'

'Don't shed too much of yourself.'

The conversation turned to books and authors. Clare had studied American literature at Bristol, and spoke knowledgeably of it. Her favourites were the women writers of the early part of the century, Edith Wharton, Emily Dickinson, Willa Cather. 'No one in England reads them,' she said. 'Except now Virago is bringing some of them back.'

When dinner was over and they were strolling back down the street, Clare said, 'How about coffee at my place?'

Billy hesitated for a moment, resisting the impulse to look at his watch. It was late now, but not that late. 'Thank you,' he said.

Her apartment was a studio, one room with an alcove for a kitchen and a bathroom you had to enter sideways. Billy sat on the sofa while Clare fixed coffee, made uncomfortable by the closeness this room prescribed and wishing he had declined her offer. She handed him a mug and sat beside him, tucking her bare legs under her dress.

'I was fortunate to get this place,' she said. 'It's owned by a friend of Bob Gottlieb's.'

'It's how this city works. We live in a rent-controlled apartment in the West Village that on the open market we couldn't possibly afford.'

'What does your wife do?'

'She's a theatre set designer.'

'And how did you meet?'

'She was studying at the English National Opera. We met at a party after a fringe play in Highgate.'

'So you came to New York for love.'

'I suppose I did. Love and adventure.'

'Two very big things.'

After a while Billy set down his mug of coffee, and now he did look at his watch, making a show of it. 'I should be getting home,' he said. He stood awkwardly, and took a few steps towards the door. Clare followed him, and then reached up and kissed him on the lips.

'Evenings can be quiet for me,' she said. 'If you feel like getting together again sometime, just let me know.'

Ellen dropped by on her way home from work, and Alice made guacamole. They sat at the table, dipping nacho chips into the pale green mash.

'So, how was the trip upstate?' said Ellen.

'Oh, it was wonderful. We just read and walked and swam.'

'Mike and I are going back to Bar Harbor next weekend. I think he's going to say something this time.'

'Say something?'

Ellen smiled gaily, and dipped her finger into the guacamole. 'Propose, I mean,' she said.

'Really? Congratulations!'

'Well, he hasn't said anything for sure. But he's been dropping hints.'

'We must meet him. I feel he's been your little secret all this time.'

'It's funny, but he hasn't met any of my friends yet.'

'Why not?'

'I don't know. Maybe it's the work thing. Or maybe this hasn't felt like a grown-up relationship until now.'

'What exactly is a grown-up relationship?'

'Well, you know, one that's out in the world.'

Alice went to the fridge and took out a bottle of white wine. 'I wonder if Billy and I have a grown-up relationship, in that case,' she said.

'Of course you do. You're married.'

'Ellen,' she said, 'if you think marriage necessarily means a mature relationship, you've got another think coming.'

'OK, I know. I'm not sure even my own parents have a mature relationship. I guess I mean something that's been... oh, I don't know... sanctified or whatever.'

'Now you're coming over all Catholic.'

'No, I don't really mean that either...' Her voice trailed off, and they sat in silence for a while.

'Billy and I talked about children when we were in the Catskills,' said Alice eventually.

'You did? When do you get started?'

'In another lifetime, it seems.'

'How do you mean?'

Alice held her glass in both hands. 'He says we're not ready.'

'But you're thirty-one, for God's sakes. When *are* you going to be ready?'

'When Billy's earning more than twelve thousand a year, apparently.'

'Didn't your parents once say they'd help out?'

'Yes. But I've never told Billy that. His pride would be wounded.'

'To hell with his pride. If you want a child you should have one. It's your body, not his.'

Alice looked up at her friend. 'It's not that he's being obstructive or anything. Just... evasive.'

'Well, he has no right to be evasive. You must tell him that.'

'I don't know, Ellen. I think this is going to take a while.'

Ellen laid a hand on her arm. 'You decide how long it's going to take,' she said.

Alice smiled. 'I'm certainly not going to be beaten to it by you,' she said, 'that's for sure.'

The narrow space of Books & Company was jammed with people, all listening with rapt attention to Peggy Massey reading from her new novel. She was a slight figure, her wispy dark hair streaked with grey, her granny glasses folded in an upraised hand. Billy looked around the room, recognizing the faces of editors and publicists from Knopf, but not knowing any of them by name. Clare Rowley was there, as he knew she would be, leaning against the shelves and now and then glancing in Billy's direction. She smiled opaquely, and Billy smiled back. Peggy Massey came to the end of her act, and Billy moved across the room.

'Can I get you a glass of wine?' he said to Clare.

'Thanks.'

They slid into an alcove, and stood for a few moments watching people queue to have their books signed by the author.

'So there are some civilians here, then,' said Billy.

'Civilians?'

'I mean people who aren't either from the publishing house or friends of the writer.'

'You've been to a lot of these things.'

'I suppose I have.'

'Why did you come to this one? Do you know Peggy Massey?'

'No. I was just curious.'

'In that case there's not a lot of point in sticking around. I have a bottle of wine at my place, and some salad fixings.'

He looked at her thoughtfully. 'Thanks,' he said.

They walked down Madison Avenue and across to her apartment. Once they were inside, Clare opened the bottle of wine and set about making supper.

'These readings are catching on, aren't they?' she said.

'It always used to be that only poets read from their work. Now fiction writers are at it too.'

'With mixed results.'

'Some people are better at reading than others.'

'But is it a good idea? Poetry started out as a spoken thing, but shouldn't fiction be savoured on the page, in the voices inside the reader's head?'

Billy looked at the shelves. 'I don't know,' he said. 'If it sells books, then it must be a good idea.'

'It sells books to the people who would have bought them anyway.'

She cleared the magazines from the coffee table and set down a salad bowl. They sat on the sofa, balancing their plates on their knees.

'So when is it you leave?' he asked.

'At the weekend.'

'That soon?'

'My two months are up.'

'And it's been a good experience?'

'Certainly. I've learned a lot. And I've met editors and agents it would have taken me years to get to know otherwise.'

She stood and took the three steps it needed to cross the room to the record player, putting on a John Coltrane album. Its cool, restrained tones were quite at odds with Billy's mood, with his sense that something was about to happen, something he was unable to resist. Though the volume was low the music filled the room, and their conversation stuttered. Clare cleared the plates and bowls, dumping them in the sink. When she sat down again she gazed at him very directly. Billy placed his wine glass on the table and leaned across to kiss her.

She took his hand in hers, leading him to the bed, and silently they took off each other's clothes. Billy felt himself to be in a trance, all conscious thought banished from his mind. Clare's body was as finely contoured as he had known it would be, her breasts shining white against the tan of her belly and shoulders. He hadn't made love with anyone other than Alice for years, and the sight of this unfamiliar flesh thrilled him. She lay on the bed and reached up with outstretched hands. Kneeling above her, he let his hands roam from her neck down to her thighs. She opened herself to him, and suddenly he was on top of her, clutching at her hair, kissing her wildly. Neither of them said a word until it was over.

After a few minutes she raised herself and put on a robe. Billy felt exposed now, and he pulled on his underpants and trousers.

'Coffee?' she said.

'I think I'd better be going.'

'I'm sorry. I've kept you from your wife.'

'Is that supposed to make me feel better or worse?'

She stepped towards him and kissed him lightly on the lips. 'I'll be gone by the weekend,' she said.

In the taxi speeding towards home, Billy gazed out of the window at the city. It was night now, but the electric night of Manhattan, the night that defies the dark. What on earth had he done, and why? He had done it for no more meaningful reason than that he could. But how would he face Alice? He heard Clare's words ringing in his ears: 'I'll be gone by the weekend.' He must never do anything like this again.

On Saturday they had a night out. Alice wanted to see a new film, *Body Heat*, and before going to the late screening they had supper in Chumley's. Billy gazed up at the walls, at the book jackets and photographs of writers. It was corny, this place, but nonetheless he liked it.

'Billy, I've decided,' said Alice after they had ordered. 'I'm going to get a job.'

'What kind of job?'

'A friend of Ellen's is looking for a PA. He's an interior designer, has a studio in SoHo.'

'A PA? Are you sure?'

'Sure I'm sure. We need the money. He's offering twelve thousand five hundred a year.' She smiled ruefully. 'That's five hundred more than Random House is paying you.'

'But you'd have to give up the theatre altogether.'

'Of course I would.'

'Oh, Alice! You can't do that.'

'I think I have to.'

The waiter brought a dish of antipasto, and Billy forked a slice of ham onto his plate. For the past few days he had ducked any attempt Alice made to talk to him about anything other than the everyday. He was mortified by what had happened with Clare Rowley. Should he confess? But it had been only one night, and even as they sat there, Clare would be on the plane back to London. Alice would be devastated if he told her. As if she didn't have enough to worry about as it was.

'I guess you've talked this over with Ellen,' he said.

'Sure. It was when I told her I'd decided to get a job that she mentioned this guy.'

'And does she think it's a good idea?'

'No.' Alice raised her glass to her lips. 'She thinks I should stick it out in the theatre.'

'That's what I think too.'

She gave him a hard look. 'Well, I've decided,' she said. 'I have an interview tomorrow. And if I don't get this one, another will come along soon.'

After supper they walked to the cinema. The film had Kathleen Turner as a scheming rich woman who wants to dump her husband

and be even richer, and William Hurt as the credulous man she draws into her net. There were some steamy sex scenes, and images of Billy's lovemaking with Clare came back to him with terrible clarity. Intensely aware of Alice's nearness, he found himself leaning away from her. And then she threaded her arm in his, drawing him back. When they got home, Alice draped a shawl over the bedside lamp, turned to face Billy, and began to take off her clothes. He hesitated for a moment.

'That film got me going,' she said. She stepped forward and kissed him, unbuttoning his shirt as she did so. 'Am I as sexy as Kathleen Turner?'

Billy's shirt fell to the floor. 'Much sexier,' he said, as he took her in his arms.

Five

The offices of Zimmerman & Chang were in a loft overlooking Greene Street. An uninterrupted open space, its exposed brick walls were painted a brilliant white. Glass partitions separated the workstations, and brightly coloured leather sofas stood facing brushed steel coffee tables. Here and there were sculptures in bronze or wood, abstract shapes that reared towards the ceiling like exclamation marks. Alice sat just outside Henry Zimmerman's area, surveying the plans that lay on her desk. His current project was a new restaurant in Tribeca, and he was about to meet the client.

Zimmerman called to her and she handed him the plans. 'Sit in on this, Alice,' he said, 'and take some minutes.'

Henry Zimmerman was a tall man in his mid-forties. He wore a black linen suit and an open-necked white shirt, and frameless spectacles that glinted in the fluorescent lighting. Everything about him and his company spoke of money and style. Alice had worn her smartest clothes on this first day, but still she felt dowdy. There was nothing in this place that had not been calculated for visual effect, and she found it all very intimidating.

The client was a Los Angeles-based restaurateur who was setting up an Asian–Californian fusion place. He had apparently told Zimmerman that he wanted something 'blue', and judging from the plans he was getting a space that might as easily be an aquarium as a restaurant. He approved them, and after the meeting was over Zimmerman invited Alice to have a sandwich. 'We'll order out,' he said. 'I encourage our people to stay in the office at lunchtime. It breaks your concentration too much when you go outside.'

When their pastrami sandwiches arrived they sat on one of the sofas.

'So, is it anything like set design?' he asked.

Alice smiled. 'The principles are the same,' she said. 'You have a space, a theme, a budget and a client. The rest is up to you.'

'Exactly. I hope we can draw on your experience.'

'But I won't be designing anything.'

'Sure. But we're a team here, we all bring to our work everything we've done and seen.'

'I'll do what I can.'

After lunch she found herself gazing out over the water towers on the roofs across the street. Had she really left the theatre now, after all these years? According to Paul the door remained open at the Public. But he had recently been given a commission at Steppenwolf in Chicago, and without him she was sure nothing would break for her. By now she was beginning to suspect that she had made a mistake, and was uncertain what to do about it. She had never worked in an office before, and it was the strangest feeling. Strange too was the sense that what she was doing was wholly determined by other people, that notwithstanding Zimmerman's little homily, nothing she thought or felt about things would matter in the least.

At the end of the day she walked slowly home, stopping at Zito's to buy bread for tomorrow's breakfast. It was a rainy, misty day, and there was an autumnal chill in the air. Ahead of her the tall buildings in midtown disappeared into the cloud, truly scraping the sky now. Rain added a new dimension to the city, the reflections of the buildings in the sheen of water plunging downwards in counterpoint to their height. New York in the rain was like a modern Venice.

Once she was home she looked in the refrigerator to see what there was to eat. On an impulse she put on her coat again and headed for Balducci's. She must do something creative this evening – she must not let the day go by without expressing herself somehow. She bought shrimp and apples and snow peas, and some Dijon mustard and crème fraiche. And as she strode back to the apartment she felt something of herself returning.

'You may have to go and see him in Arizona,' said Russell Williams.

'I'd enjoy that,' replied Billy.

'It wouldn't be a vacation, I can assure you of that.'

They had been talking about John Blueeyes's book. Billy had now read its thousand-odd pages, and it was clear that it needed a lot of work. It was not just too long – it was meandering, often hectoring in tone, and sometimes it bordered on the incoherent. When later Billy caught up with Ivan Moskovitz in the kitchen, he told him about it.

'It's a mess,' he said.

'And the guy's a nightmare, so I hear. Still angry about what was done to his people all that time ago.'

'If it means a trip to Arizona I'll be happy to take him on. I've never been out West.'

'Don't get your hopes up. He probably lives in a trailer park.'

Billy returned to work. The office was quiet once again, several of the editors being in Frankfurt for the book fair. He had been at Random House for three months now, and knew his way around. But more than this, he knew he had found his vocation. Why had it taken him so long to recognize that book publishing was where he belonged? He would make a go of this, would somehow draw attention to himself and get the promotion Ivan was now on the verge of. And then he would become what Williams had referred to as a 'star editor', working on important books that would win prizes and be reviewed on the front page of the New York Times Book Review. It was simply a matter of time.

His reveries were interrupted by a phone call. It was his mother, and her voice was tinged with the sort of anxiety Billy recalled only too well.

'Your father has been diagnosed with throat cancer, Billy.'

He gripped the receiver in his hand. 'Where is he?'

'In the hospital. The doctors think an operation won't be necessary, but he's going to have to undergo radiation therapy.'

Billy leaned back, running his hand through his hair. 'How's he taking it?' he asked.

'Oh, as you'd expect.' There was a note of bitterness in Margaret's voice.

'How is that?'

She was silent for a few moments. 'He's got it into his head that he's being persecuted somehow. Just when things are going well for him, fate deals him another blow.'

'I've never heard Dad talk of fate.'

'Only when he's in trouble.'

Billy cast his mind back to Sarah's wedding. He had sensed a hoarseness in his father's voice. And then there was the chain-smoking. Now that he had absorbed this news it dawned on him that it was hardly surprising.

'When does the therapy begin?'

'On Monday. He's going to be in hospital for several weeks. They're feeding him through a tube.'

'And then?'

'Well, he should be all right. But there's a risk he'll never come off the tube, apparently, and a remote chance he won't be able to speak again.'

'Oh, Mum,' said Billy wearily. 'This is terrible. How about you?'

'How about me?'

'Are you OK?'

'Yes. Sarah and Tom are coming down. Is there any chance you can be here too?'

'I don't know. It's pretty busy at the moment. If I came it would be for only a few days.'

'Please, Billy,' she said. 'It would make such a difference.'

As she said the words he wondered who it would make the difference to, whether his father or Margaret herself. But there was no question he must go.

'I'll talk to my boss,' he said.

'Thank you. Call me as soon as you can.'

He put down the phone. All thoughts of heading west were banished now from his mind. He must be on his way home again.

He was able to get a few days off, and flew to London. This time there was no one to meet him at the airport, and he had a tedious journey by bus to Wells. He went straight to the hospital.

'God, I hate this place,' said Jim as he sat down at his bedside.

Billy cast his eye around the ward. There were eight beds, occupied mostly by middle-aged men. One of them was hawking and spitting into a metal bowl. He seemed to be wholly occupied by this process, as though it were a task.

'You always did,' said Billy. 'Even when Tom was born you didn't want to come here.'

'Well, I came.'

'I know.'

His father looked terribly thin to Billy, his skin sallow and loose under his jaw. It was only a few months since he had last seen him, but he had changed utterly. The image of Tom lying in his bed in the Royal Free returned to him. There had been so much pain lately.

'So what happened?' he said.

'I came home one evening, Margaret put dinner in front of me, and I found I couldn't swallow. Haven't done since.'

'So all your nourishment is coming through the tube?'

'If you can call it nourishment. Filthy green muck.'

'And what's the radiation like?'

'Oh, you don't feel anything. The worst of it is they lock you in this mask-like thing, so you can't move. The Man in the Iron Mask, that's me.'

'How long will it go on?'

'A couple of weeks. Then with luck I can start eating and drinking again. They say nothing tastes very good for a while, though.'

Billy tried to imagine what it might be like not to eat or drink. For Jim there was hardly a moment when he wasn't bringing something or other to his mouth, usually a glass or a cigarette. This must be hell for him. And what did he do all day? A television burbled quietly in the corner, but too far away to see or hear clearly. There were no books on the bedside table, just a copy of the *Daily Express*. The crossword puzzle bore the marks of two answers.

'So how's it with you?' said Jim.

'Good, thanks. I've got a proper job now.'

'You said. Going well?'

'Yes. It's what I want to do, where I want to be.'

'And Alice?'

'She's got a proper job too. But I'm sad about that. I think she should stay in the theatre.'

They talked on for twenty minutes or so, and then Billy stood to go. As he walked away from the hospital he wondered how much longer he should stay. In a way he had already fulfilled his duty to his father. What would they say to each other when he visited again? What had they ever had to say to each other?

Rather than go straight to the house he kept on walking, to the High Street and Market Place. As the last time he was here, he felt a powerful sense of dislocation. This little medieval city was where he had spent his teenage years. Now it had about it an air of unreality. At Sarah's wedding he had told himself not to appear too worldly.

Nonetheless, as he passed people on the street he found it hard not to feel that lives lived in Wells were somehow of less consequence than those lived in New York. Why was that? What possible justification was there for it? He knew there was none at all, that it was absurd to think in this way. But still he felt stultified here, still he wondered how many days he would have to endure before he could return to the place he now called home.

The next day Sarah and Tom drove down in Sarah's car, and together with Billy and Margaret they went to visit Jim in the hospital. There was something inhibiting about the presence of so many people at the bedside, and conversation was desultory. Jim seemed in a good enough humour, though, and grateful for the attention. Afterwards they returned to the house, and Margaret and Sarah prepared supper. When they had sat down Margaret said, 'He asked to see his solicitor today.'

'What for?' said Billy.

'He's going to alter his will.'

'Alter his will? To what? From what?'

'I don't know.'

Sarah looked searchingly at her mother. 'Do you mean you don't know what's in Dad's will?'

'No. Should I?'

'Of course you should.'

Billy and Sarah exchanged glances, Sarah giving him a supplicating look.

'You're his wife, Mum,' said Billy. 'And you are, or should be, his sole beneficiary. I don't understand what he's doing. And I'm going straight back to the hospital after supper to find out.'

'Of course you aren't, Billy. You'll do no such thing.'

Sarah laid down her knife and fork and groaned softly. 'If he's cutting in any of his floosies, I'll kill him myself.'

'I won't listen to that sort of talk,' said Margaret firmly. 'Your father is seriously ill. Please show some respect.'

'Respect has to be earned,' said Billy. 'If he's doing anything that would disadvantage you, then you and we need to know about it.'

They had all stopped eating by now. Margaret picked up her wine glass and said, 'A toast. To your father's speedy recovery.'

'Stop it, Mum,' said Sarah. 'Stop running away from things. Billy's right – we have to confront him about this.'

Margaret replaced her glass on the table and folded her napkin. Making to get up from the table, she said, 'I'll go, then. Since you all seem to consider this so important, I'll go to the hospital.'

Billy stood up and took Margaret's hand in his. 'Sit down, Mum,' he said. 'Let's talk about this.'

She turned back and sat down heavily on her chair.

'It's time we talked honestly about him,' continued Billy. 'It's time this family came to terms with itself. Now let's eat supper, and then we'll talk.'

They ate in near silence, and then Billy and Tom did the washing up.

'What floosies?' whispered Tom. He had been practically silent throughout dinner, following the conversation abstractedly.

'Do you mean you don't know? The last one was only a few months ago, around the time of Sarah's wedding.'

'No one tells me anything.'

They joined Margaret and Sarah in the sitting room. Billy took the whisky bottle from the sideboard and offered it around, but only Tom accepted. He poured generous measures, and took a gulp before he sat down.

'Mum,' he said, 'none of us wants to embarrass you. But over the years you've talked often enough to Sarah and me about Dad's affairs. They have to stop now. It's time for things to change.'

'Isn't this a conversation for after he's well again?'

'I won't be here then, I'll be three thousand miles away.'

'Very well.' She looked at Sarah and Tom, and then at Billy. 'I think I need a little of that whisky after all.'

He stepped across to the cabinet, while his mother sat looking down at her hands. Taking a sip, she placed the glass on the coffee table.

'You think he's been a bad husband, don't you?' she said. 'That's what you all think.'

'He's made a lot of mistakes.'

'As has everyone.' She looked at each of them, her expression turning a little defiant. 'Do you think you can understand other people's marriages?'

'This isn't just anyone's marriage, Mum,' said Billy. 'It's our parents'. We ought to know something about it.'

'Then you know the things he's done for me. You know how he picked himself up after the bankruptcy and got back on his feet. He went through a terrible time. You and Sarah were too young to understand, and Tom wasn't even born. A man should never have to suffer the humiliation he endured then.'

'I'm not denying that,' said Billy. 'But it isn't the point. The point is that he's had one affair after another during your marriage. That's a betrayal.'

'You're being too harsh. And anyway, he's always admitted them.'

'Has he admitted the latest one, the girl in the office in Bristol?' asked Sarah.

'Not yet. But he will.'

Sarah looked once again at Billy, a look of exasperation on her face. 'He will,' she said. 'In his own time.'

Margaret remained silent for a few moments. 'He has always loved me,' she said finally. 'That's something that only I can know.' She looked up at them again, and there was a kind of serenity in her now.

Billy stood and went across to the window, gazing out into the garden. The leaves were scattered on the lawn, the evenings drawing in. There was a white dress of his mother's on the clothesline, and as he watched it flapping in the wind, suddenly his thoughts turned to Clare Rowley. He clutched at the glass in his hands. After a few moments he turned back into the room.

'I suppose you're right, Mum,' he said. 'No one else can really understand.'

———

Paul was back from Chicago, and Alice met him at Raoul's for a drink one evening after work.

'How was it?' she said.

'It was a blast. Chicago's such a great city. And working with Gary Sinise was exhilarating.'

'I've always wanted to go to the Steppenwolf.'

'It's a company, an old-fashioned theatre company. There aren't many of those around any more. Everyone pitches in.'

'And what now?'

'I'm seeing Joe Papp next week. He gave the *Antigone* to someone else. But there's a new David Hare play coming up. That would be perfect.' He looked at her over his glass. 'You must come with me.'

'No,' said Alice flatly. 'Thank you, but no. I've left the theatre, Paul.'

'But that's nonsense! You've taken a break, you've paid the rent. The theatre is everything to you, surely?'

'It was.' She sighed, and fiddled with her ring. 'I can't put up with the insecurity any more. This job...' Her voice trailed off, and she took a sip of her drink. 'This job is nothing much, but I know that it'll be there next week, next month – next year if I want.'

'But Alice, it's just a job. You had a career.'

She took Paul's hand in hers and squeezed it. 'I'd rather not talk about it.'

Paul looked at her thoughtfully. 'OK,' he said after a few moments. And then, 'How's Billy?'

'He's in England. His father's been diagnosed with throat cancer and he's gone to see him.'

'That's terrible.'

'Yes. And it's not as if Billy has an especially good relationship with him. They're very different. And they're three thousand miles apart.'

'I'm three thousand miles from my father, and it doesn't feel like far enough.'

'You never see your father.'

'Exactly.'

They ordered another round of drinks. Alice had no desire to return to the empty apartment. But being with Paul was less easy now than it used to be. For quite a while he had been her colleague and her friend. Would they drift apart now that they were no longer going to be working together? That would be a great shame.

'What do you know about boats?' she said.

'Boats?'

'My boss has a commission to design a clothes store at South Street Seaport. They want a nautical theme.'

'Don't ask me, sweetheart. I get seasick easy.' He leaned towards her, his expression turning suddenly earnest. 'I haven't told you about the tests, have I?' he said.

'I didn't like to ask.'

'I'm OK. I'm in the clear.'

'Thank God for that.'

'But others aren't, including one of my old boyfriends.'

'I'm sorry.'

Paul shrugged. 'We had a good time while it lasted.'

'That's not the way to look at it, though, surely? You have just as much right to relationships as anyone.'

'Yes. And it seems that anyone has just as much right to the consequences. They're no longer talking about it as just a gay disease.'

'No?'

'Obviously they don't understand it properly yet.'

'So we'll all be heading for the clinic.'

'I wouldn't imagine you have anything to worry about. You're married, after all.'

'So marriage is a defence?'

'I mean you're monogamous.'

Alice smiled. 'How do you know?' she said.

'I know you well enough by now.'

No sooner was Billy back in the office than Russell Williams was asking him to go to Arizona.

'I haven't got the time,' he said. 'And someone needs to go through the manuscript with him page by page.'

'When do I go?'

'Let me talk to John first. He isn't going to like being palmed off onto an assistant.'

'You can tell him I've been editing for years,' Billy replied, bridling. Williams was beginning to get on his nerves now. Either he was a secretary or he was an editor; but Williams seemed to expect him to be both.

'I'll talk to him.'

He went out to lunch with Ivan, and told him about the trip.

'He's dumping it on you,' said Ivan. 'The word is the sales people think the book should be cancelled.'

'When did you hear that?'

'While you were in England.'

'Well, I'm going anyway. The furthest west I've been so far is the Catskills.'

'Where exactly does Blueeyes live?'

'In the middle of nowhere. The nearest town is Chinle, I think.'

'That's in the Navajo Reservation. Don't tell him he lives in the middle of nowhere.'

Over coffee Billy asked Ivan what he was up to.

'Jason's asked me to work with him on Hamilton's Lowell biography.'

'Why you, and not Carla?'

'Because I wrote my dissertation on Lowell. Because I know every fucking thing there is to know about him.'

'That's great.'

'It sure is.'

Billy looked out of the window. 'We're pretty fortunate, aren't we, to have jobs like this.'

'It beats working. I just wish they'd make up their minds about my promotion. That and pay us decently.'

'That's the downside.'

'It's lousy, the money we earn.'

'You can always go to law school, or do an MBA.'

'No. I'll just become president of the company.'

'And pay people just as badly as you're paid now.'

'Worse.'

After lunch Billy went to the reference library and pulled out an atlas. He would have to fly to Phoenix, and then rent a car and drive over the Superstition Mountains. Ever since he arrived in America he had wanted to go out west, and now he had his chance. For the rest of the day he was quite unable to concentrate on his work, so excited was he by this prospect. And wanting to share it with someone, he walked up the corridor to talk to Joe Fox.

Joe's office was like that of all the other editors save for one distinguishing feature, a pile of yellowing copies of the *New York Times* that sat on a corner of his desk. When Billy had asked Ivan about this he had said that Joe used them as a kind of screen, so that people passing by couldn't see him. Like Joe's foraging for cookies and chips, this struck Billy as yet another instance of his peculiar charm.

'Ivan says the book is a dead duck,' said Billy.

'Probably,' replied Joe. 'But it doesn't matter. Go to Arizona and have a good time at Random House's expense.'

'That's exactly what I intend to do.'

Joe took a cigarette from a packet of Camels and lit up. 'How is your father?' he said.

'He's pulling through.'

Billy watched as Joe drew deeply on the cigarette, and Joe seemed to sense his gaze.

'I suppose I should take a hint from him,' he said.

'A hint?'

'About avoiding throat cancer.'

'I'm sure that won't happen to you.'

Joe smiled wryly. 'No, the drink'll get me first.'

———

'Let's see *My Dinner with Andre*,' said Billy one Sunday afternoon. The clocks had gone back, and suddenly the evenings stretched out before them.

'Is that the one with Wally Shawn in it?'

'Yes.'

'Don't they talk about the theatre a lot?'

He rested his arms on her shoulders. 'Is the theatre going to be off limits now?' he said gently. 'Are we supposed not to mention it?'

'I'm sorry. Sure, let's go.'

It was one of the most disturbing films he had ever seen. It consisted entirely of a conversation over dinner between Shawn and Andre Gregory. Gregory was a well-known theatre director, and he seemed to have had some kind of breakdown. Much of the conversation was about his visit to Poland and his attempt to create an improvisational company in some woods there. Gregory's nuttiness was contrasted with Shawn's nerdiness. For a while all Shawn seemed to do was giggle and utter banalities in his high-pitched, squeaky voice. But then the whole thing deepened, and they began to sound like sages. There was a lot of talk about the creative life, and the tyranny of work and careers. And then they moved on to the subject of marriage. Very soon Billy was feeling intensely uncomfortable, and leaning away from Alice in the way he had the last time they saw a film. 'To have a real relationship with another person that goes on for several years,' said Gregory at one point, 'well, that's completely unpredictable.'

Afterwards they had a bite to eat. It seemed clear to Billy that Alice was as unsettled by the film as he was, and he wondered whether for the same reasons. For her all the talk about the integrity of the theatre must have been hard to take. Their conversation skittered, and Billy realized they were not looking at each other very much. As they waited for the bill, an understanding dawned on him as to what he must do.

He had been struggling with this ever since he returned from England, wondering whether to tell Alice about Clare. The conversation with Margaret, Sarah and Tom about Jim's affairs had been haunting him. As had Tom's words about his becoming more and more like his father. Well, one way in which he could avoid such a fate would be to be honest with his wife. When they were back in the apartment he said, 'There's something I have to tell you.'

They sat down on the sofa, and he held her hands in his.

'A few weeks ago I slept with someone,' he said.

Very slowly, she withdrew her hands from his. She said nothing, waiting for him to go on.

'It happened once. After the Peggy Massey reading.'

'Who was she?'

'A British editor, over here on an exchange programme. She went back to London a few days later.'

'Was she pretty?'

'Alice…'

'I'm just curious, that's all.' She stood, and went to the kitchen for a glass of water. When she returned, she sat at the very end of the sofa. 'Why?' she said after a while.

'Why? I don't know why.'

'It's not as if we haven't been having sex lately.'

'I know. And it's not as if our sex isn't lovely, because it is.'

'Then you have to figure out why.'

Billy leaned his head back onto the cushions and stared at the ceiling. 'Have you never been tempted by anyone else?' he said.

'Not seriously, no.'

He looked back at her. Her expression was grave, and she seemed wholly composed. There were no tears, no reproaches. He had known she would respond in this way.

'I'm sorry, Alice. That night I told myself I will never do anything like that again. I promise.'

'Don't.'

'Don't promise?'

'Yes. It's meaningless. What did you promise me when we got married?'

'I'm not going to do anything like that ever again.'

She stood, and looked down at him. 'I'm going to bed, Billy,' she said. 'Why don't you stay up for a while?'

He sat listening to her brushing her teeth, wondering for the hundredth time why he had slept with Clare, and what it meant, if anything, for his feelings for Alice. A few minutes later the lights in the bedroom went out. There was so much more he had wanted to say, about his love for her, about his regret. What would they say to each other in the morning? He gazed across at the bedroom door. Surely she would forgive him. Surely she would.

———

But she didn't. Billy slept on the sofa, and the next morning Alice asked him to move out for a while. And feeling unable to argue with her, he decided he had better do so. But where to? He went to work, and very soon found himself gravitating towards Joe Fox's office. Joe wasted no time in suggesting he put up with him, and Billy gratefully accepted. At the end of the day he went back to the apartment, picked up some clothes, and took a taxi uptown. Joe was out for the evening, but the superintendent of the building let Billy in.

The following day was a Friday, and in the afternoon he travelled with Joe out to Sagaponack. It was only when they were sitting in the garden that they were able to talk about things.

'You shouldn't have told her,' said Joe.

'No?'

'What good will it do?'

Billy shrugged. 'I don't know,' he replied. 'It's just that I'm haunted by the idea that I'm following in my father's footsteps. He's had many affairs. And it seems he's always ended up telling my mother about them.'

'Then he's as much of a chump as you are.' Joe looked out across the garden. 'But you're talking to a twice-divorced man. You probably shouldn't listen to me at all.'

Billy took a sip of his gin and tonic, and then, inhaling its powerful ether, another, longer one. Maybe he would get drunk tonight, he thought.

'I suppose I don't like the idea of secrets,' he said.

'Don't we all have secrets?'

Billy thought back yet again to the film he had seen with Alice, the film that had prompted him to confess. Andre Gregory had said at some point that the closer you got to another person the more mysterious they became.

'I have plenty of secrets,' he said eventually. 'But I still don't like them. They weigh on me.'

'They weigh on all of us.' Joe lit up a cigarette. 'Look, this'll be over in no time. My hunch is that by Monday she'll be asking you to come back.'

'I hope so.'

'And if she doesn't, then ask her. Get down on your knees if you have to.'

Billy smiled wryly. 'And worship her?'

'Sure. A little worship goes a long way.'

They fixed supper, and Billy drank a lot of wine and then went straight to bed. He spent the weekend raiding Joe's bookshelves, and walking on the beach. Everything that really matters in life is so fragile, he thought. Indeed the more it mattered, the more fragile it became. And his marriage mattered, it mattered greatly. He was tempted to call her from here, but decided she needed a little time. What would she be doing at this very moment, and what would she be feeling? He longed to hear the sound of her voice, and he longed to be able to make up, to put all this behind them. But times like these had a logic and a timetable of their own. For the moment he would be thankful of Joe's company, and for a roof over his head.

For Alice too the city was a place to escape that weekend. She took the train out to Greenwich to stay with her parents. It struck her as odd, this sudden urge to see them – it wasn't as though she were especially close to her mother and father, and certainly she had no intention of confiding in them. How did people deal with moments like this, moments that must arise in most marriages? Alice suspected that her wish to go to Greenwich was more to get away than to return to home and hearth.

The more she thought about it the more extraordinary Billy's betrayal seemed. Wasn't this the kind of thing that happened when

387

marriages were in trouble? Nothing in their life had prepared her for this dreadful confession of his. She had always supposed that her husband was better than that. Now she had to come to terms with the realization that he wasn't, and that like so many men he was able to seize an opportunity, to seize on a probably lonely woman, so as to sate a momentary lust. This was surely the worst moment of her life.

It was a windswept evening, and she was grateful for the warmth of the car as Hal drove to the house. Her mother gave her a hug, and she lingered in her room for ten minutes or so before coming downstairs to join them again.

'What a nice surprise,' said Barbara. 'It's a shame Billy can't be with us.'

'He's up to his neck in work, Mom. He'll be glad of a weekend without distractions.'

'And how is his work going?'

'Very well. He's off to Arizona next week to work with an author. Everything seems to be happening very fast for him.'

Hal handed her a glass of red wine, and she stretched out on one of the sofas.

'Glad to hear it,' he said. 'It's about time.'

'He's a good editor, Dad.'

Hal took the pitcher of martini in his hand and poured the cloudy liquid into two large glasses, handing one to Barbara. Alice watched them appraisingly, considering how they looked and how she felt about them. Her father looked hale and her mother looked wan. So no change there, she thought.

'How about your new job?' asked Hal.

'Oh, it's fine. It's a pleasant office, and my boss is a nice guy.'

'So have you really left the theatre?'

'Yes. That's it now. It was fun for a few years, but it's just too insecure.'

They sat down to supper, and conversation circled around other members of the family, around whether Alice and Billy would come for Thanksgiving, around how cold it was for the time of year and what a bitter winter everyone was saying was in store. Afterwards Barbara and Alice did the dishes. As she was wiping the surfaces Barbara said, 'Let's sit down for a moment, dear.' They sat at one end of the kitchen table, Barbara methodically working hand cream into her skin and then passing it to Alice.

'Put some on your face,' said Alice. 'It looks dry.'

'I use lots of cold cream before bed. It doesn't seem to make much difference, though.'

'You should talk to Dr Rose. Your skin looks quite chapped, and winter has hardly begun.'

Barbara touched a hand to her face, and then laid it on Alice's arm.

'Your father and I have been talking,' she said. 'Don't you think that now is the time to be starting a family?'

'Oh, Mom,' replied Alice wearily. 'We have so much else to think about right now.'

'Of course. But you're going to be thirty-two soon.'

'I know. We talked about it when we were in the Catskills, and Billy was clear he thinks we need a few more years.'

'But that was before you took this new job. Don't you have benefits now?'

'I guess so.'

'And remember what your father told you about money. We'll take care of all the hospital costs, and then we want to buy you a place. It's time you got out of the city, Alice. There are some lovely new homes going up around here that are perfect for a young family.'

Alice worked the cream into her fingers, and then wiped it from her wedding ring. She looked up at her mother. Should she say something? Should she say that Billy had just told her he'd been unfaithful, that she had thrown him out, and that now was not a time for her to be thinking about sharing a child with him? No, of course she shouldn't.

'I doubt we'd want to leave the city,' she said instead. 'The commute can be hell. And we both still love being in the middle of things.'

'Well then, an apartment in the city. That's your choice.'

'I don't know, Mom. Now doesn't feel like the right time.'

'I waited too long before having you.'

She looked into her mother's eyes. 'What does that mean, exactly?' she said.

'Just that I was very tired a lot of the time. You don't have the same energy in your late thirties as you do in your twenties.'

'Sure. But all that's changed, you know that. Women are waiting longer and longer. And the doctors know more about what's going on, it's safer.'

'I do know that. All I'm saying is that there's a time for everything, and this feels to us like the time for you to have a child.'

Alice leaned across and kissed her mother's cheek. 'We'll talk about it again sometime soon, Mom,' she said. 'But not just yet.'

———————

Until now, Billy's knowledge of America extended as far as the narrow strip from Boston to Washington. As he looked out of the window of the aeroplane at the Appalachian Mountains, he was gripped by a sense of adventure. The mountains gave way to hills, and then, beyond the Mississippi River, to the plains of Missouri and Oklahoma. He kept the airline map open in front of him, trying to identify the places they were passing over. Eventually the plains gave way to a scrubby kind of desert, and in the distance to the north he could see the peaks of the Rockies. This was America. Not quite sea to shining sea, but almost. When the plane landed in Phoenix he could barely wait to get into his rented Chevrolet and light out for the territory.

He drove along the freeway through the suburban sprawl of the city, and before long the Superstition Mountains came into view. Soon he turned north, the road climbing up dry arroyos towards a pass, and then dipping into a canyon dotted with juniper bushes and pine trees. Rock faces the colour of rust soared up into the sky.

He drove on, through gentler canyons and around high ridges, turning east on the interstate and then seeing signs for the Painted Desert and the Petrified Forest. He looked at his watch. It was by now late afternoon, and darkness would soon be coming on. Perhaps he could detour on the way back.

Shortly after he had turned north again towards Chinle he saw an old Native American at the side of the road who extended his thumb and gazed at him with an imploring expression. Billy had hitched a lot when he was younger, and anyway this was now Navajo country. He braked and waited for the man to shuffle up to the car.

'Chinle?' he said.

'Sure,' said Billy.

The man was carrying four plastic bags, and they clanked as he got into the passenger seat. Billy could see that they contained beer and whisky bottles and nothing much else.

'Where have you come from?' he said.

390

'Gallup,' said the old man. 'Been stocking up.'

'Can't you get booze in Chinle?'

'Nope. No alcohol on the reservation.'

He was probably about seventy, his grey hair crew-cut, his skin nut-brown, and his expression was one of ineffable sadness. He stared straight ahead as they drove, making no attempt at conversation.

Away to his left Billy could now see lofty buttes and long, sweeping mesas, the classic terrain of the south-west. 'You have a beautiful land,' he said.

'Yeah?' The man's gaze followed Billy's. 'Beautiful if you don't have to live here, I guess.'

They lapsed into silence, until the man took out a bottle opener, flicked the top from one of the beer bottles, and offered it to Billy.

'No thanks. Not while I'm driving.'

'Mind if I do?'

'Go ahead.'

It was an hour before they reached Chinle, an hour in which the landscape continued to enchant him. It reminded him in some ways of Morocco, the first foreign country he had ever visited. But his responses to it were muted now by his passenger, who sat dolefully staring at the road ahead, swigging from the beer bottle.

John Blueeyes had told Billy to call him from the trading post in Chinle, where he would come to meet him. He parked the car, said farewell to his passenger, and walked towards the store. Outside was a stand selling crafts and jewellery and weavings. The woman minding it looked at Billy incuriously. He smiled and said hello, but she made no reply. He called Blueeyes, who said he'd be with him in fifteen minutes, telling him to look out for a pick-up. When it swept into the parking lot, Billy walked over to greet him.

He was a big man, probably in his mid-forties, with long, glossy black hair. He wore the standard western outfit of plaid shirt, faded jeans and suede boots, but otherwise he could not be anything other than a Native American. His mouth was turned down sharply at the corners, and there were deep clefts in his chin and his cheeks.

'Welcome to the Navajo Nation,' said Blueeyes.

'Thank you.'

'Where's your car?'

Billy pointed towards the Chevrolet.

'Follow me, then.'

They drove out of the little town in convoy, Billy trying to keep pace with Blueeyes while dodging the swirl of sand and dust the pick-up raised. After ten minutes of driving north they turned off onto a side road, which quickly became a dirt track. Sagebrush lined the way, and tumbleweed rolled across it here and there. Up ahead was a stand of white-barked aspen trees, and beside it a double-fronted mobile home, resting on breeze blocks. Ivan had been almost right, he thought. Blueeyes parked the pick-up beside a dome-shaped structure built of logs and mud. Billy pulled up alongside, and together they entered the mobile home.

'Drink?' said Blueeyes.

'Thank you.'

'There's iced tea, cranberry juice…'

'Iced tea would be fine.'

It was immediately clear that Blueeyes lived alone. There were native weavings and pottery, but otherwise it was wholly functional, and there was no mistaking this for anything other than a bachelor's place. They sat in rocking chairs, Billy waiting for Blueeyes to take the lead.

'It's kind of strange that my book should be edited by a Brit,' he said eventually.

'Yes?'

'Without the Brits, who became the Americans, there wouldn't have been a Long Walk.'

'I suppose not. But the Spanish were here before that.'

'We took care of them.'

There was an awkward pause, and then Billy said, 'You've written an important book.'

'Thank you. Not so important that you don't think I should re-write it.'

Billy hadn't yet attuned himself to Blueeyes's tone. Was he angry with him over the editorial suggestions he had proposed, or was this just the way he usually spoke?

'I hope I'm being helpful.'

'Let's talk about that tomorrow.'

Billy looked around him, and asked about the hut.

'That's my hogan. It's our traditional home.' He stood up. 'Let me show it to you.'

In the fading light they walked over to the hut. Blueeyes drew back a blanket that covered the doorway, and they stepped into a dark space. Looking up, Billy saw a smoke hole in the centre of the dirt roof. The floor was covered with sheepskins, but otherwise it was quite bare.

'This is the way our ancestors lived,' said Blueeyes. 'It's important for us to remember.'

'I've been reading about Navajo mythology,' said Billy. 'It's fascinating.'

'You may call it mythology. We call it our story.'

Billy looked at him through the gloom. They had spoken on the phone twice before now, and judging from these conversations Billy had been sure he would have to tread carefully. He was even surer now.

'I'd like to hear it,' he said. 'Your story.'

'I will tell it to you. And then you can tell me yours.'

Over supper Blueeyes recounted the story of the Navajos' origins, of the trickster Coyote giving fire to the First Man and First Woman, of how they then carried it through different worlds until they reached this one, the Glittering World. There was not a trace of irony in Blueeyes' telling of this tale. By now Billy knew better than to ask how this version of events might have been informed by the reality, that of an Asiatic people crossing the land bridge of what was now the Bering Strait and then moving south. He was being initiated, he sensed, into the ways of the Navajo.

The next morning they began work. Blueeyes's starting point for his book was that the American version of the Long Walk was extensively documented, from US Army archives, from newspaper chronicles, from photographs, while the Navajo version was largely undocumented and untold. In Billy's view Blueeyes had taken too much licence, had failed to justify many of his assertions, and sometimes appeared to play fast and loose with the facts. As they went through the manuscript page by page, Billy drawing on his notes, it quickly became clear that Blueeyes was unwilling to accept more than a handful of Billy's suggestions. At lunch he said, 'Let me take you to the canyon. You have to see for yourself.'

They drove in Blueeyes's pick-up to the Canyon de Chelly, the place from where the Long Walk had begun. As they skirted the rim, Billy could see red sandstone cliffs that fell a thousand feet to the floor of the canyon, deeply scored by wind and water. They stopped at an overlook, and got out to survey the scene. The river snaked between grassy fields and groves of cottonwoods. Sheep grazed in little fields, and here and there were orchards and willow trees. It was a haven, a beautiful haven.

'We'll walk down to the White House,' said Blueeyes.

'The White House?'

Blueeyes smiled, the first time Billy had seen him do so. 'Don't worry,' he said, 'Ronald Reagan won't be at home.'

They took a path that descended steeply into the canyon, Blueeyes now and then pointing out a landmark.

'Kit Carson and his soldiers came through here setting everything afire,' he said. 'It was the dead of winter, and they knew the Navajo wouldn't be able to forage outside the canyon. They shot anyone who resisted. And then they started to round them up and take them to New Mexico.'

'But why? Why then, I mean. It was the middle of the Civil War.'

Blueeyes shrugged his shoulders. 'Why?' he said. 'Because of Manifest Destiny, because their God had a plan for them to conquer the continent and the Navajo stood in their way.'

'It still seems extraordinary, when the Confederates were holding out and the Union couldn't yet be sure of winning the war.'

'They lashed out. Violence was in their nature. It was part of the American character. Still is.'

'You think Americans are more violent than other peoples?'

'Sure. They have this idea of violence as a regenerative force.'

Soon the White House came into view. It was a kind of pueblo, constructed inside a deep fissure in the sandstone walls, and it stood out a brilliant white against the red of the cliffs.

'It was built by the Anasazi,' said Blueeyes, 'the people who were here before the Navajo. They were here for a thousand years, and then suddenly they left.'

'Were they driven out too?'

'No. It was probably a drought. Then about three hundred years ago the Navajo moved in.'

'So they haven't been here very long, then.'

Blueeyes raised a hand to the brim of his hat and looked up at the sky. 'Long enough,' he said.

They began the steep climb back to the rim. Before they got into the pick-up Billy stepped over to the edge of the cliff and gazed eastwards, towards New Mexico. What must it have been like to be led at gunpoint away from this magical place? he thought. No wonder Blueeyes was still angry.

———————

'Congratulations!' said Alice, holding aloft her glass of champagne.

'Thank you,' replied Ellen. 'I can't quite believe it.'

Alice looked around the bar of the St Regis Hotel and thought how appropriate it was that they should be celebrating Ellen's engagement in a room that itself resembled a wedding cake.

'Have you set a date?' she asked.

'April fifteenth.'

'And where?'

'In a church in East Orange, near Mike's parents' place. He's Catholic too.'

'I don't think you've told me that before.'

'Not that it matters. But he is.' Ellen took a long draught of champagne. 'And how is it with you? How's Henry treating you?'

'Fine. He's a nice guy, as you said. But I don't think he knows quite what to make of me.'

'He told me you're doing a great job, that you're already indispensable.'

'That's good of him.'

Ellen scooped up some peanuts from a silver bowl. 'And Billy?' she asked.

Alice hesitated for a moment. 'You're always snooping, Ellen,' she said.

'Hey, you're my best friend.'

'I know. I'm sorry.' She looked down at herself, at the black silk dress she had chosen to wear. She was feeling strangely confident this evening, even light-headed. 'He told me he slept with someone else a while ago,' she said.

Ellen looked at her in astonishment. 'He did?'

'She was a British editor on an exchange programme. Fortunately she seems to have gone straight back to London.'

'Oh, Alice, that's terrible!'

'Not the kind of thing you want to hear when you've just got engaged, I guess.'

'No, it's not that.' She leaned across and touched Alice's arm. 'I'm just so sorry, that's all.'

'Well, we've had a while to get over it. And tonight I've decided to forgive him. I kicked him out for a few days, and then he went to Arizona to work with an author. I asked him to come back only this morning, and tonight will be the first time we've seen each other since then.'

They drank another glass of champagne, but Alice's words had robbed them of their gaiety. In the taxi heading downtown she reflected on what she was about to do. She was very sure of it now. Two weeks ago she had stopped taking the pill. She had told no one of this, and she intended telling no one. Tonight she was going to seduce her husband, and the next part of her life would begin.

Billy was already at the table in Chumley's, and he had got started on a bottle of Chianti. They kissed tentatively, and then, before Billy could say anything, she said, 'No more apologies. For either of us. Let's just start again.' Billy smiled, a smile of relief, and she took his hand. It was the first time they had touched in what seemed a very long time.

After they ordered, Alice told him about Ellen's engagement, and later Billy recounted his experiences in Arizona. He had already shaped them into a narrative, she thought, with him at its centre. Why did men do that? The way he told it, you might imagine he was the first outsider ever to enter the Navajo world. Or was it simply that he had a literary imagination, a need to make everything into a story? This conversation felt like one between strangers, not husband and wife. But after a while the champagne and the Chianti began to make her indulgent. She had her plan, and she was quite sure now that she would go through with it.

When they entered the apartment she led him straight to the bedroom, lighting a candle and then turning to face him. He took her in his arms, kissed her gently, and then slid the straps of her dress from her shoulders. Taking his head in her hands, she kissed him long and hard. This is my husband, she thought as he laid her on the bed. This is my husband, and I love him.

396

Six

In the days just before Thanksgiving, Billy was feeling pretty good about things. John Blueeyes had relented over many of his editorial suggestions and was in the process of whittling down the manuscript to a manageable seven hundred pages. At home, he and Alice had made up, and the Clare Rowley episode seemed to be firmly behind them. His father was out of hospital, and eating and drinking again. And Tom had announced he was returning to New York to visit a 'new friend'. Billy could now look forward to four days off. After spending Thanksgiving with Hal and Barbara, they were borrowing Barbara's car and heading for a cottage in Maine. So it was with a spring in his step that he walked with Ivan Moskovitz towards the diner on Second Avenue that had become their lunchtime haunt.

Ivan seemed in nothing like the same spirits as Billy. As he poured tomato ketchup liberally over his hamburger he said, 'These people. They really get to me sometimes.'

'Who?'

'Jason. Anne. When the fuck are they going to give me my promotion and that office? It's been empty for a month now.'

'Maybe there's some kind of budgetary restriction. Have you talked to them?'

'Sandy has. He says they have more important things on their mind.' He looked at Billy with a strangely fevered expression. 'What could be more important than my promotion?'

Billy couldn't tell whether Ivan was being serious, and was uncertain how to respond. He smiled, and immediately decided he had got the register of his smile wrong somehow.

'OK,' said Ivan, 'maybe the new Proust translation is a little more important. In the grand scheme of things.' He reached for the ketchup bottle again, and this time he doused his fries. After several lunches with Ivan, Billy had become convinced he had no sense of taste at all.

Ivan stared at his handiwork. 'I went to Iowa City this past weekend,' he said after a few moments.

397

'What for?'

'Friend of mine is doing the creative writing course there.'

'Did you see anything of Dan Blessing?'

Ivan looked up from his plate, but remained silent. He was seldom lost for words, and his expression put Billy on the alert. It was as though Ivan were wrestling with something he hadn't yet resolved.

'Yeah, I met Blessing,' he said. 'Interesting guy.'

'He's a good teacher.'

Ivan laid down his knife and fork in the bloody mess of his plate and said, 'Blessing asked after you.'

'I hope you told him I'm doing fine.'

'Sure. But then he told me some things.'

By now Ivan's expression was thoroughly evasive. Having lost interest in his hamburger he sat sideways in the booth, not looking at Billy, and signed to the waitress. Suddenly Billy knew what was coming, and while Ivan ordered coffee, he prepared himself for what he was about to say.

'What sort of things?'

Ivan turned back towards him. 'That you used to boast about having dropped out of college. That you spent years working in bookstores before you got into magazines. That you must be at least thirty-two. Those sorts of things.'

Billy pushed his plate away from him. 'OK,' he said. 'And what if all those things are true?'

Ivan shrugged. 'Hey, it's nothing to me.'

'Listen, Ivan. I came to New York at the age of thirty-one. I hadn't exactly had a brilliant career. Blessing gave me a break, and now Random House has given me another.'

'You don't need to justify yourself.'

'I just want you to know the facts.'

'OK. So now I know the facts.'

When their coffees arrived the conversation reverted to its usual mode, one of gossip and speculation about people at the office and in publishing generally. As they were leaving the diner Billy said he had an errand to run, and they parted at the corner. Once Ivan was out of sight, Billy let out a long, slow breath. He walked aimlessly down Second Avenue, trying to clear his head in the wintry air.

What a fool he had been to suppose that in a world as small as this,

his lies about his past would go unnoticed. When he had told Clare Rowley she had simply been amused. But Ivan was a different proposition altogether. It was with a sense of dread that he walked back to the office and took the elevator to the eleventh floor.

When he reached his desk, there was a message from Jason. He walked slowly up the corridor to the corner office and put his head around the door. Jason was reading the share prices in the *Wall Street Journal*.

'Read much Pritchett?' he said.

'V. S.?'

'Yes.'

'A few stories. *A Cab at the Door.*'

'Good. We're publishing his collected stories on the spring list. Will you write me a blurb?'

'Of course. When do you need it by?'

Jason looked at his watch. 'Five?' he said.

It was while they were in Maine that Alice first sensed she was pregnant. Her period was twelve days late, she felt a slight sense of nausea she couldn't shake, and when she put on her bra in the mornings her breasts seemed tender. If she were right, it was all happening very fast: she must have conceived that first night they had made love again. When she was back at work she went to the drugstore and bought a pregnancy kit. Deciding not to risk taking it home, she put it in a drawer of her desk. At the end of the day she went into the bathroom and opened it. As she sat gazing at the vial of urine standing on the window ledge, she knew she was right. And sure enough, eventually the plus sign appeared. She must be pregnant.

There were suddenly so many things to think about. The first was when to tell Billy, and she havered over this. Better to be certain, better to see the doctor first. She had continued to go to the family doctor in Greenwich even after she moved to New York, and it was to him that she must go now. But that would require a day off, and a pretext. The next day she told Henry Zimmerman her mother was unwell, and he insisted she be with her straight away.

It was good to see a familiar, reassuring face. Nathan Rose was in his late sixties by now, and had been the doctor to Alice's family since before she was born. He was strong and gnarled, and still reminded Alice of the oak tree in their garden, just as he had when she was a child.

'If you think you're pregnant, then you probably are,' he said when she gave him the news. 'And you're young and healthy, so there's no reason why it shouldn't have happened fast. But let's do a couple of tests and see.'

An hour later, after she had submitted to a physical examination and a battery of questions, Dr Rose told her she was indeed going to have a baby. On the train back to New York she gazed unseeingly out of the window. That her decision had so quickly borne fruit was thrilling, and terrifying. She was going to be a mother. But as the train pulled into Grand Central, all she could think about was that Billy had as yet no idea that he was going to be a father.

There was only one thing to do, even if it was trite. She went to Balducci's and bought a pheasant and an apple pie, and on the way back home she picked up some winter roses. In the kitchen cupboard there was a bottle of Zinfandel someone had given them recently, and in a drawer some candles she had forgotten to take home for Thanksgiving. By the time Billy showed up, the apartment was a sanctuary of warmth and light.

He kissed her and said, 'It's only Wednesday, you know.'

'Sure I know. But it's so cold out, and I just felt like making something special.'

They sat down to eat. Billy had been looking tired and strained these past few days, and when he spoke about his work he seemed to lack his usual enthusiasm. Alice talked about Henry Zimmerman's latest assignment, the offices of a fashion designer, and of her suggestion that they cover the walls with the kind of fabrics the designer was famous for. When they had eaten they sat on the sofa, savouring the wine.

'Billy,' said Alice after a while, 'you said a while ago you had something to tell me. Well, now I've got something to tell you.'

He smiled. 'I guessed as much,' he said.

'I'm pregnant.'

He placed his glass on the coffee table. 'When?' he said. 'I mean, how?'

'It must have happened the night we went to Chumley's for dinner, the night I saw Ellen.'

400

'You mean the night we made love for the first time in almost a month.'

'Yes.'

'But you hadn't come off the pill, right?'

'The pill isn't completely safe, you know that. Lots of women on the pill get pregnant.'

He picked up his glass again. 'So what are you going to do?'

'I want to have it, Billy.'

He sighed, and leaned back in the sofa. 'But we talked about this not so long ago,' he said. 'We agreed we weren't ready yet.'

'We *said* we weren't ready. But it was abstract then, and now it's real.'

He looked at her earnestly, and then took her hand. 'Alice, it's too soon. You know that. You need to settle into your job, and I need to get a raise. And those things are going to take time.'

She slid her hand away from his. 'Are you saying you want me to have an abortion?'

'Well, yes.'

'I can't believe I heard you say that. If you loved me...'

She looked away from him, and tears started in her eyes. She had been trying to remain composed, but now all her feelings overwhelmed her. Billy reached out to her again.

'Of course I love you,' he said. 'And I want to have a family. But not now.'

She stood up, and suddenly she was sobbing convulsively. Billy took her in his arms and held her close, stroking her hair.

'I'm sorry,' he said. 'Let's talk about it again tomorrow.'

'I don't... I don't want to talk about it,' she said. 'I want to have a baby. I want to have *our* baby.'

'Let's think about it,' he replied. 'Let's just think about it.'

'I don't want to think about it either.'

'Well, we have to. We can't just sleepwalk into this.'

She broke away from him. 'I'm not feeling very well, Billy,' she said. 'Will you do the dishes?' And with that she went into the bedroom alone, just as she had the night Billy told her about Clare Rowley, and shut the door behind her.

———

He sat at his desk in a state of utter turmoil. His conversations with Ivan and Alice had unsettled him so much that he was quite unable to concentrate on his work. At lunchtime he headed for Park Avenue, wandering northwards. It was a crystalline winter's day, and here, unlike the other avenues of the city, there was light and space, a dome of clear blue sky.

What was he to do? Ivan knew something that had the potential to threaten his career, and Alice was set on having a child. Only a week before, everything had seemed to make sense; but now the doubts and fears he had felt after the closure of *Narratives* had returned with a vengeance. A question kept gnawing at him, and he wasn't sure of the answer. That question was very simple: who was he? Was he a thirty-three-year-old Englishman who should be settling into his mature life, or was he a twenty-eight-year-old quasi-American who was still figuring things out? And how and why had he got himself into a situation in which this question might have to be asked?

For the moment there was no answer forthcoming. He looked at his watch, and then glanced up to see that he was already at Sixty-fifth Street. He turned around and headed back to the office. As he was walking down the corridor he saw Joe Fox appear at his door.

'Hi,' said Joe. 'I hear you saved the Blueeyes book.'

'Have I?'

'That's what Williams says.'

'I'm glad, then.'

'Come on in for a moment.'

Joe sat behind his desk, and Billy stretched out on the threadbare sofa.

'Williams might even be able to persuade the sales people to sell the damn thing now,' continued Joe.

'It's an important book.'

Joe lit up a cigarette, and as he did so Billy said, 'Can I talk to you about something personal?'

'Go ahead.'

Billy paused for a moment, and then said, 'Alice is pregnant. We hadn't planned it, but she wants to have the child. I don't think we're ready, and I've told her so, but she seems determined.'

'No one's ever ready,' replied Joe, blowing smoke towards the ceiling. 'You must have heard people say that. Certainly I wasn't ready when my first son was born.'

'But Joe, we live in a tiny one-bedroom apartment. Alice has just started a new job, and I'm finding my way here.'

'You're going to be fine here. That's already clear.'

'But not for a while. We simply can't afford a child.'

'The other thing everyone says is they can't afford it. That's not the way to think. Do you want to have a family?'

'Yes, but…'

'Then start now. Have you considered how Alice will feel if you pressure her into having an abortion? These things can come back to haunt you.'

'I don't want to pressure her, I want to persuade her.'

'She may not see the difference.'

Billy smiled, and made to get up. 'Thanks, Joe,' he said. 'I appreciate your advice.'

'The advice of a man who seldom sees any of his four sons. Talk to someone else, someone with a better track record.'

'I didn't know you had four sons.'

'Exactly. I see the one who lives in Princeton, and we get along. But the others…' Joe stubbed out his cigarette. 'Anyway, enough of this maundering. Go home and tell Alice you're going to be a father.'

'You should be a designer,' said Henry Zimmerman. 'I mean a designer here.'

'I appreciate the thought. But I'm not sure.'

'We would pay for you to go through Parsons. They have evening courses.'

'That's very kind of you.'

'Think about it. You're doing a great job, but your talents are being wasted. I could really use you creatively.'

When their conversation was over, Alice buried herself in work. Her thoughts were very far from being an interior designer – the only interior she wanted to work on was that of a new apartment. She called Ellen to see if she could meet her for a drink. But Ellen was at home, having been to the church that day with Mike. She suggested that Alice come to Hoboken, and at the end of the day Alice took the train under the river. They walked from Ellen's place to a new store that had just opened, and which Ellen clearly wanted to show off. It was called the

Unicorn, and was a bookstore, café and art gallery in one.

'See what's happening here?' she said as they sat down at a table. 'Not even Manhattan has a place like this.'

It was a large space with a balcony area above. There were precious few books, and those there were stood face out on the shelves so as to create the illusion that they were full. Upstairs was an exhibition of hideous oil paintings. But the espresso machine made good coffee, and they shared a slice of cake.

'They'll need some time to get this place right,' said Alice.

'Sure. But isn't it neat?'

'It's fun.'

Alice stirred sugar into her coffee.

'When did you start doing that?' said Ellen.

'What?'

'Taking sugar.'

'Oh... just recently.' She looked up at her friend and smiled. 'I'm pregnant,' she said.

'You are? That's wonderful!' Ellen reached across and embraced her.

'It would be if Billy thought so too.'

'He doesn't?'

'I told you about the conversation we had in the Catskills. Well, he's still saying it's too early.'

'But you're pregnant now.'

'Yes.'

Ellen looked at her perplexedly. 'He's not going to ask you to get rid of it, is he?'

'He already has.'

'Oh, Alice!' She thumped the table with her fist. 'What did I say to you? It's your body, not his.'

'Take it easy, Ellen. It's his marriage as well as mine.'

'Screw him. Have the baby.'

Alice licked her spoon. 'He's worried about money, and I haven't yet told him that my parents want to buy us a place.'

'Then tell him.'

'But first I want him to want a child. I mean I want him to feel we can make it work whatever our means.'

'Alice, you're so dreamy. If he knows the money side of things is going to be OK, surely he'll change his mind?'

'Maybe.'

Alice gazed across the store. There was one other customer there, and the waiter seemed to be doubling as a clerk behind the bookstore desk.

'You have to tell him,' said Ellen. 'You have to tell him now.'

'He isn't going to like the idea of taking money from my father.'

'Well, he'd better get used to it. He's going to be taking money from him after he keels over, right?'

Alice smiled. 'My father is almost completely pickled,' she said. 'He's going to last forever.'

When Russell Williams shut his office door so as to talk to him, Billy felt a rush of fear. He had been edgy lately, and liable to construe the unlikeliest things as signs that he was about to be challenged.

'Jason wants to talk to you after the holidays,' said Williams. 'He wants you to apply for the position of associate editor.'

'Me?' asked Billy incredulously.

'I can't say I'm very happy about the prospect of having to train up another assistant so soon, but there it is.'

'But that's Ivan's job, surely? He's the obvious candidate.'

'Ivan has been invited to apply too. But let's just say that in Jason's view, Ivan has some issues he needs to address.'

'Issues?'

Williams looked at Billy with an expression of uncertainty. 'Look,' he said, 'I shouldn't be telling you this. But Jason thinks Ivan is not a team player.'

Billy stared past Williams into the gloom of the December afternoon. He couldn't for a moment imagine Jason speaking that way. Surely, if there were a problem, it was that Ivan was too much like Jason, not too little – too clever, too supercilious, too ambitious.

'Well…' he replied, not sure what to say. 'I'm flattered. But Ivan isn't going to like this.'

Williams shifted a pile of papers on his desk, trying in vain to conceal his evident discomfort. 'If you want my advice, you should go for it,' he said. 'The feeling around here is that you're clearly an editor. It's not as if you arrived wet behind the ears.'

Billy returned to his desk. Aware of Ivan's gaze, he turned towards him. Ivan's hasty averting of his eyes told him everything he needed to know.

'Coffee?' he said.

'Sure.'

'I'll fix it. Why don't you come around in a couple of minutes?'

By the time Ivan arrived in the kitchen Billy had filled two mugs. He handed one to Ivan.

'What are we going to do?' he said.

Ivan looked at him with an expression that seemed very like disgust. 'What are we going to do?' he said. 'Fight to the death, like men. *Mano a mano.*'

'I didn't ask for this.'

'You didn't need to. You've been doing great work ingratiating yourself with everyone around here.'

'Knock it off, Ivan. I've just been doing my job.'

'So have I.'

Billy took a sip of coffee. The pot had been brewing since before lunch, and it was sour to the taste. 'Tell me,' he said, 'have you got some kind of problem with Jason?'

One of the other assistants came in and filled her glass with water from the cooler. Sensing the atmosphere, she quickly left the room. Ivan put down his mug and said, 'We had what you might call a difference of opinion over the Lowell book.'

'What kind of difference of opinion?'

'About the extent of the influence of his Catholicism on his work.'

Billy laughed now, a laugh that sounded unexpectedly bitter.

'You're a piece of work, Ivan, you know that?' he said. 'You can never win arguments like that with Jason.'

'I did win. That's the fucking point.'

'Does *he* think you won?'

'I doubt it. But I know I did.'

'And this was when, six weeks or so ago, just when the question of who would succeed Morris was coming up?'

'Yeah, I guess so.'

There was a moment's silence, and then Billy said, 'I can't not go for this job, Ivan. You know that.'

'Yeah. And maybe I can't not tell Jason about a few stories you told so as to get in here in the first place.'

'You'd be a heel if you did that.'

Ivan gave him a challenging look. 'I would, wouldn't I?'

Billy put down his mug and stepped across to the door. Then he turned to face Ivan again. 'Do your worst,' he said. 'I'm going for this job.'

———————

Tom's new friend was a photographer named Marcia who lived in the Chelsea Hotel, and it was there that Billy went on the Saturday before Christmas to meet him. He passed under the striped awning and announced himself at the desk, and was asked to go to the tenth floor.

When he entered the apartment, Tom gave him a bear hug. He looked radiantly well, a different person from the one Billy had collected from the Royal Free Hospital only a few months before. A woman stood in the background, her whorls of hair silhouetted against the big window.

'This is Marcia,' said Tom.

'Hi.'

She was a diminutive figure, but there was an intensity about her that made her loom larger somehow. She wore corduroy pants and a man's shirt, and her round, pretty face was clear of make-up. 'Beer?' she said.

Billy looked around the room. There was very little furniture, but the walls were covered with photographs.

'You're in the same line of work, I see,' he said.

'Yes,' she called from the kitchen.

'She does great stuff,' said Tom. 'Take a look.'

There were a number of portraits, including Andy Warhol, Laurie Anderson and Keith Haring. And then there were stranger things, a photograph of a wall on which was stencilled 'The silence of Marcel Duchamp is overrated', and a naked woman posing as the Statue of Liberty with the words 'Illegal America' superimposed over her body. Tom's enthusiasm for them was evident, as were his feelings for the woman who had made them.

They sat swigging beer, and then Marcia said, 'I'm sure you two have a lot to catch up on. I have some things to do. Why don't you go and have some brunch?'

They went to a coffee shop across the street and ordered French toast.

'It's good to see you,' said Billy.

407

'It's good to see you.'

'So, how did you meet Marcia?'

'She was staying with a friend in Whitechapel, and we met at an exhibition.'

'Sounds rather like the way I met Alice.'

'Yes.' Tom looked up at him. 'Isn't she gorgeous?'

'She sure is. Is this serious, then?'

'For me it is. We're going to spend Christmas together, and then... well, we'll see.'

'She's older than you.'

Tom smiled. 'She's twenty-seven,' he said. 'Does that matter?'

'Oh, I don't mean that. It's just interesting. All your previous girl-friends have been so much younger.'

'She's my muse. She's already had a big influence on my work.'

'And how is the work?'

'It's great. I have a commission from the NME to do some photos of Richard Hell.'

'Richard Hell?'

'Don't ask.' Tom stretched his arms and sat back in the booth. 'But how are things with you?'

'Oh, fine. I went to Arizona to work with an author, a Native American. It was fascinating.'

He hesitated for a moment, wanting to confide in Tom his anxieties about Ivan and the interview he would be having with Jason. He had been waking up in the middle of the night in a cold sweat, thinking about what it would mean if he were fired from Random House. His career really would be over then. And his marriage?

'Alice has left the theatre, she told me,' said Tom before he could say anything more.

'Yes. I wish she hadn't. But she says she came to the end of it.'

'So this new job of hers?'

'It's all right. They've suggested she train as a designer, but she doesn't seem to want to.'

'She should, shouldn't she?'

'I think so.'

Their French toast arrived, and when the waitress had left them, Billy said, 'Tom, Alice is pregnant.'

'Hey, that's great!'

'I'm not so sure.'

'How do you mean?'

'I think we're not ready, but she wants to have it. We're in a stand-off at the moment.'

'So it wasn't planned?'

'No.'

'I wasn't planned.'

Billy smiled. 'I remember,' he said. 'I was so excited when you turned out to be a boy. I was ready to leave home if you were a girl.'

'Glad I didn't disappoint you.' Tom stirred his Bloody Mary. 'And you shouldn't disappoint yourself now,' he said.

'Disappoint myself?'

'By missing this moment. You'll be a great father, Billy.'

'I doubt that. I've still got too much to do for myself.'

'You'd be crazy not to have this child.'

Billy looked out at the passers-by, all swaddled against the cold. A man and his young son were carrying a huge Christmas tree between them, the little boy holding the top end. 'Maybe you're right,' he said. 'Maybe you and Alice are right.' He looked across at his kid brother, who all of a sudden seemed very grown-up. Was Billy's saying he wasn't ready for fatherhood really about money and security, or was it about something else altogether, this nagging question of who he was? And if it were the latter, did anyone *really* know who they were? He looked out into the street again. Maybe it was time he did some growing up of his own.

They had done hardly any Christmas shopping, and arranged to meet after work at Saks to buy things for Hal and Barbara. Alice had insisted that Billy be involved, even though she knew he hated it. His own family had to make do with cards. They met on the ground floor, in the perfume and toiletries department.

'How was your day?' asked Billy.

'Oh, fine. Apparently the fashion designer loves the idea of fabric on his walls.'

'Good for you.'

They strolled towards the elevators, declining offers to sample eau de cologne.

'And yours?' said Alice.

'Fine too. Williams has commissioned a new biography of Sherman. Sometimes I think that man lives in the Civil War. With Lincoln as his god.'

They got out at the men's department.

'What shall we get my father?'

'What do you get the man who has everything?'

'You get him something that he'll enjoy, something he'll feel sentimental about.'

'A drink?'

She took his hand in hers. 'Cufflinks,' she said firmly. 'Over here.'

When they were through, Alice suggested they walk to Rockefeller Center to look at the tree and the ice rink. She loved Christmas, no matter how crass some of it had become. The rink was crowded with skaters – screaming teenagers, parents with their children. As they leaned over the railing Billy put his arm around her shoulders.

'I guess next year we'll have to go to FAO Schwartz for some shopping too,' he said.

'FAO Schwartz? But we don't know any children.'

He turned to her and smiled. 'Maybe by then we will,' he said.

———

The day the office closed for the holidays no one was doing very much work. The party had taken place the previous evening, and several people were looking the worse for wear. For Billy the atmosphere was still charged with tension. He had an appointment with Jason for the second week in January, a few hours after Ivan's. But in the past few days, doubts had crept in. He had told Ivan to do his worst, and now this was precisely what he feared Ivan would do. Was it not wiser to let Ivan have it, and to bide his time? Surely another opportunity would come up before too long. He wanted to talk to Joe about it, but how could he do so without confessing that his life at Random House was based on a lie? When later Joe passed his desk he asked if he were free for lunch. Joe suggested they go to Elaine's.

'I'm not sure whether I should apply for this job after all,' he said once they had ordered.

'Are you kidding?' replied Joe. 'Why?'

Billy looked helplessly across the room. 'I don't know – maybe

I'm not ready yet. Maybe I should spend more time getting the hang of things.'

'You had the hang of things even before you started. Ivan has nothing like the editing experience you have.'

'I suppose so.'

Joe stirred his drink and made to put the cocktail stick in his mouth, but then thought better of it. 'May I be blunt?' he said.

Billy looked up at him, startled. 'Of course.'

'Seems to me you're like the boy who didn't want to grow up. First you don't want to be a father, then you don't want to take the kind of opportunity at work that doesn't come up very often.'

Billy sighed. 'I've already accepted fatherhood,' he said.

'So accept promotion too. You were saying you don't have enough money to start a family – so take the raise.'

'I guess you're right. But if I do so, it'll be the end of my friendship with Ivan.'

'You know what's going to happen to Ivan? He'll do a PhD and go and teach English in a college.'

'Do you think so?'

'He's too much of a purist, too much of an intellectual snob.'

'You could say the same things about Jason.'

Joe snorted. 'Jason is an entrepreneur. And he's very interested in money.'

Their soup arrived, and Billy picked up his spoon. 'I'll see how the interview goes,' he said.

'You do that,' replied Joe.

———

'When shall we tell them?' said Alice, turning from the window of the train to face Billy.

'After my first martini.'

She squeezed his arm. 'It's me who's going to tell them, not you,' she said.

'Sure.'

She looked back out of the window at the lights of the suburbs as they passed by. Since Billy had told her about his change of heart, she had been in a constant state of dizzy confusion. Should she now admit to him that she had willed this all along? Surely she couldn't.

In which case it would be her secret for the rest of her life.

The house was blazing with Christmas lights. Once they had settled in, Hal mixed his pitcher of martini and Barbara poured a glass of wine for Alice.

'I'll just have some tomato juice,' said Alice.

'Tomato juice?' asked Hal. 'At this hour?'

'It's what I feel like, Dad.'

They raised their glasses, and Alice took Billy's hand in hers.

'Mom, Dad,' she said. 'I'm going to have a baby.'

A broad smile creased Barbara's wrinkled face. 'Oh, darling, that's wonderful!'

Hal stepped over to them and clinked his glass with theirs. 'Congratulations! We were talking about this just the other day, your mother and I.'

Alice smiled at him, and then at Barbara. 'You've been talking about it for a year or more,' she said.

'Well, it's what we've wanted for you.'

They talked about the practicalities, Alice wondering whether Hal would bring up the matter of buying them a place, and hoping he wouldn't. Did he have enough tact to let some time go by before broaching that? She hoped so.

After dinner Alice and Barbara sat together in the kitchen, just as they had the last time she was here.

'How are you feeling?' asked Barbara.

'Oh, the usual, I guess. You know – tired all the time, going to the bathroom every half hour, nauseous.'

'Morning sickness?'

'No, I don't throw up. I just feel like I want to.'

'How far along are you?'

'Six weeks. The first scan will be soon after the New Year.'

'A summer baby. They're the best.'

'Are they?'

'Oh, I know you'll be uncomfortable in the heat toward the end, but... well, I just like the idea of babies coming into a world that's as warm as the one they've left.' She stood up and carried their glasses across to the sink. Turning back towards Alice she said, 'You must have been trying when we last talked, when I said that now was the time to have a child.'

412

Alice looked down at her hands. 'I couldn't say anything, Mom,' she said. 'I wanted to be sure.'

'Of course. But what I mean is, you took my advice.'

'Yes,' replied Alice. 'In a way I did.'

Billy and Ivan had barely spoken to one another since their encounter in the kitchen. He guessed it must be obvious to everyone in the office that the tension that existed between them must be resolved as soon as possible. But Jason had been away since the holidays, and there was still a week to go before the interviews.

In the rare moments when he was able to think clearly, Billy had been running everything through his mind. If Ivan really was planning to tell Jason about Billy's lies, then that would hardly reflect well on him. Indeed, it might be enough to decide Jason that Ivan was not the sort of person he wanted around as an editor. But the risk that nonetheless Ivan might go ahead and say it was too great for Billy to ignore. Should he pull out? There were perfectly good reasons for him to do so. And if he did, how long would be it be before another vacancy arose? But the real question was whether he could live with this lie for the rest of his life. Surely one day he would be found out. This was such a small world, as Ivan's meeting Blessing and Billy's meeting Clare Rowley attested.

Every time he thought about it he came to a different conclusion, until finally he knew what he had to do. Two days before the interviews were due to take place he turned to Ivan and said, 'Are you free for lunch?'

'Sure,' replied Ivan uneasily.

They went to the diner on Second Avenue and ordered hamburgers as usual.

'I'm going to tell Jason myself,' said Billy.

'Tell him what?'

'Tell him I dropped out of college and lied about my age. You're off the hook.'

'Are you sure about that?'

'It's the only way.'

Ivan sat back in his seat, the plastic squeaking as he did so.

'OK,' he said. 'Deal.'

413

'And once I've said all that, I'll say I really want this job and can do it well.'

'Sure.'

'And you know what? My guess is Jason won't give a damn.'

'About your lies?'

'Yes.'

'We'll see.'

Their hamburgers arrived, and Ivan began the ritual of baptizing his with ketchup. Then he looked up at Billy.

'Did you know the government just announced that tomato ketchup is to be classed as a vegetable?' he said.

'Are you serious?'

'Yeah.'

'But tomatoes are a fruit anyway, not a vegetable.'

Ivan picked up his glass of water and raised it in an ironic toast. 'Welcome to America,' he said.

———————

The walk from the apartment to St Vincent's Hospital was a short one, but long enough for Billy to feel his stomach lurching with anxiety. Until now he had been a bystander, but he was about to step into the terrifying world of obstetrics, and about to see his child for the first time. He held Alice's hand tight as they waited to see the doctor, letting go only when the nurse had led them into the scanning room. Sitting in a canvas chair, he watched as the nurse spread a film of clear gel over Alice's stomach. Was she showing? They had been debating this for a week or two. Alice was convinced she was by now bloated, but Billy wasn't sure he could see much difference yet at all.

'This is going to be real easy,' said the nurse. 'We're just going to move this transponder over your tummy, and you'll see your baby on the screen.'

It was the strangest image, quite obscure, and not looking very much like a baby. Its head seemed as long as its body, and its limbs were as yet the slightest of protuberances. But it was a life, and more than this, a life Billy had tried to destroy. By what right had he done so, and by what reason?

'Some say it looks like a shrimp at this stage, and others say it's a peanut shell,' said the nurse.

414

The obstetrician came into the room and said, 'Let's take a look, shall we?'

Billy stood and held Alice's hand again, smiling at her with what he hoped was reassurance while the doctor studied the screen. 'Looks good to me,' he said after a couple of minutes. 'No signs of any trouble at all. No heartbeat yet, but that'll come soon.' Alice breathed out gently, and Billy brushed back her hair and kissed her forehead. Her skin was damp with sweat.

The nurse dried Alice with a towel, and she stepped into the bathroom. The doctor shook Billy's hand and said, 'She's going to be fine. This one's going to go like clockwork.'

He went out into the corridor, and sat on a sofa gazing into space. People came and went, some of them in a great hurry, but he registered none of them. The image of Alice's baby on the screen, this tiny, nascent shape, crowded his mind. For the moment it was the merest thing. But it was also his future. He was going to be a father.

Wanting

'I have wanted only one thing to make me happy, but wanting that have wanted everything.'

Hazlitt, *Literary Remains*

One

Billy took a sip of lemon vodka and gazed around the restaurant, at the dark wood panelling and the musicians' gallery above their heads.

'This place was founded by three White Russian dancing girls,' he said, 'after they fled the revolution.'

'You're an incurable romantic,' said Chloe.

'No, I'm an incurable *nostalgic*.'

'Can you be nostalgic for something you haven't experienced?'

'I'm sure you can.'

Chloe reached across with her fork to spear one of his piroshki. 'I'm sure you can,' she said.

She chewed the piroshki tentatively, a slightly quizzical expression forming on her features. For Chloe, food was merely a garnish to the more important matter of conversation, and the discreet observation of other people.

'So, tell me about this book you're going to look at tomorrow,' she said.

'It's a set of Scriptures. It's a palimpsest, and that's one of the reasons it's so valuable.'

'A palimpsest?'

'The text was written over an earlier one, which had been erased. Parchment was hard to come by in those days, and scribes often reused it. Palimpsest is Greek for "scraped again".'

'And Andrew Blackwood has asked you to authenticate it?'

'I don't have the expertise for that – this is a long way from modern first editions, after all. No, he asked me to confirm that it is where the owner says it is, that's all.'

'And then he'll come here himself, take it back to London and sell it for more than he paid for it.'

'Precisely. That's how we live. The dealer here will have done just the same.'

'Will Andrew's buyer sell it on for more than he's paying him?'

'Of course.'

She sat with her fork poised in the air, as if deliberating whether to swoop down once more onto his plate. Her silky black hair framed a face that even in August was alabaster white. Everything about it was fine yet bold, the red of her lips, the sea-green of her eyes, the jet of her eyebrows.

'Don't worry,' she said. 'I'm not going to accuse you of profiteering.'

'If we could make a living from creating things, as you do, then we would. But we can't, so we have to buy and sell them instead.'

'Don't be sententious,' she said. 'It makes your mouth pucker. And don't forget that we're actually on holiday.'

By the time they left Rejans it was nearly midnight, but the Istiklal was still thronged with people. There was something gaudy about this street nowadays, and the rococo buildings looked down on the shops and restaurants with an air of disdain. When Billy first came to Istanbul twenty-five years ago this great artery of the European quarter possessed a shabby elegance that was by now quite lost.

They turned towards the Pera Palas hotel. Out in the Bosphorous a ship sounded its horn, a melancholy leviathan passing in the night. Having collected the key they stepped through the wrought-iron gates of the lift and sat down on the red velvet seat for the ride to the third floor. Their room was named after Nubar Gulbenkian, the oil magnate. 'I don't suppose he actually stayed here,' Chloe had said when they arrived. It was quite small, full of the ponderously dark and heavy furniture so favoured by the Turks, and it had no air conditioner. The curtains billowed in the gentle breeze as Billy closed the door, and the roar of traffic on the boulevard filled the room.

They made love in a languid sort of way. A full-length mirror faced the bed, and now and then he caught sight of their reflections, the satyr and the nymph. Afterwards he lay back in silence, withdrawn into himself. How long before she tires of this, he wondered; how long before she turns to a younger man? It was too hot for sleep, and he didn't know how long it was before eventually he drifted off. The moment of his waking, however, he could be precise about: the phosphorescent glow of the alarm clock told him it was two minutes past three when the earthquake began.

For a few moments he had no idea what was happening. Then he gripped Chloe's arm tightly and said, 'Stand in the bathroom doorway.' They staggered across the room, and stood clasped in a naked embrace as the walls shook around them. It was hard to see anything, but he heard pieces of plaster fall from the ceiling, and the wardrobe door rattled ominously. Half a minute passed, and he knew enough about earthquakes to be convinced that another half minute would surely send this building crashing to the ground.

Only when it ended, a few seconds later, did he begin to consider what they should do. He had been in a state of paralysis throughout, incapable of thought, incapable even of fear. He tried the lights, but the electricity was down.

'Let's get out of here,' he said. 'There may be aftershocks.'

In the corridor they met other guests, their faces turning towards them with expressions of perplexity as much as shock. 'Outside,' said Billy. He took Chloe's hand as they descended the stairs, determined not to run.

Nearby was a park, and they sat on a bench facing back towards the hotel. He looked around him, calculating the distance from the surrounding buildings, wondering whether they might fall. The park rapidly filled up, and they sat for a long time in silence, unable to communicate either with the crowd or with one another. At five the song of the muezzin began, floating towards them from the mosque. People started to collect their things and go, and after a while Billy suggested they do the same. In the blacked-out hotel the staff seemed unconcerned, nonchalant even. But lying in bed and trying vainly to sleep, he found himself wondering whether the rumbling noise he sensed came from the cars below, or from another shock that would send them tumbling out of their bed.

He slept fitfully, and in the morning they went down to the restaurant for a breakfast of eggs, olives, bread and coffee. Their fellow guests seemed hushed by the events of the night, as were they. Chloe studiously peeled the shell from a hard-boiled egg and dipped it into the salt. 'It's eerie in here,' she said as she bit into it.

Out on the street, life was back to normal. They walked to the Istiklal, and then east towards Taksim. At a corner there was a small pile of masonry, the only evidence they could see of the earthquake. The shoe-shine boys dodged the trams, and simit sellers carried shoulder-high their wooden platters of crescent-shaped loaves. In the cafés the backgammon players were already intent over their boards, drinking tea from small vase-shaped glasses. They turned off the Istiklal and headed downhill for a block towards Cihangir.

The window of the Krantz bookshop was filled with books bearing titles in Arabic and Latin. Lev Krantz was a man of about seventy, Billy guessed. His head was shiny and hairless, and there were liver spots on his temples. He shook their hands and bowed ever so slightly. And then, ushering them into a back room, he clapped his hands and ordered a youth to go out for tea.

'I am very pleased to meet you, Mr Palmer,' he said. 'You have come a long way.'

'I'm always happy to come to Istanbul,' replied Billy. 'I came here several times when I was younger. It's a fascinating city.'

'It is the crossroads between East and West. Everyone has come through here at one time or another.'

'And it shows. All the civilizations have left something.'

'It could also be said that Istanbul itself is a kind of palimpsest. The Romans, the Greeks, the Ottomans, Atatürk – they left things of their own, but they also did their best to erase the past.'

They sat down on narrow wooden chairs. The youth brought them tea, and they balanced the little saucers in their hands.

Billy relaxed into his chair. 'I once took a water taxi across the Bosphorous with some Americans who when we reached the Asian side produced a shaker of dry martini and some glasses,' he said. 'I told them these must be the only martinis in history that were mixed on one continent and drunk on another.'

Krantz smiled gravely. 'Very droll, Mr Palmer,' he said. He brandished a set of keys and stepped across to a safe. When he picked up the book that lay inside he did so with the utmost care. He placed it on the desk, and Billy stood to inspect it.

The Latin text of the Scriptures had been superimposed by that of another, the Jerome Vulgate. Over time the original text, which would once have been completely effaced, had begun to appear again, a ghostly presence which, though not immediately apparent, was nonetheless unmistakable when he looked closely. Krantz handed Billy a magnifying glass, and he turned some of the pages.

'The original is probably eighth century, from Alexandria. And the later text is eleventh century.'

424

'How long have you had it in your possession?'

'I bought it from a dealer in Bursa a few months ago. It has made its way by stages through the East, and now it will make its way to the West.'

Billy examined it intently. He was not experienced with this sort of thing; but when Blackwood had asked him to take a look, since he was going to be in Istanbul anyway, he had promptly agreed. This little errand added spice to their visit.

'The usual imaging would have to be done,' he said.

'We have the facilities for that here. Please tell your friend that I can make the necessary arrangements.'

Krantz returned the book to the safe, and when they had finished their tea, Billy and Chloe took their leave. Back out in the street Chloe said, 'There's something faintly ridiculous about all this.'

'Ridiculous?'

'The way you two were treating it, anyone would think it was the Crown jewels.'

'It's precious.'

'I suppose so. But it's also just a few sheets of parchment.'

They returned to the hotel, collected their bags, and took a taxi to the airport. In the departures hall Billy noticed a photograph on the front page of the local evening newspaper. It showed a scene of terrible destruction in a place called Izmit. He asked the man behind the counter to tell him more.

'Earthquake,' replied the man in English. 'Many dead. Many, many dead.'

He looked at the photograph again. He was unable to understand the headline, but in the text of the report he saw the figure of five thousand. Five thousand dead? But how could that be, when they themselves were unscathed? Izmit must have been the epicentre. Billy was appalled by the realization that he had spent the day on commerce while not far away thousands of people had died or been made homeless. As they waited to board the plane, once again he sensed rumbling noises. They were from the planes, of course. But by now he wanted very urgently to be away from here and up in the sky. If he couldn't be sure of the ground beneath his feet, what could he be sure of?

425

He pushed open the door to Andrew Blackwood's shop, setting off the familiar tinkling sound of the bell. It was several minutes before Blackwood appeared, shuffling from his tiny office at the back. He was studying something closely, and after they shook hands he handed it to Billy. It was an edition of Pound's *Quia Pauper Amavi*, the Egoist Press special issue.

'The usual misprint on page thirty-four, corrected by Pound,' he said.

Billy turned to the page, and saw Pound's handwritten correction of 'wherefore' to 'wherefrom'. Turning back to the endpaper he read the inscription, 'To R, Princessa (?) de S. F., not to be confused with her daughter-in-law, EP, anno X'.

'Anno X?' he asked.

'Nineteen thirty-two in the Fascist calendar.'

'Ah. Very nice. How much?'

'Now that would be telling, wouldn't it?'

Billy handed the book back to Blackwood, and he held it to his breast. A small, dishevelled man, he was wearing the tweed jacket with leather patches coming away at the elbows that he wore every day of the year. His thatch of dark hair hung down over his forehead, not a single grey one to be seen despite his sixty-odd years.

'Shall we go to the pub?' said Billy.

Blackwood looked at his watch. 'Certainly,' he said. He disappeared into the basement, the place where he lived, surrounded by yet more books, the ones he couldn't bear to part with.

They walked to the pub, passing Peter Jolliffe's Ulysses bookshop, which along with Blackwood's was one of the few antiquarian shops left in Museum Street nowadays.

'So you escaped unhurt,' said Blackwood when they were seated.

'Yes. But it was bloody terrifying, I can tell you.'

'Twenty thousand dead, that's what they're saying now.'

'I know. But in Istanbul itself, no one. We had no idea until we were leaving.'

'So what does it feel like?'

'How do you mean? It feels like an earthquake. Everything shakes like hell.'

'Were you afraid?'

'Not at the time, no. It's sort of unreal – you can't quite believe it's happening.'

'Welcome home then, back to dear, safe Blighty.'

'I tell you, it's things like that which make you glad of this place.'

Blackwood sipped his beer. He never drank more than a third of his glass, but always insisted on buying pints anyway. 'And the palimpsest?' he said.

'It's probably the real thing.'

'They don't come up very often these days. I'm going to have to look into its provenance pretty closely.'

'I wouldn't expect Krantz to part with it cheaply. He strikes me as someone who will know all about Sotheby's and the rest.'

'Perhaps I'll go out there and take a look at it myself.'

Billy looked thoughtfully at his old friend. Blackwood seldom went anywhere, not even to the provincial auction houses, relying on runners to find books for him. That he should take himself off to Istanbul seemed out of character somehow. The palimpsest must have fired his imagination. Either that or he had his customer already lined up.

To some extent Billy owed his business to Blackwood. After his five years at Maggs, and when he discovered to his astonishment that his old boss Roy Urquhart had left him his entire library, it was Blackwood who had sold him his mailing list. Suddenly, and quite unexpectedly, he was able to set up on his own. Blackwood often muttered how cheaply he had sold Billy his list; but the fact was that this had been only a starting point, that by now Billy had his own clients and sources. Nevertheless, he would always be grateful to this little man who by now was one of the few friends he still held on to.

He looked down, and Blackwood, taking this as a prompt, poured some beer from his own glass into Billy's.

'Two thousand five hundred,' said Blackwood.

'Two thousand five hundred?'

'That's what I'm going to ask for the Pound.'

———

He sat at the back of the auditorium, as he always did at Chloe's concerts, listening to the strains of the Adagio of Beethoven's F Major Quartet. Beethoven had apparently had in mind the burial vault scene in *Romeo and Juliet* when he composed it. Gazing up at the stage, he watched as Chloe gracefully drew her bow across the strings of the

427

cello. He could imagine her as Juliet; but he had some difficulty imagining himself as Romeo.

St John's, Smith Square was almost full for this midweek recital. In the months since he first met Chloe he had attended all the London concerts the Wulf Quartet had given, and had always sat as far from the stage as possible, thinking that he didn't wish to distract her. Watching her now, though, seeing the intensity of her engagement with the music, he wondered whether anything at all would distract her.

After the interval they played another Beethoven quartet, and then the second violinist left the stage and the others played Schubert's String Trio. When the concert was over Billy went backstage to collect Chloe and her cello, and took them both to the car.

'That was lovely,' he said as pulled out into the road.

'Was it? Leo wasn't at his best tonight. He started the Allegro of the F Major far too fast, and the rest of us had to catch up.'

'I didn't notice. But then I wouldn't.' In a lifetime of going to concerts, Billy had never been quite sure he could tell the difference between one performance and another. When audiences stood and roared their approval, were they responding to the music or to the occasion, to the reputation of the players?

'Billy, I had some good news today,' she said.

He looked across at her. There was still enough light to see her expression, and it was one of even greater concentration than usual.

'Yes?'

'Hofmann has got me my first solo concert. I'm going to be playing the Bach Cello Suites at the Wigmore Hall at the end of next month. Valeria Mankiewicz has dropped out, and I'm her replacement.'

'That's wonderful.' Billy stopped the car at a red light, and leaned across to kiss her. 'Have you told Leo?'

'Not yet. I didn't want to tell him tonight.'

'Will he be OK about it?'

'He has to be.'

Leo Wulf, the founder and leader of the quartet, was a show-off and a martinet. Billy didn't care for him at all, and had christened him a cut-price Leonard Woolf, a joke that Chloe affected not to find amusing but which he knew she did.

'It's only a matter of time before you leave, anyway. He knows that.'

'We'll see.'

Chloe looked out of the window as they headed north through Kentish Town, and a silence gathered. Now and then Billy reached across and held her hand for a few moments, between changing the gears. He glanced at her again, sensing that she had retreated into her own world, the world of music, but also the world of ambition, the world of the future. She was twenty-eight, the same age Alice had been when they first met. The same sort of age that most of his girlfriends had been since his divorce. He had become an exponent of the tiredest cliché of them all, the older man and the younger woman.

They drove up the hill towards Highgate, and Billy stopped in front of the house in Holly Lodge Gardens where Chloe lived with her aunt. He opened up the back door of the estate car and pulled out the cello.

'Friday night, then?' he said.

'Yes.'

'I'll cook supper.'

He kissed her good night, and watched her step through the gate. They had never spent the night together after a concert, at her insistence. 'I'm too wound up,' she would say. Getting back into the car, he drove towards Pond Square. It was quite dark by now, the endless evenings of summer having faded. Upstairs in the flat he poured himself a glass of whisky and put on a CD of the Beethoven quartet. It was a way of keeping her with him still.

———

When the doorbell rang, Billy stood up from his desk and stretched his back. He had been cataloguing all morning, and if he spent any length of time at his typewriter nowadays, stiffness set in. He spoke into the intercom and pressed the buzzer to let in his customer. By the time Joe Mullan had ascended the three flights of stairs he was wheezing heavily.

Mullan was an immensely fat man, his thighs encased in bright red trousers, the sleeves of his pink shirt rolled up to reveal soft, hairless forearms. Sweat glistened on his face, and the few threads of hair he had left stuck to his neck and ears. He sprawled on a sofa, and proceeded to take off his shoes and rub his feet.

'Why don't you have a shop, Palmer?' he said. 'These stairs are a killer.'

'I don't need a shop, Joe.'

Mullan could scarcely reach his toes, and the effort of massaging them seemed to require almost as much energy as the effort of getting here. 'A lift, then?' he said.

'In this building?' Billy went into the kitchen to put on the kettle. 'Just consider your visits to me to be much-needed exercise.'

Mullan was Billy's Kingsley Amis collector, and whenever he called, Billy was reminded of Amis's novel *One Fat Englishman*. The fashion for complete collections of single authors was pretty much over, but there were still people who wanted a copy of absolutely everything certain authors published. Mullan had been missing one item, *Fantasy Poets No. 22*, to which Amis had made a contribution, and Billy had at last been able to track it down for him.

Billy handed him a cup of tea.

'Well?' he said.

Billy crossed to his desk and picked up the book, handing it over. Mullan wiped his hands on a handkerchief and then caressed the dust wrapper, before gently opening it up.

'The edition ran to three hundred copies,' said Billy. 'But they're hard to get hold of now.'

Mullan was unable to take his eyes off it, leafing through its pages. 'How much?' he said.

'A hundred and fifty.'

'Come off it, Billy.'

'I'm sorry, Joe. If I offer it out it'll easily fetch that.'

Mullan closed the book, and stroked it again. 'Oh, all right,' he said glumly. He picked up a leather briefcase and extracted his chequebook and a Mont Blanc pen.

They talked on for a while, Billy telling him about the private library he had recently bought and was now cataloguing. The books lay in boxes on the floor, more than he could possibly shelve; but his stock had been dwindling lately, and he needed to replenish it. Mullan eventually stood to leave, and Billy wrapped the book in brown paper. He watched Mullan from the window as he walked slowly across Pond Square. Then abruptly Mullan sat down on a bench and unwrapped the book. Within a few moments he was crying like a child.

Billy turned back into the room. There were times when he hated this business, and hated himself for being in it. But Mullan's tears were surely tears of joy, not tears of woe. He had made him happy.

He sat down at his desk again, casting his eyes over the catalogue slips and the books he was describing, thinking back to how he had got into this. When he'd returned from New York, having divorced from Alice, there were no editorial jobs of the sort he'd had at Random House, and so when Ed Maggs invited him to join his venerable firm he said yes. He had begun his working life in a bookshop, and now he returned to one. A few years later he had the bright idea of proposing to Roy Urquhart that he sell the archive of his literary magazine, The Bystander, which Billy himself had worked on in his twenties. Since this contained almost thirty years' worth of letters, manuscripts and drawings, it raised a considerable sum, setting Urquhart up for his retirement. But Roy Urquhart was destined to enjoy only two years of his newly found prosperity, and when he died Billy discovered that he had made him his sole beneficiary. Along with his wonderful library, which became the kernel of Billy's business, came the flat in which they were housed. It was ten years now since Billy moved in. At the time he could scarcely believe his luck.

He stood again and crossed to the window. Mullan was gone, and the little square was empty, as it so often was. He would probably never see Mullan again now: he had got what he wanted.

———

On Sunday mornings they would get up late and go to Café Rouge for breakfast, spreading the papers out across the table. The Observer had a story about an earthquake a few days earlier in Athens.

'A hundred and fifty dead and five hundred injured,' said Billy. 'Nothing like as bad as ours, at least.'

Chloe looked up at him. 'Ours?' she said.

'You know what I mean.'

She returned to the newspaper, and then their omelettes arrived.

'What time is your flight tomorrow?' asked Billy.

'Nine. I'll need to stay at Pru's place tonight, and be off early.'

'And when is the first concert?'

'Tuesday, in Salzburg. Salzburg, Vienna, Prague. Into the lion's den.'

'The lion's den?'

'Playing Mozart in Salzburg? They're pretty demanding. We had a very cool reception the last time we were there.'

'But they've asked you back.'

'Yes.'

431

He watched her as she inspected her omelette. He would miss her, as he always did when she was travelling; he had learned a frightening dependence on her. But she had her own life to lead. He reflected not for the first time how like Alice she was. Not physically – they were quite different – but in her dedication to her art. Alice had had to forsake the theatre just before Michael was born, but later she had reinvented herself as an interior designer. What would happen when Chloe wanted a child? Well, he mustn't worry about that: someone else would father Chloe's child, someone not yet on the scene.

After breakfast they took a walk, crossing the square and heading for Hampstead Heath. Highgate was surely the only village left in London now, a hilltop redoubt against the depredations of the city. They passed the bench where Joe Mullan had sat down and wept, and Billy told her about him.

'There's something erotic about book collecting, isn't there?' she said.

'I suppose there is.'

'Are there any women book collectors?'

'Very few.'

She took his arm in hers, and smiled. 'You know, before I met you,' she said, 'I thought books were for reading.'

'Collectors have usually read the books already.'

They strolled past the ponds and into the open expanse of the heath. Ever since Billy first came to live in London, after he dropped out of university, he had sought refuge here. To live a stone's throw from it, as he now did, seemed a great blessing.

'Come to Vienna next weekend,' said Chloe suddenly. 'I'll be free after Saturday night's concert.'

'I've promised Sarah I'll have lunch with them on Sunday.'

She hugged his arm. 'You can have lunch with them any Sunday, surely?'

'Why would you want me around?'

'Why?' She looked up at him. 'Because I like being with you.'

He stopped to gaze up at the trees above their heads. It was a luminous September day, the heat of the summer having evaporated now, the chill of autumn yet to come.

'Why do you like being with me?' he said.

'That's the sort of question teenagers ask each other, surely?'

'Teenagers and old men.'

'You are not old. How many times do I have to tell you that?'

He turned to face her. 'A lot of times,' he said.

They came to Parliament Hill, and stood gazing across the city. To the east Billy could just make out the circular structure of the Millennium Dome, London's new white elephant. When he was young it amused him to think that by the year 2000 he would be more than fifty years old. Now that he was practically there, it wasn't amusing at all.

'Seriously, Chloe,' he said, 'I want to know why you're with me. It's quite unnatural, you know.'

She looked up at him. 'I'm with you because you're interesting,' she said. 'I'm with you because you appreciate me. I'm with you because you don't feel you have anything to prove.'

'And you're with me because I make no undue demands.'

'Is that what you think?'

Billy shrugged. 'It's where we are in the arc of our lives that's so different. You're climbing up one side while I'm slipping down the other.'

She kissed him on the cheek. 'You think too much, that's your problem. Can't you just enjoy what we have?'

He smiled. 'I'll try,' he said.

He drove to Sarah and John's house in Barnet, pulling up in the drive beside a new red Jaguar. John appeared in the doorway as Billy was getting out of his own rusty Volvo.

'Smart, eh?' said John. 'Picked it up yesterday.'

Billy looked the car over. It seemed to crouch rather than stand, truly living up to its name. His thoughts went back to the Mark Eight his father had had before the bankruptcy. As a boy, Billy had loved the smell of all that walnut and leather. Cars didn't interest him now – his own was simply a workhorse – yet he couldn't help but admire the grace of this expensive piece of machinery.

'Very nice,' he said.

'Sarah won't dare drive it, says she'll stick to the Renault.'

They stepped inside the house, and Sarah appeared from the kitchen. He hadn't seen his sister since before the summer, and she was as brown as a nut, her fair hair bleached by the Italian sun. They sat down for lunch, the kids appearing from the computer room and acknowledging Billy without exactly greeting him.

The conversation stuttered and started, the kids occupied with their own talk. Billy had often reproached himself for being such a lousy uncle. Rob was seventeen now, two weeks younger than his own son, April fifteen, and Stephen thirteen. Any chance Billy had had to get to know them seemed to have been forfeited years ago, and by now they were complete strangers. They ate the roast beef and apple pie with what seemed like great haste, and were soon back at their computers.

'What do they do on those things?' he said.

'Play games,' replied Sarah. 'Watch DVDs. It keeps them out of trouble.'

'They're very excited about Y2K,' said John.

'Now what is Y2K, exactly?'

'You don't know?'

'I've heard of it. But I've no idea what it means.'

'The millennium bug. All the computers in the world are set to dates in which the year begins with a one. Many people think that when the first of January comes around, the entire system will crash.'

Billy took off his glasses and polished them with a handkerchief. 'I'd better carry on with my typewriter, then.'

'I don't know how you get by without a computer. Don't you need the Internet?'

'Seems to me I can get by perfectly well without it. So far as I can tell, the Internet is a mixed blessing in my world. Yes, you can post your catalogues on it, but at the same time it's standardizing prices.'

'How?'

'People can look up all the available copies of a certain book, and compare.'

'Isn't that reasonable?' said Sarah.

Billy smiled. 'Not in a business in which differences in value represent the margin we're all living on, no.'

John helped himself to another slice of the pie. 'I'll never understand your business,' he said. 'In my world things have the same value to everyone.'

Billy looked down the table at him. He was ten years older than Sarah, almost sixty now, and was already thinking about selling up his accountancy firm and retiring. He had gone grey, but otherwise seemed quite youthful. Billy couldn't comprehend the idea of retirement, it terrified him. What would John do when he got up every morning, mow the lawn once more?

'Have you talked to Mum and Dad lately?' asked Sarah.

'No. But I'm going down there next weekend.'

'Dad's been having trouble with his throat again, having difficulty swallowing.'

'Really? That sounds bad.'

'Mum's worried he may have to have more radiation therapy.'

'It would help if he'd give up the smokes and the booze, as his doctor told him to.'

'That's a lost cause, you know that.'

John stood to clear the plates. While he was in the kitchen, Sarah said, 'And Chloe?'

'She's in Austria on tour. Gone for two weeks.'

'She's always travelling.'

'Yes. And I don't think that's going to change. She has her first solo recital at the Wigmore Hall in a couple of weeks' time.'

'Good for her.'

Billy looked out of the window over the sloping lawn. 'I suppose so,' he said.

'It's time you were with someone nearer your own age, Billy.'

'Do you think I don't know that?'

'Well do something about it, then.'

'Sure. Answer one of the personals in the *London Review of Books*. They all seem to be about my age. My age and quite mad, that is.'

'Don't be unkind. They're lonely, like a lot of people.'

'I'm sorry.'

She reached across and took his hand. 'You must be prepared to lose Chloe,' she said.

'I know. I prepare myself every day.'

———

Sam Cummings was one of Billy's drinking partners, and they didn't come any more thoroughly soused than Sam. Billy often wondered how he managed to hold down his job as a copy-editor at Faber. They would meet after work at the Queen's Larder pub next to Faber's offices, and often still be in their places at closing time.

'All right, then?' said Sam when they met one evening.

'Generally,' replied Billy.

Sam's long, tapered, nicotine-stained fingers rolled a cigarette. His movements were slow and methodical, and his grey eyes possessed the alcoholic's steady gaze.

'Still searching for that first edition of *Ulysses*?'

Billy smiled ruefully. A signed first edition of the Shakespeare and Company *Ulysses* was the Holy Grail of modern first editions bookselling. But they seldom came up nowadays, and when they did they were prohibitively expensive.

'I was thinking just the other day,' he said, 'about when Donald Klopfer at Random House told me the story of bringing a copy into New York, in nineteen thirty-two, and having to persuade the customs officer to confiscate it.'

'Why did he do that?'

'Random House wanted to publish it in America, but to do so they had to win a court case. The best way to contrive one was to get a copy taken from them and try and get it back.'

'And they succeeded.'

'The first American edition was published the next year.'

Sam put a match to his cigarette. 'Nothing like that ever happens these days,' he said.

'So what *is* happening these days?'

'Oh, Faber's fine. I'm working on an edition of Sylvia Plath's journals. Fascinating.'

Billy watched his friend drag on the cigarette and then raise his glass of beer to his lips. Sam might be only a copy-editor, but nonetheless he inhabited a world Billy had once supposed to be his own. In his thirties he had spent six years working in New York as an editor. He sometimes felt he had sleepwalked into bookselling, lightly accepting Ed Maggs's offer and soon realizing that he had irrevocably set the course of the rest of his life. What might have happened if Faber had offered him a job back then? Would he now be at the centre of literary London? There was no use speculating about that now.

'Any news about the archive?' he said.

'No. It's still languishing underground somewhere near Tottenham Court Road.'

'It needs cataloguing. It needs sorting out.'

'Why don't you talk to them about it?'

'Oh, they won't listen to me. But what a gold mine Faber's archive would be.'

'It'd be like selling the family silver.'

'That's exactly what it would be like. And look how many families sell their silver.'

It had been months since he last saw his parents, and as the car hummed along the motorway he found himself brooding over this. There never seemed to be very much to say, and he had come to view these visits as little more than a means of escape from the city, and from the demands of the sort of conversation that required some effort. In the strange state of mindlessness that driving always seemed to induce, his thoughts strayed from one thing to another, from Chloe and her forthcoming concert to the image of Joe Mullan crying on the bench below his flat, and then to memories of the hotel bedroom in Istanbul, and the sensation he had felt then of being unmoored from reality. There had been yet another earthquake earlier that week, in Taiwan, which had killed over two thousand people. He couldn't remember there ever being such a rapid succession of devastating earthquakes. What was going on in the world?

He pulled off the motorway and wended his way along the country roads towards Wells. After a while the towers of the cathedral came into view. The great west face, the most beautiful façade Billy knew, had been cleaned a few years ago, its stone miraculously turning from black to cream, the expressions on the faces of the saints and the gargoyles coming alive again. In Market Place the stalls were set out on the cobblestones, selling local produce nowadays in just the way they might have done in the Middle Ages. Despite the bustle, and the procession of cars, he could never escape the feeling that in coming to Wells he was turning back the clock. He had lived here in his teens and gone to the Blue School. If there was anywhere he could call home, it was here.

His mother stood in the porch as he pulled into the drive, and he gave her a hug. Jim remained in his armchair, and as Billy entered the sitting room he knew that his father was already appealing to his sympathy. As he had aged, and as the empty years had stretched on, he had become increasingly prey to the self-pity that had always lurked within him.

'How are you feeling?'

'Bad. It's coming back.' His voice was hoarse, as Billy remembered it being years ago before he was given radiation therapy for the throat cancer.

'What do they say?'

'They're monitoring it closely,' said Margaret. 'They're going to tell us within the next few weeks if he needs an operation.'

'I am not having an operation, Maggie. I've told you and I've told them. I'd rather die than go around with a bloody box in my throat.'

'You'll do what the doctors tell you,' said Billy.

'To hell with the doctors.' Billy sat down on the sofa, and his father stared at him defiantly. 'Drink?' he said after a few moments.

'Thanks. I'll fix them. Gin and tonic?'

As he handed his father the glass he took a close look at him. He was still slim, and handsome despite the wattles that had formed under his chin. His hair was pearly white, tidily cut and combed. But there was a querulous look in his eyes that never quite went away. Billy sat down again and looked around the room. On the shelves were Jim's videos, dozens of them, all the films of his youth and his life as the manager of the local cinema. Tucked alongside them were Margaret's books, the Austens and Brontës, and then the Jilly Coopers and Joanna Trollopes.

'There was a sign outside the Regal saying it's going to become a discotheque,' said Billy.

Jim grunted. 'It's about time it was something again. It's been closed for years.' He smiled wanly. 'Maybe they'll bring Bert out of retirement to run it.'

'How is Bert?'

'Bored out of his mind, like the rest of us.'

'Didn't he take up a hobby or something?'

'Scrabble. He's the captain of the local team. They go off to places like the Isle of Wight and have tournaments.'

'That's right. Good for the brain.'

'If you say so.'

Jim picked up a packet of cigarettes, and then, sensing Margaret's disapproving stare, he tossed it back onto the table.

'How about you, dear?' asked Margaret.

Billy shrugged. 'Oh, fine,' he said. 'There's not much to say, really. I've been cataloguing that library I bought in Norfolk. It's a lot of work.'

'How's Chloe?'

'She has a solo concert in a couple of weeks' time. Her career seems to be taking off.'

'When are you going to marry her?' said Jim.

'Never, of course. She's more than twenty years younger than I am.'

'You need to be married, Billy. You're mouldering away, like your books.'

'I don't *need* to be married, not at my age.'

'Your age is precisely why you need to be married. You'll need someone to look after you before you know it.'

Billy picked up his glass and swirled the clear liquid. 'When I need someone to look after me I'll hire a nurse,' he said.

Diminutive though she was, and seeming to be shielded by the cello, Chloe filled the stage of the Wigmore Hall. The Bach cello suites were one of the most demanding in the repertoire, six unaccompanied pieces, with nowhere to hide if she made a mistake. Billy sat in the very last row, surveying the audience. There were a few empty seats, and no doubt some people at least had stayed away when they learned that Valeria Mankiewicz would not be playing. But still it was practically a full house, in what was surely the finest setting Chloe could expect for her solo debut.

The rhythms of the music were hypnotic. This was an algebra of sound, precise, logical, and yet thrilling. Chloe's head dipped as she played an arpeggio, reared back for the gigue, her long black hair scintillating in the light from the arc-lamps. She played the first three suites, and then left the stage for the interval. In the bar Billy bumped into Hans Hofmann.

'Potentially as good as du Pré,' he said, beaming.

'She's that good?'

'I'm her agent. What do you expect me to say?'

He was wearing evening dress, the double-breasted jacket concealing his wide girth. With his brilliantined hair and gold-rimmed glasses he looked like a man quite out of time, a *fin-de-siècle* impresario.

439

The later suites were as mesmerizing as the first three, and there was loud applause at the end, Hofmann standing to clap, turning to the rest of the audience as he did so in order to encourage them to do the same. Chloe bowed gravely, but she was unable to suppress a broad smile of triumph. She played a brief piece by Britten as an encore, and then it was over. Chloe Walston had made her entrance.

They gathered in a nearby restaurant afterwards, Chloe, Hofmann, Leo Wulf, who in Billy's view should have stayed away, a woman from the Wigmore Hall, and Billy himself. Hofmann immediately took charge, ordering champagne and proposing a toast to his new star. Billy found himself sitting on the opposite side of the table from Chloe, and next to Wulf. After they ordered food, Wulf turned to him and said, 'That's that, then.'

'Yes.'

Wulf drained his champagne glass. His ridiculous, tousled hair cascaded over his shoulders, and even in this light Billy could see the dandruff on his jacket. 'Hans can't wait to get started now,' he said. 'And I hear Mankiewicz may be out of action for a while.'

'What's the problem?'

'She's been diagnosed with leukaemia.'

Billy looked across at Chloe, who was being fawned over by the woman from the Wigmore. She had said barely a word to him since he had gone backstage. He caught her eye and they smiled, but then Hofmann claimed her again, refilling her glass and placing his arm around her.

It was late when they left the restaurant, and the first cool breath of autumn was on the air. Billy wrapped her cloak around Chloe's bare shoulders and held on to her as they walked to the car. Their conversation was desultory as he drove towards Highgate. Over dinner everything had been said about Chloe's performance that could be said, and now there was a coda of silence. He pulled the car up outside her aunt's house and took the cello from the back, placing it against the wall. Chloe folded herself into him, nuzzling against his chest.

'Thank you for being there,' she said.

'Why would I not be there?'

She leaned back and looked at him earnestly. 'You're very good to me, Billy,' she said.

'I want to be, at least.'

'No, you are.'

He kissed her lightly. 'When will I see you again?'

'There's Cardiff on Saturday. Sunday evening, maybe? But I'll be tired.'

'Let's see how you feel. Call me when you get home.'

She turned and picked up the cello. There were no lights on in the house, and she made her way carefully to the door. As she stepped through it she turned to wave, and Billy waved back.

Two

The letter had aroused his curiosity, and as he waited in the flat for its sender to arrive, he wondered what sort of person she might turn out to be. 'Dear Mr Palmer,' she had written, 'I have a number of letters from my grandmother to Aldous Huxley which demonstrate that he fathered a child with her – my mother. Would you be interested in seeing them? Yours faithfully, Gloria Beckinsdale.'

In the days since he replied, saying that certainly he would be interested in seeing the letters, he had re-read the relevant chapters of Sybille Bedford's biography and had generally tried to recall what he knew of the period. The University of Texas held the Huxley archives, including correspondence between him, his wife Maria, and his lovers Nancy Cunard and Mary Hutchinson. If these letters were genuine, there was an obvious place to sell them.

Gloria Beckinsdale was a woman quite out of time, wearing a dark green twin-set and sturdy brown shoes. She sat on Billy's sofa sipping tea, now and then wringing her hands in a nervous gesture that she clearly couldn't control. She was probably in her mid-forties, rather large, her pale face given definition by heavy black spectacles.

Billy sat reading through the letters. They were all on blue notepaper with a printed address in Chelsea, and sent to Huxley at the Condé Nast office in Holborn, where he was then working on *Vogue* magazine.

'How did your grandmother come to know him?' he asked.

'She was a secretary at Chatto & Windus, his publishers, working for Frank Swinnerton.'

'And how long did their relationship last?'

'Well, one must judge that from the dates of the letters. The first was written in February nineteen twenty-two and the last in October.'

He looked at her as closely as politeness would allow. She seemed an improbable descendant of a writer who had been known as something of a libertine, being plain, fussy, and clearly ill at ease in this room full of books. But there was an arresting quality to her, a kind of gravitational pull, which he could define only as a kind of yearning.

'When did they come into your possession?'

'My mother died in the spring, and I found them among her effects. Apparently Huxley returned them to my grandmother when their affair ended, and my mother came into possession of them when Granny died.'

The letters were full of references to people and places, and at first glance they seemed plausible. Frank Swinnerton had been Huxley's editor. Huxley's wife was mentioned frequently, as were Ottoline Morrell and Virginia Woolf. Huxley and Diana Beckinsdale had apparently met regularly for lunch at the 17 Club and the Isola Bella restaurant in Frith Street. One of the letters contained breathless and somewhat inarticulate admiration for Huxley's first novel, *Crome Yellow*, which had been published at the end of the previous year. It all seemed to add up. And yet, as Billy fingered the paper and glanced at Gloria Beckinsdale out of the corner of his eye, something told him these letters weren't the real thing.

'You live in Richmond,' he said.

'Yes.'

'May I ask what you do?'

She placed her cup on the table and wiped her mouth with a lace handkerchief. 'I work in a flower shop,' she said, and as she uttered the words she wrung her hands again.

'That must be very pleasant.'

'Yes, it is.'

He looked down at the letters. There was one dating from September in which Diana Beckinsdale revealed that she was pregnant, and asked Huxley what she should do. But the following letter, though it was imploring, made no reference to any reply from Huxley, and as Billy considered this, and the general lack of any reference to anything Huxley might have said in return, his doubts were strengthened. 'I would need to spend some time with them,' he said. 'Perhaps I could visit you at home one day and sit with them for a couple of hours. Would that be possible?'

'Naturally. In the meantime, I've brought you photocopies.'

She reached into her handbag and produced a sheaf of papers. Billy collected up the originals, and they made an awkward exchange.

'If it's not an impertinence, how did you feel when you discovered that Huxley was your grandfather?'

'Oh, shocked at first. But then… well, proud, I suppose. I set about reading all his books, and they were rather good.'

'And what do you wish to do with the letters?'

At this she leaned forward, as if about to share a confidence.

'I imagine a future biographer would find them valuable,' she said. 'I don't think my grandmother's relationship with Huxley has come to light before.'

'And what about money?'

'Oh, that's unimportant. I simply want Granny's part in Huxley's life to be acknowledged.'

They talked for another ten minutes or so, Billy gently probing into her life and that of her mother. After she left he turned on the reading lamp and settled down to read the photocopies of the letters in full. They were very well done, the style and syntax exactly of the period. He picked up Gloria Beckinsdale's letter to him and compared the handwriting. Whoever had written these letters addressed to Aldous Huxley, it was not Gloria Beckinsdale herself. So why was he so sure that she had come across some blank sheets of old notepaper and made up this sly, faintly salacious correspondence? Was it Gloria Beckinsdale herself he wasn't sure about, a lonely middle-aged woman who worked in a flower shop?

It was when he came to one of the later letters that he found the telling mistake. It referred to the character of Mary Bracegirdle in Crome Yellow, and to her almost certainly having been based on the painter Carrington. But the name written was Leonora Carrington, not Dora. Billy racked his brains. Wasn't there an artist working nowadays called Leonora Carrington? He was sure there was. At any rate, it was too glaring an error to let pass. It seemed certain proof that these letters were fakes.

He thought again of the prim yet oddly passionate woman who had sat on his sofa drinking tea and telling him a tall tale. Why on earth had she done it? Did she need the validation that an illustrious fore-bear might bring? He supposed that Diana Beckinsdale had indeed worked at Chatto, and had known Aldous Huxley or at least met him. And he supposed that the rest was the product of her granddaughter's overheated imagination. But surely she must have known that her deceit would eventually be discovered? Forged inscriptions on the title pages of books were one thing, but a forged correspondence was quite another. He stood up, and deposited the photocopies in the waste-paper bin. He would wait a couple of days before writing to Gloria Beckinsdale to express his regret that he didn't feel able to respond to this intriguing opportunity.

———

He stood at the counter in the kitchen, stuffing a garlic mash under the skin of the chicken breast. It was a fiddly task, and his hands would stink for days afterwards, but this was one of his favourite dishes. There was an element of ritual to his roasting a chicken on Sundays, one of the few rituals, it seemed, that were left. Chloe lay on the sofa listening to Rostropovich play the Dvořák Cello Concerto. The clocks had gone back that day, and suddenly winter was upon them.

She had called from Cardiff two days earlier to say that Hofmann had landed her a world tour, Valeria Mankiewicz having called a halt to her career on the eve of her departure for Japan. There hadn't been time to talk about things properly, and Billy wanted to wait until they saw each other before he learned the details. But Chloe was in an agitated state, trying to wind down after the concert the previous night and at the same time to prepare herself for an adventure which would surely define her future career. She had resigned from the Wulf Quartet on the train returning from Cardiff that morning.

'Leo was furious,' she said.

'Naturally.'

'He doesn't own me.'

'He thought he did.'

She raised herself from the sofa and joined Billy in the kitchen, lifting the lids from pans and sniffing the aroma of the chicken.

'He'll find someone else,' she said.

'He will. But not as good as you.' He reached across and kissed her hair. 'He's known for a while he would lose you. But that won't have made it any easier.'

'I was tired of the quartet. I want to try out new things.'

'So what will you be playing on the tour?'

'It's all solo stuff, and the repertoire's actually quite limited. Bach, of course, Kodály, Berio. But I'm going to have to learn fast.'

'And you leave for Tokyo the week after next.'

'Yes. There's just the concert at the Purcell next Saturday, and then I must get ready to go.'

Later they sat down to eat, Billy carving the chicken and serving Chloe a plate.

'How long will you be gone?' he asked.

'Three months. Japan, China, Australia, America, and then eight cities in Europe.'

'That's a long time.'

'You could join me somewhere along the way.'

He looked at her doubtfully. 'You said that about Vienna. You know I feel I'm in the way when you're working.'

'Is that what you think?'

'Look at the night at the Wigmore. I just have to surrender you.'

'I'm sorry.'

They ate in silence for a few moments, Billy willing her to ask something about him, about what *he* had been doing. He was convinced that she found his work absurd, this bartering in books and manuscripts. And then there was the fact that his relationship with her was quite separate from the rest of his life. What would she make of Blackwood and Cummings? And what on earth would she make of Joe Mullan and Gloria Beckinsdale?

'My American millionaire is arriving next week,' he said eventually.

'Yes?'

'I think I've found a Louis MacNeice volume he'll want.'

'Good.'

He poured some wine, the burgundy dancing in the candlelight, and watched her as she raised the glass to her lips. Was this the last supper? he wondered. When they went to bed she was passive, uninvolved, and afterwards she fell straight to sleep. Perhaps she was simply tired. He lay in the darkness, listening to the steady rising and falling of her breathing, thinking about the wintry nights ahead he would be spending alone.

Ronnie Aldridge handed Billy the copy of MacNeice's *Poems*, and he turned it over in his hand. The inscription read, 'To Cecil, From a position of "armed neutrality". Louis MacNeice, 4th December 1935'. There was some foxing on the pages, and the lower corners of the binding were slightly bumped, but otherwise it was a pristine copy.

'Where did you find it?' he asked.

Aldridge smiled enigmatically. 'Spalding,' he said.

'All right.'

Aldridge was a runner. He scoured the country for books, going to provincial shops and auction houses, places where interesting things might be tucked away, their owners unaware of their true value. He was about Billy's age, very thin, with lank grey hair and a scruffy beard. His eyes had the hunted look of the obsessive.

'A hundred and fifty,' said Billy.

'Two fifty.'

'Two.'

'Done.'

He wrote out the cheque. 'Got anything else?' he asked.

'Not up your street, no. Came across some nice Waverleys the other day in Aberdeen.'

'You get around.'

'You know me, always on the move.' Aldridge put an index finger to his mouth and gnawed at it. 'What are you in the market for?'

'Someone's looking for a good first of *Rogue Male*.'

'Difficult, that,' replied Aldridge, losing interest in his fingernail.

'If you see one.'

Aldridge stood to leave, and Billy shook his chafed hand. He had been buying books from this man for years now, but he was always glad to see him go. He watched him cross the square to where his van was parked, the van that Billy knew contained all his worldly possessions. Where would he be off to now? he wondered.

Two days later he put on a suit and tie and took the bus down to the Garrick Club. He had been a somewhat reluctant member for a while now, Roy Urquhart having put him up and, with little apparent difficulty, got him in. In the bar he was gazed upon by Garrick and Kean, by Olivier and Gielgud, their portraits given pride of place on the walls. There weren't many actors there nowadays, probably because they couldn't afford it. Most of the current members were lawyers, and a few publishers. Billy went there not so much to fraternize as to impress certain of his clients, especially the Americans.

Jack Ziegler entered the bar, and they shook hands. Ziegler ordered a club soda, and they sat on the guard rail of the fireplace.

'Good to see you,' said Ziegler.

'When did you get into town?'

'Yesterday. Here today, gone tomorrow.'

'That expression always reminds me of what Alfred Knopf said about books being returned to the publisher by booksellers.'

'Gone today, here tomorrow.'

'Precisely.'

'Did you know Knopf?'

'No. He died soon after I arrived at Random House, and anyway he was far too grand to speak to someone like me.'

They went down to the dining room and sat at a table near a window. Ziegler shot his cuffs. He was about the most elegant man Billy had ever encountered. His clothes all came from Jermyn Street, but nonetheless he could not have been anything other than an American. There was a sleekness to men like him that the British could never emulate. Ziegler was a banker, high up in Chase Manhattan. He was also an assiduous collector of twentieth-century poetry, with fine collections of Eliot and Pound and Lowell. Billy had once visited his apartment on Fifth Avenue, and it was a temple of books. Ziegler had a special interest in the poets who were collectively called 'Macspaunday' – MacNeice, Spender, Auden and Day-Lewis. He had at least one copy of every single book they had published, but he was always looking out for association copies, books by one of them which were inscribed to another. The MacNeice that Billy had bought from Aldridge was just such a book.

Over lunch they talked about books and their owners, about what Bauman's on Madison Avenue was offering at the moment, about the latest auction at Sotheby's. Afterwards they took coffee in the dark space under the stairs, sitting in brown leather armchairs. Billy went to the cloakroom and brought back the MacNeice. He watched as Ziegler leafed through it.

'"Armed neutrality",' said Ziegler, smiling. 'The phrase Day-Lewis used about MacNeice in his review.'

'Yes. MacNeice was never as committed to communism as the others, was he?'

'Sat on the fence.' Ziegler looked up at him. 'How much?'

'Eight hundred.'

'I'll send you a cheque.' Ziegler slipped the volume into a pocket. 'Coming over any time soon?'

448

'As a matter of fact, yes, next month. My son is thinking of going to Vanderbilt University in Nashville, and I'm taking him there just before Thanksgiving. But I'll be in New York for only a day or so.'

'Drop by my place if you have time. I'll show you my prize new acquisition, a copy of the Spender edition of Auden's first collection.'

'The SHS edition?'

'Yes.'

'There were only thirty copies printed. They never come up. How did you get your hands on one?'

'I paid a lot of money, that's how.'

'To another collector.'

'Right.'

'Do you mind my asking how much money?'

Ziegler smiled. 'I certainly do,' he said.

———————

Billy's younger brother Tom lived in a converted warehouse just off City Road. He had recently returned from Rwanda, where he had been on an assignment, and he wanted Billy to see the photographs. Billy parked the car and ascended the stairs to the top floor. It was a vast space, painted a dull white, with a few sticks of furniture, a fridge and stove, and at the far end a developing room. The walls were hung with prints and negatives of his recent work. It was more a laboratory than a home; but then Tom's life had always been something of an experiment.

'Have a look,' said Tom once Billy had taken off his coat.

There were photos of men with arms or legs missing, of young women with babies that were the tribute of rape, of villages still devastated all these years after the genocide. They were harrowing.

'What is it about Africa?' said Billy. 'Somalia, Eritrea, now here…'

'It just keeps drawing me back.'

'It's because it's a mess, that's why. You like messes.'

Tom ran his hand through his long dark hair. He was lean and tanned, and looked nothing like his forty years. He was wearing what looked like fatigues, as if he were ready at any moment to jump on a plane again.

'It's not a mess, it's a tragedy,' he said.

Billy stared at one of the photos, but remained silent.

449

'Coffee?'

'Thanks.'

Tom put on the kettle, and Billy sat in the only comfortable chair.

'How are things with you?' asked Tom as he opened the jar.

'Don't ask.'

'Why?'

Billy sighed. 'Business is flat. I need something interesting to happen. And now Chloe has pushed off for three months.'

'Where to?'

'Everywhere. She's taken on a world tour after a famous cellist dropped out. She'll be on the front page of the *Sunday Times* Culture section before we know it.'

'That's great.'

'For her, yes.'

Tom handed him a mug and sat down on a kitchen chair.

'You're doing OK, though, aren't you?'

'Am I? By what measure?'

'Come on, Billy, you're all set up. Seems to me you have a pretty cushy life.'

He sipped the coffee. 'I know I have a cushy life, Tom,' he said. 'But it doesn't seem like enough.' He looked up at his brother. 'And besides, any life is going to seem cushy compared to the one you've got.'

'But it's my own, like yours – I don't answer to anyone.'

'Your life is a hundred times more exciting than mine.'

He stood up and inspected more of the photographs. A few of them were almost pastoral, of forests at dawn, lakes at sunset. Tom was a gifted photographer.

'How are things with Molly?' he said as he returned to the chair.

'Over.'

'How long was it this time?'

Tom gazed up at the ceiling. 'Three months,' he said.

'For God's sake don't become what I've become.'

'And what's that?'

'A middle-aged divorcee, fooling around with women too young for him, unable to settle down.'

'I've never been married.'

'All right, a middle-aged bachelor then.'

450

'I'm not the settling down type, you know that.'

'What's OK when you're in your thirties is not necessarily OK when you're in your fifties.'

They lapsed into silence, both looking down the length of the room.

'You and Chloe have been together for a while now, though,' said Tom eventually.

'It'll soon be a year.'

'And you love her.'

'Do I?'

'Well, don't ask me. Do you or don't you?'

Billy looked thoughtfully at his brother for a few moments. 'Neither of us has ever used the word "love",' he said. 'It seems like a ticking bomb to me, primed to go off at any moment.'

Tom smiled. 'I think a good explosion is exactly what you need.'

Billy stayed for an hour or so, during which time they talked about the family, about what would be happening at Christmas. Tom was close to Sarah in a way that Billy seemed not to be nowadays, and close to the kids. His work impressed them, of course, his travelling, his credits in the newspapers. Their talk of Rob turned Billy's thoughts to Michael, and his trip to America. He was apprehensive about it, as he always was just before he went to New York. The last time he was there Alice had had no time to talk to him at all, and Michael had been as monosyllabic as ever. He must connect with his son somehow. Maybe the trip to Nashville would accomplish that.

'So did you go to Istanbul?' asked Billy as he sat with Andrew Blackwood in the Museum Tavern.

'No,' replied Blackwood. 'I talked to Krantz on the phone a couple of times, and it seemed pretty clear he just wanted someone to give him a price before he trotted off to the auction houses. Bastard.'

'You can hardly be surprised. If it's the real thing, Sotheby's will have a field day with it.'

Blackwood gestured airily with his hand. 'I thought he might not know what he was about.'

'I told you, he's canny.'

'Oh, well. I tried.' He sniffed at his glass of claret. 'I see there was another earthquake in Turkey.'

'In a place called Düzce. Nearly a thousand dead.' Billy took off his glasses. 'All these earthquakes. Is someone trying to tell us something?'

'It's nature's way of preparing us for the millennium.'

'Is it going to be that bad?'

Billy went to the bar for another round of drinks, and then proceeded to tell Blackwood about Gloria Beckinsdale and the letters to Huxley.

'Poor thing.'

'Yes. It made me feel lousy for a day or two. Who was it who said that a gentleman doesn't read other people's letters?'

'Whoever it was, he wasn't a bookseller.'

Sam Cummings appeared in the doorway, and Billy beckoned him over. While Billy bought him a pint of bitter, Cummings set about rolling a cigarette.

'I think I've got us into the archive,' he said when Billy returned to the table.

'Yes?'

'I told them I needed to consult some Hughes stuff for this edition of Plath's journals we're publishing next year.'

Billy glanced at Blackwood, whose ears had pricked up at the mention of the word 'archive'.

'The Faber archive?' asked Blackwood.

'Never you mind,' replied Billy.

'Uh, oh,' said Cummings, licking the cigarette paper. 'Sorry I spoke.'

'I'm not going to barge in, if that's what you think,' said Blackwood. 'But, Billy, if you need any help…'

'I'll ask for it.'

Billy looked at his companions, and could sense a long night beginning. He thought of the flat, and of the fact that there was nothing in the fridge. And then he thought of Chloe, wondering where exactly she was. She should have left Tokyo by now. Beijing? Shanghai? Wherever she was, it was a long way away.

'Let's go and have something to eat at the Greek place,' he said.

'Steady on,' replied Cummings. 'I haven't finished my first drink yet.'

'When you have, then. I'm hungry.'

The taxi sped along the freeway towards the tunnel, the driver jockeying with the other cars. Billy looked at the nameplate and read the words 'Amit Singh'. When he lived in New York in the eighties all the taxi drivers were from Puerto Rico; now it seemed they were from India. The city came into view, the snaggle teeth of the skyscrapers in midtown. He had to explain to the driver where the Mayflower Hotel was, and to haul his bag from the trunk without his assistance when they arrived.

He had a couple of hours before he was due at Alice's apartment, and took a walk in the park. It was very cold, and the winter sun glittered on the lake as he made his way northwards towards the Great Lawn. It was while they were walking in Central Park that Billy had first told Alice he wanted to come here to live. Six years he had spent here, trying to become a sort of honorary American. In many ways it had been a good time. But when he looked back on it, he wondered how it was that he had ever supposed it could last: America seemed as foreign to him now as anywhere in the world.

He left the park at Eighty-sixth Street and headed east towards Alice's place. She had just got back, and was taking groceries from a brown paper bag. He kissed her on the cheek, and she told him to go into the living room. Sunset was just wrapping up over New Jersey, and he stood for a few moments watching its final act.

'Good flight?' she said when she joined him.

'The usual. I'm waiting for the day when you can be beamed across, like they do in Star Trek. You step into a booth in London, and seconds later you step out of one in New York.'

'Not in our lifetime, I don't think.'

Billy sat down on a sofa. 'Michael around?'

'He's spending the evening with friends. Says not to wait up for him, he'll see you in the morning.'

'We have to be at La Guardia at nine.'

'He knows. Would you like a drink?'

'Thanks. Just a glass of wine.'

She stood and left the room, Billy's gaze following her. She hadn't changed a bit in the years since they parted, still slim, her hair its natural auburn. She had made a new career for herself in interior design, and now had her own studio, employing a dozen people. Like him she hadn't remarried. Why was that? he wondered. And why, while he was about it, had they divorced in the first place? Sometimes he thought the real reason he had returned to England was mere homesickness.

She handed him a glass of white wine. 'How are you, then?' she asked.

'Fine.'

'That's it? Just "fine"?'

'Tired. Is Michael up for this trip?'

'He seems excited.'

'I thought I'd take him to Shiloh, to the battlefield. It's a couple of hours' drive from Nashville.'

She smiled. 'Still fighting the Civil War.'

'I'm just interested, you know that. Remember all those books I had to work on at Random House?'

'I certainly do. Many a lost weekend.'

'I'm sorry.'

'You've already apologized, a few times.'

He looked around the apartment. Alice had redone it since he was last here a year ago, and it seemed to have a vaguely Mexican theme. 'How about you?' he said. 'Work going well?'

'I can't keep up with it. For a while business was slack, but now everyone seems to have money again and want to spend it.'

'Good.'

He thought back to the time when they lived here together, in a rent-controlled apartment in the West Village. Alice had worked in the theatre as a set designer, and when that hadn't worked out she had gone into interior design, reluctantly at first, to make a living, and then enthusiastically. But by that time their marriage was cracking up. Alice as a career woman was an idea he had had to get used to in the years since they divorced.

He stayed for an hour, and then, pointing out that it was already past midnight for him, he took a cab back to the hotel. Looking out of the window at the lights of the city, he thought back again to his time here, to his marriage, to what he had believed was going to be a career in publishing. Sometimes he felt he had been wearing a mask during his years in America. He had lied about his age, about his education, had tried to reinvent himself. But in the end he had remained himself. Was that a failure, or a success? Certainly it was not a cause for regret. If there was anything Billy had come to understand in recent years, it was the futility of regret.

———

He picked up Michael in the morning, and they headed for the airport. His son had grown since Billy last saw him, and now stood over six feet tall. They were awkward with each other, Michael at one point saying, 'It's Mike, Dad. Nobody's called me Michael for a long time.' On the plane they made hesitant conversation, Billy asking him how he was doing at Dalton, who his friends were, whether he had a girl-friend. Michael's responses were bluff and uninformative. He had been just three years old when Billy returned to London. No wonder they found it hard sometimes to know what to say to one another.

They picked up a car at Nashville airport and drove to the hotel, which was just near the university. Michael's meeting with the admissions officer wasn't until three, and they had lunch in the hotel restaurant. Afterwards they walked to the campus, and strolled across the grounds towards the engineering school. He left Michael in the office and took a walk, heading for the park nearby. It was a grey, chilly day, and he was glad of his coat and scarf.

After the interview Michael seemed pessimistic about his prospects.

'Why?' asked Billy.

'I don't know. They kind of asked me the wrong questions.'

'What are the right questions?'

'The ones I know the answers to.'

In the evening they went to a country and western bar in town. Billy was determined to give his son an experience of the south. Michael drank cokes while he knocked back several glasses of bourbon. Bourbon was not a drink he especially cared for, but this was Tennessee after all. By the time they went to bed he was feeling quite drunk.

In the morning they set off, driving down the Natchez Trace Parkway towards Shiloh. For mile after they mile they drove through the woods, with very little to detain the eye. Michael had the radio on all the time, switching from one station to the next as they cut across the country. Eventually they arrived at the battlefield, and stepped inside the visitor centre. Billy hadn't appreciated how large the place was, and that they would be required to drive around it rather than walk. There were mercifully few other visitors, though, and once they

455

were doing the rounds it seemed they had the place to themselves. They stopped at the first site, and read the sign explaining what had happened. His civil war history coming back to him, Billy started to get interested.

'The Confederates thought they could deal a hammer blow to the Union,' he said, 'driving them away from the Tennessee River. And they almost succeeded. Grant and Sherman won the day in the end, though.'

'Who was Sherman?' asked Michael.

'Who was Sherman? You've heard about Sherman's March, surely?'

'Nope.'

'Through Georgia. Setting fire to Atlanta. You must have seen *Gone With the Wind*.'

'Nope.'

They moved on to the next place, the sign telling them about the Confederates' early morning advance. They caught the Union army unawares, but they lacked the weight of forces to carry their attack through. Every sign told of the casualties, the dreadful numbers of dead and wounded.

'The Civil War was one of the cruellest in history,' said Billy. 'They had very destructive weapons, but no morphine yet, and men suffered horribly.'

'I guess so,' replied Michael.

'So what did they teach you in school about the Civil War?'

'I don't recall much. Lincoln won, and freed the slaves.'

'He healed the country. At least, he began the healing. Sometimes when I've been travelling in the south, seeing Confederate flags flying still, I've wondered how long it's going to take.'

'Come on, Dad, the North/South thing ended a long time ago.'

'Did it? Slavery only really ended in the sixties, surely?'

They continued on their round of the battle sites. Without a map it was confusing, and by the time they returned to the car park Billy wasn't sure just how much they had learned.

'Let's get some lunch,' said Michael. 'There's a McDonald's we passed just before we came in.'

'I am not eating in a McDonald's, Mike, you know that.'

'The fried chicken place, then.'

'That's more like it. Fried chicken, grits and gravy.'

456

Michael smiled. 'You know, you're kind of a southerner yourself.'

'I'm English. We have a lot in common.'

'I guess so.'

He went to Wells for Christmas, joining the Friday exodus from London and sitting in a traffic jam on the motorway for an hour or more. Billy hated this time of year, but there was nothing to do except to get through it. Once he had gone to Morocco, a place he loved, thinking to escape it all, but even in a kasbah in Ouazarzate he had come across a Christmas tree.

He was barely inside the door before Margaret led him to the kitchen, whispering urgently.

'You have to talk to him, Billy,' she said. 'The doctors have told him an operation is unavoidable, but he refuses to listen.'

'I will. But not just now. Let me have a drink and settle in.'

After breakfast on Christmas morning he suggested to Jim that they take a walk. 'You don't get enough exercise these days,' he said.

They strolled towards the High Street and Market Place, stepping into the grounds of the Bishop's Palace. The swans were gliding in the moat, preening their feathers, ducks scooting around them.

'I know what you're going to say,' said Jim as they sat down on a bench. 'And you can forget it.'

'You're quite sure?'

His father looked at him dolefully. 'I'm going to die, Billy,' he said.

'You don't have to, at least not yet.'

'Yes I do. You know what? I've had enough.'

'You're seventy-eight, for God's sake. You're young.'

'There's nothing left now.'

'What about your wife? She doesn't count, I suppose.'

Jim sighed. 'You'll never understand, will you?' he said. 'Any of you. I've loved Maggie all my life. But I'm no use to her now, I'm no use to anyone.'

'That's nonsense.'

'Is it?' He gave Billy a hard stare. 'Old age is hell, Billy. You'll find out soon enough. Your body doesn't work properly, you can't tie your own shoelaces, the days are endless…'

'Read some books, then.'

Jim looked into the distance. 'You know me – I was never a reader. Anyway, my eyes are giving out too.'

A young family passed them by, the boy riding a new bicycle. Billy thought back to their first Christmas in the cottage in nearby Coombe, when he was ten years old, and to his finding a bike in the hayshed and wondering who it was for. His father had told him there would be no presents that year, but then miraculously there was, a beautiful steed that would take him anywhere he wanted to go.

'You can't just decide to die,' he said. 'You have a responsibility, to yourself if to no one else, to live for as long as you can.'

'Don't get all philosophical with me, son. I'm no stoic.'

Billy looked at his watch. 'Sarah and the gang will be arriving soon,' he said. 'We'd better get back.'

They stood up, Jim shaking both his legs before he started to walk. On the way home they remained silent, until they saw the red Jaguar in the drive. Jim hadn't seen it before, and suddenly he became animated, opening the front door of the house and shouting to John that he wanted to take the car for a drive. John appeared, and looked at him sceptically.

'Are you insured?' he said.

'Of course I'm bloody insured. I'm also a good driver. Come on, let's have the keys.'

Billy watched as his father reversed the car out of the drive, John looking anxiously into a wing mirror from the passenger seat. He went into the house and greeted Sarah and the kids, reminding himself that he must call Michael later. Looking at his watch again, he saw that it was noon. He went to the cocktail cabinet and poured sherry for himself and for Sarah and Margaret. His mother looked at him searchingly, but he couldn't meet her gaze.

'Let's play charades after lunch,' he said. 'I haven't done them in years.'

———

He lay on the sofa, listening to the brooding tones of Sibelius's Seventh Symphony and wondering whether there was any point in going to bed. There would be fireworks at midnight, and much as he wanted to get some sleep, he knew he wouldn't be able to. When the symphony ended he went into the bathroom, catching sight of himself in the mirror. When he was young he had looked in the mirror for signs of character. Now he looked only for signs of decay. The grey hairs were confined to his temples for the moment. But something odd had happened to his mouth in the past couple of years, a turning down at the corners. Was it due to mood, or simply to gravity?

He drew back a curtain and looked out across the square. It was half past eleven, and on an impulse he put on his coat and descended the stairs to the street. Heading for the heath, he turned up his collar and made his way down the hill.

It was an overcast night, the light of the city colouring the clouds a dirty yellow, the lattice of leafless trees stark black against them. The water in the ponds had a dull sheen, like pewter. It was only when he arrived at Parliament Hill that he encountered anyone else, a knot of people who had clearly gathered for the show. He stood there for ten minutes, surveying the city as it pulsed below him. At midnight the fireworks went off, but they were nothing like what he had expected. He had read there would be a river of light, extending from Greenwich all the way to Chelsea, but this seemed no more impressive than any old fireworks night. The revellers around him popped champagne corks and toasted the new millennium.

The new millennium. Billy had been obstinately referring to it as the new century. A millennium was a pure abstraction, meaningless really. All of the people standing around him now would be dead before the twenty-first century was out. But the millennium it was, appropriated by everyone from the government down to the dry-cleaner around the corner that had recently changed its name.

He started to walk home, obliged along the way to wish some of the revellers a happy New Year. What would the year bring for him? Very little, as far as he could tell. Once back in the flat he closed the door with a sense of relief. Another New Year's Eve spent alone, another year gone.

Three

The first few days of January were hard for him. Nothing was happening, the holiday season seeming now to extend over almost three weeks, and the weather was foul. The silence in the flat – the silence in his life – became oppressive. He thought often of Chloe, of where she might be and how she was doing. She had called him a couple of times since she went away, sounding elated by the success of the tour, and had left a message on Christmas Day, but that was all.

One morning he called Hans Hofmann to find out where she was, and Hans gave him some dates, and details of where she would be staying. She was in Italy – Milan that day, Florence the next, and then Siena. Her Siena date was for the coming Saturday. She had often enough in the past invited him to join her when she was working abroad. Well, he would take her up on it now. He booked a flight and a hotel room, choosing to stay not where Chloe was staying but nearby. The day before he set out he left a message at her hotel to say that he was coming, that he wouldn't attempt to see her before the concert, but that he hoped they could have supper together afterwards.

He was suddenly galvanized by the prospect of this journey. When he was in his late twenties he had taken three months off from *The Bystander* one summer and spent them in the Chianti hills, working in the vineyards of an old abbey. He hadn't been back since, and he recalled the beauty of the countryside and the intensity of light and sound in Siena. He had gone there for the Palio, the medieval horse race around the main square that was the focus of the city's year. It would be quiet now in January, but it would be nonetheless pleasurable.

He picked up a car at Pisa airport and drove along the *autostrada* to Siena. He had never driven in the city, and the moment he passed through its western gate he got lost, remembering that this was not a place for cars. Eventually he found a car park, and walked to the hotel. His room overlooked the cathedral, and he stood for a while on the balcony taking it all in, the city itself and the glimpses of the country beyond. The black and white stripes of the cathedral struck him as being Moorish as much as Christian. Otherwise the buildings were a soft reddish-brown. Surely Siena was the only city in the world named after the colour of its stone?

He walked to the *campo* and had a drink in a bar. He recalled this scallop-shaped square as being a kind of theatre, the audience sitting at café tables all around it. Now, in the chill of winter, it had turned in on itself, and people walked hurriedly across it rather than lingering on its margins. He stepped back through an archway and entered the Chigi Saracini, where Chloe's concert would be taking place. It was a twelfth-century *palazzo*, containing an art gallery and a musical instrument museum as well as a concert hall. He sat in the gallery looking down on a sparse audience, and waited for Chloe to appear.

When she took the stage Billy felt a flutter of nervousness in the pit of his stomach. There she was, a few feet away, yet otherwise she seemed very remote. Had he been foolish to come all this way uninvited?

She played some Bach, and then Kodály, and Billy couldn't help but sense that she was not at her best. The applause was polite but nothing more, and quickly the Sienese were putting on their fur coats and heading for the door. The building was as much a labyrinth as the city itself, and it took him a while to find the dressing rooms. Nor did it help that his Italian had almost abandoned him. '*A sinistra... a destra... sempre diritto...*' He could do directions, and he could order in restaurants, but that was about it.

'Hello, Billy,' she said, almost shyly.

They kissed and embraced, and he stood back to take a look at her. Under the make-up she was clearly exhausted. She had been travelling for more than two months now, and it showed.

'Hello. I hope you don't mind...'

'Of course not. It's lovely to see you.' She sat down and took off her shoes. 'But I don't know how much time we'll have. Gianni, the promoter, is taking me to dinner, and in the morning I have to leave early for Rome.'

'I should have tried to talk to you first.'

'No, don't say that. I'll ask Gianni if he minds you joining us.'

He walked out into the courtyard and waited for them there. Gianni was a man in his thirties, tall and with flowing black hair that was very

461

like Chloe's, wearing a dark suit and a bow tie. Chloe introduced them, and Gianni smiled broadly.

'It's good of you to have me along,' said Billy.

'You are very welcome.'

They went to a restaurant on the far side of the square. Gianni told them precisely what they should eat – *crostini*, followed by wild boar – and ordered a bottle of Chianti Classico.

'I know this wine,' said Billy when it came. 'I spent a summer in their vineyards.'

'When was that?' asked Gianni.

'Seventy-seven.'

'That was a good year.'

'For me it was.'

He looked across at Chloe, and she gave him a tired smile. It was past ten, and clearly she would rather be in bed by now. Gianni turned to her also, and then to Billy.

'She is wonderful, yes?'

'No, Gianni,' said Chloe before Billy could reply. 'She is not wonderful. She played badly tonight, you must know that.'

Gianni looked at her gravely. 'You are wonderful,' he said. 'Yes, you made some mistakes. But your feeling for the music...'

Their conversation stuttered after that, each one of them sensing the awkwardness of the occasion. Billy sat reproaching himself for having barged in like this. Very soon Chloe began to yawn, and Gianni signalled for the bill.

'I will leave you,' he said to them. 'You know your way back to the hotel, yes?'

'Yes.'

Gianni looked at Billy. 'And I'm sure Mr Palmer will be happy to escort you.'

Chloe took his arm as they walked through the darkened streets to her hotel. At the entrance he kissed her good night, and said he would return the next morning for breakfast. When he did so, Chloe looked as tired as she had when he left her. They went to the breakfast room and took a table.

'How many more places?' he asked.

'Four. Rome, Geneva, Lyons and Paris.'

'You must be ready for it to end.'

462

She smiled. 'It's been a great experience,' she said. 'But yes, I'm ready for it to end now.'

'And will you have a chance to rest when you get home?'

'Hans has already lined up some concerts. He wants to get me doing the concertos – you know, Elgar, Dvořák – but of course that requires orchestras. I think he's being too ambitious.'

'It's his job to be ambitious.'

'I know. But he has to be realistic too.' She toyed with a croissant, and then looked up at him. 'Billy…' she began, and then, 'I'm going to need some time to myself when I get home. Do you mind?'

'How much time?'

'I don't know. I'll have to see.'

He laid a hand on hers. 'Just tell me when it's over, Chloe,' he said. 'It's up to you.'

She withdrew her hand, and then placed it on top of his. 'I don't mean that,' she said. 'I just mean I need some time.'

'But that's how it will be, isn't it? You'll tell me you need some time, and then you'll discover that the time you need is the rest of your life.'

'Don't say that, please.'

'What else am I supposed to say?' He looked at her intently. 'I shouldn't have come here. I'm sorry.'

'No, you should.'

'I shouldn't. Now, you need to pack your bag. What time is the train?'

'In an hour.'

'I'll ask at the desk for a taxi.'

He walked back to his own hotel, wondering what he might do now. His flight home was not until the following afternoon, and suddenly he had no wish to stay on in Siena. He checked out of the hotel, threw his bag in the boot of the car, and drove northwards towards the Chianti hills. He had no idea whether Count Donato and his wife would still be living at the abbey, but something was drawing him back there.

The landscape was bare now, and grey-brown but for the pines and cypresses. Smoke curled from the chimneys of the farmhouses, and cords of wood lay stacked against their walls. This was a land in hibernation, the grapes and olives having been harvested, the bright yellow *ginestra* of spring yet to flower. After the village of Castellina he looked

463

for the white road leading to the abbey, the Badia a Campomaggio, and it was further than he remembered. When the sign came into view he swung onto the dusty track and drove slowly through the oak trees until the abbey came into view.

It was a thousand-year-old building, originally a Benedictine monastery, a tower rising above its walls. Billy parked the car and entered the courtyard, gazing down into the well and up at the shuttered windows. Memories of his summer here came rushing back, of spending time in the cellars bottling and labelling, and the backbreaking work in the vineyards when the harvest came around. But it had been a magical time.

He knocked on the main door, and heard the sound of dogs barking in response. After a minute or so it was opened, and a young man of about twenty-five stood before him. The last time Billy had seen Andrea Donato he had been four years old.

'I'm sorry to disturb you. Do you speak English?'

'Yes.'

'I stayed here once years ago. I was wondering whether your father and mother might be in.'

The young man led him to the cloister, inviting him to sit in a high-backed chair. A few moments later Piero Donato appeared.

'Is it Billy?' he said, beaming. '*Che sorpresa!*'

'It's something of a surprise to me, too,' replied Billy, shaking his hand. 'But I was nearby, and…'

'I am delighted to see you. Unfortunately Mariella is in Milan. But come, let me give you a drink.'

Piero Donato would be seventy-five now, but he looked as vigorous as ever, his silver hair swept back from his forehead, his face and hands deeply tanned. Billy followed him from the cloister into the refectory. The room was cold, and Billy imagined the place must be hard to heat in the winter.

'A glass of vin *santo*?'

'Thank you.' He looked up at the frescoes on the ceiling. 'This is all just as it was when I was here.'

'And just as it will always be. I don't suppose anything much has changed in our lives either. Andrea has been learning viniculture, and will take over soon. But otherwise…'

'And Mariella is well?'

464

'Very well. She will be sorry to have missed you. But tell me about yourself. How long ago was it you were here?'

'Seventy-seven. I was twenty-nine.' He smiled ruefully. 'Now I'm a little older.'

'As are we all. So tell me about your life.'

They sat down, and Billy gave him a brief account of his doings in the past twenty-odd years. It didn't sound like very much, the way he described it. It was strange to be speaking to Piero as one mature man to another. When he was in his late twenties he had still had a lot of growing up to do, and his relation to Piero, such as it was, had been one of teacher and pupil. As they talked, he sensed that he was slipping back into that relation, was adopting the pose of a still-young man.

'You must take a tour of the place,' said Piero after a while. 'And then stay for lunch.'

'I mustn't detain you.'

'But I insist.'

'Very well. Thank you.'

Piero called to one of the staff and asked for lunch to be served in half an hour. Then they walked through the formal gardens to the winery, and on to the chapel. Billy lit a candle, and it flickered in the gloom. When they returned to the house Andrea joined them, and they sat down to eat. His father explained to Andrea who Billy was.

'You used to run about the place naked, I remember,' said Billy. 'Like a cherub.'

Andrea smiled politely, and Billy decided he would lay off the reminiscences. A woman entered bearing a tureen of soup and ladled it into their bowls.

'Billy has spent his life in books,' said Piero. He turned towards him. 'You must see the library before you go.'

'Yes. But all your books are in Latin and Italian, as I recall.'

'I'm not proposing to sell them to you.'

'My interest in books extends beyond buying and selling.'

'Of course. But you are a merchant, Billy, like me, I can tell.'

'A merchant?'

'Yes. We know about fine things, but we also know their value.'

They ate the soup, and then guinea fowl, and then returned to the refectory for coffee. It was past three by the time Billy took his leave. He had no idea where he would stay that night, but he set off anyway

465

towards Poggibonsi and the main road to Pisa. Piero Donato's words stuck in his mind as he drove, about his being a merchant. It was not a word he had ever thought might apply to him, and it had taken a foreigner to suggest it. Was that what he was, really? The Merchant of Highgate, he said out loud to himself as he turned onto the *autostrada*.

The weight of things seemed all the greater after his return. He had made a mistake in going to Siena, and the only thing the trip had accomplished was to reinforce his sense that his relationship with Chloe was coming to an end. There was very little post on the doormat when he got home, and no messages on the answering machine. Andrew Blackwood and Sam Cummings were too busy to get together, and once again he found himself languishing in the flat, with only the tedious task of cataloguing the Norfolk library to occupy him. He called Sarah, and a couple of days later drove up to Barnet for lunch. John was at the office and the kids at school, and there was an unaccustomed calm to the big house.

He wasted little time with pleasantries, saying, 'I'm losing it, Sarah,' as she handed him a drink.

'What do you mean?'

'I mean nothing is making sense any more.'

'That's nonsense, Billy.'

'Is it? I'm divorced, my son is on another planet, I have hardly any friends, and my lover is about to leave me. All I can look forward to is an uneventful middle-age leading to decline and decay.'

She looked at him earnestly. 'Let's sit down,' she said.

They walked through to the living room. It was a glorious day, the winter sun flooding through the conservatory windows.

'What did she say in Siena?' asked Sarah.

'That when she comes home she'll need some time to herself.'

'Sounds fair enough to me. This tour must have taken it out of her.'

'Wouldn't you think she might need me *more* in that case, not less?'

Sarah gazed out across the garden. 'She's an artist, Billy,' she said. 'Artists are different, you know that.'

'I shouldn't be with an artist. I should be with someone as limited as I am.'

'Don't be so hard on yourself. You're not limited.'

'My imagination is limited. And I'm a coward – I haven't seized the opportunities that came my way.'

'You're sounding like your own obituarist now.'

'All good obituaries are written well before the subject drops dead.' He took off his glasses and kneaded his eyes. 'You know what is the hardest thing to bear, in the end?'

'What?'

'The fact that no one needs me. If I weren't here, it would make very little difference to anyone.'

Sarah was silent for a few moments, and then she turned to him and said, 'You're depressed. You need to see someone.'

'I'm not going to see any quacks, Sarah. You know my views about therapy.'

'You're more of a fool than you think you are, then. I'm not talking about years of psychoanalysis or anything like that, just a friendly talk.'

'I'm having a friendly talk now.'

'Yes, and look what good it's doing you. You're not hearing me, Billy. You're listening, but you're not hearing.'

He sighed heavily. 'I'm sorry. Everything has just got on top of me all of a sudden. I must be SAD.'

'Clearly you are.'

'I mean as in Seasonal Affective Disorder. That's what they call it, isn't it? Lack of light.'

'Go somewhere where there's more light, then. You can afford it.'

'I've just been somewhere like that.'

'Not far enough. And too complicated. Take a holiday somewhere warm.'

'By myself?' He picked up his glass. 'I'm sorry. Let's change the subject. How are you?'

'OK. Worried about Dad.'

'Yes.'

'He's determined to die, isn't he?'

'It seems so.'

'In which case you had better plan on being around for a long time.'

'Why?'

'You'll be the patriarch of the family.'

He smiled. 'Some patriarch,' he said. 'Maybe I should grow a beard.'

The Faber archive was beneath a nondescript building near Tottenham Court Road. Sam Cummings spoke into an entryphone, and a man in blue overalls appeared and led them to a lift. The cage doors clanged shut, and they descended into a kind of underworld, walking along corridors which were like those in a Tube station.

'They say these tunnels connect with Goodge Street,' said Cummings.

They went on for a hundred yards or so, eventually coming upon an orange-painted door with 'Vault No. 6' stencilled on it. Cummings brandished a set of keys and opened it up. The vault was about thirty feet by fifteen, and lined from floor to ceiling with green box files.

'This is it?' asked Billy.

'Apparently. The more modern stuff is in the basement at the office. But this lot goes back to the beginning.'

Billy ran his eyes over the names on the files. 'Let's take a look at the Golding,' he said.

Cummings pulled one of the William Golding files from the shelf, and they stepped outside the vault to where there was a small table. The first thing in the file was Golding's letter offering Faber a novel called *Strangers from Within*.

'The original title of *Lord of the Flies*,' said Billy.

'Just as well they changed it.'

Billy picked up the letter. It was sent from Salisbury in September 1953, and began simply, 'I send you the typescript of my novel "Strangers from Within", which might be defined as an allegorical interpretation of a stock situation.' More interesting than the letter itself, though, was the scrawl in another hand in the top corner, which read, 'Absurd, uninteresting fantasy about the explosion of an atom bomb on the Colonies. A group of children who land in jungle country near New Guinea. Rubbish & dull. Pointless.' It was signed 'R'.

'Famous in Faber legend, that one,' said Cummings.

'Who was "R"?'

'No one. It means "reject".'

Billy glanced through later correspondence, coming upon a letter from Charles Monteith, who had become Golding's editor, congratulating him on securing an American publisher for the novel. In his reply Golding wrote that he was glad to have an American publisher, 'because I've always wanted to see the Grand Canyon'.

'A rare moment of levity for Golding, I suspect,' he said.

'He was youngish then.'

A Tube train rumbled nearby, sounding as though it must be above them.

'You wanted to look at the Hughes stuff,' said Billy.

'Yes.' Cummings replaced the Golding file and returned with one of Ted Hughes material. As he did so Billy could feel a tide of exhilaration rising inside him. When Cummings had first spoken of the Faber archive, Billy had described it as a potential gold mine. He had been more right than he knew. Joyce, Eliot, Pound, Auden, Beckett – all the Faber greats were here.

The Hughes file contained a carbon copy of a letter from T. S. Eliot congratulating him on winning the Guinness Prize and praising *The Hawk in the Rain*.

'I'm going to have to spend some time with all of this,' said Cummings. 'I'd better ask if I can take files back to the office.'

'It's wonderful stuff,' said Billy.

'It certainly is. But as I said, they'll never sell.'

'Can't you at least ask? Faber can always use cash, surely?'

Cummings clapped his hands together, and a cloud of dust flew into the air. 'I'm not sure,' he replied. 'It's tricky. And you just want to make money out of it.'

'Of course I want to make money out of it. But I also know what this kind of thing is worth, in literary terms as well as money terms. I'd respect it.'

Cummings smiled sardonically. 'I'm sure you would,' he said.

———————

Chloe had called him the day after she got back, but it was more than two weeks until they saw each other. She had spent some of that time at her parents' house near Oxford, but nonetheless Billy fretted over her continued absence from his life. They met in the Flask, the local pub, and sat alone in a dark, low-ceilinged nook which must once have been a store for barrels of beer.

'You look rested,' he said.

'In this light, I expect I do.'

'No, but really. What have you been doing since you got back?'

'Nothing much. Some practice – I've got a recital in Edinburgh next week – otherwise very little.'

'Good.'

She ran a hand through her hair, and Billy sat looking at her, not knowing what to say now. This felt more like a first date than a conversation between lovers of long standing. In the silence it began to dawn on him that this was the last chance he had left, the last chance to hold onto her. He had never imagined he would say the words that came to him so forcefully now, but taking her hand in his he said, 'Chloe, will you marry me?'

She looked at him incredulously. 'What are you talking about, Billy? You know I'm not ready for marriage.'

'I'll take that as a no, then.'

She looked at him questioningly. 'Why ask now?' she said. 'We haven't seen each other properly for months. Don't we need to slip back into things gently?'

'I'm afraid that we won't slip back into things at all. Remember what I said in Siena? You're slipping away, not slipping back.'

She raised her glass to her lips, and then turned to face him. 'Billy, this is madness. I don't know what possessed you. Did you propose to Alice in a pub?'

'I proposed to Alice in bed.'

She set down her glass and folded her arms. 'I think you might have been more considerate,' she said after a while.

'And I think you might have been more considerate. When a man proposes marriage, he'd like to be taken seriously.'

'Then he should be serious. If you want to be married again you should think about what that would mean for your wife. It seems to me that all you can think about is how sorry you're feeling for yourself.'

He gazed at her levelly, and suddenly he was furious with her. 'Has it occurred to you that if I'm unhappy then you may have something to do with that?'

For a few moments she didn't respond, and then she said, 'I don't think you know yourself. You're fifty years old, Billy, and you don't seem to have worked out even the simplest things about yourself.'

'Such as?'

She reached for her coat, and then stood up. 'Such as the fact that you're too bound up in your own problems to appreciate other people. Such as the fact that you can't accept a loving relationship for what it is without burdening it with unrealistic expectations.'

'I'm sorry.'

'I'm going home. I'll call you sometime.'

He watched as she ducked under an archway, and then she was gone. A young couple sat down on the other side of the long table, and he took this as a signal to leave. Back in the flat he poured himself a large measure of whisky and put on a Sibelius CD. He could always be relied on, Sibelius, the haunting melodies speaking to him in a way that nothing and no one else could. So, he thought as he lay on the sofa, it's over. He needn't concern himself with Chloe any more. She would surely not call him, and once again he would be free.

'Heaney won the Whitbread, then,' said Billy. He was standing in Andrew Blackwood's shop, leafing through a copy of *Death of a Naturalist*.

'Yes. Ever dealt much in his stuff?'

'Sure. He sells well these days.' He turned to the famous first poem, 'Digging', and read out, 'Between my finger and my thumb, The squat pen rests. I'll dig with it.'

'Wonderful music,' said Blackwood.

'It's a nice metaphor for writing, isn't it, digging?'

'It's a nice metaphor for bookselling, too.'

'I suppose so. Digging, treasure hunting.' He looked around Blackwood's shabby room. 'Do you not sometimes think this is a mad way to make a living?'

Blackwood looked up from the papers on his desk. 'No madder than most other ways, I'd say. In fact, a great deal less mad.' He gazed thoughtfully at Billy. 'Do I detect a little angst in you these days?'

Billy returned the Heaney to the shelf. 'I think you probably do,' he said.

'Nothing a drink can't fix, I trust. To the pub?'

Blackwood closed up the shop, turning the sign from 'Open' to 'Back in ten minutes'. Over the years, Blackwood's notion of ten minutes had challenged many a would-be customer.

'How was the Faber archive?' he asked when they sat down in the Museum Tavern.

'Oh, quite interesting,' replied Billy cagily, thoughts of the letters he had read from Golding and Hughes returning, and of the extraordinary opportunity they presented. 'It needs cataloguing, though, as I said. And anyway, they'll never sell, and if they did they'd probably go to Maggs or Quaritch. There's nothing in it for me.'

'If you were able to get your hands on it, though, you'd be set for life.'

'But I won't.'

Blackwood sat back in his chair. 'So what's the problem?' he asked.

'What's the problem?' How could he express his feelings about things to someone whose life was even more constricted than his own? Andrew Blackwood's world extended from the basement under the shop where he lived to the pub they were now sitting in; he couldn't recall an occasion for ages when he had ventured further.

'Don't tell me, middle age is the problem.'

'*Late* middle age, that would be.'

'You're talking to someone of sixty-four.'

'Maybe I just need to get through the next thirteen years. Then I can have a serene old age.'

Blackwood laughed sardonically. 'Serene?' he said. 'That's a good one. No, it's books as consolation, Billy, that's all you can expect. You know your real problem?'

'What?'

'You don't enjoy reading any more. I never hear you talk with any enthusiasm about books you've read.'

Billy took a draught of his beer. How right Blackwood was.

'I've spent my entire life in books, Andrew,' he said. 'And when I was young I read so as to learn how to live. But that's a long time ago now.'

'Consolation,' replied Blackwood. 'I never fail to take comfort from reading of the idiocies of other people.'

'Cold comfort, I'd call that.'

'Warm at least, in my case.'

'You know what I would have liked to be?'

'I can't imagine.'

'A composer. The English Sibelius. Writing something that speaks directly to the soul.'

'You *are* in a bad way. I've never heard you use the word "soul" before.'

'All right, the heart.'

472

Blackwood assumed a thoughtful expression. 'Never heard you use that word, either.'

Billy looked across at him, and then down at their glasses. 'Are you going to drink that beer or not?' he said.

——————

He met Tom for lunch in the Quality Chop House in Farringdon Road. Tom had been at the offices of the *Guardian* discussing an assignment.

'Where to this time?' asked Billy.

'Texas. Now that it seems Bush has the nomination wrapped up, they're sending a writer to do a story on the dynasty. I'll be doing the pictures.'

'What, no war? No famine?'

'I do a lot of different things.'

'I went to Texas once. All I remember is a bumper sticker on a pick-up truck that read, "Welcome to Texas. Now go home again".'

'I won't be staying long.'

Billy looked around the restaurant. It was one of his favourite places, a working men's café that had been taken over by a chef and turned into something interesting without losing its original charac-ter. They sat on wooden benches, sharing a booth with two City types. On the glass of the windows was stencilled 'Progressive Working-class Catering' and 'London's Noted Cup of Tea'.

Tom ordered a Bloody Mary and said, 'Sarah tells me you're down in the dumps.'

'That sounds about right. Even more than she knows, in fact – Chloe's just left me.'

'Welcome to the club.'

'Well it was inevitable, wasn't it? It was only a matter of time. Once she took off on that world tour I was sunk.'

'Sarah thinks you should be with someone nearer your own age.'

'Of course I should be with someone nearer my own age,' said Billy irritably. 'As should you. Anyway, she's one to talk – John is ten years older than she is.'

'Ten years, not twenty.'

'All right, all right.'

The waiter brought them steak and kidney pies and mashed pota-toes, leaning across the City types to serve them.

'I'm going to stop over in New York on the way back from Dallas,' said Tom. 'Maybe I'll say hello to Alice and Michael while I'm there.'

'Sure. See if you can talk to that son of mine, get something out of him.'

'I haven't seen them in three years or more.'

'He'll be going to college in the autumn.' Billy reached for the mustard. 'It's funny the way you and Alice have stayed in touch. She was so doubtful about you early on.'

'Don't I remember. But there were things about me to doubt. I was mixed-up in those days.'

'As I'm mixed-up now.'

'You're not mixed-up, Billy, you're just going through a difficult time. Things will look up soon enough.'

'I'd be interested to know how.'

Tom laid down his knife and fork. 'It needs to start with you,' he said. 'No one's going to be able to help you unless you're willing to be helped.'

'You sound as though you're slipping into American already.'

'There you go again.'

Billy smiled. '"There you go again" was Ronald Reagan's catch-phrase when I was living over there. He'd come up with it whenever anyone criticized him.'

'Now there was a man with a sunny outlook on life.'

'Sunny with occasional thunderstorms for those who were poor or lived in Central America.'

Tom looked over Billy's shoulder towards the windows. Drops of rain were beginning to speckle the glass. 'Who said April was the cruellest month?' he said.

'T. S. Eliot.'

'Well, he was wrong. February is the cruellest month. February in London is just grim.'

'Don't tell me I need to go somewhere warm, Tom – Sarah's already tried that one. It's not the answer.'

'OK, I won't. But you had better start coming up with some answers of your own.'

———

He spent the next few days completing the cataloguing of the Norfolk library. It was tiresome work, but not without its satisfactions. Handling each book, he had to decide what to say about it, its condition, its singular features. What had Graham Greene said about cataloguing – that it was like writing a novel, that you had to know what to put in and what to leave out? After an hour or so his hands were grey from the handling of these dusty books. The library, which had been that of a country squire, had been full of unexpected treasures, good quality Wodehouses and Bensons and Christies.

The doorbell rang, and it was Aldridge. Billy wasn't expecting him, but he invited him up anyway. Aldridge was looking more than usually scruffy and agitated.

'Got something for you,' he said, reaching into a plastic bag.

'What is it?'

'*The Unfortunates*. Excellent copy.'

He handed Billy the book. In fact it was not strictly a book but a box, with a strange amoeba-like design on its cover. B. S. Johnson's novel had been published in unbound sections, with an invitation to readers to read them in whatever order, between the first and the last, they wished. Billy opened it up, and saw the football match report that was printed on the inside of the box.

'It's all right,' he said, 'but you know these aren't worth a great deal nowadays.'

'They can only go up.'

'I'm not sure I'm interested.'

'Come on, Billy, you can easily flog this for a ton. Give me fifty quid for it.'

He looked at Aldridge for a few moments. Clearly he was down on his luck. Billy didn't particularly want this book, but something told him he should buy it anyway. He fingered the box again.

'It's sticky,' he said.

'Is it?' Aldridge reached across to touch it. 'You could say it's literally unputdownable, then.'

'I'll give you thirty.'

'Fifty.'

Negotiating with Aldridge was never difficult. They settled on forty pounds, and Billy gave it to him in cash. There was a kind of hunger in Aldridge's eyes as he counted the money.

He watched Aldridge from the window as he walked to his van, and suddenly he felt unutterably weary. What was this fetishizing of books all about? It was ridiculous, surely, just as Chloe had remarked in Istanbul. He looked at the copy of *The Unfortunates* again. Johnson had been an experimentalist, and a tortured soul. Like many writers he had committed suicide. Not such a bad way to end things, especially if the idea of the alternative seemed intolerable.

He had thought about it once or twice in the past, had flirted with it like a prospective lover. He could never go through with it, of course. But sometimes, when he considered the prospect of the rest of his life, it seemed quite rational. He had nothing to look forward to except more of this. And what was this, exactly? A living, though hardly a vocation. A family he saw very little of nowadays. A couple of friends he got tight with now and then. What did it amount to? Not very much. The image of the palimpsest in Istanbul returned to him. A life wasn't like writing on parchment, of course, it couldn't simply be erased. It was what it was. But there was something about the logic of suicide that seemed comparable. With a single dignified act you might wipe the slate clean.

He stood and crossed to the sideboard, pouring himself a glass of whisky. Thinking this way had rattled him, and he needed steadying. He didn't usually drink in the middle of the day, and certainly not whisky; but at this particular moment he knew he must still these wayward thoughts.

———

'It's not for sale,' said Cummings. 'Official.'

'You talked to them?'

Cummings nodded. 'They want to have it properly archived, and moved to a place where scholars will have access to it.'

Billy looked around the pub. He had known this would be the answer, but nonetheless he felt deflated by it. To have been able to work on that remarkable material would have been a privilege and a pleasure.

'I keep on thinking about it,' he said.

'So do I. It's history.'

Billy picked up his glass of beer. 'You know what was so interesting? The handwriting, and the different kinds of stationery, the letterheads.

The telegrams, even. How is anyone going to write the life of a present-day writer?'

'I suppose there'll be a databank of emails somewhere.'

'Not the same, though, is it? Not so idiosyncratic, not so revealing of character.'

'Maybe not.'

'If writers today *have* as much character, that is.'

'Surely they do?'

Billy looked doubtful. 'It's too easy for them nowadays,' he said. 'Too easy to get published, too easy to make money from writing.'

'That's not true. Faber doesn't publish any more novels than it did fifty years ago.'

'No?'

'And anyway, for every box file devoted to a great writer there must have been hundreds for writers who turned out to be not much good after all.' Cummings began the ritual of rolling a cigarette, and then looked up at Billy. 'You should read some of our younger writers. They're good.'

'After I've read everything else.'

'You're living in the past, Billy.'

'Blackwood told me my problem is I don't enjoy reading any more.'

Cummings looked at him pensively. 'You don't enjoy *anything* any more,' he said.

———

He went back to Wells for a weekend, and persuaded his father to join him for a drink. But Jim wouldn't venture further than the Rose & Crown, a couple of hundred yards up the road.

'They've told me if I don't have the operation then the only alternative is to feed me through a tube,' he said as Billy placed a pint of bitter in front of him. 'Like they did when it first came up.'

'That's not going to be much fun, is it?'

'It bloody well won't be.' Jim raised his glass. 'Cheers,' he said. 'Maybe for the last time.'

'Have the operation, then,' replied Billy exasperatedly.

'No. I told you at Christmas – I'm not doing it.'

'All right, have it your own way. You'd better savour this pint in that case.'

477

'I will.' Jim looked moodily around the little pub, and then at Billy. 'What's new with you?' he said.

Billy sighed. 'I can't say things are exactly very good with me either,' he said. 'Chloe's dumped me, for a start.'

'Just as you expected. You should find someone nearer your own age.'

'That's what everyone is telling me. But it's a bit rich coming from you.'

Jim's eyes narrowed. 'I've been married all my life to a woman three years younger than me.'

'Yes, and you've had countless affairs with younger women.'

'Countless? Come off it, Billy.'

'All right, quite a few. How old was that waitress from Goody's? Eighteen?'

'I was in a bad way then. And I apologized to your mother later.'

'Sure.' Billy looked reflectively at his father. He had been a handsome man, and had strayed many times. Margaret had always been forbearing, more so than Billy or Sarah felt she should have been. But then, other people's marriages were always a mystery. Other *people* were a mystery.

'You should have stuck it out with Alice,' said Jim after a few moments. 'I always liked Alice.'

'We came to the end. I woke up one morning, looked at her face on the pillow, and knew I didn't love her any more.'

'Love is a knack, Billy. Strikes me it's a knack you don't have.'

He thought about this for a moment. Hadn't he been in love with Chloe? And hadn't he told himself he'd been in love with other women before her? Or had he, really? Maybe his father understood things better than Billy had given him credit for.

'Love is something that lasts a few months, you know that,' he said. 'And then it becomes something else.'

'Yes, and it's the something else you need to be better at.'

It was the strangest sensation, being lectured by his father about matters of the heart. Billy had always considered Jim to be at best errant and at worst downright disloyal. But he was right – he had been married to Margaret for more than fifty years. As they walked back to the house, Billy stopping often to let his father catch up, he found himself spiralling once again into a vortex. All the fears that had been preying on his mind since Aldridge's last visit returned. He was not a whole person, never had been and never would be. And if that were really so, then what was the point of his life?

Four

He set out from the flat on a bright morning to walk to the post office, holding in his hand a carefully wrapped copy of Larkin's *The Whitsun Weddings* that he was sending to Jack Ziegler. Wrapping books in such a way as to withstand the rigours of long journeys was one of the arts of bookselling. The big dealers had people who did nothing other than lovingly pack books in layer after layer of bubble wrap, brown paper and cardboard. It was a lesser art, but nonetheless one that Billy took some small satisfaction from. There had been times in the past when he wondered whether he ought to take a course in bookbinding or something: now there was a higher art altogether.

He passed the old dairy that was now an art gallery and the four-square Victorian building that housed the Highgate Society. In the post office there was a queue of three people, all of them old and all of them clearly wanting not just their pension payments but also a discussion about their pension payments. As he was idly gazing at one of the posters, a youth came up behind him.

'I was here first,' he said.

'I beg your pardon?'

'I was here first, I said. Take your place in the queue.'

He was tall and rangy, with acne spots on his long, lean face. There was a sort of deadness in his eyes.

'I *have* taken my place in the queue,' replied Billy. 'What does it look like?'

'But I was here first. I was just filling out this form.' He waved a piece of paper in the air.

'So you weren't ready to join the queue, then.'

'I was here first,' he said again dully.

'Look,' said Billy, irritated. 'If you don't know what a queue is, let me tell you – it's a line of people who are ready to be served.'

By now their conversation was attracting attention, and the people in front of Billy shifted uneasily. Suddenly the youth reached out and grabbed the package from Billy's hand.

'What the hell do you think you're doing?' said Billy, raising his voice now. 'Give that back.'

'Get in your place in the queue and I will give it back.' There was menace in the boy's expression, and it dawned on Billy that now he had a real problem. How could he maintain his dignity while not giving in to this oaf? He made a lunge for the package, but the boy smartly drew it behind his back. Slightly off balance, he fell against the boy, and then a hand was appearing fast on his other side, shoving him hard. He fell heavily, and his glasses went skittering across the floor. Quickly he retrieved them, and turned to face the boy again, who by now had taken up his position in the queue. He looked towards the counter, but it was clear that the woman behind it was studiously ignoring their altercation.

The boy handed him back the package, and Billy had no choice but to take it. 'You should learn some manners,' he said. 'At your age, too.'

Billy looked at him angrily, realizing there was absolutely nothing he could do. 'Listen, young man,' he said. 'You may think you can just barge in wherever you feel like it, but one day you'll come across someone who won't stand for it.'

The boy sneered. 'Unlike you,' he said.

'I'm fifty years old. I'm not in the business of getting into fights with people less than half my age.'

'Very wise, old man.'

With this the boy turned to face the counter. Knowing that he couldn't simply stand behind him until it was his turn, Billy brushed himself down and stepped out into the street. His heart was pounding as he walked back to the flat, and as soon as he was safely home he poured a glass of whisky and sat in the armchair. He could feel a bruise forming on his hip, but otherwise he seemed to be all right. Yet it took him a long time to calm down.

He could think of nothing else but this humiliating encounter. In the normal course of his life he was entirely insulated from this sort of thing. Whenever he read in the papers about senseless violence he always thought with a shudder of relief that it was the sort of thing that happened somewhere else, and to someone else. This had been nothing, of course, a shove, a clumsy fall, and it was over. In some parts of London people were killed for less. But it had shaken him to the core.

Gradually his heartbeat steadied, and he sat at his desk. But he was

481

quite unable to concentrate on anything, and after a while he poured himself another glass of whisky. Jolts of anger coursed through him, and he had visions of knocking the boy down, beating him up. Trying to master his feelings, he thought about calling someone, but he was sure he'd be told he was overreacting. He glanced at the package, and knew he couldn't face another journey to the post office today. Taking a copy of Montaigne's essays from the shelf, he opened it at random.

Michael rang a few days later, his bi-weekly phone call. These conversations were always stilted, and Billy found them generally difficult. But there was something especially remote in his son's tone of voice today.

'How are things shaping up with Vanderbilt?' asked Billy.

'I'm not going to go to Vanderbilt, Dad.'

'You're not?'

'I'm thinking of going to Stanford. They have a better engineering school.'

'Have you seen it?'

'No. Mom's taking me there next week.'

'And how does she feel about the prospect of your being three thousand miles away?'

There was a moment's silence, and Billy could sense the shrug of his son's shoulders. 'I'm gonna be a ways away wherever I am.'

'I suppose so.' He paused. 'And what's new otherwise?'

'Nothing much. The Knicks lost on Saturday.'

They talked on for a couple of minutes, and then Billy asked Michael to put Alice on the phone. Alice seemed unconcerned over the Stanford idea. There wasn't much else to say, and soon enough Billy was gazing at the phone as it sat back in its cradle, and then out of the window over Pond Square.

In the past few days he had been bored and listless, unable to concentrate on his work and unwilling to talk to anyone unless he absolutely had to. Images of the youth in the post office flashed through his mind now and then, before he suppressed them with other thoughts. He decided he needed to get away somewhere for a few days, somewhere bracing, and he thought of the highlands of Scotland. He had often walked in the hills up there. He took out the

482

atlas and scoured both it and his memory for a good place for some walking. It didn't take long to find – Ben Damph, on the shores of Loch Torridon. He booked a flight to Inverness, a car, and a room in the Torridon Hotel, and immediately his spirits began to lift.

───────

As his departure for Scotland approached, his thoughts turned repeatedly to Chloe. It was six weeks or so since he had last seen her. Her parting words had been that she would call him sometime. And as they had both known would be the case, she had not done so. In wandering from room to room in the flat his attention had several times been caught by the Vanessa Bell drawing framed in the hallway. It was the original of one of her designs for the dust wrapper of Virginia Woolf's *A Room of One's Own*, and Chloe had often said how much she loved it. He should give it to her, he thought. And on the day before he was due to leave, he wrapped it in paper and walked down the hill towards Holly Lodge Gardens.

It was a blustery afternoon, and the daffodils in the gardens bent to the wind. He stood outside the gate, hesitating for a moment. Was this really a gift he held in his hand, or a reckoning? He thought to turn back, but then he saw her in a window, and knew he had to go in.

Her aunt was not there, and she led him into the sitting room.

'How are you?' she said.

'All right. You?'

'All right.' She hesitated, glancing at the package.

'I've brought you the Vanessa Bell you liked so much.'

She looked at him with a puzzled expression. 'Is this a peace offering?' she asked.

'You could say that.'

'I can't take it, Billy.'

'Why not?

They were standing several feet apart, Billy holding out the package. She had not invited him to sit down, nor offered him anything. After a few moments he began to think of them as two figures in a tableau, frozen in their odd attitudes.

'Why not?' She gestured impatiently. 'You just don't seem to be able to get it right, do you?'

He propped the package against an armchair. 'No, apparently I don't.'

483

She sighed heavily. 'Why don't we have a drink sometime?' she said. 'Next week, perhaps. But I can't take this from you now.'

'No, of course you can't.'

She stepped across and kissed him on the cheek. 'I'm sorry,' she said. 'I know you're unhappy, and I'm sorry. But this isn't the way out of your unhappiness.'

Within a few moments he was back out in the road, the package tucked under his arm, the wind trying its best to part him from it. He looked up at the trees, swaying above him. They were budding now, and would soon leaf into the iridescent green of spring. He looked back at the house, feeling foolish. As he trudged back up the hill to Pond Square, Chloe's words rang in his ears. 'You just don't seem to be able to get it right, do you?' she had said. Well, it was time now that he did start to get it right, way past time in fact.

The road from Inverness meandered towards the west. At the lower end of Loch Maree he turned sharply to the left, and from then on it was a single-track road with passing places. The mountains reared up on either side, rocky excrescences in strange, sometimes twisted shapes, their flanks still covered in snow. It was a barren yet beautiful landscape, the end of some kind of world.

The Torridon Hotel was a Victorian shooting lodge, complete with turrets and a clock tower. He checked in, and was led to a room overlooking a croquet lawn. On the far side of the loch was a great wall of red sandstone that reared up into the sky. He went back downstairs to the library, and spent half an hour snooping around. It had clearly been assembled in about 1935 and not added to since. He found a set of Walter Scott's novels, took down a copy of The Antiquary, and headed for the bar. Ordering a whisky, he sat on a sofa looking out towards the peaks on the other side of the water. The book in his hand had many uncut pages, suggesting that it had been found as unreadable by others as Billy found it now. The whisky brought a flush of warmth to his face. He looked over at an elderly American couple who appeared to be the only other guests in the hotel. The man was wearing tartan trousers and a bright yellow jumper, and was talking to the boy behind the bar about how his ancestors had fled the clearings and emigrated to Ohio.

In the wood-panelled restaurant he ate smoked salmon and lamb,

484

and afterwards he asked for another whisky. He was quite tipsy by now, his thoughts random and disconnected. Going back upstairs, he lay on the canopied bed, opening the Scott again and leafing through it until he could no longer keep his eyes open. He slept uneasily in the overheated room, and was glad when first light came. After breakfast he put on his boots and his waterproof, and set off for Ben Damph. Half a mile up the road a path led between rhododendron bushes into a wood of pine and larch. The ground was carpeted with soft, shiny moss, and a stream tumbled over rocks close by. Once he had cleared the tree line he looked back across the loch, and saw a curtain of rain heading his way. He put up the hood of the waterproof and made his way across a flat moorland, and after a few minutes sleety rain began to hit him in the back. Soon he was gaining height, the path becoming rockier and harder to follow. The rain passed, and brilliant sunshine cut through the mist, glinting on the snow. This was exactly the kind of clarity, of light and of mind, he had been hoping for.

He was nearing the ridge now, the last twenty minutes or so being a scramble. A cairn told him he had come out at roughly the right place, and then he was strolling across the snow-covered saddle towards the steep drop on the other side. When the mist fleetingly cleared the views were breathtaking, Loch Torridon behind him, little Loch Damph ahead, and to the west the northern end of Skye. It was very cold up here, and the wind tore at the flaps of his waterproof.

The exertions of getting there had concentrated his mind, but now that he had regained his strength and his breath he began to take in his surroundings again. He stepped across to the edge, and gazed down over the drop to the little loch below. And as he did so, the thoughts of suicide he had been flirting with lately came unbidden, as it seemed, to his mind. It would be very easy for him to take a step too far, and very easy for those he left behind to suppose that it had been an accident. He would know nothing of it after his head first struck rock. He sat down to collect his thoughts. Was he serious about this? Had he come all this way for a reason, a reason he couldn't bring himself to acknowledge? Or was he simply being self-dramatizing? Who had not stood on the edge of a precipitous drop and wondered what it might be like to fling himself over it?

He took the three steps it needed to come to the very edge, balancing himself in the wind, trying to imagine just how bad the first moments would be, how filled with pain. He was so close to the edge now that the slightest shift might send him over. And then, very gently, he drew back.

————————

Andrew Blackwood placed two pints of beer on the table and said, 'How was Scotland?'

Billy looked around the Museum Tavern, at the familiar faces of the drinkers. 'It was a tonic,' he replied. 'Fine weather, comfortable hotel, lots of single malts.'

'You did some climbing?'

Billy smiled briefly. 'Not climbing, Andrew, not at my age. Walking, with a bit of scrambling now and then.'

'Collecting Munros.'

'I just went up a mountain I know well. It's enough to collect books, without getting into mountains.'

They sat in silence for a few moments, and then Blackwood said, 'I made a good sale yesterday.'

'What?'

'Borges's *Labyrinths*, the first English translation from nineteen sixty-two.'

'Anything special about it?'

'Inscribed to Anthony Burgess, "the English Borges".'

'Not in nineteen sixty-two, though.'

'No, much later.'

'Burgess used to say that Borges was "the Argentinian Burgess".'

'Yes. He liked arguments.'

'You know my favourite remark of Borges's? Remember Beckford's *Vathek*? Beckford was living in France, and he wrote it in French, and someone else translated it into English. Borges said the original was unfaithful to the translation.'

Blackwood's features creased into a smile. 'Reminds me of the fact that in Italian the words "translator" and "traitor" are just one letter different.'

'"*Tradutore*" and "*Traditore*".'

'Exactly.'

Billy looked down at their glasses, at his half-empty and Blackwood's still almost full. Everything was the same as it had always been. But for him at least, something had now changed. His trip to Scotland seemed to have marked a turning point. He must make sense of things now. There was really nothing else he could do.

The letter was written in a fine, cursive hand. 'Dear Mr Palmer,' it read, 'I believe you have sold my father, Thomas Wyatt, a number of books in recent years. As you may know, he died recently. As his only daughter I am his literary executor, and I would be grateful for advice as to how to go about the business of selling his archive to a reputable institution. In going through some of his correspondence I came across a letter from you which appears to indicate that you might be able to help. At any rate, I look forward to hearing from you. Yours faithfully, Catherine Wyatt.'

There was a telephone number on the printed sheet of stationery, and he immediately called it. Catherine Wyatt was soft-voiced and hesitant on the phone. They arranged for Billy to visit her at her father's house in Somerset the following day. It was only when he put down the phone that he noticed for the first time the full address – Milton House, Coombe. Coombe was the village he had lived in for much of his childhood. He tried to recall where Milton House was; but he hadn't been back for twenty years or more, and couldn't place it.

Driving down the motorway, he reflected on all the things he knew about Thomas Wyatt. He had died in January, and the *Guardian* had run a full-page obit. Famous in the sixties and seventies as a novelist and travel writer, by the mid-eighties he had fallen silent, and remained so for the rest of his life. His early novels were drawn from his experiences in the navy during the war. Then, after he moved to Italy, he wrote about rural life in Puglia, and the Mafia in Sicily. He must have returned to Britain some time in the sixties, and his later work was mostly set in Somerset. Billy had met him once, about five years ago, when he bought some Hemingways from him. He was white-bearded by then, and suffering from the emphysema that would eventually kill him.

He made his way towards Coombe, turning off the Glastonbury road and suddenly realizing that he was in the landscape of his boyhood. When Milton House came into view he saw that it stood just back from the road he used to take to school. He had passed this house every day for years.

It was a large, many-gabled place, the front door arched like that of a church, a tall elm tree shading it from the spring sunshine. He pulled the iron doorbell and heard a tinkling sound from within. A few moments later a slight figure peered out at him. She led him through to a room at the front, and from the bay windows he could see a patchwork of fields, and in the distance Glastonbury Tor.

Catherine Wyatt offered him coffee. She was probably in her early forties, but there was something girlish about her that made her seem much younger, her dark blue skirt and cardigan rather like a school uniform. She had slow, dark eyes that seemed to latch onto him somehow, and which seemed at odds with the general shyness of her manner.

'Thank you for coming down,' she said.

'Thank you for writing to me.'

'You met my father, I think?'

'Yes. We had lunch at the Garrick. He had to be lent a tie.'

'He thought ties were nonsense.'

'So do I. But the Garrick has rules.'

She poured coffee from a white pot. 'Shortly before he died he asked me to take care of his archive,' she said.

'I'm surprised he hadn't made arrangements sooner.'

'He wasn't sure it had much value. It had been so long since he last published a book that he felt he'd been forgotten.'

'But he had an illustrious career. He won prizes, his books sold all over the world.'

'Once, yes.'

'So what did he say to you about it?'

'Just that I was to make sure it found its way into the right hands.'

'But he didn't express any preference?'

'No. He was very unwell for the last years of his life. I don't think he considered it very carefully.'

There was something apologetic about Catherine Wyatt, her every statement seeming to be tinged with regret. She had composed herself on the sofa as though she were a stranger in this house, rather than, as Billy assumed, its owner.

'Do you know what the archive contains?' he asked.

'All of his manuscripts. Carbon copies of letters to his agent and editor, and to other writers, especially Graham Greene. He was an inveterate letter writer.'

'Good. Anything else?'

'He didn't keep a diary, as such – he seemed to express himself mostly in his letters. But he wrote journals when he was travelling. Itineraries and tickets. Photographs. He kept things, you see.'

Billy smiled inwardly. From the moment he had read Catherine Wyatt's letter he had sensed this might be something interesting, and everything she was saying confirmed his suspicions.

'Well,' he said, 'it's very simple. Either you sell to a library in this country, the British Library or the Bodleian or some such, or you sell to one of the American universities. And unless your father expressed a preference, it comes down to one thing: money.'

'I don't think that matters very much, Mr Palmer. It's more a question of ensuring that the archive is properly cared for and made available to anyone who is interested.'

'I'll have to review it all before I can advise you.'

'Then I look forward to learning your advice.'

She stood, and he followed her from the sitting room to a large book-lined study.

'What about his library?' he asked.

'Oh, I think I'll keep that. I shall have a lot of reading time now.'

It was with a sense of high excitement that he sat down at Thomas Wyatt's desk. He had worked with just three archives of this sort in the past, including Roy Urquhart's. They didn't come along very often, and when they did they were usually snapped up by the experts, people like Rick Gekoski. It seemed merely chance that Catherine Wyatt had come across Billy's letter to her father about the Hemingways and written to him rather than to anyone else.

She showed him where everything was, and then left him to it, closing the study door behind her. It was mid-afternoon by now, and he would simply take stock of things and form a view of what might be here. The real work of going through every sheet of paper would have to wait.

Catherine Wyatt had left a copy of the *Guardian* obituary on the desk, and he began by re-reading it. It was important to have a sense of the general outlines of her father's life. Born in Taunton in 1915, he went to Marlborough and Kings College, Cambridge, and then became an English teacher at Downside. It was a very conventional beginning for a writer. But then came the war, and his years in the navy, first in a destroyer escorting convoys from America, and then in motor torpedo boats in the Adriatic. Wyatt's first novel, *The Thunder Gods*, was drawn from his Atlantic experiences, and his second, *Night Passage*, from his Adriatic. He married in 1952, and a few years later he and his wife moved to a village in Puglia, not far from the town of Brindisi where he had been based during the war. His next few books, novels and travelogues, were all set in Italy. But in 1964 Wyatt's wife died suddenly, and he and his then small daughter Catherine returned to England. Wyatt's later books dealt with Somerset history and folklore, in the form both of novels and of personal reminiscences. Billy recalled reading one of them, *The Levels*, years ago.

Wyatt won the James Tait Black and Hawthornden prizes, and was shortlisted for the Booker with his last novel, *The Age of Rust*. But he seemed always just to miss out on grand success, and in the early 1980s he fell silent, never to publish again. Like Sibelius, thought Billy, after *Tapiola*. Was there a mystery here, which the archive would reveal? He hoped so. If this were to be worth a substantial sum then there would have to be mysteries, and the solutions to mysteries: letters to hitherto unknown lovers, preferably famous; fights with other writers, also preferably famous; manuscripts of unpublished books, preferably scandalous. Though he hadn't yet discussed terms, it was customary to take twenty per cent of a sale such as this. Could he make it worth a lot of money? Well, he would soon find out.

Catherine Wyatt had set it all out in good order, and it was easy to see what and where everything was. Billy recalled someone saying that Cyril Connolly's archive had been found in bin bags, in a terrible state. There would be no such difficulties here. The manuscripts and galley proofs were arranged on a long table, and Billy recognized the titles of most of them. The correspondence had been sorted into Manila folders, each bearing a date, as had the reviews. And then there were photograph albums, and the bric-a-brac Catherine Wyatt had spoken of, the travel tickets, the brochures, the theatre programmes. All of this was likely to be of less interest, but he would have to comb through it carefully anyway. It was the correspondence he was most interested in. Wyatt had known Greene and Powell, among others. What else would he find when he delved more deeply?

After an hour or so he opened the study door and called to Catherine Wyatt.

'Thank you for preparing everything so well,' he said. 'I'm probably going to need two or three days here. Will that be possible?'

'Of course. Come back whenever you wish.'

'Early next week, then.'

She made tea, and they sat once again in the sitting room, looking out over the garden and the fields.

'You've read the letters yourself, I take it?' he asked.

'Only the very recent ones, so as to know who I should be in touch with.'

'Really?' He was unable to suppress a note of surprise.

'They were his, not mine.'

'But you're his executor.'

'That doesn't grant me the right to read them.'

'And yet you've given me the right to read them.'

'That's different. Your interest is professional.'

He took up his cup of tea, and after a few moments said, 'Didn't your father once claim kinship with the other Thomas Wyatt, the poet?'

Catherine Wyatt smiled. 'I think he did so because he felt he ought to, that to share such a name and not make something of it would be a pity. But there are no records to prove it.'

He gazed towards the tor. 'Why did he not write again after *The Age of Rust*?' he said. 'After all, it was one of his most successful books.'

'He said he had nothing left to say. He'd always drawn directly from his experience, and I think he felt he'd emptied the well.'

'So what did he do with his time?'

'He read. And until the emphysema slowed him down, he walked. He led a very simple life towards the end, monastic almost.'

'And was he alone?'

'Oh, no. My aunt Hilda, who brought me up, lived here until she died three years ago. And then I came back.'

'To look after him.'

'Yes.'

'Back from where, may I ask?'

'I lived in Teignmouth, in Devon.'

'And what did you do there?'

'I was a teacher in the local primary school.'

He watched as she replaced her teacup on the tray. Poor woman, he thought. She was clearly a spinster, and having led her life in the shadow of her father, she now appeared destined never to escape it.

'Will you stay in this house?' he asked.

'I doubt it. It's far too big. But it's too soon to say.'

He looked out of the window once again. 'I lived just up the road for a while when I was a boy.'

'You did? Where?'

'It was called Fosse's Farm then, but Fosse must be long dead. Almost opposite Coombe Hall.'

'Of course – I know exactly where you mean.'

He looked at his watch. 'I must be getting along,' he said. 'I think I mentioned that my parents live in Wells.'

As he drove the short distance he thought with relish of the prospect of spending a few days the following week back at Milton House. This was potentially really something, the Wyatt archive, and he would make as much of it as he possibly could. It was exactly what he had been needing.

———

Jim sat stony-faced in his armchair, a copy of the *Daily Express* lying on his lap. The atmosphere in the house had been strained since Billy arrived, an ominous silence wrapping itself around them. Billy looked towards the door to see whether Margaret was within earshot, and then turned to face his father. A strange contraption stood beside his chair, a transparent tube hanging from it idly.

'So how long have you got, then?' asked Billy.

'Three months, maybe six.' Jim's voice was quite distorted now, and speaking was clearly an effort.

'And everything's coming through that tube?'

Jim nodded. He had lost at least a couple of stone since Billy last saw him. He was wasting away.

'How is Margaret about it all?'

'You'll have to ask her.'

In all his life he had never known an encounter with his father as hard as this. Nothing in his childhood, when Billy felt always at odds with him, or in his adolescence, when he yearned to be free of him, compared with the silent horror of this moment as he regarded his father for what would surely be one of the last times.

'Are there things you want to do before you go?'

'Like what?'

Billy shrugged. 'I don't know – revisit a favourite place?'

Jim gestured towards the machine. 'Can't go far without that,' he said.

The silence returned. After a while Billy said, 'Your affairs are in order, I take it?'

'Yes. Margaret inherits everything. And Tom is the executor.'

Billy had forgotten about this. In the years when he lived in America his father had decided to bestow this task on his younger brother. It seemed odd now, somehow, but there it was. And with Margaret getting everything, what did it amount to anyway? He recalled Sarah's words about his becoming the patriarch of the family. That was an odd thought too – what did that amount to? Reading the eulogy at the funeral, perhaps, but beyond this?

Margaret entered the sitting room, and fussed over Jim for a few moments. When she returned to the kitchen Billy followed her, saying he needed a glass of water. The expression on her face as she looked up at him was grave but composed. He put his arms around her and kissed her cheek.

'This must be hell,' he said.

'No, please don't think that. I just want him to enjoy his last days as much as he can.'

Billy wanted to say that they both knew about Jim's pleasures, about how his condition now denied him all of them. He was simply unable to occupy himself, needing always to be diverted by someone or something else. But there was no point in stating what was obvious to both of them.

'It could come at any time,' he said.

'I know. And afterwards, well, I shall have you and Sarah and the children, and Tom.' She smiled. 'Maybe the amateur theatrical society will give me the role of Lady Bracknell, or some other dowager.'

He hugged her again, and suddenly there were tears in his eyes. Turning away from her he went upstairs to his room and sat on the

493

bed, gazing into space. His father was about to die, and his mother would be alone. What had he said at Christmas, that Jim had a responsibility to himself if to no one else to live as long as he was able? How hollow those words sounded now, how pious. His father was going to die. But in the meantime he must steel himself for the weekend, and for the business of keeping him amused.

———

His thoughts turned continually to Chloe, and to the difficulty of their last meeting. He wanted to see her again, not so as to try to rekindle things, but so as to say goodbye properly. His relationship with her had mattered too much, however briefly, for its passing not to be marked somehow. He wasn't quite sure how to handle things, and in the end he suggested they take a walk on the heath. They met near the ponds and walked to Parliament Hill, sitting on a bench overlooking the city. He raised his face to the sun, which even now, at the end of April, was radiating a curative warmth.

'I wanted to apologize,' he said.

'For what?'

'I don't know… for getting things wrong, I suppose.'

'Perhaps we both did.'

'I expected too much from you. I forgot that you have a life to lead.'

She placed a hand on his, but then quickly withdrew it. 'Why don't we simply accept that we gave each other something for a while, but that it could never have been for very long.'

'I think that's what I mean.'

He looked away towards the tall buildings of the City and Canary Wharf, and the big wheel on the South Bank. London had changed so much in the past few years.

'Then let's move on, as they say,' said Chloe.

'Yes, let's move on.'

'How are things? How is work?'

'I've been asked to sell Thomas Wyatt's archive. Ever read him?'

'He wrote a novel set in Rome, didn't he?'

'*When in Rome.* About a young Englishman trying to find *la dolce vita.*'

'That's right. He didn't succeed, as I recall.'

Billy smiled wryly. 'No, he didn't succeed at all. Anyway, Wyatt died in January, and his daughter has asked me to take care of his stuff. I've

494

only taken a brief look so far, and I'm spending a few days next week down there so as to evaluate it.'

'Down where?'

'Oh, I should have said. It's in Somerset, in the village we moved to after my father went bankrupt.'

'The village where you were happy.'

'Yes, the village where I was happy.'

'That must be rather nice.'

'I haven't had a chance to explore yet. The last time I was there was when I showed Alice around, soon after we met.'

'Then you must take a nostalgic walk. Since you're such an incurable nostalgic.'

Billy thought back to the evening in Istanbul when he had said those words. How long ago that seemed now.

'And you?' he said. 'Where next?'

'America again. Hans has a new tour lined up. I'll be in New York in two weeks from now, doing the Elgar concerto at Carnegie Hall.'

'Now that is something I would have loved to hear.'

She turned to face him. 'You will hear it, soon enough,' she said. 'Hans has also got me a recording contract, and the Elgar will be the first piece I do.'

'Congratulations.'

'Thank you.'

A boy dashed past them, trying in vain to loft a kite. It was immensely complicated, with several sails, and it failed to respond to the boy's persistent tugs.

'Thank you, Chloe,' he said, 'for some lovely times.'

'Let's stay friends, shall we?'

'Yes. I'd like that.'

———

He returned to Somerset, staying the night with Jim and Margaret and then turning up at Milton House early the following morning. Catherine Wyatt led him to the study and brought coffee. Now the real work of appraising the archive would begin.

There was correspondence with friends from his teens onwards, and references to juvenilia, short stories and fragments of a novel started while he was teaching at Downside. Then came a great lacuna during the war years, with very little except for a few letters from his parents in reply to letters from him which were all missing. It was not until 1946, after he had been demobbed and returned to England, that things became interesting. Billy came upon a letter to Connolly at *Horizon*, offering a short story, and one from Connolly in reply, accepting it. He stepped across to the table where the manuscripts were, and saw a copy of the issue of the magazine in which the story had run. It was about a sailor who falls overboard in the middle of the Atlantic, and the captain who must decide whether to risk the rest of his crew by turning back to rescue him. Clearly Wyatt was limbering up for his first novel.

The letter to Graham Greene offering him *The Thunder Gods* was dated 4 February 1948. In those days Greene was a director of a publishing firm, even though he was already well established as a novelist and screenwriter. Billy read Greene's reply.

Eyre & Spottiswoode (Publishers) Ltd., 15 Bedford Street, London W.C.2

15th March 1948

Dear Mr Wyatt,

I very much enjoyed reading your novel *The Thunder Gods*, which seems to me to represent the terrible experiences of those brave sailors who ensured that the vital convoys got through in the early years of the war in an extraordinarily vivid manner. There is something almost Melvillian in your portrait of Petty Officer Oldcastle and his bullying of Nash. I recall Connolly mentioning your story, & this book very much realizes the promise that story held out.

We would be pleased to publish this book next spring, & are able to offer an advance against royalties of £100. Perhaps you would like to drop by our offices next time you are in London, so that we may meet. In the meantime I will arrange for a contract to be sent to you.

Yours, Graham Greene

The correspondence continued, and after the two men met, their letters began 'Dear Greene' and 'Dear Wyatt'. *The Thunder Gods* was published in February 1949, and the file contained many reviews, all yellowing now but still quite legible. Wyatt was hailed as an exciting new voice, his novel the best by an English writer yet to come out of the war.

By the time of the second book, *Night Passage*, Greene had left Eyre & Spottiswoode, recommending that Wyatt go to his own publisher, Alexander Frere at Heinemann. The files began to bulge from then on, Wyatt writing to Anthony Powell and Lawrence Durrell among others, as well as to Roy Urquhart at *The Bystander*. He took on a literary agent, David Higham, and there were quite a few rather prolix letters from him regarding the terms of contracts with Heinemann, and with Doubleday in America and publishers in Europe.

The personal letters were not so interesting. Wyatt married Mary Sanditon in 1952, but they appeared not to write to one another very much. It was only after Wyatt and Mary moved to a house near Otranto, in southern Italy, that the correspondence began to blossom again, Wyatt writing frequently to Greene still, who continued to take an interest in his work, and by now to William Golding, whose own career as a novelist was about to begin, with the famous letter to Faber. This was good, substantial stuff, Billy thought as he went through it, but not exactly very thrilling. There was no hint of any personal tensions or indiscretions. Perhaps it was simply too early in Wyatt's life for that.

Lost in this world of the 1950s, he became lost in the present, and was surprised when Catherine Wyatt knocked on the door and announced that lunch was ready. He followed her to the dining room, where she had laid out salads and cold cuts.

'A glass of wine?' she asked.

'Not while I'm working, as they say. But thank you.'

They sat down at the table.

'How is it going?'

'Very well. As you said, your father was a good correspondent, especially from Italy.'

'He felt isolated there.'

'Why did he go?'

'Oh, I think he wanted to have the sort of expatriate life that so many writers had lived. And he was nostalgic for the days when he was based at Brindisi during the war.'

'You lived near Otranto?'

'Yes. Horace Walpole would not have recognized it, though.'

It was a moment before Billy understood her meaning. Then he recalled Walpole's Gothic novel *The Castle of Otranto*, a wonderful confection, full of ghosts and giants and living statues.

'Do you go in for that sort of stuff?' he asked.

'Oh, yes. *The Mysteries of Udolpho, Melmoth the Wanderer, The Monk* — they're all a little mad, but I love them.'

'Jane Austen had fun with them in *Northanger Abbey*.'

Catherine Wyatt smiled shyly. 'I *was* Catherine Morland when I was young. And not only because we shared the same Christian name.'

After lunch Billy decided he would take a walk before returning to the archive. It was a fine day, spring in full flush now. From the house he turned up the hill, and immediately came upon Folly Lane. He had quite forgotten about Folly Hill, the scene of so many of his boyhood adventures. The farmhouse cottage where they had lived in the years after his father's bankruptcy was quite unchanged. He thought of knocking on the door, but decided against it. Then, turning back, he stood at the gate from where he had first seen Glastonbury Tor. The tor had captured his ten-year-old imagination, and in the months before Jim finally agreed to take him there, it had come to signify everything that seemed to matter to him. He recalled thinking that it followed him wherever he went.

In the village he found the little school he had gone to. It had long ago become a house, and only a sign indicated that it had ever been a school. He had been subjected to the usual initiation rites, and for a while had been bullied by another boy; but he had been happy there, as Chloe had said — he had gained a freedom he never had in Bath, when his father was in his pomp and Billy attended an expensive private school.

As he made his way back towards Milton House he heard the racket of starlings, and suddenly what appeared to be thousands of them were flying from a big tree. They flew closely together, changing direction rapidly, so that they resembled a great fishing net cast across the sky. By the time he returned he felt as though the mystery and magic of this beautiful place had insinuated itself once again into his imagination. He was seeing it through the eyes of a boy, through the eyes of innocence. All morning he had been immersed in the 1950s, and now he was returning to his own 1950s. Had that been a more innocent time? No, it was him who had been innocent then, not the world. But as he sat down again at Thomas Wyatt's desk, he couldn't wait to get back there.

Five

It was not until the second day that he found the letters between Wyatt and his wife. They were not in the folders where the rest of the correspondence was arranged, but in a box file, tied up in red ribbons. Billy's curiosity was immediately aroused. The letters from Wyatt were carbon copies of typewritten sheets, and those from Mary were handwritten. The first was from Mary.

Flat 6, 125 Kensington Church Street
London W8

5th April 1955

Dear Tom,
I have found a flat, at least for the time being. You may write to me here. There is no phone, & please don't assume I am withholding any number from you. I think it best that we communicate by letter for now.

I have thought & thought about our last conversation, and I am as bewildered & sad about it as ever. You seem unable to understand what my life has been like these past three years. You have your work, & it is all-consuming. And I have had a draughty house to take care of and no one to talk to. I need this time in London, need my friends, & perhaps I need some work too. I don't know how long this will take, & I ask you to bear with me. Peggy tells me she will be down your way in a week or two, & would like to drop by. She is not an emissary, & please don't think this — she just wants to say hullo.

I hope things are going better with An Agreeable Man. You must always remember that the difficulties you have had with it stem from the fact that it is so personal. Bradshaw is you, after all.

Do write soon.

Your loving wife, Mary

Billy immediately took up the next letter, Wyatt's in reply.

Farm House
Midsomer Norton

10th April 1955

My precious Mary,

I cannot tell you what a relief it was to have your letter. Kensington
Church Street! Did Malcolm fix that up for you?

I am as lonely as Adam, & can't stop thinking about you, can't shut
my ears from the sound of your final words. I know I am selfish –
writers are, they must be. But I love you dearly. Please come back. I will
write only in the mornings, we will go for walks in the afternoons, &
I will try to cook dinner sometimes. And I will not be so grumpy. But
I can't live in London. I've never been happy there, & never will be.

The garden is in its glory now. It misses you terribly. And it's warm
enough to sit out on the bench for an hour or so after lunch.

Please phone me sometime – borrow Peggy's or Malcolm's phone.
I long to hear the sound of your voice.

Your ever loving husband, Tom

The correspondence continued in this vein, Wyatt imploring, Mary
unyielding. Wyatt proposed going to London, but Mary forbade it, or
at least forbade a meeting. There were five or six letters on either side
before the one that changed everything. Billy sat rigidly to attention as
he read it.

125 K.C.S.
12th October 1955

Tom,

I am going to have a child. Don't ask who the father is – I will never
tell you, & anyway he didn't & doesn't mean anything to me. I hate the
idea of abortion, & I am going to have it. If this means the end for us,
then so be it. If however you can find it in your heart to forgive me,
then I am willing to try again, and willing to say to the world that this
child is yours. But I do not want to return to Farm House. Would you
want to go abroad for a while? You've always spoken wistfully of Italy.
Will you run away with me?

I am very sorry. I know how much I have hurt you, & how much this news will hurt you more. But there it is. I am placing my life in your hands, in a way that will mean far more than marriage vows ever could. I have been a fool.

Your loving wife, Mary

Billy read Wyatt's reply, in which he struggled to suppress recrimination in his eagerness to have Mary back. The last letter was from him, in early December, making arrangements for their departure to Brindisi. 'Let's be gone before Christmas,' he wrote, 'and have Natale instead.'

He laid down the letter and looked out of the window. This was all quite extraordinary. Extraordinary because so far as he was aware no one had any inkling of it except for the protagonists themselves; and extraordinary for its implications. Catherine was not Thomas Wyatt's daughter. But did she know this? She had spent the past three years devotedly looking after him in his dying days. Clearly she adored him. She had told Billy that she had not read the letters, that they were private. And her mother had died when she was eight years old. The overwhelming likelihood was that she did not know her parentage. The only living person who did, apart possibly from the unnamed natural father, was Billy himself. He sighed heavily. This stuff was fascinating, and would no doubt add to the value of the archive both to a library and a biographer. And he was now its sole custodian. He looked towards the door, and then at his watch. In half an hour he would be sitting down to lunch with Catherine. What on earth was he going to say to her?

––––––––

'Tell me something about yourself,' he said as they sat at the garden table.

'There's very little to say.'

'I'm sure there isn't.' He smiled. 'And I need a break from your father for a while.'

She smiled in response, and composed her hands in her lap. She really was a very diffident woman, he thought as he waited for her to begin.

'Well, I was born in Italy. Puglia was undiscovered in those days. It's become a bit of a tourist destination now, more's the pity. There were cliffs tumbling into the sea near the house – it was almost like being in Cornwall. It was idyllic, and like all idylls, it didn't last.'

'Your mother died.'

'Of breast cancer. It came on very suddenly. Father couldn't face staying in Italy, and he bought this house. He remained in it for the rest of his life.'

'So you lived here from the mid-sixties?'

'Yes.'

'Where did you go to school?'

'The Girls' Blue School in Wells.'

Billy ran the dates through his mind. 'I went to the Boys' School,' he said. 'We might have overlapped.'

'I was there from sixty-seven to seventy-four.'

'We just missed each other – I left in sixty-seven.'

'And then a couple of years later both schools moved, to that ugly new building on the other side of Portway.'

'I'm glad I missed that.'

'I lost heart a little after that. And my favourite teacher, Diana Mogg, retired.'

Billy looked away towards the tor, a sharp outline in the sunlight. 'That name rings a bell,' he said. 'Diana Mogg?'

'She taught English and Drama.'

'Of course. She directed my mother in a couple of plays at the Byre Theatre. *Private Lives* was one of them.'

'She was very strict. But I adored her.'

'Is she still alive?'

'No, she died ten years ago or more.'

'I must tell my mother next time I see her.'

Catherine served lunch, Billy wondering all the while about the letters between her parents he had just read. The responsibility of knowing their contents weighed all the more heavily on his shoulders as Catherine spoke about herself. She went on to talk of having been raised by her aunt, of her life as a primary school teacher in Devon, and of her decision to return to Milton House to look after her father when the aunt died. It seemed a very uneventful life. There was no talk of men, no hint of marriage. She was not unattractive, though something in her manner said that she thought herself so. And she was clearly far

503

too intelligent to have been satisfied with teaching little children. As he brooded over all this, it occurred to him that the letters between Catherine Wyatt's parents represented the very antithesis of the letters Gloria Beckinsdale had shown him. She had claimed an illustrious ancestor, while Catherine Wyatt had apparently lost one.

When lunch was over he went back to the study to resume work. Wyatt was corresponding regularly with Anthony Powell by the sixties, and there was some good stuff on Powell's *A Dance to the Music of Time* sequence and the books Wyatt himself was writing then, his novel *Swimming Against the Tide* and his book about the Somerset levels. Powell lived not far away, near Frome, and it was evident that they visited one another frequently. There was a tone of crustiness to their letters, of regret for a halcyon past and bewilderment over the fashions and mores of the time.

Alexander Frere had handed the responsibility for Wyatt's books over to a new editor, James Michie, and Michie proved to be a garrulous correspondent, full of gossip about literary London. Billy had the impression that Wyatt couldn't decide what he thought about society. He had turned his back on it from an early age, and yet he seemed sometimes to yearn for it. A note of irascibility was entering into his letters about publishing arrangements by now, and Michie's replies were clearly intended to be soothing.

Time flew, as it always did when he was working like this, and when he looked at his watch it was past six. He must get back to London that evening, since he had an appointment with a customer the next morning at the flat. By now he wanted more time here, and he would return the following week. In the car driving home he turned over in his mind everything he had learned about Wyatt. The silence after his last novel in the early eighties remained puzzling. He had been rather taken with James Michie's style, and he wondered whether he might look him up. Michie must be retired by now, but that needn't matter. He would track him down, he decided, and see what he knew.

———

Michie offered him lunch, and on the Sunday Billy went to the Chelsea Arts Club to meet him. Surrounded by people in corduroy and polo-necked jumpers, they sat in the spacious bar drinking red wine. Michie was in his early seventies, Billy guessed. He had a finely sculpted face and kindly, mischievous eyes that hid behind heavy glasses Sellotaped at the bridge. The fingers of his soft left hand were curled inwards, as though he were holding a pen. Billy told him of his visits to Milton House.

'A lovely place,' said Michie.

'Yes. I spent some years of my childhood nearby.'

'Tom was always happiest in the country.'

'He doesn't seem to have spent much time in London.'

'Oh, he came up now and then. We would have lunch, but it would take him a couple of hours to relax.'

Michie drank deeply from his glass.

'There's one thing I'm curious about above all else, and that is why he stopped writing.'

Michie gazed at him thoughtfully, and it was several seconds before he replied.

'I don't know how much I ought to tell you,' he said. 'But it will be in the archive, since we wrote about it.'

'I haven't got that far yet. I'm still in the seventies.'

Michie picked up his glass again. 'It was all due to his daughter's novel,' he said eventually.

'Catherine Wyatt wrote a novel?'

'Yes. *The Ties of Blood* it was called.'

'I had no idea.'

'It was the only thing she ever wrote, so far as I know.'

'And what happened to it?'

'Now that's a long story. Shall we go through to the dining room?'

They were the first to be seated, at a table in a dim corner. Michie ordered a bottle of house red and two plates of roast beef. Once again he sat for a few moments looking very directly at Billy, clearly considering how much to tell him.

'She sent it to me first,' he said. 'I'd never met her, but of course I was the only person in publishing she knew of.'

'And was it any good?'

'It was first rate. It was about the relationship between a father and daughter. The father is a famous actor, and the daughter is dominated by him, can't see a way to live a life of her own.'

Billy eased back into his chair. Of course, he thought – of course Catherine Wyatt had written a novel.

'Did you offer to publish it?'

'Certainly. But then she went quiet, and for a long time. It was three months or more before she wrote to tell me she had decided not to permit it to be published.'

'I think I can guess what happened in that time.'

'I'm sure you can. She felt bound to show it to Tom, and he hit the roof. But of course in *The Age of Rust* he himself had written a novel about a father–daughter relationship.'

'I haven't read it yet.'

'It's the obverse of Catherine's book. It's quite striking. Tom wasn't a monster, but he was certainly demanding, and Catherine was always in his shadow.'

'So she withdrew it in the face of his objections.'

'And Tom never wrote another word of fiction.'

The waiter arrived with the bottle of wine, and Michie waved his bird-like hand in protest when asked whether he wanted to taste it. Billy sat reflecting on what he had just told him. Presumably neither novel made any mention of the daughter not having been the natural child of the father. He must read Wyatt's book tonight so as to find out.

'Why did he give up, do you think? He was a novelist to his finger-tips. And he had drawn directly from his experience in all his writings.'

'Precisely. When he read Catherine's novel he understood what it's like to become a character in someone else's book.'

'You know what Kundera said, don't you? That the novelist destroys the house of his life and with the stones he builds the house of his novel.'

'The stones had become too heavy for Tom to pick up.'

Two vast plates of roast beef were placed in front of them, the meat so red as to seem practically raw. Michie stared at it with an expression of mild distaste.

'This is remarkable,' said Billy. 'And you mentioned that he wrote to you about it?'

'Yes. He wrote about the anguish of falling out with Catherine, and then later he wrote me long letters about the impossibility of writing.'

'This was when, eighty-two, eighty-three?'

'Around then, yes.'

Billy cut up a piece of beef and chewed on it meditatively. The next morning he would be driving back to Somerset, to Thomas Wyatt's archive. He could hardly wait. They did their best with the beef, and then returned to the bar, where Michie lit up a foul-smelling cigar. When they had exhausted the subject of Thomas Wyatt they moved on to other writers and books. Billy recalled that Michie was a poet and a translator, of Catullus and Horace among others. But he wore his erudition lightly. By the time Billy said goodbye he had been thoroughly charmed by this man. And he was grateful, too: James Michie had unlocked a mystery.

The Age of Rust was a novel about a middle-aged writer and his sensitive and troubled daughter who has a nervous breakdown after her mother dies and her father remarries. There were clearly some elements of autobiography in it, and others, such as the writer remarrying, that were fictional. Had Catherine Wyatt ever had a nervous breakdown? he wondered as he laid the book down on the table. He poured a glass of whisky and sat gazing across the room towards the bookshelves. So many stories, so many lives. The daughter in the novel was sustained by books, by Austen and the Brontës, George Eliot and Hardy. He recalled Catherine saying she loved Austen. This task had now turned into a quest, an adventure. He finished off the whisky and went to bed, looking forward to his return to Milton House in the morning.

Once Catherine Wyatt had greeted him and left him alone in the study he turned immediately to the files from the early eighties. It meant skipping several years, but he had to find the stuff about Catherine Wyatt's novel before he went any further. And as he searched through the sheaves of letters, finding himself soon in 1985, he knew he wasn't going to find it. The correspondence with James Michie was regular until about eighty-two, and picked up again in about eighty-four, but in the interim there were barely three or four exchanges, and about nothing of any consequence at all. The pattern was the same with his agent, Bruce Hunter, who some time earlier had taken over from David Higham. In Hunter's case there simply wasn't much to write about, since Wyatt wasn't working on any book. But still Billy was quite certain, with the sixth sense he had developed in these matters, that things were missing. There was only one explanation for this: Catherine Wyatt had removed them. And if she had removed them then contrary to what she had told him, she must have read them. Had she read the entire archive, or had she gone straight to the period and the letters she was looking for?

For a while he lost his concentration, so wrapped up was he in these speculations. And then he told himself he must return to work, and went back to 1977. The correspondence with Wyatt's contemporaries was rich in details about his work and theirs, and he was soon immersed once again.

Over lunch Billy found it difficult to get a purchase on any conversation. He was becoming increasingly intrigued by Catherine Wyatt, and at the same time increasingly unsure what to say to her. He asked her about her tastes in literature, and she spoke of the very authors in *The Age of Rust* – Austen, the Brontës, Eliot, Hardy.

'I stopped at Henry James,' she said eventually.

'That's where I *started*,' replied Billy, 'at least professionally speaking.'

'I love the big novels. One gets lost in them.'

Billy smiled wryly. 'I prefer the shorter stories,' he replied. '*The Turn of the Screw*, *The Aspern Papers*.'

'Ah, *The Aspern Papers*. So have you come to any conclusions about where I ought to offer my father's archive?'

Billy looked across at her, trying once again to take her measure. Was she in fact more worldly, more calculating, than she appeared to be? She was wearing a white summer dress on this unseasonably warm May afternoon, and she seemed to have done something different with her hair. The mousy look that had struck Billy so forcibly was gone now.

'Well, as I said at the beginning, you basically have two choices. You can sell it to the British Library, in which case you won't get very much for it but you'll have the satisfaction of having kept a sort of national treasure in this country. Or you can sell it to an American library such as the Ransom, in which case you will probably get a great deal more.'

'And what sort of things does the Ransom library contain?'

'What does it *not* contain would be more to the point. The director has been busy for years buying absolutely everything in sight. He's an expert on Joyce, but he has more twentieth-century American and British archives than anyone by a long way.'

'It sounds a little overwhelming.'

'I'm sure it does. But it's all wonderfully laid out. I went there once, and it was fascinating. Frankly it's a better resource than the BL.'

'And they would pay more, you said.'

Billy was silent for a moment, before replying, 'I want to give you disinterested advice, Miss Wyatt. I want you to do what you think is best.'

'Do call me Catherine.' She made to pick up their plates. 'Let's wait until you've finished before we decide.'

'Of course.'

'And how much longer will you need, do you think?'

'At least another two days, possibly three. It's taking a little longer than I expected. I have to be in London on Wednesday, though.'

'Would you like to stay the night? There are plenty of rooms. That way you can continue as you wish.'

'Thank you. I will.'

He returned to the study, taking up where he left off. But as he sat reading, his mind continually strayed to thoughts of Catherine Wyatt. Who was she, and what did she want? He really couldn't make her out at all.

'That's quite a story,' said Andrew Blackwood.

'It certainly is,' replied Billy. 'The question is, what the hell do I do?'

Blackwood raised his beer glass, and the mat it had been standing on fell to the floor. He reached down to pick it up.

'You have to confront her, don't you? You have to tell her about the letters between her parents, and ask her about her novel. It would be unprofessional to do anything else.'

'Come off it, Andrew. Unprofessional? I'm dealing with someone's life here.'

'You're dealing with two people's lives, and the most important one is Thomas Wyatt's. Think of posterity.'

'That's a biographer's job, not mine.'

'But a biographer is going to be dependent to a great extent on this archive. If it's incomplete…'

Billy stared at him moodily. Of course he was right. But how was he going to confront Catherine with these things?

'Tom Staley would definitely be interested if it includes the stuff about the daughter's parentage and her novel.'

'I know. I've told her about the choice between the Ransom and the BL. But she has to decide.'

Blackwood shrugged his shoulders. 'Another round?' he asked.

'I'll get them.'

When Billy returned to the table with their drinks, Blackwood gazed down at his hands and said, 'I'm going to have to pack up, Billy.'

'Pack up? Why?'

'Rent review. I've known for a while it was coming. I just didn't know how much.'

'And?'

'Five hundred a month more.'

'Oh, Andrew, that's dreadful!'

'It certainly is. I simply can't afford it.'

'So what are you going to do?'

Blackwood looked across the room and then back at Billy. 'What can I do?' he said. 'Sell my stock and wait for my pension. Five months more.'

'But you can't. This is your life. And where will you live?'

'I'll be eligible for a council flat.'

Billy slid his hand around his glass. 'How much have you got in your pension?'

Blackwood smiled ruefully. 'I don't have a pension,' he said. 'I'm talking about the state pension.'

'But that's only about a hundred pounds a week.'

'Something like that.'

'Well, you can't live on that, surely?'

'Why not? Plenty of people do.'

Billy stared at his old friend in silence for a few moments. Blackwood had lived and worked in his shop for thirty years or more, and Billy had always assumed he would have to be dragged out of it feet first.

'I'll take care of it,' he said.

'What do you mean, you'll take care of it?'

'I'll pay it. I'll pay the difference.'

Blackwood looked at him in astonishment. 'You can't possibly do that,' he said.

'Yes I can. I can afford it. And I owe everything to you. Without you I wouldn't be in business myself.'

'Yes you would. You'd have found someone else to buy a mailing list from.'

'I found you.' He took a long draught of beer. 'Give me your bank details, and I'll set up a standing order. And stop playing with that drink, and let's go to the Greek place for something to eat.'

———————

Sarah had been shopping in town, and she dropped by the flat on her way home. Billy hadn't seen her in a long time, and there was much to catch up on.

'Are you missing Chloe?' she said after a while.

'Not as much as I expected to.'

'Good.'

'Yes, I suppose that is good.'

Her eyes rested on the boxes that still contained much of the Norfolk library. Billy had finished the cataloguing, but still he had nowhere to shelve much of it.

'And what's new with work?' she asked.

'Ah. I wanted to talk to you about that.'

He made a pot of tea, and when they were sitting down he told her the story of the Wyatt archive, omitting nothing.

'So what do I do?' he asked finally. 'Andrew Blackwood says I have a responsibility to tell Catherine Wyatt about the letters between her parents.'

Sarah looked at him sternly. 'I'd say you have a responsibility to burn them all and never mention them,' she said.

'I thought you might say that.' He looked at the boxes piled in the corner of the room. 'That really would be a responsibility, destroying someone else's letters.'

'But they're all entirely personal, yes? There's nothing in them relating to Wyatt's work, so far as I understand you. What purpose can be served by telling her about them?'

'I don't know. But they're sitting there, in their red ribbons. They're her property. And don't you think she has a right to know who her father was? Or wasn't?'

Sarah tossed her hair impatiently. 'How do you think she'll feel if at her age, with no one in her life, she discovers she wasn't her father's daughter?'

Billy made a gesture of despair. 'I know. It's a quandary.'

'Burn them,' said Sarah emphatically.

'I'll have to think about it.'

He offered her more tea, asking her now what she thought about the business of Catherine's novel.

'Perhaps she wanted to preserve her father's honour. Perhaps he doesn't come out of it very well.'

'And perhaps she wanted to remove all trace of a youthful indiscretion of her own. She's not the only person who has written a novel she'd prefer to forget about.'

'Well, you can't ask her about it, can you?'

'Maybe not.'

Sarah sipped her tea meditatively. 'I talked to Mum yesterday,' she said after a few moments. 'Dad's fading fast now, apparently.'

'I had better go and see them when I'm back in Somerset next week.'

'We had all better see them as much as we can. I don't think he has much longer to go.'

'How are the kids about it?'

'Oh, I don't think they understand that this is really it. And none of them has ever been close to Dad.'

'He never seemed to show much interest in any of them.'

'I think April was his favourite.'

'He always did prefer girls.'

Sarah smiled. 'He didn't prefer me.'

'Yes he did.'

'Billy, you haven't a clue, have you? You were always the one he loved most.'

'But we fought all the time.'

'Precisely. He needed that.'

'Needed to fight?'

'Needed to test himself.'

'Hmm. I'm not so sure.'

Sarah looked at her watch. 'I must be getting on,' she said. 'The kids will be back from school soon.' She stood, and Billy kissed her on the cheek. 'Do go and see Dad,' she said. 'I think you and he need to spend some time together.'

He reckoned he had two days' work left in the archive. He was sorry it was coming to an end – it had been the most enjoyable task he had known in a long time. As he sat in the study he sensed that he was consciously slowing the process, and savouring it. But he had passed the period of greatest interest by now. In the late eighties and the nineties Wyatt became a less faithful and less sympathetic correspondent, his tone crotchety and vain. He was a writer who couldn't write, and he complained about this bitterly to anyone who would listen.

At lunch Catherine Wyatt suggested they take a walk, so that Billy could show her the places of his childhood. He gladly accepted her suggestion, and they set out towards Fosse's Farm. A rain shower had rinsed the landscape clean, and now the road shone brightly in the sunlight.

'It's this one,' he said as they came upon the little house.

'It's not called Fosse's Farm now,' replied Catherine. 'An American has bought up everything around here. He's raising very exotic breeds of cattle.'

They stood in front of the house for a few moments, before turning down Watery Lane.

'So tell me about your time here,' she said. 'I know hardly anything about you.'

He glanced across at her, and she smiled. The shyness had all but vanished now, and she was so much easier to talk to.

'We came here in fifty-eight,' he said. 'I was ten years old. My father had had a Jaguar dealership in Bath, and it went bust. Bankruptcy was a serious thing in those days, and he ended up taking a job with my mother's uncle in a clothes shop in Wells.'

'What was it called?'

'Underhill's. It's long gone now.'

'But I remember it. I remember my aunt buying me a school uniform there.'

'Yes? The uncle had a stroke, and my father ran it for a while, before the owner of the Regal cinema hired him as manager. A few years later he was discharged from bankruptcy and he bought the place. And by that time we'd moved to Wells.'

'So you had an idyll of your own, then, when you were here.'

'Yes. It was a good time.'

They turned onto the lower road back to the village. The tor loomed in the distance, the sentinel of his childhood.

'I've been thinking about the archive,' she said after a while.

Billy had been lost in a reverie, thinking back to his days in this lovely place, and her words brought him back sharply to the here and now.

'Yes?'

'I'd like to sell it to the British Library. It should stay here rather than being pored over by a lot of earnest American postgrads.'

'I think that's the right decision. I'll talk to the man who handles their modern stuff next week. He'll need to come down here to evaluate it for himself, of course. But I'll take him through it.'

'Thank you.' She looked up at him. 'I shall miss having you around the house,' she said.

'I shall miss coming here. But with my parents in Wells, perhaps I might visit you sometime.'

'That would be very nice.'

'Have you thought any more about selling the house?'

'No, I can't bring myself to.'

'Maybe you should stay, in that case.'

'Perhaps. It'll be lonely, though, wandering from one room to another.'

He stole another glance at her, wondering how to reply. What would her life be like once all the things that followed on her father's death were settled? Did she have friends? Clearly she had no close family.

Before he could reply she said, 'I'm sorry. That sounds rather self-pitying. If I stay at Milton House I shall remind myself every day how fortunate I am to live in such a fine place.'

'I hope you'll stay there.'

She turned to face him. 'In that case I will,' she said.

Billy and his father sat watching the final scenes of *From Russia with Love*, and when it was over Billy rewound the tape and sprung it from its trap.

'Only the first three Bond films were any good,' said Jim.

'And only Sean Connery was Bond.'

They had seen these films together at the Regal, in the days when Jim was the manager there, and Billy used to joke to friends that this had created the only bond that had ever existed between them.

The films seemed preposterous now, but not so preposterous as the new ones.

'A bloody tailor's dummy, that Pierce Brosnan, if you ask me,' said Jim.

He had not left the house in the time since Billy had last seen him, tied as he was to the machine that silently dripped fluid into his stomach for hours every day. It sat beside him now, like a school chemistry set but far more sinister. Jim was thinner than ever, his voice a soft croak.

'What was the last thing you saw at the pictures?' asked Billy, immediately regretting his choice of words. But then what was this time about if not last things?

'Haven't the faintest. Years ago, before the Regal shut down.'

'I haven't seen anything in a while either.'

They sat in silence for a long time, Billy thinking about pouring himself a glass of whisky but deciding against it, not wanting to give his father any further reminders of what he had lost. Earlier, Jim had remained in his armchair while Billy and Margaret had eaten supper. Now Margaret was out in the garden, 'making the most of the longer evenings', as she had said.

'Billy, I want to apologize for something,' said Jim eventually.

'Apologize?'

'Yes. I want to apologize for not taking you to the tor when you wanted to.'

Billy let out a nervous laugh that was more like a cry. 'The tor?' he said. 'But that was forty years ago.'

'I know. And there hasn't been a year that's gone by since without me thinking about it. I was a selfish bastard.'

Billy looked at his father incredulously. Had he really stored up this memory for so long?

'You were having a rough time.'

'No excuse. I took it out on you.'

Billy thought back to those times, and then to the walk that very afternoon with Catherine Wyatt. When he was ten years old the tor had come to symbolize all of his hopes and ambitions. They hadn't had a car until after Uncle Reg died and Winnie had given them his; but even then Jim had found reasons not to take Billy to the one place above all that he longed to go. When finally they had done so, on a blustery March day, it had been an almost ecstatic moment. Now, looking across at his stricken father as he recalled it, he had to fight back tears.

'I was there today,' he said when he had composed himself. 'Saw the farmhouse and the old school, and the tor. Nothing's changed, really.'

'It was a salvation, that place. God knows where we would have ended up otherwise – a crummy hostel in Bath, probably.'

'I always thought you hated it.'

Jim's features registered a fleeting, sour smile. 'It wasn't the place I hated,' he said, 'it was everything else – that terrible job, the bike ride into Wells on freezing mornings…'

He seemed about to go on, but then stopped himself. Stopped himself, Billy thought, before this litany became too much for him. It was the humiliation that had been hardest to bear – Billy had always understood that, even at the age of ten. The humiliation of failure.

'And then you made it all good again, you got the job at the Regal.'

'I suppose so. Can't complain about what's happened since.'

A question formed in Billy's mind, but he hesitated before asking it.

'What would you have wanted if you hadn't gone bankrupt?' he said finally. 'What would your life have been like?'

'I'd have been rich. I'd have built a chain of Jaguar dealerships.'

'And?'

'And what?'

'Margaret? Us? Would that have been any different?'

'I'd have provided for you better.'

'We wouldn't have been any happier. At least I wouldn't. Coombe was the best place I ever lived in.'

Jim smiled again, only now it was a softer smile, of resignation but also clearly of relief. Billy could sense his feelings welling up in him again, and he stood up from his chair and crossed the room. And then he did something he hadn't done since he was a child – he kissed his father on the forehead. Jim looked up at him, tears welling in his eyes. Billy turned away, towards the window.

'I'll call Margaret in,' he said. 'It's practically dark out there now.'

'You do that, son,' replied Jim. 'And then for God's sake get yourself a drink.'

———

By mid-afternoon the following day his work in the archive was finished. He had formed a view as to its value, but the problem remained of the letters between Thomas and Mary Wyatt. The box file sat squarely on the table on the far side of the room. Surely Catherine Wyatt had at the very least looked inside it? The rest of the archive had been arranged in such an orderly way that it seemed impossible she might be unaware of this part of it. He was bound to broach the subject; but how?

She made tea, and they sat out on the terrace.

'I'll call Chris Fletcher at the BL next week,' said Billy, 'and invite him to come down here.'

'Thank you.'

'I've no doubt he'll want to take it, so it's just a question of the price.'

'I'm not very concerned about that, as I've said.'

'Nevertheless we may as well get as much for it as we can.'

'I will leave that to you.'

It was practically summer now, and the sun was giving out what felt to Billy like a fierce heat. He shifted his chair so as to be in the shade of the big elm tree, and in doing so he came quite close to Catherine. She was wearing the white summer dress again today, and the sun seemed to have brought out faint freckles on her shoulders and arms. He hesitated for a moment, and then said, 'Catherine, there's a box file of letters between your parents. It's separate from the other files. I've been wondering...'

She looked at him very directly. 'I've been wondering too, when you were going to mention it.' She laid a hand briefly on his, in a gesture that he felt was uncharacteristically intimate. 'I haven't read them,' she said. 'I saw that the first is from my mother, from London, and I think I know what they must contain.'

'And may I ask what you think that is?'

She sighed deeply, and then turned away from him, shielding her eyes with her hand.

'Letters about their... their difficulty. And letters about me.'

'About you?'

She turned back to him. 'I've known that Thomas Wyatt wasn't my father since I was sixteen,' she said. 'It was him who told me.'

Billy let out a long, slow breath, all the tension in him suddenly easing. 'I wasn't sure...' he began.

'You have been very tactful. And I'm grateful for that.'

'The question I'm bound to ask, though, is whether you want these letters included in the sale.'

She took up his cup and poured more tea. 'I must apologize, Billy. I've placed you in a difficult position. I think I wanted you to take responsibility for this somehow. The truth is I don't know whether to include them. I would rather they weren't made public, but at the same time I recognize that they probably have to be.'

'It was an important moment in your father's life.'

She smiled. 'And in my mother's,' she said.

'I didn't mean…'

'No, I know.' She was brisk now. 'It's my father's – I mean Thomas Wyatt's – life you're interested in, not my mother's.'

'I'm sorry.'

'Please don't be.' She brushed some crumbs of cake from her dress. 'It's me who should apologize. I haven't been entirely honest with you.'

They finished their tea, and Catherine walked with him to the car.

'I'll call as soon as I've spoken to Fletcher,' he said.

'I'll look forward to that.'

He opened the car door, and as he did so she stepped forward, reached up, and kissed him on the lips. It was almost shocking in its unexpectedness. Not knowing how to respond, he ducked into the car. The window was open, and he said goodbye to her and backed out of the drive. As he drove up the hill towards the main road he brought his fingers to his lips, and let them stay there for a long while. Last night he had kissed his father, and now had come another impulsive kiss. He was so shaken up that he could barely concentrate on the road ahead.

Six

His mother's voice was quite calm as she told him of Jim's death. 'He just faded away,' she said. 'He had no strength left at all.'

It wasn't until the next day, when she greeted him on the doorstep of the house, that it hit him. Having felt at first quite unaffected by this news, and having driven down the motorway listening abstractedly to the radio, it was only when he held his mother in his arms that the tears came. And they were tears for her, not him, he knew very well.

Tom and Sarah were already there, and within an hour the solicitor had come by, and then the vicar. There was so much to think about. But Jim had prepared well for this, and everything was in its place. It seemed strange that it should be Tom who had to deal with the practicalities and not him. 'You will speak the eulogy, won't you?' said his brother, and Billy felt he was being assigned a role.

They all stayed the night, and Sarah prepared a simple supper. The conversation was restricted to the things they needed to consider – there were no reminiscences or regrets. Billy thought of proposing a toast to their father, but the mood was wrong somehow. In the morning Sarah and Tom returned to London, and Billy and Margaret were suddenly alone.

'I'd like to see him,' he said.

'So would I. I'll call the undertaker.'

The chapel of rest was a couple of miles out of Wells, and they drove there late in the afternoon. The undertaker led them to the chamber where Jim's body lay. As they entered the darkened space Margaret took Billy's hand in hers, clutching at it.

He was dressed in a dark suit and tie, and he lay with his hands folded at his waist. He seemed very pink, and Billy suspected that the embalmer's art had been employed. Somehow he didn't seem very like his father at all, more like an impostor, someone who had been asked to play the role of cadaver. Billy reached down to touch his hand, and was shocked by how cold it was. He leaned over, and for the second time in a week he kissed his father on the forehead. Margaret tightened her grip on his hand, and then she too kissed him.

The sunlight was blinding when they stepped outside. In the car Margaret said, 'Thank you, Billy. I needed to see him one more time. And I couldn't have done that by myself.'

He took her hand in his once again. 'And I need a drink,' he said. 'Let's go to the Swan.'

Back in the city he parked the car and they walked to the hotel. Billy ordered gin and tonics, and they sat in armchairs near the window.

'How was he at the end?' he asked.

'Oh, very dignified.' She thought for a moment. 'Not serene, exactly – I don't think that's a word I would ever have used – but accepting.'

'He had willed it, after all.'

'He only willed the timing of it, Billy. He didn't will death itself.'

He gazed at his mother and said, 'You always loved him,' and these words choked him like none he had spoken hitherto.

'Yes, I did. And I know you often didn't understand that.'

'It's not that I didn't understand it, it's that I sometimes felt he didn't deserve it.'

'Who deserves to be loved?'

Billy smiled weakly. 'In my experience, probably no one,' he said.

'No one and everyone.'

Billy stirred the ice in his drink. 'When I saw him last week he apologized for not taking me to the tor when I wanted to go there.'

'He often spoke about that.'

'Did he really?'

'Oh, yes. You see, you meant the world to him. You were his eldest son.'

'I can't really believe that. We were so different. He never really understood my life.'

'You were his eldest son.'

They returned to the house, and Billy offered to fix something to eat. As he stood over the stove, stirring the spaghetti, thoughts of his father flashed through his mind. How would he best remember him? he wondered; what would be his abiding image? It would not be the last one, he decided, of him lying in the chapel of rest. No, it would be the windswept figure on the top of Glastonbury Tor.

Leaving Wells in the early evening of the next day, he passed the sign for Coombe, and before he knew it he had turned, and was heading along the narrow, winding road to the village. He hesitated for a moment before pulling into the drive of Milton House, but then there he was, climbing out of the car and ringing the doorbell. Catherine blushed as she welcomed him in, and they didn't touch each other. She offered him a drink, and spilled wine onto the tray as she poured it out.

'I've been in Wells,' he said as they sat down on the terrace, she on the bench and he in a deckchair. 'My father has just died.'

'I'm so sorry.'

'He knew it was coming. In fact he brought it on. He'd suffered from throat cancer for years, and he just got tired of all the pain and the treatment.'

'What age was he?'

'Seventy-eight. He'd had a good run.'

She sipped at her glass, clearly finding it hard to look at him. He had flustered her, dropping by unannounced like this.

'Were you very close?'

'Not at all. Sometimes we seemed like complete strangers.'

'Nonetheless it's sad, the death of a parent.'

'As you well know.'

'He wasn't strictly my father, of course.'

'But he was. He brought you up. And you never knew your natural father.'

'No.'

She seemed to be shaking a little now, and she put down the glass and stilled one hand with the other.

'I think you must have had a very different relationship with your father than I had with mine,' he said.

'Yes?'

'You were both literary people. My father never read a book – it never occurred to him to do so.'

She looked at him now, an expression of concern softening her features. 'You sound a little angry with him,' she said.

Billy smiled ruefully. 'I expect I do. There was always plenty to be angry about. But do you know the funny thing? The last time I saw him he apologized to me.'

'You made up, then.'

521

'Not made up, exactly. That would have required a kind of eloquence we weren't really capable of. He apologized for something that happened more than forty years ago.'

'What was that?'

He turned to look towards Glastonbury. 'I think I told you how fascinated I was by the tor,' he said. 'When I was ten years old I wanted to go there more than anything. But he wouldn't let me. The things in life that *he* wanted were all out of reach, and he couldn't bring himself to give me something that I wanted.'

'That sounds harsh.'

'I'm sorry. I expect I'm sounding like a ten-year-old again.'

'In some ways we'll always still be ten years old.'

'Yes.'

She took up her glass again. 'When I was ten I was still trying to come to terms with the loss of my mother. That and living in this strange country called England.'

And that was all it took. Swept up by feelings of tenderness that caught him unawares, he moved across to the bench and took her in his arms. Their kiss was a kind of exhalation, a letting go. When eventually they went back into the house, awkwardness overtook them again, an awkwardness that came and went throughout the evening as they ate supper and sat afterwards. She offered no invitation to him to stay – beyond a certain moment it was clear that he would. And when they ascended the stairs it was wordlessly still. It was soon very evident that she had not done this in a long time. It was gentle and slow, and afterwards she covered herself up very quickly.

'You're beautiful,' he said, as though he had only just realized this was so. And he *had* only just realized it. Why had it taken so long?

'And so are you.'

Billy snorted. 'Thank you, but whatever else I may be, it certainly isn't beautiful.'

'I'll be the judge of that,' she said, and she reached out to him once again.

The funeral was in St Cuthbert's Church, the place where Sarah had twice been married, and where Rob and April and Stephen had all been baptized. Jim had set foot in it on these occasions and no others, so far as Billy could recall; but nonetheless this was the place most fitting for his farewell. There were pitifully few people present besides the family. Jim had been retired for many years, and the worthies who might have turned up when he was the manager of the Regal, a citizen as well as a neighbour, were mostly gone themselves by now. And he had never had many friends. Bert Dampler was the sole representative of Jim's working life, sunk into late middle age now, barely a hair left on his head, his soft mouth and chin having quite collapsed into the folds of his neck. Dampler had spent his entire working life at the Regal, taking charge when Jim was promoted by Rank to area manager. He greeted Billy lugubriously, mumbling his words of condolence.

Billy read the eulogy he had composed. It had taken him much time and effort, as he tried to strike the right note. He wanted there to be no cant, no false pieties. And yet as he had written it, as he described the life of this man who had never fully known himself or fulfilled himself, he was overcome by a strange sense of affection for him. His had been a life that Billy himself could not have borne; and yet it had still possessed some meaning. He looked at the faces of Margaret and Sarah and Tom, of Sarah's children and of Michael. This was what Jim had brought about, this was his legacy; and it was not nothing.

It was a damp, close day, and it began to rain as they assembled to watch the hearse drive slowly away. Jim was to be cremated, at his own request, and the ashes scattered in an apple orchard near Coombe. Billy had expressed surprise on learning this, and Tom told him he made this request only days before he died.

They walked to the Swan, and set about the buffet lunch. Bert stepped over to Billy's side, munching on a sandwich.

'He was a fine man,' he said.

'Thanks, Bert.'

'He was a good boss to me. Always saw me right.'

'Yes.'

'He didn't deserve it, what happened to him.'

'I suppose no one deserves cancer.'

'No, I don't mean that.' Bert was gazing at him earnestly. 'I mean the bankruptcy. He didn't deserve to be shamed like that.'

'Those days were different, weren't they? Nowadays it's a badge of honour to have gone bankrupt. People do it time and again.'

'He never got over it.'

Billy looked at him with renewed attention. 'No?'

'No. It was like a stain he couldn't get rid of. He used to talk about it all the time.'

Billy had no idea his father had been so open with Bert Dampler. 'What did he say?' he asked.

Bert shrugged. 'That everyone had been so hard, so unforgiving. Everyone except Margaret, that is.'

He looked across the room to where his mother was talking to Sarah's husband John, and then back to Bert. 'Did he think I had been unforgiving?'

Bert averted his eyes. 'Yes,' he replied. 'He did.'

Billy felt a surge of irritation course through him. 'I was a kid, Bert,' he said.

'No, later. He said you never really understood what it had been like for him, even when you were grown up.'

'Oh, Christ.' Billy sat down on a chair. 'Of course I understood.'

'I expect you did.'

'Maybe I just never told him so.'

Bert looked down into his glass, which was empty now. 'I think I need another one of these,' he said, and with this he patted Billy on the shoulder and walked off towards the bar.

It was Sarah who sensed Billy's distress. 'Let's get some air,' she said to him, and they stepped across the road and onto Cathedral Green.

'It's all very real now, isn't it?' she said as they sat down on a bench. 'He's really gone.'

Billy looked up at the façade of the cathedral. 'It's odd,' he replied. 'I didn't think I'd miss him, but now I think I will.'

'You'll have to be him. I mean you'll have to be the head of the family. Remember what I said about being the patriarch?'

'I'm not sure what that will amount to, besides proposing toasts at Christmas dinners.'

'So just do that, then.'

They sat watching the tourists come and go. A few yards away a couple of boys were playing football. 'No ball games on the green,' Billy shouted.

'Shut up, Billy,' said Sarah. 'They're not doing any harm.'

He turned towards her, smiling apologetically. And then he said, 'I think I've met someone.'

524

'You think you have?'

'Well, I *have* met someone. Something has happened. It's Catherine Wyatt.'

'Really? But that's wonderful!'

'Perhaps it's nothing more than the fact that we've spent so much time together lately. But I think it is more than that.'

'I'd like to meet her.'

'You will, I'm sure.'

'How do things stand with the archive?'

'Oh, that's all done now. I just have to go back with the man from the British Library, and state a price.'

'What about the letters about her?'

He took off his glasses and wiped them with his handkerchief. 'Apparently Wyatt told her he wasn't her natural father when she was sixteen. She claims she glanced at the first letter from her mother and, knowing what the rest must contain, she didn't go any further.'

'And her novel?'

'I haven't broached that. And I don't intend to. She doesn't know about my lunch with Wyatt's editor.'

'You said you felt you had a responsibility to say something.'

'Did I? The letters between her parents were different – they were there, under my nose. I have only James Michie's word for the novel. I can't very well say to her, "What about those letters you removed?", can I?'

'I suppose not. But what I mean is, is she an honest person? If you're going to be involved with her...'

He looked at her thoughtfully. 'When it comes to fiction,' he said, 'I don't think honesty enters into it. It's a shadow world, Sarah.'

'Is it? I suppose you should know.'

'The only honesty you can expect from writers is on the page, believe me.' He turned towards the Swan. 'We'd better be getting back,' he said. 'There are still a few people I should talk to. Being the patriarch now, and everything.'

———

It was only in the car driving back to London that Billy found himself alone with Michael and able to talk to him. Alice had sent her regrets, and sent their son. Michael had travelled down from London with Tom, and then had cleaved to Sarah's kids throughout the funeral and the wake party.

'So, you're all set for Stanford,' he said as they drove out of Wells.

'Yeah.'

'I'll come out and see you sometime, once you're settled in. I haven't been in California for years.'

'Sure. It's a pretty boring place, though, Stanford.'

'But San Francisco is just a bus ride away.'

'I guess so.'

They drove on in silence for a little while, Michael staring fixedly through the windscreen at the road ahead. Eventually he said, 'How're you feeling, Dad? OK?'

'You mean about my father?'

'Yeah. That was a nice speech.'

'I suppose I wanted to honour him, and that's the only way I could do so.'

Michael looked across at him. 'What was he like, anyway?' he asked. 'I only met him a couple times.'

Billy thought for a few moments, and then said, 'He was an ordinary man, Mike. Like a lot of men.'

'You didn't get on too well with him.'

'We were different.'

'So you're not an ordinary guy, then.'

Billy returned his look. 'What makes you say that?' he said.

Michael shrugged his shoulders. 'You said he was ordinary, and you were different.'

'I'm ordinary in different ways, that's all.'

'I don't think you are ordinary. I think you're kind of unusual.'

'You do?'

'Yeah. With your books and all. And you were a hotshot once, weren't you, at Random House?'

Billy smiled wryly. 'I don't know what gives you that idea. I was an editor, one of many.'

'Why did you quit?'

'You know why I quit. Your mother and I came to the end of the road, and it seemed to make sense for me to come back here.'

Michael looked away from him, out of the passenger window. They were heading for Bath now, through rolling hills. 'I kind of wish you'd stuck around,' he said.

'Thanks. But we've been through all that, haven't we?'

'We went through it when I was about twelve. Things are different now.'

'I suppose they are. You're different, certainly. Before we know it you'll be a man.'

And before Billy knew it, he said to himself, Michael would be speaking the eulogy at his funeral. What would he say? Dad, I hardly knew you? Dad, I wish you'd stayed?

After another silence Michael said, 'What're we gonna do before I head back to New York?'

'What would you like to do?'

'I heard they have this thing at the Science Museum, a kind of earthquake experience. You go into a room and it shakes.'

'The Kobe earthquake.'

'Yeah.'

'You'll have to go without me, Mike – I've had my earthquake experience, in Istanbul, and it wasn't very entertaining.'

'Oh, right. I forgot.'

'But let's go. I can look at something else while you're doing that.'

'Cool.'

'Then let's hope you don't find yourself in a real earthquake one day, in California.'

A few days after Michael had returned to New York, Billy went back to Milton House. He had spoken to Chris Fletcher at the British Library and made a date two weeks hence for him to take a look at Thomas Wyatt's archive. When he had told Catherine of this over the phone she asked if in the meantime he would like to come down for the weekend.

He had been thinking about her a lot, indeed was quite unable to banish her from his mind. But when he arrived at the house it was a couple of hours before they were able to be easy with each other. Billy wondered whether she had been asking herself the same question he had been asking: was this serious, was this it? Catherine was fully ten years older than any woman he had known in recent years, and only a few years younger than him. What could be more natural, and more astounding, than the fact that this might be the start of something that mattered greatly to them both? And how dreadfully serious and self-conscious this awareness seemed to make them as they sat together over dinner.

'How was your father's funeral?' she asked.

'Oh, it was all right, I suppose. It's over, that's the main thing. What was your father's like?'

'It was in the cathedral. Lots of the great and the good came, people I barely knew or hadn't seen in years.'

'It sounds very different from mine.'

'It took me a long time to organize, and a long time to get over.'

'Was there no one to help you?'

'Not really. He had cut himself off from so many people in his last years. But nonetheless they felt they should come. It was as though he had actually died many years earlier.'

He reached across the table and held her hand in his.

'What are we to make of old age?' he said. 'How can we make sense of it?'

'We can make it productive, I suppose. But neither your father nor mine quite knew how to do that, it seems.'

'No. So much depends on what has gone before.'

'We shouldn't be hostages to our past. We ought to be able to reinvent ourselves, if necessary.'

'I'd quite like to reinvent *myself*.'

'As what?'

He smiled. 'I've always wanted to be able to compose music. But that's the sort of thing you can't just summon.'

'Perhaps you should write.'

He shook his head sadly. 'You should only write if you're compelled to,' he said. 'It shouldn't even be a matter of choice. There are quite enough books in the world as it is.'

She poured more wine into their glasses. 'Then perhaps you don't need to reinvent yourself at all. You have work you can do for as long as you want.'

'I know. I'm very fortunate. But it's strange work in many ways. Sometimes I feel it's quite unhealthy, this obsession with old books and manuscripts.'

'You don't seem the obsessive type to me.'

'Not compared with some of my peers, no.'

'Surely to have the sort of knowledge and discrimination you have is a fine thing.'

'Now you're flattering me. All I've done is to spend a lot of time surrounded by books. There's no great talent involved.'

'I think you underestimate yourself.'

She made to clear the plates, but he took her by the hand again. 'Let's go to bed,' he said. 'I'll do this later.'

Their lovemaking was surer this time, an understanding between them beginning to grow. Afterwards they lay entwined in each other's arms.

'You must come here as often as you wish,' she said. 'You must consider this house your own.'

'I could never do that.' He kissed her. 'But I will come often, nonetheless.'

'Remember the palimpsest you saw in Istanbul?' said Andrew Blackwood.

'Of course,' replied Billy.

'It's coming up at Sotheby's next month, with a reserve price of a hundred thousand pounds.'

'You should have gone after it.'

'I never really intended to – you must have known that. I thought it might give you something amusing to do in Istanbul.'

'Thanks for your consideration.'

Billy looked around the pub at all the familiar faces. How many times had he sat here with Blackwood talking about books? It was one of the constants in his life, as reliable as sunrise and sunset.

'What's the latest with the Wyatt archive?'

'She's decided to sell it to the BL. Chris Fletcher is coming down there with me the week after next.'

'He'll give you a good price for it, won't he?'

'I think so. They do seem to be trying harder these days, the BL people.'

'They've lost so much abroad.'

'Exactly.'

'And what about the mysteries?'

'Well, one is cleared up. Catherine has known since she was sixteen that Wyatt wasn't her father. She says she was aware of what the letters between him and her mother must contain, but hadn't actually read them.'

'And you believe her?'

'Yes I do.'

'And will they be part of the deal with Chris?'

'They have to be.'

Blackwood looked down into his almost-full glass. It was getting near the moment when he would offer Billy half of it, and Billy finished off his pint and sat waiting expectantly.

'And the novel?'

'She hasn't mentioned it. And nor will I.'

'Chris would jump at all that, surely?'

'Well, he isn't going to have the chance.' Billy looked at his friend sternly. 'And I don't want you mentioning it to him, all right? You're not supposed to know.'

Blackwood picked up his glass and dutifully poured some beer into Billy's. 'You're beginning to sound a little sanctimonious about it, if I may say so.'

'Am I? I'm sorry.' He paused for a moment. 'That may be because I seem to be falling in love with Catherine Wyatt.'

Blackwood smiled knowingly. 'Yes,' he replied, 'that would explain it.'

'She's a very intriguing woman.'

'Clearly.'

'And a lot more attractive than I first took her to be.'

'A woman's attractions can remain hidden for a long time.'

'And be all the more attractive for that.'

Blackwood looked at him reflectively. 'Does this mean you'll be moving to Somerset and abandoning your friends?'

'Absolutely not. Well, we haven't talked about anything like that yet. And I've got a business to run, remember?'

'You can run a business like ours from anywhere these days. You just hook up to the Internet.'

'Perhaps. I can't really imagine doing this kind of work anywhere other than the place where most of the customers are, though.'

'Well that's a relief. I don't think I can face seeing Sam Cummings by myself.'

530

'How is Sam? Haven't seen him in ages.'

'He's dried out, that's why. He's on the wagon.'

Billy looked at him in astonishment. 'No, really?'

Blackwood nodded. 'Really. He went into some kind of coma a few weeks ago, and the doctors told him that was it. I'm surprised you didn't hear about it.'

'I've been a little distracted. Is he OK?'

'He's fine. This is probably the best thing that's ever happened to him.'

'Well, I'm damned.'

'We mustn't let it influence us too much, though. Another round?'

———————

It was an odd sensation having someone else in the flat, someone who was there beside him when he woke up in the morning. It had been little more than six months since Chloe had last lain in his bed; but still somehow the presence of Catherine was electrifying. She had come up on the train the day before, and he had ushered her into his London life quite tentatively. After breakfast they went for a walk on Hampstead Heath, and he sat with her on a bench on Parliament Hill surveying the city, just as he had with Chloe.

'I've never spent very much time in London,' she said.

'Like your father.'

'We were never city people.'

'I've lived here most of my adult life. Apart from my years in New York.'

'You're at home here.'

'Yes, I am.'

She curled herself into him, and he kissed her hair.

'I don't want to take you away from it,' she said. 'I mean…'

'I think I'd like to spend more time away from it anyway.'

'You could come to Milton House for the weekends, perhaps.'

He looked down at her. 'What are you going to do now, Catherine?' he said. 'Now that things with your father are done.'

'Oh, I shall continue to do what I've been doing ever since he died.'

He looked at her questioningly. 'And what is that?'

She smiled. 'You must have guessed. I've been writing.'

'Writing what?'

531

She sat up, and turned to face him. 'I wrote a novel once,' she said. 'And then I burned it. Now I'm writing another one.'

'Another one or the same one?'

'Both. A story that has stayed with me, but which needs a different telling now.'

He returned her gaze. Was now the moment to say he knew about her first book? No, that was still for her to decide. His conversation with James Michie must remain a secret.

'I'd love to read it,' he said.

'Oh, I shan't show it to anyone for a while. But when I do, it will be you I show it to first.'

'I probably haven't been very nice about writers, now I come to think about it.'

'You've been candid. The thing you said that struck me most was that writers need to feel compelled to write, that they should have no choice in the matter.'

'And you feel compelled?'

She brushed her hair away from her face. 'Yes, I do.'

'You know how hard it is, don't you? The writing itself, and then the judgement of others.'

'I think I do. But I'm not going to dwell on how hard it is.'

They sat for a while longer, and then walked to Kenwood House for a late breakfast. The rest of the day flashed by, and in the evening they went out to dinner. This was very easy, he thought, being with Catherine, very easy and very natural. And when they went to bed, all their earlier modesty was swept away by what he could only describe as passion. When the next day he saw her onto the train at Paddington he felt a sense of loss, and could think only of the next time he would see her, just a few days hence. He didn't like the thought of her alone in that big house. But at least he knew she would not be quite alone, that she would have the world of her book.

The doorbell rang, and it was Aldridge again. Billy was about to leave for Somerset, and he was anxious to get away before the Friday afternoon traffic jam. He let Aldridge in, but didn't invite him to sit down.

'Got a perfect set of Proust,' said Aldridge excitedly. 'First editions of the Scott Moncrieff translation.'

532

'I'm not interested,' replied Billy. He waved a hand towards the boxes of books from the Norfolk library that stood against the walls. 'I'm stocked up at the moment.'

'But look, Billy,' said Aldridge, handing him a copy of Swann's Way: Part One. 'They're gorgeous.'

'No,' said Billy flatly. 'I'm sorry. Try Andrew Blackwood – he's a big Proustian.'

Aldridge looked crestfallen. 'All right,' he said.

Billy looked at his watch. 'I have to leave, Ronnie,' he said. 'I'm late already.'

He bundled Aldridge out of the door, and then hurriedly packed a bag. But the traffic was not as bad as he had feared, and he made good time. It was still early as he turned onto the Glastonbury road. Ahead of him the tor shone in the bright midsummer light, and rather than turn off towards Coombe he kept going, parking the car and heading for the gate that led to the path up the steep western slope. As he ascended it he passed groups of people coming down, some of whom encouraged him, saying, 'Only a bit further now, and it's lovely when you get to the top.' He was out of condition, and wheezing heavily by the time he made it.

There were very few other people there, and he was able to sit in his favourite place, looking out north and west towards Coombe and Wells. He hadn't done this in quite a while now, and he had forgotten how broad was the view, and how clear, in the right light, were the landmarks. The farmhouse where they had lived was just about visible, and Milton House stood out clearly.

What an extraordinary time this has been, he thought, these past few months. He had fallen into the depths of despair, and then it seemed he had been hauled out of them again. Now it was up to him to ensure that he never again lapsed back. It was also up to him to ensure that Catherine would not join the company of women whose love he had played for and then lost. This must be it, he said to himself, not because it's easy or convenient, but because it's right.

He had come a long way since he first stood on the top of the tor forty years ago with his father. But he still had a way to go. He looked once again towards Coombe, his boyhood and his old age stretching away before him.

To find out more about our books, to meet our authors, to discover new writing, to get inspiration for your book group, to read exclusive on-line interviews, blogs and comment, and to sign up for our newsletter, visit **www.portobellobooks.com**

encouraging voices,
supporting writers,
challenging readers